SIL

Visit Paul Henke on his website
for current titles and future novels at:

www.henke.co.uk

or email Paul at

henke@sol.co.uk

SILENT TEARS

Paul Henke

My very best wishes,

Paul Henke.

GOOD READ PUBLISHING

First published in 2003 by Good Read Publishing
A Good Read Publishing paperback
Reprinted in 2009 by Good Read Publishing

10 9 8 7 6 5 4 3 2

A CIP catalogue record for this title is available
from the British Library

ISBN 1 902483 11 5

Typeset by Palimpsest Book Production Limited,
Grangemouth, Stirlingshire
Printed and bound in Poland by Polska Books
www.polskabook.pl

Good Read Publishing Ltd
Balfron
G63 0RL

This book is dedicated to my daughter Louise who wrote her first novel at age 17 and is about to start her English Literature degree. I am very proud of you and know you will be a great writer.

Acknowledgements

For all the feedback and encouragement from the readers of the first two *Tears* books. To Anna Riera in Spain for her invaluable help and to Dr Eva Mithoff for her medical expertise. To my son Richard for keeping my website up to date and for helping his luddite Dad with all things technical. To the members of FOCUS who have welcomed me as a member – it is a delight to be part of such a pro-active and enthusiastic group. Thanks also to Bruce Macauley and his team at Macauley Creative for their design and creativity. To all the book shop managers around the country who give me such a warm welcome at book signings. And finally to Craig and Ruth Morrison and the staff at Palimpsest – as helpful as always.

SILENT TEARS

Prologue

SIR DAVID GRIFFITHS personally greeted his guest on the steps of Fairweather. The man had travelled a distance and the evening of August 21st 1968 was unseasonably cold and wet. Closing the door against the elements, Sir David led the way across the wide hall and into his study. A discreet bar stood in the corner of the large, warm, book lined room.

'Whisky, Prime Minister?'

'Thank you, Griffiths.' The stockily built, grey haired PM waved his pipe briefly. 'Do you mind?'

'By all means.' Sir David poured two large malt whiskies and set down a small jug of water.

The PM ignored it, taking a mouthful of the peaty malt.

'So the Russians have invaded?'

Trust Griffiths to get straight to the point. 'Yes. We heard the news a few hours ago. Did you catch the BBC?'

'No. I was at a late supper and when we returned I went straight to bed. I'm not as young as I used to be.' An understatement by the eighty-seven year old.

The Prime Minister nodded distractedly. 'Hundreds of thousands of Russian troops invaded, led by hundreds of tanks and supported by a few token units from other Warsaw Pact countries. Damnation – those poor Czechs. Imagine how frightened and confused they must be. Soldiers in the street, tanks smashing through everything. Their frontiers crossed by the people they saw as their allies. I feel as though I've let them down. Particularly Dubcek. He was counting on us to support him.'

Sir David shook his head. 'There was nothing you could have done about it. Nobody could. We cannot go to war with Russia over Czechoslovakia. The die was cast in 1945 when we sold out eastern Europe to Stalin. Only time will undo the great harm that was done then. You mustn't blame yourself.'

Relief flooded into the PM's eyes as he looked up from inspecting the carpet and he set his gaze on the tall, slightly stooped, old man standing in front of him. The Prime Minister was aware he was in the presence of one of the greatest men of the century. Sir David Griffiths had helped to shape events on a world-wide scale. He had been, indeed still was, an advisor to Prime Ministers, Presidents and Kings. His knowledge of world affairs was encyclopaedic, his memory infallible. The PM permitted himself a small smile. Hearing Griffiths' words eased his conscience. Others, his Cabinet and his political advisors, had said as much, but hearing the same reassurances from Sir David Griffiths he could almost believe it.

'The Czechs are trying to stop armour with their bare hands. Arrests, abductions . . . the killing is horrendous. No trials, no mercy.'

Sir David nodded. 'Precisely as I forecast.'

'Dubcek was one of the first arrested. There was nothing we could have done about it. Was there?' The tone was pleading, hectoring, his Yorkshire accent rasping in its self-righteousness.

Sir David heaved a sigh, feeling genuinely sorry for the PM. 'Probably not,' he said heavily, knowing it was untrue. That was what galled him. A great deal could have been done but all efforts had been too little and far too late. Throughout his life he had been dealing with vain, self-seeking, stupid men and women who never saw beyond the next election. With few exceptions they were, at best, mediocre, at worst – he shuddered, banishing his thoughts. There was no point in going over the past. It was over. The PM had a thousand other burdens to shoulder, not least of all the appalling state of the British economy. To take one problem away might be a kindness, even though his instinct was to tell it the way it really was. Russia would never have invaded if the West had been prepared to back the Czechs properly. Every opportunity had been given to Johnson, the American President, but he was being dragged into southeast Asia. Vietnam was a war that could never be won. His advice to the President was that it would lead to grief. The fact that Johnson agreed with him was of little consolation. Sir David took a sip of whisky. It burnt its way down his throat and hit his stomach in an eruption of acid. He added a lot more soda and tried again. Old age, he thought, was hellish.

'Prime Minister, there is nothing to be done. We will make the usual noises in the United Nations and the Russians will ignore us. There will be crocodile tears, loud lamentations and gnashing of impotent teeth and when it's all over nothing will change. We have to move on.'

'That's all?'

'Certainly, that's all. You have other problems to cope with. Eastern Europe, I repeat, was sold out by an old man and a dying President two decades ago. It's too late now to do anything about it.'

'Hindsight says we should have heeded your advice,' said the PM.

Sir David waved a self-deprecating hand, realised that he was still standing, dominating the room, and sat down in a leather chair opposite his guest. 'That's history. The present and the future is what must concern us. What news of Africa?'

The two spoke for a few minutes about the meeting scheduled to take place on board *HMS Fearless* between the British Prime Minister and Ian Smith, the Prime Minister of Rhodesia. The meeting was to be held on September 9th, at Gibraltar.

A short while later Sir David saw his guest out. He was walking thoughtfully back to his study when he saw a figure standing on the stairs.

'It's a bit late to be wandering around the house, isn't it?' Sir David asked, pleasantly.

'Sorry, sir,' replied the reporter. 'I couldn't sleep and was coming down to look for something to read. I hope you don't mind?'

'Not at all. Well, now we're both awake, why not join me for a drink?'

'I'd like that, sir. Thanks.' Tim Hunter followed the older man into the study. He was a reporter for *Time* magazine and was staying at Fairweather, chronicling the history of the Griffiths family.

'Help yourself,' Sir David waved at the bar.

The reporter poured himself a bourbon and added ice and soda. 'Good health.' He raised a glass in salutation.

Sir David acknowledged the gesture and took a sip. 'How goes the work?'

'I'm wading through the latter part of the twenties. The miners' strike and the national strike intrigue me. Your attitude to them. Not one of, shall we say, a capitalist?'

Sir David chuckled. 'It was a dilemma, I can tell you. My heart said one thing and my brain another.'

'Is that why you went to South Wales? To try and solve the problem?'

'Solve it? No.' He shook his head. 'Solving the problem was way beyond me. The economics of the situation were so stark that it was useless. Either the taxpayers subsidised coal as a national requirement or . . .' he trailed off, the reporter waiting in anticipation. Sir David shook his head. 'Read it all and make up your own mind,' he said. 'To more important matters. What are your intentions with regards to my granddaughter?'

The unexpected question caused the reporter to pause with the glass halfway to his mouth. He gulped.

'Don't look so surprised,' said Sir David, kindly. 'I may be old but I'm neither blind, nor a fool.'

'No, sir. That's obvious. I take it that was the British Prime Minister I saw leaving?'

Sir David nodded. 'There's nothing wrong with *your* eyesight either.'

'Can you tell me what he wanted?' Hunter knew that he was pushing his luck.

'Just a chat. That's all. Just a chat,' Sir David replied, vaguely.

Hunter smiled, thinking he had moved the conversation away from dangerous waters. 'Like all the others who drop in for a "chat"? I've never seen so many dignitaries beating a path to one door before.'

'They come to sound off. To see . . .' he paused and smiled sadly. 'Maybe to see if the old man still has it in him? Let me tell you something about getting old, young man. Something nobody tells you. Up here,' he tapped the side of his head, 'you're stuck in a time warp. Somewhere in your twenties, maybe your thirties. The body grows old and decrepit while, if you're lucky, the brain stays as fit as ever. You think the same. Experience has shaped your thoughts but your head still says you can achieve all the things you used to be able to do. Then one day, suddenly, you realise it's not so. That's when you know you're old. The mind begins to catch up with the body. So now I dispense words of wisdom to anyone who thinks I have something useful to contribute.' He smiled, sadly. 'So? What's the answer?'

'Sir?'

'My granddaughter, damn it!'

Caught out, Hunter stuttered, 'S . . . strictly h . . . honourable, sir.'

'Really?' Sir David raised a cynical eyebrow.

BOOK 1

David's Story

1

Spring 1926

I STOOD ON THE platform and smiled at my wife. Although Richard was just over a year old, Madelaine had already regained her slim figure. Her hair was becoming more auburn than red, and the corners of her eyes carried a few more wrinkles but she was as lovely as ever.

'I hope the visit is successful,' she said.

'We'll see. I don't hold out much hope but I'll give it my best shot. A strike is in no one's interest.'

Madelaine nodded towards a paper vendor. 'He's saying the strike is imminent.'

'Bad news sells papers. Look after the baby.'

Madelaine smiled, her face transformed with an inner contentment. Motherhood suited her. 'You always say that. Hurry back. We'll both miss you. Good luck, darling.'

'All aboard!'

'I'd better go. The railways, like time and tide, wait for no man.'

I pecked her on the cheek, received a tight hug in response and climbed into the train. As it began to pull away I just had time to open the window and wave farewell. A cloud of smoke from the engine wafted towards me and I hurriedly closed it again and went in search of my seat. It seemed to me I was always saying goodbye for one reason or another.

As a weapon of the working class, the rallying cry of 'General Strike' is highly effective and puts fear into the hearts and minds of the government. My task was to secure a peaceful settlement with the miners of South Wales but I had very little hope.

In truth, I did not want to go back. Llanbeddas, the village where I was born, was in turmoil and I was expected to help pour oil on troubled waters. I had left the valley behind in time and soul nearly three decades earlier. My return in 1911 had been little short of a fiasco. Now, fifteen years later, the government hoped I might be able to help improve the worsening situation. If South Wales could be brought to heel, the fonts of wisdom in Whitehall spouted, then so could the remainder of the coalfields. I disagreed. Furthermore, in spite of being born and brought up there, I had little influence with the place and its people.

I was travelling first class, all expenses paid by the government. Not that I needed the money, of course, simply as a matter of principle. If they wanted me to haul their chestnuts out of the fire then they could pay me to do it.

Initially I had rebuffed all attempts to coerce me to travel to Wales. However, the guarantee of a safe seat in Kent at a by-election due in nine months convinced me otherwise. It was Churchill, in his usual fashion, who had finally persuaded me.

'Listen, Griffiths, I can assure you of the seat. If the miners don't return then no matter. The seat is still yours. I give you my word.'

'How can you be so certain?' I asked.

He frowned, looking up at me from under a wrinkled brow, a fat cigar clamped in his right hand. 'Certain of what?'

'That there'll be a by-election,' I replied, frowning in turn.

'Silvers is being given a peerage and kicked into another place. In the New Year's Honours list. Hence the by-election in nine months.'

'And if another seat comes up in the meantime?'

'Ah! An interesting question.' Churchill looked uncomfortable for a moment but then answered truthfully. 'Fact is, another one or two seats are already spoken for. Favours have to be repaid,' he added, puffing contentedly on his cigar.

His words didn't surprise me. That was the way of the political world. Utterly corrupt in an almost honest fashion. Part of me loathed the system, but powerful forces were dragging me inexorably into a political career.

I was fully briefed for Wales but nothing could have prepared me for the emotions the valleys would unleash within me when I arrived.

It had been noon when the train pulled out of Paddington. Civilisation in the form of a dining car had been added to the trains a few years earlier and I was booked for the early sitting. I took my briefcase with me. Settling at the white-clothed table with a sea of silver laid out before me, I opened my case and lifted out my papers. These were not the official memoranda and inter-office notes of the government, but a stack of newspaper clippings. I had instructed my staff to acquire newspaper articles from all over the country. Local newspapers that formed a part of the mining community reflected the miners' views. Those in other regions were, on the whole, against them. Nationally the press was split down the middle, the Labour newspapers supportive, the Tory against. Two facts did not surprise me. The first, the total bias of the reporting and the second, its inaccuracy. Newspapers sold, not through facts but emotions. They could arouse such fierce passions that arguments spilled over into violence. *It was my job to stop it happening.*

Whilst reading the various papers I absent-mindedly broke a bread roll and ate it. As a steward took my order I became aware of the three men sitting directly across the aisle from me and looked over. I was surprised to recognise Arthur Cook, the secretary of the Miners' Federation and two of his cohorts. Cook was a rabid left-winger and a syndicalist – his aim was to amalgamate the miners across Britain under one union. A short, heavily built man, nattily dressed in tweeds, his waistcoat pulled taut across his bulging stomach and a watch chain of gold dangling from the button hole to his left hand pocket, Cook's neat, grey moustache bristled with anger.

'The men will never accept the recommendations,' he said angrily, leaning across the table to make his point.

I looked out the window, not wishing to draw attention to myself. I was sitting diagonally, about six feet away. Cook spoke in a loud undertone to the two men opposite him. I could hear everything that he had to say and, as I took no notice of him, he ignored me. The other two, with their profiles to me, were difficult to hear and understand but I did catch the odd word and phrase.

I guessed they were George Barker and Noah Ablett who, more than a decade earlier, had formed the Unofficial Reform Committee advocating one, all-inclusive national union for mineworkers. 'The Royal Commission want to abolish the minimum wage set in 1924. Right?' Cook continued. There were nods from the other two. 'They also want to reduce wages. Well, it's not on. The lads won't accept it.'

I was listening intently. Cook, as usual, was being selective with the Commission's findings. What he said was true, but there was also a great deal of good contained in the report. Cook was failing to mention the compulsory profit sharing for miners and paid annual holidays of two full weeks a year. Far from perfect, but I knew it was the best deal available. If Cook wouldn't buy into it then I saw no chance of avoiding a strike.

The steward came and served me an indifferent game soup which I ate distractedly, still tuned into the conversation taking place across the aisle.

'So we push for a general strike,' said Cook. 'We have no choice. We've got nearly a million men working in the coalfields. If we call an all out strike we'll be able to drag the rest of the unions with us. The TUC will have to follow.' Cook pugnaciously prodded his forefinger on the table in front of him. He stopped talking when the steward appeared and placed soup in front of the three men. His tirade was replaced with the slurping of soup and I stopped listening for a few moments deep in thought. A general strike was the last thing the country needed. Europe was a mess, India was being rocked by riots between Hindus and Moslems and the African continent lurched from crisis to crisis. In the Middle East our troops faced skirmishes across vast areas of land from the Sudan to Iraq. We were already having problems paying our soldiers and seamen. On-going subsidies to the railways and the mining industry were bleeding the country dry and other industries had begun demanding financial support from the government.

I picked listlessly at a piece of beef while the conversation opposite resumed. 'We aim for a general strike in six weeks,' said Cook, 'if we don't get the government to back down. Agreed?' Barker and Ablett hesitated. 'Agreed?' he said, angrily. The two men nodded. 'Good. That's settled. Now we can enjoy the rest of our meal in peace.'

I tuned out once more and concentrated on my food. I needn't have bothered. It didn't improve just because I was now thinking about what I was tasting. A half bottle of claret was the meal's only saving grace. That, and what I'd learnt.

The three men left the carriage a short while later and after an interval, I followed. Standing in the corridor outside my compartment I realised we were pulling into Temple Mead station, Bristol. I entered my compartment and sat down, in deep thought. Cook was an honest man, fighting for what he passionately believed in. The problem was, in essence, very simple. Cook was wrong. If I ran the Griffiths empire in the way the country was being run then we would be bankrupt in no time. It was impossible for the government to continue to cross-subsidise failing industries. The figures whirled through my head as I considered my mission. Eventually, as the train pulled out of Bristol, I fell into a fitful doze. I was aware of the train going through the tunnel under the River Severn but took no notice of the Monmouthshire countryside as we drew out the other side. Newport came and went and I finally awoke when the train pulled into Cardiff station.

The platform was bustling with crowds yelling cheerfully, people climbing on and off the train. Good natured shoving and jostling were the order of the day. I felt a pressure on my hip and swung round just in time to grab a small hand with my wallet.

'Let me go!' The hand belonged to a runt of a boy who squirmed in my grasp. His face and hands were grubby, as were the tattered clothes he wore. As I snatched my wallet back, he twisted and escaped my clutches, darting through the crowds. I thought fleetingly of giving chase but what was the point? I was hardly going to have him arrested.

In the huge open space in front of the station I hailed a taxi and gave the Angel Hotel as my destination. The city owed its existence to one thing – coal. The coal dust-ridden rivers Rhondda and Taff met at Pontypridd as thick, black sludge that poured down to Cardiff. The rivers Rhymney to the east and the Ely to the west washed millions of tons of coal every year. The valleys, with their rich seams of coal, spread across South Wales like tentacles, whose head and brain were located at Cardiff. The docks which had grown up over the previous three hundred years were a massive complex of locks, wharves and warehousing. Huge quantities of coal were piled high in open, rat-infested compounds and the grime of coal dust lay everywhere. When a north wind blew it wasn't too bad, but when it became a southerly, the dust spread across the city. Coal fires added to the smog and filth. Like most industrialised cities across Britain there was abject poverty and great wealth. I found it a depressing thought, more than two decades into the twentieth century.

Our roots were here. But of my father's four brothers only Uncle William was still alive. I was looking forward to spending some time in his company. He lived in Rhiwbina with his wife, Nancy. I had last seen him at Mam's wedding to John Buchanan, my step-father. The other relatives I had rarely seen in thirty years. David and William had become partners in a shop they had opened in Rhiwbina. They had prospered and, on Uncle David's death, they had owned seven stores in the city and a further eight across South Wales.

My dear step-father, John Buchanan, had been under the impression that my uncles had combined their resources and were all in partnership together. That had been far from the case. My Uncle Albert had stayed in Llanbeddas and worked in the mine. He had died there in a pit accident. Uncle Huw had become a union representative and had ended his working life working in an office and attending miners' rallies. Between them I had fifteen or sixteen cousins, none of whom I would recognise if they passed me in the street. I felt guilty at the thought.

The Angel Hotel was a large, Victorian building on the outskirts of the city, on the road to Rhiwbina. Recently, a new rugby ground had opened nearby, called Cardiff Arms Park. Being Saturday, a game was in progress. I could hear the cheering and yelling as I alighted from the taxi.

'Cardiff are playing Port Talbot,' the taxi driver said when I enquired.

I paid the fare and thanked him. As I hefted my portmanteau, singing broke out in the stadium and the hairs on the back of my neck stood on end. For Scots the world over the sound of the bagpipes has that effect. For me it was the harmonious sound of tens of thousands of Welsh voices raised in song. I recognised the battle hymn, *Men of Harlech*.

I was humming it to myself when I stepped through the swing doors into the opulent foyer of the hotel. The two men standing just inside the door had a certain familiarity I couldn't place.

2

THEY WERE STANDING closely together, watching me, my own uncertainty reflected in their faces. The taller stepped forward and said, tentatively, 'David?'

I nodded, taken aback.

He smiled and thrust out his hand. 'Welcome to Wales, boyo. We're your cousins, Rhodri and this is Dafydd.'

I placed them immediately. Rhodri was Uncle Albert and Aunt Gwyneth's son and Dafydd was Huw and Mair's. They were both tall, strong looking men. Rhodri was a year older than me, Dafydd, two years younger. The calculations flitted across my mind as the memories came flooding back.

We shook hands. I felt the rough, callused grips of the two miners and smiled. It was good to see them.

'Let me check in,' I said, 'and buy you two a drink.'

They both nodded. I realised that they were ill at ease. Mistakenly, I presumed they were unused to the grandeur of the Angel. I went across to the reception, signed the register and asked the receptionist to have a porter take my bag to my room. Back in the foyer I shepherded my cousins into the large lounge bar on the first floor.

They asked for Worthington Pale Ales and I joined them. While we waited for the drinks to arrive a short, uncomfortable silence fell between us. Despite our blood ties, I was aware the two men were strangers. I began wondering how they had known that I would be there. The awkward silence was interrupted by the arrival of the waiter, who added the drinks to my room bill.

'*Iechyd da,*' I raised the light beer and sipped. Over the rim of the glass I took a closer look at my cousins. Their well-pressed suits were shiny, the cuffs of their shirts frayed. Both wore white scarves around their necks. They had on heavy, black highly-polished boots. I was acutely aware of my Savile Row suit, spotless white shirt and light leather brogues. It was almost as though we lived on different planets.

Neither man said anything and I broke the ice. 'It's an unexpected pleasure to see you both,' I began, 'but I'm a little confused. What are you doing here? Not that I'm ungrateful,' I added, 'but apart from Uncle William I hadn't told anybody in the family that I was coming.'

Rhodri nodded. 'That's right.' He said nothing further.

I realised at that moment that this was no friendly family gathering. I did what I always do in such circumstances. I kept quiet.

'So what do you have to say to us?' asked Dafydd, belligerently.

'Don't play us for fools, boyo,' Rhodri added, angrily. 'If you think you're here to break us, then think again.'

'Break you?' I frowned.

'The strike,' hissed Rhodri. 'We're one hundred percent. Solid. What's been offered is not enough. We can't feed and clothe our families as it is, look you. A cut in wages and increase in working hours will break some of us.'

'An extra hour a day,' said Dafydd, bitterly. 'That's nearly a whole working day in the week. It can't be done. We work till we drop already.' Coughing in his agitation, he took out a grubby handkerchief and wiped his mouth.

I felt pity for them both. Mere months between us, yet already they were worn out, killing themselves under the ground, digging a living out of the hell of the mines. I had a horrendous flashback as I sat listening to them, remembering the strike of 1890 and its aftermath. Nothing had changed in over thirty years. I felt chilled and saddened at the thought.

'Hear me out,' I stopped. I felt I owed them an explanation, though doubted it would make an iota of difference. I began again. 'Face facts. The mines are losing money hand over fist. The government has subsidised uneconomical pits for nearly nine months at a horrendous cost. It simply cannot go on. Seventy three percent of all coal is being produced at a loss. British industry is paying for it, at a terrible price . . .' I saw the look on their faces and paused. These men lacked the foresight to see the outcome of their strike, the political power which would be unleashed against them.

'Why should we care?' asked Rhodri. 'Our only interest is feeding and clothing our families.'

'I know,' I said, harshly. 'But at what cost? Never mind everybody else. Is that it? As long as you're okay then to hell with the rest of the workers in Britain?'

'What do you care about the workers?' Dafydd asked angrily. 'You capitalists suck the blood out of us. You with your fancy houses and cars and soft jobs. What do you care?'

I could have hit him. Instead I took a deep breath and tried again. 'I care. More than you will ever know or understand,' I said. 'But that doesn't change the facts. The drain of the coalfields on the British economy is becoming untenable. We are unable to pay our servicemen, and our ships are currently sitting in harbour because we have no coal in our bunkers.'

'The servicemen are no concern of ours,' Dafydd said. 'We're on the breadline as it is. We cannot give anymore.' He coughed again.

I was not surprised to hear the words, merely saddened. 'Look, you may know that I'm involved in many businesses.' I did not say that I owned the companies, or at least large parts of them. It would have been tactless to parade my wealth too conspicuously. I knew I had an uphill struggle as it was. 'At the last count there were more than fifteen thousand men and women working in them. Other companies in which my bank has invested have workforces exceeding two, maybe three hundred thousand people. Each business has to be profitable. Surely that's self-evident?'

'Not to me it isn't,' Dafydd said, his anger simmering beneath the surface of his words.

'Where's the money to invest in new machinery otherwise? Where are the new plant and new products coming from? Who would pay the wages and the dividends?' Immediately I knew I had made a mistake.

'Dividends!' Rhodri hissed the word. 'Sucking the lifeblood from the workers. Paying the rich at the expense of the poor.' They used the same words. A mantra of hate against anyone who did not fit their image of themselves.

I decided it was time to display some anger myself. I leant forward and prodded the table with my finger, emphasising each point. 'First of all, nobody owes you a living. The strategic value of coal has been overplayed. Yes, we need coal for our ships, yes, we need coal for our industries, yes, we need coal to keep our people warm but *not* at the expense of the huge subsidies we are having to pay.' At each word shadows passed across the faces of the two men sitting in front of me. 'If one of my companies fails then we cut it out. An unprofitable business is like a cancer. It will kill everything it comes into contact with. We can operate, we can change, invest, if we think there's a chance of the business surviving. But at the end of the day, if it isn't profitable, it has to go.'

'Are you saying the mines are finished?' Rhodri asked.

'No, I'm not,' I said more calmly, allowing the anger to seep out of my voice. 'I'm saying we need to find solutions. Sir Herbert Samuel came up with a number of good ideas. I'm here to discuss those ideas with the miners.' Sir Herbert Samuel had chaired the Royal Commission that had looked into the question of the future of the coal industry. He, Sir William Beveridge and others, including myself, had made radical suggestions. They included reducing the minimum wage to earlier levels and adding an hour to the working day. If jobs were to be preserved at the current level then wage cuts were the only solution. There was another, of course, but I had to keep my powder dry on that one. It would not be popular in some quarters.

'Why not get out? Leave? Find work elsewhere?' I suggested. It was a grave error.

Dafydd was scandalised. 'Sell out our friends and their families? Leave and go where? Do what? Mining is all we know.'

'You're both young and still fit enough to do anything you want.' I had been sitting back but now I leant forward again, emphasising my point. Mustering my arguments, I continued. 'There's a whole world out there. You don't have to grub down a mine for a pittance. I can get you jobs anywhere in Britain. The whole family can get out. I . . .'

Dafydd stood up, righteous indignation seeping from every pore. 'You can go to hell, *Sir* David Griffiths,' he sneered. 'We don't need or want your charity. You're a traitor to your class and your family. We'll stay and fight you and the rest of the rotten bosses. Tell the government that, if they want a fight, the South Wales coalminers are ready for one. Come on, Rhodri.' With that he stalked out of the hotel, his cousin at his heels.

Sighing, I beckoned over a waiter and ordered a large whisky and soda. I'd made a complete hash of talking to them and needed to rethink my strategy. Where did the two of them fit into the picture? Had they been there representing only themselves or did they really speak for the other miners? If they did, then my mission could well be over before it had begun.

Pensively, I took a sip of my drink. I needed information and my Uncle William seemed a good source. He might be getting on in years but, if his letters were anything to go by, his mind was still as sharp as ever. I asked the porter to arrange a taxi and I abandoned my drink to stand outside in the fresh air. There was a yell and a loud roar from behind the walls of the rugby ground but I couldn't tell who had scored. Then the voices broke into a rendition of *Cwm Rhondda* and the hairs on the back of my neck stood out again. My roots were firmly and deeply entrenched in the Welsh valleys, no matter how much I tried to deny them. I had to find a solution. That was all there was to it.

A taxi drove up alongside and I gave the driver my uncle's address. I settled back to watch the scenery as we headed for Rhiwbina, a small village on the edge of the city. We covered the two miles in a few minutes. I paid the fare, climbed down from the car and stood in the driveway, looking at the house. My uncle had done well for himself. His home stood in an acre or more of ground and was set back fifty yards from the road. The drive was well kept, the lawns immaculate and the flowerbeds appeared to be well tended. Like my father, Uncle William had escaped from the valleys and coal mining. Unlike my father, he had stopped when he had reached Cardiff while we had journeyed as far as America.

I paused outside the front door and rang the bell. A few seconds later a parlourmaid answered with a polite, 'May I help you?'

'I'm here to see Mr Griffiths.'

'Is he expecting you, sir?' She stepped back, allowing me to enter the vestibule and then the hall.

'I'm his nephew . . .' I began but was interrupted by a roar.

My uncle came striding across the hall, his hand outstretched, gripping mine and shaking it warmly. 'David, my boy, how wonderful to see you. Come in, come in.' William ushered me across to a closed door throwing it open. I followed him into his study. At eighty-two he was still hail and hearty. Stooped, his almost bald pate was covered with liver spots, his hair a thin white fringe. I declined an offer of a drink but gladly accepted a cup of tea. The room was lined with books, nearly all fiction, from classics to contemporary literature. I saw that, like me, William was a fan of PG Wodehouse, a comic writer of genius. One complete section was given over to Russian writers and a second to American authors. I realised that all the books were categorised by country and that there were a few unusual translations of Chilean and Portuguese writers. I was further surprised to learn that my uncle had read most, if not all of them. We exchanged small talk, mainly about the family, until the tea arrived. I was only too delighted to have the chance to show him the latest photograph I carried of my son Richard. I had another one of the family – Madelaine, Susan and Richard together.

Astutely he asked me, 'How does Susan get on with her new brother?'

I pondered the question for a few seconds and shrugged. 'Fine, I think.'

'No resentments?'

'I wouldn't say so. At least none that I've noticed. And if there had been I am sure Madelaine would have mentioned something to me.'

He nodded. 'Good. It can often be difficult for siblings with different mothers or fathers to live in harmony with each other. Petty rivalries and jealousies can so easily turn into something else. Hatred even.'

It was something Madelaine and I had discussed but there didn't appear any cause for concern. My daughter Susan had been born out of wedlock. Her mother had died in a gunfight in America years earlier – the same fight that had killed my father. I looked at the photograph of the three of them and smiled.

'He's a good looking boy, David. He's got your father's colouring and his looks. But I can see a lot of Madelaine in him too.'

'Just as long as he doesn't inherit her stubborn streak.'

Uncle William raised an inquisitive eyebrow.

I shrugged and muttered, 'The woman's too damn opinionated. Always questions everything.'

My uncle burst out laughing. 'She's strong-willed, beautiful, intelligent and educated. Which is precisely why you married her. And if you were honest you wouldn't want it any other way.'

I smiled back. He was right and I had the good grace to agree.

Cup and saucer in his hand he stared at me and changed the subject. 'I take it you're here to negotiate with the miners?'

I nodded. I told him about my conversation with my cousins.

'It doesn't surprise me. The biggest problem is not one of wages. We need an end to restrictive practices.'

Although I was aware of the problem, my uncle was an astute man, who thought things through. I was intrigued. Placing my cup and saucer on a low table, I sat back. 'Please explain.'

'The demarcation between jobs is unbelievably rigid. Say you're a face worker. You know they're the highest paid men in the mine?'

I nodded.

'Right. At the coalface there is a huge diversion of labour. Depending on the mining system used you can have holers, hammer-men or drivers, remblers, loaders, timberers and several other groups. In longwall mining, which is what they have at Llanbeddas, holers and loaders are separate classes of worker. In the past they helped each other. But not any longer. A driver can be waiting for a loader to finish before he can carry on. I'll give you another example. A chain cutting tool breaks so they have to send for a fitter to repair it.'

I nodded again. That seemed perfectly reasonable to me.

'But the fitter can take an hour to get to the face,

diagnose the problem and get back with the right part. Lost production? Anything up to half a shift.'

I raised my eyebrows in surprise. 'Why not have spare parts or even second machines available close by? Then the problem wouldn't arise.'

'Too simple. A second machine is expensive, spare parts too. A fitter needs to make the repair.'

'But why?'

'The system started as a way to protect jobs. If you're a face worker and can repair a broken tool then who needs a fitter? But now the system is entrenched. Productivity per man is lower than it was twenty years ago – in spite of mechanisation. In the Cwm Colliery at Beddau they've even introduced a conveyor belt, the first in Wales and *still* they can't make the pit viable.'

'So we change the system.'

'Believe me, David, the unions have enormous power and vested interests so they'll fight to keep things as they are.' Uncle William continued, sounding more like my grandfather with every word. 'They have a million men under their control. If they call a strike they can escalate it into a general strike and possibly topple the government. It's heady stuff. Power with little or no responsibility.'

'What's the solution?' I asked.

He surprised me with his answer. 'That's your job. I'm only giving you the facts.'

'Thanks, Uncle William. How do you view the fragmentation of the coal industry? There are hundreds of mines all over the country.'

'There are nearly three thousand mines, many of them so small as to be uneconomical. The government only agreed a national wage policy because of the war. We desperately needed every pound of coal we could get. The miners milked the situation for all it was worth. It was called strategic supplies.'

'I agree we had no choice. We needed the coal for the ships and the steel industry in particular. Miners were exempt from being called up. They exploited the war only to get a national wage. Do you remember the fuss in 1921 when the national strike was called by the Triple Alliance?' I asked him. 'Back then employers wanted to reduce wages as well.'

'That's right. In reality we're still facing the same problems. Nothing was resolved then and nothing will be now. In my opinion we need a national arrangement, where the coalfields are administered by an overseeing body. Until that happens I think we'll lurch from crisis to crisis.'

It was a radical idea and one worth considering, but right then it wasn't on the cards. We discussed the situation for a while longer but we were unable to come up with concrete proposals for my meeting with the miners' leaders the next day. I would have to play it by ear.

My aunt was away for a couple of days visiting her sister in Llandrindod Wells and so we had the house to ourselves. I had declined an invitation to stay as I wanted the freedom to come and go as I pleased and to hold meetings where and when I liked. Although Uncle William wouldn't have objected I didn't wish to tax him too much. I wasn't sure whether he was relieved or not. I agreed, however, to stay to dinner.

'What about Rhodri and Dafydd?' I asked when we sat down to eat later that evening.

'What about them?' Uncle William cut a slice of beef, added enough mustard to take the roof off your mouth and chewed it with relish.

'Where do they fit in? Are they union representatives?'

'Dafydd represents the Llanbeddas colliery. Rhodri follows Dafydd around and helps whenever he can.'

'Is Dafydd the leader at Llanbeddas? Or is there someone else?'

'Good question. There are others. He was sent, I suspect, because of the family connection. The union boss is a man called Colin Lewis.'

The name rang a bell. 'Any relation to Lewis Lewis?'

'Grandson. But, unfortunately, not a chip off the old block. Devious. A liar. Looks out only for himself.'

We finished our meal and returned to the study, this time with a glass of port for my uncle and a malt whisky for me.

'Any more advice?' I asked.

He shook his head. 'I am flattered to be asked, but, no. I've thought about the problem but there is deep intransigence on both sides. I've had to shut seven shops in fifteen years because they weren't paying. If I hadn't we could have been bankrupted. But if the uneconomical pits are shut or amalgamated with others then tens, maybe hundreds of thousands of miners would be put out of work. That's a social price too great to pay.' He paused and sipped his port.

'So what does the government do? You know that we cannot pay our sailors and soldiers? The country is going bankrupt.'

He shook his head. 'No! That's where you're wrong,' he said vehemently. 'A country isn't a business. Print more money. Come off the gold standard and put the country back to work. Send the women back home and let the men have their jobs back.'

I shook my head. 'It's not as easy as that. The women have found a new freedom . . .'

He held up his hand. 'I know, I know, I know. I've heard the arguments on the radio, read them in every newspaper. Churchill has put us back onto the gold standard but that's an artificial pin to the country's wealth. Print more money . . .'

I interrupted him. 'That would lead to inflation. The problem would get worse.'

'In the long run, but we have short term problems to solve. Crank up British industry, lend money through the banks and modernise and by the time we have a bit of inflation the real problems will be solved.'

I shook my head. 'If it was only that easy,' I said sadly, enjoying the debate for all that. My uncle applied a cold logic to arguments forged by being a small businessman for much of his life. Getting up to replenish my glass from the sideboard I noticed a section of books I hadn't seen earlier. A quick glance showed that they were on accounting and economics.

'Have you read these?' I waved a hand at the twenty or so titles.

'Most,' he nodded. 'Interesting stuff. For every one that says one thing another will say something else. I finish one book that advocates the gold standard and I think, that's right. Then I read a second that says the opposite and agree with it. At the end of the day I've had to make up my own mind. There are a couple you should read.' He pulled himself up out of his chair and ambled across. Pulling two titles from the shelf he handed them to me. One was by John Maynard Keynes, an economist, and the other was by Gunnar Myrdal, a Swedish sociologist and economist. 'Keynes' book is particularly interesting because he's analysed coal production in some detail. A year ago the average profits on a ton of coal was six pence. To retain our exports of coal, now that we are back on the gold standard, we need to reduce prices by one shilling and nine pence a ton. Remember that we are the least mechanised coal industry in the world. So how are prices reduced? Only by reducing wages. Read the books. They argue from the same standpoint and arrive at different solutions. Myrdal is still only in his early twenties but he makes a few valid points.'

'Thanks.' I placed the books on the table to take away with me.

'The price per ton of coal in 1920 was one pound fourteen shillings. It's now eighteen shillings. The economics of the industry are mad,' he continued.

I nodded. The facts had been explained to me in laborious detail back in London.

The telephone in the hallway rang and Uncle William left the room to answer it. When he came back he was looking extremely grave.

'Llanbeddas. There's been an explosion at the mine. One of the tunnels has collapsed. Hundreds of men are trapped below ground.'

3

MY FAMILY HAD left Llanbeddas in 1890, leaving behind a community devastated by the loss of the school and the death of its children, including my sister, Sian. Memories of that day lived with me constantly. Now I was back in Llanbeddas to find the village once more blighted by the mine.

It was a scene from hell. Outside the gates to the colliery, a short distance from the house where I had been born, hundreds of people were milling around. My throat was constricted and my stomach felt leaden as more memories surfaced.

I helped Uncle William through the crowds, his advanced age persuading people to be courteous and to step aside. Even so, it took a long time to get near the pit. The winding gear stood out starkly against the cloudless night sky. There was none of the usual noise of the night shift – machinery and chimneys belching steam and smoke in equal measure. Yards from the gates we were forced to stop. The mass of people was solid. Voices carried across the still night as people tried to get more information. Other pits in the area had been called up and rescue squads were being bussed and lorried in from all over the valleys. So far only a handful had arrived.

I turned to the woman beside me. 'Do you know what's happened? How many are trapped?'

She shook her tear stained face. 'Don't know, bach. All the face workers of Iswyn shaft are caught, maybe more. Dear God,' she put her hands over her face and sobbed.

Awkwardly I put my arm on her shoulder. 'Take it easy. They'll get out.'

'My . . . my husband . . .' She gulped and tried again. 'My husband and three boys are down there. The youngest only started last week. On his fifteenth birthday.'

I felt a chill down my back. Fifteen and down a mine. What a stupid waste. What was ahead, if he survived? A life of hard work, heavy drinking and a short old age.

A yell from behind made me look over my shoulder. A convoy of lorries was approaching, horns blowing to clear their way through the throng. Miners from the other pits, pulled off shift, were arriving. The front lorry was travelling at a snail's pace, the driver leaning out of the window, waving his arm, encouraging people to move aside. Standing on the running board, hitching a lift, yelling at the crowds to move, was Rhodri. We saw each other at the same time. Our eyes locked. The lorry edged nearer until I could reach out and touch it.

'Well, David,' he sneered, 'what are you doing here, you waster? There's nothing you can do to help. Go back to London and tell your masters we won't give in. Second thoughts,' he threw down the challenge, 'prove you're a man and come and help. We need every able bodied man we can get.'

I hesitated for a second. I might know little about mining but I could hump a pick and shovel. I stepped to the side of the lorry and climbed onto the running board alongside my cousin. More than likely other members of my family were trapped underground. The least I could do was help as best I could. Rhodri looked over his shoulder at me, his eyes met mine and he nodded, saying nothing. The lorry reached the gates. They opened and we passed inside. The crowds of women, children and old men stayed out, aware that there was nothing they could do to help. Except pray.

We jumped down from the lorry and walked briskly across the yard to a large building capable of holding two hundred or more men standing shoulder to shoulder. There were thirty or forty already gathered and from what they were saying I understood that they had been on the day shift. Most of them had come either from their beds or from the Wheatsheaf, the local pub. News of the disaster had sobered them quickly.

We stood in silence. Many glanced at me in my city garb, some with hostility. There was little talking.

'What's happening?' I asked Rhodri.

'We're waiting to find out what's going on. There's no point in going off half-cocked. The engineers have gone down to assess the problems.'

It was clear to him that I had not understood. 'Mining engineers, they're in control of the whole of the pit. Reporting to the manager. They make the decisions about blasting and digging. We need to know the scale of the problem before we can do anything.'

'Are those maps of the mine?' I nodded to the side where large sheets of paper were pinned to the blank, yellow painted walls.

Rhodri wandered across with me in tow. 'The problem is here. In Iswyn.' He traced a finger down a shaft and along the straight.

'How far is that?' I asked.

'The shaft is thirteen hundred feet deep. The roadway goes along here for nearly a mile. There are gobs here,' he touched a square, 'here and here.'

Gobs, I knew, were large underground caverns, left over from the old bank system of mining. Pillars of coal were left unmined to prevent the roof from caving in as the miners cut deeper into the coal system.

I was looking at a red line and another set of drawings. 'I take it that this is the water level. Here's the roadway. This is the horse gate. Is that to allow ponies to pass?'

'Something like that.'

'The water level,' I stated the obvious, 'is above the workings.'

He nodded bleakly. 'That's why we have very little time to get them out. If the pump's stopped then we have less than twenty-four hours.'

'How many pumps are there? How do they work?'

'There's only one. It's steam driven. An old Newcomen. It's reliable most of the time.'

'Most of the time?' I raised an eyebrow.

He held up his hand. 'They're expensive to replace. It's a well tested machine designed a hundred years ago.'

'A hundred years!' I was aghast. 'There's nothing newer or better since then?'

'That's the way it is down here, David. Water isn't a particular problem. The owners recently spent a lot of money on a new winding engine. It increased the amount of coal we can lift from three hundred tons a shift to a thousand. That was what we needed.' I realised that he was now talking to hide his nervousness. He paused, 'Dafydd's down there. So are Huw and Peter.'

I had to think for a moment. 'Huw is Dafydd's brother? Peter's yours?'

He looked bleakly at me. 'You know the family, I'll give you that,' he said, heavily.

'Christ! There must be a way to get them out.'

'Along with two hundred and eighty other men.'

I looked at him in shock. 'So many?'

'It's labour intensive work. This colliery alone employees fifteen hundred men.'

There was a commotion at the door as three blackened, weary men appeared.

'That's Clifford Giles, the manager,' Rhodri nodded in their direction. 'The other two are engineers.'

Whatever they were about to say was not good news. They were looking grim. I turned away and studied the maps once more.

'Men,' Giles had no need to raise his voice the room was so silent. 'Men,' he repeated, gulped and went on. 'The fall is from three gate onwards.'

There was an immediate outcry and Rhodri, standing next to me, shook his head and looked down at the floor.

'How bad is that?' I asked.

'Pretty bad. We don't know how far the fall extends nor what caused it. If it was a backfall, one behind them, sealing them in, then it may only be a short distance. On the other hand it could stretch all the way to the face.'

'What does that mean?' I asked.

'It means . . .' Tears sprang to his eyes, 'that they're all dead.'

'Is there no hope?'

'How the hell should I know?' he spoke harshly. 'We live in hope all the time. Every day we go down that stinking hole we hope to finish the shift. To get out alive. Men could be trapped in any one of a dozen places and still be living for now. But let me tell you something, boyo, they are very aware of the water seeping in. They are also aware of the air running out if they're trapped in a gob.' His shoulders slumped, the fight going out of him.

By this time the men were getting organised, putting on helmets, checking safety lamps, collecting picks and shovels.

'Are you coming?' Rhodri asked.

I shook my head, my thoughts elsewhere.

'Coward,' he said in disgust and stalked off. I watched as the men filed out and along a passage to the pit head. I heard the winding gear jerk loudly and the machinery begin operating. Still I stood and studied the map, tracing the roadways and the ventilation shafts. More men began to come in from other mines. I grabbed one by the arm.

'Tell me something,' I said, ignoring his puzzled look at my suit and tie. 'How wide is a ventilation shaft?'

'How wide?' he repeated. 'Depends, look you. As narrow as a bore hole, say six inches, to a downcast and pumping shaft. Say three feet.'

'This one, how wide is it?' I pointed.

He shrugged. 'I can't say. I don't know this mine but it looks like a downcast and pumping shaft so I'd guess anything from three to perhaps four feet.'

'So that's a way down?' I asked excitedly.

He gave me a pitying look. 'Don't talk daft man. How do you go down a thousand feet? You need the winding gear.' He walked away.

True, my knowledge of mining was limited and I didn't know enough to work out what to do. But I also didn't have the blinkered approach they had. I was used to looking at a problem from different angles. If the scale of the disaster was as bad as they feared then it would take a month of Sundays to dig out the collapsed tunnel.

My ignorance also allowed me to think of a different solution. Uncle William could tell me what I needed to know without either patronising me or treating me like a complete idiot.

I went outside. There was now some semblance of order and people had resigned themselves to waiting.

I found Uncle William next to the fence, a little apart from the main throng.

'What's happening?' he asked, worry and fear etched deeply into his face.

I shook my head. 'I don't know. They've gone down to begin digging. It appears to be one hell of a problem. There could be hundreds of yards of collapsed tunnels. How in God's name can such a thing happen?'

'An explosion caused by firedamp,' he suggested.

I nodded. Ventilation was a constant problem in the mines. Fresh air was critical for safety. The mines produced methane and as little as five percent mixed with air could result in an explosion.

'If they've stretched the longwall too far,' he continued, 'and hit a fault then there could be a partial collapse that has transmitted along the whole wall and brought the lot down. They use sprags to prop the wall up until they're ready to collapse the lot.'

'What's a sprag?'

'A short wooden prop. The miner digs a deep slot at seam level as much as six or even eight feet into the coal. He lies on his side digging with his pick. It's called holing out. The sprags prop up the seam until they're ready to collapse the lot, often with explosives. When the area is abandoned, the explosion does its work and they go back in to get the coal out. In this place they use what they call an endless rope system. Full trolleys one way, empty trolleys the other.'

Uncle William paused for a second, tears in his eyes. 'The men may be safe in one of the gobs. That's what we're all hoping for. That's what all these men, women and children,' he gestured around him, 'are praying for. The problem is, if the cut was long and hit a fault something could have set off a relatively small explosion, say firedamp going up, and that's ruptured along the seam. A small accident quickly becomes a nightmare. Do you know where Britain's worst mining disaster took place?'

I shook my head.

'Thirteen years ago at Senghenydd. Four hundred and thirty-nine miners died. An explosion followed by a major collapse.'

Senghenydd was down the valley, a mile or two from Pontypridd.

'That means it's the same coalfield. A fault ten miles away could be duplicated here. That's common. Everyone here knows it. Which is why I suspect they're going to go in along the road.'

'I still don't understand.'

'They think the men are dead and they want to save the mine.'

The callousness of it appalled me. 'What about air into the mine?'

He shrugged. 'Depends on the distance from the winding gear where the main shaft is located. The main vent is half a mile up the valley.'

'Look, supposing there are still men alive at the face. I understood from looking at the map that they are in a large mine area. A gob. What if the collapsed wall was behind them?'

'It's not very likely,' William said dubiously.

'Uncle, it may not be likely, but is it possible?'

He stroked the side of his chin, deep in thought. 'I guess so. But what good will that do? There's no way to get down.'

'Yes, there is. Down the ventilation shaft.'

'But that's a thousand feet,' he protested.

'I know, so everyone keeps telling me. Look, where's the damn shaft?'

'Walk straight past the yards and keep going. You'll come to a tall brick building. Like a square chimney about fifty feet high. It sits over the shaft and houses the fan.'

'A fan? I thought the vents were just holes in the ground.'

'There are some bore holes. At the bottom of them are iron baskets where coal is burnt. It's called an upcast and the heat makes the bad air rise. Next to it is a down-cast and fresh air is sucked in. But they aren't much use further along the underground roadway. You need a proper ventilation system. In the ventilation shaft chimney a giant fan sucks the bad air out and forces fresh air down.'

'I've got this idea. What if there are men trapped at the end? Right down by the ventilation shaft. Isn't there some way we could get them up?'

William looked sadly at me and shook his head. 'If they are there they need the fan on, to keep the firedamp down at less than five percent. Not only is there a risk of an explosion with firedamp but it eventually chokes you to death as the air turns bad.'

'How long will they last? How long do they have to get through from the main shaft?'

'Depends.'

'Damn it, Uncle William. Depends on what?'

'The water level. This is a wet mine. It's now operating way below the water table and the river Taff. If certain pumps have been put out of action then it'll flood in a day or two.'

'What does that mean? They get wet feet or wet knees?'

'They get wet heads,' he said. 'They'll be dead.'

'Then it has to be worth while looking to see if we can get down the air shaft.'

He thought about it for a moment and said, 'You might be right. The only problem is, the men are now working to save the pit. They must get the water pumps back in action before the lower levels are flooded. Otherwise the mine could be lost forever. It's been a lot of years since I worked here but nothing much has changed. See that building over there?' He pointed to a low brick structure a hundred yards away.

'Yes.'

'It houses all kinds of tools and equipment. See if you can find wire cutters and a couple of safety helmets. I'll meet you further along the fence. Near the main ventilation shaft. You can cut the wire and let me in. I'll come with you.'

'Are you sure?' I asked, aware of his age and lack of strength.

'No, I'm not sure,' he said with some asperity, 'but you need someone with you who has an inkling of how things work. If you want to know, I helped to install a similar ventilation system at Bedwas colliery half a life time ago.'

I nodded, grateful for his offer, and quickly crossed the rough ground to the door of the building. It was wide open and a few men were entering and leaving, carrying various tools and pieces of equipment with them. If anybody was curious as to why I was there and who I was, nobody said. They were too preoccupied to bother with me. As William said, I found safety helmets, wire cutters and Davy safety lamps. I checked the spirit level in the bottom of the lamps, found two that were reasonably full, grabbed what else I needed and rushed out.

The ground underfoot became rougher the further along I went. Soon I could see the tall, chimney-like building. I estimated it was fifteen feet square and sixty feet high. I found Uncle William standing next to the fence and quickly cut through the strands of wire. He stepped through and we hurried across to the door. There we paused while I lit the two Davy lamps. Designed principally to detect firedamp, the light they gave was poor, but it was better than nothing. The door was unlocked and I pushed it open.

The noise inside was tremendous. The system was driven by a steam engine automatically fed through a coal hopper at one end. As the piston pumped back and forth it turned a huge backward-bladed centrifugal fan about twenty-five feet in diameter. The copper legend on the side proudly proclaimed it a Waddle Patent Fan made in Manchester. The guarantee written underneath said that the fan moved 200,000 cubic feet of air through a mine every minute.

My uncle pointed and I followed his finger. A belt drove the fan which sat at the top of the ventilation shaft and turned horizontally. The blades were twisted, sucking the air up the shaft from below. Another shaft allowed fresh air to be drawn, replacing the bad air sucked out. The fan was turning very slowly.

I pointed at the door and we went back outside. 'Is that its normal speed?'

'No. At full speed you can't see the blades. But then air is sucked into the pit from other openings. It's moving slowly because other exits are blocked. At that speed the downshaft keeps the area immediately beneath the shaft fully ventilated. It's just as I thought. The same as Bedwas.'

'Can I get down there?'

'Down the shaft?' He frowned when I nodded. 'In theory. But how?'

'If one man is still alive down there then we have to try and get to him.'

'But the air, even at that speed,' he spoke slowly, voicing his doubts. 'The blast will smash you back and forth against the side of the shaft.'

'How wide is it? Three feet in diameter? What happens if we shut down the fan for a few minutes?'

'If there are men still alive at the bottom the air will go bad in ten, maybe twenty minutes. The methane build-up in this colliery is bad. Really bad. That's why the ventilation system is so good.'

'I have an idea.' I explained my plan. Reluctantly he nodded.

4

WE WENT BACK to the pit head. It was eerie, looking at the silent, strained faces of the people. The vicar had appeared and he began saying a prayer, loudly beseeching God's help.

Uncle William spoke to a few people, all women. Some shook their heads, others nodded. Reluctantly, in dribs and drabs, a small group of them walked over to where I was standing.

'Mr Griffiths said that you have an idea. That it might work,' said one harsh voice, raw with emotion. 'Who are you, anyway? You in your fancy clothes. Why are you helping us?'

'Because I'm from here. This was my village too,' I replied.

'You're not local,' said a woman, who looked to be about my age. 'I'd know you.'

'Well, I know you, Beth Thomas. Cliff's younger sister.'

She gasped. 'Who are you, then?'

'David . . . Dai Griffiths.'

There was another gasp and a few more sharp intakes of breaths. 'Dai Griffiths? Evan and Meg's boy?'

'That's right! Now, can we get on? We're wasting time.'

There were murmurs of assent. 'Tell us what you want us to do,' said an old man on the edge of the crowd.

I explained my idea, elaborating on whatever Uncle William had said. 'Do you understand?'

There was a chorus of agreement and we got to work. There were eight woman and three old men. The woman ranged in age from early twenties, I guessed, to around fifty. Compared to the women of the same age that I knew, these looked at least ten years older. They lived a hard life and I thanked my lucky stars we had emigrated to America when we did. Mam was still a handsome woman, unlike her neighbours of old.

Taking three of them with me, we raided the equipment store and tottered outside with our haul. Uncle William and one of the other men had gone in another direction. A short while later they reappeared driving one of the coal dumpers, a smaller version of a farmer's tractor, used to pull single trucks of coal down to the wash rooms. There the dirty coal was washed out by the river Taff. Which was why the river was a stinking cesspool of black running water inhabited only by rats.

Although the rope and chain of the winding gear had long been replaced with steel wire, there was still a huge requirement around the mine for rope of different length and thickness. Stacked in a corner of the shed were rolls of one inch hemp. The Dundee manufacturer's label guaranteed a breaking strain of three tons and was six hundred feet long. The rope was wrapped around a wooden spindle with a hole through it. I grabbed a crowbar, shoved it through the hole and leant backwards, dragging the reel over onto its edges. While that one was being rolled out I pulled a second over. We heaved them into the back of the truck towed behind the tractor and trundled towards the ventilation shaft.

We had to get down to the bottom of the pit, fast. If there was anybody down there, we needed to get them out quickly. What if there were a number of men trapped? Carbon monoxide was one of the gases that seeped out of the coal. It was odourless but deadly. That was assuming the firedamp didn't kill them first.

Inside the ventilation chimney a metal ladder was fixed vertically to the wall. I climbed it, trailing a length of rope behind me. When I reached the roof I straddled a beam and hauled up the end of the rope. Tied to it were a snatch block, a six feet length of chain and a heavy duty clump block. I wrapped the snatch block around the beam and fed it onto the chain, fixing it in place. It hung down with the clump block dangling underneath the beam and above the ventilation shaft. Feeding the rope through the clump block, I climbed back down to the ground, pulling the rope with me. In the meantime Uncle William and one of the other men had spliced two ropes together. We now had twelve hundred feet of rope.

Another snatch block had been fixed at the door and the rope was passed through it and out to the tractor. At ten feet intervals short lengths of half inch sisal rope had been tied to the hemp and the ends had been made into a loop using a bowline. Ten of them were tied on. The bowline loop fitted over my shoulders.

'Ready?' Uncle William asked me.

I nodded, dry mouthed with fear. I hated the thought of being underground.

'We're agreed on the signals?' asked Beth.

I nodded again, cleared my throat. 'Yes. Let's get going.'

We had to move fast. I needed to give certain signals to tell them when to stop lifting or lowering. So we were running a length of bailing string, thin, tough and light. My end was tied to my left wrist.

I gave the signal and the message was relayed by four people to the tractor. The tractor moved forward and I was lifted into the air, the rope jammed under my shoulders. I hung over the down shaft, alongside the turning blades of the fan. One of the men operated the controls of the steam piston pump and it came to a halt. The whirling blades stopped and the huge volume of air being sucked down the shaft ceased flowing. Quickly the order was passed and I was lowered slowly down the shaft. As soon as my feet were inside the speed of descent was increased. I had a Davy lamp strapped to

my waist and the faint light gleamed off the side of the
tin lining the shaft. Time was of the essence. If there
were men below I needed to get to them before the gases
built up to a dangerous level. Yet we had to stop the
pump because the power of the air being sucked into
the shaft would have battered me against the sides. If I
continued my descent at the speed I was going and hit
the bottom of the mine, I would either sprain my ankles
or, if I was unlucky, break a leg or two. We were working
to fine tolerances. The distance between the bottom of
the shaft and the mine floor was ten feet. However, we
had taken every precaution we could. The rope had been
measured and marked every one hundred feet. When the
nine hundred feet marker was showing at the top they
would slow the tractor down. I was moving at about two
feet a second but not in a smooth comfortable ride. The
tractor slowed, picked up speed, jerked and braked as
the driver drove towards the tower. The rope was digging
into my armpits, the air was becoming heavier and I
was sweating and fearful. I lost track of the time I
dangled there but then I realised that I was moving more
slowly. I heard voices and looked down. It was pitch
black. I yelled.

'Anyone below? Hey, down there!'

A voice came booming up the shaft. 'What's
happening?'

'I'm coming down to get you out. Stand clear.' Relief
flooded through me. There were men alive down there!

I realised that I was finally out of the shaft and gave
a tug on the signalling line. Immediately I stopped being
lowered and hung, twisting in the air, surrounded by
blackness with only the faint light of my lamp showing.
I gave another single tug and moved very slowly down.
As I did I became aware of being surrounded by men.
My eyes, now accustomed to the dark, opened wider in
disbelief at the sea of blackened faces that looked back
at me. My feet hit the ground and I gave a double tug.

The rope stopped and I stood there, the rope snaking around my feet.

'Who the hell are you?' asked a burly miner.

'That can wait.' I reached up and gave four distinct pulls on the rope, the signal was repeated and almost immediately there was movement in the air as the fan started. The rope bucked like a writhing snake, proof if it was needed, that it would have been dangerous to have attempted the descent with the fan in operation.

There was a sigh of relief and a voice said, 'Thank God for that. Another five minutes and I reckon we'd have been in trouble from the firedamp.'

'Who are you, man?' another miner asked. 'I've never seen you before.'

'My name is David Griffiths. Look, we need to get you out of here. How many of you are there?'

'A hundred and forty-eight. I'm Llewelyn Thomas. I'm the fireman for this area.' That made him responsible for safety in this section of the mine.

Somebody shouldered his way through the crowd. 'Dai? Bloody hell, it is you!'

I looked at the haggard and lined face before me and realised it was Cliff, my childhood friend. He had aged a great deal since I last saw him, what . . . fifteen, sixteen years earlier?

'*Noswaith dda*, Cliff,' I said in Welsh. 'It seems I'm always having to get you out of one scrape or another.' There was a swell of laughter, a release of tension.

'Good evening, Dai,' said Cliff, holding out his hand. We shook warmly. 'I won't ask what you're doing here. You can tell me in the Wheatsheaf. We didn't expect anyone to come down the ventilation shaft, I can tell you. When the fan stopped we thought it was all over for us. The firedamp and the carbon monoxide builds up fast in this part of the pit.'

'I know. The fan is on for ten minutes and will then stop. We need to be ready to send you up. Ten men at a time. See here.' I lifted up the rope and shone my lamp on it. 'You stand in this strop and hold tight. The ride up will be fast. Anybody injured who cannot hold on goes up in the bight in the end. Is there anybody hurt?'

'Aye,' said Cliff. 'At least ten who won't be able to stand. This is going to take hours.'

'Well if you've anywhere to go, don't let me keep you.' My smile took the sting out of my words.

'Are they coming through the main roadway?' somebody asked.

'How far along can you go from here?' I asked.

'About half way to the next gob,' answered Thomas.

I tried to remember the map of the mine and let out a heavy sigh. 'That means there's at least half a mile of tunnel down,' I said.

The men were stunned.

'Look, we can talk about it while we get ready. Get ten of the men lined up here. As the rope travels up the first man puts his foot in the loop. When the last man is clear I'll give the signal and they'll speed up the tow. When the men are clear at the top they'll send the rope back down. The fan will operate when there are no men in the shaft.'

Just then the air stopped circulating.

'Right,' said Thomas. 'You men get ready. Bring Saul. He's got a broken leg and an injured arm. He goes on the end.' Used to discipline and obeying orders, quickly the men stood in line. The rope was passed along and each stood with a foot in a strop. The man Saul was carried over and the bowline passed around his shoulders. He was conscious but in obvious pain. 'What about you?' Thomas asked me. 'Aren't you going?'

'In a while,' I replied. 'Anyway, I know the signals.' I gave a pull on the bailing string and the rope started to ascend. The first man rose slowly out of sight. Within a minute and a half the last man, Saul, was raised, moaning, from the ground and I gave three sharp pulls. We watched him accelerate away. I heaved a sigh of relief. So far, so good.

'If they don't open up the mine soon then we could lose it,' said Thomas. 'And if half a mile of tunnel has collapsed they'll never get to the next gob in time.'

'How many men are likely to be there?' I asked.

'I don't know. Fifty or sixty. The gobs tend to survive a fall, the damage being down in the tunnels.'

'What about air at the other gob?' I asked.

'Bore holes only. The circulation caused by this fan sucks the air down the bore holes and along the main shaft. Also, the air isn't as bad back there. Not so much firedamp in the coal.'

'If we get more of the men away and get some room down here, can we start tunnelling back along to the next gob?' I asked.

'No,' was the short reply. 'We need proper gear, including chocks and sprags for support. Some of the pillars have collapsed, which is why we had this disaster in the first place.'

I coughed. Already the air was becoming stale, the smell peculiar to a coal mine catching at the back of my throat. I wiped sweat from my brow and took off my coat. My pristine white shirt was turning black before my eyes.

'The next group of men up sorts the gear we need and sends it back down on the rope, tied off at each strop,' I said. 'In the meantime we get organised and start digging into the tunnel.'

I could see them hesitate. They were brave men but they'd been through a great deal already. Now rescue was staring them in the face and I was asking them to risk their lives by tunnelling along a collapsed seam.

It was the fireman, Thomas, who carried the day. 'You're right! We've got picks and shovels and a few sprags. We go in low, on our bellies. Tell them to drop more sprags down. We'll get started.' He gave a hacking cough, the thickening air getting to him and some of the others. There was a slight draft and then the air began to circulate again and we could breathe properly once more.

Seconds later the rope appeared, the end coiling on the floor. One of the men grabbed the end and passed it out. It bucked in his hands. Another ten men got ready and another injured man had the bowline placed around him. Ten minutes later the rope stopped jerking, the fan stopped and I gave the signal. The men slowly ascended the shaft and as the last man left the ground I gave three sharp tugs and watched as he accelerated out of sight. This time it took a few minutes longer to get the air back on and when it did start again we took in deep lung fulls, cleaning the carbon monoxide and firedamp out of our bodies.

We stood clear of the bottom of the shaft and waited. The rope appeared and a few minutes later it rained sprags. Luckily none of them connected with anyone's skull or they would be dead. After a few minutes they stopped falling and we were able to collect them and pass the supports along to the tunnel. This time the fan ran for fifteen minutes before it stopped. Another eleven men passed safely out of the mine. I stood with the bailing string in my hand sending the signals back and forth. I was dog tired, scared half to death and feeling increasingly claustrophobic. I vowed I would never go down another mine as long as I lived.

I thought of Madelaine and Richard. An image of my mother came to mind followed by Susan, my daughter, who was now sixteen. My mind wandered and memories flooded in. Before I left London Madelaine and I had been arguing about Richard's future education. John Buchanan was adamant that the friendships Richard made at the 'right school' would stand him in good stead all his life. I pointed out that I hadn't needed such connections. Was I wrong? I brought my thoughts back to the present with a start.

Now that thirty three men had gone up the shaft the

air lasted longer and there was more room to move. I learned that there had been a warning of sorts when the tunnel had collapsed and many of the men had been able to run into the gob along the roadway. How it had started no one knew but it seemed that one of the pillars had collapsed.

Cliff came over to speak to me. '*Diolchiadau*,' he said. 'From all of us.'

'My pleasure. How's it going back there with the tunnelling?'

'No problems, look you. It's loose coal. That has its own dangers but with the sprags we can get in quickly. There have been three open areas so the collapse isn't solid. If there's anybody left alive we'll get them.'

'Good.' The air started circulating again and the rope appeared. Another load of sprags rained down and we collected them and passed them over to the men who were worming their way through the tunnel.

Another hour passed. Another two loads of men were sent aloft. Sixty six men had gone so far. There was a shout from the tunnel and the message came back that they had broken through to the other gob. Men were there, still alive.

Soon the gob we stood in began to fill up again. Fifty seven miners came worming their way through the tunnel, exhausted, hardly able to stand, some with injuries ranging from sprained wrists to a broken leg. There were also five bodies.

The laborious process continued slowly. Men went up the shaft until there were only eight of us left standing. Finally, I too, went back up the shaft standing in a loop, my arm wrapped around the rope. When I reached the surface I was surprised to find that a new day had dawned.

Exhausted I climbed onto the edge of the shaft and was helped down. One of the woman, tears on her cheeks hugged me. I nodded my appreciation.

Uncle William came over and took my hand. 'Well done, my boy, well done.'

'Any luck at the main shaft?'

'They've got some men out. They reached the first gob and are half way to the second. So far they've recovered a dozen bodies, maybe more. The last I heard was they've hit a real bad patch of tunnel and been forced to slow down.'

'How many are still missing?' I asked.

'Fifteen,' was the reply.

'There are still five bodies at the bottom of this shaft,' I said.

'I know. They're going down for them.'

Cliff joined us. He looked like an old man, a hacking cough catching in his throat. 'We're going to send gear down the ventilation shaft and start working the tunnel from this end. A complete clean out. It's possible, if they can get the pumps working again soon, the mine can be saved. The water will stay away for about another day. After that it'll be too late. The old sough can't take any more.'

The sough, I knew, was the old drainage tunnel which connected the mine workings with the Taff. It had been keeping the water down but it wasn't enough. Without the pumps the pit would flood and it would never recover. The mine would be abandoned because it would be too expensive to reopen.

'You're going, Cliff?' I asked.

'After I get a few hours sleep. Dai,' he looked embarrassed, 'I don't know what to say.' He choked on the last word. 'If it hadn't been for you . . .'

'Forget it. I happened to be in the right place at the right time. And I had a good deal of help, otherwise we couldn't have managed.' I indicated my uncle and the others still standing around the outside of the ventilation building. They were dazed with fatigue, half asleep, wanting to leave but, at the same time, afraid to go. I helped them to make up their minds.

'Go home, all of you,' I spoke loudly. 'There's nothing

more we can do. Get some rest. You've got a mine to save after you get some sleep.'

Somebody called, 'Three cheers for Dai Griffiths. Hip, hip . . .'

Embarrassed and hearing the cheers through a fog of tiredness myself, I led the way towards the main gate. I needed sleep and a large whisky and not necessarily in that order. I was stopped at the gate by Dafydd. He was as white as a sheet and appeared to have been crying.

'What's up?' I asked.

'It's Huw. He's dead.' Tears filled his eyes.

It took me a few seconds to realise who he meant. 'Huw? Your brother?'

'Who else?' he asked harshly.

'Sorry, Dafydd. I'm not thinking straight.' I shook my head, sadly. 'Was he married?'

'Yes. Christ, Dai, you know so little about us. Why don't you go away again and not come back?'

'Wait a moment, Dafydd,' said Uncle William, 'if it wasn't for David we wouldn't have two hundred men on the surface right now. Men who will make the difference as to whether or not the pit survives.'

'Maybe,' retorted my cousin, 'but he's still not welcome. We'd have got to the men along the main roadway in another day or two. Sod off, Dai,' he looked at me, 'back to London.'

I nodded as though agreeing with him and turned away.

'Come on, David,' said Uncle William, sadness deep in his eyes. 'I'm glad Mair and Huw aren't alive to see this day. It's time we went home.'

I followed him out of the pit and up the road. We reached the main Pontypridd to Merthyr Tydfil road and trudged towards the car. We passed the mean, drab houses lining the street. I knew exactly what each one was like inside. I had lived in one until I was ten. Then we'd gone to America. The memories washed over me. I knew I couldn't return to Cardiff just yet.

'Wait for me in the car, Uncle, please. I must go and pay my respects.'

He nodded, understanding fully. I turned to the left and went up past the next and then the next row of houses. The road was steep but flattened out at the top. At the end was the chapel. I went into the graveyard and quickly found the headstone.

Dearly Beloved
Sian
Daughter of
Evan and Megan Griffiths
Born 29th July 1882
died tragically 14th October 1890

Suffer the little children to come unto me.

I stood with my head bowed, a lump in my throat. Sian's death changed our family's destiny. I could still see her and, by a quirk of memory, it seemed to me that I could still hear her, calling, laughing.

Her grave was still being tended by some kind person though I doubted it was Lewis Lewis, the old man who used to look after her headstone. He had to be long dead by now.

'Well, little sister,' I whispered, 'here I am again. It's been a long time since I spoke to you.' Tiredness and the emotion of the last twenty four hours brought tears to my eyes. 'It's time I brought you up to date on what's been happening. You know Da's dead of course, because he's with you right now. Mam married John. You never knew him. He's a great chap. He does wonders for Mam, though she misses Da dreadfully. For years John has been smoothing the path for us, quietly working away in the background. He has done it out of friendship for us all and love of Mam. It wasn't until Da died that he declared his love for her and asked for my blessing. It had all come as a shock but in the end I was happy for him to marry Mam, Sian, provided it was what she wanted as well. I needn't have worried. Mam was the first to admit that she was the most fortunate of women to have married, loved and been loved by two men. Particularly men like Da and John Buchanan. In other ways, Mam says that the price we've paid for our success is too great. But is it really? Oh, I don't mean with you leaving us too soon. That was always a price too much. But look around you. Look at the lives of the people here. Poverty, hard work and an early death is all that there is for most of them.' Light headed from weariness I rambled on, caught up in my own memories. Finally, I swallowed the lump in my throat, finished all my news and stood to go.

At the edge of the graveyard I looked out over the valley. The winding gear was a mile away, dominating the landscape. I looked down at the skeleton of the school. The rain that summer of 1890 had been almost without end, causing the slag heap to wash down like a black tide of death onto the village school. I remembered the sound of the children singing. Of seeing Sion and looking frantically for Sian. I remembered the day a million tears had been shed.

I looked back at her grave, my eyes misting over before I walked away.

5

THE MEETING WAS postponed and I spent the period in and around Cardiff. This was not the time to confront the miners of South Wales. The Llanbeddas pit was saved, opened and operational again. Two more men had been found alive. Eighteen had died and thirty six had been injured, five seriously. The remainder were expected to recover fully. The *South Wales Echo* made a fuss about my involvement and made me out to be some sort of hero. I found it highly embarrassing and tried to play down my part. Some of the people in Llanbeddas helped stoke the fuss and I was under the spotlight for a couple of days. Much was made of my background and my father winning the American Presidential election only to have the cup of success dashed from his lips in such a tragic manner. Naturally, much was written about our wealth and eventually unkind comparisons were drawn between my lifestyle and that of the people of Llanbeddas and other mining villages across South Wales. As a result, any goodwill I may have engendered quickly dissipated.

The Prime Minister sent a telegram congratulating me in one sentence and reminding me why I was there in the next. It was a week before I travelled up the valley again. This time, a meeting was called in Pontypridd's Town Hall. On the agenda were proposals for the future of the mining industry in South Wales in particular but also in the rest of Britain in general. I was expecting a stormy reception. The hall was packed with miners. The meeting was being held on a Saturday to allow as many men as possible to attend. They had travelled from all over the valleys, from as far east as Cwmbran, Neath and Glyn Neath in the west and north west, and Merthyr Tydfil and Tredegar in the north. Not only miners appeared but shopkeepers and other small business owners. If a mine closed the whole valley died and that would be disastrous for thousands of people. Only those men with union cards were allowed into the hall. The remainder stayed outside, packing the streets. I estimated at least two, perhaps three thousand had arrived and only three hundred of them were in the hall. This had not been the way that we had hoped to negotiate a deal with the miners but it was all I was being offered. A public meeting or an all out strike. My aim was to avoid the latter while at the same time agreeing a financial and working package that would save the industry, preserve as many jobs as possible and at the same time, most importantly, save the government's face. My problem was, I could see both sides of the argument.

Chairs and a table had been set up on a stage. There were five of us, myself and four union representatives. It would be, as I expected, a one-sided argument. Gradually, the men fell silent until all that was to be heard was the shuffling of feet and the coughing of a miner as he cleared his lungs. Watching that sea of faces I saw basic similarities. Not in their features but in their expressions. Many wore a white scarf around their necks and a flat cap on their heads. There were no smoking signs around the walls but the men ignored them and most of them were rolling their own cigarettes. Their eyes were hard, antagonistic, a lifetime of brutality mirrored in them. Yet I knew these men for something more. I had been born and brought up amongst them, at least for my first ten years. I knew that they represented communities of great compassion and love. Life might be hard – was hard – but they loved and nurtured their families above all else. They had stayed. Men like my cousins and their wives and their children. And we had left. We had abandoned them. I was startled by my thoughts. The tentacles of the life I had left behind all those years ago reached out now, wrapped themselves around me and dragged me back. These people, my people, needed help. And I could give it to them. If they would only listen. What could I do? Invest in some other industry? Bring other employment to South Wales? The thought took root and I became excited by the idea. If a pit had to close then perhaps there was something else that I could do after all. With all the resources I had available . . .

'Order, order,' shouted the union boss, Colin Lewis, standing up and addressing a now totally silent audience. 'Let's get started.'

'That's why we're here,' said some wag in the audience. There were a few chuckles.

'Right! You all know that we are here to talk about the offer we have had from the government. Whether we accept an increase in work as well as a cut in pay.'

He got no further. There were yells of outrage from the men and minutes passed before he could be heard again. Finally, Lewis' voice rose above the hecklers. 'Now, it's no good going on like that, look you! If you can't or won't listen then we will have to have this meeting in private. Or you can sit there and listen to what is said. What's it to be?'

Silence reigned once more.

'Most of you know the men up here but for those of you who don't let me introduce them. On my right is Mr Cook of the Miners' Federation. He has said of this offer, "not a penny off the pay, not a minute on the day".' There were cheers and I glanced at Cook to see an irritated look flash across his face. I suspected he did not like having his thunder stolen but his quote was often repeated in the newspapers. 'Next to him is Dafydd Griffiths, the union representative for Llanbeddas colliery. He's known to many of you . . .' there were more cheers. The third man who was introduced said nothing throughout the meeting and was greeted by no more than a half-hearted cheer. I forgot his name as soon as it was announced.

'On this side is Sir David Griffiths.' There were a few isolated cheers. 'He's known to many of you as he comes from Llanbeddas. Some of you will even remember his father, Evan.' That was a jolt. I hadn't expected my father's name to be mentioned. What would he think about all this? About my role? I shook the thought away. We had left Wales precisely because he had wanted a better life for us and he had been strong enough to go and carve one in America. Mam too, for without her we wouldn't have succeeded as well as we had done. 'Now, you all know what he did for us at the mine last week. He helped to save a few lives,' the understatement was greeted in silence, 'but that doesn't give him the right to dictate to us what we do in the future.' Lewis' words were greeted with a roar of approval. In a week I had gone from being the local hero to 'helping to save a few lives'. Anger bubbled up. I hadn't expected any medals but at least, if they were going to mention my help, they should do so honestly. My sympathy for the miners was starting to wane.

The entire meeting was a disaster. Cook was cheered to the rafters when he threatened a strike and I was booed when I tried to explain the economic realities of the pits. Cook lied about the prospects for coal mining throughout Britain and especially for the collieries of South Wales. When I explained that two thirds of pits lost money I was greeted with yells of, 'Liar!' and when I spoke about the huge losses per ton of coal I was shouted down. Many of the men in the hall knew I wasn't lying. The figures had been quoted often enough in the papers and had been debated between the unions and the mine owners for months. Sent down to Wales to try and explain the harsh facts in a way that was acceptable to the miners, I was failing miserably.

Sick of the boos and catcalls, I stood at the front of the stage with my arms crossed. I watched them, my eyes sweeping across the audience, holding the looks of individuals until the noise abated. Gradually the hall fell silent.

'Now listen to me,' I said loudly. 'I was asked to come here to explain what will happen if we can't agree a settlement.'

'Sent, more like, David Griffiths,' a voice called from the packed hall. 'We'll go back and tell your masters we aren't giving in. We don't accept their offer.' Yells of encouragement followed. Despair washed over me. I was wasting my time. I glanced at Cook and saw the self satisfied look on his face. That made me angry.

'For God's sake and your own, listen to me,' I yelled. I strode across the stage and pointed at a few faces, calling their names. When they were quiet I continued, 'This country simply cannot afford to keep subsidising your jobs. The money doesn't exist.'

'Yes, it does! You've got enough, according to the *Echo*. We'll have some of yours.' There was laughter and jeers.

'You must know men,' I tried again, 'that the price of coal has almost halved in the last five years.'

'Stop the imports, then,' somebody called.

'It's not as simple as that,' I began, but was drowned out again by voices. I let them finish and continued. 'The coal industry is now international. America, Germany and Poland produce more coal per man than Britain.' The jeering got louder. I waited for the noise to stop. 'Our pits have to be modernised. They could be profitable . . .'

'Take away our jobs, you mean,' a voice called out.

'No!' I said angrily. 'I mean that we save jobs by mechanisation. We have more ponies per man in the pits than anywhere else in the world. One pony for every twenty-five men. In America it's as low as one in sixty. In Germany . . .'

'This isn't Germany or America,' a man shouted. 'This

is Wales. We keep our jobs, our money and our hours!'
There were loud cheers and the meeting fell apart
completely. Attempts to restore order were futile. They
wouldn't have listened in any case. I turned my back to
the hall and looked into Cook's smirking face. It took
will power not to put my fist into it. I knew something
the miners didn't; the fighting fund they had been
contributing to was controlled by Cook and his men. The
union leaders would not be facing hardship this summer
if a strike was called, though the miners would.

The meeting broke up and the men went out to tell the
miners thronging the streets. There were loud cheers. The
fools! Didn't they realise that only further hardship and
poverty lay before them? I knew the government. They
would not, could not, give in this time. Despondently I
turned to go, to find Dafydd standing in front of me. His
words surprised me.

'I'm sorry you had such a hard time of it.' He held out
his hand.

I took it and we shook. 'You know this will lead to
trouble, don't you?' I asked.

He shrugged. 'We eat and breathe trouble. Along with
poverty and hardship. Especially for anyone who's hurt
or loses his job. We're fighting for justice, David.' The
set of his jaw, the intransigence in his eyes told me I was
wasting my time but I tried anyway.

'Dafydd, the government doesn't wish to see you out
of a job. Any of you.'

'Rubbish! That's exactly . . .'

I interrupted him. 'Wait a moment, will you? What's
the advantage to the government if you can't work? If we
cannot, as a nation, produce coal to compete in the world?
The government exists on taxes. It needs people working.
Everybody. Right now there's talk of a world-wide slump.
If that happens, what then?'

He looked uncomfortable for a moment and then said
angrily, 'The hard earned concessions we fought for

during the war are being taken away from us. We're fighting for what's ours.'

'Look!' I interrupted. 'Don't talk to me about fighting. I've fought for my businesses and companies all my working life. So did my father. So does my brother, Sion. We don't strike and make demands. We sort the problems, find the solutions. Nobody pays us if we don't work. We don't have a fund to fall back on to pay our bills.'

'You don't need one,' he said, the bitterness ingrained in his voice. 'You're one of them, keeping the working man down. Grinding our faces into the poverty . . .'

'Shut up!' I said savagely. 'You know that's not true. We dragged ourselves up by the bootstraps, like Uncle William. Your father chose to stay in Llanbeddas that was all. Nobody forced you down the pit. You chose it.'

'It was expected of me,' anguish broke through his voice. 'My father expected me to join him. Not at the top, not by becoming an engineer but at the coal face. Do you think I wanted it? It was a . . . a great honour to follow in my father's footsteps. To have the privilege of working at the face. With the men.' He coughed, his agitation upsetting him, his handkerchief the recipient of the filth he spat up.

All at once I felt sorry for him, though he would neither welcome nor appreciate pity. They were immensely proud men. I knew then that I was wasting my time.

'All right, Dafydd, but mark my words. No good will come of a strike. Cook says there will be national support. Well, I can tell you there won't be.'

'What are you talking about, man? Of course there will be. Arthur's already got pledges from the other unions. The big three will come out behind us.' If the dockers, transport and steel unions came out on strike then effectively a general strike was in force and anything could happen.

'You might get a week or two's support and then they'll go back.'

'How can you know?' he asked contemptuously. 'I'm telling you what Arthur told me last night.'

'Cook's lying. How I know is not relevant. Just believe me. You'll be isolated within days. At most a couple of weeks. Once you are then God alone knows what will happen.'

'I don't believe you,' he turned away, our conversation at an end.

'Hard luck!' Cook called to me as I turned to leave. I ignored him. 'The best man won.'

Turning my head I gave him a look of contempt. It was totally wasted.

Outside the day had turned windy and rain threatened. I walked down to the river Taff and stood on the bridge, looking down at the filthy water. On the other side of the bridge was a well laid out park, a gift from the mine owners of the valley. I heard footsteps and felt a presence alongside me.

'Don't take it to heart, David,' said my uncle. 'The outcome was inevitable.'

I looked at him. 'God help them, Uncle William.'

He nodded. 'There's nothing you can do about it, now, *bach*. No one can say you didn't try.'

'You might be right.' Standing on the bridge, looking at the park, an idea had been forming. 'When we came through Taff's Well and followed the road up the valley, we passed a lot of empty land. Who does it belong to?'

He looked surprised. 'I don't know but we could easily find out. Why?'

'What if I bought it and opened a factory or two. Could we find alternative employment for some of the men?'

He laughed. 'David,' he said, regaining control of himself, 'that's the daftest thing I've ever heard. Basic economics: first, you find a product to manufacture, then you open a factory.'

I looked at him, mulishly I said, 'There must be a suitable product somewhere.'

'Factory work is for women,' said my uncle, 'You'll never get a miner to work in a factory. It's not for a man.'

There was a great deal of truth in what he said but times were changing. Perhaps I could create employment for women. If the men were on strike then any wage was better than none. And it wouldn't be slave wages either. I'd see to that. I sighed. Uncle William was right. Apart from having no product to manufacture, no factory and no land to build it on, the time scale would be of no use if a strike was called soon. I dismissed the idea.

'Come on,' said Uncle William, 'let's take a stroll in the park.'

Later that day we returned to Cardiff. I had thought about going back to Llanbeddas but decided against it. There was nothing more I could say or do. It was time I returned to London to report and face the music.

I yearned to be with Madelaine again.

The miners came out on strike later that day. My uncle and I were drinking whisky in the Angel Hotel when the news broke.

Three men entered the lounge discussing the issue and what it would mean. 'How did you get the news so quickly?' I asked them.

'It's on the wireless. I caught it just before I left the house,' one of them replied.

'Damn!' I said, with feeling. 'Was there anything else on the news?'

'Indeed,' was the reply. 'The TUC has called a General Strike of essential services in sympathy.'

'So soon?' I queried.

The man shrugged. 'That's what it said on the news.'

I checked my watch, surprised to see it was nearly 7.45pm. It had to be after 7pm as no news was allowed to be broadcast before that time, in spite of the plea by John Reith, the managing director of the British Broadcasting Company to the House of Lords, to allow news bulletins throughout the day.

'What I don't understand,' I said frowning at my uncle, 'was how could they call the strike so quickly. We only met this morning.'

My uncle grimaced. 'What better time? They called the strike after you left and the message spread across the valleys within hours. Cook probably already had the other coalfields lined up. South Wales led the charge, I suspect.'

At that moment a newspaper boy came in calling, 'Extra! Extra! Miners' strike called. Extra!'

I bought a copy. When I finished reading I handed it to Uncle William. The strike was solid from South Wales to Kent, the Midlands and north to Scotland. If the TUC went on strike it would be the first General Strike in British history.

With a heavy heart I ordered another round of drinks.

Early the following morning I left Wales to return to London. I met with the Chancellor of the Exchequer in the members' bar in the Houses of Parliament before lunch.

'Well, Griffiths,' said Churchill in his gravelly voice, 'it appears your journey was a complete failure.'

I nodded. 'That about sums it up. What I still don't understand was how quickly events moved forward. Even though I didn't succeed, surely more time would have been needed to call a strike.'

'I agree,' said the Chancellor, 'which is why I think it was a set up. Cook always intended the strike to go ahead, no matter what you may or may not have achieved in South Wales. The rest of the coalfields were poised waiting to come out.' He beckoned to a waiter and ordered a glass of port. I declined. It was too early in the day for me. 'Well, at least we tried.' Reaching for his cigar case, he added, 'That's what counts.'

'I thought being successful was what counted,' I argued.

He looked up in surprise, puffing on his cigar. 'What? Good grief, of course not. Nobody expected anything other than the outcome we've got. But at least we can tell the newspapers that we did everything in our power to avert a strike. Even sent a special envoy to Wales to talk to the miners' leaders.' He chuckled. 'Nothing more we could have done.'

I looked at him in surprise. 'I went there in good faith, man.' I leant forward. 'Damn you, you used me.'

He looked at me, puzzled. 'Of course we did. Surely you understood what was going on?'

The look on my face was sufficient answer.

'Griffiths, I am surprised. I thought you were more politically astute than that.'

I looked into his puzzled eyes. 'I went there,' I said angrily, 'to try and avoid a strike and the resultant hardship that will fall to the miners and their families.'

He blew out a long stream of smoke, looked at the end of the cigar, twisted it in his fingers and then looked at me. 'In that case, Griffiths, more fool you.'

6

I WAS STILL POLITICALLY naive compared to heavy-weights like Winston. When I thought it through, he was right, of course. Hell would freeze over before a miner voted Conservative and so the party needed to concentrate its efforts on those who were described disparagingly as 'middle England'. It was a term of abuse that had appeared in the Labour supporting newspaper, the *Mirror*. But it described accurately those people whose continued support was needed for the party to flourish.

'What do you think will happen?' I asked.

'Oh, there'll be a General Strike before the week is out,' Churchill said blithely. 'We'll write to the Trades Union Congress and protest. They'll make suitable noises and in less than a fortnight they'll all be back at work and the miners will be isolated.'

'Winston,' I hesitated, put off by his look from under beetling eyebrows but then continued, 'how can you be so sure?'

His answer took me by surprise. 'I have friends in high places. Or, to be more accurate, low places. We have been expecting something like this from the miners for some months. I have been in private talks with the TUC, with Arthur Pugh.'

'The TUC chairman?'

'And a highly pragmatic man. I explained that the government could not allow the strikers to win. He said that the TUC would have to show solidarity with the miners. We agreed a compromise. They'll be out for a week.'

'When will they start?'

'Wednesday.'

'And the miners?'

'Will be isolated.'

The conversation turned to other matters and shortly afterwards I left. I walked to Waterloo and took the train. I was looking forward more than ever to getting home.

Had we been living in France, Fairweather, my home, would have been called a chateau. Here in England, we understated everything and hence Fairweather was merely a 'house', like any terraced two up and two down. Except we had ten bedrooms, a bathroom and two separate water closets. The public rooms included two withdrawing rooms, a ballroom and a library. There were servants' quarters at the back, a large garage and the property was surrounded by fifty acres of land. We had built a runway shortly after moving in, big enough to take the Griffin II, a six-seater passenger plane. My brother Sion usually arrived by plane which delighted my daughter Susan. A competent pilot and navigator, she flew whenever she had the chance.

Two hundred yards away and closer to the main gates stood the dowager house. It had been the residence of the last owner's widow whose son had inherited the property. According to local scandal the son had drunk the estate away and broken his mother's heart. Whatever the truth, the dowager house was a sturdy, four bedroomed property with three public rooms and a study. Mam and John lived there half the year. The remainder of the time they spent either in London, for the season, or in Switzerland, for the pure air and waters. Two servants from the main house went down whenever Mam and John were in residence. For shorter visits we kept rooms for them in the main house.

The Waterloo train deposited me in Brighton where I took a taxi to Ovingdean. A short while later I was dropped at the front door of Fairweather. I paid the fare, took my

bag from the driver and was hefting it in my hand when
the door flew open and Susan, with a squeal of delight,
ran down the steps to give me a hug. I hugged her back
and marvelled how much she had grown in the six weeks
she had been away. She was tall, with an oval face, a
straight nose and a wide mouth. Her mahogany coloured
hair was cut short and wide blue eyes, normally full of
mischief, looked solemnly at me. Her pale blue dress was
cut in the latest fashion but to me she still looked like a
tomboy.

'Hullo, Father,' she greeted me.

'Father?' I queried. 'I thought you called me Dad.'

'Not any more. That's terribly plebeian,' came the
startling reply. She hooked her arm through mine and
walked with me up the steps.

I handed the bag to Gibbs, my butler, who welcomed
me home with a polite smile and said, 'The mistress is
in the small drawing room, sir.'

'Thank you, Gibbs. Any visitors?'

'Yes, sir. Your mother and Sir John are here and your
brother will be arriving tomorrow.'

I nodded my thanks and turned to Susan, 'So that's
why you're home, young lady,' I said. 'Your Uncle Sion
is arriving.'

She shrugged nonchalantly, not fooling me for an
instant. 'I may have heard something to that effect,' she
replied.

I grinned and gave her arm a pat. 'May have heard
something, ha! You just want an opportunity to fly.
Shouldn't you be at school?' I frowned half remembering.
'No! You're meant to be some place else. Where?'

'Staying with a girlfriend for the hols. It's half-term.'

'That's it. I knew you had something planned. You
shouldn't cancel on people because you get a chance to
fly,' I admonished her gently.

'I didn't,' she protested with wide-eyed innocence. 'The
house I was going to has been quarantined following an

outbreak of measles. Gloria's younger brother is covered with them. Ugh!'

'Gloria?'

'My friend. Instead, she's had to come here. And here she is.'

I was introduced to a tall, plain girl who, I subsequently learnt, was captain of hockey and netball at the Brighton College for Young Ladies. Gloria turned out to be articulate, extremely bright and from a wealthy family. She was Susan's best friend.

'David!' Madelaine greeted me when I walked into the drawing room. She hurried across and kissed me warmly. I embraced her tightly. It was good to be home. I greeted Mam and John before Madelaine hustled me to the nursery where I could talk to her and spend time with Richard, now a year and two months old.

The following morning Sion arrived in the Griffin III with his wife Kirsty and their two youngest children, Louise, nearly six and Paul three. Their eldest, Alexander, was away at Winchester boarding school. Kirsty had been horrified when he had gone initially, but it had been his own wish to do so. According to Sion it was as a result of reading *Tom Brown's Schooldays*, but whatever the reason, Alex appeared to be thriving.

After lunch Sion and I went flying in the Griffin with Susan and Gloria. Susan took the controls.

It was a beautiful day. The sun was shining, there were lamb's wool clouds dotting the blue sky and a gentle breeze came in off the sea. Susan lined us up at one end of the runway and opened the throttles. Gloria sat next to me in the first two seats with her eyes agog and glued on the back of Susan's head. I couldn't tell if she was frightened or merely astounded at her friend's ability. As usual I was filled with a mixture of pride and trepidation as my daughter lifted the plane into the air like a veteran. We swooped upwards as gracefully as a bird. The plane's

engines sounded sweet and healthy in spite of the fact
that the Griffin III had been in service for nearly seven
years.

I stood up and leaned over the pilots' seats to get a
better view through the cockpit windows. 'The engine
seems a lot quieter,' I commented to Sion who was seated
on Susan's right.

Sion turned to me with a smile. 'Glad you've noticed.
We've used something called fibre glass. Horrible stuff
if you get it on your hands. It can cause the devil of an
itch, but highly effective for sound proofing. We've put
it on the floor and walls of the passenger cabin and the
floor in here. It's an inch thick.'

'Doesn't the weight make a difference?' I asked.

'No, that's the beauty of it. The stuff is as light as a
feather.'

'What about fire risk?'

'It's fireproof,' was the surprising reply. 'Take a close
look at the engines,' he suggested.

I looked at each wing with a puzzled frown. 'What am
I looking at?'

'The engines are covered.'

'So they are!' I looked in surprise. 'But I thought that
caused over heating.'

Sion laughed. 'So did we all. We've known for some
time that the engines cause drag because of their shape.'

I nodded vaguely. I seemed to recall he had said something along those lines. He had his head craned round
and was looking at me but glanced forward to look at
Susan, the instrument panel and where we were heading.
Apparently satisfied he turned back to me. 'Peter and I
discussed it *ad nauseam*.' Peter Cazorla was Sion's right-
hand man at Biggin Hill where the aeroplane manufacturing business was located. 'We thought the open engines
caused drag. We built a cowling, which has vents in front
to let air in. The surprising result is that the engines have
a lower temperature than when they were open. It has

also added ten, maybe fifteen percent, to our top air speed and increased our range. We're considering other methods of lowering the drag.' He shrugged nonchalantly and grinned. 'We'll just have to see.'

Aeroplanes were Sion's passion. He was probably one of the most knowledgeable people alive on the subject, and was continuously surprising me. I personally had no interest in them, apart from the fact that flying provided a quick way of travelling long distances. I thought it was highly dangerous. As if to prove my point first one and then the other engine made a spluttering sound and cut out. My heart missed a beat, hit the back of my teeth and settled down to a mighty thumping.

The plane began to glide as Susan coolly flicked switches, pushed in and pulled out on a hand pump and then shoved the joy stick forward. The increased speed turned the propellers, an engine coughed and burst into life, followed closely by the second one.

'Well done, Susan,' Sion said loudly. 'You followed procedure exactly.'

'Thanks, Uncle Sion. But I was ready for it. It's not the same as when its unexpected.'

'You knew?' I asked incredulously.

Susan looked over her shoulder, smiled and then burst out laughing. As did Sion. 'You didn't?' She turned to look at Sion, her eyes sparkling with mirth. 'Unc! You didn't tell him?'

Sion laughed so hard I though he would bust a gut. 'No! I wanted to see his face.' He gasped for air. 'It was a picture.'

'Thanks, Bro,' I said. Relief and anger fought within me. Relief won and then I laughed too.

'It was a practice,' said Susan. 'There are a number of manoeuvres I need to be able to do and emergencies I need to cope with before I can go it alone.'

'Go it alone?' I queried. 'Without Sion?'

'Of course, Father. What else? I'm not learning to fly

to be mollycoddled all the time. I want to go alone. Fly solo. To be,' she looked at me with exasperation, 'a pilot.'

I nodded. I understood, or at least I thought I did. Even so the prospect filled me with dread. Susan was head-strong, obstinate and brave. Any one of those traits could and probably would, get her into trouble one day. I smiled through my worry. She had, unfortunately, inherited all the Griffiths' family characteristics which had been getting Sion and me into one scrape after another all our lives.

We flew across the Channel, went down to wave top height at Boulogne and flew back to England. Susan piloted and navigated at the same time with only an occasional word from Sion. When we lined up on the runway at Fairweather Sion cut the port engine and made Susan land with only the starboard engine running. We went in at an angle and just feet above the ground she slewed the plane to starboard to line up on the strip. The Griffin III plonked down and rolled smoothly along the slightly undulating track. She worked the brakes and the plane came to a dead stop.

'How was that, Unc?' she turned to Sion.

He smiled at her and said, 'Susan, you're a natural. I couldn't have done better myself. One day soon you'll be ready to fly without me.'

'Hear that, Dad?' she turned to me, a wide grin plastered across her face. In her excitement she forgot to call me father.

I nodded, pleased for her.

'What do you think, Gloria?' she asked her friend, who had said very little throughout the flight.

'I think,' said Gloria, 'that you're stark, raving bonkers. But it was fantastic!'

We climbed down from the plane and the two girls went off, arm in arm, chattering gaily. Part of me felt a twinge of envy at their carefree youth. I glanced at Sion and, from the look on his face, guessed he was thinking along the same lines.

'What a wonderful time to be young,' he said.

'When? In the middle of a national strike, inflation and unemployment? Less than a decade since millions died in a rotten war and many more millions died of influenza?' I shook my head. 'The fact is, Sion, any time is good to be young.'

'Isn't that the truth, David.'

On that philosophical note I helped him to pump petrol into the plane from the storage tank at the side of the barn. The barn had been converted into a workshop and hangar for whenever Sion visited but it also held the paraphernalia needed to look after the gardens and grounds of a fifty acre estate.

Madelaine was gardener, supervisor and architect. With a head gardener and three under gardeners to boss around, she was in her element, but I was the first to admit that she was doing a wonderful job. She'd had three large glasshouses built, out of sight of the house, where she grew all manner of exotic plants from orchids to herbs. The front lawn was immaculate and could be used for half a dozen croquet matches played simultaneously. The intricate maze she designed had been planted the previous year. The three feet high yew was growing at a foot a year. In two or three years it would be ready. I smiled at the thought. What great fun it would be for Richard and his friends.

Further away from the house the grounds were still uncultivated fields. We had stables that held half a dozen horses and we needed paddocks for them to graze. Even so, over forty acres were still to be landscaped. Madelaine had plans for a gazebo and an ornamental pond. I gladly let her get on with it. In the distance I could see the English Channel, the sea barely moving in the calm air. It was a beautiful, clean place to live and I couldn't help but contrast it with Llanbeddas. I was as content as my restless soul would allow.

With a mountain of paperwork to attend to, I was about

to walk along the patio to the side entrance that led straight
to my study, when I was called to the telephone by Susan.

I took the call in the hallway. 'Hullo? David Griffiths
speaking.'

'David? It's Llewelyn.'

'Who?'

'Llewelyn. Your cousin. William's son.'

My mouth went dry. He would only be telephoning
with bad news. He had two sisters, Lilwen and Llywela,
both of whom lived around Swansea. 'What's happened?'

'It's my father. He's died.'

'What!' I was shocked. 'He seemed well enough only
three days ago.'

'The doctor said it was his heart. The stress and excitement of what happened at the mine proved too much for
him.'

'Hell. I'm so sorry.' Guilt washed over me. I should
have left Uncle William out of it. He had laboured too
hard for a man of his age and sedentary habits. 'I shouldn't
have let him . . .'

Llewelyn cut me off. 'It wasn't your fault. Father
wanted to help. All yesterday he talked about it.'

'When's the funeral?'

'Thursday. Will you come? And ask your mother as
well?'

'Yes, of course.'

Llewelyn had worked in his father's shops for a few
years, before having a year of cramming and becoming
articled to a firm of solicitors. Thanks to his father's money
and influence he had eventually trained to be a solicitor,
passing the exams with flying colours. His mother's letters
to Mam in America came back to me, keeping us up to
date with family matters. We exchanged a few more words
and I hung up the receiver. I found Mam sitting with John
in the conservatory. They had a tea trolley nearby with
thinly cut cucumber sandwiches and two pots of tea, one
Indian, the other Earl Grey. I broke the news to Mam.

She put down her cup, tears filling her eyes. 'Poor Nancy.'

'What do you want to do, Meg?' John Buchanan asked. 'We can go down to Wales tonight if you wish.' He was a tall, heavy set man still in good shape for his age. He had spent a lifetime at sea, much of it in command.

Mam shook her head. 'I'll only be in the way. Nancy has her two daughters, her son and enough grandchildren to keep her company. No, I'll wait until the funeral. David, please send a telegram with our condolences and say that we will be there for the funeral.' She sipped her tea. 'That makes Nancy and me the last of our generation,' she spoke sadly.

'David,' John said, 'can I have a few minutes of your time?'

'Certainly. Now?'

'Yes. Let's go into your study.' He placed his cup down and excused himself to Mam.

I grabbed a couple of cucumber sandwiches and he followed me from the room.

'Drink?' I offered when he closed the door behind us.

'No thanks. I've been mulling over what you said about alternative employment for the miners in Wales.'

'Oh?' I sat on the leather chesterfield opposite John. The previous evening, after dinner, I had confided my exasperation about the situation in Wales.

'Did you know that the British Broadcasting Company now has ten million listeners? Its education programmes alone are heard in over a thousand schools.'

I nodded. 'I read about it last year.'

'The other day John Reith, the managing director of the BBC, was complaining to me about the lack of wirelesses available to buy at a reasonable price.'

I looked at him blankly. I still didn't see where this was leading.

'Wirelesses. All sorts of shapes and sizes. Why not,' he sighed in exasperation, 'build wirelesses in South Wales?'

I sat bolt upright. 'The idea has a lot of merit,' I spoke slowly, thinking fast.

'Apart from getting someone to build and design the sets, there's also the small matter of finding a factory, setting up the business, finding outlets and so on.' He paused and added, 'And of course there's the biggest problem of all.'

I frowned. As if the few he'd already mentioned weren't enough to contend with.

'The entrenched attitude of the miners to any other kind of work apart from mining. Working in a factory does not fit with the image they have of themselves. It's women's work.'

Uncle William had said much the same. I nodded slowly. 'What if the wages are high enough?'

He shrugged. 'That doesn't solve the problem. Their lives and their friends and family are all wound up, no, cemented together by the work they do as miners. It's a way of life, not just a means to earn a living.'

I nodded. 'You're right of course, but how do you know?'

'I saw it at sea. Men who were excellent able-bodied seamen hating being promoted to leading hand or petty officer because they left behind what they knew. Some were naturally ambitious and took it in their stride, others quickly reverted to the lower rate. I suspect your miners will be the same.' He grinned. 'They can't all be a David Griffiths.'

'Many of them have the Griffiths' blood in them and they may be persuaded.'

'I wouldn't count on it,' he replied dryly.

Our conversation had set me thinking. A plan of sorts began to take shape. I knew I would have to make it seem as if they were doing me a favour and not the other way around.

We travelled by train to attend the funeral. We formed quite an entourage, with Mam and John, Madelaine and me, Sion and Kirsty, the children and Susan. Sion and Kirsty had brought their nanny, Carmen, with them. She was Peter Cazorla's eldest daughter. Her father had been with him from the beginning of his aircraft building enterprise. In fact, all Peter's family worked for Sion, one way or another. His wife, Maria, was the cook and housekeeper, his two sons, Raphael and Juan were engineers and his youngest daughter, Rosa, helped her mother. Carmen had inherited her father's looks and her mother's brains. A pity, as she was short, dark haired, round faced, plump and prone to a hairy upper lip. But she had a wonderfully joyful personality, nothing was ever too much trouble and she had the patience of a saint with the children. She was also bringing them up to be bi-lingual in Spanish and English. At twenty-four and with no obvious suitor in her life she appeared content with her lot. The question of a nanny had been raised between Madelaine and me but we'd reached no decision as yet. There was plenty of time, although the ability to speak a second language would come in useful to Richard someday.

With the youngsters it was impossible to keep the journey a solemn affair. We had met at Paddington Station and had the entire first class coach to ourselves. The ladies sat in one compartment with the children, while we men sat in another. Within minutes the door opened and Louise and Paul came in, wanting Grandfather John to play. Carmen stood behind them shrugging helplessly. With a martyred air and a twinkle in his eyes John left and was soon rushing up and down the corridor with the kids, chasing them or being chased.

Just as we pulled into Reading, much to John's relief, lunch called a halt to their playing. We had a cold buffet of chicken and pork pie, a salad – an early lettuce from Madelaine's hot house – and a bottle or two of white wine. After lunch, John pleaded weariness and the children left him alone. We sat and talked in a desultory fashion until we arrived at Newport. Collecting our belongings we prepared to alight at Cardiff.

The sky was overcast and rain was threatening. We sent the children with Carmen to Uncle William's house while we took taxis to St. Mary's Church, Whitchurch, and joined the congregation. It was a solemn affair. The church was packed and flowers filled the entrance. Two front pews had been reserved, the second one for us. As we took our place Rhodri came to speak to Sion and me.

'Aunt Nancy asked if you would be pall bearers. The hearse is on its way from the house and will be here in a few minutes,' he said, without so much as a welcome.

Nodding, we excused ourselves and went back out into the light drizzle that was now falling. We stood silently alongside Rhodri, Peter, Huw and Dafydd. A few moments later two black horses with black plumes appeared, pulling the hearse. The coffin on the back reminded me of my father's funeral and I felt a lump in my throat. I exchanged glances with Sion. I could see the memories flooding back to him too. I hated funerals. The other four looked on stoically, not prepared to show any emotion.

Behind the hearse walked Llewelyn and a number of other men. A black car followed. In it sat Aunt Nancy and her two daughters, Lilwen and Llywela.

The hearse stopped alongside us and the undertaker, dressed in black with a top hat sporting a long black ribbon, climbed down. The flowers were removed and we took our places to carry the coffin inside. We easily lifted it to our shoulders and walked slowly up the steps and into the church. As we entered the organist struck up the Funeral March and so the ceremony began.

When the service was over only the men and my aunt went to the graveside. The women left to return to the house. There was food and drink to organise. Cars and taxis had been ordered by Llewelyn and after the burial we were driven back to the house. People of all ages and walks of life appeared to pay their respects. How well they'd known Uncle William dictated how long they stayed. Ham and cheese sandwiches were offered in abundance, as were bottles of beer and whisky. Sherry was available for the ladies but woebetide any of them who asked for one. Tea was the preferred beverage. Otherwise people would talk!

Mam and Aunt Nancy sat together, the last of their generation. I suspected they were reminiscing as they sat like dowager duchesses at one end of the room, breaking off from time to time as somebody came up to pay his or her respects to Aunt Nancy. The afternoon wore on. It was neither pleasant nor unpleasant, neither sad nor happy. My uncle had reached a ripe old age and now he was gone. We were there to pay our respects and that was all. I felt a pang at his passing but death comes to us all in the end. We just hope and pray it doesn't come too soon.

With a whisky and soda in my hand I went to find Llewelyn who was talking to two women in a corner of the room. He was a tall, good looking man, a few years younger than me. 'May I have a word?' I asked.

'David! Of course. Do you remember my sisters?'

I hadn't until he introduced them. Llywela was tall, dark haired and pretty, while Lilwen was short, plump and had frizzy brown hair. After only a few minutes in her company I realised that Lilwen had a bubbly personality that more than made up for her dowdy looks. Even at this solemn time her natural enthusiasm for life and mischief shone through. We exchanged pleasantries and a few memories and the two girls left us to check on their children.

'What can I do for you?' Llewelyn asked.

I briefly outlined our ideas to open a wireless factory in the area.

'And how can I help?'

'Can you find the land, negotiate the purchase, arrange planning permission and so on, somewhere around Ponty?'

'Actually I can do better than that,' he said, stroking his chin. 'Planning permission has just been passed en bloc for an area near Taff's Well to build an industrial estate. There are already two or three factories there and I believe there will be room for at least a further twenty or thirty. Planning permission is automatic. The size of the unit is down to the purchaser.'

'Will you act for us?'

'Certainly. I'd be delighted.'

There was a burst of laughter from the kitchen and we both looked in that direction. John was holding court with half a dozen of the family.

'Imagine, the Earl of Guildford in my Mam's kitchen. It seems,' said Llewelyn, 'that even we Welsh can't resist the aristocracy.'

I laughed. 'Hardly that. He's only an Earl.'

'Precisely,' Llewelyn laughed.

His laugh brought me up short. I had never seen John as aristocracy. I just saw him as a man who had achieved much in his life and had been granted his just rewards. Now, through the eyes of my cousin, I saw the future. When I inherited the title, as John's adopted son, I would become different. I'd become an aristocrat. It gave me a cold feeling down my spine. I didn't want it and the thought gave me a shock.

7

THE EARLDOM LEFT me in a dilemma that I would have to deal with at some time in the future. Now, I needed to sort out other, more urgent matters.

'Who will you get to run the business?' Llewelyn asked.

'I don't know yet. I was hoping maybe Rhodri or Dafydd.'

He was well trained and didn't so much as blink but I could see from the tension in him that I had said the last thing he had expected. He breathed out slowly and then said, 'I'd never have thought it of you, David.'

'Care to expand?'

'That you were a fool.'

'They're family,' I said, anger simmering beneath the surface of my words.

'They may be our cousins but they're stupid. They could have got out of the mines years ago. My father kept offering them good jobs, from managing a new shop to being a district manager looking after three or four. The wages were twice as much as they earned in the mines and they would never have had to get their hands dirty again. They told him to forget it. They were born miners and they would die miners.'

Deep down, I wasn't surprised.

He paused to gulp a mouthful of whisky. His tone softened when he continued. 'I tried to persuade them as well. It was no good. If anything, they resented my interference. They live in a tight knit community and they'll die there. If they die sooner rather than later then they'll tell you their fate is in the lap of God. They go to chapel regularly, pray often and live just above the poverty line.'

'I'll try and persuade them.' Another idea took root. 'May I ask you something? And if it's none of my business please say so, but I have a reason for asking.'

'Certainly,' he nodded and smiled.

'Your father's will. Was the estate mainly left to your mother or are you three benefiting as well?'

He looked at me in surprise, thought about it and shrugged. 'There's no harm in telling you, I suppose. Mam's been left with more than enough to live on. The rest is being shared between the three of us. There are a few bequests to old employees but nothing much.'

'Is the estate considerable?'

'Reasonably so. A drop in the ocean compared to your wealth, of course, but we could all live off the money for the rest of our lives if we were careful with it. Why do you ask?'

'Thanks for being so blunt with me. I'm going to try and convince the others that they should come and work in the factory. I'll offer them shares and incentives and see what they say.'

'I can tell you what they'll say. David, I meant it when I said that they're stupid. You can't make a silk purse out of a sow's ear and I'm afraid our cousins fall into that category.'

'That seems a rather harsh judgement.'

'I'm sorry, David, but it happens to be true. My training as a solicitor taught me to be honest and to confront the issues. But if you must, go and find out for yourself.'

On that note I left him. I found Rhodri alone in the front parlour and put my offer to him.

Narrowing his eyes he gave me a look that bordered on hatred. Through clenched teeth, his face white and his hand holding his glass shaking with anger, he said, 'Go to hell. Take your filthy money and go back to London. We don't want it. We never accept charity.'

'It isn't charity, man. You'll work as hard as you do down the pit. The only difference is you'll earn three times as much money and . . .'

'Money! Money! Is that all you can think about? What about friends and loyalty? The strike is just taking hold and you want us to abandon them? You disgust me.' On that note he spun on his heels to walk away.

I grabbed him by the arm and he tried to pull away from me. I could feel the solid muscle beneath the coat but I wasn't going to give an inch. I think my grip surprised him because after a few moments he stopped and looked me in the face. 'The TUC will go back in one week and you'll be isolated,' I snarled at him. 'So don't tell me about loyalty or the camaraderie of the workers. I'm giving you a chance to better yourself. If you don't want it for yourself then take it for your family because believe me things are going to get a lot tougher before they get any better.'

He pulled violently at his arm and I let him go. 'You're daft in the head, Dai Griffiths. You always were. The strike is solid.' With that he walked away.

I thought about talking to the others but decided against it. To hell with them.

I'd done my best. John walked into the room and joined me. I recounted my conversation with Llewelyn and Rhodri. He was not in the least bit surprised.

'So what now? Are you going to abandon the idea?'

'What? Of course not. The plan is still a very good one. The management might be different, that's all.'

John smiled and lifted his glass in salutation. 'That's what I thought.'

I laughed in return. 'Excuse me a moment,' I said. 'I must have another word with Llewelyn.'

While John went off to sit with Mam I found my cousin. 'You were right.'

He nodded. 'It was considerate of you nevertheless.'

'At least I tried. Listen a moment.' I told him about the Trades Union Congress arrangement with the government. 'So you see, things will get exceedingly tough for them. I have an idea though. Can you arrange a letter to each of them telling them that your father left them a thousand pounds in his will? I'll make sure you're in the funds by next week.'

'Why don't you just give it to them direct?'

'I don't want them to know it's from me. They're prickly enough as it is.'

'I don't suppose they'd throw it back at you. Even they aren't that stupid.' He paused, 'All right, if that's what you want but I'd better warn you, they won't keep the money. They'll give it to the miner's fighting fund to share with the others.'

I saw with clarity that he was right. 'I'm damned if I'm going to allow that to happen,' I replied, feeling thwarted.

'You could let me give them say, two pounds a week. That'll be enough for them to live on but leave nothing over to give away. Once the strike is over I'll give them the remainder, if that's what you want to happen.'

I thought about it and nodded. 'All right. But, better still, give it to their wives. At times like this they're much more pragmatic. And I still intend to go ahead with the factory. I'll give jobs to those miners who want to leave the pit, even if our own family won't accept them.'

'All right. But most importantly who do you get to take charge? As of now you have a sentimental idea and no business plan.'

He was right, of course. I was launching a new enterprise for all the wrong reasons. As was often my problem, my heart was ruling my head, but I knew it was the right thing to do.

'You?' I suggested, tentatively.

Llewelyn burst out laughing. 'No thanks. I'm flattered

but that was an offer made of desperation. I also enjoy the law. I can make a difference to people's lives. Anyway, you need somebody who knows what they're doing.'

'Leave it to me,' I said with confidence. 'I'll sort it out.'

We returned from Wales the following day and I immediately tracked down a wireless manufacturer in Hounslow by the simple expedient of reading the maker's label on a set I had in my study. Under the guise of wishing to purchase a number of sets I made an appointment to visit the following day.

The factory was a long low building surrounded by a wire fence topped with barbs. Notices warned of guard dogs at night. I was surprised at the security. I parked my Charron-Laycock two seater next to a door marked 'Enquiries' and climbed out. I placed my hat on my head and went inside. I knocked and entered to find a middle-aged lady seated at a desk, typing.

'May I help you?'

'I have an appointment with Mr Carruthers.'

'Ah, yes, Sir David.' She stood up and practically curtsied. A knighthood has its advantages sometimes. She showed me into an adjoining office.

The room was stark; no money had been spent on frills. The man sitting at a scarred, paper-strewn desk stood and offered his hand. He was my height but more heavily built. His hand was rough and callused. I learned later that he had apprenticed as a carpenter.

'Take a seat, Sir David.'

I looked around. The chairs were wooden, as battered as the table and each piled high with paper. He smiled, unfazed, and lifted a pile from one chair and dumped it on top of another.

'What can I do for you?' He had a deep voice, almost a growl. His brown eyes twinkled with pleasure and I had the ludicrous thought that if you pasted a white beard on him and put him in a red suit he'd make a good Santa Claus.

'I wish to buy a dozen wirelesses. Before I do I want to make sure of the quality of your work.'

He bristled visibly. 'It's second to none.'

'I'm sure. Out of interest, how many wirelesses do you make?'

He sighed. 'Not enough, truth to tell.'

'Oh? Why's that?'

'The demand is huge. Not for the great big ornamental contraptions *we* make but for the basic wireless that will receive the BBC. Most houses can't take the ornate pieces of furniture wanted by the upper classes. Sorry, no offence.'

I smiled. 'None taken. Why don't you make the simpler wireless and sell more?'

'It's not as simple as that. If we fit a wireless into a cabinet we can sell it for seventy-five pounds.'

I pursed my lips in surprise. 'That's a great deal of money.'

'It takes two months or more to make one. They are highly crafted, beautiful pieces of furniture. The final price we get reflects the work. But,' he held up his finger, like a school master admonishing an unruly class, 'the real profit is in the wireless itself.' He was warming to his theme, excitement bubbling through him. 'The components cost us . . .'

He finished his lecture fifteen minutes later. The raw materials to make a wireless cost less than three pounds. Put together to receive the BBC it sold at between ten and fifteen pounds. Carruthers' problem was he couldn't make enough of them to cover his costs. He needed bigger premises. With half the factory making the cabinets he just didn't have the space. The high prices he could charge for the cabinets made ends meet. It was, he admitted, very frustrating. He thought that every home should have a wireless set. I wasn't so sure but I liked his evangelical approach to the business.

'Where are you from?' I asked a short while later, when his secretary brought us a cup of tea.

'Originally, Liverpool. Then Birmingham. I came into a bit of money and ended up here. Why?'

'Oh, no reason. I was trying to place your accent. Are you married?'

He frowned, his cup halfway to his mouth and looked keenly at me. 'You're asking these questions for a purpose.'

Which was very astute of him. I wondered what I should say in reply and thought, what the hell! 'Yes, I am. If you had a factory with as much space as you needed and funding to do as you wanted, how much bigger would the business be?'

He blew out his cheeks, thoughtful surprise written across his face. 'How big do you want it?'

I then proceeded to tell him my plans for the factory in Wales.

When I finished he said, 'So you aren't really here to buy wireless sets?' His tone hovered somewhere between angry and curious.

'Oh, I'll buy them all right. But I have a better idea. How do you fancy running my factory in Wales?'

His jaw dropped and he leant forward. He was about to say something, thought better of it and leant back again. 'Why should I?'

I proceeded to explain. As usual, when it came to deals like this, I ensured that there was plenty in it for the key players. When I had finished he looked at me keenly, then said abruptly. 'Come on. I'll show you around.'

He gave me a guided tour. The factory had fifty employees. Half of them were craftsmen building cabinets, twenty made the wireless sets and the remainder were involved in finishing and packaging. By the end of the tour I'd another idea.

Back in his office I made a suggestion. 'Keep the cabinet makers here,' I said, 'and expand that side of the business. Take all wireless production away and ship in the finished sets.'

We discussed the matter at great length and night was falling when we came to an agreement. We shook hands on the deal and I made an appointment for Carruthers to meet me at the bank in three days time. I gave him my card and left. It wasn't often that I made a mistake in judging a man. This happened to be one of those times.

The next few days I was busy at Griffiths, Buchanan & Co, our bank at Hill Street in Mayfair. I had a series of meetings that lasted all day, discussing policy and making plans with my good friend Angus Frazer and other members of management. Angus had a bundle of titles he refused to use. He was the Earl of Strathperth and a Laird with estates and business interests near Dundee. We had saved each others lives so often we'd lost count. Throughout the Great War we had been in one jam after another and we had both survived thanks more to luck than anything else. I explained my ideas for the factory in Wales and received approval to continue with the project. If they had turned it down I would have used my own money. As it was, I preferred to use the bank. It seemed a sure-fire business and my duty was to make money for the investors.

That week the TUC announced they were going back to work and the miners were isolated.

Spring turned into summer. We spent a holiday on my new boat, *My Joy II*, another William Osborne I'd had built to replace the *My Joy* which we'd unfortunately lost in Germany. We took delivery at Deal on July 15th and set about putting her through her paces.

She was extremely well constructed. The oak ribs were only twelve inches apart and the hull was built of Canadian rock pine, a very hard, tough wood that came from trees which had taken an eternity to grow. The single Perkins S6 diesel was the ultimate in modern engines and, although she was thirty-two tons dead weight, the single screw could push her narrow beam through the water at eight knots. She was sixty feet bow to stern, twelve feet wide but drew only four feet six inches at the deepest part of her draft. The length of her keel was a solid single piece of oak that was as hard as iron. She was amazingly strong and was more like a small ship than a boat. *My Joy II* was a twin masted motor sailer and carried a jib, main sail and mizzen.

The wheelhouse was set a third of the way from the bow and was large enough to sit four or five people. The wheel itself was situated at the front on the port side and on the starboard side was the brass handle used to move the engine from ahead to astern. A compass was set next to the wheel and had been swung so that it pointed to magnetic north. After the compass was installed tiny magnets were added to compensate for the effect of any metal in the boat, from the engine to rivets and brackets. A compass which hadn't been swung could result in an error as high as fifty degrees or more.

There were three entrances to below decks. The first was a hatch in the bows and led down to the forward sail lockers and two cabins, one to port and the other to starboard. A toilet and shower were also found there. The wheelhouse was directly above the engine room and there was an access hatch from one to the other when a seat in the wheelhouse was lifted.

Six steps led from the wheelhouse down to a corridor that ran fifteen feet towards the stern. On the port side was the navigating office which held the chart table, books and equipment necessary to plan a safe passage from Britain to the other side of the world. To starboard was a comfortable cabin that held two bunks, a wardrobe and a wash-hand basin. At the end of the corridor a door opened into the saloon that included a galley and dining area stretching the full width of the boat, that ran for another fifteen feet. A coal burning stove heated the place, allowed for food to be cooked and supplied hot water. It was a beautiful room, wood-lined in teak with a table large enough to seat eight people in comfort. Above this space was an eight-foot long, double-sided skylight that hinged in the middle and gave the room plenty of airy light. Aft of that was another door that led to a short corridor and a dog ladder to the upper deck. On either side were two cabins, each with a single bed, well fitted out and comfortable. The one to starboard was mine; the one to port was Madelaine's.

The hull shape was very clever. Osborne's had taken a sleek destroyer and made a design one quarter of the size. Hence the boat's speed – eight knots on the engine and, sailing with the wind from the right quarter, capable of achieving thirteen knots. I fell in love the moment I set eyes on her.

We went to sea with a crew of Sion, John, Susan, Madelaine and myself as well as two people from Osborne's. After five hours I declared myself satisfied with her performance. More importantly, Madelaine announced that she was happy with the 'domestic arrangements' as she insisted on calling them. The stove worked and the water was hot. The coal bunker was ingenious. It was supplied from a hatch on the deck and could be accessed by lifting an ornate flap and the coal was then shovelled into the top of the stove. According to Osborne's, a full bunker would last three or four weeks.

Madelaine made a reluctant Susan help her unpack boxes of gear for the galley and cabins. By the time we returned to the boatyard *My Joy II* was almost ready for a long voyage. I happily signed for the boat and the two men from the yard left us. All that was needed was a complete store of food and drink, a top-up of the diesel tanks, situated all the way aft, and to fill-up with fresh water.

Osborne's, acting under my instructions, had supplied a full set of charts, navigational equipment, books and even pencils. We christened her that night. Not by smashing a bottle of champagne over her bows but by drinking a quart or two while sitting in the saloon.

Prior to departing for the Channel Islands the following morning we were joined by Kirsty and Mam. The children were left at home. Kirsty had brought Paul and Louise to Fairweather with Carmen, who was only too happy to look after Richard as well.

It was a beautiful summer's day. There was a light breeze from the southeast, the sky was blue with hardly a cloud and the *My Joy II* felt like a thoroughbred horse with the bit between her teeth, raring to go. We headed south past the white cliffs of Dover, the mizzen and mainsail set, the engine at three-quarters revolutions. Being a motor-sailer, without the bite of the screw, her shallow draft would cause her to skim across the water, making it virtually impossible to hold to a steady course.

I stood in the wheelhouse, getting a feel for her, seeing how she reacted to the wind.

'Well?' John asked, a smile on his face, a mug of coffee in his hands, hiding the itch I knew he was feeling to get hold of the wheel.

'See for yourself,' I offered.

With alacrity he put his mug in the specially designed holder alongside the wheel and took my place. He tentatively moved the wheel, watching the sails, glancing at the compass. I took my hand-held compass and shot up three easily identified objects and plotted our position. We were two miles off the coast, heading 190 degrees and, according to my calculations, making good seven knots. The boat was as steady as a rock, a slight pitch the only sign that we were heading into a gentle swell from the west. The others, having hoisted sails, were busy examining every nook and cranny.

'The mizzen holds her steady,' John announced, 'and the mainsail adds about a knot and a half to her speed. Perhaps less. We should try a foresail and see what it does. However,' he added, 'at thirty-two tons, in this breeze, I wouldn't have thought it would make much difference.'

'I agree.' Reaching out I raised the lever that controlled the speed of the engine. It immediately picked up and we could feel her move perceptibly faster. At the next fix I estimated we were doing closer to nine knots.

Much to our amusement it wasn't long until Susan appeared, desperately wanting to get her hands on the wheel. John and I exchanged wry smiles and shrugs and he let her take control. She was in her element whether it was sailing or flying. We sat on folding deckchairs on the open space behind the wheelhouse and watched the world go by. It was very pleasant and restful. Quite literally the calm before the storm.

8

WE HAD TACKED a few times during the night, intending to pass close offshore to Cap de la Hague. The wind shifted to the west and storm clouds began to brew on the horizon while at the same time the barometer began dropping. I tapped it a few times but the pressure kept heading south. The wind picked up in short, sharp gusts and in the middle of the forenoon we had to batten down the hatches and stow away all moveable gear.

By noon Cherbourg was twenty-one miles to port and almost directly south of our position. We had a choice. We could continue with our present heading with the sea and wind to starboard and risk the storm, or we could tack and run with the wind and head for Cherbourg. It was no contest. This was a holiday. We elected for a night alongside and immediately turned thirty degrees to port and headed for shelter. Now it became interesting sailing. With the wind on our starboard quarter we watched as the speed crept up, fix on fix. We began to edge towards ten knots when the wind began gusting twenty to twenty-five knots. We changed the foresail for a spinnaker and, as the canvas filled and lifted, the *My Joy II* seemed to thrill to the wind and picked up speed. I estimated we were doing twelve knots when the entrance to Cherbourg's harbour became visible. We passed the outer buoy, and then the first of the port and starboard hand buoys that led us along the estuary and through the outer wall. We dropped the sails and I let Susan take us in. She expertly took us alongside the inner harbour where we tied up.

The nearest restaurant and bar was a hundred yards away. *L'Auberge* served fine wines and good food. The atmosphere was jolly and the place was packed with holiday-makers. At an adjoining table two youths made eyes at Susan and sent her into fits of giggles. We exchanged a few words with their parents. Their family name was Boucher. They were a party of eight, two families aboard a large yacht, sailing from Dunkirk to Spain. They too had looked at the weather and wisely decided to wait out the storm. We saluted each other, congratulating ourselves on our fore-sight in entering harbour when a storm force ten was blowing up the Channel. Soon we joined parties. We swapped sea stories and family histories and had a most enjoyable evening together. The two lads, Simon and Phillipe, were cousins, who vied with each other in paying attention to Susan and after I received a few nasty looks from Madelaine and Mam I did my best to ignore them. One of the fathers, Jacques, was about my age. He was well informed on world affairs and we had a lively discussion. I practised my French, while he spoke fluent, though heavily accented, English. We both agreed that Europe was still in a mess after the Great War and that we seemed incapable of making life better for the majority of people. I wasn't as big a pessimist as Jacques but it was a close run thing.

The frivolities ended just about midnight and we said our farewells. Going out into a wind-and rain-swept night we hurried back to the boat. On board we lit the candles and had a final nightcap. Although we had electric lights, they were supplied by generator attached to the engine and rather than have the noise of the engine we elected to use the candles. While we sat companionably, Sion suggested an improvement to the boat – to power the lights using a bank of batteries and keeping them topped up whenever the engine was running.

The wind howled through the rigging and battered against the side of the hull but the boat barely noticed. She sat serenely alongside, unaffected by the weather.

We went our separate ways to bed. When I closed the door to the salon behind me I showed Madelaine a modification I hadn't shown the others. The walls of our cabins could be folded back and her bed slid across on rails to fit snugly with mine. She giggled with pleasure when she saw it. A desire to protect Madelaine's modesty had kept me from letting the others know about the arrangement.

By the following morning the storm had blown itself out and we set sail early, deciding we would have breakfast once we were at sea. Our friends from the evening before had already departed. There was a long, uneasy swell from the west, a result of the storm, but with the mizzen set, the boat sailed smoothly over it. We were heading straight into the wind, pushing along at a steady seven and a half knots. The glass had settled and a depression had moved on, trailing wind and rain in deceptive squalls. It was eighty miles to St. Helier and we had all day to get there. Once we were in the passage between Alderney and Cap de la Hague we hoisted the main and fore sails and added three knots to our speed. I intended to take us between Sark and the western side of Jersey giving us more sea room and a run before the wind straight into St. Helier.

Sark was on the starboard beam about ten miles away when a red flare erupted in the sky directly ahead of us. Susan spotted it as she was on the wheel while we were sitting below drinking cups of tea.

'Dad! A flare!' she called down.

John, Sion and I piled into the wheelhouse, grabbing binoculars, searching the horizon.

'Where was it?' I asked, the glasses glued to my eyes.

'Directly ahead. There! Another one!'

The red flare made a graceful arc high in the sky and sank back into the sea. I pushed the fuel control lever all the way over and *My Joy II* began to slowly pick up speed. John and I went out on deck and began to fine tune the sails, trying for every tenth of a knot we could squeeze out of her. If people were in trouble then speed was of the essence.

We scanned the horizon with the binoculars, searching for other ships and boats that could also come to a possible rescue but saw nothing. I estimated that we were now doing eleven and a half to twelve knots; a superb speed in such a sea and wind. The heavy, narrow bows sliced through the water like a dolphin and we dashed onwards. Sion stood in the bows – the eyes of the boat – an arm wrapped around the forestay for balance.

'Got her!' Sion yelled a few minutes later. 'Blue hull, low in the water. No! She's turned. She's lying on her side. There are people sitting on the hull. I can't make out how many.' He fell silent, eyes glued to the binoculars. 'Go ten degrees to port,' he yelled.

Susan altered our heading and looked to see if we needed to adjust the sails. They would do. We hit a particularly deep trough and dipped down out of sight for what seemed like half an age but was only a handful of seconds before the bows came high out of the water. I wasn't watching Sion but rather searching the water beyond him but I noticed his sudden jerk.

'Good God! I think it's the same crowd we met in the restaurant. The Bouchers. They haven't seen us yet.'

I grabbed the Very pistol, broke open the barrel and thumbed in a cartridge. I held the pistol above my head and fired into the wind. The green burst of light mushroomed above us.

'They're waving,' Sion yelled.

We were about half a mile away and the yacht's hull was clearly visible, riding up and down in the long swell. Luckily the waves had eased a good deal but I could see that they were still splashing and washing over the bedraggled people sitting forlornly along the hull. I counted heads and frowned. There were two missing. I looked more closely. I couldn't see the boys' grandparents.

'Ahoy, there!' Sion called. 'Stand by and we'll come alongside and help you on board.'

'*Faites attention*!' Jacques replied. 'Throw a line. My parents are trapped inside the hull.'

'Are they alive?' I asked.

John had taken the wheel from Susan. Her natural ability could not compare to John's knowledge and experience, earned after a lifetime at sea. He brought the boat to a stop with the wind and the upturned hull lying along the port side of the *My Joy II*. Jacques and his cousin, Pierre, helped the two women and the two boys on board. Madelaine and Kirsty took them below. They were all shaking with cold and fear, mumbling their thanks, exhausted. Jacques rapped a tattoo with his knuckles on the hull and was immediately answered by a faint knocking.

'They still live,' he said. Fear for his parents replaced the worry he'd been harbouring for his wife and son. '*Qu' est-ce qu' on va faire*?' He looked up at us helplessly. Now the others were off, the hull floated a little higher in the water but not by much. Nearly ten feet shorter than the *My Joy II*, she had a wider beam and taller masts.

'Get two lines from your boat,' I ordered. 'One from the bow, the other from the stern. We'll hold her fast against us while we work out what's to be done.'

The two men were tired, fumbling the ropes. I climbed down onto the hull and sent them aboard *My Joy II*. The hull was awash and slippery underfoot and I marvelled that they had not been swept into the sea. I was already soaked as I struggled with a rope around the bowsprit which I passed up to Sion. He tied it off on the aft mooring cleat. I edged my way forward and as I did so the hull lurched and I fell heavily to my knees, gripping the side of the hull to prevent myself from sliding overboard. When the boat steadied again I inched my way aft. Sion threw me another line. I reached into the water and felt the edge of the deck, fumbling around until I felt a guard-rail stanchion and tied the rope to it. It was inadequate but the best that I could manage.

I rapped on the hull and was rewarded with a faint knocking. I looked up at the faces gazing bleakly at me.

'That was a feeble response,' said John.

I nodded. 'We need to hurry. Any ideas?'

'Can't you cut through the hull?' Susan suggested.

It was John who replied. 'We could but it would be a difficult and dangerous task. The hull will be three-quarter inches thick. If it's teak, which it looks like, then it will be as hard as iron. It'll be a hell of a job to cut a hole big enough.'

'What about going in through the deck?' Sion suggested. 'At least that'll be thinner. And it's probably oak. Ask Jacques,' he added as the Frenchman came on deck.

He confirmed the deck was oak. A far softer wood, it would still be a difficult task to cut through. There was also another problem. As soon as we breached the hull any air would escape and she would lose buoyancy. The arrangements with the two ropes would swiftly prove inadequate.

'Where are they?' I asked nodding at the hull.

'In the cabin behind the forepeak,' Jacques replied, mournfully.

'What on earth happened?' John asked.

Jacques shook his head. 'I don't know. We were sailing easily enough. The wind and the sea were running on our beam. Suddenly there was a loud bang, the boat shuddered and went over before I could do anything.'

'When was this?' I asked.

'Just after lunch. My parents had been taking a siesta. I was at the helm enjoying the breeze and thinking about altering course when, pouf!' He shrugged eloquently. 'The others were all in the saloon and came up straight away. I tried to get into the forward part but the door is jammed. Then the boat began to sink and I climbed back out.'

'How tightly is it jammed?' Sion asked.

Jacques shrugged again. 'I cannot say for sure but I suspect something is stuck behind it.'

'Susan,' I said, 'fetch the log and a pencil from down below. I want Jacques to draw the inside of the boat so that we can see what we're up against.'

A few minutes later we had a sketch of the boat. Sion pointed to the problem. 'That door to the head has come open and jammed across the entrance. We could use a crowbar and work on the door.'

'Sion,' I said, heavily, 'you know aeroplanes but not boats. We don't carry crowbars.'

Sion was not put off. 'Something like it then. What about an axe?'

'We have one in the engine room, above the door,' I replied. 'That might work. Any other ideas?'

'Not an idea, an observation,' said John. 'What if gear has come loose and is blocking the passage. Is that possible, Jacques?'

'Anything is possible, but I doubt it. I am an experienced yachtsman and I ensure that everything is stowed away at all times.' The Frenchman spoke stiffly, affronted at the suggestion.

'I had to ask. Now, who's climbing inside?' John put the question to the small group.

'*Moi, bien sûr*,' said Jacques. 'They are my parents.'

'I'll go with you,' said Sion. 'Two of us will have a better chance than one to get in. We may need to carry the old folk out. All right?'

Jacques nodded, relief etched into his face.

I hurried below, grabbed the axe and returned on deck. Sion and Jacques had taken off their shoes and socks and were tying ropes around their waists. I handed the axe to Sion.

'No heroics, Bro',' I said. 'If there's any danger get out.'

He raised an eyebrow at me. 'Like you would, you mean?'

'Yes. Just like me.' We swapped inane grins.

Trapped in the hull, two main problems faced the grand-parents. The air would be going bad and water would be seeping in. Time was running out. Sion and Jacques climbed over the stern and onto the hull. I watched them duck through the companion way and heard them splashing and cursing. A few seconds later we could hear the thump of the axe.

It seemed to last a long time but in reality could only have been a few minutes. There was a yell of triumph and then Jacques' voice calling, 'Maman! Papa!'

At that moment, the capsized hull moved and turned turtle. The cause of the problem came clear. I suspected the keel had been made from pig iron. It was common to have it fixed to the hull with long, heavy bolts holding it in place. Poor maintenance or an accident at some time may have weakened the bolts. Whatever had happened had left them unable to take the strain. The loud bang Jacques had heard earlier was the shearing of the bolts. Now the keel had dropped off and the yacht had gone over. The guard-rails on the stern broke away and the yacht sunk, held in place by the rope tied to the bowsprit and the cleat on *My Joy II*. As the weight came on the rope we began to heel over dangerously. My mouth was suddenly dry with the fear of capsizing. My fear galvanised me into frantic thought. The way out of the sunken yacht was through the aft companion way. They had to dive down to get out!

I had to get Sion out if I could, but what to do? By now Madelaine and Kirsty had come on deck and they stood side by side, shock rendering them speechless.

After a few seconds, Kirsty whispered. 'Dear God, let him be saved. David,' she paused, 'David, what can we do?' She looked beseechingly at me.

If the rope broke the sunken yacht would plunge to the bottom of the sea. We were leaning more to port as the water continued rising in the hull and were now in real danger of turning turtle ourselves as the deck canted at an angle I estimated to be nearly forty-five degrees.

'John!' I suddenly yelled. 'Get me a rope.' I began stripping off my shoes and outer garments. 'I'll dive down and tie the end to an aft cleat. Tie another length of rope to the forestay securing ring. I'll pass this end up to you and you secure it on the starboard side. We then cut the rope holding the boat. Understood?'

He nodded. 'Right. Good idea. I see what you're trying to do. Only hurry up.' He handed me the end of a length of rope and I dived cleanly into the water, swimming down along the vertical hull. The cold was a shock but I kept swimming, aware of how little time we had. I reached the stern, found a deck cleat and quickly secured the rope. With bursting lungs I headed back to the surface. I hit the fresh air gasping.

'Haul tight and cut the other end,' I shouted. I clambered up the starboard ladder and onto the deck. Water pooled at my feet and the cold left me gasping. Madelaine brought a blanket and draped it over my shoulders while I stood watching John cutting the rope securing the hull. He sawed at the rope with a sharp knife. The strands stretched and unravelled as the weight of the sunken yacht pulled on the rope. Suddenly it parted and the bows sank beneath the sea. *My Joy II* lurched upright and, as the weight came on both ropes, either side of her hull, she settled with the bows down about three or four inches. She was a stable platform once again. Shucking off the blanket, I climbed over the side, took a deep breath and dived down. The companion way was about five or six metres down and I quickly reached it. The salt water was clear but stung my eyes. Just as I reached the doorway somebody appeared and blocked the entrance. The person stood there, swaying, and I grabbed whoever it was and swam for the surface. I literally had a dead weight in my hands. Hitting the surface, I gasped air and pulled the old woman alongside me. Her eyes were closed and she did not appear to be breathing. John threw down a line. I tied it around her and, with him pulling and me pushing, we got her on board.

Just then, other heads appeared alongside me as Sion, Jacques and the old man arrived at the surface. We helped M. Boucher onto the *My Joy II* and the three of us clambered up after him. He sat retching, gasping, dragging air into his lungs, shivering. Mam came on deck with more blankets and placed one over his shoulders. Kirsty did the same for Sion, giving him a big hug, relief in her eyes.

'You all right?' I asked him.

He nodded, taking deep gulps of air. 'It was touch and go there for a minute. When the hull shifted I thought we'd had it. There was a bit of air still trapped but it was leaking out fast. If the boat hadn't dropped when she did I doubt we'd have made it. The swim down was too difficult for the old folks. As it is . . .' He looked over at the inert form lying on the deck.

John was working like a Trojan. He had the old woman lying on her front, her head to one side, and was pumping her arms up and down as fast as he could in a desperate attempt to get air into her. He kept at it and we sat and watched while hope faded. Finally, with sweat pouring down him in spite of the evening chill, gasping for breath, he stopped.

'It's no use,' his head hung down. 'It's no use.' He looked up at us. 'I'm sorry.'

The only sound was a quiet sob from the old man. Jacques and Pierre were given the task of wrapping the body in a piece of canvas while we cut the sunken yacht free and drifted away from it. Susan, ashen faced, engaged the engine and turned us around to head towards Jersey.

It was a sombre group that eventually arrived in St. Helier. When we moored alongside the wall I could not help but contrast our mood with the previous night's happiness.

9

GRANDMÈRE BOUCHER WAS buried in a small cemetery in St. Helier. The only people in attendance were her family and ourselves. After a service performed by a local priest we retired to a nearby hotel. She had been sixty-six, had brought up five children, three boys and two girls. Jacques' brothers had died in the Great War and his two sisters during the flu epidemic that followed. Their family had been struck with one sort of tragedy or another throughout its history. Grandpapa was nearly seventy and had, overnight, become a shadow of his former self.

We sat and talked in a desultory fashion about their intentions. Although Porto had been their initial destination we learned that it was merely to re-supply with water and fresh provisions. Their final destination was Cádiz in Spain. They had bought a fish canning factory and were moving there, lock stock and barrel. Most of their possessions were being sent by rail but, owning a yacht, they had decided to sail south.

'What will you do now?' I asked Jacques.

He shrugged, about to say something but then appeared to change his mind. He took a deep breath and said, 'We go on. We have nothing to go back for. This is all that is left of my family. There was only unhappiness in the village we left and so we now have to start again.'

I nodded. It was a concept my family understood. It was what we'd done when we left Llanbeddas for America a quarter of a century earlier. With a shock I realised that it was actually thirty-five years since we had left. I told him briefly about the tragedy that had led to us emigrating. With the sharing of confidences and family histories a bond was growing between us.

'*Et votre père?*' I cast a quick glance at the old man. He was sitting with his head bent, his hands between his knees, saying nothing, taking no part in the conversation.

Jacques shook his head sorrowfully. 'I don't know. He seems to be in shock. I can't get him to talk. He'll do what he's told but will not move or talk. I hope he'll get better as time goes by. I had a doctor look at him yesterday and he says the same thing.'

'If there is anything that we can do,' said John, 'you have only to ask.'

'You have been kindness itself,' said Pierre. 'Once we have our new passports we can get away. The Consulate will issue them sometime tomorrow once they have received references from my bank. Thanks to you we have money which I will repay as soon as we get to Spain. We will take the ferry to St. Malo and the train to Paris. There we will catch the train for Cádiz. We will arrive even earlier than we planned. Luckily the boat was insured. I shall complain to the shipyard that built her and see what they have to say. How those bolts came to break is a mystery. It should never have happened. However, the yard may be able to shed some light on it.'

A short while later we made our way back to the *My Joy II*. We had said and done all that we could. We spent the night alongside and set sail the following morning, before the dawn. I loved that time of day. John and Sion helped me to take the boat out, leaving the women asleep. Once we were at sea I had the helm while John went below to make bacon sandwiches and a cup of tea. We sat in companionable silence in the wheelhouse, watching the sun appear over the horizon. There was a gentle swell from the west and a steady southeasterly breeze. We had only the mizzen sail up as a steadying sail and were pushing along on the motor. Once we passed the western end of the island we planned to turn to the north north-east and hoist the main and jib.

The wind stayed steady from the same quadrant and we ran smoothly along once we turned towards Brighton. We neither tacked nor jibed throughout the day, running at a steady nine to nine and a half knots. It was a very pleasant cruise, the kind I liked, when I could jokingly say it was calm enough not to spill the gin and tonics. For all that, we were sombre for the most part, our memories fresh with the tragedy that had befallen our French friends. We arrived safely back in harbour and returned home.

The following morning I received a telegram from Jacques. His father had gone missing on the ferry to St. Malo. It was presumed that he had fallen overboard and drowned. I showed the message to Madelaine.

'Poor Jacques,' she said, sadly. 'Was it suicide, do you think?'

'Probably. I'll write to him with our condolences.'

There would follow years of exchanging letters, cards and telegrams. A postal friendship grew that one day would have enormous consequences for both families.

Throughout the summer the miners' strike continued. Across the country there were bitter scenes, with miners' leaders accusing the other unions of betrayal. Fighting often broke out but luckily resulted in nothing more than bruises and black eyes. I arranged for money to be passed to the family in Llanbeddas using Llewelyn's firm of solicitors in Cardiff. In the meantime plans to build the wireless factory were proceeding smoothly.

A firm of architects had been employed to design the factory and they were working closely with Carruthers. I then received a letter from Llewelyn informing me that building had started.

On August 8th I attended a meeting at the bank. John, Angus and myself met with the directors of the Southern Railway Company. We had finalised plans to raise

£3,000,000 to electrify two hundred and thirty miles of track. The electricity was to be supplied by a third rail which would replace the overhead electric system used in some areas of Southeast England. At the same time older steam trains would be replaced with electric trains. They were cleaner, faster and cheaper to run. Sitting with us round the large table at Griffiths, Buchanan & Co. were three men from the board of directors of the railway company. All three were corpulent, smug and wealthy.

'Are you sure that everything is in place?' asked Lord Petersfield, their chairman.

'Yes, sir,' I replied. 'We have completed the paperwork with all other lenders. We will remain the lead bank with half a million. The remainder is shared out as agreed in the last report. You can make the announcement today as planned, just in time for tomorrow's newspapers.'

He nodded, his jowls shaking as he reached a hand for the telephone sitting on the table. He picked up the receiver. 'Get me Mayfair 222.' He hung up. No please, no thank you. Just curt orders. I had been dealing with him for six months and found him abrasive and utterly lacking in charm or manners.

'It's just as well you concluded your end of the bargain, Griffiths,' he looked at me. 'Otherwise I'd have had your guts for garters.' He turned to the two men with him. 'We'll adjourn to the Ritz for luncheon. To celebrate.' He looked across the table. 'It can be your treat.'

I was ready to tell him to go to hell when John clamped a hand on my arm and smiled. 'It'll be our pleasure, Petersfield.' As a Baron himself, the conventions meant that John had no need to be obsequious to the fat toad sitting opposite me. I did not look at John but conjured up a smile. It was still only 11am and far too early to think about lunch or any other meal. I resigned myself to the thought that John and Angus would be away for the rest of the day. I knew it was good business to wine and dine wealthy clients but it was something I did not subscribe to often. I let John do most of our entertaining and, if he needed somebody else to boost the party I often suggested Angus.

I managed a gracious smile. 'I'll join you later,' I said. 'I have other business to attend to.'

The phone rang and Petersfield swept it up with a fat hand and placed it to his ear. 'Hartfield? Send out the press release. Oh, and make sure the BBC get a copy as well. Don't argue man, just do it.' He slammed down the receiver, heaved himself to his feet and led the way to the door without a backward glance. His fellow directors did the same and in their wake went John and Angus.

I leant back in my chair, reflecting on the meeting. It was a good deal for the bank, provided the railway company could meet its obligations. There was no reason to suppose that it couldn't. I left and went to my office. Pulling files from my in-tray, I began to work.

There were loans to approve, deals to conclude and business proposals to assess. We had a filtering system which meant that by the time any proposal reached me it had passed numerous stringent tests. These were based on viability, management strength, cash-flow and market-ability. A businessman could design and produce the best widget in the world. If nobody wanted widgets then the idea was a waste of time, money and effort. Our current portfolio of investments included newspapers, shipping, light and heavy manufacturing, land, forests, a distillery in Scotland, property in Scotland and southern England, aircraft manufacturing and soon, aircraft passenger services. The bank was stretched but not too thinly. A number of accounts were giving cause for concern but had not yet become serious. Action would need to be taken to ensure they did not. I made notations on the files. Most importantly, the debt/equity ratio of the bank was healthy and our cash reserves were within banking guide-lines and regulations. I sent a message to the hotel that I'd been unavoidably detained but would join them for

coffee later if it was at all possible. Naturally the opportunity never arose.

When John and Angus made an appearance around
4pm they were the worse for wear and I ordered coffee.
I knew them both to be hard headed and capable of
holding their liquor so I was somewhat surprised to hear
their slurred speech and see their unsteady gaits.

'Petersfield,' said Angus, 'wouldn't take no for an
answer. I . . . We,' he corrected himself, 'kept refusing
more brandy but he kept ordering it. For a peer of the
realm he's an uncouth lout. He was becoming more and
more rude the more he drank. It was a relief when we
finally poured him into a taxi.' He leant back in his
chair and closed his eyes. 'I can't believe,' he spoke in
a strangled voice, 'that I've drunk enough to make the
world spin. Christ.' He heaved himself to his feet and left
the room.

'What about you?' I turned to John.

'Don't ask. Never again, David. Thank goodness our
dealings with him are over. All we need do now is monitor
the account. Is all the paperwork complete?'

I nodded. 'It's not often such an arrogant and disagree-
able man becomes chairman of a large railway company,
but he seems to have done it.'

'His contacts are legion. He's delivered on many large
and lucrative deals across the City. And don't forget, we
still live in an age when a title opens many doors.'

I grinned. 'How could I forget?'

John quickly ran out of small talk and retired to his
own office. I finished just before 6pm and called John to
tell him I was leaving. There was no reply and I assumed
he'd already left the building. An hour later I was on the
Brighton express and heading home. I was looking
forward to seeing my son and spending a quiet evening
with Madelaine.

On Wednesday, August 18th, I was lucky enough to
be at The Oval for the fifth test match against Australia.

England regained the Ashes after fourteen years with a victory by two hundred and eighty-nine runs. We celebrated late into the night. I learned that on the same day the miners had re-opened negotiations with the government to end their three month strike. Six days later riots broke out among the miners and the troops were sent in. The contrast between my life and the hardship and poverty of the working classes never failed to move me. I had been concerned about a cricket match and they were unable to feed their families. I felt ashamed but angry as well. The miners needed to understand that times were changing and changing fast. They needed other forms of employment.

I decided to pay a visit to Wales and see how the factory was coming along. I arrived a few days later to a wet welcome at Cardiff. Llewelyn met me at the station and drove me to Taff's Well.

'You can see,' said my cousin, 'that we'll be ready to start putting in the production equipment within the next day or two. We've finished the offices.' He led me from one room to another.

I took a look around. Carruthers' office looked about twice the size I remembered from the plans but I said nothing.

'How long will the rest of the work take?' I asked.

'We are on schedule for six weeks time,' Llewelyn replied.

'Can we hurry it up?'

'Possibly. We're waiting on machines from America that make the valves. Everything else will be ready within the next three weeks.'

'I'll see what I can do,' I said. 'I'll contact a friend of mine in the States. Get me the details and I'll try and expedite the order.' My friend, Sonny McCabe, had worked for us many years earlier. When we left the USA after my father died, we had sold our business interests there. Sonny had been able to buy the retail business thanks to a preferential arrangement and was still going from strength to strength. He had been a close family friend, and though the passage of time and distance had loosened our ties, we still remained in regular contact. 'What else will you be needing?'

'Manpower.'

'What? I thought recruitment was going on apace.'

Llewelyn shook his head. A windy-hammer started up and he yelled. 'Let's get out of here. I'll tell you all about it.'

I'd seen all that I'd needed to and we left. We drove past Castell Coch – Red Castle – the Victorian folly built in the middle of the 1870s by the architect William Burgess for his friend, the third Marquise of Bute, reputedly the richest man in Britain.

'The problem we have is that very few men are coming forward to volunteer to work at the factory. I've had a number of adverts in the Pontypridd Observer and the Western Mail but with little result. Quite a few women have asked for a job and for the more delicate work I've agreed to hire them but we still need at least two hundred men.'

'What will be the total workforce? Three hundred?'

'And twenty. Plus office staff. It will be quite an operation once it gets started. The problem is, we'll be over budget.'

I wasn't surprised and so I merely nodded.

'Considerably over budget,' he added.

'Oh?' The modifier got my attention. 'How much over?'

'Ten thousand pounds,' came the shocking reply.

'How in hell did that happen?'

He shrugged. 'I've got all the invoices and estimates. It seems to me that all the original estimates were low. There's nothing pointing at one particular error, just many small adjustments. Each one was tiny but they add up to a lot of money.'

'All right. I'll take a look back at your office.' I could

find nothing wrong and in the end I had to agree the additional expenditure.

'What are we to do about workers?' I asked.

Llewelyn shrugged. 'We can tackle the problem from a different angle.'

'How?' I frowned.

'Hire more women. Let them earn good money. Naturally, you won't have to pay them as much as men, so there'll be a huge saving on the wages bill. I've done some figures. Look.' He took out a large sheet of paper. 'I asked a friend of mine what he thought and he agrees. At present we'll be breaking even in eleven months and gradually but steadily moving into profit thereafter. With lower wages we get there two months faster.'

I checked his figures. I was impressed. My cousin had given it a lot of thought. 'What's this item here?' I pointed at the heading – Transport.

'I had an idea. What if we ran our own bus service from the outlying districts to the factory? It would be free for our employees. That way we'd create a lot of good will for very little cost.'

I nodded. It made sense. 'Where do we get the buses?'

'Second hand. They don't need to be pristine. After all, they'll be stuck in the factory most of the day, idle.'

'What about the wages for the drivers? We don't want them loitering around all day doing nothing.'

'Easy. The drivers will also be fitters, mechanics and handymen. It'll be part of their duties. We need such people in any case, to keep the machinery in the factory running.'

'Excellent. You've thought of everything.'

'Hardly. But I've enjoyed the problem. Makes a change from thinking about the law all the time. Anyway, it was something to do in my spare time.'

'May I have this?' I pointed to the sheet of paper.

'Certainly. It's no use to me. You might like this as well.' He handed over a bundle of neatly typed paper.

'What is it?'

'It's the names and addresses of the men and woman who have asked for work. Here's a map of South Wales. Compare them and let's see if you come to the same conclusion I did.'

'Thanks.' I placed the papers in my briefcase. 'How about dinner?'

He nodded. 'Eight o'clock suit you?'

We arranged to meet at the Angel Hotel, the only establishment I knew in the city.

I went to the Angel and in my room I laid out the map. I spent the best part of half an hour poring over it, reminding myself of names and places. Memories came back, some good, some bad. I traced the railway line and remembered the time the scabs had been brought in and the train derailed. I'd been, what? Ten? Yes, ten. Cliff and I following the men. I shuddered. It had been a bad time.

Llewelyn had made it easy for me. He had split the applicants' names up by gender and it took less than fifteen minutes for me to see the picture. The women who had applied for jobs were local or in the valley, some from Llanbeddas. The men who had applied were all from other valleys or travelling from as far afield as Port Talbot, Swansea and Monmouth. Not a single man had applied for a job from within the region where we had established the factory. I frowned, lay on my bed, hands behind my head and thought deeply. It was evening when I woke up.

Llewelyn met me at eight and we drove to a new restaurant in Rhiwbina. He asked me what I'd deduced from the lists.

I fiddled with my wine glass, which held an indifferent claret, and said. 'The women have no problem applying for a job. Quite the reverse. Large numbers have applied from the Rhondda and Taff valleys. But for the men it's different. If they apply, they're abandoning their friends and families. They are,' I paused, thought about what I was going to say and plunged on anyway, 'abandoning their roots, their heritage?'

Llewelyn nodded. 'It's why some of our own family didn't leave when they had the chance.' Llewelyn stopped, drained his glass and added, 'It's what defines them as men.'

I nodded. 'They would rather starve than do something that is seen as a betrayal of their community. It's a form of tribalism.'

Llewelyn nodded, and beckoned to a waiter to clear our dishes. 'Sorry about the food and wine. The place was recommended to me by a friend.'

'Never mind. We'll try the cognac. It may make up for it.'

It didn't. A short while later we were in Llewelyn's car driving back to the city. 'What do you propose to do?' he asked above the noise of the engine.

'I don't know. What if I approach Rhodri and Dafydd and make an offer? Or the others. They can't be more alienated than they are now. The reality is, I hardly know them. But they're family.'

'I agree, but there's a better way. Offer the jobs to their wives. Give them good jobs. Make them supervisors. Accounts clerks. That way you can pay them a bit extra.'

It was an idea worth pursuing.

10

'CARRUTHERS MIGHT HAVE a good deal to say about it all,' I said.

'He's left much of the hiring to me. He's still busy at his old place, grooming his replacement. Don't misunderstand, he hasn't been shirking. He's been down quite a number of times to meet with the architects and builders. The man has a lot of ideas, seems to know what he's doing. He says he'll help with the interviews for the senior positions. Which makes sense.'

I nodded, saying goodnight. After careful thought I had made up my mind. I intended staying in Wales another day.

The following morning I visited Aunt Nancy and borrowed the car. It was the first time I'd seen her since Uncle William's death but she seemed to be coping. She admitted that having the family about her helped a good deal. Soon I was driving north past the new factory. Passing streets of houses, I drove into Pontypridd. The roads were busy with tram cars and buses and the pavements were packed with people. I realised that it was market day and the town was ringing with the sounds of stall holders shouting out their wares. I parked the car at the far end of the town and walked back. In the new covered market place I found a stall that sold faggots and peas. I bought a bag, threw on salt and vinegar and stood watching the throng as I ate my food. Provided I didn't think too carefully about the ingredients I enjoyed the simple meal.

Half a dozen urchins came round the corner. They were dirty and bedraggled. One ran past, grabbing an apple off a stall. The stall-keeper didn't notice and I couldn't bring myself to alert him. Seeing he wasn't being pursued the boy stopped and began munching the fruit with obvious relish. His friends clustered round and demanded a bite but the boy finished it, core and all. They were skinny and obviously hungry.

'Hey, you,' I beckoned to the boy who'd eaten the apple.

He looked at me nervously, ready to bolt.

'Fancy some faggots and peas?' I asked.

'Huh?' His small, freckled face was a picture of astonishment. 'Here, what's your game?' he asked, suspiciously. His friends with him were lined up either side of him.

'No game,' I replied, 'No strings attached. You all look like you could do with a good feed.'

A few seconds later I was buying faggots and peas for all eight of them. Two minutes later the numbers had swollen to twelve and before I'd finished I'd bought meals for twenty-two children. There were a few girls amongst them but it was hard to tell under the grime. I also bought them a bottle of lemonade and gave them each a shilling. Their gratitude made me more determined than ever to try and talk sense into my cousins.

I returned to the car and continued my journey, driving over the Taff and alongside the river towards Abercynon and Treharris. As I approached Llanbeddas I stopped short of the houses, parked off the road and walked on. I paused and looked down the valley. At ten years of age I had stood on this very spot and looked south towards Cardiff, my escape route from the drudgery of a life in the mines.

Further along the streets, I took a detour to visit the house I'd been brought up in. My memory of the place had been distorted by my youth and the passing of time. It looked so tiny. I wandered up to the church and finally to the graveyard. I could never visit Llanbeddas and not talk to Sian. I leant against an adjoining headstone and quickly brought her up to date with what had been going on in the family. Not out of any morbid feeling – it was something I had to do. I used Sian's spirit as a conduit to Da, and took great comfort from thinking of them together. I wasn't even sure I believed in God anymore but on the few occasions I'd spoken to Sian I'd left the graveyard with a feeling of peace. Minutes passed in contemplation till I shivered and looked up. A cold wind was blowing down the valley and with it I could see the rain clouds gathering. I made my farewells and left.

I realised that I didn't know Dafydd's address. The first person I asked told me. Within minutes I was outside his door. I paused. Now that I'd come this far I was unsure whether or not I should go on. Angrily I took a grip on myself and lifted the knocker. Before I could drop it, the door opened and a young girl stood in front of me. She was as startled as I was.

'*Prynhawn da,*' she said. She managed a hesitant smile. She was pretty, with black hair and big eyes. She was also skinny, but her clothes, though worn, were clean.

'Good afternoon,' I replied. 'Is your father in?'

She shook her head and switched smoothly to English. 'He's on the picket.'

'*Diolchiadau,*' I said in Welsh. She looked at me in surprise. Hesitatingly I continued in Welsh asking if her mother was in.

She laughed.

'Why are you laughing?' I asked.

'Sorry, your accent,' she replied. 'Yes! She's in.'

I was about to ask if I might speak to her when a woman appeared in the doorway.

'Who are you talking to, Myfanwy?' she asked. She stopped and stared at me for a few seconds. 'Oh! It's you! What do you want?' Her tone was not welcoming. She looked at the girl. 'Go and tell Da that his cousin David is here.'

Myfanwy goggled at me, nodded and left.

'Betty,' I began, 'I've come to talk to Dafydd.'

'I didn't think you were here to . . . Never mind.' Abruptly she remembered her manners. 'Would you like to come in?' Betty gestured at the short hallway that I knew led to a living room.

'Thank you. After you.' I followed her in. Five paces would take me past the sitting room. The room would only be used on special days or when visitors arrived. Betty opened the door.

'If you don't mind,' I said, smiling, 'I'd rather sit in there.'

'Suit yourself.'

The living room was fifteen feet by fifteen feet. Against the window stood a table. Next to it was a chair and along the opposite wall was a two-seater sofa. The door led to a small kitchen and beyond that was a tiny courtyard. A stone outhouse contained the toilet and tin bath which had to be filled by hand with hot water boiled on the open fire in the living room. A second shed held the free coal all miners received. I knew that upstairs were two small bedrooms, replicas in size and shape to the two downstairs rooms.

Her natural hospitality asserting itself, Betty offered me a cup of tea.

I was about to say no but changed my mind. 'Yes, please. That would be nice.'

A black kettle sat warming on the oven to the side of the fire and she adjusted it to come to the boil. A pantry under the stairs held her china and other household goods. The place was clean, worn and threadbare. My memories of the poverty we had faced when I was a child hadn't been distorted by time. Mentally I shook myself. This family's poverty was a direct result of the strike. They had been out for months, living on the breadline, not knowing where their next meal was coming from. Suddenly I felt ashamed that I had agreed to take a cup of tea.

'It's all right, Betty,' I said, 'you needn't bother. I . . .'

She interrupted. 'We aren't so poor that I can't offer a cup of tea.'

'But it must be very hard for you.'

Betty pressed her hands together over her white apron, protecting her dark dress. Her hands were rough and red from scrubbing clothes and floors. I was aware that the people of the mining villages aged young. Her beauty was fading yet she could only have been in her late thirties. She was thin to the point of gauntness, yet her eyes were bright and fierce. Within her, I could see, burned a strong will. She epitomised the brave women of South Wales.

'You have no idea.' She hesitated, then added, 'But we'll never give up. Never. We'll fight to the end.' Pursing her lips, she busied herself putting out cups and saucers.

'Does Dafydd feel the same way?'

'Even more than I do.' Her voice was taut, barely audible. 'Why are you here?' She looked me in the eyes.

I wondered for a moment whether or not I could trust her. 'I'm here to offer Dafydd a job. Out of the mine. In a factory. A senior job with good money.'

Her intelligent eyes registered total surprise. She sat down on the chair opposite. 'Out of the mine?' Her voice was a whisper. She was looking at me, hope gleaming in her eyes. 'Good money?' and I nodded. Suddenly hope faded and her shoulders sagged. 'He won't take it. He won't betray the others.'

'The real betrayal,' I said, with feeling, 'is to his family. Look at this.' I waved a hand about me. 'Betty, my servants live in better conditions. There's a whole world out there. Go and grab it for you and your family before it's too late.'

She sat up in indignation, anger turning her back rigid. I thought she was about to argue but then the fight went out of her and she sank back. Bending her head she lifted her pinafore to her face. I realised she was crying.

Immediately I was on my knees by her side. 'Shush, *cariad*, shush. There's no need to carry on so.'

After a few minutes her sobs subsided. 'You'd better go. Before Dafydd gets here. He'll be angry. Let me try and work on him. What is this job, anyway?'

Briefly I told her about the factory. When I'd finished she looked pained. 'They won't listen, David. None of them will.' She paused. 'What about . . .' she stopped and then continued. 'What about me? Is there a job for me? Anything will do. Just so that I can bring in some money.'

I patted her hand and stood up, now she had herself back under control. 'Not any job. A good one. I promise you. How about something in accounts? Can you add up?'

I wasn't being patronising and Betty knew it. Education was good as far as the age of thirteen or fourteen and then for many in the valleys it tailed away. For the boys, their only objective was to get into the mines as quickly as possible. As for the girls . . . I realised with a start that I did not know what happened to the girls. Married at sixteen, children at seventeen, I supposed.

'I stayed on at school until I was seventeen,' Betty replied. 'When I left I got a job in a shop in Pontypridd. Serving behind the counter I was for three years before I married Dafydd. Now look at me. I want better for Myfanwy.' She wearily looked around the tiny room. 'I can add, subtract, divide and multiply. They say, I have a gift for it.'

'A gift?' I asked, puzzled.

'Try me. Ask me to multiply two numbers.'

'Eight times four,' I said.

'Don't be silly, David. Give me three or four digits.'

'Two hundred and twenty six times four hundred and five.' As I spoke I was writing the numbers down on the back of an envelope I took from my pocket. Betty gave me the answer before I could finish the calculation. 'Ninety one thousand, five hundred and thirty is right,' I said in awe. She had given the answer out of her head. I tested her again and then for a third time.

Betty was enjoying herself immensely. When she gave the third answer correctly I put away my pen. 'That's amazing.'

She shook her head. 'That's as may be, except it's never done me any good. Except as a trick at Christmas parties.'

'Look,' I continued, 'I still want Dafydd to go and work there as well. In the meantime if you want a job in accounts, I'll arrange it for you.' I told her about the arrangements we were making with the buses and she nodded approval.

'No one's going anywhere,' shouted Dafydd, standing in the doorway, glowering at me.

'It's work, Dafydd. A job in a new factory in Taff's Well,' I explained.

'We don't want your stinking job. We want our own jobs, here in Llanbeddas. We stay here and fight for what's ours.'

'You don't even know what the work entails yet. Why dismiss it out of hand?' I asked, anger stirring in me.

'I don't need to know. Get out and take your traitor's job with you,' he snarled.

'Look, Dafydd, be reasonable. I'm here to offer you a job with good money and better prospects.'

'Get out! My side of the Griffiths' family doesn't betray their friends. We don't run away when the going gets tough. We stay and fight for what's right!'

I lost it then. 'You pompous ass,' I turned on him. 'Look at this hovel! You're fighting to keep your family in poverty. Don't be a fool all your life. Get out of the mines before they kill you too!'

His anger boiled over and he took a swing at me. The small room left no space for him to move and it was a clumsy effort. I caught his fist in my hand. It turned into a pushing match. He brought pressure to bear on my

upheld hand and I held his fist in front of my face. His
was the strength born of physical labour but I still had
the natural strength I'd inherited from my father. His face
mottled with rage and his arm began to tremble. I shoved
it away and he stepped back a pace.

'Dafydd,' I spoke softly, 'never do that again. The next
time you won't get off so easily. I came here in friendship, to offer you a better way of life. Now you can go
to hell.' I turned to Betty. 'The job is still there if you
want it.'

'Get out, Griffiths,' said Dafydd. 'And take your lousy
job with you.'

I didn't look at him but was watching Betty. Tears
welled up in her eyes and her hand was at her throat. I
reached into my pocket, withdrew my wallet and counted
out four five pound notes. It was all the money I had on
me. I placed it on the table. 'This is for you, Betty. Not
for the strike fund.'

I turned to go. Suddenly I was swung round by the
arm. Caught unawares I was about to defend myself when
Dafydd grabbed the money and stuffed it into the top
pocket of my coat.

'We don't need your bleeding charity. Now get out.'

I shrugged his hand off me, reached into my top pocket
and withdrew the notes. Looking him in the eyes I folded
the money as tightly as possible and threw it onto the
fire. The coals had been dampened down and no flames
were showing but the unfurling white notes immediately
began to smoulder. I walked out without another word.

From Betty's cries I was sure she had rescued the money
from the fire. Dafydd yelled at her to leave it there but she
replied harshly. I left them to it and walked out into the
damp street, turning up my coat collar against the falling
drizzle. With a heavy heart I walked away. I'd handled the
situation badly and I knew it. Throwing the money in the
fire was arrogant and indefensible. I was determined.
Llewelyn would make Betty an offer she couldn't refuse.

I passed a few people I thought I recognised but chose not to acknowledge them. I was in no mood. If the men couldn't see beyond the mine then they were doomed. One day the coal would run out, or become so uneconomical the pits would close. I forced myself to stop thinking about it. I had my own problems to deal with. It was time to get back to the bank.

I arrived in London late in the day. I had missed the last train to Brighton and settled for staying at the United Services Club. There were plenty of friends I could have called on but decided I wanted a quiet night. Standing at reception I felt a heavy hand descend on my shoulder. I looked round and broke into a grin.

'Angus! What are you doing here?' Angus was my age, thick set, brown hair turning grey at the sides. In keeping with his position at the bank he was normally dour looking but now he was smiling. He was, without doubt, my closest friend.

'I was working late. A couple of things at the bank I needed to attend to.'

'Problems?'

'Nothing substantial. A few difficulties with two of the sovereign loans.'

I was aware that every time the bank agreed a sovereign loan, where we had loaned money to a government, we had fronted the business but spread the risk by only taking a small percentage. Our real profit had been in the fees. 'Which loans?'

'Spain and Italy.'

'Tell me about it over a drink.' I sent my bags up and we went into the bar. Over a couple of whiskies he gave me the background to the problems. 'Damn fascists. This is all their doing,' I said angrily.

'Maybe. Maybe not. They're causing trouble but there's a backlash of anti-Communist and anti-Socialist feelings which are rife across Europe. Anyway, I think I've sorted the problems. We've extended Italy's repayment terms by

five years and I'm arranging for more money to be loaned
to Spain.'

'In effect lending them more money so they can pay
their interest.'

Angus shrugged. 'Got a better idea? If we called in
the debt and they stuck two fingers up at us, what could
we do?'

I shrugged. He was right. There was little we could
do about it. 'What else is happening?'

'Sion is planning on building a sea plane.'

'He is?' I was surprised.

'He thinks the way ahead is to have a trans-Atlantic
flying service. A large plane, carrying a few passengers
across the Atlantic. He's sent me a proposal. Thinks it
would make a lot of money.'

'Is he after a loan?'

'Certainly, what else?' Angus paused with his glass
raised to his lips.

'He may be my brother,' I said, 'but that doesn't mean
he gets a loan for any half-brained idea he may have.'

'Of course not. But as it happens it's a sound business
proposition.'

'There are no aeroplanes capable of such long
distances.'

'True. His would be the first. Look, let's not argue
about it. I'll show you his proposal and you tell me what
you think.'

'He's over-extended already,' I replied.

'Maybe. But Sion never misses a payment. He has a
good business building planes for the military and the
new Griffin already has advance orders.'

'I know, but he still has the problem of no depth in
his management structure. Which means he's working too
hard.'

'Like us, you mean?' Before I could protest Angus
raised his hand. 'All right, I don't disagree. O'Donnell is
doing a good job as his chief test pilot. Perhaps it's time

he was promoted to a desk job and someone else took over his role. Talk to Sion about it. After all, with twenty-five percent of the shares we do have some say in the matter.'

'All right. I'll speak to him tomorrow. Now, what about a late supper?'

The following morning I was at my desk in the bank, dealing with a mountain of paperwork. The phone rang and I lifted the receiver.

'Sir,' said my secretary, 'I have Mr Churchill on the line for you.'

'Thank you. Put him through.'

'Griffiths? That you?' he asked brusquely.

'It is. What can I do for you, Chancellor?'

'That seat has come up. In Eastbourne. Do you want it?'

11

I WAS TAKEN COMPLETELY by surprise.

'No humming and hawing, Griffiths. Do you want the blasted seat or don't you?'

'Well, yes. If you put it like that.'

'Good. The selection committee is meeting in three days time. A private room in the Savoy. Be there for eight pm.' He hung up.

Churchill was always in a hurry. He forever gave the impression that great events of state were taking place and he was needed immediately in order to save the Empire. I grinned. I liked the man enormously.

Other candidates were interviewed for the sake of form, but I passed through the selection process 'on the nod'. I spent a pleasant half an hour sitting in front of the six man election board where my achievements were quickly recounted. At the end of the interview, the chairman escorted me from the room and said, 'It's yours. This is just make believe.'

I received written confirmation two days later. Madclaine and I sat in the drawing room having a cup of coffee, discussing what we should do.

'At least there'll be no need to move,' she pointed out. 'Your constituency is only just along the coast.'

'That's a bit presumptuous, isn't it?' I teased her. 'I haven't actually won the election yet.'

'I took the liberty of going to the library. The conservative majority was over fifteen thousand last time. Somehow,' she said dryly, 'I don't think that even you could manage to squander that amount of votes.' She smiled at me.

'True. But I still intend to apply myself to the election. I'll get to work on newspaper articles and see what editorial coverage I can drum up.'

'You'll be spending much more time in London, David. Frankly, I don't relish the idea of seeing you even less than I do now. We need a town house.'

'Good idea. I'll speak to John, see what he can suggest.'

The summer ended and drifted quietly into autumn. We took a week's break in a cottage on the outskirts of Torquay, just Madelaine, myself, Susan and Richard. Unlike our friends and acquaintances we did not travel with an army of servants. The much discussed nanny still hadn't material-ised. It was a pleasant holiday consisting mainly of long walks and playing in the sand. The weather was kind although not warm enough to go swimming. As soon as we arrived back home I was cast into the middle of events.

The factory opened two weeks late but was quickly in full production. Llewelyn had met with Betty in Pontypridd. He offered her the job of senior book-keeper, much against Carruthers' wishes, as it was a role normally filled by a man. However, I over-ruled him on this occa-sion and, though he didn't like it, he was prepared to put up with my decision. Betty's new salary was as much as Dafydd earned after a full week at the coalface. A long time later she told me that when she accepted the job she told Dafydd she was earning half her actual pay. She hadn't wanted to hurt his pride.

Turnover surpassed our initial forecast. The basic wire-less sets sold as quickly as we could produce them. Carruthers ceased wireless production in his old factory and bought in our sets at cost price plus ten percent. He expanded the cabinet-making side and was very happy with the arrangement. Although we had competition, the market was insatiable and business was booming.

For a while I persuaded Sion to put his plan for a trans-Atlantic flying boat on hold. But there was no holding him back when, on 1st October 1926, a pilot named Alan Cobham landed his sea plane on the river Thames at Westminster. He had completed his record breaking 28,000 mile round trip to Australia. Cobham's De Havilland 50 biplane had taken twenty-nine days to fly across Europe, the Middle East, India and the Dutch East Indies. When he was interviewed by the *Times*, Cobham said that sea planes were the most suitable for long journeys as they could land in areas without airstrips. Sion's imagination was fired again. This time I lost the argument.

The miners' strike continued with serious unrest gripping the country. When the TUC conference debated giving financial aid to the miners there was a small riot that led to the conference being adjourned. But for all the strife a lot of good things were happening to the country. The Northern Line extension from Clapham Common to Morden opened. The seventeen-mile tube from Morden to East Finchley via Bank was now the longest tunnel in the world.

In November I attended the Imperial Conference in London, a momentous occasion. It was announced that from now on Canada, Australia, New Zealand, South Africa and Newfoundland would be self-governing dominions. Under the Crown they would have equal status with Britain as members of the British Commonwealth of Nations and be masters of their own destiny.

In deference to Irish Nationalists, the Irish Free State also became a Dominion but the King was no longer its sovereign. New legislation was to be passed in the House of Commons to implement the changes. India, however, was to remain a dependent country. The King's title now became, 'George V, by the Grace of God, of Great Britain, Ireland and the British Dominions beyond the Seas, King, Defender of the Faith, Emperor of India'.

In front of an audience of Empire and Commonwealth

leaders, Edward, the Prince of Wales, unveiled a plaque in Westminster Abbey honouring the one million men of the Empire killed during the Great War. It was a moving and solemn event which brought tears to the eyes of the strongest men and women there. I stood holding Madelaine's hand as the words 'Lest we forget them' were spoken. They echoed in my mind for a long time afterwards.

During the autumn, although a quarter of a million miners went back to work, in South Wales they stood fast. A riot left forty-seven people hurt when miners clashed with police at Glencymmer Colliery, near Port Talbot. It was reported that sheer luck prevented actual deaths. The most damning evidence against the miners' strike came when it was shown that 15.4 million tons of coal had been imported and had cost the industry three hundred million pounds. Three days later the miners caved in and went back to work.

I was still acting as an advisor to the government and so naturally I attended the meeting convened on 11th November between the miners' leaders and the government.

When Cook, Barker and Ablett arrived in the after-noon they stuck initially to their original demands. In the face of the government's and owners' implacable attitude they gradually yielded point by point. I realised about midnight that this was all grandstanding. Cook expected to lose. But he had to lose with a show of a tough fight.

'You've had the men out for six months,' I spoke bitterly, 'and you've achieved nothing. Worse, you've caused enormous hardship and put dozens of pits in jeopardy. The result is pit closures and tens of thousands of jobs lost. The longer you stay out the greater the losses will be.'

Cook regarded me with barely veiled contempt. 'We're fighting for a bigger cause than a few pits and a little hardship,' he retorted. 'We're fighting to save an industry. To give men a decent wage for a fair day's labour.'

The union representative and I were standing together at the end of the room helping ourselves to coffee. I looked down at the short man and said in a low voice, 'Don't give me that twaddle.' I'd play their negotiating game to get the right result but I wanted Cook to know what I really thought. 'I was on the train six months ago and heard you talking. I saw you travel first class and then move down the train to get off at Cardiff from the third class carriages. You're a fat, lying toad. Fighting for a job means working hard to keep a pit open and viable. Not striking when the only possible outcome is pit closures. Fair pay for a fair day's work – that I go along with completely. *You're* nothing but a charlatan.'

Cook spluttered angrily and drew himself up, his chest expanding as he prepared to remonstrate with me. Just then my name was called and I left the odious man standing there, bathed in indignation.

The miners conceded to raising the working shift from seven to eight hours. Next they agreed that pay and benefits could be negotiated locally and not nationally. The unions stated that in exchange for keeping wages at pre-April levels they would do all in their power to get the miners back to work. When presented with the economic facts of the northern coalfields this agreement was amended to exclude Durham, Northumberland, Cumberland and North Wales. One concession was wrung by the miners. It was decided that an independent tribunal be given six months to examine and vary regional agreements.

At precisely 3am Cook and his entourage stepped out to meet with waiting reporters. He announced the end of the strike but gave no details. Another unwritten concession allowed him by the government was the right to put as much gloss on the settlement as he wished. At the end of the day, after enormous hardship and heartache, the battle was over. Neither side won. In fact, everyone lost. Not only the miners and the government, but British industry as a whole. Furthermore, the country's balance of payments had taken a pounding. Britain was sinking further into debt as each year passed.

I was offered the task of heading up the tribunal but when I pointed out my vested interests – my family in South Wales – I was allowed to step aside. I had no intention of drinking from that particular poisoned chalice.

On a personal note the problem of finding somewhere to live in London was solved by John. He still owned his house in Mayfair and he offered it to us. When I protested, both Mam and John quickly rounded on me and I had to agree it was a sensible arrangement. I had been staying at the club and not only was Madelaine becoming upset but I was also missing her and Richard. He had begun to talk and was adding to his vocabulary every day. The house in Mayfair had been manned by a skeleton staff but now I arranged for John's butler, Beech, to hire some help and to get the place ready for our use in the New Year.

As 1926 ended Britain was planning to send thousands of troops to China to protect foreign and British nationals. Fascism was rising in Germany and Italy at an astonishing rate and rioting was continuing in India.

In contrast, we had a wonderful Christmas at Fairweather. I persuaded Aunt Nancy to accompany Llewelyn and visit us. Initially Mam had been a little diffident about the prospect, but once they arrived she came round. Talking about Da wasn't awkward or distressing once the subject was broached and Nancy understood what good friends my father and John had been for so many years. She was, to all appearances, genuinely happy for Mam.

Llewelyn was engaged to be married to a pretty young woman from Penarth, named Rosemary. She and Susan got on famously, finding a mutual enjoyment in riding to hounds. The Boxing Day meet was a roaring success.

In spite of the problems around the world, when we welcomed in the New Year it was with an optimistic heart.

*   *   *

I won the Eastbourne by-election with an increased majority, using the same tactics I'd used in my father's Presidential race in America and during the Tory victory at the last General Election. It had been on a far smaller scale but it had been effective nonetheless. When I walked into the chamber I was greeted with a thunderous roar of approval from the government benches which was very gratifying. I took the oath in Parliament with alacrity.

After my swearing in I sat and listened to some of the debates. I was keen to make my maiden speech which was scheduled to be in ten days time. A labour member from Leeds was boring the House to death with statistics about jobs in the north and my mind wandered. I was suddenly in awe of the majesty of the place. That chamber had witnessed hundreds of years of historic decision making. Even the dispatch boxes opposite each other, in permanent confrontation, had been designed to stand two swords lengths apart, as a symbol that the weapons used in the House were words, not arms.

On the day of my maiden speech I glanced up at the visitors' gallery. It was filled with family and friends. Even Peter Cazorla and his family had made the journey.

'The House calls Sir David Griffiths to the despatch box.'

Order papers were waved about amidst cheers and of course, boos from the opposition. In fact the usual cacophony of noise, like a zoo awakened late at night. Smiling, I waited for the noise to abate and began.

I had been practising for weeks and I spoke without reference to my notes for a full half an hour. Following the theme: 'This land, fit for heroes.' I covered many issues, following no party line. I made enemies that day on both sides of the House. I also made friends.

The main thrust of my speech was the inexcusable inequality in living standards for the men and women of Great Britain. There were calls to switch sides but I forged on, explaining that big business was the only way forward.

We needed to create wealth before it could be distributed. No one had the right to a job for life and no one should expect others to pay for their way. I highlighted the need for profits while at the same time the equal right of all sectors of society to participate in the benefits. I received a good deal of audible support from Churchill. When I finished and sat down there was cheering from the public gallery and, much to my surprise, a smattering of applause from the press gallery. I had hoped that my speech would be favourably covered, pulling out every trick I could in my now considerable portfolio of tricks. I didn't make the front pages, but my maiden speech was widely reported the following morning in the national newspapers.

'Look at this,' said Madelaine, excitedly. 'Sir David Griffiths is proving that he is no poodle of this government and is very much his own man. A thoughtful speech left the Parliament divided, not along party lines, but along a clear divide of conscience. Sir David spoke passionately . . .' she went on, while I contentedly buttered a piece of toast.

After the speech it came to my ears that Churchill considered it one of the finest maiden speeches he'd heard in decades. I thanked all well-wishers with due modesty, aglow with their praise. However, I knew it was only the beginning. A back-bencher has little power in Parliament. That rests with ministers and, to a lesser extent, with the committees operating across a wide spectrum of issues. I wanted to get onto both the War Committee and the Committee for Industry. My predecessor had been on neither and I was hoping that a vacancy would arise.

'You've made quite a hit with the papers, darling,' Madelaine commented, pouring us both a cup of tea.

I related much of what I had learned in the past two weeks as a parliamentarian, keen, as ever, to hear Madelaine's views. 'Do you know that the House doesn't sit until the afternoon to enable many of the MPs to work at other jobs. Some of them have lucrative directorships . . .'

Madelaine interrupted me. 'Or have a bank to run.'

I smiled. 'I admit the hours suit me. But it's a ludicrous way to run a country. We have late-night debates that go on until midnight, the division bell rings, we vote and all adjourn to the bar. We're paired off and my opposite number and I will agree which way we're voting and if it's against each other, which normally happens as it splits along party lines, we both agree not to attend. Major issues are debated and decided in the house with less than thirty MPs in attendance.'

'What about listening to the arguments and then deciding which way to vote?'

I laughed. 'Nobody listens to the arguments. The decisions have already been made by the Whips.' When she raised a quizzical eyebrow I explained. 'The Party Whips have already decided which way to vote. We get our instructions from them.' I shook my head sorrowfully. 'If we ran our businesses like we run the country we'd be bankrupt by the end of the year.'

I was interrupted at that point by Richard rushing in with Sarah, his new nanny. The girl had been with us only a few weeks but was proving capable and pleasant. In her early twenties, Sarah was homely, but with a twinkle in her eyes and a ready smile. Richard wanted to share his latest accomplishment with us – reciting the first two lines of 'Baa Baa Black Sheep'. We laughed and applauded him then I took him on my shoulders back to the nursery, Richard making gee-up noises while I pranced and neighed like a horse. I left for the bank with a smile on my lips and a heart full of contentment.

Staying in the town house meant I had only a few minutes walk to my office. When we had first opened the bank it had been on the ground floor of a four storey building. Now we occupied all three floors of a property on Park Lane that was tailor-made for our purpose. When I arrived I found my steps echoing across the marble floor of the main banking area.

When I reached my office I began working through the files my secretary had placed on my desk that morning along with the mail. It was all fairly routine. Coffee was brought into me while I worked and then, just before lunch, Angus appeared.

'I have to go north. Matters of the estate. I'll take the sleeper train.' As well as his job at the bank, Angus was a Laird and land-owner of a considerable chunk of Scotland. Usually the estate ran without his assistance.

Nodding, I said, 'No problem. How long will you be away?'

'Just tomorrow. I've a problem with a couple of the tenants.'

'I thought that's what your manager was for?'

He shook his head. 'It's a dispute between two of the farm tenants. Only the Laird can decide what's right or wrong.'

'What's the dispute about?' I was intrigued.

'A bull escaped from one of the farms, crossed to another and serviced a number of cows. Ownership of the calves is being disputed.'

I couldn't help grinning. 'How do they know the bull did it?'

Angus grinned back. 'Two ways. The colouring of the offspring and the fact he was caught on the job.'

'So what will you do?'

He shrugged. 'No idea. I need to get all the facts. Make a decision, then make a ruling.'

'Sounds like a court and you're the judge.' I was half joking but Angus took it seriously.

'Precisely. Which is why I have to be there.'

'How many calves are involved?'

'It looks like three.'

'Pity.'

'Why's that?'

'If it had been two you could have given them one each and that would have been the end of it.'

'I'd already thought of that. But what do I do about the third one?'

'Toss for it? Head or tails?'

Angus shook his head. 'David, you really need to take this seriously. These calves are worth a great deal of money, especially if they're from stock like ours. They can be worth a small fortune if they begin to win prizes at the international shows. A champion can sell for over two hundred pounds.'

I looked at him in complete surprise. 'That much?'

'Certainly. We sell our best bulls to South Africa and Argentina. They're in great demand. So it's a serious business.'

'When will you be back?'

'I'll take tonight's sleeper up and tomorrow's back.'

'Can't be helped, I suppose, but we need you here.'

'I know. But I've no choice, believe me. There's nothing that can't wait until I get back.'

I had an idea, 'Why not get Sion to take you? If you get there this afternoon you could be back first thing in the morning.'

Angus looked doubtful. 'I suppose so. But Sion's so busy I doubt he'll have the time.'

'If I know my brother he'll jump at the chance. Flying is his life blood.'

'All right. Let's ask him.'

I instructed my secretary to try and get Sion on the telephone. Angus and I discussed bank matters for a few minutes until my brother was put through. I put the proposition to him.

Sion was silent for a few seconds. 'I'll need to rearrange a few things but I don't see why not. What time does Angus want to leave?'

'As soon as possible. He can be with you in two hours?'

I made the query with raised eyebrows to Angus who nodded. 'Yes. He can be with you by midday.'

'I'll be ready.'

We exchanged a few pleasantries and I broke the connection. 'I wonder how many other landowners would like to fly instead of taking the train?' I asked pensively.

'No idea. But you know what Sunday night is like on the train south. The first class bar is packed. Many of the regular commuters are in the Lords but there are also a lot of Commons MPs as well. They travel north on Thursday nights, do constituency work on Friday and Saturday and return Sunday or sometimes Monday.'

'If there was an early morning flight on Monday they could have another night at home.'

'For those who want it. For many it's another night away from their mistress,' Angus said cynically.

I nodded. 'True. But there are many who are just too old, or have too much integrity, to be playing away from home. And they might like another night or two with their families. If the plane left on Thursday night it would be two extra nights.'

'Except it wouldn't work in the winter. The nights are too long and night time landing is a hazardous undertaking. Hell, *daytime* landings are bad enough.'

'Do you think they'd be too scared to try the service?'

'I wouldn't say that. I can sound out members of the Lords and you do likewise in the Commons. If we do get enough takers, what are you proposing?'

'To set up a regular charter. You talk to Sion about it on the flight north. I'm sure the Griffin III can carry fifteen or sixteen passengers. He'll have to cost it. But it may work.'

On that note Angus left the office. I didn't see him until the following evening when we met in one of the bars at the House of Commons. Over a large whisky I asked him about his trip.

Shrugging he smiled. 'I dispensed justice with the

wisdom of a Solomon. There's no doubt as to who the sire of three of the calves is. There's a fourth we're still waiting to see. It's not been born yet. We solved the problem by drawing the calves' names out of a hat. Each farmer got one and the third will be kept at home farm. When it's sold the cost of its keep will be deducted and the balance shared between the two who are in dispute. If the fourth calf is also involved then we'll draw the names again and one can go to each of the farms. Nobody was particularly happy. But tough.'

'It sounds fair to me.'

'I suppose it is but usually its a question of paying for the bull to cover the cow. He gets three opportunities to get the cow impregnated and if he fails, too bad. The owner of the bull gets paid. There are all kinds of implications when this sort of thing happens, all to do with the purity of the bloodlines and the genealogy of the stock.'

'Genealogy? You're joking.'

'No. Some of the great champions can be traced back hundreds of years. You'd be surprised.'

'Talking of which, how's Catriona?' She was Angus' wife. She was pregnant and there had been one or two scares during the start of her pregnancy when Angus thought she was going to lose the baby.

'Fine. She can't wait for the baby and neither can I.'

I grinned and changed the subject. 'Did you talk to Sion about flying regularly back and forth?'

'Yes. He's thinking about it. He likes the idea but he needs to work out the details. He said he'll get back to us at the end of the week.'

It was Saturday before I heard from my brother. He came up to town to talk about the idea. We met in my study.

'I need to have two pilots and I suggest a steward. His job will be to dispense snacks and drinks. I've totalled the lot and these are the figures. You can see here,' he pointed with a pencil, 'that I've compared the costs with taking the train. If ten passengers share the plane and split the price equally it'll be no more expensive than the night sleeper. If the plane is full and sixteen share then it's a lot cheaper per head.'

'And if only six or seven fly?'

'Then it's more expensive. It will be up to the passengers what they want to do. If there were ten regulars then they may wish to keep the plane just for themselves and fly with empty seats and be more comfortable. By the way, I also intend the drinks and snacks be free. It's all part of the cost.'

I liked the whole idea and said so. I could see nothing wrong with his plan.

'Except we don't know if we've enough takers to make it work.'

I smiled. 'Not so. I've already been taking soundings. And so has Angus. If everybody we've asked uses the service you'll need another plane at least.'

'So you think we should go ahead?'

'Definitely. How soon can you get started?'

'I need a couple of weeks. Even if we only use one plane we need a second as back up. If necessary we can use the second plane if there are too many passengers for one of the flights. You can see the profits on the third page of the proposal. Even with a second flight from time to time we can't go wrong. You can see the schedule I propose gives us plenty of time for servicing the planes.'

We discussed it at length. Throwing around some more ideas, we agreed that half a dozen reporters should travel free on the maiden flight. Twelve days later the service was inaugurated. Much to his chagrin Sion was not flying. It was a great success. The publicity was excellent and from the outset the plane was always full. The second plane was used fairly often and Sion was soon thinking of getting a third one as the standby. The flights flew out of a new airport located at Croydon, south of London, to Perth. After a month the flights became daily as ordinary passengers elected to fly rather than take the train. There were plenty of people going to Scotland for the shooting and hill walking. The morning flight flew north, the evening one south. Sion was even toying with the idea of two more flights a day, a morning one from Scotland and an evening one from London.

Six months later I was with Angus in Scotland when he received a telegram from Madelaine urging him to return at once. Catriona had gone into labour two weeks early. We'd been due to catch the following evening's flight but instead we rushed south on the night train. An hour after we arrived at King's Cross we were pacing the corridor of the hospital when Catriona gave birth. Much to Angus' relief both mother and baby were doing well. To everyone's great joy, the Laird's first child was a boy. That evening the plane on which we had been scheduled to fly south crashed somewhere in the Borders.

12

As SOON AS I heard the news on the wireless the following morning I telephoned the airfield. Sion sometimes filled in if he was short of a pilot and relief swept through me when he answered my call.

'Sion? Thank the Lord! What's happened?'

'I don't know. I heard about the crash an hour ago and I'm still trying to find out details. I'm getting nowhere this far away and so I'm going up right now. I'll take the two-seater.'

'Do you want company?'

He paused for a second before answering. 'I was going to take Mike.' Michael O'Donnell, ex-sergeant major and Victoria Cross holder from the Great War was Sion's right-hand man and senior pilot. 'But it would make more sense to leave him here. I'll be happy to have your company.'

Within minutes of arriving at Biggin Hill we were airborne in the Griffin, a refined version of the single seater Sion had developed for the war of 1914. Once revolutionary in design, the old plane had outlived its usefulness and its successor had been given the original name. The Griffin was a single wing, single engine plane capable of attaining a speed of 160mph. I sat behind Sion in the open cockpit, well muffled against the wind, the cold and the noise. Communication was only possible via hand signals so neither of us bothered unless it was to point out something interesting on the ground. Luckily the day was dry, but bitterly cold, which was only to be expected in December. A welcome modification Sion had installed was a heating system that blew hot air around our feet. A scarf kept my face warm and pilots' goggles kept the wind from my eyes. We'd been in the air about an hour when Sion pointed down. In the distance I could make out a town and on one side a straight, short road. On approach I saw other aeroplanes and realised that it was a flying field. Landing with a bounce we taxied over to a corrugated iron hut.

Stiffly I climbed out of the cockpit, glad to be moving. 'Where are we?'

'Lincoln. I need to telephone Mike. He's trying to get exact co-ordinates of the crash site. I'll arrange to refuel while you get us a cup of coffee.'

Inside the hut I found a lit stove with a kettle sitting on top, steam pouring from its spout. The hut was typical of the airfields dotted around the country. Pilots often dropped in for warmth and sustenance, usually in the form of a cup of tea or coffee. Facilities were free to travellers, who could help themselves. There was nobody else inside but I saw a few men walking about outside, talking to Sion. Ten minutes later he joined me. I handed him a mug of coffee.

'As soon as I've finished this I'll telephone Mike from the control office.'

'Where's that?'

'The other side of the field. About ten minutes away.'

'I'll come with you.'

We wandered outside and had a brisk walk across the frost hard ground. Planes were parked in various spots around the field, some with men working on them, others sitting idle. I noticed that none of them had the elegant sleekness of the Griffin. Indeed the plane had already attracted attention and a number of men had gathered around, looking her over. Sion was blasé on the subject.

'It always happens. Although single wing aircraft have

been around for a few years they still attract a lot of interest. Here we are.'

We entered a hut which was a replica of the one we had left. Inside there was a desk strewn with papers and a telephone. Two men and a woman were working. Introductions were made. They were obviously impressed to learn Sion's identity. I often forgot that Sion was becoming something of a legend in aviation, thanks to his exploits during the war and his state of the art aircraft design and manufacturing company.

I telephoned John. He had no new information other than to say that the police were now interested in the cause of the crash.

Sion got through to Mike, listening intently for a few moments. Looking up, he checked a chart that filled one wall. 'We're at Lincoln. We can be at Hawick in an hour. I don't see a landing site.' He paused. 'Okay. I'll phone from there.' He hung up. 'We need to get to,' Sion pointed at the chart, 'just here. According to Mike there's a landing strip halfway between Hawick and Selkirk. Although it's not shown on the chart.'

'That's right,' said one of the men. 'I've been there.' Standing up he walked across to the chart and pointed. 'Just here.'

'Good. Thanks for that,' said Sion.

'We heard what happened,' he added. 'Good luck. It's a terrible day for us all when a plane crashes. It makes the public lose confidence.'

'True. We urgently need to find out what caused it,' said Sion.

'Probably dirty fuel,' said the man.

Sion nodded. 'That's what I was thinking. It's the most common problem but we've installed some excellent filters with back-ups.'

Soon we were flying north again. Flying over the river Humber, we passed the sprawling conurbation of Leeds on our port side and then we were climbing to gain height to take us over the Fells. Sion was a superb navigator. He used every trick in the book, hitting his target points every time, knowing exactly where we were at any given moment.

A few minutes after passing over the river Teviot at Hawick we were circling a large flat field. I could just make out a path of sorts and in the distance I could see a wind sock. We landed with a bump, bounced and settled down. Sion gunned the engine and we trundled across the field to a shack on the perimeter. Cars were parked outside and when we climbed down from the plane we were met by a number of men, some in police uniform. The man in charge introduced himself as Inspector John Carrew of the Lothian and Borders Police. He was a tall, spare man with a bristling fair moustache and a receding hairline.

'What can you tell us, Inspector?' Sion asked.

He shook his head. 'I'd rather leave it to you to say, sir,' he replied in a strong Lowlands accent.

Sion and I exchanged glances. It sounded ominous. 'In that case, can we go straight to the crash site? But before we do, I need to secure the plane.'

'No need for that, sir,' replied the Inspector. 'One of my men will stay with it.' He gave an order to one of the uniformed constables and we climbed into cars and left. The country lane quickly became a track and we were soon climbing the hills with windswept moorlands on either side. A small lake was pointed out to us as Essenside Loch and about two miles further on the track petered out.

'I'm afraid, gentlemen,' said Carrew, 'that we walk from here.'

Being dressed warmly for the plane we were well kitted out to hike across the hills and we passed along a path that led ever deeper into what appeared to be a wilderness, with no living being in sight. We were accompanied by the Inspector and three of his men and we walked along in silence. A wind picked up from the west and with it came a light shower. Over the brow of a hill we stopped. We were looking down on the crash site.

It was a shallow valley. On the far side was a white-walled cottage. A stream snaked along the valley floor. There was a good deal of activity and I estimated that there were at least fifty people already there, many of them in uniform.

'Where did they all come from?' I asked waving a hand in the direction of the crash site.

'The shepherd that lives in the cottage opposite raised the alarm. When the news got out the Chief Constable received a message from the Home Office so he mobilised half our force.' It was stated matter of factly. There was no hint of annoyance or anger at the intrusion from on high.

'The Home Office?' Sion queried, looking at me.

I shrugged. 'Nothing to do with me. Perhaps John had a quiet word. Though why the HO is beyond me.'

'You mean you don't know,' the Inspector was surprised, 'the names of the people on the passenger list?'

Sion and I shook our heads.

'The Deputy Prime Minister for Northern Ireland is among the dead, as well as three members of the House of Lords.'

'Good God!' Sion exclaimed.

We began to walk down the hill. As we did, the horror of the crash site began to take on some semblance of order. On one side were stretchers laid out with bodies beneath blankets. On the floor of the valley parts of the aeroplane were being manhandled and heaped together. I saw bits of the fuselage being placed around one of the engines. Another engine lay in the distance, a lump of broken metal fit only for the scrap heap.

Sion walked around the wreckage with me at his heels. He knelt beside a piece of the plane and turned it over in his hands. He looked up at me bleakly and asked, 'What do you think, David?'

I heaved a sigh and said, 'A bomb?'

Nodding he looked at the Inspector who nodded in return. 'That was our conclusion as well. This is a murder hunt.'

More men arrived. From Otterburn Barracks came members of the Regiment of the Scottish Royal Fusiliers and soon a camp site was erected. A cook-house began turning out tea and hot food which was gratefully accepted by everyone.

'What do you intend doing?' Sion asked the Inspector. 'This is obviously out of my hands.'

He shrugged. 'We'll try and find out who planted the bomb. On the face of it,' he paused and then continued, 'it seems like Irish Nationalists. But then they always get blamed whenever something like this happens.'

There was nothing more that we could contribute. The Inspector walked back with us to the cars. We were taken to Hawick and there we booked into a small hotel. The Inspector joined us at the bar.

'I've telephoned headquarters. They are going to check who had access to the plane. Och, it's a terrible crime. All those men dead. And for what purpose?' It was a rhetorical question.

'I'm going to have to talk to the press soon,' said Sion. 'What should I tell them?'

'I think the best tack to take,' said Carrew, 'is to tell them that we're baffled. That there seems no logical reason for the crash but as soon as we know anything they'll be told. We'll withhold the names of the victims until the next of kin have been informed. That'll give us a wee bit of time to find the culprit.'

'Do you think you'll find whoever did this?' I asked.

The Inspector took an appreciative mouthful of his malt before replying. 'I don't know. We usually do. Once we start we won't stop. Especially with a case like this one. The only problem I can see is that whoever did it may already have skipped the country. Gone back to Ireland.'

'If it's anything to do with Ireland,' I said.

'I'd bet my pension on it.' He drained his glass. 'Well gentlemen, thank you for the dram. I must get on.'

When he left we sat in contemplative silence. The possible involvement of Irish Nationalists was not good news. Years before, Sion had been involved in flying escaped Nationalists back to Ireland. The experience had been nasty and Mike O'Donnell had been lucky not to be killed. 'If it is Ireland then maybe Mike can help.'

'I doubt it,' replied Sion. 'And anyway, I wouldn't ask. It's too dangerous. Look what happened last time.'

'So we leave it to the police?' I queried.

'This time, David, I think it's for the best. Don't you?'

We spent a quiet evening in the hotel. I phoned John who confirmed that he had used his influence to get things moving with the police and the army. It was looking more and more like an Irish problem though there were no firm leads.

The following morning we were about to have breakfast when Mike O'Donnell arrived. O'Donnell was Irish through and through, though he held no truck with nationalism. He believed, as did I, that independence should be won through the ballot box. There were many others who thought that only direct action would work. I understood their point of view when faced with the intransigent, bloody-mindedness of some of the establishment in England. The Irish question was a running sore that needed cauterising or it would continue to fester.

'You made good time,' Sion greeted him. 'Do you want breakfast?'

'I'm starving,' said O'Donnell. 'We drove all night, so we did. We've brought the two biggest lorries I could find.'

'Who's with you?' I asked.

'Peter, Raphael and Juan.'

The Cazorlas were the backbone of Sion's engineering

business. Intelligent, mechanically minded and hard-working, they were an amazing family to know, warm and intensely loyal. It made sense that they had come.

We waited for the three of them to join us before we started breakfast. It was a sombre affair made doubly so when we told them about the bomb.

O'Donnell asked, 'Have you spoken with the crew's family yet?'

Sion nodded. 'I managed to get hold of Stuart Aitken's father and Bob Pritchard's wife. I'll go and see them when I get back.'

I knew Aitken and Pritchard were the pilots. Stuart had flown at the end of the war and seen service in France while Bob had been flying as a hobby for three or four years. Bob had only been married six months.

'And the steward?' I asked.

'Colin Bateman. A bachelor. No family. A bit of a loner but very good company and very good at his job. He was forever telling jokes to the passengers and was very popular. I checked his records. He has a sister in Tunbridge Wells. I've still to contact her. I hate having to do it but it goes with the territory.'

There were sombre nods from them all. 'Bastards, whoever did this,' said O'Donnell with feeling. 'I'd like to get my hands on them.'

'So would I,' said Sion.

'*Madre mia*,' said Peter, 'it is all so terrible. To destroy such a beautiful machine as well. It is unforgivable.'

That was typical of Peter. He thought in terms of the aircraft, not the lives lost. It wasn't that he was callous, it was just that after seeing so much death between 1914 and 1922 – the Great War and the Influenza Outbreak – he, like many, had become hardened to the cheapness of life. Like him, his sons were excellent mechanics and loved helping to design the aircraft as well as build them.

'Do you want me to try and find out if the Boyos are involved?' O'Donnell asked in an undertone.

I stepped in before Sion. 'No. Leave it to the police. It could be something entirely different.' I paused and then added as an afterthought, 'They haven't contacted you at all, have they?' I asked him.

He looked genuinely surprised. 'No. Why do you ask?' I had great respect for O'Donnell. The tall, tough man had won his VC the hard way. He and his men had been pinned down by three German machine gun nests. He had single-handedly taken care of each one, killing eighteen of the enemy in the process. O'Donnell had saved the lives of at least fifty men that day.

'I can't help wondering, after the last time.'

He shook his head. 'No. I'm long off their list. Let me ask a few questions,' he said. 'I might be able to find out something.'

'It's just as likely not to be them,' I pointed out.

O'Donnell snorted. 'It ain't going to be the Sally Army now, is it? I'll ask. Discreetly, like.'

'Right, do that,' said Sion. 'In the meantime we've work to do. We have to get the plane down off the mountains and back to Biggin Hill. The army'll help but we'd better get up there. David, you may as well stay here. I'll go with the others.'

Sion's plan suited me. I had things to do.

BOOK 2

Sion's Story

13

SION WATCHED THE lorries depart with a heavy heart. The deaths of such prominent people would ensure maximum bad publicity. The company had lost not only an aircraft, but also the confidence of the public. Just when so many more people had been prepared to try the fledgling service than ever before. He doubted now whether he would be able to fill one flight a week. Damnation!

David and he flew north to Edinburgh. The airport lay to the south of the city. A few maintenance hangars were scattered about and a wind sock hung at either end of the runway. Half a dozen aircraft were parked there, none as modern as the Griffin. Lining up to land, Sion was thinking furiously. Had the target been one of the passengers or the company itself? It was easy to put the problem down to Irish Nationalists and leave it to the police. But suppose they were all on the wrong track? Just suppose he had enemies who were out to destroy him and the business? He shook his head. That was nonsense. Was he being paranoid for no reason? They landed with a heavier bounce than usual and taxied over to the passengers' shed.

The single storey building had been extended over the past three or four years so that now there were offices, a passenger lounge and a small room for handling parcels. Passengers carried their own cases to the plane but packages being sent as air cargo were delivered to the airport and handled by one man. The Post Office had also begun using the service for delivering letters. Air-mail had been in common use since August 1912 when flights between London and Paris had been inaugurated. Ever since the success of the New York to Washington air-mail service in May 1918 there had been talk about having a similar service between Edinburgh and London. The saving in time could be calculated in minutes rather than hours, as the train service was fast and frequent, direct from the centre of one capital to the next. However, the novelty factor amused the rich. It pleased them to be sitting in their drawing rooms boasting that they had received an air-mail letter from Edinburgh or London.

The downed plane had taken off from Perth then landed at Edinburgh to pick up more passengers and to collect sacks of mail. Identifying himself at the airport's main office Sion asked for the aircraft's manifest. He perused the names and handed the list to David.

David examined it carefully. 'I see the hand of the Irish all over this one,' he said. 'These names prove it. With the banning of Sinn Fein in the north, the tension's getting worse. Both the IRA and the Ulster Unionists want the Parliament closed and power moved back to London for diametrically opposite reasons. Either one of them could have planted the bomb. I had wondered if it was aimed at us. Or one of us. But somehow I don't see it. Do you?'

'Not really but there is a third possibility. What if there was somebody due on that plane who didn't catch it for some last minute reason?'

'Who?' David asked.

Sion shrugged. 'Angus for one.'

David was about to argue but then paused to think. Finally, he shook his head. 'I don't buy that either.'

Sion sighed. 'Neither do I. It was just a thought. Unless . . . there was somebody else due on the flight? I'll go and ask.' They returned to the counter and Sion made the enquiry. No one else had been due to fly on the plane.

'What do we do now?' David asked.

'Now we refuel and find a bed for the night. We'll leave in the morning.'

The following day, prior to take-off, Sion spent an inordinate amount of time searching the aircraft for items that should not be there – just in case. Finally satisfied they took off. They refuelled at a small field south of Leeds and by lunch time they were back at Biggin Hill.

The newspapers were full of speculation. Some arguments bore water, others were patently nonsensical. Various groups – Irish Nationalists, Scottish Nationalists, dissatisfied Ulster Unionists, Communists against business, even the jilted lover of one of the passengers – were named as suspects. There was not a shred of evidence to convict one party or another until O'Donnell got a lead.

Sion was at home in his kitchen, a large comfortable room, when there was a knock on the door and O'Donnell entered, a grim look on his face.

'I think I may have something on the crash,' he said without preamble.

'Take a seat and I'll get you a cup of tea.' Sion stood up and began pouring from a teapot keeping warm on the wood-burning stove. Without asking, he added milk and sugar and handed the mug over. 'So what have you learnt?'

'I passed the word out through my cousins. They owe me after I gave them the money to buy a post office and shop in Dublin. They've both been, shall we say, connected? On the edge of nationalism in Ireland for years. Thing is, they knew who to ask. I told them to be discreet – and that's why it's taken so long. The rumours in Ireland have been almost as mad as the ones here.' He took a mouthful of tea. 'Anyway, they had a bit of luck. Someone in the shop, mouthing off, dropping hints about the crash. Then somebody knew something else. And so it went on. Bit by bit they built up a picture.'

'So what happened?' Sion interrupted him.

'Remember when O'Higgins was assassinated, coming out of church?'

Sion nodded. Kevin O'Higgins had been the vice-president of the Irish Free State. As he lay dying in the road other men pushed through the crowd and pumped his body full of bullets. There had been talk of civil war in the IFS. The murderers had never been caught. 'What's his death got to do with our plane being blown up?'

'Everything. After the assassination the President of the Irish Free State, William Cosgrave, tried to push a tough law through Parliament, to crack down on the Nationalists. When they voted on the new law they were at an impasse, seventy-one to seventy-one. Hell, even Eamon de Valera and his Fianna Fail party turned up for the vote. And as you know, that's a first in six years. De Valera has always refused to take his seat because the peace treaty with Britain involves swearing allegiance to King George V. Only the casting vote of the Speaker saved the day for the government. Anyway, the new law has meant widespread searches for men and weapons across the IFS. As many as a hundred men are arrested and questioned almost every day. Vast amounts of guns and ammunition have been found, as well as explosives.'

'It was all over the papers,' said Sion, standing to replenish his mug.

'The Labour leader, Tom Johnson, came out against the motion, saying it would not help peace and social well-being. Cosgrave was vitriolic in his condemnation of those against the law as he, probably rightly, said there was room for only one army in the state. He went to a general election over the issue and won with a majority of six.'

'At the cost of human life – two supporters of the government were murdered.' Sion frowned.

'Cosgrave's coalition has brought out a new law, cracking down on Nationalists who refuse to see anything other than a united and free Ireland. The law has gone into force with a vengeance.'

'I still don't see what all this has to do with my plane,' said Sion in exasperation.

'A good deal of the money used to back Cosgrave's election campaign appears to have come from the British government, via the office of the Deputy Prime Minister of Northern Ireland. If De Valera had won he would have pushed for the north to join the south. As it is, with the frontier now fixed it appears that a united Ireland is out of the question. The IRA wanted revenge and blew up the plane with the DPM on board. The fact that other members of the ruling class were killed is seen as a bonus in some quarters.'

'Christ Almighty,' Sion exclaimed. 'Is Ireland to dominate everything we do? If you know all this presumably the authorities know as well.'

O'Donnell shook his head slowly. 'Of course they do, but not officially. They don't want to know otherwise they would have to take action. They also don't want the information about the British funds to become general knowledge in case it sparks even more trouble. They intend to let sleeping dogs lie.'

In his anger and agitation Sion stood up and paced the room. 'We have to do something.' He rammed his right fist into the palm of his left hand. 'Nobody blows one of my planes from the sky and gets away with it.'

O'Donnell knew better than to argue with Sion when he was in such a mood but he tried anyway. 'Think on, man. If you react the Boyos will get you. They have long memories and a longer reach. They never forgive. You know that.'

Sion looked at O'Donnell coldly. 'We just buried two damned good pilots and a steward who'd done nobody any harm. The men kill indiscriminately for their own ends without a thought for anyone else. What about the grieving families who have lost husbands and fathers because of this madness?'

'Look, Sion! If the British government can turn a blind eye and leave it alone then so can we. If the IFS can settle quietly for a few years then the Irish question will slowly disappear. It's for the best. If you cause any trouble then they'll come after you and the family. You can't risk that.'

At the thought of his family, of Kirsty and the kids, Sion knew O'Donnell was right. There was nothing he could do. His shoulders sagged. He slumped into a chair and looked at his friend, nodded and said bitterly, 'It still doesn't tell us how the bomb came to be on the plane.'

'The mail man at the airport. He's a Catholic from Glasgow. His roots go right back to Ireland. He's been working for the IRA for years.'

'Do your cousins know for sure?'

O'Donnell shrugged. 'It makes sense. Nobody else had the same opportunity.'

'Is there anything we can do about it?' Sion asked.

O'Donnell shrugged. 'Maybe. It depends what you want to happen. I can tell the police, anonymously like, and leave it to them. They may get enough evidence for a conviction. On the other hand they may not want a court case and let the matter drop for the greater good.'

Sion sat pensively for a few moments, toying with his empty mug. 'I think we should tell the police. Inspector Carrew seemed like a decent enough copper. I'll phone him.'

A few days later Sion received a telephone call from the Inspector. 'Mr Griffiths? Carrew here. I'm afraid our man did a runner. We had him in for questioning and to my mind there's no doubt he was guilty. But he had a slick solicitor who got him bail. The man has gone to ground.'

'Damn! Any idea where?'

'We're pretty sure he hasn't left Scotland. All the ports have been told to keep an eye out for him. My guess is he's holed up in Glasgow, in one of the east-end tenements, waiting for a chance to slip across to Ireland. Fenian scum.'

'Do you have a photograph of the man?'

'Certainly.'

'Send me a copy, will you? I'll distribute it as well. We may get lucky.'

'Well,' Carrew drew the word out before saying, 'I don't want anything illegal.'

'Of course not. But we have excellent contacts all over Britain.' He did not elaborate and if asked about Glasgow in particular he would have been forced to admit that he could not think of a single name in the city. He'd just had an idea.

Two days later the Orangemen of Ulster received the photograph and a message, giving them the facts. They passed the information to the Orange Order in Govan Hill, Glasgow. Two weeks later a body was found in the River Clyde, under the Victoria Bridge, snagged on a piece of wire. It was identified as the mail man wanted by the Borders police.

Carrew again phoned Sion and began without preamble. 'They found the man's body.'

'Say again?' Sion was bewildered for a moment. His thoughts had been on an innovation for the Griffin's cockpit and not on the tragedy in Scotland.

'The mail man. He was found in the River Clyde three days ago. I've just confirmed the identity.'

'The matter's closed then.'

'It would seem like it,' Carrew spoke heavily. 'But it's not the outcome I would have wanted. Personally, I like the due process of law, watching them pay for their crimes with a rope around their necks.'

'But in this case that wasn't very likely, was it?'

'Maybe. Maybe not. The Chief Constable isn't shedding any tears. I doubt anybody will be looking too hard for who did it. Don't suppose you can shed any light?'

Sion did his best to keep his voice level. 'Me? What could I know?'

'I had a stupid idea that you might have had something to do with it, that's all. Well, I'll leave it there.'

With relief Sion said goodbye to the Inspector. All he knew was that there would be no more bombs placed on his aeroplanes. The explosion on board the Griffin was quietly dropped by the British government who had a word in the ear of the newspaper proprietors. Soon the incident was all but forgotten by all but the grieving relatives; in the overall scheme of things that didn't appear to count for very much.

On the 29th of March 1928 the Suffragettes' long campaign for equality finally came to an end. The House of Commons overwhelmingly passed the Equal Franchise Bill giving all women aged twenty-one or over the vote. With great satisfaction David saw the Bill he had sponsored pass into law. It was, he thought, a fitting tribute to the memory of Emily, his first wife, who had fought so hard for women's suffrage.

In spite of the bombing there were still enough people who wanted to fly to keep the business viable. Security was still minimal and people could wander to and from parked aircraft whenever they felt like it. Later in the Spring, however, a plane bound from Paris to Croydon crashed killing all eight people on board. That dented people's enthusiasm for flying even further. Then on the 1st May that year, the 'Flying Scotsman' train service between Edinburgh and London started their daily non-stop runs. The 392 mile journey was covered at an average speed of 70mph and made air travel superfluous. Sion stopped the flights between London and Edinburgh as they were no longer profitable.

Sixteen days later Wall Street share prices plunged. 4,820,840 shares changed hands – all in the last two hours of trading. The downside was triggered by the selling of aircraft shares such as Curtis Aero and Wright Aeronautical. These were followed rapidly by Montgomery Ward, US Steel, General Motors and General Electric. With such high volumes being traded, panic selling ensued. There had been no bad economic news and experts were unable to say why the slump had occurred. The world appeared headed for a recession.

David and John Buchanan arrived at the airfield a few days later.

'Sion,' David greeted his brother, 'we're travelling to Paris for a summit of European countries at the French Foreign Ministry. We wondered if you'd care to take us.'

'When?' Sion looked up from the drawing laid out on the desk in front of him, pencil poised to make an alteration to the design he was working on.

'In the next few hours. The meeting's tomorrow. We thought we'd catch a show.'

'I'm not sure, David,' Sion replied, throwing down his pencil. 'I've a ton of work.'

'What are you doing?' John asked.

'Trying to find a way to retract the undercarriage. But it's too difficult.' He suddenly grinned. 'But we'll find the answer, won't we Peter?'

'Si, Sion. No problem.' The Mexican smiled back.

'Well, a rest will do you good. A bit of fun,' said David, 'will help your creative juices flow.'

'What's this about?' Kirsty walked into the kitchen, Paul, her son, at her feet. The child had his mother's solemn look but when he smiled his whole face lit up. His fair hair was turning brown and his eyes had darkened in colour, seeming almost black. He was tall for his age and frequently up to one sort of mischief or another. Seeing David he ran into the kitchen and squealed with delight when his uncle threw him up into the air.

'David wants me to take them to Paris. For a meeting,' said Sion. Putting his arm around her, he gave her cheek a kiss. Kirsty's heart shaped face lit up with a smile and she placed her hand to the side of his neck.

'Fifteen countries are meeting to sign a Pact for the Renunciation of War,' said John Buchanan. 'The United States of America's Secretary of State, Frank Kellogg, is behind it. He's been trying to make amends for the fact that the USA didn't join the League of Nations, which I think seriously weakened the organisation.'

'And where's the fun in that?' she asked her husband.

'They suggested a show in Paris,' said Sion, sheep-ishly.

'Why don't you go?' Kirsty suggested. 'When will you be back?'

'In two days,' replied David, putting his nephew down on the floor.

'Right that's settled then. I'll pack you a bag.' Kirsty left the room, leaving Paul with the men.

An hour later they were airborne and heading for the Channel. Two hours after take-off they landed at an airfield to the south of Paris and arranged a car to take them to the city. That night they enjoyed the semi-nude spectacle of Josephine Baker in 'Le Revue Negre' at the Folies Bergères, slapping her buttocks to the tune of 'Yes, sir, she's my baby' The beautiful singer had the audience in a frenzy. A late supper followed and it was the early hours of the morning before they retired to bed.

Nevertheless, David and John presented themselves at the French Foreign Ministry in good time where they were shown into an ornate room. There they shook hands with the other governments' representatives and exchanged small talk until the Foreign Ministers of the nations arrived. The first to sign the pact was Gustav Stresemann of Germany, using a large gold pen, which was solemnly passed from delegate to delegate. At the end a loud cheer went up. The Pact for the Renunciation of War was now binding. War had been made illegal in Europe.

After witnessing the ceremony David and John returned to the hotel and met Sion.

'I wouldn't have missed it for the world,' John announced over a glass of champagne. 'After the Great War we must ensure nothing like it ever happens again in Europe.'

'Amen to that,' said David and the two brothers lifted

their glasses in a silent toast to the future of European peace.

Sion barely noticed the 1929 election. He was too busy running his aircraft manufacturing company. The new Griffin had been ordered by the Air Force and he was trying to turn out thirty planes a month. He could always rely on David, however, to keep him up to date with political events.

'Damn MacDonald,' David said with feeling over a pre-dinner drink at Sion's.

'What's got you so fired up now?' Sion asked in amusement.

'In May the General Election ended in stalemate. We had two hundred and sixty seats, Labour two hundred and eighty-eight and the Liberals fifty-nine.'

'I seem to remember you harping on about it.'

'Well, prior to the election Baldwin and MacDonald met at Crewe and agreed that whatever happened, the Welsh Windbag, Lloyd George, must be kept out of government.'

Sion took a sip of his whisky, wondering where this was leading.

'Well, Labour reneged on the agreement and has done a deal with the Liberals. Just to hold power! *That's* why Baldwin resigned. He was not prepared to be obligated to Lloyd George but it seems MacDonald is. There's going to be ructions in the Commons, I can tell you.'

'David,' Sion said, wearily. 'The degrees of difference between one party and another is so small it hardly matters to the average working man or woman. Politics are all froth and no substance, particularly in the House of Commons.' The ensuing debate lasted most of the evening, much to their wives' annoyance.

Four months later, on 24th October 1929, Wall Street crashed. The threatened world recession arrived with a vengeance.

14

THE CRASH BECAME known as Black Thursday. Thirteen million shares changed hands and at 11.30am the bottom dropped out of the market. After meaningless reassurances by Thomas W. Lamont, senior partner of the huge J.P.Morgan Bank, the prices bounced back and some stocks ended the day higher than when they started. But Black Thursday was the beginning of the end.

Sion looked at the letter in horror and disbelief. The government had cancelled the order for the planes! He felt the rage well up within him and his hand twisted the sheet of paper into a crumpled ball. He threw it down onto the table and stomped out of the house. Taking deep breaths of the early autumn air he walked down the drive towards the factory. Their home backed onto the edge of the airfield and the rear garden led to the huge hangars where they built the Griffin aircraft. He had three styles in production although the new one, the modern Griffin IV, was the plane on which his fortunes rested. Months previously he had sold the idea of a mono-plane, equipped with the new *Rolls Royce S6* engine, to the Royal Air Force. A 'Supermarine' flown by Flying Officer Waghorn had recently won the Schneider Trophy race at a speed in excess of three hundred mph over the Solent. Despite the fact that the plane had heavy floats with which to land and take-off on the water. Sion was convinced that the way forward was to use some sort of retractable gear, to help to reduce the drag of the plane. He and the Cazorlas had been working on the idea. In the meantime, the military contracts he had managed to secure were his bread and butter. Flying and building aircraft was not the way to become rich. His all-consuming obsession had saved his life once but Sion had risked his skin many times. Financially he lived from hand to mouth, despite the company's substantial turnover. All his capital was tied up in the business and current contracts. Now this! What in hell was he going to do?

After reading the recent *Times* report on proceedings in parliament and its intention to pump more money into the economy, he didn't understand why they were now cutting back. Sion hated the idea, but decided he had better ask his brother if he knew what was going on. Maybe David could use his contacts.

It was barely 8am when he entered the echoing vastness of the hangar. A dozen aeroplanes, in different stages of construction, were being worked on by a swarm of men. He stood in quiet satisfaction as he watched the progress of the work. The plane nearest was almost complete. Three weeks from beginning to end was something of a production record and he was proud of it. Next would come the test flight of each aircraft. He often took a plane aloft but now, more than ever, he left that to Mike O'Donnell and his two other pilots. Originally O'Donnell had been hired as a business manager but that had changed when he had learned to fly. He had become Sion's right-hand man and they spent a good deal of time together. Once mere working colleagues, they had become good friends.

One of the men, perched on the cowling of the almost finished plane, waved and Sion waved back. Sound battered him from all directions. High pressure air-driven hammers, huge chain pulleys ratcheting overhead – it was enough to give a man a headache, but they were used to it now. Indeed, Sion welcomed the noise, the sound driving away his gloomy thoughts.

He wandered across to his office and closed the door, reducing the noise by some seventy or eighty percent. The room was more than just an office. It was also the design room. Along one wall were angled drawing boards. Sion studied the different designs pinned to the boards, thinking about what he was going to tell Peter and the others when they came in. Mentally he did the arithmetic. He had enough money in the company to last six months with a full crew. Existing contracts would come to an end and he would be paid. But aircraft production worked months in advance. Orders coming to fruition now had been, in reality, discussed up to eighteen months ago! He had signed a contract for one hundred Rolls Royce S6 engines, based on promises of orders from the War Office. Griffiths Aviation was, after all, on the WO's preferred supplier list. The list, although not officially acknowledged, was where all manufacturers aspired to be. For him the WO rubber stamp was not an aspiration but a necessity. With it he was guaranteed a fair share of the huge orders the War Office placed every day.

He was sure of one thing, he wasn't giving up. He had a real fight on his hands, a fight not just for himself but for the two hundred and ninety-six men and women who worked for him. He straightened his shoulders, mentally shook himself down and sloughed off the beaten feeling that was beginning to envelop him.

First of all he needed some inside information. He picked up the phone to his brother. Griffiths Aviation was still not connected to one of the new automatic exchanges and he had to go through a local operator. He waited impatiently until he heard the click of the operator leaving the line.

Sion quickly explained the situation to him.

'Damnation. I knew some orders were going to be cut back but I didn't expect it to be for aircraft.'

'You knew?' his brother was incredulous. 'You knew and you didn't tell me?'

'Hang on, Sion, we knew that there was going to be a cut-back on military spending but that was almost exclusively in new warships. Particularly battlecruisers. There will be a meeting in January, the Five Power Naval Conference. Even the King will be there. He intends to open the proceedings with a broadcast to the world about the threat of war. I helped to draft his speech, as a matter of fact. We're spending a fortune on the ships and it has to stop. We need to redirect the country's money into public works on a grand scale that will help to get our people back to work. Ramsay has instructed J.H.Thomas, the Lord Privy Seal, to pump-prime the economy.'

'How much?'

'Forty-two million.'

'That's far too little, too late. Hell, I know that and I'm no economist.'

'The problem is if you put three economists into a room they'll all come up with different solutions. As a result the Cabinet is heading for a major clash.'

'Why?'

'Lloyd George and the Liberal economist Maynard Keynes have advocated a huge programme of investment into Britain. The Labour government agreed at first but now they're back-tracking as fast as they can go. There's a fight going on between the Treasury and Sir Oswald Mosley, who's one of the Cabinet, who wants to go as far as Keynes if not further. The resultant stalemate means ineffectual government. In America President Hoover is asking Congress for huge sums of money to invest in federal construction programmes to create jobs. Before it's too late.'

'Why has the WO specifically cancelled the aircraft order?' Sion asked, homing in on his concern.

'I don't know,' said David with brutal honesty. 'It's small beer as far as War Office spending is concerned. I'll try and find out what's going on. Manufacturing means jobs, and we need to get the people back to work and fast. Before we have anarchy in the streets.'

'Do you think that's likely?'

'Yes, if things get bad enough. Already men have committed suicide in the States because they've lost all their money in the crash. The situation's not quite as bad here, but there must be an awful lot of people who are hanging on by the skin of their teeth.'

'David, if I can't solve this problem then we close in six months.'

'That's what I figured. What about exports?'

His brother sighed. 'For such a clever man you can be awfully dim sometimes, Bro. As a supplier of warplanes to the British Air Force, I'm forbidden to sell my products anywhere else.' There was no such thing as an export licence for military hardware. Not if Sion wanted to continue to supply Britain and remain on the preferential suppliers' list. He was more likely to be arrested as a traitor and end his days in prison.

'What about selling civilian planes abroad?'

'To whom? The Japanese don't buy anything from overseas, the Americans don't need to, seeing as they have the most thriving aircraft industry in the world. The French have the same problems as us. It's not even worth considering Germany, as right now the equivalent weight of a Griffin in Reichsmarks wouldn't pay for the engine alone. Their problems continue to grow in spite of the new currency.'

'There is one option,' his brother said tentatively. 'Go after the civilian market. Especially if you fix the planes with floats. Sweden, Denmark and Norway are crying out for planes to flit from island to island. There are a number of American companies after the business in Scandinavia but the word is, the buyers would prefer to deal with a European manufacturer. Give it some thought. In the meantime, I'll try and get some more orders from the Air Force, but I can't promise anything.'

Sion said, 'I'd considered chasing more civilian contracts. I was going to talk to Mike about it. A sales tour of Europe, perhaps. You've saved me the trouble by pointing me at Scandinavia.'

'How difficult will it be to modify the Griffin to take floats?'

'Not very. We did build one a few years ago. However, thanks to its added power the new S6 engine has given us some good options for a new design.'

'Such as?' David was intrigued. He knew his brother had a restless impatience and a brilliant mind when it came to designing aircraft. More importantly, he wasn't afraid to steal others' ideas if they worked.

'The plan is to incorporate wheels and floats. I'll let you know how it works.'

When they eventually finished their conversation Sion sat, compiling a list of possible Scandinavian contacts. When O'Donnell and Peter Cazorla arrived for coffee, he told them about the cancelled order. The news was greeted with stunned silence.

'*Mierda*. What do we do now?' asked Peter, running his chubby fingers through his thick grey hair in agitation.

Sion relayed David's suggestion. 'If we can pull together enough orders from overseas and maybe even alternative British companies we might be able to replace the work.'

'That's no easy task, Sion,' said O'Donnell. 'What's the biggest order ever placed by a civilian company? Six? Ten planes? We need to replace hundreds over the next eighteen months.'

'No, we don't,' replied Sion. 'In reality we need only to replace half the order. If we're careful with our costs and get rid of some of the workforce we might even get that figure down to a third. We need to look at the bottom line. The military have cut us to the bone on costs and are notoriously late payers. Agreed?'

Understanding passed across O'Donnell's face and he smiled for the first time since hearing the news. 'Of course! We get the margins higher. The few planes we've

sold to the airline companies have all made a higher profit.'
Spooning coffee grains into an enamel pot he stopped
suddenly. 'What we need is an edge. Something that'll
make our planes more attractive than the competition.'

'Such as?' Peter Cazorla asked.

'I don't know. More comfortable seats? A longer
range?' O'Donnell shrugged.

'How about,' said Sion, keeping his face a mask and
his voice neutral, 'a mechanism which allows our planes
to land on water and *terra firma*?'

Both men immediately raised protests – it could never
be done. Sion let them have their say until both eventually
ran out of steam.

'That would give us the required edge, all right,' said
O'Donnell, pouring coffee for the three of them and
carrying the mugs across to the table. 'But it's impossible.'

'Not impossible,' Sion shook his head, adding milk
and sugar to his mug. 'It's just never been done.'

O'Donnell grinned. He'd heard Sion say the same thing
on many occasions. 'You also claim we'll fly to the moon
one day.' The tall Irishman and the stocky Mexican
exchanged looks, as if there were no hope left for their
boss and his mad notions. 'Okay. If you can design a
landing gear that will cope with land and water then we'll
have a huge selling point over the other companies. But
dreaming it doesn't make it so.'

'Of course not,' said Sion, 'which is why we need
complete secrecy. No one must find out what we're up
to. You know that the other companies will do everything
in their power to steal our designs. Hell, the aircraft
industry is riddled with spies.'

The other two nodded sagely. They had used a few
underhand methods themselves over the years. 'In the
meantime we carry on as normal. Peter, you, me and
young Ralph *only* to work on the design. Nobody else.
We'll work at home. Get drawing boards put up in the
study. Mike,' he turned to O'Donnell, 'here's a list. Start

thinking where else we can sell the Griffin. Think countries as well as companies. Go to the Scandinavian Embassies in London and talk to their Trade Secretaries. We want the names and addresses of every solvent company in their respective countries who operate aeroplanes. I'll get David to arrange introductions to as many people as possible. His contacts across Europe are legion. In fact,' Sion added as an afterthought, 'so are John Buchanan's. We'll exploit every name we can. We're fighting to survive and, by God, we'll fight hard. We'll take any order no matter how small.' Pausing, he nodded, 'A combined landing system is a sure-fire winner.'

'Maybe,' said O'Donnell, 'but so far nobody has come up with a way to make one work.'

'With the military buying our planes we haven't really explored the potential. Look at these three designs. The first is the flying boat with floats under each wing.' Sion grabbed a pencil and stood at one of the drawing boards. Quickly he sketched the basic design. 'It's literally a flat-bottomed hull that will land and take-off on water with stabilising floats each side. Next we have a normal fuselage supported by two large floats. The result is a small, fast plane. Agreed?' He was rewarded with nods. 'The third is the three-wheel fixed undercarriage which is on all land-based planes. When we combine both – I know,' Sion raised his hand to forestall any protest, 'the difficulties. The unbalancing of the plane along with the extra drag is horrendous. But there has to be a solution. Imagine wheels somehow fixed inside the floats,' his hand flew across the drawing board as he drew the option, 'or a separate arrangement which is somehow removable.'

'You mean,' said O'Donnell, 'so that the plane is rigged to land either on land or water and the pilot can decide on the day?'

'No,' Sion shook his head. 'I mean we take off on land, remove the wheels and land on water.'

'Impossible,' said Peter Cazorla.

Heated arguments carried on well into the afternoon.

Ralph Cazorla arrived towards evening and joined them. He was a younger version of his father, stocky, broad-shouldered and with a sharp mind that thought exclusively in terms of flying and design. He was brought up to date with events and, characteristically, he took the development in his stride.

'Others have tried incorporating a wheel on the bottom of the floats but it hasn't worked,' he said. 'The plane is very tricky to land, especially if there's any sort of chop on the water. We need to find a way of swapping from one to the other.'

'That's precisely what I said,' said Sion, excitement in his voice now that he had an ally. 'We need to be able to remove the wheels . . .'

'Or the floats . . .' interrupted Ralph.

'. . . in mid-air,' continued Sion, uncertainly. 'The wheels would be easier.'

'Agreed,' Ralph said.

Two hours later Kirsty came in looking for Sion. The four men were still hard at it. Sheets of paper on the drawing boards had been covered with ideas but eventually discarded except for one that they kept going back to. When she walked through the door they looked at her, startled.

'Sion,' she said with exasperation, 'dinner has been ready for simply ages.'

Sion looked at his wife and then his watch. 'Oh! Sorry, Kirsty, we hadn't noticed the time.'

'Evidently not. What are you doing?'

'Looking at a new design,' said Sion, vaguely. 'Come on, we may as well finish for the night.' Collecting the sheets of paper, he folded them and put them away carefully in a locked cupboard. Sion took industrial espionage very seriously.

For the next week they discussed and argued design. O'Donnell was no longer needed. He understood what they were trying to do, but his job was to find customers, not design aeroplanes. He let them get on with it. By his estimation he needed to find buyers for sixty to eighty planes if they were to survive the loss of the military order. He had a lot of work to do.

'It's decided then,' said Sion to the Cazorlas, father and son. 'We need to be able to move the wheels. Even the whole undercarriage.' He received nods of agreement. 'If we use the flying boat design we can have the wheels on either side of the fuselage and one back here in the middle. We winch up the wheels and lock them inside the cabin. When we winch them back into position we slide this locking device over the main strut and lock it in place. The biggest problem is one of passenger comfort. The cabin will be open to the elements for anything up to ten minutes while the procedure is being carried out. In the winter and at height it will be extremely uncomfortable.'

'NACA,' said Ralph, using the acronym for the National Advisory Committee for Aeronautics in America 'has been working on this problem since the war. Heck, their wind tunnel experiments have produced some startling results which they have always shared with us. If I remember correctly they said that a completely retractable undercarriage was the best way to create the optimum flying results.'

Cazorla senior nodded. 'We still have no way of locking the wheels in position.' He spoke with irritation, the long days and short nights fraying his temper. '*Pedir paras al almo.*' In his agitation he reverted to Spanish. 'Don't expect the impossible.'

'What if,' said Ralph, excitement creeping into his voice, 'we were able to move the lot, floats and wheels, through one system.' He stood up and eagerly reached for a pencil and fresh sheet of paper. 'Right now each float is held to the wing with two fixed struts, here and here.' He drew the two vertical bars, each about a quarter way in from the front and rear of the edge of the float. 'If we moved the rear strut to here,' he sketched it at the halfway point, 'we'll have the same strength in the float. If we place the wheel strut next to it, with a hinged forward strut, we create a space no bigger than about a foot square on either side of the cabin to hold a mechanism which can raise and lower both the floats and the wheels.'

'But Ralph,' Sion interrupted, 'we'll still have the same problem – freezing wind whistling into the cabin.'

'Imagine hollow chimneys reaching as far as the roof. We have turning gear on either side of the chimney, one to operate the floats, the other for the wheels. We lock both in place by pins, here and here,' Ralph indicated points at the foot of the chimney and on the floor of the cabin. 'We can reduce overall drag by quite a high percentage.'

Sion frowned. 'Nine percent,' he spoke absently. He suddenly looked sharply at Ralph. 'That's the figure from NACA. It could work. The chimneys become a feature. We incorporate them into the cabin's decor. Or better still,' he snapped his fingers, 'disguise them with a small bookrack holding newspapers and books for the flight.' He stared at the drawing, ideas churning in his head, dismissing some almost as quickly as they appeared until he was left with a few that could just about work. If the wheel assembly was winched away and the floats tucked under the belly of the plane, then there was no doubt that drag could be reduced significantly. That would mean more speed, greater endurance and a longer flight. The crucial part of the design was being able to lock the landing gear into a place safe enough to take the sharp impact of hitting the ground. What had one test pilot waggishly called it? A controlled crash? That was it in a nutshell. Every landing was a controlled crash from which it was essential that pilot and passenger walk away safely and happily. The locking gear would have to be especially strong to deal with the weight of the impact.

The Cazorlas were obviously sharing the same thoughts. They began discussing the options. Peter Cazorla made rapid calculations on a slide rule but kept shaking his head. 'I can't get a pin strong enough. The sheer force is so great that a pin will almost inevitably break and the undercarriage collapse.'

The other two nodded in gloomy acceptance. They needed another solution. Finally stopping for the evening, Sion decided that he needed some fresh air to help him think. Outside, in the deepening gloom, he walked, deep in thought for half an hour, pausing finally under the horse chestnut trees in the corner of the airfield. There Sion bent down and picked up a fallen spiky, green chestnut and broke it open. Looking at its glossy, brown kernel he squeezed it between his fingers to test its hardness. Memories of playing conkers flooded back from his childhood. One year . . . He stopped, the chestnut resting in the palm of his hand. An image of threading the string through the chestnut sprang to mind. Rushing home he was still frantically drawing his idea when Kirsty entered the room.

'Dinner's getting cold and don't forget we're visiting Winchester tomorrow.'

'What?' Sion looked at her distractedly. He was sure he'd cracked the problem. 'What was that about Winchester?'

'We're going to collect Alex from the school. Your son is playing in the second fifteen team and then we're bringing him home for the Christmas holidays. It's his first match. Against Eton,' she added in exasperation. Her preoccupied spouse had obviously forgotten.

'Kirsty, I can't!' Sion said in dismay. 'I've got to finish this design. It's vital.'

'And so is seeing our son play rugby.' An obstinate look came over her face – one that he knew only too well. 'We see little enough of him as it is. One day won't make any difference and you know he'll be thrilled to see you.'

Sion was about to argue but thoughts of Alex persuaded him otherwise. 'You're right. I can show Peter what I've done after dinner and let him get on with it. But it'll mean working late,' he warned her.

When Kirsty awoke the following morning Sion's side of the bed was empty. She went downstairs to find him slumped over his drawing board fast asleep. She didn't know whether to be angry with him or not. For a few seconds she stood next to him, looking lovingly at his dear face. Meeting and marrying Sion had been her salvation in more ways than one. Falsely arrested for theft and soliciting, she would have faced prison had Sion not paid the fine and taken her into his home. To thank him she began working for him but, in the end, she fell in love with him. There were over ten years between them, but the difference had never mattered to her, although it had bothered Sion at first. She had spent fourteen years with this exasperating, driven, wonderful man. She sighed. How time flew.

Gently she woke him up. Groggily Sion sat up, yawned and stretched. Kirsty practically pulled him from the stool and up the stairs. An hour later, after a shave, bath and large breakfast, they were on the road. Sion was driving. The December day was crisp. The sky was blue, there wasn't a cloud and hardly a breeze disturbed the tranquillity of the morning. From Biggin Hill they had to drive through the countryside to Leatherhead and then on to Guildford. There they drove on the new road that went all the way to Southampton, a wonderful innovation called a trunk road which had two lanes, one in either direction. It was relatively straight and on some stretches Sion was able to take the car up to fifty and even sixty miles per hour. He was driving the latest Wolseley, a Straight 8 saloon. The car had eight cylinders, did sixteen miles per gallon and had a top speed of sixty-five mph. With his foot hard down the car could accelerate to fifty mph in twenty-seven seconds. Sion enjoyed driving and drove like he flew, with verve tempered by skill.

They stopped on the edge of Winchester for lunch at a country hotel before driving into the school grounds.

'You know,' said Sion, as they entered the gates, 'I've never lost that feeling of awe when I come here.' They slowly drove through the vast grounds. There were pitches laid out on both sides. Cricket in the summer time, rugby in the winter. The craze for soccer had not reached Winchester school and was unlikely ever to do so. Rugger was the game for the upper classes.

15

GAMES WERE ALREADY underway on each pitch. Whistles blew and names were called, there was cheering, yells of encouragement and a good deal of banter. The Griffithses pulled up near the front doors and were approached by a school prefect. Ticking their names off a clipboard, he pointed to the car park, informing them that tea was being served in the masters' common room.

Having been there on numerous other occasions, they knew the way, finding the common room and joining the throng of other parents. Alex's house master, Eric Small, spotted them and greeted them with a hearty handshake.

'Kick-off is in half an hour,' he told them. Contrary to his name he was a large man with a bushy, grey-streaked beard. His black gown was smeared with an unguent of cigarette ash and chalk dust, and his fingers were stained yellow from handling too much hydrochloric and nitric acids during chemistry lessons. Small's experiments were the schoolboys' favourite, as the chemicals were used in the manufacture of explosives. During the Great War Alex's house master had been a captain in the Royal Ordnance Regiment. Showing the boys how to make low grade explosives was one of the party tricks he used to keep his students interested and attentive. He achieved excellent results in the national examinations and had been instrumental in paving the way for many schoolboys to get to the university of their choice. Usually Oxford or Cambridge.

'How's Alex doing?' Sion asked.

'Very well. He's a credit to you both. An enthusiastic little tyke, I'll say that. Willing to give anything a try. He has a natural exuberance that needs . . . curbing from time to time.'

Sion smiled at the accurate description of his son.

'And academically?' Kirsty asked.

'Fair to middling, I'd say. He's lacking in application rather than brains – needs to work harder if he's to achieve the results required for a good university. But don't worry. We'll beat the knowledge into him if we have to.'

Kirsty gasped. 'You don't mean it?'

'Mean it?' Small frowned. 'Of course I do. A judicious caning when required works wonders. I don't think Alex has bent over for me more than three or four times and that's only been to receive two cuts. Some of the boys have had four or even six cuts. You know what they say, spare the rod and spoil the child. Well, that won't happen here, my dear Mrs Griffiths. Mr Griffiths, I'll see you on the field. It's pitch number two. A prefect will show you the way. Now please excuse me.' With a smile he moved to another set of parents.

Kirsty looked at her husband with a mixture of fear, anger and indignation. 'Sion, I won't have my son beaten. It's . . . it's barbaric.'

'It doesn't appear to have done Alex any harm.'

'You can't possible know that. I don't believe he'd get up to anything that warrants a caning.'

'Kirsty, there are over six hundred boys living in this school. Without discipline anarchy would reign. All human life is here, including liars, thieves and bullies. There are also some very pleasant, well adjusted lads like our son, who are a credit to their parents. Before we condemn the school and do something we may regret, like taking Alex out, we need to speak to him and find out what he did to get caned.'

Kirsty sighed while she and Sion joined another couple they knew from previous visits. Their son was in the same house as Alex and both were in the second fifteen for that day's match. They all trooped out to the touch lines to watch the game. Sion once more patiently explained the rules to Kirsty. If the ball was run over the score line the try counted for three points. If it was then converted, i.e. kicked over the goal and between the uprights, it counted for two.

Alex was a miniature of his father, stocky with black curly hair. He was playing in the second row and was always in the thick of it whenever the ball came to a stop. He had waved an acknowledgement to his parents when he had run onto the field but thereafter had feigned an indifference to their presence. This was his first important game as they were against the hated enemy – the second fifteen from Eton. It was a needle match, with old scores to be settled and new ones to be made. The ground was hard and dry and within minutes there were grazed knees and bruised shoulders. By the middle of the first half Eton was winning. Eton had two tries and a conversion while Winchester had one try and one conversion. There were only three points in it. The game flowed back and forth and then the ball went wide from a clumsy kick by the Eton captain but well inside the Winchester half. In a flash Alex darted across the pitch, grabbed the ball and ran along the touch line as fast as he could. His heart was pounding and his breath came in hard, sharp gasps as he dodged a first and then a second player. The Eton team were converging on him from all sides while two players from the Winchester side tried to catch him up to give him support.

A burly prop forward was bearing down on him and Alex felt his body cringe at the thought of being tackled by such a heavyweight. For all his bulk the prop had a good turn of speed in short bursts and Alex was within moments of being smashed to the ground. Knowing he couldn't get around the boy in front of him Alex did the only thing he could. He drop kicked the ball over the head of the prop and turned to run around him. By the rules of the game Alex could no longer be tackled. He was safe. Furthermore there was a chance he'd get to the ball before anyone else and continue his run. A try was in the offing and he could score it. His heart soared as he saw the ball drop loose. It bounced away from the touch line just as the prop smashed into Alex's side and brought him to the ground with a body-jarring tackle. His nose hit the hard earth with a crunch, spurting blood. Tears sprang to Alex's eyes as he tried to sit up. The prop, Bowen, was two years older and two stones heavier than Alex and had tackled high, deliberately trying to hurt the smaller boy. Spectators were cat-calling and a few were booing.

'I say, old chap, I'm most frightfully sorry.' Bowen spoke in a loud voice, holding out his hand to Alex in a gesture of goodwill and friendship. Smirking at him, Bowen assumed a contrite expression on his face.

Ignoring the hand Alex clambered slowly to his feet. He was winded and ached all over. Blood was still dripping freely from his nose. He wiped it with the back of his sleeve.

Having blown his whistle, the referee came over.

'I say, Ref, I'm most awfully sorry. I didn't mean to tackle him late like that. I apologise. And I offer him my hand on it.' So saying the prop held out his hand to Alex a second time who stood looking at it.

The referee was in a quandary. It had clearly been a foul tackle, executed late. He should by rights send the prop off, but that was not character forming, not games-manship. Besides which an apology had been offered.

He made up his mind. 'Right. Shake hands and carry on with the game. A free kick to Winchester.'

The prop held out his hand to Alex who regarded it with disdain. Suddenly Alex was aware that all eyes were on him. To refuse the hand would be churlish. To accept it would be acid in his soul. He had no choice. He took the hand but had to pull away sharply, looking with loathing into the face of the other boy. The look of triumph he saw there made him blink hard.

As the captain took the free kick, the Winchester team strung out across the field, ready to run as fast as they could to get the ball and mark the ground with their heel. That would get them within kicking distance of the goal.

The Winchester captain ran at the ball. He misjudged the distance and kicked the top of the ball, sending it along the ground.

'It's a grubber,' someone called.

Already both teams were converging on the bouncing ball but it was Alex who got there first. Instead of falling on it and calling for a scrum he scooped it up and ran like the wind. Straight towards the prop who had just fouled him.

He was within ten yards of scoring a touchdown. Only the Eton prop was in front of him, charging down on Alex like a runaway train. Alex jinked left and right, trying desperately to put the other boy off. He was within a few paces of being tackled when Alex swerved left and then sharp right. Bowen followed the first movement, but realising he was going to miss Alex, continued sweeping round with his leg stuck out at right angles. Alex was driving forward at the same time and his right leg hit Bowen's boot with a bone-cracking thud. Agony shot up Alex's leg. He screamed in pain and fell headlong over the line. He had scored but the sensation in his leg was beyond anything he had ever felt before. A stretcher was called and he was carried off.

For Alex the remainder of the afternoon passed in a blur. The school matron gave him a painkiller before he was rushed to the local cottage hospital. Through a daze he heard his fear confirmed. His right tibia had broken halfway between his ankle and knee. When he was eventually wheeled out of the operating theatre, a plaster cast stretched from his toes to his knee. He saw his mother trying hard to hold back the tears when she saw him.

Sion forced a smile. 'How are you, tiger?'

'I'm all right, sir,' Alex answered in a trembling voice. Tears were just beneath the surface and neither of them wanted him to shed them.

'Good lad. Well, you'll be pleased to know you're a hero. Your try made it level and your captain converted. The Eton prop got sent off so both teams played on with only fourteen men.'

'Thank you, sir,' Alex said in a stronger voice.

'If you feel up to it, old son, we can go back to school and you can see your friends. Or you can stay here. I've arranged a bed for the night for you. We'll stay in the local hotel and take you home tomorrow. Your decision, Alex . . .'

'I think I'd like to stay here, sir. It hurts . . . a bit.'

'Poor darling,' said Kirsty, kneeling by his side, 'it must hurt like crazy. So none of this stiff upper lip. It was a very nasty break. The doctor said it'll heal given time, but you need lots of rest.'

Her words of sympathy pushed Alex over the edge and the tears started. Kirsty put her arms around her son and ached for him. Alex pulled himself together after a few moments and wiped his cheeks with the backs of his hands.

'Sorry,' he said in a soft voice.

'That's all right, old son,' said Sion, a lump in his throat. 'Tell you what. Why don't we go for tea and then we'll bring you back here. Your mum and I will then go and tell your house master how you're fixed. How's that sound?'

'Sure, Dad, that'd be great.'

Sion smiled. He preferred Dad to sir.

The following morning they drove back to the school, arriving in time for the morning break. When Alex was wheeled into the dining room, where the boys were finishing their tea and scones, a great cheer went up. The head prefect personally raised another three cheers and Alex basked in the reflected glow. The second fifteen's captain came over and shook his hand and many of his friends wished him a speedy recovery. Within minutes his pristine white plaster was covered with scrawled names and messages. For a little while Alex was able to forget his discomfort but soon he was flagging. Kirsty, quick to sense his mood, insisted they leave for their meeting with Mr Small.

Their chat with Small was brief. It was end of term and most of the boys were due to leave over the next two or three days anyway.

'When can we expect him back?' Small asked.

'The plaster will be on for at least three months. Perhaps longer,' Sion answered.

'This is a bad business,' said Small. 'We are putting in a complaint to Eton about young Bowen's unsporting behaviour. It is most ungentlemanly. However, *adhuc sub judice lis est*. Translate young Griffiths.'

'Em, the case is still before the judge, sir.'

'Exactly. Though I have no doubt that the wretched boy did it deliberately. You'll have to stay home until the leg mends, I'm afraid. In the meantime I will see your masters and arrange to have work sent home to you.' He looked at Sion. 'Will that be in order?'

'Yes. Certainly.'

'*Nil desperandum*, Griffiths. You'll soon be back. I've spoken with the headmaster and he agrees that you can miss a term and return after Easter. If you have to cram for a few weeks after you get back, so be it. All right? We can pack your things and forward your trunk or we can keep everything here.'

'Forward it on please,' said Kirsty.

'That's what I thought you'd say, Mrs Griffiths. Is there anything else?'

'I think that's everything,' replied Sion. 'We'll keep you informed of Alex's progress. Good day to you, Mr Small.'

Soon the Wolseley was leaving the school gate. Alex sat in the back of the car with his leg on the back seat, propped up by pillows. Whenever they hit a bump in the road a jarring pain shot through his leg and though he tried hard not to, from time to time he gasped involuntarily. Each sound was a dagger in Kirsty's heart.

'Slow down, Sion,' she ordered, after they'd been on the road only a few miles. 'And try and miss the damn potholes.'

'Sorry. I'll do my best.' Sion eased his foot off the accelerator and their speed dropped to twenty miles per hour. It would be a long journey at that speed but it couldn't be helped. Minutes later Sion pulled over. 'This is ludicrous. We can't subject you to a journey like this. I propose we return to the hospital. You can stay there for a few days until your leg begins to mend and the pain eases and *then* we'll go home.'

'It's all right, Dad. Honest, I can take it.'

'You may be able to, my lad, but we can't,' said Sion and with that he turned the car. They drove sedately back to the hospital in the middle of Winchester and Sion went to find a nurse. Sion quickly arranged for Alex to have a room for a few days while he and Kirsty stayed at the local hotel. Alex was put on a bed and his leg raised on a pulley, to his evident relief.

'We should have stayed here from the beginning,' said Kirsty, once Alex was settled.

'You're right. But usually it's only if both bones are broken that the patient stays in bed. You heard the doctor. The tibia should help to keep the fibula in place.'

'Be that as it may, this is the right decision. We need to telephone home and let them know what is happening.'

'I think,' said Sion, 'that I had better go home while you stay here.' The new design was playing on his mind.

'I've a ton of work to get through. I must see to this concept we're working on.'

Kirsty was about to protest but knew it would be for the best. Sion would be no help, champing at the bit to return. She didn't want Alex to feel any obligation to travel until he was ready and so she nodded. 'You're right. Will you go tonight or in the morning?'

'I'll go now. I'll send Rosa with a suitcase. She can come by train tomorrow. That way you'll have clean clothes.'

It made sense and he left soon afterwards.

Alex stayed in the hospital for five days. By then the pain had eased considerably and he could propel himself without too much discomfort in the wheelchair. Kirsty telephoned Sion with the news. 'We'll come tomorrow by train. It'll be easier on Alex, rather than bouncing around in the car.

'I'll meet you at Croydon. Any idea what time?'

They arrived home in the middle of the afternoon. Sion had turned his study into a bedroom for Alex so that he didn't have to climb any stairs. Everyone made a fuss; plates of Lyons' cakes, ice-cream and comics taking up most of the evening. But Alex was tired after his journey and went to bed early. With only five days to go until Christmas the house was in a state of subdued excitement. The morning of the twenty fifth would be spent at home and then they would be travelling to Fairweather to spend the evening and Boxing Day with David and the rest of the family.

Like all youngsters who had the benefit of good food, and plenty of milk, Alex was mending quickly. His leg itched beneath the plaster and he resorted to a ruler to scratch it. On Christmas morning, Paul and Louise presented Alex with a long box tied with a ribbon. Amidst great hilarity, he opened it to find a pair of crutches.

'Hopefully you won't need them for long, son,' said Sion.

'I'll try them out.' Alex stood on his left leg, tucked the crutches under his arms and swung himself across the floor. 'Brilliant. I can get to my own bed now. Thanks, Dad.'

It was a happy party that left Biggin Hill for the south coast. Kirsty wore a new camel coat, lined in pink floral silk, to match her day dress. She was glad of her pink cloche hat, as it was a blustery day with a hint of rain or snow in the air. Carmen, the nanny, was staying home with her family although she had protested that she wanted to go with them. Even so it was a squeeze to fit everyone and all the presents into the car. They arrived in good time and were soon in the drawing room with cups of tea, scones and hot cinnamon toast.

Holiday or no, Sion had a quiet word with his brother. 'Anything on the aircraft orders?'

'No. I'm still working on it. The War Department has been demob happy leading up to Christmas. But I'll keep at it.'

'Thanks.' If he was disappointed Sion did not show it. 'How's the new design coming?'

'Fine. We're hoping to test fly a prototype in January.'

16

THE AIRCRAFT TOOK OFF with the wheels firmly locked in the down position. Once airborne Sion altered course for the southwest and Southampton Water. The wind was blowing from the northwest, about ten to twelve knots and Sion decided he would land flying into it at Calshot Castle. They had practised raising and lowering the gear fifty, sixty times, and to date it had worked smoothly. This was the crunch – the first live attempt to change the wheels for the floats in mid-air. Once they were over the Solent, Sion gave the thumbs up to Peter Cazorla in the main cabin.

Peter slid a metal plate out of the way, engaged a ratchet drive and began turning a handle on the starboard side. Smoothly the wire pulled the starboard undercarriage tight against the outside of the fuselage and a bolt locked the wheel in place. Repeating the procedure for the port wheel, he moved on to the rear wheel. Mouthing a prayer to the Virgin, he withdrew the pin holding the starboard float and turned a second handle. The float dropped smoothly away from the underbelly and when it reached the end of its travel Peter slid a thick metal plate across, locking the metal strut in place. The gear was raised and lowered with quarter inch flexible wire. When it reached the fully open position the specially modified metal plate slid into position, locking the gear down. The turning gear operated both front and back struts and two separate plates slid into position. On the port side the transition was equally smooth. Thanking the Virgin, he reported to Sion.

'Ready to land.'

Susan had arrived the night before, pleading with Sion to let her fly on the test flight. But Sion had been adamant. When Susan had learnt to fly, Sion had promised David that she would never be on board until the plane had been proven safe. But Susan never missed an opportunity to be a part of anything to do with flying and badgered her uncle until he at least let her go in the boat with Ralph Cazorla to await the plane's landing. In her presence young Ralph was tongue-tied and awkward. He was more than a little in love with Susan. Over the years he had watched her grow up, changing from a precocious if intelligent child, sometimes given to dramatic outbursts, yet filled with great good humour. She had blossomed into a beautiful young woman, strong-willed, independent and utterly unaware of her beauty.

Ralph was armed with a Very pistol. During the landing, if anything appeared amiss, he would fire the pistol and the landing would be aborted. Sion could see him as they lined up to land. He was waving his encouragement and causing the boat to rock alarmingly in his excitement. He sat down with a thud as the plane hit the water in a fine spray and came quickly to a stop. His mortified expression sent Susan into a fit of giggles. Scowling, Ralph rowed across to the plane. As the door opened, he smiled up at his father.

'Everything work all right?' Ralph asked.

'I think so. Let me climb down and take a look.' Peter and Susan exchanged places.

Sion and Susan dropped a small kedge anchor out of the door. They were in about twenty feet of water and it quickly snagged. The anchor would be useless in any sort of a blow but on the calm water it sufficed. The Cazorlas made a careful inspection of the plane, paying particular attention to the floats.

Sion stood anxiously in the doorway until Peter Cazorla shouted, 'It looks fine. Now we need to try it in reverse.'

He climbed back into the plane while Susan returned to the boat and Ralph rowed them clear. While Sion went through the starting procedure Peter stood ready to hoist the anchor aboard. When the engine was roaring healthily he hauled the anchor in and secured it in its resting place by the doorway.

Airborne once more Sion headed back to the airfield. Peter slid the plates open, engaged the ratchet and turned the handle, winding up the wire until the floats were secured hard against the underbelly of the plane once more. Without increasing the throttle Sion watched as the airspeed indicator crept up by ten knots. The reduction in drag was clear.

Near the airfield at Biggin Hill Peter pulled out the pin which held the starboard wheel locked in the up position and began turning the handle. Gravity took the wheel down and he slid the plate over, locking the wheel in the landing position. He did the same for the port and then the rear wheel. Satisfied, he slid into the co-pilot's seat alongside Sion.

'Looks okay,' he said.

Sion nodded, lining up to land. There was no warning red flare and with dry mouths they touched down. There was the usual bounce and squeal of the tyres, as they settled onto the tarmac. Sion taxied to the hangar and the plane vanished from sight. When they climbed down from the plane half a dozen of the men gathered around inspecting it. The system had worked perfectly. The locking pins and the plates only worked if the landing gear was in the correct position and so the pilot had the satisfaction of knowing that either the wheels or the floats were properly aligned for landing or after take-off.

The next stage was to incorporate the idea into the production line. In the meantime O'Donnell was to start lobbying customers. Prospective buyers could either come and see the revolutionary design or they would travel to them. Whichever way, they were in for a busy time.

O'Donnell had amassed a mountain of information on various companies, creating a list of names and addresses across Europe. David and John Buchanan had also supplied him with undated letters of introduction to senior politicians and company directors. So far O'Donnell had made appointments with twenty companies, six of whom agreed to visit Biggin Hill.

The first was due in three days time.

Back in his office, Sion sat looking at his wall chart. It was split into months and showed meetings and sales conferences far off into the future. It was based more on optimism than fact.

For weeks he had been quietly battling the insurers of the plane they had lost in the Scottish borders. Lloyds were arguing that the aeroplane operators should have checked the baggage and the plane for bombs and therefore should accept responsibility. That was nonsense, of course, but it looked as if it could go to court to settle, costing money but also precious time. As a result of Lloyds' argument some of the families of the dead passengers were considering suing him as well. So the Lloyds issue was far greater than merely the cost of the plane. If he lost he could be laid open to a lawsuit from the families of the passengers killed. In the meantime his cash-flow suffered. The bank had already sanctioned an increase in the overdraft with two provisos – one that there was a significant order for the planes from His Majesty's Government and two, that there was a pay out from Lloyds for the downed plane. He was skating on very thin ice.

Sion thought back to the good old days. With just himself, the Cazorlas and a small workforce he had actually been making real money. During the Great War, the war to end all wars, he'd had no option but to expand. The planes had been needed and he had supplied them. He smiled ruefully. Once he had set off down that trail there had been no turning back. Expansion meant borrowing from the bank and that in turn had led to further expansion. Now he was having to run to stand still. Even so he was slipping back, and needed to do something drastic. His present course of action would be a start, but it was probably too little too late. With a heavy heart he thought about his workforce. They were, on the whole, highly skilled. Most of them were good workers, with only a few shirkers. He needed some sort of criteria for keeping some and sacking others. He shook his head in irritation. There were other considerations. Last in, first out? Preference given to family men? What about the skills of the individuals and their contribution to the company? The door opened and Kirsty walked in, shrugging out of a green jacket, which, frankly, had seen better days.

He smiled and said, 'Hullo, my love.'

Kirsty crossed the room and put her arms around his neck. 'Why are you sitting in the gloom?' She asked, twiddling his hair around her forefinger.

'I hadn't noticed. What time is it?'

'Nearly six o'clock. What were you thinking about?'

'Business.' He took her hand and kissed it, standing up, putting his arms around her waist. 'But that's all the thinking I need to do.' As always her presence made him feel better. It seemed to him that he loved her more with each passing day.

'Sion, don't lie to me. There's something wrong so tell me what it is and I may be able to help.'

'There's nothing . . .' he began but stopped as she placed a finger on his lips.

'Shush. I know there is. If you don't want to tell me that's one thing but, please, don't lie.'

He shrugged. 'We've a few cash flow problems, that's all.'

She could see the worry in his eyes. Stretching, she kissed the side of his mouth. 'Tell me about it.' She sat in the chair he had vacated, removed her hat, and looked up at him expectantly. Sion sighed. He'd seen that look before. He wouldn't get any peace until she knew the full story. Taking a deep breath he explained the position.

When he had finished, Kirsty said, 'Make a list. Best and worst case scenarios. What would we be left with? When we know we can make decisions. I won't jeopardise this family for anything, Sion. If it's a question of somebody losing his job then so be it.'

Sion grinned. She reminded him of a lioness defending her young. She continued. 'We cut back to the minimum. Make savings everywhere we can.' Kirsty was thinking aloud, planning. Not for the first time Sion thought how lucky he had been to marry her. 'We'll need to sack some of the men.'

'Hey, that's my job,' Sion protested. 'I'll decide who stays and who goes.'

'Of course you do. But we need to keep only the best, the most committed.'

'True, the clock-watchers are no use to us. We'll be needing a lot of commitment and unpaid overtime will be the order of the day. A lot of them won't like it.'

'Tough,' said Kirsty, callously. 'They'll like it less when they're given their cards. I told you, Sion, if it comes to them or us then it'll be us everytime. With few exceptions we can hardly call on their loyalty. The men in turn are only loyal to themselves and to *their* kin.'

'That's the way it should be,' Sion protested.

'I agree. So we owe them nothing. We've given them work when times were good. Now times are hard we have to protect ourselves. I have an idea.'

Sion loved it when Kirsty announced "I have an idea".

'I'll spend a few days wandering the factory, making sketches. We'll say it's part of a new sales campaign. But I'll really spend my time watching them all, watching who is skiving, who's pulling his weight.'

'There's no need for that,' Sion protested. 'I know my workforce. And if I don't know the malingerers, Peter certainly does.'

Kirsty shook her head. 'How many of the men make work when the boss is on the shop floor? How many appear busy when they're actually achieving nothing? How often have you complained that a job is taking longer than it should? Is it always the same men who aren't doing their fair share?' Kirsty stood up and smoothed down her calf-length, pleated skirt, announcing, 'No. It needs a woman's eye. I'll soon be able to tell who is effective and who isn't.' She slipped her arm through her husband's. 'Now let's go and have dinner. You promised Louise a chapter of *Alice in Wonderland* before bed.'

Sion smiled, patting her hand. As always, Kirsty's steely determination made him feel better. But he wasn't so sure about her acting as a spy.

Kirsty had a rare talent. She could draw inanimate objects with almost photographic accuracy. Unfortunately, as soon as she drew a person, she ended up making a parody of the subject. She couldn't help turning the figure into an object of fun, either by exaggerating a blemish on the person's face or body, or by causing the subject's character somehow to shine through. She didn't mean to do it, it just happened. Her gift had got her into trouble in the past and she was careful not to let her drawings be seen by everybody. But there was an added benefit behind her talent. She was a keen observer of human nature.

Kirsty had spent time sketching machinery in the past and so the workforce largely ignored her. None of the men thought anything of her being there and behaved in their usual manner while she wandered around with a large drawing pad tucked under her arm. Frequently she stopped to make a sketch. At the end of each day she showed Sion what she had done and the conclusions she had reached about the men. Some came as a complete surprise.

There were, according to her criterion, thirty-three men

in total who weren't pulling their weight. Sion would have staked his life on eight of them being dedicated and hard-working.

She pointed at two of the caricatures in her folder. 'These two layabouts spent time moving stuff from one place to the next and back again. It was so . . . so . . .' she was stuck for words for a moment, 'pointless. If they had worked as hard doing their job properly they wouldn't have had so much to do. They're pathetic. It's as if they enjoy getting one over on you. On us.' She shook her head in exasperation.

'You'll always get some people who don't pull their weight,' Sion said, thoughtfully.

'And those are the ones we want to get rid of.' Kirsty said reasonably. Ten percent of the workforce could be sacked and the effect on the efficiency of the factory would be minimal. Surely, she thought, Sion can see that?

He stroked his chin and smiled at her. 'You've done a good job. All week I've been keeping an eye on some of the men you've told me about and you're right. Ellis and Filpot are shiftless. To think I intended making Filpot a foreman or at least a section leader. 'They have to go. I'll give them their cards tomorrow.'

Earlier in the week, the first potential customer for the new aeroplane had been enthusiastic, but wanted some modifications. A few more seats crowbarred in would make it more economical, he said. Could the plane cope with the extra weight? Sion sighed. The only way to find out was to fit the seats and take a flight.

Payday would have been a debacle if Kirsty hadn't thought of a solution. Normally the men went to the pay office and an envelope was handed out with their money and time sheet, showing any overtime. The original intention had been to hand out the firing notices at the same time. They had settled on sacking twenty-eight men simultaneously and Kirsty foresaw that certain individuals could cause trouble. Instead, during the afternoon, two of their trusted line-managers visited each individual's home and put a letter through his door.

That night, hours after the workforce had left for the day, Sion, Mike O'Donnell, Peter Cazorla and the two managers, Chris Peach and Geoff Falconer, waited at various vantage points around the airfield. Closing time for the pubs was 10pm, chucking out time fifteen minutes later. Shortly after that they heard the first signs of unusual activity. Sion was by the main hangar, the most likely target around the complex for men looking to cause trouble. He heard them, drunk and belligerent, loudly telling each other to be quiet in case they were heard.

'Don't worry, the bastard will be giving his whore one,' shouted Filpot.

'He can't,' said another voice, 'without help.'

There were roars of laughter followed by more hushing sounds. The men opened the gate and covered the thirty yards to the hangar. Invisible in the darkness, Sion stood behind one of the two side doors which stood temptingly ajar. The evening had started overcast but a fresh breeze had scattered the cloud and now a half moon lit the landscape. Sion counted seven, no eight men. He immediately picked out Filpot and Ellis.

'Right,' Filpot ordered in a loud whisper, 'let's get on with it. You know where the motor spirit is kept. Open the taps and let it all out. I'll let out the fuel oil for the generators.' The men stood stock still, staring past him. 'What are you waiting for?'

'Their Maker,' replied Sion, stepping out of the door, 'but they got me instead.'

Filpot whirled around, staggering slightly, his reactions befuddled with drink. He was first shocked and then delighted to see Sion standing there, all by himself.

'This couldn't be better,' Filpot snarled, crouching down and moving in a shambling gait from one side to the next. 'Now I can break your neck as well.'

Sion stood still, erect, unafraid. The pickaxe handle he

held in his right hand hung unnoticed alongside his leg. The others moved in to back up Filpot.

'It's all right lads, leave him to me. I won't need any help with this pansy.'

Filled with alcohol fuelled courage, the men stood back, forming a semi-circle, facing Sion. Filpot moved forward and when he was about four paces away Sion made his move.

Stepping forward two paces, straight at Filpot, wrong footing the bigger man, Sion swung a devastating blow across Filpot's left knee. There was a crack. Filpot screamed and collapsed, holding his shattered leg. Sion was ready with a back swing but realised it wasn't necessary.

The others stood stock still in utter astonishment for a second, until Ellis let out a yell. 'Kill the . . .' He got no further. He was felled by a blow on the back of his head.

'Look behind you,' Sion called, loudly.

The men turned. Five grim faced individuals, each armed with a stave or handle, stood ready to do battle. The men were unarmed. They hadn't come prepared to confront anyone, only to cause as much damage as possible. Their actions were born of drink. A shared grievance in the pub had ended in a spur-of-the-moment decision they now regretted.

'What's it to be?' Sion asked. 'You can walk away and go home or you can be taken in the truck to the police station. Choose the police and I warn you, you'll have to be carried.'

The men looked at each other, the fog of alcohol dissipating with the rise of fear. Sion wasn't a man to cross. They'd been fools to listen to Filpot.

'All right,' muttered Ellis, 'we'll go. But it won't be the last you've heard of us. We'll get you Griffiths. You and that cow you're married to. It was her, wasn't it? All those drawings and notes. I guessed she'd been up to something.'

Ellis didn't get any further. Sion had grown up hearing stories about Evan, his father, reacting when Meg and the boys had been threatened. Evan had gone berserk, half killing one man with his bare hands. Sion now understood those stories.

O'Donnell pulled Sion off Ellis whose bloodied body lay at Sion's feet.

'Easy, Sion, easy,' said O'Donnell, grabbing Sion's fist and physically preventing him from making one final blow.

Ellis' face was a broken mess, his nose squashed across his face, teeth missing. The other men looked on in horror. This was a side of Sion no one had seen before.

Sion stood up straight and took a deep breath. 'If anyone comes near my family I'll kill them. Do you understand?'

The men looked at Ellis and the moaning Filpot and nodded.

O'Donnell stood in front of them, the pick-axe handle he was carrying moving in rhythm, slapping against his big hand. 'Pick those two up and get out,' said O'Donnell. 'If I see one of you near the place it won't be Mr Griffiths you have to deal with but me. Understood?'

Picking up Ellis and Filpot between them, they half carried, half dragged the two men away. When they stepped into the road Chris Peach locked the airfield gate with a new padlock and offered the key to Sion.

'You'd better keep it,' said Sion. 'Open the gate first thing in the morning. We need,' he looked at the satisfied faces around him, 'a gatekeeper from now on. Let's go into the kitchen and have a dram or two. All this melodrama has given me a thirst.' He shook his head in self deprecation, 'I can't believe I threatened to kill them!'

O'Donnell put his hand on Sion's shoulder. 'Just as long as they were convinced. It brought back memories of Germany. Do you remember that run in we had with the Brown Shirts?'

They sat in the kitchen, late into the night, re-living past adventures. Chris Peach and Geoff Falconer sat agog, eyes as wide as their mouths, listening to the scrapes their bosses had survived. Eventually, commonsense sent them to bed, a busy day still loomed ahead.

They spent two days changing the seating in the plane. The extra seats reduced the leg room by about four inches but there was still space to sit and stretch out. With three engines there was plenty of power, but with extra passengers, would the plane take off and land in a reasonable distance? And what about its cruising speed and top speed? The NACA report Sion was reading made him sit up with an oath.

17

THE REPORT CONCERNED the Ford Tri-Motor, a thirteen-passenger plane known as the Tin Goose. It was a rugged, all-metal plane, powered by three Wright Whirlwind engines. The Tin Goose cruised at 105mph which was fast enough to cross America in two days. The National Advisory Committee for Aeronautics had worked tirelessly to discover the main causes of drag and to show why the Tri-Motor was, aero-dynamically speaking, an underachiever. The Ford slab-sided fuselage was partly to blame but the undercarriage and the underslung engines caused major problems. Using the NACA wind tunnel, the fixed landing gear was shown to account for a massive forty percent of the plane's drag. Using the propeller wind tunnel they also found that the engines accounted for a further thirty-three percent of total drag from the fuselage.

But NACA had made a surprising discovery. Using a specially shaped, streamlined cowling to go over the engine, they had actually enhanced cooling. Always determined to be ahead in the design game, Sion wondered how quickly he could incorporate some of the ideas he was reading about. Damn the Americans, he thought. When it came to aviation they were always at least one step ahead.

By reducing the amount of undercarriage in his last design, he had vastly improved his own drag statistics. What if there was a way of retracting it all? That would be something! The NACA report showed a diagram of the cowling and how it covered the engine. The radial engine sucked air in and let it escape through vents in the rear. Sion crossed to the drawing board and began sketching. When Peter Cazorla found him a few hours later he was still hard at it.

'Sion, we're ready for a test flight. What are you doing?'

'Here, read this.' Sion thrust the NACA report into his chief designer's hand while he continued working.

Cazorla Snr. immediately saw the possibilities and watched what Sion was drawing.

'How long to make?'

The Mexican shrugged. 'If we get started right away we might have something to fit in two or three days at the most.'

'Can we do this and still keep to the delivery date for those first planes?'

'Probably. But you're presuming we get the order. We have to be able to fly with six passengers now the extra seats have been fitted.'

'Right. Let's give it a go.' Sion picked up his flying jacket, changed his shoes for fur-lined flying boots and wrapped a scarf around his neck. He would be piloting the plane.

Originally they had planned to have six men sitting inside the fuselage, but after a lot of consideration Sion had decided it was too dangerous. Instead, each seat was occupied by bags of potatoes, varying in weight from twelve to fourteen stones. Instead of the expected sack of potatoes in the co-pilot's seat, Sion found O'Donnell sitting there.

'What are you doing?'

O'Donnell grinned at him. 'You didn't really think I'd let you go on this junket all alone, did you? You might need me.'

Sion was about to order him out of the plane but then grinned back. O'Donnell wouldn't go so why bother? The truth was, Sion was glad to have him aboard. Completing the checks, Sion walked around the plane. Her wingspan was forty-three feet, length thirty feet six inches and her height, nine feet two inches. She weighed five thousand, seven hundred pounds gross and three thousand, one hundred pounds empty. The design *should* work.

Satisfied with the external checks, Sion climbed into the fuselage and went forward to the cockpit. Except in an emergency when they could knock out the side windows, it was the only way in and out of the plane for pilots and passengers alike.

'Ready?' Sion looked at O'Donnell who nodded. 'Let's go!'

The engine fired on the first turn and the two pilots sat there, watching the oil pressure gauge, rev counter and temperature gauge. Satisfied, Sion signalled to the men outside to remove the chocks and began to manoeuvre the plane. He lined up on the runway, checked everything once more and opened the throttles wide. With a loud roar the plane moved forward, picking up speed.

The plane was only halfway along the runway when she gracefully lifted into the air. They put her through her paces, pleased with the results they were getting. Then they raised the undercarriage until it was tucked tightly against the fuselage. It was like adding a second engine. The Griffin exceeded their expectations.

They landed with a gentle thump and taxied towards the hangar. Beside the group of men waiting for them they saw two policemen.

Sion jumped down from the plane followed by O'Donnell, and walked across to them. Chris Peach and Geoff Falconer stood next to Peter Cazorla; all were looking decidedly downcast.

The officer who spoke had sergeant's stripes, a bucolic face and a slow, deliberate way of speaking. The other, a constable, was looking around, obviously awed by the planes he was seeing close up for the first time.

'It is our understanding, sir,' said the sergeant, 'that

three nights ago you deliberately and wilfully beat up two men who had come to discuss, all peaceable like, their employment situation.'

'Is that what they told you?' Sion asked, his face an emotionless mask.

'Sir, it is my duty to arrest you and take you down to the station.'

Sion nodded, looked thoughtful and nodded. 'If you wish. You'll be making a complete ass of yourself, of course, and oh, incidentally, if you do, I'll have your stripes.'

'Here! You can't speak to me like that.'

'Every man here will tell you what happened. Ask them. Then go down to the local pub. Question the others who were with them. Find out what they were doing here at nearly midnight When you've done all that, I suggest you come and apologise. Peter, have you been asked to make a statement?'

'No, Sion. They said they wanted to talk to you.'

'Take them to the canteen, give them a cup of tea and explain what happened. Afterwards, you can come and interview me.' Sion turned on his heels and walked away.

The sergeant called after him but was waylaid by O'Donnell. Sion didn't hear what was said as he marched off to his office. He needed to get to work.

Less than an hour later the two policemen, Cazorla and O'Donnell appeared. The sergeant was holding his hat, shifting from foot to foot.

'I appear,' he stopped, coughed and started again. 'I'm sorry, sir. It appears I made a mistake. Filpot and Ellis came to the station this morning and made statements. I should have checked.'

Sion nodded, unsmiling. 'Indeed you should have.' Then he smiled and stood up. 'Let's hear no more about it, shall we?' He reached into his pocket, withdrew his wallet and removed a five pound note. 'This is for the Police Benevolent Fund. Give Filpot and Ellis a warning.

Something about wasting police time. Spurious complaints. Anything you like. Just make it clear it's in their best interests to stay away.'

'Yes, sir. Thank you.' The sergeant saluted Sion, relieved. 'You can rely on us.' He turned to his young colleague and said, 'Let's go.'

Sion let out a sigh as he watched them leave. 'That could have been nasty.'

O'Donnell shook his head. 'I think the sergeant was worried in case you made a complaint against him. He almost had a heart attack when he found out who you were.'

Sion laughed. 'Thank God for family. Have you told Peter about the Griffin's performance?'

'It's all right. I saw it,' said Peter with a wide smile.

'It's better than we could have hoped for. We need to recalculate the plane's top speed and endurance.'

'That'll be a pleasure,' said O'Donnell.

'I think it's also time we used aluminium. You're finished experimenting with it?' Sion asked Peter.

'*Si*, we have finished. But it will be much work.'

Pure aluminium was too weak to use in aircraft, but when small amounts of manganese, copper and magnesium were added, the aluminium became four times stronger. The problem was it corroded too easily. Then, a few years earlier, British researchers found a way of anodising aluminium with a protective coating that stopped the corrosion. Sion had immediately embraced the new technology. Copying the Alcoa company of America, he improved on the design by sandwiching the aluminium alloy between thin layers of pure aluminium, making the plane practically corrosion free. It was the new sandwich design he now wanted to use for the water/land aircraft.

'Then the sooner we get started, the better,' said Mike O'Donnell with a smile.

The workforce toiled tirelessly and by Thursday of the

third week, the plane was ready and wheeled out from the hangar. The Griffin weighed nearly a thousand pounds less than the original, wooden design yet had the same look to her. At 10am the weather had turned from blustery to calm. The sky had a leaden look to it but the thunderstorm that had been threatening all morning seemed to have changed its mind and veered away to the north.

In preparation for the flight they tied the sacks of potatoes into the seats once more. Sitting in the cockpit at the end of the runway they watched the temperature gauge and revolutions counter. The engine was definitely running cooler. Peter Cazorla stood behind Sion and Mike while they went through their take-off checks, waggling the rudder, ailerons and elevators.

'Ready?' Sion called, opening the throttle.

'As we'll ever be,' said Mike. Peter tapped Sion's shoulder in acknowledgement.

'Let's go.' The plane accelerated quickly.

The entire workforce was standing outside the hangar, watching and praying. The Griffin lifted gracefully and effortlessly into the air. The engine had a deep throated, steady roar and the temperature remained lower than usual. The new cowling they had fitted was working and the aerodynamic changes they had made around the undercarriage also seemed to help.

Once airborne Peter winched up the wheels and said, 'Right, Sion. Ready when you are.'

They were above the blanket of cloud which covered the southeast as far as they could see. The grey and white fluff looked as though they could land on it. Sion eased the throttle open, watching his heading, his eyes darting across the gauges, checking constantly.

O'Donnell tapped the temperature gauge. 'Either this thing isn't working properly, or,' he grinned at Sion, 'the cowling is working better than we expected.'

Sion watched the revolutions increase, along with the

air-speed indicator while the temperature remained steady. The single engine roared approval, dragging the plane faster and faster. In level flight they reached 190mph and the plane steadily droned on, with still more power available.

Peter Cazorla let out a yell of triumph and thumped both pilots on their shoulders. 'What about a top speed?'

'Trying now.' Sion eased the throttle open the last few degrees and more power surged through the engine. He put the plane into a shallow dive and watched as they increased speed to 257mph. After a few minutes he eased back on the throttle and returned to level flight. His hands were clammy with sweat and he wiped them, one at a time, on his trousers.

He looked over his shoulder. 'Right, try the heating.'

Peter Cazorla slid open a panel in the fuselage on the starboard side of the cabin and immediately hot air blasted in. He pulled his hand away quickly, surprised by the heat. The additional noise was not as bad as they had expected but the air was too hot. He shut the panel and returned to the front.

'I need to rethink the design and let in more cold air. I've an idea how to fix it.'

'Good. Get it working for next week and in the meantime we'll ask the customers to come and see us,' said Sion.

They stayed aloft for five hours, Sion adjusting the throttle to see at what revolution count they achieved the most economical flight. The fuel gauge inside the cockpit was a simple capillary tube and they could see the level dropping, measured in tenths of inches. O'Donnell meticulously noted the readings. Finally low on fuel it was time to return to Biggin Hill. They plunged below the cloud cover to check on their position and Sion was gratified to see that they were within a few miles of where he had hoped to be. The town of Croydon was directly below them.

When they landed, the three men were exuberant. They had a plane of distinction.

The customers arrived on time. Two men from a company known as the Highlands and Islands Aviation Services of Scotland and based at Fort William. They were both Scotsmen, one a tall, skinny, loud-voiced man, named William MacLeod, the other smaller, with thinning reddish hair, softly spoken, named Donald Stevenson. They were taken out by O'Donnell to see the plane.

MacLeod exploded when he saw the inside of the fuselage. 'I specified eight seats.'

'We appreciate that,' said O'Donnell soothingly, 'but we think the modifications we've made will make all the difference.'

'Are you stupid man,' said MacLeod turning thunderously towards him, 'or just deaf? We need eight seats, man, otherwise it's not economical for us to run the planes. I told you that and,' he added ominously, 'it's in my letter.'

Mike O'Donnell had become the consummate salesman over the years and he bit back the retort that sprang to his lips. 'Listen Mr MacLeod, you don't understand. We've changed the flight profile of the plane so much that it is *now* economical to run. The reduction in weight and drag has improved the fuel consumption by over forty percent. As well as that we've added a heating system to keep the customers comfortable and don't forget why you were interested in the first place – it can use water and land. What's more, she needs a much shorter runway or seaway now we've incorporated the modifications. Some of the smaller lochs you couldn't use previously can now be utilised.'

MacLeod was slightly less belligerent. 'What do you say, Donald?'

Stevenson was busy with a notepad, scribbling some figures. 'On paper it makes sense. If we reduce the fuel costs by forty percent then it helps to offset the loss of revenue, but that's not enough. The extra landing sites will be welcome but I don't know if that's sufficient incentive either. Heating doesn't matter a hoot. We aren't in the air long enough to make that much difference. The passengers can always get warm again after they've landed.'

'But,' said O'Donnell, showing no sign of the desperation he was feeling, 'the increased performance means that it is now possible to fly from Fort William to London.'

'What? What did you say, man?' MacLeod grabbed O'Donnell by the arm in his excitement and squeezed his biceps. 'Did you say to London? From the Highlands?'

'Yes.' O'Donnell resisted the temptation to rub his arm when MacLeod released him. 'The better fuel and higher speed means a non-stop journey in less than four hours. Three from Edinburgh.'

MacLeod tried to hide his growing interest. If he could offer a direct flight to London there were plenty of possibilities he could take advantage of. Not only landowners going back and forth but now there were the shooting parties as well. Then there were the people looking to travel to the islands. Landing was always a problem if they couldn't find sheltered water. But that problem appeared resolved as well. They could charge a premium on some of the flights.

'We'll see. Let's get aboard and try it.' He clambered into the plane, Stevenson close behind.

O'Donnell showed them the various features and alterations that had been made, including the heating system. Peter Cazorla had reduced the air from the engine and mixed it with cold air so that it was warm rather than red hot. He was now working on a way to adjust the temperature by altering the amount of cold air in the mixture so that the passengers could vary the temperature to suit. At that point Sion joined them. O'Donnell was the pilot for the demonstration, Sion the co-pilot.

'Observe, gentlemen,' said Sion, 'underneath the seats. If you take out the tray you can slide it into holes either side of the arm rest.' He took the wooden tray and fitted the round pegs into the holes. 'This hole is to hold a glass while you have a place for any food you may wish to eat, from sandwiches to a plated meal. In the rear of the cabin we have a toilet for those planes flying say, more than three hours. In the cupboard we have racks to hold bottles,' he continued showing the various features of the plane and finally revealed the handles used to raise the landing gear.

'What happens,' asked Stevenson, 'if the pilot forgets to put the gear down?'

'They crash. However,' said Sion, 'in the cockpit there is a large sign saying "Remember the Gear". There is a landing check list as well which we recommend to all pilots. I'll show you later.'

'If you gentlemen would like to take your seats, we'll start the demonstration.'

Sion sat in the right hand seat and let O'Donnell get the plane ready. While he was doing so Sion looked over his shoulder and said, 'Do you see the white line on the tarmac?' Both men insisted on standing behind the pilots' seats to watch what was happening, rather than taking their seats as invited by Sion. They nodded. 'The next line you can just see is less than a hundred yards away. We'll be airborne before we get there.'

'I'll believe that, laddie, when I see it,' said MacLeod.

'Take your seats, gentlemen, as we'll have a steep climb.'

'Don't worry about us. Just show us what this plane can do,' replied MacLeod.

Sion shrugged and exchanged glances with O'Donnell. With the engine roaring they moved out to the runway and stopped on the first white line. O'Donnell opened the throttle, holding the plane on the brakes, watching the revs climb. He released the brakes and the plane accelerated quickly along the tarmac. After less than fifty yards the plane reached forty-five miles per hour and O'Donnell pulled back on the column. The plane lifted sharply into the air and both the men standing behind only kept their feet by grabbing hold of the pilots' seats.

MacLeod could not keep the surprise from his face. Sion quickly climbed from his seat and went into the main cabin. He showed the men how to retract the under-carriage as far as it could go and then let O'Donnell put the plane through its paces. Sion also adjusted the air vent and soon the cabin was warm enough to allow the men to remove their thick coats.

They settled at cruising speed before showing off the plane's top speed. Now came the big test – landing on water.

'Where are we setting down?' asked MacLeod.

Sion, back in the co-pilot's seat, looked over his shoulder and smiled. 'Wait and see.'

The plane was approaching London. O'Donnell banked it around Big Ben and the Houses of Parliament and, seeing a stretch of empty water, lined up to land between Lambeth and Westminster Bridges.

'This isn't legal,' said MacLeod, fascinated by what they were doing.

'Who's to stop us?' Sion asked, with a grin.

'Don't be daft, man. They'll take the registration number.'

'It's not painted on yet and few people have the gump-tion to recognise one plane from another.'

O'Donnell took them in. Crowds were gathering to watch and point. The plane landed on the water with a gentle kiss and quickly approached Lambeth Bridge. As it did, a barge appeared between the central arches, precisely where O'Donnell had planned to go. Neither Sion nor O'Donnell showed the concern and heart-stopping fear demonstrated by the other two men. O'Donnell opened the throttle and the plane shot forward until it appeared they couldn't avoid the oncoming barge. He heaved back on the column and the plane lifted into the air like an express lift. It was almost standing on its tail as they roared over Lambeth Bridge and away. Stevenson kept his feet. MacLeod slid in a heap down the aisle and came up against the rear of the cabin.

'Let's get out of here before somebody comes looking for us,' said Sion.

They headed west for a few miles until London was a blur behind them. Then they turned south. Twenty minutes later they landed at Biggin Hill. Sion had said nothing throughout the last part of the journey. He wondered if they had blown it with their show.

When they landed O'Donnell brought the plane to a halt in as short a distance as possible and then taxied to the hangar. Once inside they closed the doors and shut off the engine.

If Sion was under any strain, either from the tension of the moment or from the flying he didn't show it. Instead he said, 'What about a nice cup of tea in the office?'

In fact they settled for large whiskies to toast the placing of an order for six aircraft.

The following morning he took a telephone call from his brother. 'Sion? David. An amazing thing happened yesterday.'

'Oh, yes? What was that?'

'An aeroplane landed outside the House, on the Thames, and took-off again, just missing a boat and the bridge.'

'Which bridge?'

'I know it was you, brother dear, and so do a few others. Despite the lack of registration, your stunt didn't fool anyone. I've had a quiet word dropped in my ear to tell you not to do it again. Right?'

'Right.' Sion was grinning.

'How did it go? I presume you were showing off to somebody?'

'A customer. They placed an order for six planes.'

'Excellent. That's a good start.'

'If I can find a dozen or more orders.'

'Yes, well your little prank didn't go unnoticed. I'm hoping to push some business your way. Leave it to me. In the meantime, don't forget, no more landing and taking-off on the Thames.'

Sion smiled to himself. The powers-that-be couldn't prove he had broken any rules. If push came to shove he could always claim that they'd had an emergency that miraculously cleared as they touched down. Dirty fuel? He nodded to himself. That would do. In the meantime he'd get on with what he was good at. Building aeroplanes.

The letter the following morning came out of the blue. The Southern Counties Bank at Sevenoaks was insisting on a meeting. The agenda – the loss of the contract for the War Ministry.

18

How THE HELL had they learnt about the order being cancelled? Damnation, thought Sion, just as things were looking up. He was sure they could use the Scottish order to find many more customers. The new airliner he was now planning was a world beater. It would be able to land on water and at a conventional airport and, if his figures were correct, they would be able to carry twenty passengers. The biggest plane flying anywhere in the world was only carrying fourteen. Now this. Damn it all to hell. He needed to keep the bank off his back, but how? The family bank of Griffiths, Buchanan & Co held a good deal of stock in the company and in reality had provided the core of the finance that had got him started. However, the money for the day-to-day running of the business came from Southern Counties Bank. The overdraft was secured by company shares as well as a bond and floating charge over the company's assets. If the bank called in the overdraft he would be finished. Briefly Sion considered asking David for help and then dismissed the thought. David had done enough. If he really got stuck then he might approach his brother but . . . not yet. He'd try other avenues first. What he needed was a full order book. Or at least the illusion of one. He balked at the thought but admitted it to himself. It was cheating. But if the bank did pull the plug it was more than covered by the company's assets. Here at the plant, hundreds of people would lose their jobs. The value of the land alone, now no longer mortgaged, would repay the bank loan.

Land prices had been rising steadily in the area for the last few years thanks to a housing boom. People working in London were now wanting to live in the clean air of the leafy suburbs, away from the smog of the city. However, assets didn't pay bills, cash flow from profits did. Convincing himself that he had the moral, if not legal, right to do whatever was needed to save the company Sion began working on his plan.

When an order came in each aircraft was allocated a number and a work card. The card was placed in the left hand side of a bank of slots that filled half a wall. As each stage of production was completed the card moved along the slots until it reached the end one. This showed the plane was ready for a test flight. Normally all the slots were filled and when one emptied another took its place. This was no longer happening and gaps were beginning to appear amongst the slots. So far only the Islands and Highlands company had placed a firm order. And even that was subject to a letter of confirmation.

He'd create a myth. A lie. Sion picked up a few cards and slotted them into the board. Standing back he looked at his handiwork and allowed his conscience to make one more appeal. His determination won. Taking new cards he began filling them in. In less than an hour the board was full. It looked as though the company had sufficient orders for a full twelve months. Now all he had to do was create the same impression out on the factory floor. After all, he reasoned, a bank manager may know something about money, but he knew damn all about building aircraft.

Sion called in Peter Cazorla and issued his instructions. Peter smiled and nodded. Sion, he knew, was at his best when cornered.

The following morning when the bank manager arrived it was to a bee-hive of activity. Smithson was a stout, overbearing man, with an inflated sense of his own self-importance. He climbed from his small Austin 7, briefcase in one hand, his bowler in the other. Sion held out his hand, waiting patiently while the manager put his hat on his head, before switching the briefcase to his left hand. Finally he shook Sion's hand.

'Mr Smithson, a pleasure.' Sion smiled.

'Mr Griffiths, how do you do?' There was no corresponding smile. 'Can we get on?'

'By all means. Follow me. This is the first time you've been here, I believe?' Sion knew the answer without waiting for a reply. He stopped and held up his hand as a tractor towed an aircraft from the hangar. 'You need to have eyes in the back of your head in this place. Tread carefully.' He smiled at Smithson who merely nodded, his small eyes everywhere. Sion walked ahead with a sinking heart. This could prove more difficult than he had been hoping. What if his subterfuge didn't work? It was a frightening prospect.

Walking through the large hangar it was obvious to Sion that the activity around them was not productive. He hoped that to the bank manager it would look real.

Some of the men looked up at him and waved. On cue, Juan Cazorla came rushing over to him. 'Mr Griffiths, that's the tenth completed and rolled out. We're on schedule to reach our target of one hundred planes as you ordered.'

'Thank you, Juan. I'll let the Ministry know.' He didn't say which Ministry, implying it was the one for War. He could equally have meant the Baptist Ministry. Smithson walked close to him and Sion glanced in his direction. The manager looked suitably impressed by the activity and noise pounding around them. Windy hammers were going non-stop, as were the presses for the aluminium bodies. All the diesels in the factory were running needlessly and the noise was reaching bedlam proportions. It was a relief to reach the office and close the door, reducing the noise level considerably.

'Coffee?'

'No, thank you. I would like to get down to business.'

'Certainly. Where do you want to start?'

'It's come to our attention,' Smithson began pompously, 'that the Ministry for War has cancelled its order.' He paused sententiously and cleared his throat. 'The bank views the situation with a good deal of seriousness. We are concerned that you will not be able to meet your indebtedness.'

Sion appeared surprised. With a thundering heart he forced a smile. 'Is that why you've come all this way to see me? You needn't have bothered. A phone call or a letter would have sufficed.'

'Indeed, it would not, Mr Griffiths. It is our understanding that you are in difficulties because of the cancelled order. My task today is to assess whether or not you should continue to have access to bank money. I want to see your order book and I want to have an extended tour of the works. I shall, of course, be taking notes. You will then hear from us later this week.'

Sion leaned forward in his chair, allowing anger to seep into his voice. 'Now you listen to me, Smithson.' There was no 'Mister', this time. 'You can look all you like. If you want to withdraw the bank's support I'll take my business elsewhere. This notion that the Ministry has stopped its order simply isn't true. We were so busy that I decided to fulfil our obligations to the RAF and then withdraw from government work. We're supplying aircraft companies all over Europe with our planes and I can tell you, we make a good deal more profit from commercial contracts. We're also paid a lot quicker. So your information is both wrong and, I may add, slanderous.' Sion stood up and poured himself a cup of coffee. He thought about offering one again to the pompous bank official but decided against it.

Sion sat down as Smithson went redder in the face and ran a finger around the inside of his straining collar. Suddenly he felt much less sure of himself. The man sitting before him was a member of a family that was fast becoming one of the most influential and powerful in Britain. But he still had his duty to do. He coughed and said, 'Be that as it may, Mr Griffiths, I still need to satisfy my directors.'

Sion immediately changed his tactics and smiled, waving a hand in the direction of the orders wall. The friendly tone of his voice caught his visitor unawares. 'By all means. We use the very latest techniques for keeping tabs on the work. The cards you see along the wall represent our order book. Each aircraft that is being built reaches a certain stage of manufacture and when it does the card is moved. At a glance we can see precisely where we are with each plane. It's an idea that came from America.' Inwardly Sion smiled at the other's reaction. Anything innovative from America was considered good. 'If you count the cards you will see that we have orders for one hundred and fifty aeroplanes, some of which are nearing the completion stage. We are also about to build a new, fast airliner that will carry as many as fifteen or twenty passengers, depending on the configuration our customers demand. The profit is triple what we were getting from the Ministry, although the specification for the interior of the plane is higher. After all, bombers and troop carriers don't need much in the way of comforts.'

Smithson nodded slowly and said, 'Indeed, indeed. However, be that as it may, we wish to reduce your indebtedness to the bank by means of staged payments.' He stopped when Sion shook his head.

'I think, Mr Smithson, that this conversation has gone far enough. To be frank I have thought for some time that your bank was too small for my needs, especially as I will soon be dealing with a good number of overseas customers. And that will mean currency changes.' Sion paused, watching the manager lick his lips. Currency changes meant a good deal of additional profit for the bank. 'Yes, I've been thinking of approaching Barclays in Kensington. It's a large branch that understands the international business I'm now in. I believe the Anglo-Persian Oil company banks there. I met the Deputy Chairman of APO at a function of my brother's recently and he's put in a good word. My business with Barclays should go through on the nod, as it were.' It was true he'd met the man but the rest was pure fiction. Hell, Sion couldn't even remember his name.

Sipping his coffee, Sion watched conflicting emotions chasing each other across the other man's face. The meeting was not going the way Smithson had planned. Swallowing convulsively, he wished he had accepted Sion's offer of coffee. He was suddenly feeling parched.

'If that is all, Mr Smithson, perhaps we can dispense with your "tour of the works". After all, there are many secrets here we don't want seen by outsiders. Especially if we no longer have a working relationship.' Sion now pushed home his advantage. 'If you have the bank tell me what is needed to clear the company's debts I will arrange full and final payment within the fortnight. I shall, of course, be writing to your head office,' – now for the *coup de grace*, thought Sion, – 'to tell them how unhappy I have been at the treatment I've received.' Sion was careful not to say Smithson's name, but it was implied in the statement and the little man broke out into a cold sweat.

This could ruin his career. Damnation! He had come here to threaten Sion and here he was receiving threats himself. And powerful ones they were too. He needed to extricate himself from the mess as quickly as possible. Gulping he summoned up a ghastly caricature of a smile. 'Now, Mr Griffiths, let us not be too hasty.'

With those words Sion knew he had won. Now he had to play him like a fish, to reel him in, carefully and without too much haste, otherwise he could give the game away.

'What are you proposing, Mr Smithson? Before you tell me, let me get you a coffee.' The discussion became one of friendliness and co-operation followed by a brief tour of the factory. It continued, to the untrained eye, to be a very busy and productive place. Out of the deafening noise once more and standing next to Smithson's car Sion shook the odious man's hand. 'If you agree then we can go ahead. It will save me the time and effort involved in making alternative banking arrangements as I am,' Sion gilded the lily, 'about to fly to Moscow to discuss a big contract. Of course, I would want your bank to handle the financial transactions between Russia and ourselves. I trust you can manage that?'

Smithson nodded. 'I'll put our agreement in writing. I must say I am very impressed by what I have seen. You appear to run a smooth operation. Good day to you, Mr Griffiths.' Smithson removed his bowler and placed it on the passenger's seat when he climbed into the small narrow car. The engine started at the first touch and he drove sedately away.

Sion watched him drive out of sight, relief flooding through his body, his shoulders sagging. It had been close. Too close. He had bought some time but that was all. If he didn't deliver soon he would be out of business and this time there would be no pulling the wool over the man's eyes. He hadn't lied about Russia; exaggerated perhaps but not lied. He and O'Donnell did have a possible deal in the offing.

Returning to his office Sion began to remove the cards. Taking each one, he ripped it up and dumped the pieces in a rubbish bin. In the meantime the men returned to normal working levels. Unwanted machinery was switched off and the noise reduced to its more usual pitch. At least they could now stand in the hangar and speak to one another without yelling. When he'd finished with the cards Sion did an actual count. Forty-nine planes left to be completed. The last plane would be leaving the hangar in a month. They needed orders and they needed them fast.

In the evening he called a "conference" with Kirsty, Peter, Juan, Raphael and Mike O'Donnell.

'Fact,' said Sion, 'I can keep the bank off our backs for six, maybe eight weeks. After that we'll be finished.'

'What about David?' asked O'Donnell.

Sion shrugged. 'He's our last resort but I know they're stretched as well so I'd rather not go to him unless we have to. Okay, let's review our situation.'

'At the moment we've got three possible aircraft,' said Peter Cazorla. 'The new twenty-seater is still at the design stage. Then we've got our fighter and the new Griffin V. We know she's economical and with a cruising speed of 190mph and a top speed of 265mph she's the fastest single engine, six-seater in the sky.'

'For now,' said O'Donnell.

'That's true,' said Sion. 'But that's the point of this business. It never stands still,' replied Sion.

'No,' said Raphael, straight-faced but always the joker, 'it flies.'

The quip broke the tension, earning Raphael far more laughter than the joke deserved.

Kirsty was the first to recover. 'I've had an idea. Sion, you said a few months ago that there are rich *individuals* who can afford to buy a plane. Remember?'

Sion frowned and nodded. 'Yes. There will always be those who'd like to make their wealth more conspicuous.

'Well, why don't we run adverts in all the country set magazines like *Horse and Hound*, and *Living in the Manor*. A full page extolling the joys of owning your own aircraft. The freedom it imparts – go anywhere you like whenever you like.'

'And who,' asked O'Donnell disdainfully, 'will fly the planes?'

'They will,' was the surprising reply. 'How difficult is it to learn to fly?'

'It's not,' said O'Donnell. 'But it is difficult to become good. To be safe.'

'During the Great War,' said Kirsty warming to her theme, 'men were in the front line after eight or nine hours of lessons. True?'

The men nodded soberly, each thinking of the young pilot's life expectancy in those terrible days.

'Why not offer free flying lessons with each order? Say twenty hours of tuition after which they take possession of the aeroplane. Flying is glamorous – let's appeal to their vanity. Make it the *sine qua non* of society.'

Whether or not they understood the Latin none of the man questioned her meaning. They sat quietly thinking furiously of the implications. Sion looked at his wife with something approaching awe. 'The real benefit,' he said, 'would be instant cash. We could sell the plane like a car. What we would need to do is appeal to their snob factor. How?'

Kirsty smiled. 'I've already thought of that.' Standing up she walked across the kitchen to collect her drawing pad. Stopping briefly to open the door of her green and cream enamel cooker and check on her shepherd's pie, she returned and flicked open the pages. 'Look at these.' Half a dozen pencil drawings showed figures standing around a Griffin V. In one they were a shooting party, in another the group was wearing evening dress. There was no doubt – the drawings worked.

Kirsty took a sip of tea, now going cold. 'I know unemployment is high and the stock market crash and recession hit so many people. But, like the poor, the rich are always with us as well. There are hundreds of wealthy landowners and an equal number of businessmen all looking for some way to flaunt their wealth. They've got the house, the grounds, the swimming pools and so on. A Rolls Royce isn't enough any more. Let's turn the Griffin *V* into the ultimate status symbol.'

Sion leant across and kissed her soundly on the cheek. 'Kirsty, my darling, that's brilliant.'

'We could include personal modifications,' said

O'Donnell. 'They could have a smart bar, like you find on yachts. Even,' he stopped, laughing, and then plunged on, 'have curtains on the windows.'

'A feminine touch, now that's a very good idea, Mike,' said Kirsty. 'There are loads of women who can twist their daddies around their little finger . . .'

'Wait a second,' said Sion, 'are you suggesting we teach women to fly?'

'Of course. Look at Amelia Earhart. She's idolised by women all over the world.'

'Maybe,' Sion replied, 'but who do we get to teach the women?'

Kirsty smiled. 'Susan.'

The men looked at her in astonishment. Susan? David's daughter? She was a good pilot, of that there was no doubt. But she was only twenty and still at college.

'You've really thought this through, haven't you? asked Sion.

Kirsty shrugged. 'At first, I couldn't see how it would work. After all, planes are dirty and noisy. But with the changes you've been making, it's like taking an original old Ford car and turning it into a Daimler. You've done that with the new Griffin. Say we show a plane at . . . at Falmouth. We list the places a Griffin can land. In the bay, on the Helford, on that track at Truro.' Her eyes shone with excitement. She loved being involved with the business.

Figures were spinning around O'Donnell's head. 'With the country in such deep trouble, do you really think that even the rich will indulge in such an extravagance?'

'But that's the point,' said Kirsty. 'This is an overt way for them to display their wealth, to prove that what's happening to others isn't affecting them.'

Sion turned to the others. 'What do you think?'

Peter Cazorla hung his head sheepishly. With all these new fangled domestic appliances, vacuum cleaners, washing machines, it seemed Mrs. Griffiths had too much time on her hands. Women should, in his opinion, stay in the kitchen. His two sons Ralph and Juan followed their father's lead and said nothing. It was left to O'Donnell. He was uncomfortable with this growing movement of independence for women, but he liked Kirsty. More importantly, he liked the idea.

It was agreed. They would sell planes in the same way that Daimlers were sold. Every Daimler was made to order and they would do the same. One third deposit with the order, a third when the plane was finished and the balance after the purchaser had learnt to fly or a competent pilot flew it away. Safety was paramount. They would not take risks by selling to those who had an obvious disregard for the rules of flying. The last thing they needed was bad publicity. On this sobering thought they ended the meeting.

Two days later a photographer from *Country Life* was positioning beautifully attired models around the Griffin V, the new symbol of glamour and wealth. It appeared the following week, on the same day that the Hollywood actor, Douglas Fairbanks, was seen in cinemas all over Britain, flying his own plane.

Whilst pursuing contacts in Scandinavia, O'Donnell had also followed up the business enquiry from Russia. As far as he could tell, the contact was serious and they were invited to fly to Moscow; a flight of fifteen hundred miles, some of it across uncharted territory. Sion relished the challenge.

19

'ONLY A FEW years ago, the Russians were shooting Englishmen as spies,' said O'Donnell.

Sion grinned. 'Then we have nothing to worry about. I'm Welsh and you're Irish. You aren't getting cold feet on me are you, Mike?'

'It's a long way to go on a maybe. It's hardly as though we've got a firm order.'

'David maintains that the way has been smoothed for us. Since the Bolshevik revolution Russia has done nothing to bring itself out of the Middle Ages. Now, with Stalin's new Five Year Plan, they need a means of travelling across their huge country. There are many lakes and rivers and few airfields. It's ideal for the Griffin V.'

O'Donnell looked uneasy. 'I just have a bad feeling, that's all. From what I've read in the newspapers this man Stalin is a right evil sod. He plans to avoid widespread famine by combining all the small-holdings into collective farms – using force if necessary.' O'Donnell shook his head. 'It didn't work in Ireland and I don't see it working over there.'

Sion nodded. 'David said they're willing to pay in gold. We have to go and give it our best shot. It's too good a chance to miss.'

With a potential order for fifty planes, it was the biggest contract on the horizon. If negotiations were successful then there would be more to follow. Kirsty's idea had huge potential but it was still only dribs and drabs. A week or two in Russia could secure them orders to last months, possibly years. O'Donnell knew that Sion was right. Now that he had voiced his objections he would work heart and soul to make it work. 'What's the plan?'

'We've had confirmation that we'll be met next week in Moscow. All *we* need to do,' Sion grinned, 'is get there. We'll fit long range fuel tanks, carry spare petrol and load up with a complete set of spares, including struts and an undercarriage. We'll be as self sufficient as we can be.'

'The Russians we'll be seeing,' O'Donnell asked pertinently, 'are they underlings or decision makers?'

'Rykov. He's Stalin's right hand man, along with the Red Army commander, whose name is Vorochilov. If the deal's to be done then they'll do it.'

'Sounds good to me,' O'Donnell smiled for the first time. 'What about the other prospects here at home? We can't abandon them.'

'Kirsty will take care of them. Besides, she's eager to get more involved. She and Peter know what's needed.'

O'Donnell nodded. The recent successful advertising campaign was evidence that Kirsty was highly capable. 'I'll take her my files. Give her the names and addresses of the people we've contacted.'

'And I'll speak to David. I'm hoping he can help with flying permits across Europe.'

The evening before his departure Sion and Kirsty enjoyed a family dinner. Alex, thankfully, was on the mend and would soon be going back to school. Louise, at nine years old, hero-worshipped her older brother and sat glued to him at dinner. She wished with all her heart he wasn't returning to Winchester. Paul, just turned six, was a quiet, introspective boy who was already showing a talent for drawing and painting.

They had dinner in the gleaming, tiled kitchen. Alex asked his father all sorts of questions about the trip ahead. He appeared to have the same love of aviation as Sion and was keen to learn how to fly, though whether from a desire to please his father or from real passion, only time, thought Sion, would tell. With dinner ending, Paul announced a desire for bed while Alex pleaded to stay and talk longer with his father. Louise, of course, stayed too. Anxious as he was to secure the contract, Sion didn't relish the prospect of time spent away from his family. Alex had, for some time now, been pestering Sion for stories of his life in America. They had got into the habit of spending a little time together each evening, Sion talking and Alex listening agog to the family's early history. He was clearly impressed that Sion had survived being shot when barely older than Louise, a head wound at that. That, Kirsty observed wryly, explained a lot. Sion's tales of the Great War had the boy jumping up and down with excitement especially the part where Sion rescued David and their downed plane sank into the English Channel.

'I hope,' announced Alex, 'that I'll be able to fight in a war and be a hero. I'll shoot down lots of the enemy and get a medal.'

Sion smiled at his son. 'You may get a medal, but you take something you can never give back, someone's life. Better to live and even better to live in peace.'

'But, Dad,' Alex protested, 'war must be so much fun . . .'

Kirsty looked at her eldest with some asperity. 'When they all went off gaily in nineteen fourteen, claiming it would all be over by Christmas, nobody foresaw what would happen. Millions were killed in a hellish, brutal and bloody war. Men who should have lived happy lives. War has no place in a civilised world. Which is why we signed the treaty last year outlawing war in Europe. It is better to live without conflict, Alex, believe me.'

The philosophical argument was too much for Alex and he eventually went to bed, Louise trotting behind him, Alex still proclaiming that he was going to join the Royal Air Force as soon as he grew up and fight for Britain. The country's enemies were vague and unnamed.

But there was no doubt in the boy's mind – they were out there somewhere.

Kirsty and Sion had an early night. The following morning, bright and early, Sion and O'Donnell prepared for take-off.

Sion had letters of introduction to half of Europe, written by well-connected and powerful men within the British establishment. Many were the 'To whom it may concern' type, but others were addressed to specific people in positions of power or influence in France, Austria, Poland, Germany and Russia. When Sion protested to David that they were unlikely to be used his brother shook his head.

'Believe me, Sion, you can never be too careful. More than once I was glad to have a letter in my possession that turned up trumps in the most unlikely of places. So take them. You can never tell. How long will the flight take?'

'It's only ten hours flying time,' O'Donnell replied, 'but we're stopping en route.'

'With long range tanks fitted we'd get to Moscow in one hop. We've also sufficient petrol in the tins for an extra five hundred miles,' Sion said while they were walking towards the plane. He opened the door and pointed. 'Look.' Three of the seats had been removed and a camp bed placed along the starboard side. 'The seats can be refitted after we arrive. I don't want to risk getting to Moscow in the dark as we don't know what we'll find there. So we'll land about six o'clock and carry on in the morning. We'll take turns keeping watch. Can't be too careful.'

That made sense to David. In the evening they'd have plenty of time to set down safely, whether on land or water. A calm lake would be best, he thought. That way nobody could sneak up on them unawares. Europe, for all its apparent civilisation, was still a dangerous place especially that far east.

Kirsty had prepared flasks of soup and hot water which they stowed in special containers. Finally a hamper of food was secured on board. Then it was time to say goodbye.

Sion kissed Paul and Louise and solemnly shook hands with Alex, admonishing him to look after everyone. Alex, equally solemnly, said that he would. Putting his arms around Kirsty, Sion smiled, an ache in his heart, yet the old yearning for adventure tugged at him. Kirsty smiled back bravely, holding in the threatening tears. They both knew that he was undertaking a hazardous journey. Airfields were at a minimum, they would be prey to the weather and prone to mechanical problems. And there was no guarantee that when they arrived in Russia their efforts would be crowned with success.

'Are all the spares on board?' Sion asked Peter Cazorla, shaking his hand.

'Yes, Sion. There is even a spare engine, just as you asked. The only parts you cannot replace are the fuselage and the wings,' he smiled at his joke.

'Excellent. Ready?' he asked O'Donnell.

'Whenever you are.'

The two men climbed aboard. Sion checked the cargo, making sure it was secure. The last thing they needed was it shifting while they were airborne. Satisfied, he sat in the pilot's seat and began to go through the starting procedure. Finally he made a twirling motion with his finger to Ralph Cazorla, who swung the propeller. The engine roared into life and they sat for a few moments, watching the gauges and allowing the engine to warm through. It was not uncommon for an engine to stall halfway through take-off because it was still cold. Usually with fatal consequences.

They taxied out to the runway and Sion looked back one last time to wave to his family. Kirsty and the children were all waving madly. David raised his hand in a brief salute. Sion opened the throttle and they headed down the runway. As soon as he could he lifted the plane off the ground and turned gently towards the east. The adventure, he thought, was beginning.

It was not long before they were crossing the Channel. There was a steady breeze from the southwest, virtually no cloud and the sun was warming up the cockpit. Sion felt a thrill of excitement sweep through him – he loved the pull of the far horizons. This dichotomy had always existed within him – home-loving, family man and the adventurer. It had been a long time since he had indulged his passion for the latter. He glanced across at O'Donnell. He could see from the way his co-pilot was lazily sweeping the far distance with his eyes that he was feeling it too. O'Donnell was a born buccaneer. Sion eased his fingers on the control column and relaxed.

His father, Evan, had been the same. An adventurer who had fought and won the greatest role in the world – President of the United States of America. Thinking of his father, Sion felt himself becoming melancholic and shook himself out of it. He needed to concentrate on flying.

Beneath the wings they could see the white sails of numerous boats and as they left Ostend to starboard, they saw a regatta in progress. An hour after they had taken off they identified Rotterdam. Sion adjusted their course by a few degrees to port and aimed for Hamburg. Hopefully they would be over Rostock three hours after leaving England. They would cross the Baltic Sea in a straight line to Moscow. Without the new undercarriage they would have been forced to deviate to the south and stay over land. As it was, with Europe held in an almost stationary high pressure, there was little wind and, in an emergency, a landing onto the Baltic would not prove too hazardous – they hoped.

O'Donnell took the controls and Sion scrambled into the cabin to attack the picnic hamper. Back in the cockpit he munched contentedly on a sandwich of smoked salmon and cucumber and sipped home-made broth. His ear was tuned to the engine and both men heard it cough, a slight hiccup in the backdrop of its regular, deep roar. They

exchanged rueful glances and continued to listen carefully. Normally the ears gave the first indication of a
problem. A few minutes later the hiccup came again, this
time more pronounced. With it they saw a flicker of the
revolutions counter. The problem could be anything, from
a dirty carburettor restricting the flow of fuel, to water
in the petrol. To avoid the latter they had left the plane's
fuel tanks full after her last flight, reducing the possibility of condensation in the tanks. The Griffin's engine
was capable of spitting out droplets of water with merely
a slight change in revolutions. A few coughs and splut-
ters were no real cause for concern. When she cut out
. . . then it was time to worry. As the thought formed, the
engine coughed, picked up again and then faded to
nothing. The silence was terrifying.

O'Donnell began to adjust the trim of the plane to glide
but they were rapidly losing height. Pulling a lever to permit
a direct flow of petrol to the carburettor, Sion began operating a small hand-pump. He closed the valve and switched
on the engine. The air passing over the blades of the
propeller helped it to turn and after a few tries the engine
coughed and started again. It was a new design of theirs,
made for such an event. They had dropped fifteen hundred
feet and could clearly see the roads and fields around them.
O'Donnell scanned the area for an emergency landing
place. As Sion pumped petrol through the carburettor for
a few seconds, O'Donnell eased the plane back up,
regaining the height they had lost. The engine continued
roaring steadily and the problem appeared to have passed.

'Should we land?' O'Donnell asked.

Sion shrugged. 'Keep going. The new valve and pump
system worked like a dream, just like it did on the bench
test. We need never worry about dirty petrol again. We
should even be able to clear a blockage! Only a major
catastrophe can bring us down now, Mike. Let's get as
far as Lithuania and land. We can check the rest of the
petrol and carry on in the morning.'

'We should keep going,' O'Donnell argued.

Sion was about to overrule him when he thought better of it. Kaliningrad was the largest city on the eastern end of the Gulf of Gdansk, just inside the Lithuanian border and still a good five hundred miles from Moscow. It made sense to carry on to Vilnyus or even Smolensk before stopping for the night. 'Maybe you're right. We should make the most of the weather. It could be blowing a storm tomorrow. Head for Smolensk.'

O'Donnell nodded and they droned ever eastwards. After their makeshift meal, Sion took the controls again. O'Donnell went back into the main cabin and lay down on the camp bed. Within minutes he was fast asleep, lulled by the smooth sound of the engine and the gentle swaying of the plane. An hour later he and Sion changed places. Sion dropped off quickly and woke up forty minutes later when he felt the plane change direction and swoop down from the sky.

He was instantly alongside O'Donnell. 'What's wrong?'

'We're fine. That's the river Dnieper. Smolensk is thirty minutes flying time away. I've just checked the name of that last town. It's Orsha. According to the information I got from the Russian Embassy, we can land on the Dnieper as it's used by barges, mainly taking timber down to Kiev. But it would be better if we can find a quiet lake.'

Sion nodded. 'I agree.' He checked his watch. 'Sunset isn't that far away. We've lost over three hours of daylight flying east so we should set down soon, while we can still see. That smudge ahead must be Smolensk.'

'On the nose. Let's fly lower and see what we can find.' O'Donnell pushed the column forward and they headed gently down. The Dnieper was broad, sluggish and full of barges and boats. The heavy, slow moving craft represented a danger to the relatively fragile aeroplane and it made sense not to land there. To either side of the river the land was flat. Here and there they saw a scattered hamlet or

isolated farm with sheep or a few horses grazing. Most of
the land was pine forest stretching almost as far as the eye
could see. It was, on the whole, a bleak part of the world.

The sun was setting now, the last rays bathing the landscape in a golden light. Seeing a small lake they headed
for it, disturbing a flock of geese as they lined up to land.
The sun setting behind them was their saviour. As their
shadow fell before them they saw a blackness that was
more than a silhouette. O'Donnell opened the throttle and
pulled back on the controls just in time and they sailed
over the half-submerged tree trunk. Both men heaved a
sigh of relief. Passing low once more they checked their
landing site and went in again. The plane kissed the water,
bounced and settled. They were down and, to all intents
and purposes, safe. With the engine still running they
moved slowly across the lake until they neared the shore
and stopped, the boat drifting on a gentle breeze.

Sion opened the main door and lowered a lead weight
over the side. The edge of the lake was shallow, just
four feet of water. He pointed away from the shore and
O'Donnell turned the plane. Sion took a sounding every
few seconds until they were nearly fifty yards from the
land and had ten feet of water under them.

'This'll do.' Hand over hand he lowered a kedge anchor
on its chain, and secured it to the side of the fuselage.
The plane stopped drifting and O'Donnell shut down the
engine. After the hours in the sky, the peace thundered
in their ears. At that moment the sun vanished and dusk
quickly changed into darkness. Before settling down for
the night they pumped up the small inflatable dinghy they
carried and paddled around the plane. Everything appeared
to be in order. Sion took the petrol cans handed to him
by O'Donnell and refuelled the tanks. They ate a hearty
meal of chicken and potato salad, washed down with
warm soup. Sion took the first watch, sitting in the pilot's
seat, a rifle at the ready, the windows open, so that he
could hear anybody approaching.

O'Donnell slept like a log until Sion woke him at 1am and they changed places. The sun was rising when Sion awoke and they made a breakfast of their leftovers. Sion set up a primus stove in the doorway to make fresh coffee. Both men shaved and washed before they took-off. They intended making a good impression on arrival. Once airborne O'Donnell lay down on the camp bed and slept until Sion called him. Moscow was dead ahead.

Their instructions had been to land to the south of the city. They dropped lower. The sky was a solid mass of heavy cloud with a base of about eight thousand feet. A storm cloud shaped like a black anvil towered in the distance, forks of lightning flashing from it every few minutes. With relief Sion saw that the mass was moving away, like a huge grey and black galleon, beautiful to look at but awesome in its power.

O'Donnell tapped Sion on the shoulder and pointed. Craning his neck Sion could see a small airfield. There were no hangars, just half a dozen aircraft dotted across a green field and a landing strip, a dirt track lying east to west. The windsock was standing out stiffly, blowing to the north. With the crosswind hitting the side of the plane, it was wobbling dangerously, requiring all of Sion's ability and concentration. Less than twenty feet from the ground the wind suddenly stopped having an effect. They had passed below the summit of a small hillock and the wind was now whistling overhead. Seeing that within seconds they would be past the hill and could expect the buffeting to start again, Sion increased the angle of descent. The plane slammed into the dirt track, bounced and stayed down. Both men prayed that no damage had been done. As they continued along the track, passing the protection of the land, the wind hit the side, raised the starboard wing and took the wheel off the ground. For one terrifying second they feared the plane would flip over. But it dropped back down and stabilised.

'Hell,' said O'Donnell. 'That was too close for comfort.'

'What a stupid place to put an airfield. I'm surprised the place isn't littered with crashed aircraft.'

'It is,' said O'Donnell, pointing at a plane on the port side with a broken wing and a bent undercarriage. He pointed to a second one, similarly damaged. 'This looks like a scrapheap, not an airport.'

Taxiing over the track their initial impressions didn't improve as they neared a dilapidated shack a few hundred yards away. There appeared to be nobody around. Exchanging worried glances, they halted, Sion switched off the engine and let the propeller wind to a stop.

'I thought we were going to be met,' O'Donnell said.

'That's what the telegram said. This is the right place, isn't it?'

'As near as I can tell. Ten miles south of Moscow. And the description of the place is accurate enough. Although what the telegram omitted is far more interesting. This can't be the main airfield for Moscow. Can it?'

'I wouldn't have thought so,' said Sion his frown deepening. 'What shall we do?'

'Wait. I don't see anything else that we can do.'

'Well, we've come this far so I suppose you're right. Let's give it two hours.'

'Then what?'

'Then I'll toss you a coin to see who goes for petrol. We fill up the tanks and get ready to leave. Damn! This really annoys me. To think we've come all this way for nothing.'

'We don't know that yet. I'll make some fresh coffee.' So saying O'Donnell clambered into the main part of the plane and hunted out the primus stove. They were sitting in the cabin, cups in hand, when a battered lorry came into view and began to cough and splutter its way towards them. Behind it followed a staff car. Both vehicles had a red star painted on the side.

When the lorry drew up an order was shouted and a squad of men leapt down. They wore army uniforms of varying degrees of shabbiness. However, the rifles slung over their shoulders looked dangerous enough. The staff car drew up alongside. A corporal got out and opened the rear door. The immaculately dressed officer who stepped out was saluted by the squad of soldiers and the corporal. He returned the salute punctiliously. He appeared to be in his early forties, moustached, of average height and build but with piercing brown eyes that were never still. Their anxiety eased slightly when the officer smiled and extended a hand to welcome them.

Inviting him on board for a cup of coffee, the officer climbed nimbly inside. He introduced himself in heavily accented English as Klementi Vorochilov. 'I have the honour of being the Marshal of the Army. I am sorry not to be here earlier. We had no exact time of your arrival.'

'I had expected this to be a busy airport, so I hadn't foreseen any problems contacting you,' replied Sion.

'Alas, no. This is now disused. The main airport is to the east of the city.'

Sion and O'Donnell exchanged glances but said nothing. 'Can we get some petrol? Then we can give you a demonstration of what the plane is capable of.' Sion was keen to get on.

'All in good time,' the Marshal waved his hand airily. 'We have a dinner arranged for tonight. Business can be done tomorrow.'

Resignedly they nodded. 'But we need to refuel before we do so,' said Sion.

'I am afraid that will not be possible. Tomorrow the petrol will be brought here. Come my friends, let us go.'

'What about the Griffin?' Sion asked.

'My men will guard it. You will see. Come.'

Both men had brought a suitcase of clothes. The driver collected the cases and tied them to the back of the staff car. Climbing inside the vehicle, Sion decided he would make the most of their situation. This was his first time in Russia and he was eager to see as much as he could.

His first impressions unsettled him greatly. Peasants working in the fields wore little more than rags while the gangs who laboured on the roads, filling in holes and digging ditches were equally badly dressed. After a few miles Sion realised with a shock that many of the labourers he thought were men, wielding sledge hammers, carting wheelbarrows, were women. Their woefully inadequate, tattered clothes hung on their frames. Those who bothered to look at the car did so with dead eyes.

The car stopped at a huge hotel near the centre of Moscow. By now the rain was falling heavily, bringing with it an early dusk. Vorochilov marched into the brightly-lit foyer and went up to the desk. Seeing the Marshal the desk clerk immediately abandoned another guest and turned to him. The customer, about to protest, saw Vorochilov, paled and walked away. Sion watched the well dressed man slink into the shadows.

The Marshal returned with two keys in his hands and a tight smile on his face. 'Here we are. Compliments of the State. The bar is there.' He pointed behind them before handing over the keys. 'Let us meet there in say, one hour. We will talk about planes and business later.' There was no room for argument as he marched away. A slight figure, stiffly erect, he had a definite air of menace about him.

O'Donnell hefted his suitcase, 'Let's get cleaned up and see what the evening brings.'

In fact it brought very little. Too much vodka was drunk and too little food eaten. What was on offer was practically inedible. Beneath the veneer of opulence the true state of the hotel soon became apparent. Lights didn't work, the lift was out of order, glasses were dirty, the waiters' uniforms were slovenly. Behind the façade, the stories of Russia's economic woes appeared true. If they did win the order for the planes, would they ever get paid?

20

THE FOLLOWING MORNING, bleary-eyed and slightly the worse for wear they met downstairs for breakfast. It consisted of bread, cheese, dried meats and watery coffee.

'Let's get this over with as soon as possible,' said Sion, 'and get the hell out of here. The quicker we get back the better. Here comes the Marshal.'

Strutting towards them, a smile on his face, Vorochilov looked as though he'd slept the sleep of the innocent. 'Good morning, my friends. As soon as you are ready I will take you to the airfield. I would like a trip in your fine plane. Petrol is being delivered even now.'

'Then let's go.' Sion wiped his mouth on a grcy-looking napkin and stood up. 'We'll fetch our things.'

'Surely you will not be leaving so soon? We have much to discuss. If we want the planes we need to talk about prices,' Vorochilov raised his brows in surprise.

Sion's instinct was to fill the plane with petrol and return to civilisation as soon as possible. As it was . . . they had no choice but to go through with the whole sales pitch before they could leave. It was with a heavy heart he left the hotel.

The rain had stopped although a blustery wind still blew. Driving through the city they were saddened by the beautifully designed buildings falling into decay. Although they saw many bicycles, there were few cars, the majority of the population using the trams that ceaselessly criss-crossed the city. Moscow's people all had one thing in common – a look of bone-deep weariness.

At the airfield they found the petrol already delivered and quickly filled the tanks. Without asking permission they also filled the Griffin's spare cans. While they were busy with the petrol, two more staff cars appeared, carrying senior officers of the Russian army. Introductions were made, although they had met some of them the night before.

A short while later, with every seat taken by a strapping army officer, Sion ran through the take-off procedures. When he indicated he was ready, a soldier heaved down on the propeller and the engine burst into life. Taxiing away, they lined up with the wind coming at them from about forty-five degrees to port, and Sion opened up the throttle. The Griffin picked up speed, hit 50mph, and Sion pulled back on the joystick. The plane rose gracefully into the air.

They spent the next hour showing what the plane could do. From the excited reaction of the officers in the cabin they appeared delighted at the Griffin's performance. None of them had encountered a heating system in a plane before. They praised the fact that the plane could use both land and water. But halfway through the test flight the engine cut out. Unperturbed, Sion and Mike went through the routine of pumping petrol through the system and restarting the engine. When the engine burst into life again the officers began clapping. Looking over his shoulder Sion saw Vorochilov nodding and smiling to the man sitting next to him. A short while later they returned to the airfield.

That evening Sion and O'Donnell met Marshal Vorochilov in the hotel, at the huge wooden bar that could have served fifty customers simultaneously. There were a dozen other guests and one slovenly barman. The Marshal ordered a bottle of champagne.

'Let us drink a toast,' he raised his glass, 'to our business together.'

O'Donnell drank but Sion paused. 'We have a deal? What about Mr Rykov? I thought he had the final say.'

'That is true. He has been given the details of the plane's performance. The Griffin is ideal for our purposes. To implement our Five Year Plan officials must be able to travel efficiently. All is agreed.'

'Why don't your officials use the telegraph or even send written reports?' O'Donnell asked.

'They are, shall we say, unreliable?' The cynical look on the Marshal's face explained what he meant. Or so they thought.

Getting down to business Sion asked, 'How many planes does your government require?'

'We wish for one hundred.'

'Excellent,' Sion said. 'Do you mind me asking, what was the deciding factor?'

'The way you could restart the engine.'

'As a safety feature, it's rarely needed. We're careful not to let water contaminate the petrol.'

'I am afraid that is not the case here in Russia,' said Vorochilov. 'Water is often added to petrol. A gallon of petrol with ten percent water means more profit.'

'But that's ludicrous. It could kill somebody,' Sion protested.

The Marshal nodded. 'We have had many planes fall out of the sky as a result. Here in the Soviet Union it is one of the hazards of life. Now, can we discuss delivery dates?'

'Let's,' Sion smiled, 'discuss price first.'

There was little haggling. The price had already been sent by telegram. However, the Marshal demanded a discount for quantity. They argued and finally Sion agreed to take five percent off the price.

'What about shipment?' Vorochilov asked.

'We can fly them in. Although that will take some time. Alternatively we can ship all the planes at once, in pieces, and put them together once they reach Moscow.' The Marshal was shaking his head. 'My pilots need training. I think it will be best if we send fifty pilots to

England. They can fly back, then return for the second fifty.'

Sion nodded. The problem was solved. 'What about payment?'

'We do not have enough foreign currency,' said the Marshal frowning, 'and so you will be paid in gold. Is that acceptable?'

'Agreed. But we will require a deposit with the order, a further payment when each plane is built and the balance on delivery.'

'I take it by delivery you mean when they arrive here in the Soviet Union?'

Sion shook his head. 'No. I mean when your pilots sign for them in England. What happens if a plane crashes on the way because of pilot error? I cannot be held accountable,' Sion argued.

Vorochilov beckoned the waiter to bring another bottle of champagne. And so the horse trading continued until they finally reached an agreement. An initial payment of twenty-five percent would be made with the order for one hundred planes. A further twelve and a half percent would be paid when the pilots arrived in England to fly the first fifty back, and a further twelve and a half percent would be paid on delivery to Russia. The balance of the order would be paid when the next fifty planes arrived in the Soviet Union. The Marshal drove a hard bargain but on the face of it a fair one. Neither Sion nor O'Donnell could see anything wrong with the arrangement.

They shook hands and the Marshal again beckoned to the waiter. 'I will have the papers delivered here tomorrow. We need a real drink to cement our deal. Vodka from the Black Sea area, the finest in the Soviet Union.'

'I'll give you a contract to take away with you,' said Sion. 'Please have the necessary signatories look it over. You will see that it is our standard contract. All we need to do is make the necessary changes as we've agreed.'

'I will see to it,' said Vorochilov.

The following morning five pages of typewritten script arrived at the hotel. It was in Russian.

'Flaming hell, Cyrillic alphabet,' said O'Donnell. 'It might as well be double Dutch.'

'We'd better get this independently translated,' said Sion, angry at the delay. 'I'll ask at the desk.' Neither man trusted the Red Army Marshal.

A few minutes later he was back. 'I've been given directions to a translation service not far from the hotel. Do you want to come?'

'Sure. I've nothing else to do.'

Sion and O'Donnell left the hotel and, for the first time, walked the streets of Moscow, getting a closer look at the people. The pavements were packed with throngs of humanity hurriedly going about their business.

'They don't look very happy,' assessed Sion.

'Does anybody in London?'

'Fair point. But they seem so down-at-heel. I've never seen so many people so badly dressed. Look at that woman over there,' he indicated with his head. 'She's wearing little more than rags.'

'Selling matches, too. That sort of thing ended in London years ago. Before the war.'

'How can an economy that can't look after its people afford to buy our planes?'

O'Donnell looked uneasy. 'I don't know. That's why we've got a contract.'

The sign over the door offered translations in over twenty different languages. Entering, they found themselves in a small office where a harassed young woman was busy typing. She looked up and painted a smile on her face.

'*Ví gararet-ye pa-Angleeske?*' Sion stumbled over the words.

'Yes, sir. How may I help you?' Her accent was pronounced but her English was perfect.

'We have a document we need translated.' Taking it from his pocket he waved it in front of her.

'Into which language?'

'It's written in Russian and I need a fair copy in English.'

'Leave it with me. I will have it ready in three days.'

'*Pazhalsta* – please' said Sion. 'We need it now.'

The woman shrugged. 'That cannot be helped. I have other work waiting.'

'It's only five pages long.'

'*Prasteet-ye* – sorry,' came the sullen reply, her smile vanishing.

'I need this done today,' Sion turned towards the door. 'Perhaps Marshal Vorochilov can recommend another agency.'

The woman paled. 'Comrade Vorochilov? The translation is for him?' She licked her lips, fear in her eyes.

'Yes. We've concluded a contract with your government. I cannot sign it until I see an accurate translation.'

'Many sincere apologies. I will do the work immediately.' The woman nodded vigorously.

Sion feigned gratitude. 'Oh? Are you sure?'

'Yes, quite sure. Please come back in two hours.'

'That's very kind of you,' said Sion.

Outside O'Donnell said, 'She was really afraid. Vorochilov casts a long shadow.'

To their pleasant surprise the contract was exactly as they had agreed. Reassured, Sion contacted Vorochilov and made arrangements to meet the following morning at the Marshal's office. Sion made it clear that the deposit must be paid when the contracts were signed. Again, he was pleasantly surprised with the alacrity at which the Russian agreed.

They spent a temperate night in the hotel, neither of them wishing to fly with a hangover. The following morning they met the Marshal and two copies of the contract were signed, one in Russian and the other in

English. When Sion and O'Donnell left they took with them a small chest of gold and Vorochilov's best wishes. They took-off at mid-day.

In the course of the next three hours the engine cut out five times. Finally in exasperation they landed on a small lake. It took them the rest of the day to filter the water from the Russian petrol. They stayed where they were overnight and set off again at first light. That evening they landed safely back at Biggin Hill.

Kirsty's understanding of the psychology of the rich was paying off. Over the next two months orders began to trickle in from rich individuals eager to display their wealth and status. The money coming in enabled Sion to keep his entire workforce employed while the final payment from Russia would turn a handsome profit.

The next few weeks saw them all working sixteen hours a day, seven days a week. Sion wheeled and dealed, pulling favours from their suppliers to ensure a constant flow of raw material.

Eight weeks after their return, Sion sent a telegram to Marshal Vorochilov. The first fifty planes were ready for collection. He received a telegram back stating that fifty pilots plus co-pilots were on their way and would arrive within a week. As part of the agreement, Sion had erected a string of tents near the house for them to sleep in. He expected to have them all signed off as competent to fly the planes within two days. The language barrier, however, made training more difficult than expected.

A hundred men also took a good deal of looking after, even if they were all military and mainly officers. A field kitchen had to be established, cooks hired. It became a logistical nightmare that Sion and Kirsty worked hard to solve. Initially, Sion had intended to give each man at least two hours of flying training, landing and taking-off, switching from land to water. In the end he settled for less than fifty minutes. All the officers were experienced flyers. Moreover, he couldn't wait to get rid of them.

Even so it took three days before he was satisfied that the pilots could return safely to the Soviet Union. The officer in charge agreed with Sion's assessment and paid over the next instalment of gold. They made arrangements to leave the following day, the 31st March 1930, at 2pm.

It was a cold, clear, blustery day. The planes were lined up to depart, engines had been warmed through, petrol topped up and spare cans stowed on board. Each plane carried a full set of spares, in accordance with the contract. The pilots had been briefed. The two English interpreters had worked overtime to make sure everybody understood what was needed. Sion and O'Donnell were the lead aircraft in their own Griffin.

The whole workforce stood outside, watching. When the planes began to lift off nearly three hundred voices were raised in cheer. Hands were waved and hats were thrown into the air. For the staff of Griffiths Aviation, it was a joyous occasion.

This time the approach was to an airfield north of Moscow. Neither Sion nor O'Donnell had been aware of its existence and couldn't help comparing the two fields. This one was large, flat and had two runways. One ran north to south, the other east to west. Hangars were in use, airplanes were taking-off and landing and staff were busily moving around.

Sion cast a cynical look at O'Donnell. 'So why didn't we come here last time?'

'Paranoia?'

'Probably. Seeing this lot I feel happier. I was worried about their ability to maintain the planes. The last thing we need is one of our aircraft falling out of the sky due to poor maintenance. Our reputation could be at risk.'

O'Donnell shook his head. 'Nobody would ever have found out.' He grinned at his friend. 'Maybe it's you who's paranoid.'

Sion grinned back. 'Maybe you're right. Let's get this

over with. I don't plan to stay here any longer than we can help.'

Vorochilov was there to greet them, a wide smile on his face. Shaking their hands, he said, 'Excellent, excellent.'

'Have any of the others arrived yet?' Sion asked.

'Not yet. You are the first. But look.' The Marshal pointed. A second string of planes came into view, lined up and began to land, one at a time. Pride coursed through Sion. It was a stirring sight. Each plane was a work of beauty, moving elegantly through the air. The aerodynamic changes put them at the forefront of design. At a mere seven hundred and fifty pounds each, they were a bargain.

The pilots began to congregate, excitedly talking about their individual flights and experiences. When Sion had explained the necessity for clean petrol they were sceptical. Now they were convinced. Sion had brought an extra petrol filtration unit with him which he gave to the senior flying officer as a present. Within two hours all the planes had landed safely, Vorochilov was pleased, delivery papers were signed, and the next twelve and a half percent of the money handed over.

After filtering the petrol they needed for the return flight they decided to spend the night at the airfield. Despite invitations from the other pilots to join them in a celebratory dinner they insisted that they needed a clear head for the following morning. In truth, Sion wanted to stay with the gold. At dawn, when the airfield was still asleep, they completed their pre-flight checks and lined up to take-off. It was bitterly cold outside, snow lay on the ground, the air was breathless and the day appeared perfect for flying. To the north, storm clouds were gathering at a frightening speed.

The cockpit barometer was a recent refinement. Filled with mercury it was designed to warn the pilots of changing weather. If the mercury rose, high pressure was coming in heralding fine weather. If it dropped it meant the reverse. The glass was settled when they took off and

it wasn't until they were airborne that O'Donnell noticed
it had dropped. When they'd left Moscow the mercury
had been high at 1,038mb. It had dropped below 1000.

Scanning the horizon they saw a faint grey smudge
forming at the edge of their vision, where the sky met
the land. Even as they watched it grew perceptibly.

'If we don't land soon we might be in trouble,' said
O'Donnell.

Sion nodded. 'Smolensk is twenty miles away. We can
land near there – or we can try and outrun it.'

'If we land we could be trapped for days. And we'll
need to find somewhere safe to stow the plane. Or just
peg her to the ground.'

Sion thought of the metal pegs and ropes stowed in
the aircraft. A sudden squall could easily pitch a plane
over if precautions weren't taken.

'I think we should make a run for it,' said Sion.

O'Donnell looked out of the window and watched the
grey cloud rise and darken. 'Okay. Let's get the hell out
of here.'

Sion opened the throttle and put the plane in a very
slight dive. Barely two degrees below the horizon the
plane's speed crept up. To date the fastest the Griffin had
travelled was 248mph in level flight. With the slight
incline they edged up to and hovered around 270mph.
The plane lurched and a wing dipped – the wind had
finally arrived.

'Try and get our speed over the ground,' Sion said.
'I'll let the wind take us south.'

O'Donnell's chart was drawn at the time of the Great
War. A handful of features were shown on an otherwise
almost blank sheet of paper. He managed to identify the
confluence of two rivers, checked their heading and saw
in the far distance a knoll that was also marked. Timing
their approach he made his calculations.

'Two hundred and seventy-eight miles per hour.'

'Good. Now we're past the Central Russian Uplands

the storm could be delayed by the higher land. We've also got more airspace to play with.'

The land had dropped to a height of less than 900 feet above sea-level but was now rising again. The clouds to the north were growing higher and darker as the land rose to meet them. Inside the maelstrom were high winds and a deadly combination of rain, sleet and snow. They had to outstrip it. The die was cast.

21

THE WIND PICKED up. The Griffin was now down to 3,800ft above the ground, still descending slowly but maintaining airspeed. O'Donnell identified another two landmarks.

'Two hundred and fifty-five miles per hour over the ground. How's she handling?'

'No problems. At this rate we'll be over Poland in an hour and a half.'

'It looks pretty bleak down there,' said O'Donnell staring out of the window.

Below them lay a white, undulating carpet of snow stretching as far as the eye could see. The thought of landing brought a chill to both men's hearts. It was one thing to select a suitable site, another to be forced down without any option.

The wind was buffeting them now, and the plane was skidding across the sky southwards as well as west. Sion altered their heading a few degrees right so that the wind came more from the starboard quarter, but they were beginning to rise and fall as though they were on a switch-back. Luckily their height above ground left them plenty of room but it was still a swooping, gut-tightening experience. So far only the wind had reached them. The storm itself with all its incipient dangers was still miles away. By now a huge anvil of cumulonimbus cloud, ragged, threatening, was towering over them.

'It's a big one,' said O'Donnell. 'I reckon the top's eighteen to twenty thousand feet.'

Like all pilots they had studied meteorology and knew that the lightning they could now see was caused by the formation of raindrops being swept upwards in the rising air. When the drops reached a quarter of an inch in diameter they disintegrated, liberating an electrical charge that created a difference of potential between the top and bottom of the cloud large enough to cause an electrical discharge. If it was visible it was forked lightning, and if only seen in reflection it was sheet lightning. The thunder was caused by the expansion and subsequent contraction of the air due to the electrical discharge. Light travelling faster than sound meant the discharge was seen before it was heard. Counting the seconds in between gave the approximate distance of the storm.

O'Donnell counted. 'Still forty miles away.'

'Is it my imagination or is the cloud lighter ahead?'

Peering through the cockpit window, O'Donnell examined the clouds. 'Starboard and ahead it's definitely lighter. We're outpacing it but we've a long way to go. If the wind veers another ten degrees we'll be free and clear.' Ten degrees would take the wind clockwise and help to push them even more quickly from the path of the storm.

A quarter of a mile further on, they hit a huge downdraft and began plunging downwards at an alarming speed. The altimeter unwound rapidly and Sion gunned the engine, hauling back on the steering column. The Griffin was screaming in protest and the screech of the wind was a death threat. The plane hadn't been made to withstand such a strain but she struggled valiantly. With land hurtling up to meet them, the wind came to their aid. Bouncing off the undulating land, it threw them skywards once more, passing two and then three thousand feet. Still they shot up. Four, five, six thousand and still they were heading upwards. Finally they broke through the leading edge of the wind and hit straight and level flight.

Sion was sweating, the strain of fighting the controls clearly etched on his face. 'Check our position, Mike, if you can. There's a river down there. And another one just ahead. Look to starboard. That looks like a big town about ten, fifteen miles away.'

'If our dead reckoning isn't too far out . . . then I think that's Warsaw. Which puts us about here.' He placed a finger on the chart and showed it to Sion who nodded.

'How are we doing for petrol?'

'Still half full. That tail wind probably added eighty or a hundred miles to our range. Look, the cloud is thinning. It's much lighter to starboard.'

With relief they realised that they had outrun the storm, which was now passing behind them.

'Thank God for that,' said Sion with feeling. 'Mind you, the old girl took the strain in her stride. For a moment or two back there I thought our goose was cooked. Jesus,' he shook his head in wonder, 'I would never have thought she would cope so well.'

'The plane's stronger than she looks. That much is obvious. Perhaps we should try a few violent manoeuvres, like a dive under full power.' O'Donnell, seeing the horror on Sion's face, laughed. 'Only kidding. There's been enough excitement for one day.'

Six weeks later they repeated the performance. The men who came for the second fifty planes were a mixture of new pilots and some who'd done the first journey. This time the new pilots had already practised on the planes in Moscow and so were quickly checked out. In the third week of April Sion and O'Donnell arrived back in Moscow. This time it was to collect the balance of the money – representing fifty percent of the deal, their profit and the company's future.

The ground was still covered in a winter's coat of freshly fallen snow. Marshal Vorochilov was not there to greet them this time. Instead there was a message delivered by a Red Army Colonel. The Marshal would see them the next morning at the Kremlin.

As they watched the officer leave, Sion turned to O'Donnell. 'I've got an itch between my shoulder blades which I can't scratch. Something is wrong.'

'He was distinctly unfriendly for a messenger. The big question is, what can they do to us?'

'You mean apart from put a bullet in our heads and throw us in the river with lead shoes on?'

'Apart from that.'

'They say undesirables get sent to Siberia.'

'And the thieving swine get a hundred planes for the price of fifty. We've been set up.'

'I never trusted Vorochilov I only went along with him because we needed the deal so badly.'

'We could cut our losses and run.'

'True. And return home to face ruin. I need the balance of that gold to keep the factory going while we build up the personal orders. If we return to England without it I'll have to sack sixty or seventy percent of the men.'

'So what do we do?'

'We use David and John's letters of introduction,' was the enigmatic reply.

As on the earlier trips they had arrived mid-morning. When they checked the petrol quality at the airfield they were surprised to discover that it was as contaminated with water as ever. Setting up the filter equipment they extracted the water, filling the plane's tanks and spare cans.

'So now what?' O'Donnell asked.

'Now we go to the embassy.' Sion lifted down a document case and looked through the papers. 'I thought so. This letter is for the Ambassador himself.'

The embassy was busy. They were made to wait in a queue. When they finally reached the window of a harassed young man, Sion said, 'I'd like to see the Ambassador, please.'

'So would everyone here, I assure you. If you tell me what it's about I can tell you who you can see.'

'Well, I have a letter of introduction, to hand to the Ambassador personally.'

'May I see the letter, please?' There was a little more respect now. After all, the letter might be genuine.

Sion handed it over. 'You'll see it's from the Baron of Guildford.' *Good old John Buchanan to the rescue again.*

The letter began, 'My dear Fotheringham' and nobody called His Excellency, the Ambassador, Fotheringham, unless he was a close personal friend or significantly superior in rank. 'I'll see he gets it right away.' Scrambling to his feet the young man rushed from the room. They were kept waiting a good twenty minutes before he returned, by which time the queue was stretching out the front door.

'His Excellency asks that you return in time for cocktails at seven.'

The two pilots exchanged wry glances.

'Can't we see him now? It's urgent.'

'I'm sorry, no. He's just left and has a round of calls to make before he returns this evening.'

'Damnation. All right, thanks.' Sion turned to go.

'Excuse me, sir. I was told to tell you that the affair is black tie.'

Sion returned to the window. 'We've just flown in from England. We don't have penguin suits with us.'

'Flown? By plane?' The young man asked excitedly.

'I didn't know there was any other way to fly,' Sion replied dryly.

'If you come back at six thirty I'll see about arranging dinner jackets. Leave it to me, sir.'

'That's very kind of you, thanks.'

O'Donnell and Sion left the embassy, eventually found a taxi and returned to the airfield. They checked the plane over carefully but found nothing suspicious.

'Shall we take a wander?' Sion suggested. 'See what's going on?'

'Sure. I've been wanting to take a look at their maintenance.'

The airfield was at least two miles square. There were all types of planes dotted across the field from several nations. They recognised many of them, but some were unfamiliar. None were as modern looking as their Griffin. A wind had picked up from the north and there was a sharp bite to the air, so they moved quickly into one of the hangars. There were a number of men working on the few planes stowed there.

'In the corner,' said O'Donnell, 'That's one of ours.'

Dressed in standard flying gear of leather, fleece-lined jackets, they walked across unchallenged and stopped next to the Griffin. A casual glance at the fuselage was sufficient.

'Let's get out of here,' said Sion.

Sauntering away without a backward glance, they stopped only when they were outside.

'Bloody hell, Sion. What do we do now?'

'Nothing. If we breathe a word of what we saw, we won't get out of here alive.' The Griffin was being modified as a fighter bomber. A bomb bay had been cut into the fuselage and a machine gun mounted on the front. 'So much for officials reporting on five-year-plans.'

'We stay quiet about what we've seen. Not a word at the embassy. Our government takes a dim view about selling weapons abroad. Even if we can prove we knew nothing about it.'

They arrived back at the embassy in plenty of time. The young official they'd met earlier proved to be a flying enthusiast and a great fan of Sion's exploits. He and a friend were glad to supply dinner suits and black ties suitable for the occasion. The suits were slightly tight and rather old-fashioned in style but they weren't complaining. The price was a flight in a Griffin when their owners returned to England on their next leave.

The reception started promptly. The Ambassador and his wife greeted their guests at the door, shaking hands, murmuring a welcome.

'How do you do, sir. My name is Sion Griffiths.' Seeing the puzzled frown on the older man's face Sion added, 'A friend of the Baron of Guildford.'

The frown was replaced by a smile. 'Ah, yes. And how is dear John?'

'Well, thank you, sir. You may know that he is married to my mother. My brother is the Member of Parliament, David Griffiths. And this,' he turned to O'Donnell, 'is Sergeant Major O'Donnell, VC.'

The ambassador was in his late fifties. Of medium height, he had a thick head of silvery hair and an ample waistline, testimony to the number of dinners he had to attend.

'O'Donnell, I am very pleased to meet you. Such an honour to meet someone held in such high regard.'

With no further names to throw at the Ambassador, Sion murmured, 'I must speak to you, sir. It's important.'

'Very well. Let me finish here. A footman will show you to my study. Though I can spare you a few minutes only.'

'Thank you, sir.'

Satisfied, the two men wandered into the crowd. A tray of drinks appeared under their noses and they opted for whisky and sodas.

More than an hour of boring small talk passed before they were summoned. Once installed in the book-lined study, it was another fifteen minutes before the Ambassador arrived, making his apologies.

'Now then, Griffiths, what can I do for you?'

'Sir, Griffiths Aviation has sold one hundred aircraft to the Russians. We've received fifty percent payment to date although we've delivered all the planes. For some reason I feel uneasy about being paid the balance. I simply don't trust Marshal Vorochilov.'

The Ambassador pursed his lips, wandered behind his desk and sat down heavily. 'Your instincts do you well. About six months ago a similar deal was concluded with a French company. Same terms. It was reported that their plane crashed on the homeward flight and the three men on board killed. The money was never found and the Russians, providing proof that they'd paid the balance, wiped their hands of the problem.'

'But you don't believe it?'

The Ambassador tapped his fingers on the desk and then said, 'No one in diplomatic circles did. Quite frankly, some of these Russian fellows are not to be trusted. Their war with China is getting out of hand and some senior officers are becoming antsy. Back to the problem in hand. When do you propose to leave the country?'

'As soon as we've got the gold, we'll head for the airfield. Once we get there we'll try and get airborne as quickly as possible.'

'No good, I'm afraid. Vorochilov will have a fighter up after you before you're out of sight. He can have you shot down in seconds and no one will be any the wiser. No wreckage and no bodies. But gold – that he can recover from a burnt out plane.'

'The swine,' said O'Donnell. 'The conniving, evil swine.'

'You seem to have a good feel for the whole mess, sir. Any tricks up your sleeve?'

Rather surprisingly, the ambassador proved something of a magician.

After a fitful night's sleep at the ambassador's residence, Sion was escorted to the Kremlin the following morning. Driven in an embassy car, he was accompanied by three senior members of the ambassador's staff, all with diplomatic immunity. A letter from the ambassador, congratulating Vorochilov personally on excellent trade links with Britain, rested snugly in Sion's top pocket. Nevertheless, they were kept waiting for nearly three hours before Vorochilov saw them. Gone were the façade, the jokes, the offers of vodka. The gold was handed over with barely a word.

'What are your travel plans, Mr Griffiths?' the Marshal asked, stone-faced.

Sion looked at his watch, unsurprised to find it was already 12.30pm. 'We leave tomorrow, early.'

'I wish you a safe journey.'

The tone sent shivers up Sion's spine. 'Thank you,' he said hefting the box of bullion under his arm. Back in the car Sion let out a sigh. 'Thanks fellows. I don't know what I'd have done without you.'

'You're not out of the wood yet, old boy,' said the Military Attaché. 'Driver, as quick as you can. The old airfield to the south of Moscow.'

'Right you are, sir.'

Although they kept a lookout there didn't appear to be anybody following them. Half an hour later they arrived at the field. There was no sign of O'Donnell. He had left the residency before dawn, to check the plane over thoroughly, making sure it hadn't been sabotaged in some way. Once he was satisfied it was safe, he was to fly to the airfield where they had first landed and wait for Sion there.

'Damn,' Sion said. 'He should have been here by now. I hope nothing's happened to him.'

'I hope so too,' said the MA, a tall, thin man, sporting a fashionable hairline moustache. Beneath his veneer of insouciance was a quick mind, a readiness for action. Even as he spoke he was opening the boot of the embassy car and handing out Webley Mark 6 service revolvers. The guns fired heavy .455 British Service cartridges that could stop a charging elephant. Since there was no safety device on the gun, the chamber under the hammer was normally kept empty. 'If it comes to shooting,' he smiled at Sion, 'let us get on with it.'

Sion held the gun in his right hand, familiar with its use from his time in the war. 'I'll fight my own battles.'

'But we have diplomatic immunity and you don't. The

worse they can do is deport us. *You* they can shoot. We'll give it another ten minutes and if O'Donnell doesn't turn up then we'll head for the other airfield.'

The words were hardly out of his mouth when they heard the drone of an aeroplane. Looking up they saw the Griffin turning onto the field. Bundling themselves back into the car they headed out across the field towards where the plane was touching down. O'Donnell landed, turned and trundled away to the end of the runway to face the wind for take-off. The embassy's Lagonda bounced over the hard ground after him. Pulling up next to the plane Sion climbed out and was turning to thank the others when they heard the sound of an engine racing and back-firing in the distance.

'You'd better go, old boy,' said the MA.

'Thanks. I won't forget you for this. When you get back to Blighty come and see us at Biggin Hill. That goes for all of you.'

O'Donnell was speeding along the track before Sion was in his seat. In the distance they saw two lorries racing towards them, each lorry packed with armed soldiers. The embassy car was also racing alongside them, trying to head off the uncovered lorries which were fast approaching the track.

The Griffin reached 45mph and, a good hundred yards short of the lorries, they left the ground and sailed gracefully into the air. Banking hard to port, the plane veered away from the trucks. Disgorged soldiers were already loading and firing their rifles at them. It was an empty gesture as the Griffin quickly headed away from Moscow.

'That was close enough,' said Sion. 'What took you so long?'

O'Donnell smiled grimly. 'Your instincts were right. The scratches you made on the filler cap were out of line. They'd put sugar in the petrol. I had to change the whole lot, filter fresh petrol and check all the cans. I thought I'd never get it done.'

In flight the sugar would have crystallised and quickly clogged up the engine. It would have cut out with no chance of it being restarted – ever. 'We'd better get out of Russia as fast as we can.'

'If I was Vorochilov I'd have a hundred planes strung out across the sky in a barricade from north to south directly ahead of us.'

'So would I. But he daren't shoot us down until we're clear of Moscow. So let's assume he has his flying circus twenty or thirty miles ahead and we're flying straight at them. That being the case,' Sion looked back, Moscow was already fading in the distance, 'turn north now. We're going to Finland.'

'How far is it?'

Sion was checking on the chart. 'Four hundred and eighty miles. That's two and a half hours flying.' Looking out the window, he remarked, 'And for once the weather's clear.'

'Where'd you get the gun?'

'What?' Sion looked at his belt. When he'd rushed from the car he'd tucked the Webley into his belt, forgetting to return it. It was now digging into his side, a painful reminder of their escape. 'The guys from the embassy. It may come in useful, but I think I'd better get out the Enfield as well. Just in case.'

From a hidden compartment under the floor of the fuselage Sion extracted a MkIII, Short Magazine, Lee-Enfield rifle, known as the SMLE. The magazine held ten rounds of .303 British Service cartridges and had such a smooth bolt action that during the World War German units on the Enfield's receiving end thought they were under machine-gun fire. He checked out the rifle, loaded the magazine and put an eleventh round up the spout. Back in his seat Sion began searching the horizon using binoculars, quartering the sky, looking high and low. It was empty apart from an occasional white ball of fluffy cloud. A more peaceful scene could hardly be imagined.

He looked down. The countryside was a picturesque, uniform white as far as the horizon. Sitting in the right hand seat, Sion looked out of his side of the window. Three thousand feet below the Griffin's shadow kept pace like a black crow. Above the crow flew the shadow of a hawk, ready to pounce.

22

IT ONLY TOOK Sion a second to react. 'Dive,' he screamed. 'Hard left.'

O'Donnell obeyed instantly. Pushing the controls forward in a steep dive he turned hard to port. Bullets flew down their left, like a solid rod of iron that missed by the nearest of margins. He increased the dive, their speed passing 288mph and still rising. At 450ft he pulled back hard on the column and they swooped skywards.

'There he is,' yelled Sion.

About half a mile away the Russian was also pulling up from his dive, in a modified version of the Griffin. Their opponent had a front-mounted machine gun, as well as a bomb bay. O'Donnell clawed for the sky, wanting as much room to manoeuvre as possible. Their only hope was to out-fly the Russian.

At 5,000ft he turned back to their former heading, put the plane into a shallow dive and accelerated. After the beating they'd taken in the storm both men were reasonably sure that the plane could take far more stress than they'd dared try before. They hoped the Russian wouldn't feel as confident.

'We're outpacing him,' said Sion, looking out of the side window of the cockpit. 'He's after us but not as fast.'

'Jesus, Mary and Joseph, would you look at that,' O'Donnell pointed ahead.

Turning around Sion felt his guts churn. There were two aircraft lining up to dive on them, both Griffins, both modified with machine guns.

'Take the rifle,' said Sion, thrusting it at O'Donnell. 'I'll take the plane. No disrespect, Mike, but I've been here before.' In spite of the fact that he wasn't serving in the air force at the time, he had been in his share of dog-fights during the war. 'Beside which, you're a better shot than I am.'

Sion kept the plane in its shallow dive. One of the attacking aircraft was lining up to fire straight at them as they passed underneath and in front. They were sitting ducks if he didn't do something fast. It was all a matter of timing. If he pulled up too soon the other plane could follow and get them from below. If he pulled up too late it would be all over. The two planes were about a hundred yards apart and their paths were about to cross when Sion pulled hard back on the column. At the same time he flipped the aircraft onto its wing, presenting an even smaller target. They shot past.

The other plane was to their right and closing fast, a stream of bullets whizzing their way across the sky, directly at them. In desperation Sion rammed the column forward throwing the plane into a steep dive, trying to turn inside the hail of bullets. Just when they were about to hit, the bullets stopped and they flew past, looping the loop, trying to get behind the Russians.

'There, look! They're flying straight and level, in a dive. The engine's cut out,' O'Donnell yelled.

'Right. Shoot when we get alongside.'

Accelerating as fast as he could, Sion turned the plane parallel to the Russian and levelled off less than forty yards on their right. The two pilots were too busy trying to restart the engine to notice them. O'Donnell poked the tip of the rifle out of the side window and fired, smoothly working the bolt and firing again. His second or third shot blew the head of one of the pilots apart and the plane nose dived. His comrade let go the pump lever and grabbed the column, pulling back hard. With no engine the plane's flight stalled and it began to tumble from the sky, turning and twisting all the way down.

Sion didn't wait to see the result but turned into a shallow dive, accelerating away. Not a moment too soon. The second Russian plane was already lined up and firing, his bullets missing their tail by a whisker. Sion was desperately trying to out-run the other aircraft. Imperceptibly they were pulling away. At 287mph they were flying well outside the parameters laid down in the plane's manual. The Russian pilot didn't dare take the risk.

'We're winning. That'll teach them not to filter their petrol.' The words were barely out of O'Donnell's mouth when their own engine spluttered. Both men held their breaths, their hearts pounding, their mouths dry with fear. But O'Donnell had done a good job and the engine picked up smoothly and they continued their headlong rush. 'You can slow down, Sion. We're tempting fate too much like this.'

Sion eased back on the throttle a couple of notches. Although the other aircraft continued following it never came close. Slowly but surely O'Donnell and Sion made good their escape.

'Any ammo left for the Enfield?'

O'Donnell slipped out the magazine and looked at the single round. 'One bullet. Plus the Webley.'

'Let's hope we've seen the last of them. Keep your eyes peeled.' A few minutes later Sion pointed ahead. 'There's the Gulf of Finland. And there's Leningrad.'

'And there,' said O'Donnell bitterly, 'are two Russian aircraft.' Grabbing the binoculars he focused on each plane in turn. 'One's a Fokker T-2 and the other's a Curtiss R3C-2.'

'The Curtiss is the danger,' said Sion.

The particular model of the Curtiss now directly ahead of them had won the 1925 Schneider Trophy Race at a speed of 232.57mph. The Griffin had a significant edge. The single engine Fokker was a six-seater transport built in the early twenties for the American army. Slow and cumbersome it did not represent much of a threat. Both planes were now approaching, the Curtiss easily outstripping the Fokker.

'Mike, in this weather that open cockpit must be hellish. That's always been the problem with the Curtiss. The gunner in front has to stand to shoot over the prop. A few sharp manoeuvres will throw his aim off. If we can slip past we can get away. Here he comes.'

So saying, Sion threw the Griffin hard to starboard and entered a roll. The gunner in the Curtiss was pressing the trigger of his swivel mounted machine gun when his target moved violently and he missed by a wide margin. Back on level flight Sion pushed the plane into another shallow dive and swooped clear. Concentrating on the Curtiss, Sion had missed the Fokker which was suddenly fifty yards ahead and on a collision course. There was no time for rational thought. Instinct saved them. Ramming open the throttle he pulled back on the wheel and the Griffin sailed upwards in danger of stalling at any second. If that happened both men knew they couldn't escape. They passed with only inches to spare.

'Bloody hell,' said Sion with feeling, relaxing in his seat, sweat beading his brow, his hands slippery.

'Look out!' O'Donnell yelled. 'Here comes the Curtiss.' It came pouncing down out of a clear sky like a hawk ready to snatch its prey. Bullets cut through the port wing as Sion again turned violently, this time trying to get inside the other plane's turning circle.

'Shoot at the engine,' Sion said. 'Empty the Webley when I get us there.' They flew behind the Curtiss, to one side, closing fast. The Russians, unperturbed, knowing that the Griffin was unarmed, were letting them get close. The Russians must have thought that their adversaries had a death wish. In a few more seconds they would be able to bring the machine gun to bear and it would be all over for the Griffin.

O'Donnell said, 'I've a better idea. Go above and on your port wing.'

'What are you going to do?'

'Give them a headache.' So saying he clambered out of his seat and into the back of the plane. Grabbing a spare starter motor and a can of petrol he quickly returned, just as Sion twisted the plane to port, flying at ninety degrees to the horizontal. O'Donnell opened his window and looked down at the open cockpit of the Curtiss. The pilot was looking up at him, his eyes hidden behind a pair of flying-goggles. The planes were less than fifty feet apart, the gunner was pointing at them, unable to aim his machine gun.

O'Donnell dropped the heavy starter motor and had the satisfaction of seeing it hit the wing of the Curtiss. But it passed through, leaving the aircraft still flying. The petrol can rapidly followed. Because of the planes' relative speeds it was falling ahead of the plane and in danger of missing. The Curtiss pilot saw O'Donnell pointing a rifle at him and dived. The plane's propeller hit the petrol can. The can burst open but instead of destroying the propeller as O'Donnell had hoped, it sprayed the engine with petrol. The hot, uncovered engine ignited the petrol in a whoosh of flame and the Curtiss began to spiral down, out of control.

'Nice one,' yelled Sion.

By now Leningrad was abeam to starboard and they were crossing the coast. Helsinki lay one hundred and fifty miles away on a heading of 290 degrees. Sion banked the Griffin to port and increased speed, desperate to get out of Russian airspace.

'Anything else in the air?'

'Not that I can see.' Craning his neck, O'Donnell looked around, up and down, searching for any hint of more trouble. 'Hell,' he slumped in his seat, 'We're getting too old for these high-jinks. Now what?'

'We'll land at Helsinki. We need to repair the holes in the wings before we head for home.' The plane was now flying straight and level at 250mph. The sky was clouding over but the barometer glass remained steady and there seemed no hint of rain in the layer of altocumulus that was spread around them like a woolly fleece.

On the approach to Helsinki Sion turned the plane to circle around the city. When they reached the northern side they found what they were looking for. A windsock on a low hillock indicated an airfield close by. Moments later they were flying over it and Sion was preparing to land.

Bouncing onto a dirt track that cut a line diagonally across a sward of green, the Griffin quickly came to a halt. The field was practically empty with only two old-fashioned bi-planes parked at its southern edge. A few men were loitering around watching as the Griffin taxied along the track. It seemed there was no permanent building, but two large tents could be seen in the distance. Compared to British and other European airfields this one ranked low down the scale. It suited Sion and O'Donnell. They wanted to effect speedy repairs and to get home as quickly as possible. They were still too close to Russia for comfort.

'I'll get a brew going,' said O'Donnell, 'and get us something to eat.'

'Good. I'll check the damage.' Climbing wearily down from the plane, Sion stretched, yawned and began examining the plane. To his relief the only damage he found was a line of four holes along the port wing. The bullets had gone neatly through, as if the holes had been drilled. The aluminium wing was tough but too much strain could rip it off if it wasn't repaired.

The holes were smooth on the top and jagged on the bottom where the bullet had punched through. Sion began by cutting off the biggest of the rough edges using a small saw. He had finished all four holes when O'Donnell called him and they stopped for a cup of tea and a cheese sand-wich. As soon as they had drunk and eaten, O'Donnell used a rough rasp to smooth the edges of the holes while

Sion cut squares of aluminium to cover them. Using extra-long bolts they managed to pull the aluminium patches flush to the wing, top and bottom. Careful not to over tighten the bolts, they sawed off the small protuberances of extra metal.

The work took longer than they'd expected and it was late afternoon before they'd finished.

'We'll top up the petrol,' Sion announced, 'and stay here to-night.'

'In that case I'll get a fire going. Make us a proper meal.'

'Get out the whisky as well. I'm in need of some serious refreshment.'

By now it was pitch dark, the night cloud-covered, though there was virtually no wind. They sat for a while discussing the day's events, sipping at the whisky, passing the bottle back and forth. But after a few sips and the stress of the day they were quickly tiring.

'Before we go to sleep,' said Sion, 'I'd like us to move the plane.'

'Where to?'

'Just to the edge of the track. So we can take off p.d.q. if needs be. I don't think Vorochilov will give up so easily. He must know by now that we came this way.'

'Let's get it done. I'll swing the prop and walk the field, you follow.'

Half an hour later they were settled for the night. Sion had the first watch while O'Donnell crashed out on the camp bed. It was nearly midnight. Sion found his head drooping and he jerked awake. He climbed down from the cockpit to get some fresh air and began to wander the field. He stretched his cramped limbs, trying to keep his wits about him. The moon had risen, almost full, and behind the thin clouds to the north a diffused white glow filled one quadrant of the sky. At the edge of the field was a tarmacked road and he was about to return when he saw headlights in the distance. As he watched they drew nearer.

One, no, two sets. Whatever they were doing out there, he had no intention of hanging around to find out. Turning on his heels he ran as fast as he could back to the plane.

Panting, he thumped the side of the fuselage. 'Mike! Mike! Wake up! We've got visitors. Time to go.'

O'Donnell was instantly wide awake and throwing back his blanket. He didn't wait to question Sion but crawled over the seats into the cockpit. Sion darted around the front of the plane, waited for O'Donnell's signal and swung the propeller. It burst into life and Sion was scrambling through the door even as the plane began to move. By the time he'd strapped himself into his seat the plane was approaching take-off speed. Through the windscreen they saw two cars approaching. There were a series of loud bangs but the Russians were far too late. The Griffin sailed gracefully into the air and was almost immediately out of danger.

'It seems to me, this is a hard way to make a buck, Mike. Follow the Gulf and we'll try to get to Sweden.'

The moonlight showed a silver path of water between the dark mass of land on either side. Estonia was to their left, Finland to their right.

Forty minutes later the engine coughed, coughed again and cut out. They were about to commence the restart procedure when Sion checked the fuel tank tube.

'It's empty. Damn, one of their bullets must have hit us. Keep her gliding for a few minutes while I add some petrol. We daren't land without power in the dark.' Undoing his seat belt Sion quickly grabbed a can of petrol and began to pour it into the tank. The restart worked smoothly and, once more under proper control, they looked for a place to land. By now the moon was setting and the water was darkening rapidly, becoming indistinguishable from the land. Worse, they could no longer see to set down safely. How high above the water were they? If they miscalculated they could hit so hard the plane's back would break.

'I'll put more petrol into the tank,' said Sion, 'and drop a can full onto the water.'

'All right, but hurry up. We're losing petrol at a hell of a rate.'

Both men knew how desperately serious their plight was but the solution was highly dangerous. It was imperative that they knew where the sea was relative to the plane. Flaming petrol dropped onto the water would float and burn for a few minutes, hopefully giving them time to set down. Dropping lit petrol from an aeroplane in the middle of the night through an open door was hazardous in the extreme.

Sion stuffed a towel down the spout of a petrol can. When he was ready to light the towel he yelled, 'Okay, Mike. Down to thirty feet on the altimeter and I'll open the door.'

A few moments later O'Donnell called. 'Right, Sion. Drop the petrol.'

Pushing open the door with his shoulder, Sion lit the wick, saw it was burning and dropped the can outside. When it hit the water the tiny flame was lost for a second and then the petrol exploded, the result they had both been praying for.

O'Donnell banked quickly round, checked the wind direction as best he could and began to drop towards the sea. The red and blue flames were quickly spreading across the water and as the petrol thinned the flames died. Watching from the starboard side of the cockpit, O'Donnell eased the Griffin down and, heart in mouth, gauged when they were only a foot or two above the surface before taking the power right off. The plane landed with barely a splash.

They kept an eye on the flames but the plane was quickly drifting away from any danger. 'I'll set the drogue parachute,' said Sion, 'while you get out the inflatable.'

From a locker Sion took out a folded conical piece of canvas, six feet long, with a diameter of eighteen inches at one end and only two inches at the other. A harness of ropes met at a metal ring, to which he attached a long mooring rope. Tying the end to a ring-bolt in the doorway he passed the drogue outside and lowered it into the water, arresting the plane's forward momentum.

Sion helped O'Donnell with the inflatable and then started taking soundings using a line and weight. By now the moon was fully set and the water was as black as Hades. They could see nothing, no lights, no reference points, to tell where they were or how far they were from land. The line Sion was using was ten fathoms long but he failed to touch the bottom. O'Donnell, in the meantime, had lit a safety lamp and easily found the leak.

'It's along a seam,' he said. 'A bullet appears to have caught the edge of the tank and split the metal.'

'Can you fix it?'

'Shouldn't take too long. There's still some petrol left. Pass me a can and I'll save what I can.' He drained the rest of the petrol out and handed the can back to Sion. Then he began filling the petrol tank with water. The tiniest spark near an empty petrol tank which is still full of fumes was more deadly than if it had been full of petrol. Once the tank was full he opened the draining cock and let the water flush away. Taking a piece of putty he kneaded it until it was pliant and then filled the crack. Next he took a small piece of aluminium, bent it around the tank, coated the inside of the aluminium with putty and pressed it into place over the crack. Two self-tapping screws held the aluminium in place.

'If we give it an hour or two,' said O'Donnell, 'it should hold until we get home.'

Wearily Sion looked at his watch. 'We might as well wait until dawn. It's only three hours away. If we try and take off in the dark with the way our luck's been holding we'll probably hit something.'

O'Donnell chuckled. 'The way our luck's been holding,' he corrected Sion, 'we'd come up smelling of roses. After all that's happened and we're still alive? No sirree, our luck is holding good, so it is. You get some sleep while I keep watch.'

Too tired to argue, Sion climbed onto the bed and almost immediately fell asleep. It was daylight when he awoke. O'Donnell was sitting in the doorway, his head lolling forward, snoring.

The dawn light was strengthening fast and Sion climbed off the bed and looked outside. They were in the Baltic Sea and a swell was coming in from the south. The plane was beginning to rock and Sion could see that if they didn't take-off soon it would be marginal whether they'd be able to make it. A wind was picking up from the north and whitecaps were already forming. There were no other vessels around and no land in sight. A squall of rain hit them, sweeping in through the door, waking O'Donnell. With a start he sat up.

'Time to go,' said Sion.

O'Donnell got to his feet, yawning. 'Let's fill the tank.' That was an optimistic statement. They used up the remainder of the spare cans but that left the tank less than a quarter full. Climbing out the door and down into the inflatable he said, 'I'll swing the prop.'

Sion removed the drogue. A few minutes later they were both in their seats, the engine was warming up and they were ready to go. By now the sea was the wrong side of marginal. The waves were breaking over the floats and taking-off into the wind would be uncomfortable and even dangerous. The pounding the plane would take bouncing over the waves could be fatal. Instead, Sion turned down sea and down wind. The plane's speed increased and it began to skip from wave top to wave top. The wind from directly astern was blowing a steady fifteen knots and gusting twenty. As they crept up to 75mph, Sion pulled back on the wheel and they were airborne. Immediately he began a steep turn into the wind and their rate of climb increased.

'There's land on the horizon,' said O'Donnell.

'We'd better check it out. See where we are.'

A few minutes later they were approaching an island that O'Donnell quickly identified as Gotland. During the night they must have drifted between thirty and forty miles south.

'Stockholm is an hour north,' said O'Donnell, 'and Copenhagen two hours southwest.'

They landed at the small, busy airport to the north of Copenhagen. Taxiing over the bumpy field they identified many different aircraft, mostly European but some American. Mechanics and pilots stopped in their work to watch them pass. The double landing gear was causing interest and when they'd stopped a number of men drifted across to take a closer look. Sion left O'Donnell to deal with questions while he went to find petrol.

A static bowser was at the other end of the field and an hour later they had refuelled, checked the plane for any damage they might have missed and were discussing an early departure, when . . .

'I don't believe it,' said O'Donnell. A police car's just arrived and a copper's gone into the office.'

'It might not mean anything,' Sion said frowning.

Both men exchanged tired glances. 'On the other hand,' continued Sion, 'it's better to be safe than sorry. I was about to suggest a night on the town, but we'd better get ready to leave.'

By way of reply O'Donnell strolled around to the propeller while Sion climbed into the cockpit. The engine had just started when Sion looked over his shoulder towards the office. He was in time to see the helpful manager who'd provided fuel point in their direction.

'Hurry up!' Sion yelled.

He could have saved his breath. O'Donnell was already hurrying to the door. The police car, ringing its bell, was heading rapidly in their direction, cutting off their access to the runway. Sion headed across the field. Conditions weren't ideal but he had no other choice. The land was slowly dipping away and with a shock they saw the sea ahead of them. Sion was opening the throttle fully, desperately trying to increase the revs, when the Griffin plunged over the cliff edge.

23

Down they swooped, towards the water, a millpond of grey. There was no time to change from landing wheels to floats and so they did the only thing they could – they prayed. The engine's speed was picking up, helped by the force of the air through the propeller. Even so they kept dropping. The glide turned to powered flight and, only feet above the water, they began to lift. Level flying suddenly turned into a swoop into the sky and they were safe.

Turning on a southwesterly heading, Sion said, 'Give me a course for home. The next place we stop is England. I don't trust anywhere else.'

'Keep on this heading. I'll give you a more accurate course in a few minutes.' The plane droned on then shortly O'Donnell said, 'Just over three hours flying time. When we hit the North Sea at Jutland follow the Frisian Islands, keeping them on our port side.'

Sion grinned. 'I've done that a few times. At this rate we'll be home in time for supper.'

The remainder of the flight was uneventful. The engine ran smoothly, the weather stayed kind and three hours and ten minutes after taking off they were approaching Biggin Hill. As they lined up to land a number of people came to watch their approach. Sion waggled the plane's wings, indicating that it had been a successful trip and the figures below waved in return.

When they came to a stop both men climbed wearily down from the plane. They were met by Kirsty and the Cazorlas. They had an air of gloom about them.

'What's wrong? Is it the children?' Sion greeted his wife, kissing her cheek.

'No, the children are fine. We'll tell you inside. How was the trip?'

'Let's just say,' he paused, 'we got the money.'

O'Donnell had the casket and he lifted it with a smile on his face.

'That's something, anyway,' said Kirsty. 'Come on. I'll pour a couple of large drinks and tell you what's been going on.'

With whiskies in front of all the men and a sherry for herself, Kirsty began, 'Something awful has happened. It's the bank, Sion. The recession has become a depression, whatever that means. It's in the *Times*. I don't understand it all to be honest and I doubt many people do. Maybe that's why there's a run on the banks.'

The colour drained from Sion's cheeks and he paused with his glass to his lips. 'A run?' His voice croaked and he cleared his throat. 'A run? Are you sure?'

Kirsty nodded. 'It began yesterday. David phoned to warn us. He didn't say what it would mean. They did close the doors early, which is unprecedented. Thank goodness today is Saturday and they were able to stay closed. But they have to open Monday. They have no choice.'

Sion let out a sigh. 'How will it affect us?'

'The company's shares. David says he has no choice but to sell them for whatever price he can get. We may end up with a hostile shareholder.'

'Poor David,' said Sion softly.

'What does it mean for him?' O'Donnell asked.

'Bankruptcy probably,' said Sion. 'The bank isn't limited. It's a partnership. Everything David has is on the line. The same goes for John. It was their great strength and now it's their greatest weakness.'

'I don't understand,' Peter Cazorla shook his head.

'As a partnership, David and John could boast that

their interests and the interests of their customers are inextricably linked. Any decisions they make would be good for all of them. Many customers like the idea. But if anything goes wrong then they're completely vulnerable. But why? Why Griffiths & Buchanan?'

'It isn't just them,' said Kirsty. 'It's all the banks. Because of events in America and Germany we're heading for a depression, with a lot of unemployment and firms going under. A General Strike has been called and marches are planned in all the major cities. What shall we do, darling?' It was a rhetorical question with no answer possible.

Later that evening, alone at last, Sion was deep in thought. A ludicrous idea had occurred to him which he double checked by reference to a book on metallurgy he had in his extensive library. Glancing at the kitchen clock he saw it was almost 10.30pm; David would still be about.

He dialled his brother's number. The phone was answered almost immediately. 'Griffiths.'

'David! I thought you'd be hard at it.'

'Too much to do even at this time of night. We're trying to get as much cash together as possible so that we can pay all withdrawals.'

'What happens if the bank runs out of money?'

'The bank closes and John and I go bankrupt.'

Sion let out a heavy sigh. 'Does that mean losing everything?'

'Yes, of course,' he spoke with some asperity. 'The house, the cars, the boat. It means being destitute.'

'What happens to your seat in the Commons?'

'I would have to resign my seat forthwith.'

'How many people know how bad it is?'

'The board and the Chief Cashier. No one else. So far. But that won't be for long.'

'What will the people do with the money they withdraw?'

'Maddeningly, they'll take it to another bank. The run is on all the banks. Withdrawals, both large and small, are being made all over the country. Cash is withdrawn, some banks go under, some hang on and after a few days or possibly weeks the customers realise there is nowhere else for their money and start depositing again. I just don't know if we can hold on.'

'I've had an idea, David. I was thinking about the gold I brought back from Russia and I had a ludicrous thought. Tell me if you think this could work . . .'

Minutes later David said, 'I think it could. We've nothing to lose and everything to gain.'

'We need to clean the lead. Make the gold electrolyte. The direct current is no problem as we have a transformer. The sticking point will be the number of small plating tanks. But I think we have time if we get cracking.'

'What made you think of it?'

'Peter. His first job was working in a factory in Mexico that did electro-plating. They used to coat silver with gold. Mainly for religious trinkets.'

'We'll have to move fast if we're to make it work. We have to open on Monday. Let me phone John. What do you need to get started?'

'I need the dimensions of an ingot. But there is one problem. A major one.'

It was child's play to make the moulds. Once they had twenty they began casting the lead ingots. They had enough lead for fifty. Around mid-morning David and John Buchanan arrived.

'How's it going?' David greeted his brother.

Sion wiped the sweat off his soot-blackened face with a cloth. 'There are more problems than I thought but we're solving them. The lead needs to be cleaned. It gets dipped in there,' he pointed to a large tank. 'That contains an etching solution that removes surface dirt. Even the stains left by greasy fingers. The ingot then goes into that tank where we have a cleansing and deoxidising solution. There,' he pointed to a row of small china tanks like deep baking trays, 'we have our biggest problem. Those are bread making dishes. Each ingot sits in one of those. It contains a gold electrolyte which we made using some of the gold from Russia. That transformer changes 220 volts AC into 80 amps DC. We can run as many cables as we like from it. We attach the ingot to the cathode, switch on and leave it. The gold flows from the anode and coats the ingot.'

'What's the problem?' John asked.

'The process is very slow. We need more of those dishes and more lead. Also I've discovered the difference in weight between gold and lead is very marked.' Sion picked up a well-thumbed book and pointed. 'Look at these tables. Gold per cubic inch is one point seven times as heavy as lead. If anybody who knows gold picked up an ingot he'll be able to tell immediately.'

'Why should anybody pick one up?' David queried.

Sion shrugged. 'If our bluff is called and an assayer is sent in we can't refuse a reasonable request to examine the gold. He'd be able to tell immediately that it's a fake.'

'Have you coated an ingot yet?' John asked.

Sion shook his head. 'Not yet. That's another problem. The gold coats the lead so slowly it takes forever to get a reasonable thickness.'

'We haven't got forever,' John replied.

'That's why we need more dishes to coat them all simultaneously. We also ran out of lead. Ralph and Mike have gone to see what they can scrounge. How much do we need?'

'A ton would be about right,' said John.

'A ton!' Sion stopped in dismay. 'That's impossible! We'll be a month of Sundays. Won't we, Peter?'

The Mexican shrugged. 'With sufficient ingots and tanks we can run cable from the transformer as far as we need. There's no limit.'

'What about the gold?' John asked. 'Do we have enough?'

'*Si*, Sir John. Plenty. We use very little gold. At the most two cubic inches. I agree with Sion. They'll look okay. The problem will be if anyone gets close enough to examine the bars. They will be able to tell as soon as they pick one up.'

'I guarantee it will look like a gold ingot, feel like gold if anyone runs a finger across it. Picking it up will be a different matter. We have enough gold from Russia to make two real ingots but that's all.'

'Come outside,' John said. Throwing open the boot of his car, John lifted up a blanket, displaying a complete dinner service with settings for eight people. '*Voila!* Every plate is twenty-three carat gold. My pater had it given to him when he was in India. Some rajah or other owed him a debt and he repaid it with this gold service. There should be sufficient for a few ingots. It's heavy enough.'

'That's an heirloom,' protested Sion.

'It's gone anyway if we can't pull this off,' came the honest reply. 'So just take it. Make as many ingots as you can. You're right about the problem of an assayer and I've got an idea I'll share with you later.'

Inside the hangar more containers had arrived. Heavy duty cable had been run to each container, one negative the other positive, carrying direct current electricity. Peter was busy connecting each ingot to the negative anode in each container and placing a small copper bar, the positive anode, in the gold electrolyte. As soon as the copper touched the solution the electrolysis began.

As they cleared workbenches for more containers, Sion turned to John. 'Have you thought how to maximise the publicity?

'We want to make as big a splash as possible. We'll announce in tomorrow's papers that a ton of gold is being delivered to the bank on Monday, as collateral for all withdrawals. We'll make sure there are plenty of reporters and photographers there for its arrival, so it makes the afternoon editions. When the cashiers give them their money we'll invite the customers to walk through the vault to see the gold. There'll be armed guards standing conspicuously nearby. The bank has to be seen to be rock solid.'

David added, 'We'll also start a line of depositors of our own people. Can you send some of your lads up to help?'

Sion nodded and then said, 'It could work. If anyone finds out what we've done we'll be finished, you know that, don't you? We'll be humiliated, arrested for fraud.'

David hesitated before replying. 'John and I discussed all the implications. We are currently liquidating assets to get as much cash into the bank as possible. But this is a buyer's market, not a seller's, and prices are sorely depressed. We definitely cannot cover all our liabilities if we have a run. No bank can. This is our only option. So let's get back to work.'

And work they did. All day. It was hot and dangerous handling the ingots of lead. Backs, fingers and arms ached. Dishes were bought from ironmongers all across London and brought to the hangar to be used for plating. The shortage of lead was solved by a fluke. Mike had gone to a metal merchant's to find that a disused church had just been demolished and a large quantity of lead had been removed from the roof. The problem was solved.

'When will the first bar be ready?' John asked late that evening when they stopped for a break.

'I think the first one can be taken out,' Sion replied, checking his watch.

In nervous anticipation they gathered round the first plating tank. The original lead ingot now shone like . . . gold. Sion lifted out the copper anode and the current stopped. He lifted out the ingot. The men gasped in awe.

'It looks like the real thing,' said David. 'Can I touch it?' He was looking at Peter Cazorla.

'Certainly. It isn't hot.'

David took it in his left hand and then lifted one of

the solid gold ingots they'd cast earlier. 'The gold is far heavier.'

'It won't fool an assayer,' said Sion gloomily.

John nodded. 'Which is why we need to use our own man. Somebody well enough known in the trade but whom we can trust. Leave it to me. We've fifteen solid gold ingots which we can arrange on top.'

They worked all weekend taking it in turns to sleep. Finally they were finished.

Timing was important, if they were to arrive at the bank with the maximum of fuss. At a few minutes before nine thirty on Monday morning Sion drove John and David towards the bank. Behind them was the bank's bullion van with the legend GRIFFITHS AND BUCHANAN BANK painted on the sides in yellow lettering.

Already there were queues stretching for hundreds of yards either side of the bank. In the main the people were good tempered, with only an occasional shove or yell at anyone trying to queue jump.

'There's the press.' Sion nodded at the throng of reporters who were busy with notepads, questioning people, while photographers were busy flashing bulbs along the long lines.

Sion gave the horn three short and one long blast, the agreed signal. The two company cars parked outside the bank drew away and they pulled into the vacated space.

'Let's go,' said David, climbing out of the car. If he was nervous he didn't show it. Sion grinned at his brother. He had nerves of steel. 'You ready?' David looked at Peter in the cab.

'*Si*, David.' When agitated or excited his Mexican accent came out stronger than ever. 'We are ready.'

Raphael and Juan, sitting beside their father, were wearing security guard uniforms. Both carried rifles and sidearms.

Calling on his considerable contacts John Buchanan had arranged with the Metropolitan Police Commissioner to have a large contingent of police present. As the bullion van stopped outside the bank, a dozen uniformed officers appeared and stood guard. Silence fell on the men and women in the queues.

'Our apologies, ladies and gentlemen,' said David in a loud voice. 'Bear with us please, whilst the bullion is deposited in the bank's vaults. We may be five minutes late in opening this morning.'

There were murmurings from the crowd.

'Griffiths & Buchanan has organised the bullion deposit as an act of good faith. Please feel free to view the gold in the vault at your leisure.'

Excitement swept through the crowd but not everyone was convinced. One man yelled, 'I just want my money.'

David looked at him for a second. 'Indeed, sir, you are free to withdraw your funds. But may I suggest you think very carefully before investing it elsewhere?'

By now the bullion van had been opened. Tellers from the bank appeared and small, obviously heavy, wooden crates were being carried inside. The police lined the route to the doors, their backs to the gold, looking for any trouble. The photographers flashbulbs were popping and reporters were yelling questions.

This was John's opportunity. 'All accredited newspapers are invited to the conference room on the second floor,' he said loudly. 'A statement will be issued and questions answered. Refreshments will be served once the bullion is safely stored. Photographers will be invited into the vault to take pictures.'

Crate after crate was carried in. A member of staff appeared to slip and the box he was carrying fell from his hands. There were gasps from the crowd as the box opened, allowing two of the bars to escape. The cashier pounced on the ingots in panic.

Inside the main banking hall David took Stanners, the Chief Cashier, to one side. 'Well done. That trip looked natural enough.'

Sweating profusely, Stanners nodded. Hopefully a glimpse of the gold had whetted the crowds' appetite for more. But they had to move quickly. Their reserves of cash were already very low and without a huge boost in customer confidence they would be shutting the bank's doors within a few hours. The police would then be needed for real – to stop the rioting.

The gold was taken down a wide stairway into the basement vault. Downstairs there were storage rooms for the mountain of paperwork generated by a busy bank, a wall of private deposit boxes and small rooms to allow customers privacy. Along a corridor and through a heavy wooden door was the vault itself.

The bullion boxes were deposited on the floor and broken open. The ingots were piled neatly on wooden pallets, and gradually the stack of bars grew. All the boxes were empty, the bank employees had left, and David and John surveyed their handiwork.

'We need more reflection,' said Sion entering the vault. 'Can we run a light from that socket and hang it overhead? Two would be better.'

'I'll arrange it right away,' said David. 'Are the real ingots in place?'

John nodded. 'Juan and Raphael, take your positions inside the bars, please.'

The Cazorlas, father in the middle flanked by his two sons, stood stern-faced, behind the gold, all armed. An electrician arrived and positioned two lights to shine on the gold, leaving the three Cazorlas half in shadow. The effect was startling. Locking the barred gate Sion also went up to the hall. By now the lines of people had reached the counter and busy tellers had begun honouring withdrawal requests. David and John stood in the middle, looking as if they hadn't a care in the world. Sion joined them.

'The crowd is bigger than I expected,' Sion said. 'I hope to God this works.'

David nodded. 'The tellers have been instructed to invite all customers to visit the vault and view the "mountain of gold". Hopefully, their confidence will be restored.'

Only one man was seen to stalk out of the bank. The rest were curious enough to make the trip to the vault.

'When do our people get here?' John asked.

David checked his watch. 'Another ten minutes.'

The Chief Cashier, Stanners, went from teller to teller, distributing bank notes, rearranging tills. When he was finished he joined his employers.

'Gentlemen, if the run continues, we can last perhaps another two hours. No longer.'

'Here are some of my men,' Sion said glancing at the entrance.

Two of the men from the airfield, dressed in their Sunday best, walked through the door. They looked around nervously until they spotted Sion, who gave them a nod of encouragement.

Speaking loudly enough to draw attention from the queuing customers, they began their charade. 'Safe as houses, I tell you. I'll not be taking out my money.'

'Me neither. I've never seen so much gold. We won't find a safer bank than this. Where do I make a deposit?'

'Walk this way, gentlemen,' said the Chief Cashier walking across the hall to join the two men. He led them to an empty window. 'I'll deal with this,' he said quietly to a teller who was approaching the window. The man gave him a puzzled glance and went about his other duties. Other people in the queues for withdrawals were watching carefully.

The charade continued. 'I seen the gold with my own eyes. There's nowhere safer.' Handing over a bundle of notes they waited at the window. The Chief Cashier handed back a folded sheet of paper with the money hidden inside. As Sion's employees left the bank they met two others and slipped them the cash. The money was to be used again and again.

Now the real customers were walking through the vault and hesitating. What were they to do with their money? Which bank could they trust? So far regional banks had been failing almost daily and two had gone in the city only the previous week. Who could they trust? Which other bank had as much in the way of assets? Many walked away indecisively, nearly all carrying large sums of money.

In the meantime John Buchanan had given a press interview and photographs had been taken. A special edition of the *Evening Standard* was being rushed out. John was using his influence again. But there was one sticky moment.

'How do we know the gold is real?' asked the reporter from the *Daily Mail*.

'Does the name Bernard Bernstein mean anything to you?' John countered.

Another reporter replied. 'He's the goldsmith at Samuel's in the Savoy Arcade.'

'That's right.' John was pleased he didn't need to prove the assayer's credentials. 'He'll be arriving in ten minutes to examine the gold. Will that do you?'

There was a chorus of ayes.

'Before we do, there are some light refreshments on the table. A wee dram or two to keep out the cold and to oil the brain.'

There was some good natured laughter. Reporters were known to take a drink any time, day or night, and they had a reputation to live up to. A short while later they trooped back down to the vault. There they were introduced to Bernard Bernstein, a short, fat, obviously Jewish gentleman, whose eye-glasses were as thick as his guttural accent.

Bernstein hefted an ingot in his hand and examined it closely through a magnifying glass. He found the stamp he was searching for and looked more closely. Nodding, he began to measure the bar using a special micrometer.

Carefully, he wrote the measurements down. Next he removed a set of scales from his case and placed it on a nearby table. On the left hand scale he placed weights and then positioned the ingot on the right. The needle hovered in the middle of the scale. Taking off his glasses he fished a clean handkerchief from his pocket and wiped the already sparkling lenses.

Ignoring the flashing bulbs he cleared his throat, enjoying every second of the attention and announced, 'There is no doubt that the gold is pure.'

'One hundred percent?' a reporter called.

Bernstein smiled condescendingly. 'There is no such thing. But I can say it is over ninety-nine point seven percent pure.'

Excited chatter broke out and John Buchanan stepped forward with his hand out. 'Thank you, Mr Bernstein.' The two men shook hands warmly, both smiling. More flashbulbs went off. Reporters and photographers rushed off to meet their deadlines.

Upstairs once more, John and Bernstein sat in comfortable chairs in John's office. 'I cannot thank you enough, my friend.'

'Such *chutzpah*! You are to be congratulated on your audacity, my friend. I picked up one or two other ingots and could tell by the weight that they were real.'

'Indeed,' said the Baron of Guildford.

'The tiny give away,' admonished the assayer, raising a finger, 'was the stamp. It was sharp, too clear edged. It should have been more rounded. Only slightly I grant you but it is what happens to gold. An expert can tell. I,' he emphasised the point by touching his chest, 'knew immediately that it was freshly cast. Yet I had not heard of such an amount of gold entering the country recently.'

John shrugged. 'There is still the question of your fee?'

'Ach, yes. My fee.' The round face broke into a smile.

David went across to the window to speak to the Chief Cashier. 'How are we doing?'

The man, worried to death, shook his head. 'Not good, sir. At this rate we'll be closing the doors in less than thirty minutes.'

'Hell! What more can we do?'

The Chief Cashier shrugged helplessly. 'I don't know. Pray?'

David looked bleakly at the man. 'God, Mr Stanners, helps those who help themselves. How many clerks are upstairs?'

'Thirty-three, sir.'

'Get them down the backstairs, have them mingling in the corridor to the vault. I want them stating clearly and loudly that they are leaving their money in the bank. Can you do that?'

'Yes, of course. Right away.' Hurrying from the hall the Chief Cashier wondered if it would be too little too late.

24

WHEN, TEN MINUTES later, voices were raised, David hurried across to the teller's window.

'I'm sorry, sir, I've no money,' the helpless teller was telling an irate customer.

'Can I help?' David asked.

The customer, a squat, belligerent man turned to David. 'This nincompoop tells me there is no money. But I've heard the rumours. The vault is full of gold.'

'What he means, sir, is that his position has run out. I'll have some delivered immediately. Just wait a moment.'

Going from teller to teller David quickly checked the tills. He was appalled. They were down to the last of the cash. His mouth was suddenly dry. Fear flared up in the pit of his stomach. There was nothing for it but to close the doors. He was about to make an announcement when there was a commotion at the door. Looking towards the entrance he was astonished to see his mother, Kirsty and Madelaine arrive. The women were making a great fuss and drawing attention to themselves.

Baroness Guildford was still a handsome woman. Wearing a calf length coat, trimmed in the finest mink, with matching hat, she stood imperiously in the centre of the hall. She waved a silk glove at Sion and commanded, 'You, sir, help us with this case. Do be careful. I have withdrawn my entire funds from my bank and I wish them deposited here.' Meg's distinctive voice carried around the hall. 'My friends also have extremely large deposits to make. Well, don't just stand there. My solicitors in due diligence have informed me that this bank is as safe as the Bank of England. Be so good as to escort me to a counting room.'

Sion looked at his mother and resisted the urge to smile.

Madelaine, resisting a look in David's direction, pointed at an attaché case. 'Be kind enough to carry mine as well, my good man.'

'I'll carry my own,' said Kirsty, unwilling to entrust it to anyone.

Meg looked around the hall and said loudly, 'These people obviously haven't read the latest financial reports, my dears, if they intend withdrawing funds from Griffiths & Buchanan.' She looked at Sion once more, 'Now lead the way, there's a good chap.'

The three women followed Sion through a door marked private. As soon as the door was closed they let out sighs of relief and exchanged smiles.

'Mam, what on earth are you doing?' Sion asked.

'It was John's idea. Go and see if it's made any difference.'

Sion hurried back.

The queue of those wishing to withdraw their money had dwindled to a trickle. The bank was still desperately short of cash. It wasn't enough merely to stop any more haemorrhaging. They needed money returned.

'How are we doing?' David asked John, standing with the family in the upper office that overlooked the main counting hall.

'It's touch and go. I brought in three thousand pounds half an hour ago. I just don't know. It may tide us over. Our best bet,' said John, 'is the newspapers. Sion's out now trying to find an early afternoon edition. Talk of the devil, here he comes.'

In his hands Sion carried an *Evening Standard* as well as an *Afternoon Times*. The bank had made the front page of both papers. In essence the lead stories were the same.

Griffiths & Buchanan was declared solvent, the best place for depositors to keep their money. The front page photograph of the Cazorlas standing guard over the gold made a big impact. The goldsmith's statement of authenticity was printed in full.

By the middle of the afternoon the queues to deposit money were as long as the ones to withdraw it had been. The family were emotionally drained – they knew how close they'd been to losing everything. Another run like the one they'd been through and they could still be wiped out. They needed liquidity.

Though the bank normally closed its doors at three-thirty, they decided to remain open.

The Chief Cashier joined them just before 5pm. 'What should we do, gentlemen?' He was out of breath from rushing up the stairs.

'Stay open,' said David. 'What's the situation now, Stanners?'

'All options are covered. The afternoon's deposits have returned funds to the level we enjoyed two weeks ago.'

'How far do the queues extend?' John asked.

'Right along the street, sir. What should we do?'

'Stay open. All night if necessary,' replied John. The Baron of Guildford clapped the Chief Cashier's shoulder. 'We won't forget the part you played in today's success.'

'Thank you, sir. May I ask, where did the gold come from?'

'Russia,' Sion answered quickly. 'I brought the gold back from Russia. You have my word on that.'

'I wouldn't care,' said Stanners, 'if the gold was lead coated with paint. We saved the bank, that's all that matters. I had better get back downstairs.' With a slight bow he left the room.

The family exchanged glances. 'Does he know?' Sion asked.

David shrugged. 'Probably. He's no fool. We'll need to reward him properly. In the meantime I'll let the staff know that they are on double time for as long as we stay open. Sion,' David grinned at his brother. 'It was a brilliant idea. Thanks.'

By the time the queues were gone and the last customer had been dealt with it was 9pm. Wearily the staff shut up and left for their homes, nursing their bonuses. Tomorrow was another working day.

The family left for David's town house where a cold buffet was organised and large drinks poured. 'What's to become of the ingots?' Sion asked.

'We leave them there for a few weeks,' replied David. 'Then we quietly get rid of each one. Nobody must find out what we've done. It would mean prison.'

There was a shocked silence. 'Prison?' Terror struck Meg's very soul.

'I'm afraid so, Mam. We've committed a very serious fraud against the country's banking laws. We'd be shut down overnight.'

'It isn't enough to get rid of the lead,' said John. 'We need to replace it with real gold.'

'How?' Sion asked.

'We quietly buy up gold on the bullion markets around the world. I know it's not a great investment but it does suggest stability and financial strength. We saw that today.'

'What about the bank's accounts? How will we deal with those?' David asked aloud.

'I've been thinking carefully about that,' said John. 'None of us actually claimed the gold in the vault was ours, so we don't declare it as bank assets. That way the gold doesn't show up on the balance sheet and we haven't actually committed any fraud. We'll have sailed close to the wind but that's all.'

'A case of semantics,' said Sion.

'Which makes the difference between being ruined and going to jail,' John replied cynically.

The following morning Sion and Kirsty left early. They still had an aircraft manufacturing business to run. In the car back to Biggin Hill, Kirsty read the newspapers aloud, while Sion drove. The *Times* called the Griffiths & Buchanan bank a beacon of good management in an uncertain world.

'Well done, darling,' Kirsty laughed. 'Instead of ruin it looks like the bank will go from strength to strength. It was a brilliant idea of yours.'

'Thanks. But we couldn't have managed without everybody's help.'

'That, so you keep saying, is what families are for.'

Each time David visited the factory over the next four weeks he brought lead ingots for smelting. Buying gold in the bullion markets was progressing smoothly and the fake ingots were gradually being replaced with real gold. Rumours surfaced briefly that the 'mountain of gold' was fake. Another run on the bank threatened as nervous depositors wrote, telephoned and arrived at the bank for reassurance.

David and John acted decisively, calling a press conference in the bank vault. Independent assayers were invited to examine as much of the gold as they cared to. The bullion, although substantially less than previously, was declared pure. The rumours were scotched, their origin never discovered.

Orders for aircraft were still coming in occasionally. The factory continued to survive on a knife edge. Nationally, unemployment reached two million. Troops patrolled the streets and police were often attacked by hungry and frightened people. Marches took place across Britain as civil unrest mounted. Soup kitchens sprang up and desperate men walked away from their families, unable to bear the pain their loved ones were suffering. They walked the country – solid family men reduced to itinerants looking for work, living hand to mouth. When they couldn't work they stole. Always hungry, they took refuge in drink. Cheap gin was the preferred route to oblivion. If they couldn't afford gin, methylated spirits came a close second.

Throughout 1931 matters steadily worsened. In July, Parliament proposed deep cuts in state expenditure. These included salary cuts for teachers, the police and the armed forces. Unemployment benefit was to be slashed, along with other far-reaching economies. The savings proposed amounted to £96 million and substantial tax increases were also advised. The proposals, made by Sir George May, were put before Parliament the day before the summer recess. The Prime Minister, Ramsay MacDonald, announced a cabinet committee to consider the report with a view to actioning it in the autumn. The result was financial chaos. A run on the pound took Britain to financial ruin. The cabinet was split as to what action to take. An all party 'Government of Co-operation' was proposed. Ramsay MacDonald resigned and advised the King to invite other party leaders to form a new government. The Governor of the Bank of England warned that Britain was on the verge of bankruptcy. The pound collapsed and other countries demanded gold instead of holding sterling. MacDonald, Baldwin and Herbert Samuel led the coalition and forced through severe austerity measures. It wasn't enough. In September Britain was forced off the gold standard. Sterling was devalued by thirty percent from $4.86 to the pound to $3.40.

David, of course, had his parliamentary duties to see to. He and John were advising government committees on what strategies to employ. All-night sittings in the Houses of Parliament were not uncommon, both in the Lords and Commons. They were also working around the clock at the bank. Not only did they have their own business interests to care for but also those of their customers.

Unthinkably, sailors in Invergordon mutinied against their twenty-five percent pay cut, which reduced their wages to as little as twenty-five shillings per week. Five thousand people rioted near Battersea Town Hall and postal workers brought the traffic in the west of London to a halt. Crime continued to rise inexorably.

In October the General Election was held. The National Government would stay in power but Labour was completely demolished. Only two years earlier Labour had held two hundred and eighty-eight parliamentary seats, now they had fifty-two. It was the largest reversal of fortune in political history.

In Germany reparation payments were constantly being re-negotiated while Hitler's National Socialism Party rose in power. In the election of March 1932 it took just over thirty percent of the vote. In the run-off vote one month later it took almost thirty-seven percent. Germany's unrest festered.

Back home, the troubles continued. The newspapers claimed that many of the marches led by the Communist-run, National Unemployment Workers' Movement, were funded and orchestrated by Russia. On the 30th October, pitched battles broke out between supporters of the hunger marches, which were now flash points for anti-government protest. Days of rioting followed. Five thousand police fought with youths for two hours at Hyde Park. The riots ended with fifty injuries and fourteen arrests. Scotland Yard seized literally dozens of sticks, cudgels and spiked staves.

On the same day Sion's nine year old son, Paul William Griffiths, disappeared from Biggin Hill.

25

MIKE O'DONNELL CAME running into the house.

Kirsty was sitting red-eyed at the kitchen table, her face was chalk-white. Wordlessly Sion handed over the piece of paper. Mike glanced at it quickly. He looked up, disbelief and denial etched into his eyes.

'This has to be some kind of sick joke – you're *sure* the boys aren't messing around?'

Sion shook his head. 'That was my initial reaction, too. Alex is far too grown up to play stupid games like this. Hell, he's fifteen. Almost a man. He's out with Peter and his boys combing the area.'

O'Donnell read the note again. Written in pencil on a sheet of lined paper, the writing was rounded, uneven, childish. BRING £1000 OR THE BOY DIES. WE WILL SAY WHERE TO BRING THE MONEY TOMORROW. COME ALONE. DO NOT TELL THE POLICE.

O'Donnell frowned. 'Queer amount. Why kidnap somebody and ask for so little?'

'If one thousand pounds is a lot of money to the kidnappers, then either we are dealing with very poor people or people who don't understand the real value of money.'

'You go to prison for a very long time for kidnapping. One thousand pounds isn't worth it. Ten thousand is more like it. Everyone knows the Lindbergh baby's ransom was fifty thousand dollars.'

'Unless they think I'd pay a small amount quickly and quietly.'

Kirsty looked up sharply. 'Of course we'll pay. We

have to.' She looked at Sion. 'Get the money from David if we have to. And do as they say. The Lindbergh baby was found dead two months after he was taken.'

Sion nodded. *Even though the ransom had been paid in full.* 'What's the best thing to do?' He looked helplessly at O'Donnell.

O'Donnell looked at his hands. They were shaking. 'I don't trust the police. They'll go in with their great hobnailed boots wanting an arrest more than the safe return of Paul. That isn't our priority. Neither is the money. We want the boy back, no matter what.'

Sion nodded. 'I agree. We can only wait until we hear from them. In the meantime I'll get the cash from David.'

'What will you tell him?' O'Donnell asked.

'The truth. We could use his help. Probably John's as well.'

At that moment Alex returned from searching with the Cazorlas.

'Well, son?' Sion asked.

Alex shook his head. 'We searched all the buildings. Nothing.' Only half a head smaller than his father, the boy placed a comforting arm around his dad's shoulder. 'We'll keep looking. We just wondered if there was any news.'

Peter growled. 'If I get my hands on the scum who do this.' In his agitation he broke into a torrent of Spanish. Of Sion's three children, Paul was closest to Peter. A gentle, creative child, he was always getting him to make something or to show him how something worked. Peter boasted that Paul would be a great engineer one day.

Kirsty stood up. 'I'll get you some tea. Sit down, all of you. Sion, go and make the phone call.' Kirsty looked at her husband. 'We need the money Sion. Don't fail.'

Sion nodded, a lump in his throat. He went through to his study to telephone his brother.

David arrived two hours later, with the cash, John and his mother. Meg immediately went in to see Kirsty.

Madelaine phoned to say she would be arriving in a few hours, after she collected Susan. The family were gathering, as they always did when a crisis threatened.

'Nothing more?' David asked Sion.

'No. It's far too early. We've searched everywhere. He isn't being held around the airfield.'

'When did it happen?' John asked.

Shrugging, Sion replied. 'We don't know. He went to bed last night as usual. This morning I came down to make a cup of tea and I saw the note. I thought it was a prank at first but went upstairs to look. His bed was empty.'

'Had he slept in it?' David queried.

'Yes. His pyjamas were there, so he'd obviously dressed.'

'What time was this?' John asked.

'Just before seven.' Sion frowned and then asked, 'Where is all this leading?'

'Bear with us, Sion,' his brother replied. 'We're just making sure no clue was missed. Paul had got dressed and come downstairs early. Why?'

'That's easy,' replied Alex. 'He wanted to get to the village early to collect horse chestnuts. Before the other boys lifted them. You know, from the big tree on the green?'

'No one could have known Paul would leave the house so early,' said David thoughtfully. Turning to his nephew he asked, 'Have you seen the note left by the kidnappers?'

Alex shook his head. 'Why?'

'This is it.' David held it out. 'Do you recognise the paper?'

Alex took it and looked closely. 'I think it's from a school exercise book.'

'That's what I thought. Whose books are they?' David pointed at a small pile of school books on a sideboard.

'Paul's,' Alex replied. 'He was sitting in here last night

doing some homework. We always get lots to do at half term.'

Walking across the room David rifled through the half dozen books. At the bottom he found an English exercise book. Flicking it open he found a torn page. The ragged edge matched the note left by the kidnappers.

'So you're saying,' Sion spoke slowly, 'that this was a crime of opportunity. Nobody came here to kidnap one of the children. Paul dressed, came down here and was walking out the door. Perhaps he disturbed someone in the yard. There's no indication of a break-in, no broken windows or doors. Somebody was here, looking to steal something. Maybe rummaging for food. We get enough tramps through here and it's become worse over the last six or seven months.'

'Which means we aren't dealing with hardened criminals,' replied Meg. 'That *is* good news.'

None of the men corrected her. For hardened criminals the return of the child would be a business transaction. Money for the boy. Amateurs acting on the spur of the moment could easily panic and do something stupid that they would later regret.

Sion sat down heavily at the table and placed his hand on his wife's. 'We'll get him back. If it was unplanned – where would they have gone?'

John replied. 'If it was tramps or opportunists either they've got a billet somewhere or . . .' He left the sentence unfinished.

Sion quickly stepped in. 'Or they've taken him on the off-chance they'll find somewhere.' He didn't voice his thoughts. In all likelihood they would kill the boy and hide his body. It would be easier. They could still demand the ransom.

'Let's assume,' said David, 'that they've taken him somewhere not too far away. Sion, you've ordnance survey maps of the area. Can you get them?'

Sion leapt to his feet and hurried away to his study.

With the door closed he sat down on his sofa and put his head in his hands. 'Dear God, please don't let anything happen to him. Please.' Paul was a gentle soul. He had inherited Kirsty's talent for drawing and painting and at the same time was good with his hands in a practical way. Tears sprang to his eyes and he wiped them away. He knew he had to be strong for Kirsty and the others but it was hard. If he caught the men responsible he'd . . . he didn't know *what* he would do. He was shaking with suppressed rage and anguish. Pulling himself together he crossed the room to the chest of drawers that contained his maps. He found the one he wanted and hurried back to the kitchen.

Laying out the map they stood around and looked at it. The map was six feet by four feet. 'We're here.' Sion pointed at the cluster of buildings shown on the map. 'Here's our boundary. Every building and possible hiding place has been searched. Where else is there?'

The others began to point out certain features. A disused barn, a hut, derelict buildings.

'May I make a suggestion?' said Meg. As always, when the family was in disarray, her inner strength and determination came to the fore. 'Make a list of the locations. Put a drawing pin in each place you identify. When you search the place, you can mark the pin with a touch of ink or paint. That way we won't miss anywhere. How many search teams can we organise?' She looked at her Sion.

'If we go in pairs there's . . .'

'Not enough! Each one of you, including Alex, should lead a team of three men from the factory.'

'Who'll look after things here? Co-ordinate the search?' David asked.

His mother fixed him with a gimlet eye. 'We will, of course. And probably a lot better than you can. Each team needs a runner who'll report back here. How many telephone boxes are shown on the map?'

Sion scanned the area and replied, 'Six.'

'Each one will be manned by one of our people. Make sure they have plenty of pennies.' The new coin-operated, red telephone boxes were springing up all over the country. 'Runners can go to the nearest one and phone the house direct, or come here whichever is closer. We'll then give new destinations for search areas. Have I forgotten anything?'

The men exchanged wry looks. 'Food and drink,' Kirsty said. 'I'll get soup and sandwiches organised. We'll bring them out by truck.'

Sion was relieved. It would do his wife good to have something positive to do. Bile erupted in his stomach again as he thought of the fear his son was experiencing. He turned away to blow his nose, surreptitiously wiping his eyes.

'What about arms?' John asked.

'Hold on,' said David. 'If it was an opportunistic kidnapping I doubt the kidnappers have guns.'

'Staves then? Pickaxe handles?' Peter suggested.

'Yes,' said Sion who then paused and frowned. 'And a rifle. Just in case. One for each team. Can we do that?'

'*Si*, Sion,' Peter replied. 'We have the Lee-Enfields we use for setting the sights on the planes.'

'Good. Give one to the best shot in each party. I'll go and select the men. You lot start on the map.'

Hurrying outside he made his way across the airfield. He had already mentally selected his most reliable men.

On returning, Sion found that fifty-four possible locations had been marked covering a radius of ten miles. Looking over the map he noticed the pin marking the old quarry. His pulse quickened. It would make an ideal hideaway.

His finger was trembling when he pointed at it. 'The quarry,' his voice croaked and he cleared it. 'It would be perfect. Nobody goes there and there's a hut with a stove. It's been used a lot by tramps.'

'So Alex said,' David nodded. 'Which is why we'll look there first. For every place we check we need to be careful. We spy out the land and do *nothing* to spook the kidnappers if we find them.' Looking at his watch he said, 'It's nearly midday. One team goes to the quarry. The rest of us will carry on with the plan.' He was looking at Sion who nodded. The quarry would be his first destination.

'What about waiting for the kidnappers to contact us?' Kirsty asked.

'Even if we come up with nothing we've lost nothing,' said John. 'We will definitely make contact when we deliver the money. So either way we will get to these people.'

One of Sion's team, Fred McArthur, spoke for the men. 'Don't you worry none, sir. We'll get them, don't you fret.' McArthur was a Glaswegian who had been with Sion for over three years. In his early thirties, already balding, he was a cheery individual who was fiercely loyal to Sion. Although he was immensely strong, he was an excellent engineer capable of the most delicate of work when necessary.

Sion and three of his men, including McArthur, took a car around the airfield, followed a track across farm land and approached the quarry from the south, away from the road that the quarry trucks had used. They stopped half a mile away in the middle of a wood and climbed out. Sion had a Lee-Enfield slung over his shoulder, a bullet up the spout, the safety on. Most of the trees had lost their autumn foliage and as the men walked the leaves rustled loudly underfoot.

As they approached the excavation site, they were alert for any sign of habitation. Sion held up his hand and sniffed.

'Smoke,' he whispered.

McArthur pointed. 'It's coming from the quarry. Look.' They could see a thin wisp of smoke rising ahead of them. Cautiously they approached. They were standing at the edge of the top of the quarry. The drop was steep but not impossibly so. The trees reached almost to the lip and, glancing over, Sion could see bushes and small trees precariously gripping the sides of the site. At the bottom, a good hundred feet down, was a small stone hut, next to a large, man-made lake stretching hundreds of yards around. The depth of the water was unknown, but it was certainly dangerously deep. Even as they watched, an individual dressed in no more than rags came outside, filled a billycan with water and went back in.

'What do we do?' McArthur asked.

'The only way out of the place is up the sides here or down that track,' Sion pointed to the left. 'Fred, you and Colin cover the track. Jim, you stay here and I'll go down to the hut. There are no windows this side so they won't see me unless someone comes out. I won't go in until you two have the track covered.'

Sion slithered down the side. He moved as slowly and carefully as he could but still dislodged tiny stones and earth. Finally he reached the bottom. A few minutes later McArthur signalled to him and Sion moved cautiously around the hut. It was about twelve feet by eight, windowless and had only the one door. It looked solid enough, even the corrugated iron roof had very few holes in it. Pausing at the door, Sion readied himself. His hand was on the catch when it lifted under his palm and the door began to open. Sion shoved hard and followed the swinging door inside, forcing whoever to totter backwards with a cry of alarm.

In the gloom Sion could make out two people. One was sitting on a rickety chair, the other lay on the floor where Sion had pushed him.

'Hey! What's the big idea?' He was hardly more than a youth, no more than nineteen or twenty. His clothes were dishevelled and dirty, but not torn or worn. He couldn't have been on the road for very long.

Sion signalled outside. McArthur walked towards him. Sion gave his attention to the second occupant of the hut. He was possibly younger than the first. His clothes were in worse repair and the top of his sole was coming away from his left boot. He looked scared.

'There's nothing to be afraid of,' Sion said. 'We saw the smoke and came to investigate. You're on private property.'

'Everywhere belongs to somebody,' said the youth, getting up off the floor. 'But we wasn't doing no harm.'

'So why are you here?'

'Getting warm. This is a good place if you knows it. We got some vegetables and I was going to make a broth.' He indicated the pot on the stove in the corner and the few carrots and a turnip on a dilapidated table nearby. Somebody had been there before and had tried to make the place more comfortable. A bed with a filthy mattress stood in one corner and three chairs were round the table. They had obviously been brought there over the years by the itinerants who passed through. 'We ain't done no harm,' he repeated.

Sion mustered a reassuring smile. 'I can see that. How long have you been here?'

The two exchanged glances.

'Come on, just tell me.' Sion was becoming irritated.

'Two days,' was the sullen response.

'Have you seen anybody else in the area? Earlier this morning?'

Again the two youths exchanged glances. 'No, we ain't.'

Sion knew that they were lying.

Sion looked at him closely. The boy was frightened, but what of? 'Those vegetables came from the vegetable patch at the back of my house by the airfield. Am I right?' He spoke more harshly than he'd intended and the two youths were looking really scared now.

The older one, Spike, nodded slowly. 'We was hungry,'

he justified himself. 'We only stayed a minute. As soon as those men . . .' He stopped speaking.

'What men? Tell me what you saw.' Sion took a pace towards the older youth who cowered back.

'Tell him, Spike. It's not right. We should have done something this morning.'

'All right. We did see something. We was behind the wall. We'd just got the carrots and we saw these two men arrive. They came out of one of the buildings. They were carrying something. I couldn't see what it was. Then the door to the house opened and this boy came out. He was wheeling a bicycle out of a shed when they grabbed him. One of them put his hand on his face to stop him from yelling. The other grabbed his feet. He smacked the boy one and he stopped struggling. They put the bike back and one of them went inside the house for a minute. Then they picked up the boy and left in a hurry. We . . . we grabbed what we had and ran ourselves.'

'Why didn't you yell? Make a noise? Do something?'

'We was too scared. We think one of them had a gun. A revolver. And we didn't want to get caught up in it. It's none of our business.'

'Which way did they go?'

'The opposite way to us. Towards the trees.'

'That takes them to the road. Did you hear a car or an engine?' Sion dreaded the reply.

'Yes. It sounded like a truck.'

'Could you tell which way they went?'

The two youths exchanged looks and shrugs. He swept his arm to the left. 'That way.'

'What do you mean?' Sion suddenly understood. 'You were standing this way, with your back to the trees and they went that way.' He swept his arm around and the youth nodded. South. They'd gone south. 'Thank you.'

'Mister, one more thing. Those men talked funny.'

'A strange accent, you mean?'

'Nah – foreign, like.'

Foreign? Nothing made sense anymore. The road south led to Westerham, and from there the kidnappers could head in any direction. Sion's heart felt like lead. Reaching into his pocket he took out a five pound note. 'Take this. Buy yourself some proper food. Take care.'

'Thanks Mister.' The youth thrust the fiver into a grubby pocket.

When they returned to the house other reports were coming in. Nothing unusual. No signs. Sion told what he'd learnt. A pall of gloom descended on the searchers. Meg rallied first.

'Nothing's changed,' she announced, mentally girding her loins. 'Except we look further afield. Whoever has him could keep him hidden for days, even weeks. Do we call in the police?'

'No!' Kirsty's voice was anguished. 'They said no police. I thought we agreed?' She was standing next to Alex who hugged her tightly. Kirsty responded with a hug of her own. When they had discovered Paul was missing her instinct had been to send word for Louise, who was spending the half-term at a friend's house, to return home. But commonsense prevailed. There was nothing Louise could do and they thought it better to spare her the anguish. Until they had no choice. Kirsty shuddered at the thought.

Meg crossed the kitchen and placed her arm around her daughter-in-law's shoulders. 'I only meant they'd have the manpower to search more effectively than we can. Make enquiries about a car or a van leaving the area. Perhaps find out where it's gone.'

'I don't think so, Meg,' said John. 'It occurred to me those boys at the quarry could have been talking about tinkers. Their language is Indic, isn't it?' The question was met with blank stares so he continued. 'They think nothing of coming onto people's land and begging money or food, while at the same time seeing what they can steal. A thousand pounds would be a lot of money to them *and* they would have somewhere to take Paul.'

'Are there any travellers in the area? Any gypsies?' David asked looking at his brother.

Sion shrugged. 'No idea. But I can easily find out.' Reaching for the telephone he dialled zero. 'Operator, please connect me to the police station at Sevenoaks.' There was a pause of a few moments. 'This is Mr Griffiths at Biggin Hill, I was wondering if you could help me? Are there any travellers in the area you know of?'

At the other end the duty sergeant boomed back, 'There was, sir. And a lot of trouble they was too, the thieving beggars. Nothing but complaints but they're gone now. Have they been giving you any trouble, sir?'

'Gone? When did they go?'

'This morning, sir. Funny thing. Last heard they was staying until Saturday. Then we just had a report that they'd upped and gone.'

'Where had they been camped?'

'Over by Sundridge, sir. On Lord Whitley's land. He lets them stay on condition there's no thieving, like.' He repeated his question. 'Have you had trouble with them?'

'No! Not this time. I just heard they were in the area and was about to take precautions. But if they've gone I've nothing to worry about. Any idea where they were headed?'

'The motorcycle patrol says he saw them going down the lane past Brasted Chart.'

Sion forced relief into his voice. 'Good. Excellent. Hopefully that's the last we'll see of them for a while. One more thing, Sergeant. Do they have any cars or vans?'

'A lorry certainly, sir. I don't know about anything else. It's mostly horse and carts. Beautiful most of them are. Very ornate, comfortable. And clean, I give them that. But not to be trusted, sir. Not by an inch.'

'Thank you, Sergeant.' Sion broke the connection and told the others what he had learned.

'It looks promising,' said David. 'What do we do? Attack?'

John Buchanan folded his arms and leant on the sink. 'They may not have Paul with them. They may have hidden him somewhere else. We need to follow them. It won't be easy. It's open countryside for miles around. And the lanes are narrow and twisting.'

Sion was standing at the map, tracing the roads. 'We need to see where they go. Check every crossroads.' He pointed. 'They're horse drawn, so they'll only be making three maybe four miles an hour. They can't have travelled far. The first thing we need to do is get a good look at them.'

'We need to find them first,' said John.

Sion snorted. 'Easy. Mike'll have their whereabouts ten minutes after take-off. He can hang back, high in the sky and follow their every movement. Get ready to take-off, Mike.'

The VC holder nodded, beckoned Juan and they left the house together. Juan would fly as observer.

'As soon as we know where they're going we'll take the car and head them off. We'll stop and watch them. Take stock. See how many men, women and children there are.'

'I'll get my coat,' said Kirsty. 'I'm coming too.'

'You'd better not, my love,' said Sion. 'We need you here. We could be barking up the wrong tree and it isn't the travellers. Somebody else may make contact. Alex'll stay with you.'

Reluctantly Kirsty nodded.

Alex was about to protest but seeing his father's face he too nodded.

Sion stood at the window and watched his friend take off. He waited a few minutes, thoughts of Paul flitting through his mind, before going through to his study. In the corner stood a radio transmitter, already warmed up. He spoke briefly to O'Donnell. There followed a tense wait while the plane searched the countryside. Luckily it was a clear day with very little cloud. The ornately painted caravans were quickly spotted and O'Donnell radioed back to Sion. The route the tinkers had taken was plotted on the map. They were already past Ide Hill and appeared to be heading for Four Elms, six miles away.

'Time to go,' said Sion. 'We'll telephone you if we need any help.' Kissing Kirsty he gave her a hug. She held him fiercely, tears in her eyes. He summoned up a smile and then left with David and John.

They took John's car and from Biggin Hill went through Westerham, Crockham Hill and down to the hamlet of Four Elms, where there was a major crossroads. They stopped the car on the green alongside. Knowing what to look for they easily spotted the plane in the distance, an innocuous speck in the blue skies. The tinkers were still heading their way and soon the quiet evening was disturbed by the steady clip-clop of horses' hooves coming down the lane. The first caravan came into sight. Its walls were bright yellow, the roof red and ornate paintings decorated the sides. The swarthy man with the reins in his hands was making the two horses move at a fair speed. Beside him sat a small, rather anxious looking woman.

Without glancing in either direction, he drove the caravan straight across onto the Edenbridge road. The other caravans followed closely behind, moving relatively quickly, the horses blowing, their owners pushing them on.

'Something's up,' said Sion. 'Normally they plod along quite happily. They must be going seven, even eight miles an hour. And one of the women looked as though she'd been crying.'

All in all, a dozen caravans went past. Each one decorated differently, each one beautiful and in immaculate condition. The horses too were well kept and healthy, their coats gleaming. Brown-eyed children peered out through curtains at the back windows of some of the wagons.

'Do we follow them?' David asked.

'At a distance,' his brother replied. 'They can't keep this speed up for long. One of their horses will cast a shoe or go lame or just get plain tired. They'll have to slow down. Where's the lorry?' Sion asked, clenching his fist and thumping the steering wheel hard.

'Gone ahead. This lot are chasing after it.'

John was busy looking at a road map. 'It'll be dark in two hours. I should think they'll want to be camped before then.'

Sion started the engine and turned the big car onto the road. Five minutes later they'd caught up with the back of the wagons. Sion slowed down to match the pace of the caravan and checked the speedometer.

'Seven to eight miles per hour, like we thought. I'll let them get ahead.'

Waiting was agony. The caravan went into the village of Cowden and though dusk was falling rapidly they carried on. In the village Sion spotted a new G.P.O. telephone box and called the house.

'No news this end,' said Meg. 'Mr O'Donnell radioed with your position. He's flown as far as Ashdown Forest but hasn't seen anything incriminating. However,' Meg paused, collecting her thoughts, 'the Ordnance Survey map for the forest is very interesting. The whole area is criss-crossed with tracks. It would make an excellent place to get lost in – the area is huge. There are only a few villages and there are quite a number of derelict buildings and woodcutters' huts. There's even a lake.'

'They could be heading there,' said Sion. 'It would make sense and explain their hurry. They'll be there in less than an hour. Thanks, Mam. Can I have a word with Kirsty?' He spent a few minutes reassuring his wife and receiving encouragement in turn before leaving the telephone box.

Sitting in the car he relayed what his mother had told him.

'So we follow them,' said David, 'to confirm they turn into the forest. Once they are safely inside the forest I expect they'll relax and make camp. If they do, Mike may be able to see their fires. We then move in.'

'What do you propose?' John asked. 'You boys may have grown up in the wild west of America, but England is a civilised country. We have laws. There are women and children to be considered as well. And we've no proof as yet.'

'Our priority is to find Paul,' said Sion. Biting his lip, fighting back the despair that suddenly washed over him he added, 'We do what's necessary.'

David patted his brother's shoulder. 'Hang in there, Sion. If we're wrong we've lost nothing. The kidnappers have to contact us soon. In the meantime we run with what we've got.'

Sion nodded. 'You're right.' Taking a deep breath he straightened his shoulders, resolve sweeping through him once more. 'We hope for the best and plan for the worst. Phone Mam again.'

He got through to the house. O'Donnell had spotted a lorry being driven through the forest.

26

MIKE O'DONNELL BANKED the plane. They were at ten thousand feet. The night was clear, the moon a sliver on the horizon and rising. Below, the countryside was dotted with street lamps and house lights but the area he was watching was in darkness. Juan tapped his shoulder and pointed. The plane turned sharply and both men peered down.

Juan had binoculars glued to his eyes. 'There are two fires.' Grabbing the sextant he measured the angle between the lights of Chelwood Gate and the fires. He read out the numbers to the hundredth of a degree. 'Now Crowborough and then Maresfield. Hold her steady.'

As each angle was read out the information was relayed to the house. In the study Sion plotted the figures after using declination tables to transcribe the angles into distances for the plane's height. They crossed in an irregular triangle deep in the middle of the forest.

'Got you,' he said loudly, nodding with satisfaction to his brother. 'Let's go.'

In the kitchen the men had helped themselves to hot soup and rolls. They were all similarly dressed in dark clothing, wearing flat caps.

'Are the men ready?' Sion asked John Buchanan.

'I briefed them a short while ago. They're raring to go. I told them no violence unless it's in self-defence.'

'With our overwhelming odds,' said Sion, 'it would be stupid of the tinkers to try anything. This is the spot they're camped at.' Prodding the map with his finger, he added, 'We travel by lorry to here, here and here and then we walk. We'll approach the camp at midnight. We go in nice and steady. I've got aniseed to attract the dogs and doctored meat to put them out.'

Outside they heard the plane arriving. It landed and taxied over to where they stood.

'Good work,' Sion said to Mike and Juan, shaking each of them by the hand.

In the hangar the men were waiting. There were forty-five of them, plus the Cazorlas, Mike, Sion, David and John – fifty-two able bodied men in all. Each man carried a pickaxe handle while Sion, David and John also had a rifle. If it all went according to plan, their intention was to frighten the tinkers into submission.

Sion addressed the men. 'Listen, we want no trouble. This isn't about the tinkers, it's about finding Paul. We think they have him. *If they don't*, we apologise and leave. If they do, we rescue him. That's the priority.'

There were more murmurings of agreement.

'We can't afford any slip-ups.' Sion voiced the unthinkable. 'If these people think we are closing in on them then they may decide they have nothing to lose, kill Paul and bury his body,' his voice wavered and then rallied again. 'So we'll go in nice and slow and quiet. Mike, David and I will be the advance party. We'll go along these three tracks,' Sion pointed at a diagram David had put on a chalkboard, 'fifteen minutes ahead of you. I must emphasise – my son Paul's life could be at stake and silence is the order of the day until we're on top of them. Once we're up close we rouse them out of their caravans and search them. And remember, no rough stuff. When we search, we do it without destroying their property. Do I make myself clear?' There was nodded agreement. 'If anyone has a problem with my instructions let him speak now. It would be better not to come with us.'

Nobody moved. They all knew and liked Paul. Many

of the men had seen him grow from a babe-in-arms into
a young lad.

They climbed aboard three lorries, the engines were
started and they moved out one behind the other. It was
now 10pm. It was less than an hour to get to the forest but
they would be walking the last two miles. At Groombridge
they spilt up, diverged, each lorry headed for a different
track into the forest.

O'Donnell was driving the truck with Sion alongside
and fifteen of the men in the back. They travelled in
silence, each busy with their thoughts and fears. What
they were doing was high risk but there didn't appear any
other option. It was O'Donnell who broke the silence.

'You, Sion. What do you intend to do?' O'Donnell
knew the love Sion had for his family. The man must
have murder in his heart.

Frowning, Sion looked at his friend. 'I'm going to seriously hurt the people responsible. But I'll do it alone.
You keep the other tinkers back. I cannot believe they're
all in it.'

'Of course they are,' O'Donnell retorted. 'Otherwise
one of them would have called the police by now.'

'They may be too frightened. These people are
outsiders, Mike, they live by their own rules, dictated by
their culture. But to blame them all is as ludicrous as . . .
as blaming all Germans for the war.' Even under stress,
Sion's innate sense of fairness was uncompromised.

They pulled off the track into the trees. Switching off
the engine they sat listening for a few moments. All they
could hear was the ticking of the cooling engine and a
faint rustling of the almost leafless branches of the forest.

Climbing down from the cab Sion went round to the
back of the lorry. 'Okay, men?' he whispered.

There was a murmured chorus of ayes.

'Mike'll be with you. You wait half an hour before you
follow. And remember, keep quiet.'

Slinging a gunny sack of the doctored meat over one

shoulder and his Lee-Enfield over the other, Sion started along the track. There was a frost in the air although it wasn't freezing. He moved as quietly as he could, barely discernible in the light of the waning moon. Though tempted to switch on a torch he thought better of it. He could see enough, just, to find his way to the camp without injuring himself. There were surprisingly few leaves under foot and the track was reasonably smooth in between the two wheel ruts on either side. After half an hour's march, the sound of horses neighing softly warned him he was approaching the campsite. He slowed down.

Taking a cloth dipped in aniseed he threw it ahead of him, unsure where it landed. He was rewarded with a low growl and then a harsh voice. 'Shut up, yer daft mutt. There's nobody there.'

Sion froze, his mouth suddenly dry, his heart pounding. Why was there a guard on the track? The dog made a whining sound and was repaid with a sharp slap immediately followed by a yelp. The sound came from up ahead, perhaps fifty or sixty yards away.

As silently as he could Sion stepped off the track and into the wood, moving forward slowly, aware of each tiny sound he made. In his left hand he carried the doctored meat, in his right, a pickaxe handle.

'What's that?' A loud whisper came from directly ahead. 'Sic'em. Go see what it is.'

A mongrel rushed into view only yards away, a low growl coming from its throat. Sion threw the meat straight at his nose. It landed just in front of the dog, which stopped in indecision, its nostrils assailed by the tantalising aroma of aniseed and raw meat. Growling, it sniffed the meat warily then wolfed it up. It turned its attention back to Sion and travelled two paces before stopping again. A gruff sound escaped its mouth as it stood perplexed, its legs twitching. Sion didn't move. The dog lay down, sound asleep. Sion's heart was still pounding as he listened intently for the man. After a few seconds he heard a low whistle followed by a whispered, 'Here boy.'

Moving slowly, Sion stepped up to a tree and slid behind it, close to the dog. He didn't have long to wait. He heard rustling, then approaching footsteps. From the sharp intake of breath Sion realised the tinker was standing just the other side of the tree. Stepping around the bole he came behind him and hit him over the head with the handle. The blow wasn't hard enough. With a loud oath the man sprang around, an ugly knife glinting in his hand. This time Sion didn't hesitate. He swung the handle into the man's hand, smashing the knife from its grasp. In one movement he carried through and brought his cudgel down on the man's head. This time the blow was a lot harder. The man dropped, pole-axed, and for one heart-stopping moment Sion thought he'd killed him. With relief he found the man's pulse, strong and steady. Using the knife, Sion cut strips of cloth from the man's trousers and coat and tied the inert form as securely as he could. He added a gag for good measure.

Sion continued slowly towards the camp. Within minutes he saw the dying embers of a fire. The caravans were scattered across a wide clearing in no discernible pattern. A line held the horses on the other side of the area. The animals appeared contented enough, asleep on their legs, heads drooping. A dog growled and Sion took a piece of meat from his bag and threw it into the clearing. Two dogs slinked across the ground towards the meat sniffing suspiciously. Sion threw a second and then a third piece. Both dogs swallowed the meat and were asleep within seconds. Sion waited. Nothing. Total silence except rustling in the trees.

Looking at his watch Sion saw it was nearly midnight. Taking a flashlight with a red filter from his belt, he shone it briefly across the clearing. He was answered by a red flash. David was in position. He aimed it the other way and received two red flashes in reply. John was there.

The three men waited patiently. The moon was now set and the glow from the fires had faded to nothing. The bodies of the dogs were no longer discernible. For Sion the waiting was unbearable. Paul could be nearby, in one of the caravans. Hurt perhaps, or tied up. Scared certainly. It took will-power not to run through the camp yelling his name. But they needed an overwhelming force. It was the only way.

Sion heard rustling in the trees. There was some murmuring but on the whole the men were silent. Sion flashed his torch along the track. The men stood quietly awaiting orders.

'Mike,' he whispered in his friend's ear, 'tell the others to spread out, and to wait for my signal.'

O'Donnell slipped away. The men began to walk around the edge of the clearing, staying within the tree line.

Finally, with the men in position around the clearing, 'Right!' Sion yelled. 'Now!'

The men moved in, marching up to the caravans and pounding on the doors. There were screams and yells, doors flew open and dishevelled men, rudely woken from a sound sleep, appeared. Some carried staves, others shotguns.

'Drop your guns! Drop them!' Sion roared.

Those who'd appeared in the doorways were pulled down the steps and had their staves and guns taken from them. Dark-haired women appeared, screaming abuse. The sounds of children crying and dogs barking filled the clearing.

One man recovered more quickly than the rest. He was a swarthy individual, unshaven, with a few days' growth on his face. A gold ring glinted in his left ear and his broken nose attested to the fact he'd been in a few fights. He was about the same size as Sion, fit and strong looking. 'What's this?'

'My child was kidnapped this morning,' Sion said.

A woman standing near by exclaimed and put a hand to her mouth. She was trembling, clearly scared out of her wits. Sion caught the angry looks the other gypsies cast at her.

'There's nobody here,' said the man. 'But here we go, the same old story. A child goes missing so blame the gypos. We don't know nothing about a kidnapped boy.'

In that second Sion knew for sure. 'I didn't say it was a boy.' Sion raised his voice and yelled, 'Paul! Paul!' The tinker's eyes flickered in the direction of his caravan.

'In there!' Sion pointed and O'Donnell made a rush for it, disappearing inside, only to reappear seconds later. 'He's here. He's safe, thank God.'

Sion acted without thinking. It was instinct and later he was ashamed of himself for it. Stepping towards the man he snarled, 'You know nothing, eh?' Before anybody could move to stop him, he swung the pickaxe handle. It swept through the air at knee height and smashed the man in the left leg. There was a loud crack and the man screamed. Collapsing in agony, the gypsy rolled onto the ground, holding his knee. Sion brought the handle down onto the man's hands, breaking his right wrist and cracking his fingers.

David rushed across the clearing and dragged the handle out of his brother's hands before he could do any more damage. At that moment Paul appeared. Though dirty and tear-stained, he seemed none the worse for his ordeal as he ran towards his father. Sion grabbed him in his arms.

'Are you all right?'

'Yes, Dad, now you're here.'

Sion looked proudly at his son. He'd shed a few tears but he seemed to be in control. 'Who did it?'

'It was him, Dad,' Paul pointed at the man on the floor who was writhing in agony, his woman kneeling by him. 'And him.'

Paul indicated a lad of fourteen or fifteen, who was shaking his head, backing away from Sion.

'You little scum.' Sion stepped towards the boy. He was a scrawny individual, skinny with black hair and brown eyes. When he grew up he'd be a good looking man. *If he grows up*, thought Sion.

'He made me,' he croaked.

'Who? Him?' Sion pointed.

The boy nodded. The kneeling women spoke up. 'No harm would have come to your son. I promise. We'd never have allowed it. It's not our way.'

Sion looked at the tinkers. There were about thirty of them. He felt suddenly tired. In a perverse way he also felt sorry for them. They were scared and who could blame them? They were surrounded by over fifty strong men, waiting only for a signal to smash them and their caravans to pieces. And all because of one man. One greedy bully.

'Are you this man's wife?' Sion asked the woman kneeling next to the man.

Nodding she said, 'I'm his woman. That's our son. Please. Don't hurt him again. He's not hurt your boy. We were already arguing for his return. Ask your boy if you don't believe me.'

'Is that true, Paul?'

His son nodded. 'It's true, Dad. They wanted to let me go. Only he wouldn't let them. He insisted you'd pay the ransom.'

Straddling the fallen man Sion looked down at him. 'What do you say if we fire your caravans? What do you say if I give your son a good hiding as a lesson? Eh? Tell me that.'

The man looked at Sion with loathing. 'Do your worst. The likes of you always does. I asks for no quarter and I gives none.'

'Please!' The woman begged. 'If you burn our caravans where will we live? Look at our old people. They've got nothing else. Please.'

'Please, Dad,' said Paul. 'Don't do it.'

Sion sighed. 'I won't, son. I won't punish all these peoples for the sins of one man. But let it be a lesson to you all,' he raised his voice. 'Thieving is one thing, but stealing someone's child is something else entirely.'

In the background they could hear the lorries approaching, bang on schedule.

Sion ground the heel of his boot on the man's arm. The gypsy groaned as pain shot through him. 'If you come back to this district again I will have you. You and all the rest. Leave the area and don't return. Ever. Do I make myself clear?'

'We will,' said the woman. 'I promise.' She was a handsome woman and Sion could see where the boy got his good looks.

'Get him to a hospital. Have his leg and hands looked at.'

The woman shook her head. 'We don't have any money for hospitals. We'll look after him.'

From his hip pocket Sion extracted some money. 'Here's ten pounds. I'll give it to you on condition you take him to see a doctor.' Paul was safe and sound and that was all that mattered.

'Take the money,' the man said harshly. 'More bloody fool him. It's conscience money. But don't worry, we won't be going to the police.'

Sion barely hid his astonishment. 'Go to the police if you like. You'll go to prison, I promise you that.'

'And so will you. For assault. You're . . . umph.'

'Be quiet!' The woman clamped her hand over his mouth. 'You've caused enough trouble. We'll take him to the hospital. And thank you.'

She had a quiet dignity about her which Sion found strangely compelling. He believed her. Looking closely he could see their pride, but also their poverty. Their gaunt faces were testament that they weren't getting enough to eat.

Turning to Paul he said, 'Time to go, son. Your mother has been through enough.'

BOOK 3

Meg's Story

27

Autumn 1934

WHEN YOU UNDERSTAND the past, the present becomes much clearer. These days I looked back more often than I looked forward. Perhaps those reflections added to the sense of peace I felt as I sat sewing happily in the withdrawing room. Though a lady should never tell her age I admit to seventy-four. My life and that of my family had been as turbulent and exciting as the times through which I'd lived. There had been many regrets, too many to mention, but also great joy and pleasure along the way.

I had long since come to understand the bad feeling that had existed between my mother and myself before we left Wales. I knew, too, the reason for her anger – Evan. I had just qualified as a school teacher when I met him. For me, it was love at first sight. He had stepped out of the pub at Llanbeddas straight into my path. I'd stopped, startled, looked up into his deep blue eyes and fell for him even before he doffed his cap to apologise. All I'd managed to do was nod. I was sure he thought me very rude.

From that day on I began to see Evan whenever I walked to the primary school at the end of the village. The second time I met him was at a miners' social, just before Christmas. My mother was horrified that I'd gone – she wanted me to meet a professional man, another teacher or a lawyer even. I contrived somehow to dance with him but for the life of me I cannot remember how.

My memory is becoming highly selective. Six months later we married much to my mother's fury. Thankfully my father stood by me, said it was my happiness that counted and nothing else. Father rarely went against my mother but when he did she had the sense to keep quiet. She never would accept the fact that Evan made me very happy.

Nine months and two days after the wedding, David was born. Then to add to our joy, I had the twins, Sion and Sian we named them. And what a wonder they were to me. I couldn't look at them enough. Eight years we had her before that terrible day. The day the slag heap wiped out the school and killed my little girl. Sion had survived only because his class had gone for a nature ramble. Sian had stayed back because she'd been unwell. For years I'd tormented myself, blaming myself for having sent her to school. *Everything* changed from that day. Evan's parents were murdered in a house fire. We booked passage for America. The night we left I thought Evan wasn't going to make the ship. He'd gone back to Llanbeddas to settle a score with the mine owner. When he arrived on board he'd brought Uncle James with him. I smiled. He was a wonderful old man. He'd saved Evan's life that night.

Deep in my memories I crossed the room to the sideboard and poured myself a cup of tea.

Compared to my first meeting with Evan, my first sight of John had been much more dramatic. He was Master of the ship which carried us across the Atlantic. I would never forget that storm. John was almost swept overboard and I – well, I saved him. He was plain John Buchanan in those days, not the Baron of Guildford. I knew from the first that he'd fallen in love with me but he was too much the gentleman to hint at it and I was too much the lady to let on that I knew his true feelings. We became and remained great friends for many years. Evan and he became true friends. Thanks to John we got our first start when Evan needed to borrow money for our business.

Life's roller-coaster started in earnest then. The business prospered and Evan moved into politics. Then came that other terrible time when David went missing at sea. Nearly a whole year he was away and we all thought him dead. He turned up at the house while I was putting away my best china. I broke nearly every piece when I realised who was standing in my kitchen. I had never felt such joy as I did at that moment. After his confrontation with Gunhild, Susan's mother, I lost him again when he left America to travel to Britain.

But our darkest days were still to come. Evan became a Senator. The American Constitution was changed, which allowed Evan to run for the Presidency. After a huge effort, he won, only to be cut down at the moment of his greatest triumph. Shot before he knew the result. When the boys arrived with Evan's body on the buckboard, I almost lost my wits. When he was in the earth, I knew my time in America was over. At first I thought of living in Wales but after only a few days visiting the valleys I knew I had outgrown the place though it still had its grip around my heart. You can never go back, you have to move forward. I lived with David and Madelaine, and my granddaughter, Susan, joined us. She's grown into a fine young woman. Headstrong more often than not, but beautiful as well as intelligent. They say she's like me.

John's wife committed suicide, a terrible, terrible tragedy. She chose, together with her lover, to jump off a cliff. Both women left behind a note, condemning the world for its intolerance. John was now free to remarry. It came as no surprise when he asked for my hand. At first I felt that I was betraying Evan's memory. John understood that. He even suggested adjoining bedrooms. But I'd told him that if we married it would be done properly. We would be husband and wife in every sense. I worried about the boys, David and Sion. How would they react? Of course, I needn't have concerned myself. If I was happy, they were happy. And they'd known and admired John for most of their lives. Indeed, they'd been in so many scrapes together I'd lost count. So I became Mrs John Buchanan and – when John took the title – Baroness of Guildford. Meg from the valleys was now Lady Megan and never called anything else except by the family.

Almost losing Paul – well, I know what it's like to lose a child. Kirsty was reluctant to let him out of her sight at first but the boy didn't seem any the worse for his adventure. When he returned to school he was hailed a hero by some and a blow-hard by others. He quickly learned not to be too boastful.

I sighed. If only we old ones could impart our knowledge and experience to the young. Mankind would move forward so much more quickly. Instead each generation is doomed to repeat the same mistakes. To learn for itself.

My reverie was disturbed by the telephone ringing in the hallway. A few seconds later the door opened and Beech, our butler, entered.

'The telephone, for you, my Lady.'

'Who is it, Beech?'

'The caller gave her name as Betty Griffiths,' he hesitated and then added, 'I think.'

I stood up with some alarm coursing through me. Why was Betty of all people phoning me? I hardly knew the girl. 'What do you mean, Beech, you think?'

'The accent, my Lady. I found it hard to understand. And the connection isn't as good as it might be.'

Nodding, I hurried into the hall. Beech was the worst kind of snob but ran the household impeccably.

'Betty?' I asked tentatively.

'Aunt Megan? I mean, Lady . . .' She stopped, cleared her throat and said, 'I'm sorry, what do I call you?'

It was such a ludicrous question that I chuckled. 'Aunt Megan, auntie Meg, take your pick. But certainly not Lady anything.'

I heard her sigh of relief.

'Is there anything wrong, Betty?' I felt there had to be if she was telephoning me. 'Has something happened?' I was the last of the old generation and though I had made an effort to stay in touch with Nancy and William, Mair and Huw and the others, while they had been alive, I'd lost contact with their children. I knew their names but not much else about them. I suddenly remembered that David had given Betty some sort of job in a new factory making wirelesses.

'No, it's not the family, Aunt Meg. I'm sorry to bother you. It's just that I tried to reach David and he's away somewhere and nobody can tell me when he'll be back.'

'In two weeks. He's on a tour of South America for the government. Some trade delegation or other. I can get a message to him if it's really urgent but I doubt it'll do much good unless there's something he can do from ten thousand miles away.'

The sigh this time sounded weary.

'What's the matter?'

'I'm . . . I'm not sure I should trouble you with this,' Betty began. She paused and then continued more forcefully, 'But I need to tell someone. I don't want the blame. You know I work as a book-keeper at the factory in Taff's Well?'

'Yes.'

'Last year I found some discrepancies in the figures and when I mentioned them to Mr Carruthers, the managing director, he said David knew about it. It was merely an "accounting procedure". But I've been checking since and I think something is seriously wrong. A lot of stock has gone missing as well as certain invoices. It doesn't make any sense and I wanted to check with David before I made a fool of myself.'

I could hear the uncertainty in her voice and guessed there was more to it than she was letting on. 'There's something else, isn't there?'

Betty didn't reply for a moment and then blurted it

out. 'I think Mr Carruthers is stealing. Oh!' She fell silent and then said, 'Aunt Meg? Are you there?'

'Yes, my girl, I'm still here. Before we make any wild accusations we need to have the facts. Where are you now?'

'In the factory. Mr Carruthers has left for the day. I thought this would be a good time to try and get hold of David. I tried the bank but they couldn't help me. Only told me to phone the house. But nobody was at home.'

I couldn't help a small laugh. 'Madelaine is visiting a friend and Susan is at her uncle's. But, my dear, when the bank said to telephone the house they meant the Houses of Parliament.'

'Oh! I feel such a fool,' Betty said, obviously horrified.

'Don't be. If you had telephoned you wouldn't have gotten anywhere. You need a special number. Be that as it may, it doesn't help with your problem. Is it possible for you to come here? Bring the information with you?'

There was a sharp intake of breath. 'I . . . I don't think so, Aunt Meg. I've never been to London. And I can't take any time off work.'

'What about the weekend?'

'I'm not sure. Dafydd doesn't like me working as it is. We're always having rows about it. If I was to come to London I don't know what he would do. He expects me to be here for him. He'd go doolally if I suggested wasting money on a train fare. Not . . . not that I think it'd be a waste. That's what he would say.'

Doolally! I hadn't heard the term in more years than I cared to remember. It brought back memories of the valleys and family life there. Family mattered – more than anything else. Had I been negligent, where the extended family was concerned?

'Couldn't Dafydd come with you? Explain it's business. All expenses paid.'

'That would be worse. Dafydd . . .' Betty paused. It

seemed to me she was torn between loyalty to her husband and the truth of her situation.

'You don't have to explain,' I said. 'I understand. Their pride gets in their way. They can't see beyond the mine and providing for their family.' I was about to talk out of turn though I claimed the right to do so because of my age. 'Does he resent your job?'

It was like a dam bursting. In a mixture of Welsh and English, she told me everything. How unhappy they were. How she couldn't tell Dafydd how much she really earned and how she hid her money in a Post Office savings account in Pontypridd. The resentment she'd faced from the rest of the family. How she'd even stopped buying little things to make the house more comfortable. Envy is a corrosive and hateful emotion.

'You have a daughter, don't you?'

'Yes. Myfanwy. Dafydd says it's time for another before it's too late. But I don't want to be stuck at home again. There's so much I want to do. I . . . I don't know why I'm telling you all this, Aunt Meg.'

'Probably because I understand exactly what you're going through. I was born and brought up there. I know how the people think. Especially the men. I'm only thankful I married Evan. He had ambition to spare. Betty you have so many options open to you. But now isn't the time to discuss them. We must solve the problem you've discovered at the factory. First, I need information to wire to David. I can contact him through one of our embassies, depending on where he is. John is with him.' I realised she didn't know who I meant, so I added, 'My husband.'

'Oh, yes, of course.'

'Let me think what's best to do. You obviously believe it's very serious otherwise you wouldn't have telephoned.'

'Carruthers isn't covering his tracks so well anymore and I think more money is being taken and we could have a problem with the bank soon. Unless, of course, *it is* something David knows about and the money is being used elsewhere.'

'That's a possibility,' I replied, but didn't add that I doubted it. 'Today is Wednesday. Can you call me tomorrow at the same time? I'll tell you what I've decided.'

'Yes. Mr Carruthers is usually away before three o'clock. I'm truly sorry to have called you, Aunt Megan, but I didn't know what else to do.'

'You did the right thing.' We said goodbye and I hung the receiver on its candlestick base. I went back slowly to the withdrawing room, deep in thought. I was too old to go gallivanting to Wales, far too old. Just as John was too old to be in South America. It was time he retired, even from the House of Lords. I wanted him home. But, like John, I wanted to do more than issue orders to servants. I felt a stirring of excitement. I still had all my mental faculties even if I was becoming frail in wind and limb. I made up my mind. I would go to Wales but I wanted help. That evening I telephoned Madelaine at Fairweather. Now that Richard was away at school she had time on her hands and, like me, she enjoyed an adventure. When in town, she and David occupied a complete suite of rooms on the second floor and used the public rooms for entertaining. Each of the children also had a room they called their own, though they used it less and less nowadays. The arrangement was highly convenient and I selfishly enjoyed having them around as much as I did.

The following morning found Madelaine and me ensconced in the back seats of our Rolls Royce Phantom II. I didn't drive of course, although Madelaine did. We had never bothered with a chauffeur. When I needed to be taken anywhere I usually sent for Beech. He loved driving the car and saw it as an extension of his duties. He agreed to drive us to Wales with alacrity. According to Beech the car had a top speed of 84mph. I insisted he never went above 40mph. Which I felt was quite fast enough. On the front seat alongside Beech sat a picnic hamper. We set off shortly after breakfast.

Beech had recently passed his driving test, which had just become compulsory. It had cost a maddening seven shillings and sixpence, silly really, when he had been driving us all these years. Having consulted a road map and discussed the route with Beech we decided to travel via Gloucester. The roads out of London were congested as usual. The traffic was maddening and I commented on the fact.

'It is the new thirty miles an hour speed limit in towns, ma'am,' said Beech.

'And those ugly beacons for pedestrians to cross the road,' said Madelaine. 'What eyesores!'

Out of the city, the traffic quickly thinned and we were able to make far better time. But the roads were narrow and winding. By mid-morning I was beginning to regret my impetuous act to drive to South Wales. We should have taken the train.

We stopped for lunch on the bank of the River Isis. Beech spread a blanket and Madelaine and I sat and talked while we ate cold chicken, crusty bread and drank tea from a Thermos flask. England was enjoying a mild autumn and the day was unusually warm and pleasant for the middle of October. We discussed what we might find in Wales but our conjecture was fruitless. We turned to family matters. Richard had been at school for three weeks and appeared to be enjoying it immensely, although he had bouts of homesickness. As an old and influential Etonian, John had pulled a few strings to get him a place. Being near Windsor visiting him was easy enough, although visits were strictly rationed. I didn't believe in public school, but was forced to admit that it would be good for him in later life. Schoolboy friendships lasted a lifetime and could be very useful. Madelaine understood this and had reluctantly agreed to him going.

As we arrived at Gloucester it began to rain, although

the shower quickly passed. We found a garage in the middle of the town and Beech filled up with petrol. Shortly afterwards we crossed into Wales and headed for Monmouth. Pontypool and Cwmbran followed and in the late afternoon we arrived at Caerphilly. We stopped for tea in a local hotel before finishing the last few miles. It was nearly five o'clock when we drew up outside the factory in Taff's Well.

'What I don't understand,' said Madelaine, 'is why the fraud, if there is one, has taken so long to come to light? I know David is busy with the bank and at the House, but he usually keeps a tight rein on things.'

'Don't be too harsh on him, my dear,' I said. 'This has been such a new venture that he was relying on Carruthers' experience. It seems he's misjudged the man badly.'

'I wonder if Carruthers is here?' Madelaine asked.

'I shouldn't think so from what Betty told me. We'll know soon enough. Beech, if we are still inside in ten minutes time it will mean we're staying. Kindly drive into Cardiff and get us rooms at the Angel Hotel.'

'Yes, my Lady.'

We walked slowly towards the entrance, signed "Enquiries". The place appeared deserted. I tried the door. It opened smoothly and we stepped inside.

'There's a bell by the hatch,' said Madelaine, giving it a pat with the palm of her hand.

The jingle caused the hatch to suddenly open and an anxious face peered out.

'My goodness,' it said.

I recognised Betty's voice immediately. 'Hullo, my dear. I know we're not expected but I've brought Madelaine with me to look at the books.'

'My goodness,' she repeated. 'I'll . . . I'll open the door.'

Having introduced Madelaine, we followed Betty into an office. She still appeared dazed. 'Can I offer you anything? A cup of tea, perhaps?'

'Thank you, but no. We had tea a short while ago.'

'Please, sit down.' Betty indicated a chair. 'I'll get you something to sit on, Madelaine.' Betty was back in moments with a straight-backed chair. 'I was just about to telephone you, Aunt Meg.'

I smiled, looking at her closely. Betty was a good looking woman, with a lot of character. I remembered David describing her as very thin but she'd put on weight over the last few years. 'I decided that if you couldn't come to London we had to come here. It would be easier all round. Why is it so quiet?'

'The factory stops at four-thirty. I was just finishing some paperwork before calling you. I've been making copies of files ever since I became suspicious. Only . . .' she paused.

I finished the sentence for her. 'Only you're not sure we'll be able to understand them.'

'No offence, Aunt Meg.'

'When Evan and I started out, I was his book-keeper. I can read a column of figures as well as the next person. So why don't you show me what you've got?'

Removing my reading glasses from my leather clutch bag, I put them on while Betty fetched the files.

'It'll save time,' she said, 'if I work through them with you, skimming the accurate accounts and highlighting the problems.'

She started laying the files on the desk between Madelaine and myself and began pointing out discrepancies. Invoices for goods not received, payments for work not done, and many more wirelesses were leaving the factory than were being invoiced for. There had been a systematic, wholesale fraud, committed against the company, going back as far as the opening.

'My goodness!' Betty exclaimed. 'Look at the time. I must go.' The clock on the wall showed it was nearly a quarter to eight. 'Dafydd will kill me.'

'We'll take you home,' Madelaine said. 'Beech will be back from the hotel by now. May we keep these files?'

'Yes, of course. What do you intend doing with them?'

'Inform David,' I replied, standing up. Suddenly a meal and an early night were very appealing. 'Tell him what we've discovered. Or rather what *you've* discovered,' I corrected myself. 'After that I've no idea but with David you can be sure there'll be no half measures.'

While Betty locked the factory gates we waited by the car. The dear girl was wide-eyed at the prospect of riding in a Rolls-Royce. Madelaine sat in the front with Beech. Betty sat tentatively on the seat beside me, bolt upright, as if afraid she would damage the leather upholstery if she sat back.

'Relax, my dear. Enjoy the ride,' I smiled encouragingly. As a family we appreciated the finer things in life, and tried hard not to take them for granted. After all, we had come so close to losing everything. Seeing Betty's reaction, I dearly wished I could do something for her.

'Why don't you leave Llanbeddas?' I began. 'I can guarantee you a much better life in London if you wished, away from the mines.'

She looked bleakly at me and shook her head. 'I can't,' she spoke hardly above a whisper.

'Indeed, you can,' I replied fiercely. 'I'm an old woman and perhaps I shouldn't be interfering but I left Llanbeddas when I was ten years younger than you. It was such a . . . a relief. There is so much to see and do beyond the valleys. A whole world that doesn't revolve around coal.'

In the glow from the passing street lights I saw her smile. 'You sound just like David.'

'I do?' I was surprised for a moment and then I laughed. 'I suppose I must do. We think alike about so many things. Sion too.'

'You must be very proud of them.'

'Yes. Yes, I am. They've achieved so much. But they've had the opportunity to do something with their lives. My dear,' I took her hand in both mine, 'think of Myfanwy. What do you want for her? These are the thirties. Anything is possible for a determined young woman these days.'

Tears sprang to Betty's eyes. 'I know. Every night I go to bed, I pray that she doesn't get stuck in a rut like me. Education, that's the key. Women are even going to university. There's such a whole new world out there.'

We were passing through Pontypridd, along the main street, a place I hadn't visited in many years. How many years? I shook my head. Senility, I thought, was setting in. A few more miles passed in silence, before Betty spoke.

'The problem is Dafydd.' Now she had said the words, stepped over the boundary between wifely duty and disloyalty, there was no holding her. She became animated. 'He's jealous. Of everything and everybody. He hates to see people bettering themselves, moving up in the world. He disguises the fact by being an active member of the union but in truth he's scared.'

'Of what?' I was intrigued.

She shrugged. 'Of everything. Frightened of change, I think, in the end.'

'We all are,' I replied, much to Betty's surprise.

'You? Frightened of change? Of anything? I don't believe it.'

'My dear, when we left Wales we were all terrified. We had no idea what we were headed for. We hoped and prayed for a better future. But that's all we had. Hope and prayer. I have had a long and interesting life but there's been a huge amount of heartache along the way. A lot of joy, yes, but a lot of pain as well. Without the one you cannot experience the other. We all change as we grow older, some for the better, some for the worse. Some of us grow with each challenge that comes along and surmount whatever hurdle we're faced with. But each time you succeed you become stronger, more sure of yourself. Does that make any sense?'

'Yes, Aunt Meg, it does.' Her pale face was animated

and she sat forward in the seat. 'Like the challenge of working in the factory. Each day I'm asked for solutions to problems instead of Mr Carruthers. Every week he relies on me more and more to make decisions when he's away.'

'What other management is there?'

'There's a production manager, a buying manager and a sales manager. But because I look after the financial side it all comes to me. So I see everything that's going on.'

'That's a lot of responsibility,' I said, smiling at her enthusiasm.

'I enjoy it.' The simple statement spoke volumes.

'May I speak bluntly?'

Betty nodded warily. 'If you wish.'

'I don't think it's a question of wishes but of necessity,' I said gently. 'You're moving on with your life. You're making things happen. Today has been an example. You uncovered a serious crime and had the courage to do something about it. As a result we are sitting in this car, having this talk. Our actions can have life changing consequences. You're being made to confront your future whether you like it or not as a result of your actions. I don't think you'll ever be content again if you don't do something purposeful with your life.'

She was obviously thinking carefully about what I'd said. After a few seconds she nodded. 'Aunt Meg, you've put into words thoughts I've been suppressing for months.' There was real anguish in her voice when she said, 'I cannot continue to live the way I do now. In that poky little house, in those filthy streets. Waiting for my man to come home, listening to him coughing his lungs out, living life with no hope of a better future. Working in the factory I've had contact with people all over Britain. It opened my eyes, I can tell you. I'd look at the map on the office wall, to find place names on orders and invoices. I dreamt of clean towns, clean rivers, clean air

. . . of being away from the filth of the coal dust and the oppression of the mine.' She took a deep breath. 'I must get away.'

'I'll help you,' I said. 'And tell me to mind my own business but I need to ask. What about Dafydd? Do you love him?'

She looked at me bleakly. 'I don't know,' she whispered. 'God help me, but I don't know any more. What shall I do?'

I shook my head. 'Betty, that's not for me to say. I'll do all that I can for you but you have to make your own decisions. I know it seems like I'm an interfering old biddy but I want what's best for you. If you tell me you want to stay in Llanbeddas then so be it. You can continue to work at the factory and travel back and forth. If you want more I can help you there too. But I cannot tell you what to do.'

'I know that, Aunt Megan. But Dafydd wants me to stop working in Taff's Well. I get home too late if he's on the day shift and he has to get his own bath and make his own food.'

'What about the money you take home? Doesn't that count for anything?'

'In some ways it makes it worse. I actually earn more money than him but I deliberately take home less than he does. The rest I put in a PO account. If he ever found out,' she shuddered, 'I don't know what he would do.'

'He doesn't hit you, does he?' I was thoroughly alarmed at the thought.

'He's slapped me a few times but that's all. But I probably deserved it.'

'Nobody,' I said fiercely, 'deserves to be hit. Betty, *cariad*, let me know what you want to do and I'll respect your wishes.'

'Thank you, Aunt Meg. What do we do tomorrow?'

The question surprised me. 'Why, nothing. I'll contact David and give him the salient facts. He and John will

be in North America all next week. He'll be home the
week after. It can wait until then.'

Betty seemed disappointed.

'A few more weeks won't matter. Not after all this
time.'

Reaching into my purse I extracted a calling card. 'Our
address is on the card. You can write or telegram me if
you need to.' Looking out the window I realised our
journey was almost over. 'We'll be at Llanbeddas shortly.
Thank you for all you've done. I really appreciate it.'

'No, thank you, Aunt Meg. You've helped me more
than you can know. I've put off making decisions long
enough. There have to be changes not only for Myfanwy's
sake but also for my own. Does the driver know where
to go?'

'No. You'd better tell him.' I slid back the glass
partition which had allowed us our privacy. 'Beech, Mrs
Griffiths will tell you the way.'

Leaning forward Betty gave directions and a few
minutes later we drew up outside her house. I knew it so
well that when I looked I was transported back nearly
forty years. I realised I had tears in my eyes and a lump
in my throat. I reached for a handkerchief and repaired
my face while Betty climbed out of the car. Madelaine
got out and came into the back with me.

'Thank you so much,' Betty said. With that she went
through her front door.

'Are you all right?' Madelaine asked.

'Yes. I was suddenly swamped with my memories.
Pardon me, my dear, but I have something I need to do.
Beech, take the next right. Go to the top of the hill and
I'll direct you from there.' I sat back watching the drab
streets unfold. I continued giving directions until I told
him to halt. I turned to Madelaine. 'I hope you don't
mind. But I couldn't leave without visiting her.'

Getting out of the car I spoke quietly. 'I'll only be a
moment or two. Come with me, if you like.'

Much to my pleasure, she agreed.

I held onto her arm as we walked through the cemetery. Unerringly I took us to the spot. Kneeling down I read the inscription on Sian's grave although it was carved in my heart.

Bending down, I picked a few stray weeds away from her grave, although I could see it had been well tended. I looked up at Madelaine. 'Though we lost her all those years ago, it seems like yesterday. Help me to my feet, there's a dear.' Madelaine steadied me as I stood up. 'If I could turn the clock back I'd make a pact with the Devil himself to have her with me. I would even have stayed in Llanbeddas and given up everything we've accomplished.' Although my eyes were dry my chest was tight and my heart thumped uncomfortably. 'But we can never go back. We can only go forward. But oh, how I wish she was here with us. Come Madelaine, we should leave.' I smiled at her and thought how lucky David and Sion were to have married Madelaine and Kirsty. Both women were like daughters to me but there still a black hole in my heart for Sian.

The suite of rooms we had at the Angel Hotel came with a personal maid and an hour after leaving the graveside I was lying in a hot bath, letting the cold seep out of my tired limbs. While I lay there I couldn't help wondering if I was an interfering old woman who should mind her own business. Perhaps, because of my age and experience, I had a duty to say what I really thought. With a sigh I decided I didn't have an answer.

In my nightdress and dressing gown I went into the sitting room. Madelaine was there presiding over a light supper. We had dismissed the maid as we wanted privacy to talk. Nowadays I allowed myself one glass of white wine in the evenings and I sipped my drink with unfeigned pleasure.

'I've looked more closely at those papers Betty gave

us,' Madelaine said, spearing some cold lamb onto a fork. 'By my calculations, Carruthers has been defrauding the company by about seven or eight thousand a year for the last few years. He started with a smaller amount but it became serious three years ago.' She paused with a glass to her mouth and mused, 'I'm still dumbstruck David didn't see this a long time ago.'

Ever the mother, I leapt to the defence of my eldest son. 'Too busy? Too trusting? A bit of both?'

Madelaine nodded. 'I suspect you're right. I remember when he first appointed Carruthers. He was so full of praise for the man. Now this. When do we return to London?'

'I'm in no hurry, my dear. If you don't mind, I was thinking that I would like to stay for a few days. See some of the sights. Have you ever visited Wales before?'

28

I SPENT THE NEXT few days unashamedly immersing myself in my Welshness. I spoke the language at every opportunity and we visited as far west as Carmarthen, where we stayed the night, and as far north as Llandrindod Wells, the spa town. I found that I was extremely proud of my heritage, a feeling I had suppressed for many years.

From Llandrindod Wells we returned to London. We journeyed all day, but Beech was in his element driving us across the countryside. The following evening we were preparing to sit down to dinner when Beech entered the drawing room. It was a family gathering – Sion, Kirsty, Louise and Madelaine, with Susan expected at any minute. Normally, my forthright young granddaughter came right in without waiting to be announced and so I was a little surprised when Beech appeared. I was even more surprised by his announcement.

'Mrs Betty Griffiths and em, Myfanwy, my Lady.'

Betty appeared nervously in the doorway with Myfanwy hidden behind her mother's skirts. Betty's obvious anxiety wasn't helped by the curious stares from the family.

I hurried to my feet. 'My dear, what a surprise! Do come in. And Myfanwy, come and have some cordial. Louise, my love, get your cousin a cordial.'

'Yes, Grandmama. What sort would you like?' Sion's daughter, Louise, approached Myfanwy with a smile and pointed to the sideboard. 'Come and look.'

Hesitatingly Myfanwy stepped forward and looked up

at her mother. Quietly in Welsh, Betty encouraged
Myfanwy to join Louise.

'Can I get you something?' Sion asked.

'No. No thank you. I'm sorry,' she looked at me, tears
forming in her eyes. 'We shouldn't have come. But I
couldn't think where else to go.'

'In that case, let me get you something to drink, tea –
or something stronger – and you can tell us all about it.
Now, what would you like?'

Betty hesitated. 'Do you have a port?'

'Beech, get Mrs Griffiths a port, please.'

'Yes, my Lady.'

I took hold of Betty's hands and exclaimed, 'You're
freezing! Come and sit by the fire. We'll soon have you
warm. Kirsty, please tell cook there are two more for
dinner.'

'We couldn't . . .' Betty began.

'Hush, my dear. Of course you can. You're family and
family is always welcome in this house. Ah, thank you,
Beech.'

Betty took the proffered glass and sipped the rich, red
wine.

'Now, tell us what has happened.'

'This morning just after I got to work Mr Carruthers
sent for me. He was furious. He knew all about your visit.
About the files, the figures I gave you, just everything. I
was fired, he said, and we would never be able to prove
anything against him. He had me thrown out of the factory
before I could even get my personal belongings. He was,'
she paused and took a gulp of port this time. 'He was
very rude. I couldn't understand how he knew so much.
Every last detail of what we said and what we'd done.
At first I thought you or,' she looked at Madelaine, 'you,
had told him for some reason. But that didn't make any
sense. I was so upset. On the bus home I wondered how
on earth he had found out so much. Then it came to me.'
She paused, biting her lip, holding herself together.

'It was Dafydd,' I said, understanding.

She nodded. 'He came home from the day shift. When he saw me he smiled, said I'd not be leaving him to fend for himself anymore. I knew then for sure he'd told Carruthers.'

'Did he say why?' Sion asked.

Betty nodded wearily. 'He spouted the usual jealous bile, about all of you and David in particular. I tried telling him how good you'd been to me. To us. But he wasn't having any of it. I went into the dresser and took out my Post Office book. I showed him how much I'd saved. A fortune. Nearly four hundred pounds. He went as white as a sheet and threw the book onto the fire. When I tried to get it he grabbed hold of me, made me watch my book burn. Then he stormed out of the house.' Betty paused and tears began to roll down her cheeks.

Sion put his hand on her shoulder. 'The money isn't lost, Betty. You can claim it back from the post office.'

She wiped her cheeks with the back of her hand. 'It's not just that, Sion. Carruthers will do his best to hide his tracks. I know he will.'

'Don't worry, we'll take care of him,' said Sion. 'We'll update David by telegram this morning. Early tomorrow we'll go to Wales and take control of the factory.'

'Take control?' Betty asked, a gleam in her eyes.

In the meantime, practicalities needed resolving. 'Did you bring any clothes with you?' I asked.

'A few. As soon as Dafydd left the house I packed a case. It's mainly Myfanwy's stuff. We left as soon as she came home from school. We came on the train. A taxi brought us from Paddington. I wasn't sure it was the right place until I saw Mr Beech at the door.'

'You did the right thing coming here,' I assured her. 'Madelaine, please tell cook we will be delayed by twenty minutes. Kirsty, could you show Betty to the yellow room? Myfanwy can have the room adjoining.' I looked at the girl. She and Louise were talking animatedly together.

Louise at fourteen was a head taller than Myfanwy who I knew to be ten years old. For all that, with their dark colouring and curly hair it was obvious that they were related. 'Or she can sleep in Louise's room. We'll leave it to the girls to decide.'

They decided to share. While Betty and the children were out of the room I said to Sion, 'That's torn it.'

He nodded. 'We need to stop Carruthers doing too much damage.'

'What can he do except try and doctor the files?' asked Madelaine.

'I think it's gone far beyond creative accounting,' Sion replied. 'He may steal everything he can lay his hands on, including any funds at the bank, and scarper.'

The possibility hadn't occurred to me. 'We need to know who can sign company cheques,' I said. 'Betty will know.'

She joined us a few minutes later. Madelaine had lent Betty a dress, a full length yellow gown, with ruched sleeves and kick pleats from the knee. When she crossed the room she gave a shy smile.

Myfanwy, quiet until now, announced in a loud voice, 'Gosh. Mam, you look nice.'

It broke the tension. Sion said as much and we all agreed. Betty relaxed when Beech offered her a second glass of port. I had no illusions about how difficult it must be to come into our company, when all you were used to was life in a mining village. I remembered in 1890 being on board ship for the first time. How awkward I felt at the Captain's table for dinner. The borrowed glad rags John had organised for me, so we could sit in first class. I remembered that evening so well, especially the efforts John made to make Evan and me feel welcome.

We were about to go in to dinner when Susan arrived, breathless as usual. She came striding through the door, carelessly throwing her coat to Beech, who deftly caught it, and demanding a Bourbon Manhattan.

'First of all, young lady,' I said with some asperity, 'don't throw your coat to Beech like that. And secondly, what on earth is the outlandish drink you asked for?'

'Beech doesn't mind, do you Beech? It's a game we play. He caught it, so I owe him a quid. If he'd missed, he'd owe me one. What's the tally so far, Beech?'

'You now owe me twenty-one pounds, miss.'

'See, Gran? I'll settle up at Christmas, just as I always do. And a Bourbon Manhattan is the latest drink in all the clubs. Do you know what it is, Beech?'

'Yes, miss. American whisky and Vermouth.'

'Don't forget the ice and a twist of lemon,' said Susan.

'No, miss,' Beech smiled.

It seemed to me there was another game going on. He left the room and I turned my attention to Susan.

'This is your cousin Betty. My dear,' I smiled at Betty, 'this is my granddaughter, Susan.'

'How do you do?' Betty asked politely. She was looking shocked, a reaction very common in those who meet Susan for the first time.

My granddaughter was, without doubt, a beauty. Her full, expressive mouth was often smiling but became a thin line when she was angry. Her dark blue, restless eyes often seemed focused on far horizons.

'How do,' said Susan. She took out a packet of cigarettes and offered one. 'Care for a gasper?'

'Susan,' I said loudly. 'You will not light one of those filthy things in here. You know my rules. The smoking room is the place. Or the snooker room after dinner, if you must. Although it is no place for a lady.'

Susan shrugged. 'Dear Gran,' she smiled at me, 'loves the sinner, hates the sin.' She put them away again. 'So what brings you to town, Betty?'

Betty replied. 'Business. I work for your father.'

The penny dropped with Susan and she looked across the room at Myfanwy. 'Betty! The wonder woman who does the books at the wireless factory. And you must be

Myfanwy. What a gorgeous little girl.' Susan crossed the
room and gave the girl a swift hug and a kiss. Myfanwy
was looking at Susan in awe. 'Do you know that in my
room I've got a dolls' house and a load of dolls? Did Louise
tell you? She used to play with them when she was younger.
What do you say we go and have a look after dinner?'

'Oh! Yes, please. That would be lovely.' Myfanwy was
looking at Susan with complete adoration. Susan had a
knack with people. She could put them at ease and have
them eating out of her hand within minutes of meeting
her.

Turning to Betty she said, 'I had no idea you were
coming otherwise I'd have been here to greet you. Thank
you Beech,' she accepted the glass and took a sip. 'Perfect.
That's another quid but I'll catch you out one day, mark
my words.'

'Yes, miss. Cook said that if you don't go in now, my
Lady, she won't be responsible for dinner.'

'Thank you Beech.' I stood up and said to Susan,
'Betty's visit was unexpected but very welcome. We'll
tell you over dinner. And you can tell us where you've
been. To one of your radical political meetings I suppose?'

Like every girl her age, Susan had dutifully made her
debut in London. For a while she had devoted herself to
the social whirl of balls, dinners and entertainments so
popular with her set, but the attraction had soon waned.
Over the last few months it was apparent from her conversations that she wanted more from life than gaiety and
endless tennis matches. Her interest in politics had grown.
David and John enjoyed debating with her – Susan's
insight and integrity impressed them no end. For all her
attempts to shock us with her behaviour, Susan was a
very decent, compassionate young woman.

'Oh, Gran,' Susan tucked her arm through mine and
we led the way into dinner, 'of course that's where I've
been. And jolly good fun it was too. Some thugs at the
back threw vegetables at us and we threw them back.'

I tried to keep the alarm from my voice but another memory was stirring, of a riot at a political rally Evan and I had attended thirty years earlier. We too, had been politically motivated, had wanted to make a difference. It was history repeating itself.

The three course dinner, miraculously saved by cook, was followed by cheese and biscuits. As Sion was the only man present we didn't leave him with his cigar and port. The situation at the factory was too pressing.

'It seems to me,' said Susan, 'that we need to stop this man Carruthers before he robs Dad blind.'

'We're all agreed there, my girl,' I said. 'But what's the best course of action?'

'Thankfully,' said Sion, 'Madelaine and I have power of attorney over David's affairs. It's a precaution we took some time ago. His affairs are too complex to be left alone should anything happen to him.'

'I was doing some calculations on the train,' Betty offered. 'I estimate there's at least ten thousand pounds worth of finished wirelesses waiting to be shipped. Add the stock for parts, and that's at least another three thousand pounds. It's an awful lot of money. He could steal it,' Betty continued. 'And I wouldn't put it past him.'

'My very cynical son agrees with you.' I smiled at Sion, who winked back. Betty was proving even cleverer than I had first thought.

'What's the fastest way to get there?' I asked. 'Train?'

Susan was so fanatical about flying we all adored teasing her. Smiling sweetly at me, she rolled her eyes and didn't bother reprimanding me. 'If we drive to the Hill, at about seven ack emma, we can be in Cardiff by around nine, nine-thirty.'

'Ack emma,' I reproached her. 'Where do you learn such nonsense? If you mean seven a.m. please say so.'

Susan grinned at me and I couldn't help a small twitch at the corners of my mouth. She had such a big heart and

was so full of mischief I feared for her future. God help
the man who married her.

'In that case,' I said, rising from the table, 'I, for one,
need an early night.'

'You aren't coming, are you, Mam?' Sion asked. 'You
mustn't overdo things.'

'Nonsense, Uncle Sion,' Susan replied, 'of course she's
coming. You wouldn't miss it for the world, would you,
Gran?'

I smiled at my granddaughter. In many respects she
knew me better than the rest of the family put together.
Perhaps because we were so alike. 'Naturally I'm going
with you. But I need my rest. Sion, please make the
necessary arrangements for cars in the morning and taxis
when we get to Cardiff. Betty, may I suggest Myfanwy
stay here with Louise?'

Betty looked a little worried. 'If you're sure it's no
trouble.'

'Of course it's no trouble,' said Susan. 'Myfanwy, why
not come and see my dolls? You'll be able to play with
them tomorrow if you like.'

Susan took both girls with her while Betty and I
exchanged smiles.

'I will see you at six-thirty sharp for breakfast.'

'Mam,' said Sion, 'are you sure you want to come? So
early?'

'Sion, I've told you, I wouldn't miss it for the world.
I may be an old woman but I'll stop kicking when I'm
in my wooden overcoat.' On that note I went to my room.
Before retiring, I checked an entry in my *Who's Who*, a
very useful publication to have. On the way I passed
Susan and the two girls exclaiming over her dolls' house.
I smiled. Susan had a wonderful way with children.
However, she had made it very clear that she would never
be satisfied with several babies and a perfect home. I just
wished she wouldn't be so involved in politics. She was
so passionate about issues. Why couldn't she support the

Liberals or the Conservatives? Not the fools she was mixed up with. The Socialist Workers Party *my foot*!

I was awoken all too soon with a cup of tea. I concluded my toilet and went downstairs. I found Betty in the dining room, uncertainty written in the way she was standing.

'Betty, my dear, because of the early start breakfast is under those covers.' I gestured at the tureens on the sideboard. 'I will content myself with a piece of toast and another cup of tea but the others will have a hearty meal. Flying always makes them hungry.'

'Flying? What on earth do you mean?'

I looked at Betty in surprise. 'Why, we're flying to Wales.'

The look on her face was priceless.

'You mean you didn't know?'

Shaking her head, she said, 'I didn't understand what you were talking about so thought it wisest to say nothing. I've never flown before.'

I smiled encouragingly. 'You'll love it, I promise you. Now, why don't you take a look under the covers and choose something to eat?'

The others joined us a few minutes later. Sion and Susan spent breakfast discussing the flight and I could see that Betty was even more startled to discover that Susan was a pilot as well. I think the poor lamb was in something of a shock when we finally left the house to drive to Biggin Hill.

At the airfield we found that Sion had warned Peter Cazorla and he in turn had passed a message to Mr O'Donnell. The Griffin was ready for departure. I liked Mike O'Donnell very much. Not only was he a man of proven courage but I knew him to be kind and courteous – if a bit of a rogue with the ladies. He fussed over me, making sure I was comfortably seated while we listened to Sion and Susan arguing as to who was doing the flying. Seeing that he wasn't going to win, Sion gave in with good grace and let Susan pilot us.

Throughout, Betty kept quiet and if she was nervous she didn't show it. 'Are you all right, my dear?'

'Yes, thank you, Aunt Meg. This is all too exciting for words.'

'You sit here, miss,' said O'Donnell. 'I'll point out some of the sights as we fly over, if you like.'

'Thank you,' said Betty. 'Oh! We're moving.'

A short while later we were in the air. Dawn had brought with it a clear and cloudless day. One could see for miles and while O'Donnell pointed out places of interest to Betty I couldn't help thinking that the world was a very beautiful place. There was so much to see and do. I had seen so much and done so much I should have been satisfied. But I wasn't. Even now I felt a stirring in my blood.

'Are you enjoying yourself?' I asked Betty.

'This is wonderful. I never knew it would be like this.'

Madelaine helped Kirsty to distribute mugs of coffee from a Thermos and we munched on biscuits as we passed over Swindon. Soon we could see the Bristol Channel and the coast of Wales. It was a wonderful sight and we stared avidly, drinking in the scene. Landing at Cardiff, we touched down as lightly as a feather. I congratulated Susan on her flying prowess. Glancing at my watch I saw that it was still a few minutes shy of nine o'clock.

Sion had sent a telegram to the airport manager and two taxis were waiting for us. Soon we were on our way to Taff's Well. As we neared the factory Betty was becoming more and more agitated.

'Don't worry,' Sion assured her, 'if Carruthers is there, we'll soon have him out of the place.'

Betty nodded, a heavy frown on her pretty face. The more I saw, the more I liked her. Her husband, Dafydd, might have been a Griffiths, but he was a nincompoop nevertheless.

We drew up outside the factory. It looked peaceful enough. The cars were on hire for the day and they parked out the front while we went to the door marked enquiries. Much to our surprise the door was unlocked and we entered.

'I wonder who's here?' Susan whispered.

'It can only be Mr Carruthers,' said Betty. 'He and I were the only ones to have keys. He took mine from me when he dismissed me.'

The offices were empty.

'He must be in the factory,' said Betty. 'It's this way.'

We followed her through a door marked 'Authorised Personnel Only' and into a large works area. The large doors at the rear of the factory were standing wide open.

Sion and Mr O'Donnell were hurrying towards the open doors. I followed at a more sedate pace. A large removal truck was parked outside. Men were carrying boxes into the back of the truck. It was almost full. When I arrived an altercation was taking place between Sion and a thick-set man I guessed was Carruthers.

'You will not remove a single wireless from this factory. You men,' Sion pointed at them, 'put those back and empty the lorry. Now!'

The three men stood indecisively, each with a box in his hands, looking at Carruthers for guidance.

'I'm the Managing Director of this company,' Carruthers said in a loud and overbearing voice. 'Now get out of my factory before I call the police. As for you,' he pointed at Betty, 'I'll have the law on you. You're a thief. I can prove you've been fiddling the books.'

Betty gasped. 'That . . . that's a lie. You're the thief. I've proven it.'

Carruthers looked at us craftily. 'So you say, but I can prove otherwise. Now are you going?'

Sion replied, 'The only one leaving is you, Carruthers. But unlike the way you treated Mrs Griffiths we'll give you the courtesy of clearing your desk. You've got ten minutes.'

'On what authority?'

'On my brother's. I'm Sion Griffiths.'

'I am not leaving.' Carruthers stood very close to Sion his face only inches away from my son's. Sion didn't bat an eyelid.

'Get out of here before I throw you out,' said Sion.

Carruthers looked strong although not very fit. He was an inch or two shorter than Sion. 'You aren't man enough,' Carruthers said with barely suppressed fury.

One moment Carruthers was menacing Sion and the next he was on his back, winded. Sion was standing with his hands on his hips looking down at the odious fellow.

Carruthers climbed warily to his feet. Sion took Carruthers by the lapels of his coat, turned round and knelt down and Carruthers went flying over Sion's shoulder and hit the floor with a loud thump. This time the man had the good sense not to try and get up.

When he got his breath back, Carruthers shouted to one of his sidekicks, 'Send for the police. They'll throw this lot out.'

'Mam,' Sion looked at me, 'can you telephone the local Sheriff?'

'Yes, of course. Betty, please show me the way to the nearest telephone.'

Glancing back I saw Carruthers climb awkwardly to his feet. He was no longer looking quite so bombastic.

I produced my little black book, as my children jokingly called it, and was soon connected to the county Sheriff. As the chief administrative officer for the county, responsible for the mandates of the court, he wielded a good deal of influence as well as power. From 'Who's Who' the evening before I knew his name was Colonel Stephen S. Montague, late of the Household Guards, who now farmed a huge area in the Vale of Glamorgan. He had been highly decorated in the Great War.

'Baroness Guildford?'

'Yes, Colonel. I have need of a little assistance.'

I briefly explained the problem and he promised to

get onto it right away. Hanging up the telephone receiver I saw Betty looking at me agog. I smiled. 'It is the perk of rank, my dear. It took me a long time to get used to it.'

Betty tentatively returned my smile. 'I bet there's nobody you can't speak to in the whole country. You didn't believe him, Aunt Meg, did you?"

'Not for a moment. And neither did the others. So don't give Carruthers another thought.'

Relief flooded over her face and she smiled more brightly this time. 'Thank you for that. It means a lot to me.'

I found the others in Carruthers' office. What a difference from Betty's utilitarian work space! It was large, well appointed, with a Chesterfield, matching furniture and a bar, of all things.

'I've spoken to the Sheriff. He's getting the police.'

Now that he was faced with the reality of the situation, Carruthers wasn't so cocksure. He had seated himself behind his desk and was fidgeting with the pens and inkwell set.

Betty came in carrying a tray and Madelaine helped her serve tea. They didn't offer one to Carruthers.

'I suggest,' said Sion, 'that you start getting your personal belongings together.'

Carruthers scowled at him malevolently. 'We'll see, shall we? Wait until the police get here. I know the local inspector. We play golf together. He'll soon settle your hash for you. And yours,' he glared at Betty.

Betty quailed but her hand was steady enough as she poured the tea. The woman had backbone, of that there was no doubt.

'Two cars have just pulled up outside,' said Mr O'Donnell. 'I'll go and welcome them.'

A few seconds later he showed our visitors in, a smile plastered on his face. 'Lady Megan, may I introduce the Sheriff? Sir, The Baroness of Guildford.' Montague took

my hand and bowed formally. He then introduced me to
the Assistant Chief Constable, whose name I didn't quite
catch, with apologies that the Chief Constable was unable
to be there due to a prior commitment.

They both turned questioning eyes on Carruthers who
was looking decidedly pale.

'I have here,' said Sion, 'a copy of my power of attorney
for you to inspect. Also this telegram which I received
from my brother late last night. In it you can see that he
wishes Mr Carruthers to be suspended on full pay, pending
an investigation. The situation has changed, however. This
morning we caught Mr Carruthers filling up a removal
lorry with wirelesses.'

'I told you they're for an order we received,' Carruthers
butted in.

'Show us the paperwork,' Sion said.

'I'll do no such thing.'

'If you cannot produce the paperwork to prove the
shipment then I will assume you're stealing the items in
question,' said the ACC.

In a foul temper Carruthers pulled open a drawer and
threw a sheet of paper onto the desk. 'Read that.'

The Assistant Chief Constable glanced over it and
handed it to Sion, 'It appears in order.'

Betty marched across the room and took the sheet.
'This is nonsense,' she announced. 'There is no such
company.'

'Meddling busybody!' Carruthers shot back. 'Quite
clearly, it's an order for one thousand wireless sets to be
delivered as soon as possible to Basingstoke.'

Betty stood her ground. 'There is no such company.
We shipped sets to this address six months ago and never
received payment. I telephoned the number on the top.
It doesn't exist.'

'Of course it does,' said Carruthers, although not with
such bluster this time.

'Try the number, Sion,' suggested Betty. 'You will find

there is no sound on the line. She was white-faced, nervous, but sticking to her guns.

Lifting the receiver Sion dialled. He hung up and tried again. 'Nothing.'

We all looked at Carruthers. Now he was the one who was looking scared. 'There must be a simple explanation.' He was licking his lips, his nervousness plain to all. None of us believed him.

'What would you like me to do, sir?' The Assistant Chief Constable asked Sion.

Sion shrugged. 'Can you arrest him?'

'I can. Will you press charges?'

'Definitely,' Sion replied.

The ACC said, 'In that case, you're under arrest. I'll get one of my men.' He stood at the window and signalled to an officer sitting in the car.

'You won't make it stick,' said Carruthers. Picking up a briefcase, he began to place items into it.

'Wait a second,' said Betty. 'I'm . . . I'm sorry, Aunt Meg, but shouldn't we see what he's got in the case? Papers or anything?'

I was looking at Carruthers face and I caught a look of fear on it before he began to bluster again. The policeman wordlessly took the briefcase and emptied its contents. Betty picked up a chequebook.

Flicking the pages she said, 'This is the company's.'

'I . . . I didn't know it was there,' Carruthers said quickly. He cast a malevolent look at Betty who returned his stare with equal dislike.

'Somehow,' said Sion, 'I don't believe you.'

Betty still wasn't finished. 'The car belongs to the company. Where are the keys?'

'You're coming with us, so hand over the keys,' said the ACC.

Carruthers ungraciously threw them onto the desk. 'I'll get you,' he said venomously but who his remark was directed at I couldn't tell. It seemed to be to the room in general.

The police officer took him away and I turned to Colonel Montague. 'I cannot thank you enough. You've been a great help.'

'My pleasure, my Lady. Only too glad to be of service.'

Sion shook his hand. 'Now that he's gone, may I offer you a drink from Carruthers' rather well-stocked bar in the corner?'

Montague and the ACC declined. We exchanged more pleasantries and they bade us farewell.

'Tell me, Sion,' I asked, 'how on earth did you throw Carruthers like that?'

'Jujitsu. It's a Japanese form of self-defence when you use your opponents weight and strength against him. I've been doing a bit of practice, but that's the first time I've used it in anger.'

'You must show me, Uncle Sion,' said Susan. 'I can see it coming in useful, fighting off suitors who won't take no for an answer.'

'What happens to the workers now?' Betty asked, ever the practical one.

'The factory opens as usual,' said Sion.

'But who'll run it?' Betty asked. Unfortunately she was taking a sip of tea when Sion replied.

'According to David's second telegram, you will.'

She nearly choked, poor thing.

29

NATURALLY IT WASN'T as simple as that. I realised Betty would need a good deal of support if she was to manage the factory and sort out her home life. I felt responsible and took it upon myself to help. I had spent years being a member of, or chairing, one committee or another, usually fund raising for charities. When John retired, I quit most of them, although one or two that were dear to me I kept on. With John away, apart from my busy social life, I had nothing onerous to do. He and David would not be back for at least another fortnight, possibly longer.

After Sion's dramatic announcement Betty was, I could see, fearful and yet determined to make a go of it. What I particularly liked was her lack of false modesty.

I said, 'Betty needs to find somewhere to live and she can't do that if she's busy running this place. We need to have a full audit of the company if we are to get to the bottom of the problem that Carruthers has created, and we need to counter any accusations that he might make against Betty.'

Betty looked crestfallen. 'In all the excitement I'd forgotten about Dafydd and Llanbeddas. I was thinking about going back home.'

'Is that what you want?' I asked.

'I ought to give it another try. It's the least I can do. I cannot give up fifteen years of marriage just like that.'

I nodded. It was a sentiment I wholeheartedly approved of, though I had my doubts. Betty was expanding her horizons daily, taking on new challenges. Dafydd would be left behind, unless he was prepared to get out of the mine and leave Llanbeddas. But that wasn't something I could tell Betty. She needed to learn it for herself.

'What about Myfanwy?' Betty asked.

'She can stay with me for as long as you wish,' I replied. 'But she needs her own friends. She needs her mother, as well. But a few days alone with Dafydd might help you.'

'Sion,' said Betty, 'we need to change the locks. It's possible that Carruthers has another set of keys. And we need to unload the lorry. And I need to sort out the situation with sales and deliveries.' As the enormity of what lay ahead finally dawned on her, I could see doubt in her face.

'You'll be fine,' I encouraged her. 'And remember, your salary will be the same as Carruthers.'

Betty looked at me in disbelief. 'So much?' She shook her head. 'What will Dafydd say?'

'Don't tell him,' suggested Sion.

Betty shook her head. 'There'll be no hiding the facts from Dafydd now.' She sat up straight. 'I cannot believe that I will be the managing director even if it is only for a short time. But if I am earning that much money I want to spend it.'

I smiled. That was a reaction I approved of. 'Why,' I asked puzzled, 'do you say "only for a short time"?'

'Well, until David gets back and he can find the right man for the job.'

I shook my head. 'If David thinks you're the right "man" for the job you'll keep it.'

That afternoon, Madelaine and I left the others to get on with things at the factory. I wanted to visit David Morgan's, in Cardiff, the Harrods of Wales.

Madelaine and Betty were of a similar size. I was looking to buy a business suit suitable for a woman in her new position. We returned to Taff's Well laden with parcels.

We found Betty in her office. The desk was strewn with sheets of paper, old letters and buff coloured files. 'These files will take a lot of sorting,' she said. 'How was the shopping?'

'Oh, fine,' I replied. Stacking the boxes and bags on a chair I announced, 'These are for you.'

'For me?' She was pleased, though surprised. 'What are they?'

'Open them and see,' said Kirsty.

Dressed in a dark blue jacket and matching skirt, white blouse and scarf, Betty exclaimed, 'It's beautiful! Oh, I know, the ladies. There's a proper mirror in there.'

'You didn't mind?' I asked tentatively as we followed her.

'Mind? Why should I mind?' Betty was genuinely puzzled.

'My presumptuousness in buying you clothes. Some women would take offence.'

'I'm not one of them, Aunt Megan, believe me.' Standing in front of the mirror she exclaimed, '*Daioni*,' she lapsed into Welsh but quickly changed. 'Goodness, look at me!'

'You look like a managing director,' Madelaine said.

A short while later, with the locks changed, we left to return to the airfield. Mr O'Donnell had volunteered to stay behind to look after the place until a night guard could be hired. Sion wasn't going to take any chances and I couldn't say that I blamed him.

The flight back was uneventful. Betty was very quiet the whole way until we were lining up to land. 'Everything is different now, isn't it?' She finally commented. 'I can never go back.'

'You can,' I replied, 'but you will be discontented for the rest of your life.'

'It's like this plane journey. This morning I was as excited as a child at Christmas. This afternoon I've sat here thinking about the factory with hardly a glance outside.'

I had noticed her distraction. 'It's natural, my dear. If you let yourself, you grow into these things. That has been my experience.'

'But Dafydd won't let himself grow,' she spoke softly.

I said nothing. There was nothing to say.

We left Sion and Kirsty at Biggin Hill and the four of us travelled up to town. Susan drove with Betty alongside her. She explained how the gears worked and how to use the foot brake and how to steer. Along with the job she had also inherited Carruthers' car. We arrived home in time for dinner and a huge welcome from Myfanwy and Louise. They had, it seemed, spent the day baking with Cook.

On Sunday morning I sat with Betty in the drawing room. She had been making a list of things she needed to do. I saw that it ran into pages.

'I don't think I'm capable of doing all this,' she said to me.

I had been reading the *Sunday Times*, delighted to see that I knew nobody in the obituaries section. I put the paper down and looked over my reading glasses at her. She had the good grace to look uncomfortable.

'Capable? Of course you are, which is precisely what you wanted me to tell you. Susan is going to Wales with you for a week or two while you find your feet. Sion can manage without Mr O'Donnell for a few days and he has agreed to stay to help as well. A local hotel has been booked for all of you. I know it is a new experience, my dear, but money is not an issue. All your expenses will be paid by the company. You are to find a maid who can also help to look after Myfanwy. Tomorrow morning I will contact my solicitors here in London to give me the name of a reputable firm in Cardiff. It will be their task to find a house for you.'

'A house? Where?'

'I've no idea. I've told them how much we are prepared to pay, so we will have to see what they come up with.'

Betty frowned at me. 'In rent, you mean?'

'My dear, you cannot rent a suitable house. No, you must purchase one. I thought five hundred would be enough. Of course, if . . .' I paused. 'What on earth's the matter?'

Betty's mouth was agape. 'Buy a house? That's ludicrous! Who on earth buys a house?'

'Anyone with any sense,' I replied dryly. 'It makes a good place to invest your nest egg in the post office. We aren't talking about a palace. A nice house somewhere near Taff's Well, in a little village, perhaps. Don't worry about the balance,' I added. 'I shall be paying it.'

'What? But you can't do that. I'm already indebted to you for so much.'

'Betty, it's quite the reverse. We owe you a good deal. Or at least, David does. If it makes you feel any better have it as a loan and you can pay me back over the next few years. Interest free, of course.'

'I just don't know what to say. How to thank you. What about hiring a maid? I wouldn't know a good one from a bad one.'

'You can leave that to me. I've a good deal of experience in that direction. Now, what do we do about Myfanwy?'

'In what sense?' Betty asked.

'About her schooling. I'm a great believer in education. And that applies to girls as well as boys. It's important to instil the idea of further education into them from an early age. That way they'll get to university without much effort.'

'University? Myfanwy?' There was utter shock in her voice.

'Why? Don't you think she's bright enough?'

'Yes, yes I do. Oh, it's too much to take in. Just too much,' and suddenly she was weeping softly.

I comforted her and she soon dried her eyes.

'Sorry. That was very silly of me.'

'Such a lot has happened in a remarkably short space of time. But once you get to Taff's Well you'll be so busy you'll hardly have time to think. I'm also coming with you – until John gets back.'

'But, Aunt Meg, are you sure?'

'Of course. I'm thoroughly enjoying myself. While you sort out the factory I'll look at houses. Don't worry, I won't make a decision for you but find five or six I think are suitable and you can choose. I will also interview for a maid.'

That afternoon Susan drove back to Wales with Betty while Myfanwy stayed with me for another day. She was a charming child. Confused by what was happening to her but also taking it in her stride. We followed by train and departed at a civilised hour. We spent part of the journey doing word and number puzzles. She struggled a little with her English while helping me to remember my Welsh. Anything involving numbers she could do as well as me. In actual fact, better than me!

In the early evening we arrived at Cardiff to be met by Susan. She took us to a small country hotel near Taff's Well where I quickly settled in. I had a living room as well as a bathroom attached to a comfortable bedroom. I announced that I would be staying put for a day or two to regain my strength. I'd done far too much running around.

And stay put I did. But there was nothing to prevent a firm of Cardiff solicitors from coming to see me. A scruffy assistant with pimples brought a dozen or so particulars on houses of which I thought one, possibly two, were suitable. I sent him away again with clear instructions as to what I was looking for. The following day he was back with another four possibilities.

I had the hotel supply me with a local map and I checked each location. Caerphilly, Church Village, Pentyrch, Efail Isaf, Creigiau and Whitchurch. All close enough to the factory and at the right price. Church Village even had a primary school although Myfanwy only had half a year to go before she went to senior school. When she did, according to the wife of the hotelier, Whitchurch School for Girls was the place to go. With that in mind I had Susan drive me to Whitchurch. As soon as I saw the house I knew it was all wrong. I didn't bother making an appointment to see the inside.

At the end of the day I'd seen four houses I thought suitable. One I particularly liked. It was the end of three in the pretty village of Efail Isaf. There were green fields as far as the eye could see, the house had a sensible garden and a good sized orchard. The factory was about three miles away over a hill and easily accessible by car. The village itself, though small, was joined to the main road to Pontypridd, seven miles away.

When Betty arrived at the hotel later that evening she was exhausted, as were Madelaine and Mr O'Donnell.

'Woman's a right slave-driver,' he said, when we met in the lounge for a pre-dinner drink. I had a small sherry while he opted for a well-deserved whisky.

'I'm no such thing.' Betty smiled at him. There was genuine warmth in the look she gave him, 'But I do thank you for all your help. I'll be sorry to see you go.'

'You don't need me. I've spoken to your management team and they seem a pretty decent bunch.'

'Were there any problems?' I asked. 'About having a woman in charge?'

'When I asked if any of them would like to take on the responsibility of sorting out Carruthers' mess they quickly declined. The sales manager reckons it's a poisoned chalice. They appear to be giving Betty their grudging support which is about all she can ask for right now. After all,' he raised his eyebrows and looked at her, 'you still have to prove yourself.'

Nodding fiercely, she said, 'I intend to. But I also need to get my life sorted out. I don't want to stay here a moment longer than necessary. Driving lessons are going well, aren't they, Susan?'

Susan said, 'You're a natural.'

I showed Betty the houses I'd found and described the villages they were in.

'Which do *you* prefer?' she asked me shrewdly.

'The one in Efail Isaf.'

'Then why don't we drive out that way tomorrow and take a look? Kill two birds with one stone, so to speak.'

The following morning we sat in Carruthers' car, a Wolseley 9-hp saloon. It was white with a black trim. I was informed that it had a top speed of 59mph. Susan threw in a lot of other technicalities that went straight over my head. I sat in the back while Betty sat behind the steering wheel. Susan began issuing instructions.

We finally left the hotel with a jerk and a clang, Susan grabbing the wheel to steer us onto the road. After her initial nerves, Betty appeared to settle down and we went along smoothly enough. In ten minutes we were over the hill and approaching Efail Isaf. The first building we came to was the Tabernacle Chapel. We stopped at a junction before turning left, with much grinding of gears. On our right were terraced houses and then we stopped at a further junction with a pub named the Carpenters' Arms on our left. We turned down the hill, passing high hedgerows, until we came to another row of houses and I indicated the one for sale.

The house was named 'Anghorfa', and the street name was Heol-y-Ffynnon. 'It looks very nice,' pronounced Betty.

I opened the car door. 'We had better take a look,' I began alighting from the car.

'We can't do that,' said Betty aghast. 'Surely we need an appointment?'

'Yes, manners suggests that we should,' I replied. 'But there's no harm in knocking on the door and asking when it would be suitable for us to call.'

The front garden was a tiny plot, well stocked with flowers. Five paces took me from the gate to the front door. I rang the bell. It was answered by a middle-aged woman in a pinafore.

'*Bore da*,' I greeted her. When I explained in Welsh why we were there, she was most welcoming and invited us in.

The house consisted of four rooms downstairs with a kitchenette added on the back. Upstairs were three bedrooms and a bathroom. I could see that Betty was enchanted with the place.

Outside were a shed and a coal house. The rear garden was mainly planted with vegetables and at the bottom stood a greenhouse and other sheds. The orchard held a mixture of eating and cooking apples as well as three pear trees. It really was a very pretty place. Standing in the orchard we heard the sound of a train whistle.

'The train goes to Cardiff as well as Pontypridd,' said the lady of the house. 'The station is half a mile along the track.'

'Well, my dear,' I looked at Betty, 'what do you think?'

'It's lovely. But can I afford it?'

'Of course you can,' I replied. 'I understand the price is five hundred and fifty pounds?'

The woman nodded.

'Here is my card.' I handed her one of my calling cards. 'The name of the firm of solicitors acting for my niece is written on the back. Kindly inform your solicitor that we have a deal and we will pay the full asking price. Does that suit you?'

Looking at my card she read my name. 'This is a trick,' she said. 'Lady Megan, Baroness of Guildford indeed. You should be ashamed of yourself. I don't care what prank you're playing but you can leave my house immediately.'

Our reactions were so different it was comical. Susan burst out laughing, I spluttered indignantly and Betty became angry.

The householder looked perplexed.

'Just tell your solicitor to contact my solicitor, my dear.

But I am not the purchaser. My niece, Mrs Griffiths is.'
On that note we departed.

Three days later the purchase was confirmed and an
entry date was set for six weeks hence. On the same day
Dafydd came to the factory.

I was in Betty's office, to say my goodbyes. David and
John had sent a telegram. They had crossed North America
by train and were now on a liner from New York. It would
be arriving in Southampton in three days and I wanted
to be in London to meet John. I was missing the old boy.
A firm of auditors were also arriving later that day, recommended by the bank, and I thought it best if I wasn't
around to get underfoot. When the question of a maid
came up, Betty demurred. She said she'd wait until she'd
moved in before making any decisions. I suggested that
she might find a local girl or woman to do for her, as
that would save having somebody living in.

We were wording an advertisement for the local shop
window when we heard a loud yelling from the reception area and the door was flung open. Dafydd stood in
the doorway, in a towering rage. He had obviously been
drinking.

'So this is where you are, you bitch. Carruthers told
me I'd find you here.'

'Dafydd! Sit down, please. Let's talk about it.'

'There's nothing to talk about. I want you home where
you belong. Where any wife should be. You can forget
all this nonsense about running a factory. They're only
using you. The whole rotten family, especially that swine
David Griffiths.'

I sat up straight, ready to do battle on behalf of my
son but Betty gestured to me with her hand.

'Dafydd, the only thing the family has done is give
me a wonderful opportunity.'

'Me! Me! Me! You selfish cow. What about us? What
about "honour and obey until death do us part"? You took
those vows, Betty.'

'I did,' said Betty, white spots of anger showing in her cheeks, 'but they don't mean I have to give up the chance to better my life or Myfanwy's. And you could be a part of it too, if you weren't so pig-headed.' Standing up she made soothing gestures to him. 'Dafydd, *cariad*, let's not fight. Come and be a family again. Myfanwy wants that very much.'

'She might, but what about you?' His speech was slurred and there was a terrible tension in the man. He stepped away from the door and I could see Susan in the corridor. She suddenly disappeared.

'Where will you live, eh? Tell me that?'

'I'm getting a house nearby. You can live there with us. If you want to stay in the mines then there's a colliery nearby. The Cwm. At Beddau.'

'Beddau? I'm a Llanbeddas man, through and through. I was born there and I'll die there. As will you. You're coming back with me.'

Betty had stepped around her desk to try and placate him. Dafydd suddenly stepped forward and grabbed her hand. Pulling her roughly to him he slapped her tired face and raised his hand to hit her again. Betty screamed while I sat there, too stunned to move. Susan came through the door carrying something in her hand. As Dafydd's fist came down, Betty pulled away and he caught her on the back of her head. Betty fell to her knees and Dafydd drew back his foot to kick her. Susan rushed over and hit Dafydd across the head with a length of wood. Unfortunately she didn't hit him hard enough.

Still holding onto Betty he turned his rage on Susan and lashed out at her with his fist. Susan ducked. He missed and she kicked him on the shin. By now I had recovered my wits and was searching frantically for a weapon. Carruthers had been a smoker. His ashtray still lay on the desk. It was made of cut glass, solid and heavy. Picking it up I stepped over to Dafydd, who had his back to me, and brought it down with a satisfying clunk onto the top of his head. He dropped to the floor while I stood looking at my handiwork, feeling shocked, though not a little proud.

Betty pulled herself awkwardly to her feet, a hand on the back of her head.

'Are you all right?' I asked.

She nodded, tears welling up in her eyes. 'And you?'

'I thought I was,' I said, sitting down suddenly, 'but I'm not so sure.'

'I'll get you some water,' said Betty.

'I'll get it,' Susan went to the door, 'you sit down.'

Betty shook her head sadly. 'I'd better get a doctor to him. Make sure he's all right.'

'What about the police?' I asked.

Betty shrugged. 'A fight between husband and wife? They'll say it's none of their business. And if they did come it will only cause a stir, especially if your name is mentioned.'

The thought had also occurred to me. 'The last thing I want is to see my name in newsprint for assault. The Baron would be shocked. Is Dafydd still breathing?'

Betty knelt by her husband and checked his pulse. 'Yes.' She felt his scalp. 'He's got a bump but there's no blood. Thanks, Aunt Meg.'

I grimaced. 'It was nothing.' I was still holding the ashtray and replaced it on the desk. I felt short of breath and I could feel my heart pounding. Adventure was one thing, this was something else entirely. Susan returned with a glass of water and a cup of tea, both of which I accepted gratefully.

'What will we do with him?' she asked.

'Help me to put him on the couch,' said Betty. 'He's much the worse for drink and will probably sleep for a while. It's the best thing for him.' It wasn't easy lifting a heavy miner but between them they got Dafydd to the chesterfield and laid him out on it. He began snoring loudly.

'I think,' I said, 'I had better stay a while longer. One more day won't matter. We need to prevent Dafydd attacking you again. Perhaps a bodyguard.'

'That's ludicrous,' Betty protested. 'He'll be as right as nine pence when he's slept off the drink. I know him well enough.'

'But there could easily be another time,' I argued. 'His rage was . . . was terrifying.' I had been about to say murderous. I didn't want to frighten Betty but I had seen it in his eyes. Dafydd had intended doing her serious harm and any regret afterwards, once he'd sobered up, would have come too late. My mind was made up and I telephoned Sion. I explained the situation and asked if we could borrow Mr O'Donnell for a few more days. Sion agreed at once. My next call was to the solicitors in Cardiff.

I am, by God, no snob, but a title has its uses. When I need to use my name and connections I do so with utter ruthlessness. This was one of those times. I had the firm's senior partner called from a meeting, agreed what was needed, and thanked him. He promised he would have the papers with us within the hour.

Betty sat at her desk, still shaken, an untouched cup of tea at her elbow. 'What am I to do, Aunt Meg?' Tears formed and rolled down her cheeks. 'I didn't want this. I never wanted this.'

'I know, my dear. But the choice is clear. You can go back or you can go forward.'

Taking a handkerchief from a pocket she blew her nose and replied. 'Go back! Never! Not after this.' She looked around the office. 'I love it. The cut and the thrust.' She spoke more fiercely, 'And I want to make a success of my life.'

'It's like a drug,' I said gently. 'Once you've tasted it you want more. David has ambition by the bucket load. As does Sion, though his ambition is secondary to his first love, flying. Dafydd, although a Griffiths, doesn't appear to have any. It's ironic that he married a woman who does.' I changed the subject. 'By this afternoon you will be in possession of what is called a court injunction, issued by a high court judge. Dafydd will, by law, have to leave you in peace. If he doesn't he can be arrested and jailed. You would only have to show the papers to a police officer for him to remove Dafydd immediately.'

'You can do that?' she asked in awe.

'Not me, my dear. The solicitor suggested it. Apparently he can arrange it. Your position has its privileges but it also has responsibilities. There are far too many people working here who will lose their jobs if you don't get to the bottom of the fraud committed by Carruthers. It's imperative we find out how far the rot has spread. If the losses are too great, David may be forced to close this place.'

Betty said, 'I know. And the figures are horrendous. I just don't know how Carruthers kept it all hidden so well. He was juggling money back and forth between three different banks as far as I can see. And the inventory bears no relation to the stock sheets. I've got the two storemen checking everything. Of the completed wirelesses, we have less than twenty percent of the figure in the books. It's a mess.' Betty managed a smile. 'I might not have this job very long.'

I nodded grimly. 'If that happens, I am sure David will be able to find something else for you.'

'I don't want anything else. I want this,' she spoke fiercely.

30

THE AUDITORS ARRIVED a few hours later and swept into the place as if they owned it.

Dafydd eventually woke with a groan, sat upright and put his head in his hands. When he looked around him he saw four unsmiling faces. Closing his eyes he lay back and said nothing.

'What do you have to say for yourself?' I asked him.

He looked blearily at me. 'Mind your own business, you old cow.'

Mr O'Donnell kicked him on the sole of his shoe, hard. 'And you mind your manners when you speak to her ladyship.'

I didn't translate the colourful abuse Dafydd heaped on Mr O'Donnell. This time Betty told him to behave himself.

'You're coming home with me,' he said to her. 'And when you do I'll give you the hiding of your life. This is finished here, do you understand me?' Pointing a finger at me he added, 'And you can keep out of this as well, your Ladyship,' he spoke sneeringly. 'This is between a man and his wife. You've no right to interfere.'

'Dafydd,' I said sorrowfully, 'I'm just glad your parents aren't alive to see what a loathsome creature you've become. But as to not interfering I'm afraid you're too late.' I threw an envelope into his lap. 'This was delivered ten minutes ago.'

'What is it?' He didn't bother opening it.

'It's what is called an injunction. It warns you to stay

away from Betty. If you don't you'll be arrested and sent to prison.'

'You can't do that,' he said venomously.

'I can and I have.' I was sitting only a yard or two from him and I saw the hate in his eyes. He launched into a tirade of claptrap about the power of the rich and how they oppressed the poor. I didn't disabuse him of his ideas. I knew there would be no point.

Betty couldn't help arguing though. 'Grow up, Dafydd. You're talking rubbish. I'm about to buy a lovely house in a pleasant village and you could share it with me and Myfanwy. Instead you choose to work down the mine with your friends, enduring hardship and danger for what? Some perverted ideal? A life of poverty and a sick old age? You're stupid, Dafydd, just plain daft.'

'You've never understood,' he said bitterly. 'I can't let my friends down.' In a last, childish act of defiance, Dafydd ripped the injunction to shreds.

'You're a fool,' said Betty. 'If you break the terms of the injunction, Dafydd, make no mistake, I will have you arrested. Now kindly leave. I have a factory to run.'

I think it was that last sentence more than anything that finally got through to Dafydd. He stood up with a look of shock on his face.

'You haven't heard the last of this,' he said over his shoulder. I think he would have slammed the door if Mr O'Donnell hadn't caught it and followed Dafydd out.

Betty straightened her suit and her shoulders. 'If you should need me, I'll be with the auditors.' Nodding she left the room

Susan and I exchanged rueful smiles. 'I think our Betty is a lot tougher than she looks,' she ventured.

'Perhaps. Even so, I'm glad Mr O'Donnell will be around to look after her for a while.'

The following day I left Wales, travelling by train to Paddington, where I was met by Beech. I spent the next two days resting, planning a welcome home dinner for

John and wondering whether my interference in Betty's
life was for good or ill. I fervently prayed it was the
former.

It was almost eight o'clock when John finally arrived
home. We had a cocktail before dinner, and regaled each
other with our stories. The trade talks had been a great
success and business almost concluded when Sion's
telegram had arrived in Mexico City. David had cut short
their visit immediately. The quickest route back to Britain
was a three day journey by train to New York, then a
liner to Southampton. Being the Chairman of the shipping line, John had no difficulty in procuring suitable
staterooms. During the voyage they had rested from their
almost sleepless dash across America.

I smiled affectionately at him. He was still a handsome man. His hair was grey and thinning but he still
held himself straight. And if he was getting a little stout
around the middle, what of it? It was more to put my
arms around.

Over port I told him something about my adventures.
When he heard that I had knocked Dafydd out with a
glass ashtray he burst out laughing.

I was indignant. 'What's so funny?'

'My dear old thing, it's priceless. The Baroness of
Guildford laying someone low with a clout across the
head?' He laughed again. 'Wait until I tell them in the club.'

'John! You can't! It's undignified!'

'I disagree. It shows there's life in you yet, m'dear.'

Three days passed before David returned from Wales. He
looked tired.

'How bad is it?' I asked him once he had a cup of his
favourite Earl Grey tea in his hand.

He avoided answering. 'What gives this tea its distinctive oily texture and smell?'

'Bergamot. It's a kind of orange. The factory. How
serious is it?'

'Pretty bad. The auditors are almost done. It looks like a fraud amounting to over twenty thousand pounds.'

I paused with my cup near my lips. 'Can you survive it?'

'I'm almost sure we can. Thank God Betty is such a genius with figures. Even the auditors were impressed with her rapid grasp of the situation. I'll arrange for the bank to extend a temporary facility. She's convinced they can trade out of the problem, although it'll take a year at least.'

'What about Carruthers?' John asked.

David shrugged. 'We're proceeding with the prosecution. We'll try and recover as much of the money as we can. But I don't have much hope.'

'What a scoundrel,' I said with feeling. 'After all you had done for him.'

My son shrugged. 'To an extent I blame myself. I gave him too much leeway. The auditors are building a solid case against him. I'd better be going. Madelaine is expecting me for dinner and I've hardly had a moment with Richard since I got back. He's home for the midterm. I've brought him a baseball bat and glove from America. What he'll make of them I don't know.' With that he departed for Fairweather.

Things were relatively quiet on the home front for a while. Politically, especially internationally, the situation was dire. The Nazis were making frightening noises in Germany, Mussolini was strengthening his grip on Italy and Austria had recently become a dictatorship under the fascist, Engelbert Dollfuss.

Spain lurched from one crisis to another. There was armed fighting in Madrid and an assassination attempt made on Alejandro Lerroux, the Prime Minister. Catalonia, having declared itself an independent state, was ruthlessly suppressed when a warship carrying a battalion of the Spanish Foreign Legion from Morocco arrived. To my astonishment, despite all the unrest in that benighted land, people still travelled there for their holidays. Indeed dozens of British people were caught up in the troubles and some even lost their lives.

I followed events as best I could. I was aware that rural Spain suffered great poverty. Vast estates were rented to peasant farmers who subsisted on one or two crops, usually olives and grapes for wine. The harvests were not always good, but the rent still had to be paid.

Some areas, like Catalonia, were semi-industrialised. Farms nestled uneasily amidst small factories producing mainly textiles and leather goods for export all over Europe. The region was a hot-bed for the flourishing trade union movement which caused much of the area's problems.

Knowing of the country's unrest, I was taken aback by an invitation to visit the Boucher family in Cádiz, Andalusia. This was only fifty miles from the British crown colony of Gibraltar. I was tempted to accept. It seemed to me that a little sun before the winter would be very pleasant. Loath though we were to admit it, John and I were getting older. How many more opportunities would we have to travel abroad, especially with the worsening international situation?

John agreed we should go. One of the Buchanan Shipping Line's banana ships called in at Gibraltar for bunkering and we could travel on board her in great comfort. The invitation had been extended to the whole family but they were all too busy. All that is except for Susan, who agreed instantly to come with us.

We set sail on the first day of November. The ship sailed regularly between London and Equatorial Africa to fill up with a cargo of bananas. On the outward journey she occasionally carried items such as cars and lorries but often sailed in ballast. Apart from the crew's quarters and officers' cabins there were also six luxurious staterooms. These were in great demand, mainly from diplomats travelling to new posts in Africa. Each stateroom was

really a small suite, consisting of a sitting room, bathroom and two bedrooms. The best hotels could boast
nothing finer. As chairman of the line, John was given
the very best accommodation.

John, Susan and I stood at the taffrail, in the stern, and
watched a wet and blustery London slip away. We waved
merrily to David and Madelaine who had come to see us
off then strolled to the main saloon for a cup of tea. Leaving
King George V Dock at ten o'clock, just before high tide,
we had no need to bother with the lock and sailed serenely
into the main river. I stood at a window on the starboard
side and watched the docks passing by. It was an incred-
ibly busy place with ships moving up and down the river
almost constantly. There were innumerable barges, some
towing others in a long convoy, ferrying the provisions
needed to keep a great capital like London alive.

Whilst we enjoyed our tea a steward was unpacking
our cases. Indeed, he would be at our beck and call, day
or night, throughout the voyage. The richly-furnished
saloon stretched almost the width of the ship, with a
promenade deck surrounding it. A table stretched halfway
from the back of the room and could comfortably seat
twenty-four people. A discreet sign informed passengers
that the well-stocked bar would open at 18.00. In the
meantime, if one was thirsty or in need of alcoholic
refreshment, a steward would appear and serve you at the
press of a buzzer.

I sensed a presence and looked to see John at my
shoulder. 'Whenever I'm on a ship,' he said, 'I think of
that first time we met.'

I smiled. 'So do I. A lifetime ago. Do you know, I can
remember the past, the distant past, so much better than
I can remember yesterday.'

'I'm reliably informed it's a sign of age. Are we wise
to be taking this trip, Meg? You are all right?'

'Of course I am. Whatever put that idea into your
head?'

'It's just you seem a little breathless sometimes. And you have a habit of placing your hand just under your left breast.'

I hoped my smile was reassuring. 'I'm just making sure my heart is still beating. That I'm still alive.' The truth was, of course, slightly different. I was getting a little breathless and my heart did seem to pound and race a little. My physician maintained it was merely a sign of my age and quite normal.

We stood watching the shore for a while longer. Susan had been taken on a tour of the ship by the First Officer who was paying her more attention than I thought appropriate. She looked effortlessly beautiful in a blue floral day-dress with white collar, cuffs and belt, with tiny flower buttons from neck to hem. By the time I was her age I was married with three children.

As if reading my mind, John whispered in my ear, 'I don't know what she's going to do with her life, but she'll be no ordinary woman. You mark my words.'

The ship was pitching slightly and John said, loudly, 'We're passing Sheerness and Southend. It'll be the North Sea shortly. Do you fancy a rest before lunch?'

'If you don't mind I think I'd like to visit the bridge.'

He took my arm. 'Let me show you the way.'

On the floor above were the staterooms. Forward of those lay the Captain's quarters. A staircase led to the bridge directly above. John introduced me to the Captain, or Master, as he was known. His name was Richard Farringdon, a distinguished looking man, in his late forties, married with two grown-up children. One was following in his father's footsteps and was a third officer in the Buchanan Shipping Line, while the other was a midshipman at Dartmouth Royal Naval College.

'Dickie and I were on the same ship, what was it . . . thirty years ago?'

'At least, sir. I was a third and you had just been made Master. It was your first command, I seem to remember.'

'So it was. Do you remember . . .'

I left them to their reminiscences and walked across to the chart table. A young officer was busy making a cross on its surface.

'Is that where we are?' I asked.

Blushing, he stammered a reply to the effect that it was. 'We'll be a . . . altering c . . . course in t . . . ten minutes.' He pointed at a pencilled track and explained when we would be passing North Foreland before turning south.

The other person on the bridge was the man on the wheel. He was following a compass heading, his hands constantly moving, mere fractions of a degree. Aware of my scrutiny, he asked if I would like to try it. I looked at John and Mr Farringdon, who nodded and exchanged smiles. I'd show them.

Within seconds we were wandering off course and the sailor had to correct it. Despite my best attempt I couldn't keep us on a straight course. 'Bother, I give up. Here, young man, you'd better have it back.'

'Not so easy, is it?' John asked.

'*He* makes it look very easy.'

'That's because he's had a lot of training,' said Mr Farringdon. 'Sir, I'll be honoured if you and Lady Megan could join me for a drink before dinner. Say nineteen hundred?'

'Yes, I should think that will suit. I see from the manifest all the staterooms are full.'

'Yes, sir. Two of the passengers are missionaries, I think. And one is a diplomat travelling with his wife to Freetown in Sierra Leone. But no doubt you'll get to know them all in the course of the next few days.'

'I'm sure we will,' John replied.

We left the bridge and went to our rooms. 'How many passengers are there?' I asked.

'Eighteen.'

'But I thought there were only six state rooms.'

'There are, each with two bedrooms. Some passengers are sharing cabin space. Susan, for example, has somebody in her second bedroom. Another woman.'

'What about us? We're only using one room.'

'Rank has its privileges. The company knows better than to put a third party in with us.'

Over lunch we met the other passengers. Susan was indeed sharing her stateroom with an elderly spinster who was joining her recently widowed brother to take over his household in Volta. I did not envy her the six hundred mile trek she faced from Freetown across country.

The remaining passengers were as varied as you would expect. Among them we met a diplomat, an odious little man, in his early forties I thought, well groomed, though continuously preening himself. I felt it apt he wore a waistcoat of peacock green. He was, I learned with some surprise, our new Ambassador to Guinea. From the instant he learned that John was the Baron of Guildford, a member of the House of Lords and Chairman of the shipping line to boot, he spent much of the voyage toadying up to us. I learnt more than I cared to about the problems of Africa, the Diplomatic Service and the rights of native Africans.

I loved being at sea, cocooned away from the stress of modern life, relaxing, enjoying a good book or merely resting quietly. After dinner we broke up into smaller groups. A foursome of bridge started for small stakes. The younger set, including Susan, played gramophone records, jazz and suchlike, while I sat with a newly-married couple emigrating to Sierra Leone. Donald was a mining engineer, about to take up a management post in a diamond mine.

The sounds of Duke Ellington and George Gershwin were a pleasant background to the evening. We retired early, the gentle movement of the ship inducing a deep sleep at the end of the day. I awoke to the sound of a horn sounding every minute.

'What on earth?' I turned to John, aware that he was awake beside me.

'Fog horn. It's common, if we have a flat calm, for fog to appear in the early dawn in the Channel. It'll burn off later when the sun comes up. We must be somewhere around Falmouth, round the Devonshire coast anyway.'

I got out of bed, put on my silk wrap and went over to the window. Drawing back the curtain I saw nothing but a dense grey. It was a real pea-souper.

'I think I'll get dressed and go for a walk,' I announced. 'If I find a steward would you like a cup of tea?'

John glanced at the bedside clock. 'It's six forty-five. Tea will be arriving at seven. I've already arranged it. Tea in bed, breakfast at eight-thirty. An ordered routine. I must say that it's good to be at sea, especially on one of our own vessels.'

I smiled at him. I had to agree. Just at that moment, life was very good.

Many of the passengers had their breakfast in their rooms while we opted for the saloon. Afterwards we went up to the bridge.

The Master greeted us with a cheery, 'The fog's lifting already. I can almost see the bow.'

I peered forward but could make nothing out.

'Unfortunately we've been at slow ahead since around 4am but that can't be helped.'

'Any other ships around?' John asked.

'Mmm. We've passed a few, heard them clear to port. I've got lookouts posted all over the ship, listening. Including down aft. We don't want some idiot coming too fast up our stern. We're in radio contact with eight vessels all told and we have their positions, courses and speeds. Those coming up channel are only dead reckonings but even allowing for a wide discrepancy there's no danger.'

John went over to the chart. 'The Lizard is eight miles away. Have we got her fog signal?'

'Yes. Very faint but clear.' If he was irked by John's questions he didn't show it. 'Once a Master always a Master, eh, Sir John?'

John pulled a face and replied. 'Sorry. I can't help it. But it's nice to know the ship is in such capable hands.'

'Thank you for those kind words. I was well trained, as you know.'

Unlike a cruise ship there were no organised activities, dances, entertainment, other than what we made ourselves. The cliques of the night before regrouped after dinner and the evening repeated itself. The Bay of Biscay was notorious for its rough weather but we sailed serenely across with barely a ripple on the smooth glass of the Atlantic swell. By the third day we were settled into a comfortable routine. Even the weather was becoming warmer. Strolling the upper deck before lunch and tea was very pleasant.

Although Susan appeared to be enjoying the voyage, a day out of Gibraltar she was champing at the bit to get ashore.

'It's all very well,' she said, 'to indulge in a hedonistic lifestyle but it does pall after a while.'

With a straight face I formulated a suitable reply. 'According to the Greek philosopher Atistippus, any pleasure is the only good.'

Susan laughed out loud. 'Good old Gran, someday I'll catch you out.'

We had played word games for years. One of us would use an unusual word and the other would have to top it. Simple fun and it helped to keep my mind from atrophying.

'When do we see Gib?' she asked, tucking her arm in mine as we walked the deck.

'According to John not until we are around Tarifa, that's the southernmost tip of mainland Spain. We'll be less than two hours out then.'

'I'm looking forward to getting to Spain. I want to see

for myself what's going on. One hears and reads such awful things and we don't really know what's happening.'

'Young lady, I didn't bring you all this way to get involved with Spain's political problems. And besides, they are mostly in the north and the east.'

'I know.' She changed the subject adroitly, aware that I was upset. 'Are we staying in Gib a while or are we leaving immediately for the Boucher's place?'

I didn't want a row and so I went along with her. 'We're staying for one night at the Europa Hotel. I gather there is a special dinner tonight, in our honour. A sort of farewell.'

Her response was unguarded. 'Another soirée of gluttony and outrageous snobbery. How tedious.'

'Is your attitude really so condescending, or are you putting on an act?' I asked with some asperity.

'I'm sorry, Gran but it's all too much. In Spain there are thousands experiencing real hunger. Look at us. The food we've been offered in the last five days would have been enough to feed a small Spanish town for a week.'

'Don't exaggerate, young lady. I will not apologise for the comfort we live in. If we gave away everything we have we won't change a thing. The poor will always be with us. And don't forget where we've come from. Our lives have not been easy. We've paid a high price for our wealth and we very nearly lost it all. I don't hold with all this socialist nonsense. Communism is failing in Russia as we speak.'

'How can you say that? Socialism is the only hope for the world. We need a better redistribution of wealth. Workers paid a fair day's wage so they can live in dignity.'

'It's all very well condemning the status quo, Susan, but money has to be earned. It's not our inalienable right, as some socialists seem to think. Come, let us agree to differ and go and get changed.'

On that more cordial note we went to our staterooms. She worried me, my granddaughter. A kind heart and a headstrong personality were, to my way of thinking, a disastrous combination.

It was our last day and I was up early, as were a number of the other passengers. Although it was November, the day was as balmy as an English May. To port and starboard were Morocco and Spain. I felt a stirring in my blood. Dawn was breaking, darkness receding, the stars fading. At a latitude of thirty-six degrees the sun came up quickly.

There it was! On the port side, rising over thirteen hundred feet into the air was the Rock of Gibraltar. The northern Pillar of Hercules. The gateway to the Mediterranean. The white rock was marvellous to look at, somehow a symbol of the might of Britain the world over. I was, I realised, still a romantic at heart.

'It's a wonderful sight, isn't it?' John said, joining me. 'Come to the starboard side and smell the air.'

Dutifully I wandered across and sniffed. There was something different in the air – indefinable but there.

'That, my dearest Megan, is the smell of Africa. Decaying, rotten, adventurous Africa. It becomes more noticeable still as you head south, past the northern deserts, but it's there all right. Of course it comes mainly from the jungle. Hundreds of thousands of years of vegetation. With the wind from the south like it is this morning you can smell it here. Shall we go in to breakfast?'

We ate early as we would be arriving at Gibraltar at eight o'clock. The harbour was mainly a base for the Royal Navy but, at the northern end, merchant ships put in to take on provisions, either coal or oil but always water. The ship would not sail again until the afternoon and so there was no hurry for us to disembark. Our cases were packed and arrangements had been made to have them taken to the Europa hotel.

In the middle of the morning we made our goodbyes and set off to explore Gibraltar.

31

THE FOLLOWING MORNING we sat in an open horse-drawn carriage and crossed the border into Spain. We carried on through the border town of La Linea and drove along the coast to Algeciras, five miles away. We were deposited at the railway station, our cases given to a porter and the carriage left to return to the hotel.

The train journey to Cádiz was stunning. The track went south to Tarifa before following the coast to the north west. After a few miles it crossed inland over the low plain. In the distance we could clearly see hills rising into the far mist.

As we were rattling across a river, the Rio Barbates, John demonstrated his knowledge of naval history. 'This river leads to Cape Trafalgar. It's just a few miles further along the coast. It's where Nelson had his victory and met his death on the twenty-first of October eighteen hundred and five. He fought and beat the French *and* the Spanish, a fact that is often forgotten. People always think of the battle in terms of beating the French alone. But of course we were also at war with Spain in those days.'

The journey progressed pleasantly. A little while later we passed over the salt marshes near San Fernando where salt had been extracted since Roman times. There were several other sights to be seen and admired. At lunchtime we pulled into the railway station, situated alongside the main port, which was used as a base for the Spanish treasure fleets of old.

Jacques Boucher was waiting there for us. There had

been a regular and lively correspondence between our families ever since the tragic events at sea nearly a decade earlier. The Boucher family had remained very grateful to David and Sion for the rescue attempt despite the accident's tragic outcome. Jacques was now fifty-five. He was the same height as John, an inch under six feet, but a lot thinner, his narrow shoulders and an upright bearing making him seem taller than he was. He was tanned, had brown eyes and hair as white as chalk. By nature Jacques was a happy creature. He was smiling now as he embraced us. Standing next to him was a young man, taller than his father, with wider shoulders. He was almost too handsome, with dark brown hair, determined chin and intense brown eyes. Phillipe was a year older than Susan.

'Marie-Claire apologises that she is not here to greet you as she is supervising lunch. But I can tell you she is very excited to welcome you to our humble home. The car is outside.'

Our luggage filled the boot and what was left over was strapped onto the roof. The car was large and John, Jacques and I easily fitted into the back. Phillipe drove with my granddaughter, Susan, sitting alongside. Susan looked stunning. She had dedicated the last few days on board ship to sun-worshipping, covered in walnut oil. Her light tan contrasted beautifully with her white, calf-length dress and black hair tucked prettily behind her ears. Wherever she went, heads turned.

A charming host, Jacques kept up a commentary on the area as we drove. Cádiz, it seemed, was the oldest town on the Iberian Peninsula, dating back to Phoenician times around the 11th century BC. It was situated on an isolated rock at the end of a six mile promontory. It was a hugely important port and had been from the time of the Romans.

'The road leads to El Puerto de Santa Maria,' said Jacques, 'a town eighteen kilometres north of here. Our canning factory has done well. I have been able to buy a vineyard where we grow grapes for wine and where we make sherry. It has become a great passion of mine.'

We nodded. We'd gathered as much from his letters.

'More than a passion, Papa,' said Phillipe, over his shoulder, 'a great love affair.'

Jacques chuckled. 'Perhaps. But after the stink of the canning factory, the clean sweet air of the vineyard and the heady aroma of the cave is a highly pleasurable change.'

'Did you say cave?' I queried.

'Yes. It is where we store the bottled wines. You will see very soon.'

'What about the unrest there's been in the country?' John asked.

I noticed a tensing of Phillipe's shoulders, his smooth, brown hands gripped the steering wheel more tightly. Jacques gave an uneasy shrug.

'It's difficult to say. So far, most of the trouble has been in the north and the east. But it has been terrible. The country is splitting into two factions, Nationalists and Republicans. On each side there are many smaller parties and interest groups. Some are prepared to work for democratic change. Others demand a violent uprising. Spain is in a dreadful mess but there are many men and women of good intentions working for a fair and just solution.'

Phillipe interrupted his father, obviously furious. 'How can you suggest such a thing, Papa? How much more must the poor of Spain take? The rich become richer as the poor become poorer. We need real reforms before we see any lasting solution to problems this country is facing.'

'I agree,' said Susan. 'There is far too much suffering across Europe. Greedy capitalists living off the sweat of the labour of the multitudes. Russia has the right idea.'

Phillipe threw her an admiring glance. Was it my imagination, or was she sitting more straight-backed than usual? She smiled back.

In the back we each had our own thoughts. The young were so idealistic.

'Uncle Sion brought back terrible stories from Russia,' Susan continued. 'It's certainly no paradise on earth. But they need time to achieve their objectives. 'Russia is so vast, so medieval in many areas that it will take time to educate the masses properly. And that's what it all comes down to. Education and opportunity.'

'Precisely,' said Phillipe. 'Tax the wealthy and redistribute it to the poor.'

'Phillipe,' Jacques said sharply. 'That is enough of that communist nonsense. We have guests and I am sure they do not wish to hear your radical views.'

We had all been speaking English. Phillipe lapsed into rapid Spanish but was sharply rebuked by his father.

'I apologise for my son's bad manners. He should know better but unfortunately I, how do you say? Spared the rod too often?' He continued when John and I nodded, 'And now it is too late.' Jacques smile was forced, white patches of anger showing on his cheeks. The political divide was obviously an open wound but how far and how deep it went was impossible to tell.

After driving for about twenty minutes, we turned inland onto a secondary road.

'It's not far now,' said Jacques. As we rounded a bend he added, 'There it is.'

On a low hill, facing south, was a beautiful white building with a red tiled roof. Far from a humble dwelling, it looked large and substantial. It was surrounded by terraced rows of vines, stretching far up the hill. We drew up outside the front door and Phillipe blew the horn. The door was flung open, servants came to take our luggage and Marie-Claire appeared to greet us with a smile. I knew her to be fifty-one but she looked a good ten years younger. She was the same height as me, with brown hair, parted in the middle, held back with beautiful tortoiseshell combs. I noticed a few strands of grey beginning to show at her temples. She had a voluptuous figure, wide set brown eyes and a full-lipped, expressive mouth. From her letters I knew she was a rare creature – on the whole, happy and contented with her lot. There were few people who could claim to feel as she did.

We crossed a broad veranda and entered into a large open hallway, with various doors and a wide, sweeping stairway leading off it.

Marie-Claire said, 'Would you like to freshen up? Or are you ready to join us for an aperitif before lunch?'

John and Susan opted for the drink whilst I went to freshen up. Phillipe led them away while I followed Marie-Claire upstairs. The room she showed me into was lovely. It had two double beds, a large oak wardrobe and a wash-hand basin in a corner. The walls were white and hung with interesting paintings. The high ceiling also boasted a fan which turned lazily, circulating the air. Outside our room was a balcony wide enough to accommodate a table and four chairs. The view to the south was spectacular. I could see a town to the left, a wide expanse of ocean and Cádiz on the right.

'Let me show you the bathroom. When you are ready I'll take you downstairs or would you prefer a tour of the house first?' Marie-Claire asked.

I could see that she was eager to show me around and so I suggested the tour. I freshened up and followed her around. The house was built around a central courtyard. The left wing housed her family while the right wing was the home of Pierre, his wife, Augustine and their son, Simon. The two wings were joined together by the public rooms, consisting of a huge kitchen, a dining room, a library and a large lounge.

'The servants live in separate quarters out the back nearer the winery. We have two maids and a cook. Their husbands work with Jacques making wine and sherry. I've no doubt he'll show you his side of things later. Come, let us join the others.'

Marie-Claire led me outside and around to the back of the house. There I was greeted by Pierre, Jacques' cousin whom I remembered well. He was a year younger than Jacques, his grave demeanour in stark contrast to Jacques' cheery disposition. His thinning black hair framed a round face and a small moustache. His eyes were dark and intense, but for now his austere look was softened by a welcoming smile. He kissed both my cheeks and then turned to his wife, Augustine. A small, slim woman, her hair was fair and tied back with a black velvet bow. She greeted me with a beaming smile and a kiss on both cheeks. Holding my hands, she looked me up and down.

'You are looking younger than ever, Meg. Welcome to our home. We hope you have a wonderful time with us.'

'Thank you, Augustine, that's very kind of you. I'm sure we will. This looks delicious.'

The sons, Phillipe and his cousin, Simon, who was yet to arrive, had both spent a year in America and spoke excellent English. The older generation spoke accented yet idiomatic English which showed how highly educated they had been.

On the patio a long, wide table stood groaning under the weight of platters of food. Jacques gestured to a number of bottles on a side table.

'These are all made from grapes grown here. We have two different sherries, a white wine, and a red wine. This sherry,' he picked up the nearest bottle, 'is a fino. It is very dry, slightly acidic and is served ice cold. This second one is an amontillado and has matured for three years longer than the fino. It isn't quite so dry but it is also served very cold.'

'I'll try the amontillado, please,' I replied.

The others all had a glass in their hands and were appreciatively taking small sips.

When Jacques handed me a glass he said, 'This is known as a *copita*. You can see how the glass tapers towards the brim which allows the aroma to fully develop. The amontillado is eighteen percent alcohol while the fino is only sixteen percent. We blend the wines here and add the brandy which we buy in from a vineyard near Jerez de la Frontera.'

I took a sip. The sherry was amber in colour, slightly tart to the tongue and quite refreshing. 'Why, how delicious!' I exclaimed.

From Jacques' delighted expression, I could see he was pleased with my reaction. 'We add a wine from Montilla,' said Jacques, 'hence the name, *amontillado.*'

'Let's change the subject,' said Marie-Claire, kindly, 'otherwise Jacques will go on about it all day. Tell us about your trip.'

We were glad to do so over a lunch of cold meats, cured hams, fresh fruit and various cheeses. We were offered the vineyard's white or red wine which I declined, opting for cold water. John took a glass of red and made appreciative noises.

On the surface everything appeared very pleasant but within a few days I realised there was an underlying tension. I thought at first a clash of interests between Jacques and Pierre was to blame but soon knew that wasn't the case. Pierre was happy to run the family canning business while Jacques' passion was the winery and vineyard. The canning of fish, mainly pilchards and salmon, was the basis of their fortune. They had bought the vineyard merely two years earlier because they had wanted the house.

Its location was ideal as it took only fifteen minutes to drive to the cannery and it had everything the two families wished for. They had been together for so long they never considered buying separate homes. Only after they had moved in did Jacques begin to take an interest in wine making. The grapes had been cultivated on the land for centuries but the original winery had fallen into disrepair and the grapes had been sold to other sherry makers in the district. Jacques invested a great deal of time and money and brought the art back to the estate. The sherry we had drunk had been made in another winery using estate grapes. I was astonished to learn that a good sherry took from five to eight years before it was ready for drinking.

Jacques insisted on giving John, Susan and me a tour of the winery. It was while we were standing in the low, brick-lined, long building known as the cave, that I dared ask Jacques what was wrong.

Smiling sadly at John and me, Jacques replied, 'It is Phillipe and Simon. What is happening is polarising the country. Brother against brother, father against son. It is truly tragic and we worry so for them.'

'Where do you stand?' John asked.

Jacques shrugged. 'I do not agree with socialism or communism. I believe in a republic but am indifferent to whether there is a monarch or not. The boys, though, have all the passion of youth. They are true believers in socialism, and cannot understand why we don't want to change Spain as passionately as they do. So we argue. They, in turn, hide their involvement. The reason you have not yet seen Simon is because he is up north. Have you heard of the *caballeristas*?'

John, always fascinated by politics, said in a low voice, 'They are the followers of Largo Caballero, the leader of the Socialist Party.'

Jacques nodded. 'He wants a bloody revolution and sees himself as the Spanish Lenin. There's another man on the left named Indalecio Prieto. He was a minister in the parliament and he wants a more gradual approach. In effect, a revolution without bloodshed. There is no love lost between the two men. Simon has gone to help Caballero who has only just been let out of prison. Phillipe wishes to join him too. So far we have persuaded him to stay here, but one day we will be unable to stop him.' He shook his head sorrowfully and then shrugged, changing the subject.

Jacques was so obviously making an effort to be cheerful, we went along with the charade. 'These, my friends, are called *soleras*,' he pointed to a vertical row of five barrels. 'Each row has a blend of grape of the same quality and as you can see there are twenty-one rows. I have bought in blended grapes from the area, added the necessary amount of brandy and now the wine is fermenting. The oldest and closest to drinking lies along the bottom. When it is ready we draw off the bottom cask, move each cask down and put the youngest wine on the top. And so the process continues. In four years we will have wine we can call our own. In the meantime we are blenders and bottlers.'

'Do you have a bottling plant?' John asked.

'Yes, but not here. We ship to a plant not far from the canning factory. Once it is bottled the sherry is ready for selling. The wine we make and intend to sell is laid down for two years in the bottles. The sherry we sell to *bodegas* all over the region.' We had seen the wineshops which often stocked groceries too. 'We are using the same outlets we have for the canned food to try and sell the sherry and wine and are beginning to make progress. Let me take you to the presses.'

He led us to another building in which there were large wooden vats, not deep but big enough to allow five or six people to stand. 'We still press the grapes using our feet. I am looking to install a more modern method either next year or the year after, but this year we did it the old fashioned way. We all took turns. I had to hire a considerable number of casual workers to get the wine pressed in time. The liquid runs along these channels and into these large barrels called tuns. Here the first fermentation takes place. The content is called must or stum.'

Jacques continued the tour until we reached a small cellar with racks of bottles. 'These are last year's wines. They are a selection for control purposes. We need to find the best time to open a bottle. Most wines are drunk relatively young, a year or two, maybe three after pressing. Some vintages can be laid down and improve with age. Most don't. So we open and mark the bottles in this book. Here, taste this red.'

Jacques drew a cork and poured us a glass each. He showed us how to swirl the glass and what to look for when smelling the wine. Finally we tasted it. He and I spat it out, John swallowed his. We both murmured our appreciation. Jacques was inordinately pleased with our response.

'Over there are the stables. Do any of you ride?'

'I adore horses,' said Susan.

'In that case I must get Phillipe to introduce you to ours.'

'What about you, John? Or you Megan?'

John still rode but I hadn't done so for several years. Although I thought John was getting too old to go fox hunting, he still enjoyed the sport although I saw no merit or pleasure in it myself.

Each night we dined in the house itself as there was a distinct chill in the air once the sun had set. On our fourth day we were just sitting down to eat when there was a commotion at the front door. The men were about to see what was happening when the dining room door swung open. A bloodied figure stood there, swaying. Pierre jumped to his feet, throwing over his chair, while Augustine went white with shock.

'Simon,' his mother whispered.

32

THE YOUNG MAN staggered into the room and fell into a chair at the table. He was covered in dirt and blood, his clothes torn, and he looked exhausted.

Jacques ordered a maid to fetch a bowl of warm water and a towel. 'What has happened, Simon?' he asked.

I could see that under the grime Simon was round faced, a little overweight, with black hair and intense, brown eyes. 'We were at a meeting in Seville. The *cedistas* attacked us.' He shuddered and put his hands to his face. When he looked up his cheeks were wet with tears. Gathering his wits, he continued. 'They came in with staves and bottles. There was a fight. I took a blow to the head and must have gone out cold. They set fire to the hall. Someone dragged me out through a side door.' He paused and took a gulp from a glass of wine. The maid appeared with the basin and a cloth and Augustine began to clear the blood from his head.

'Sit still,' his mother said through clenched teeth. There was an understandable mixture of fear and anger in her voice though she treated the boy's wound gently.

'What happened then?' Pierre asked. His eyes showed more anger than fear and his hands were opening and clenching as though he wanted to grab hold of somebody and teach them a lesson.

'We got into a back alley but were seen, so we ran. We met more of our men and retaliated.' Simon sat up straighter, a touch of pride in his voice. 'We gave some of them a good hiding. But then more *cedistas* appeared with guns. They shot at us and we were forced to run again.'

'Guns!' Jacques repeated, thunderstruck. The others, too, gasped in horror. 'This is the escalation we feared.'

'Simon,' Pierre spoke harshly, 'you must stop this nonsense before it is too late. People will be killed.'

'It is already too late, Papa. Falangists and Marxists have been fighting and killing each other for years.'

'Yes, in the north, but not here,' his father argued. 'We don't want trouble here in Cádiz. Let them play their politics in Madrid and Catalonia and wherever else they care for it. We will catch fish, make wine. Let the troubles blow over.'

His son drained his glass, winced when his mother touched his cheek with the damp cloth and said, 'We cannot. There is too much at stake. The freedom of the people is above the life of one man.'

'Don't talk such rubbish, Simon,' Pierre retorted. 'We live in a democracy. We vote for our leaders. This is Europe not Africa or South America. I forbid you to take part in any more meetings. You must concentrate on the business. The family. Your home.'

Simon struggled out of the chair, still white with pain and exhaustion. 'Our struggle is greater than business and family. We have to fight the church and the army. If the right wing get to power, all will be lost. I am going to my room. Thank you, Mama.'

Walking away, he lurched slightly, regained his footing and continued out of the room. The rest of us looked at each other in shocked silence.

'I'll go and see if I can do anything for him,' said Phillipe.

'I'll help you,' said Susan. Before I could think of something to say to prevent her she was out of the room.

A pall of gloom settled over us as we sat down at the table. Wine was poured and we drank it gladly as we gathered our thoughts. Both Marie-Claire and Augustine were clearly upset while Jacques and Pierre were angry.

'Who or what,' John asked, 'are *cedistas*?'

It was Jacques who replied. 'Members of the *Confederación Española de Derechas Autónomas*, the CEDA. It is a right wing group led by a man named Gil Robles.'

John nodded. 'I've heard of him, of course. I remember now. Wasn't the party formed only recently?'

Jacques said, 'Yes, in nineteen thirty-three. It started as a Christian Democratic party, moderates working for a better system. But Robles quickly became a rabble rouser. Soon he was sounding more like Hitler than a democrat. Recently, when he's giving a speech, his audience have been chanting for the *Jefe*. The Leader or Chief. They rail against Jews, heretics, freemasons, liberals and Marxists. Both in and out of parliament Robles has been making speeches about abolishing the political movements of the working classes and outlawing trade unions. His intention is to acquire power like Hitler, using constitutional means.'

'If he does, what will it mean to you?' John asked.

'We don't know,' was the honest reply. 'Except I would prefer them to the Marxists and communists. The left wing socialists will bankrupt us if they have their way. At least with the combined parties of the Radicals and CEDA we know where we stand.'

'I thought, what's his name . . . Lerroux? who formed the Radical party began dirt poor and quickly became rich. I understand he's as corrupt as they come.' John frowned, deep in thought.

'That is true,' said Pierre. 'But the Radicals are on the side of the landowners and businesses like us. If there's an uprising, what's to prevent the masses from taking everything we've worked for?'

'At least Simon is safe for now,' said Marie-Claire, obviously trying to save the evening in her quiet, dignified manner.

Eventually we ate. It was a gloomy meal, despite Marie-Claire's efforts. The conversation reverted constantly to Spanish politics. Neither Susan nor Phillipe rejoined us.

The following morning Simon made an appearance. He was very like his father, but with an air of superiority about him.

Simon was helping himself to a breakfast of bread, cold meat, cheese, jam and fruit when Jacques attempted a joke. 'It's just as well you have a thick head. Otherwise you may have been hurt.'

Simon managed a smile and riposted, 'I inherited it from my father, sir, which is your side of the family.'

Jacques smiled good-naturedly. 'Are you up to going to work today?'

'Yes, of course.'

'Good. But don't work too hard,' said Pierre. 'A knock on the head can be nastier than it seems. If you begin to tire, stop and rest.'

'Yes, Papa.'

That seemed to be the end of that. Simon departed for the canning factory, Pierre went to Huelva to meet the captain of a fishing boat and Jacques went to the winery. Phillipe took John, Susan and myself for a tour along the coast. We stopped at a small restaurant overlooking the Atlantic for lunch and sat outside in the autumnal sun. It was a cloudless day, there was no wind and the view was magnificent. I had no intention of spoiling the afternoon with talk of politics but Susan brought the subject up.

'Did Simon say what he plans to do next?' She addressed Phillipe.

Shrugging, he replied, 'Support the party, as before. We must keep the Popular Front in power, to give them a chance to bring in reforms.'

'Why?' I could see that my idiocy annoyed him but he was too polite to do other than smile and explain.

'The government is a coalition, a hotch-potch of many different parties, which, I have to admit, do not sit well together. They include the Marxist Socialists, the Spanish Communist party, the Liberals and the Spanish Socialist party. They, together, represent the left, the Republic and, most importantly, anti-fascism.'

'The coalition won't last,' said John, breaking a piece of bread and cheese in his hands.

'Why do you think that, Sir John?' Phillipe asked.

'We, in the British parliament, have a shrewd idea about what is happening in Spain. You can't keep together a coalition where one side believes in bloody revolution and the other advocates gradual change. It won't work.'

'But the alternative is unthinkable. Even now the *africanistas* are plotting a military coup against the government.'

'Who are they?' I asked, confused.

Susan chipped in. 'Oh, Gran, they are the army officers who have served in Africa in the Spanish colonies. They are anti-left, pro-monarchist and pro-Nationalist.'

I nodded wisely. 'Most army officers are,' I said.

'Lady Megan, the two main pillars of old Spain were the Church and the Army. When the Republican Left came to power under Manuel Azaña in 1931 he tried to reform both of them. He retired thousands of officers on full pay, a very expensive endeavour, causing a lot of resentment. The army's officer corps has been reduced to highly trained professionals who have been or are serving in Africa. Azaña attempted, in a new constitution, to separate the Church and the State. But he didn't go far enough for some of the anti-clerics in the *Cortes*, as the Church was left with its own schools and was allowed to continue religious teaching in state schools. The Church is in the pockets of the big landowners. They forged an unholy alliance, with the clergy preaching against communism and socialism at every opportunity. That in turn is alienating the peasants.'

My head was spinning. 'I take it the Army and the Church are lined up on the side of the Nationalists?

And angry with the government because of the new reforms?"

Phillipe nodded. 'I believe we are sitting on a powder keg with a lit match. It will go bang – only we don't know when.'

'So you and Simon support the Republicans?' John asked.

Susan replied for him. 'Of course they do. Anybody with any sense would.'

'Anybody with any sense,' I said, 'would lay low and let the drama play itself out. A civil war will lead to many deaths, terrible hardship and families fighting each other.'

'But there are important principles at stake,' Susan protested.

I interrupted her. 'Now listen to me, young lady, it's so-called principles that cause most of the problems. When we arrived in America nearly thirty years after *their* civil war there was still bitterness and anger. More Americans were killed then than during the Great War. The South didn't recover for decades. And the North fought for one of the greatest principles it is possible to imagine. Freedom. The freedom of a whole race from slavery. Families took years to heal their bitter wounds. Some never did and never will.'

'What should they have done?' Susan asked. 'The North was right to fight.'

'The North was forced to fight,' I replied. 'There should have been more negotiation. More talking. War might have been avoided. It may have taken longer but the blacks would have had their freedom.' I paused, willing her to understand. 'We fought the Great War for the same reason. Look at the result! Millions dead and for what? We should have had *more* dialogue. Let me tell you something else. Wars are fought by children.' If I sounded bitter I couldn't help it. There had been so much suffering. 'I still remember the doughboys marching to their ships, singing their songs, ready to cross an ocean, to fight in countries most of them couldn't find on a map of the world. And I was with Evan when the coffins came back. Draped in their country's flag, sealed to hide the pitiful remains of their mutilated bodies. Did you know that the majority of those killed were men under twenty-five? The older generation, the men who caused the war, were safely behind the lines.'

'Gran, it won't be like that this time,' Susan protested.

I looked at her bleakly. There was dread in my heart. If an intelligent girl, an outsider like Susan, could be influenced, then there was no chance for the Spanish people. 'Susan, Phillipe, believe me when I say that once the conflagration starts there will be no stopping it until one side or the other wins. And that will result in many, many needless deaths.'

'Many are prepared to die for the cause,' Phillipe spoke proudly.

John spoke for me, using the words I was about to utter. 'Spain is a democracy, Phillipe. It should sort out its problems in one way only. Through the *Cortes*.'

With that the subject was dropped and we continued our tour. In the late afternoon we drove down the mountain road from Arcos De La Frontera. Rounding a bend we were forced to stop by a roadblock straddling the highway.

'What on earth is going on?' Susan asked.

The make-shift barricade was a cart placed across the middle of the road with two large barrels at either end. Four armed men stood by it, roughly dressed, unshaven and sporting long moustaches. I felt a twinge of fear and lifted a hand to my mouth. John placed his hand on my arm and gave a reassuring squeeze.

'Take it easy, my love,' he said. 'Let me handle this. Phillipe, say nothing. You are our chauffeur. Until we learn who they are and what they want.'

We drew up in front of the cart. Three of the men remained there, rifles held across their chests, while one man approached the car. To say I didn't like the look of them is something of an understatement.

Opening the car window John leaned out. 'What's the meaning of this?'

The man immediately bristled with anger and let loose a torrent of Spanish.

'What did he say?' John asked Phillipe.

'He demands to know who we are, where we are going and where we have been.'

'Ask him who he represents and by what authority he stops us.' If John was nervous or worried he didn't show it. Phillipe spoke at length and received a short reply. Phillipe looked distinctly unhappy as he turned to John.

'They are Falangists, looking for enemies of Spain.'

'What the hell does that mean?' John asked.

'It doesn't matter,' answered Phillipe. 'They want to know who you are. What should I tell them?'

John plastered a smile on his lips and said to Phillipe, 'The Falangists are monarchists, right-wing?'

'That is correct.'

'Then tell them exactly who I am. The Baron of Guildford. This is the Baroness. Tell them I am a personal friend of the King of England and that King Alfonso has been a guest in my house.'

Phillipe translated and almost immediately a change came over the gunman. But he said something to Phillipe who looked at John.

'Sorry, Sir John, but he asks if you can prove what you say.'

John took some papers from a jacket pocket, his passport as well as a letter written in Spanish. The gunman read them and handed them back. He gave a poor imitation of a salute, gestured to the others and the wagon was wheeled to one side. We drove slowly through and on our way.

We were silent for a few minutes. 'I don't like the look

of this,' said John. 'Roadblocks and armed ruffians . . . it bodes badly for Spain.'

'I agree, Sir John,' Phillipe replied, a frown on his forehead.

'What was the letter you showed him?' I asked.

'We have been accredited to the embassy in Madrid. Diplomatic immunity. I arranged it just in case.' He paused, 'As always, it's not what you know, but who.'

We had an uneventful journey back to the vineyard and over drinks that evening recounted our adventures.

'Perhaps it is time for you to leave Spain,' said Jacques.' It is becoming dangerous.'

'Oh no,' Susan said quickly. 'It's too soon.'

She cast a quick glance at Phillipe and I thought, *so that's the way the land lies*, but I kept my counsel.

John agreed with her. 'Speaking for Meg and myself, we're having a wonderful time and we aren't afraid of a bunch of thugs so, if we're still welcome, we'd like to stay.'

'Of course you're still welcome. I didn't mean to offend you in any way. My house is your house and always will be.'

'Thank you for that,' I smiled at him. 'And no offence taken. But we won't run away. There is still so much to see. We haven't even sampled the delights of Cádiz yet.'

'You're quite right, my dear,' said John. 'So we'll stay a while longer if that's all right with you?'

'I'm delighted,' said Jacques. 'I had hoped to discuss exporting my sherries to England.'

Phillipe rose to fill Susan's glass and I caught the smiles they exchanged. As she thanked Phillipe, Simon came in. This was the first time I had seen him since the morning after his dramatic entrance and he appeared none the worse for wear. It seemed he had spent the day in the region of Extremadura on company business.

During dinner Simon brought the conversation around to his recent trip. 'It was no surprise to see the poverty amongst the peasants,' he pontificated. 'It's truly horrendous. But do you know what they've done? They've taken over the estates of the absentee landlords. And the government has done nothing to stop them.' He chuckled. 'More power to them, I say.'

'They won't get away with it,' Pierre replied. 'The Civil Guard is being strengthened and will make a move soon.'

'What sort of move? And how do you know, Papa?' Simon looked at his father through narrowed eyes. I wondered what he'd really been doing in Extremadura. I doubted it was solely company business.

'The government has decided that the situation is intolerable. When the Guard is ready, they will move in a concerted operation to remove the squatters.'

'You can't call them squatters,' Simon argued. 'They are trying to feed their families. The land is lying unused.'

'It isn't their land,' Pierre argued.

'The people who own the land inherited it from their ancestors who raped and pillaged Spain over centuries. Land is sitting fallow while women and children starve.'

'I've noticed when it comes to socialist arguments,' said John, 'that it's always women and children who are starving and not men. Why is that?'

Simon looked daggers at John. 'That is not what I meant. Men are starving too. It's simply . . .'

'. . . more emotive to use women and children as an example,' John finished for him. 'That still doesn't make it right to seize the land.'

White spots of anger were showing on Simon's cheeks and he controlled his temper with difficulty. 'What else are they to do? Starve?'

His father protested. 'The government is bringing in reforms as quickly as possible. Even now Madrid is pushing through a bill for land reform. It's at the top of the agenda.'

'Papa, Papa,' Simon shook his head sadly, speaking as

though to a slightly retarded child, 'Madrid can bring in any law it likes. It won't be actioned at the local level. And that is where the problem lies. The whole of southern Spain is made up of the *latifundios*.' Simon addressed John and me, 'The agricultural methods of these huge estates are so old that they cannot even feed the peasants who work the land. The workers only have employment for a few months of the year. The rest of the time they go hungry. We have landless labourers, impoverished tenants and low agricultural productivity. As a result the country is a seething mass of anger and resentment.'

'But you must be patient,' argued John. 'The present government is *for* reform. It's against the old-style landowners, it supports trade unions and is trying to improve matters in the way you seem to be advocating.'

Simon nodded. 'It is true but the reforms go too slowly. The government is hampered on all sides. The stranglehold of the Church and the Monarchists in the regions is almost total. Laws just aren't enforced. And how do you make something happen if the powers-that-be in the town and village won't agree to it? Who do you turn to?' Angrily Simon took a deep drink of wine and replaced the glass on the table.

I saw that he had a point.

'Catalonia has modernised,' protested Pierre, 'and so will the remainder of Spain. And when it does, we will have a fairer society. But it has to be a gradual change or else we will have anarchy. There is far too much unrest as it is.'

'But that's because things are changing too slowly,' Phillipe broke in. 'Every reform is fought bitterly by the Church and the Catholic middle classes.'

'No good will come of forcing change,' said Jacques.

John said, 'I think you're right. However, steps should be taken to enforce laws passed by the government, otherwise a good deal of discontent will result.'

'The Right are fighting back,' argued Phillipe. 'Not

legally, but by disrupting legitimate meetings, causing fights that result in the Civil Guard being called out.'

Simon interrupted. 'And when they appear, what happens then? They break the heads of the Republicans. Innocent people who wish for nothing more than to better their wretched way of life. The Civil Guard are acting on the orders of the local Nationalists, in spite of the fact that the government increased their numbers to protect the very people they are attacking.'

'Listen to me, Simon, Phillipe,' said Pierre in a placatory tone. 'We must remember we are not Spanish. We are foreigners. Let the Spaniards sort out their own mess. In the meantime we will obey the laws, pay our taxes and look after our workers.'

'Bury your head in the sand if you will,' his son argued. 'But . . .'

'Enough!' Pierre spoke harshly. 'We have guests and I am sure they are becoming bored by our conversation. Let us change the topic to more pleasant matters.'

Simon was about to argue but saw the look on his father's face and thought better of it. The talk became more general, but there was an underlying tension for the remainder of the meal. Throughout the political interchange Augustine and Marie-Claire had said very little. I could see in their eyes their sadness and an understandable fear for the future. It was always left to the women to pick up the pieces during and after a war.

Three days later we were eating our meal alfresco on the patio. With the dusk came horror.

33

SIX MEN APPEARED around the corner of the house. They wore bandannas over their faces and carried rifles. Without warning, Pierre leapt to his feet with an oath. I looked over my shoulder and was suddenly very afraid. My hand went to my mouth. Though I managed to keep my composure it took a great deal of will-power. John's response was a slight start and then he sat still, watching. When I looked to him he smiled encouragingly and touched my arm.

Jacques let loose in a torrent of impassioned Spanish. Their reply was lost on me, but from Marie Claire's sharp intake of breath I guessed this was more than merely a robbery. One of the men pointed a handgun at Pierre's head and drew back the hammer.

'What do they want, Pierre?' John asked in a steady voice. At that moment I loved him more than ever for his calmness and bravery.

'They want Simon. They mean to take him with them. To stand trial.'

'Trial?' John repeated scornfully. 'Then why do they come like thieves? Why do they hide their faces?'

The man pointing the gun at Pierre replied in good English, 'Stay out of it, Englishman. That is none of your concern. He will be tried before a military court – before being taken out and shot.'

Augustine let out a low wail and began pleading with the men. She should have saved her breath and her dignity.

John spoke again. 'From the way you're talking you appear to have found him guilty already.'

'He supports the enemies of Spain,' spat the gunman. 'The Republicans who undermine our monarchy and our church.'

'He speaks out against you but he doesn't bear arms,' John argued. 'That is the right of any man living in a democracy. He merely supports the government.'

'They are not our government,' came the harsh reply. 'Enough discussion. Who are you to question me, Englishman?'

'My name is John Buchanan. I am the Baron of Guildford, a personal friend of your King. These are my diplomatic papers.' John took out his passport and handed it over with the letter. The gunman read them, made a short bob of his head by way of a salute and handed them back. The gesture was not lost on either John or myself.

The gunman turned back to Simon. His voice was that of a man who expected to be obeyed. 'Come with us.'

Simon was a deathly white but he stood up calmly enough. Augustine threw her arms around him, wailing in her native French. Simon disentangled her arms and replied in English. 'Do not be alarmed, Mama. I will stand trial and they will have to let me go free. I have nothing to fear.'

It was an obvious lie but I admired him for trying to calm his mother.

Both Pierre and Jacques continued to argue with the men, but to no avail.

'What are the charges?' John asked in a clear voice.

The Bouchers and the men with the guns looked at him. He repeated the question.

'My orders are simply to take him before the military tribunal.'

'Don't act as though you have any legitimacy,' John continued. 'When you leave we will call the Civil Guard. They will hunt you down.' John was baiting the gunmen. I wondered what he was trying to achieve.

The men appeared singularly unconcerned.

There was a further exchange in Spanish as the men began to leave, taking Simon with them. We followed them around the house. The next few moments were very tense. I was fearful that a gun could go off either unintentionally or on purpose. Someone might be injured or, God forbid, killed.

There were two cars parked a hundred yards or so from the house. They made their way towards them. Two guns were pointed at Simon at all times, the remainder at us. One of the gunmen ordered us to stay and we stopped following.

'Mother of God, stop them,' said Augustine, anguish in her voice, as the gunmen reached their cars.

'Phillipe, get the guns,' ordered Jacques.

While we stood watching the men climb into the cars, Phillipe ran back to the house. As the cars pulled away, we entered the hallway. Phillipe appeared from the cellar, carrying four rifles.

He gestured with one to John who nodded and took it from him.

'John, you mustn't,' I protested. 'You're too . . .' I saw the look on his face and stopped.

'We must hurry,' said Jacques.

'May I make a suggestion?' John said. 'There is no way of stopping the cars without somebody being seriously hurt or killed. We need to know which way they are going. Those men had the look of soldiers about them. I think they're Army.'

'I agree,' said Pierre.

'Where are the nearest garrisons?' John asked.

'There is one in the south, at Vejer De La Frontera and another in the north, at Arcos De La Frontera. They are the closest,' answered Pierre. 'So, depending on which garrison they're from they'll either go left or right on the main road.'

'May I suggest you take the horses and cut across country to the main road and see which way they go? I think Phillipe should come with me in the car, to show me the way. I intend to stay unnoticed, but if they spot me they won't dare shoot. Even in these desperate times, a diplomatic passport means something.'

'What are you planning to do?' Pierre asked.

'I will make serious political noises at the garrison where Simon is taken. This is an illegal act. Let us not forget that fact,' John replied.

The Bouchers stood uncertainly.

'Hurry, for God's sake, before it is too late,' Augustine said.

Pierre and Jacques exchanged nods. They turned and ran for the stables. John and Phillipe ran out of the front door and climbed into the car. I was looking down the hill and along the valley. In the distance I could clearly see the other two cars and the dust trail they left behind. When I looked back at John's car, now pulling away with spinning tyres, I was puzzled to see three heads in the car. Suddenly I was aghast to realise Susan was with them. I called after her but it was too late. The car shot away, Phillipe at the wheel.

Marie-Claire, Augustine and myself sat nervously in the house, overwhelmed with worry and fear. Pierre and Jacques returned nearly two hours later. The nationalists' car had headed towards Arcos De La Frontera, thirty kilometres to the north. Speculation was pointless and soul-destroying but we indulged in it anyhow. It was dark when lights finally appeared on the track and wove slowly towards the house. After an agonising wait it finally drew up outside. With a feeling of immense relief and cries of great joy we saw Simon climb out with the others. Augustine began to gently weep into a handkerchief. Pierre put his arm around her shoulders while they stood and watched their son approach.

We gathered in the lounge. John began the tale but was constantly interrupted by Susan and Phillipe if he omitted some detail. As a result he shrugged and left it to them. They told their tale with gusto, each correcting the other whenever a detail wasn't quite accurate.

When their car reached the road they saw Pierre standing on a low rise pointing north. They turned right and Phillipe quickly caught sight of the army cars. He slowed down, to let them stay comfortably ahead. They appeared unaware that they were being followed, and went straight to the garrison at Arcos.

The garrison was an ancient fort, built in the time of King Philip II, to house soldiers trained to fight Christianised Moors, known as Moriscos, and to spread the terror of the Inquisition. Now it was used to train regular soldiers, many of whom had seen action in Africa.

As soon as the two cars went through the fort entrance, Phillipe drove up to the gates. John presented his credentials and told the guard that he had an appointment with the garrison commander. An officer was sent for, who also checked John's credentials. Realising they were genuine, he became immediately obsequious and waved the car through, indicating the office of the commanding officer.

The two cars they had trailed were parked outside the same building. Phillipe jerked the car to a stop and they piled out, rushing up the steps and into an office. Seated at a desk was a bespectacled soldier, reading files. He looked up in surprise, asking them their business.

Phillipe was about to reply when they heard a thud. A moan escaped from behind the door opposite. Though the soldier stood to stop them, they rushed across the room. Throwing open the door, they stormed into a large office. An immaculately dressed senior officer was sitting behind a desk in a corner. Simon lay on the floor, groggily pushing himself erect, while three of his captors stood nearby.

'*Qué significa esta intrusión?*' The officer commanding the garrison stood up, bristling with indignation. He was of medium build, black hair cut short, a neat moustache reaching the corners of his lips. According to the sign on his desk his name was Colonel Segismundo Casado.

'Pardon my intrusion,' John said, 'but do you speak English?'

'Naturally. Now what are you doing in my office?'

'We have come for this man.' John pointed at Simon, who had now risen to his feet.

'That is not possible. He is under arrest. I suggest you get out.'

'Not before you have seen my papers and heard what I have to say,' John replied.

The colonel spoke in rapid Spanish and one of the gunmen drew a revolver and cocked the hammer. It made a loud and frightening click.

'Leave my office or I will have you shot as intruders.'

'I don't think so,' said John. 'Allow me to introduce myself. I am the Baron of Guildford, a member of the British House of Lords and I travel with diplomatic immunity. I am a personal friend of King Alfonso, who has dined on more than one occasion at my house. This young man was taken at gun point, illegally, from his parents' house. We were there and witnessed it. You have no jurisdiction over him and I demand he be released immediately.'

'You are in no position to make demands, Baron,' said the colonel.

'Colonel Casado, I am and I do. Others know of my presence here. Even now representation is being made to Madrid as to my whereabouts and those of my grand-daughter,' he nodded towards Susan. 'If you try and prevent us leaving with this young man there will be hell to pay. If any harm befalls us, you will find yourselves in serious trouble. At best your army career will be finished. At worst you could go to prison for a long time or even be hanged. Will you sacrifice your career? For this one man?' John spoke with utter confidence, and if he was nervous he didn't show it.

The colonel understood only too well the protection afforded by diplomatic immunity. They stood in a silent tableau for a few moments while Casado weighed up his options.

John's next words clinched the decision. 'If you let us all walk out of here and leave, then I give you my word nothing further will be said about this incident.'

Simon began to protest but Phillipe interrupted him and told him to be quiet.

'I have your word?' Casado looked with narrowed eyes at John.

'You have my word.'

The colonel opened a cigar box, removed a long, slim panatella, gripped it between his white teeth and used his thumb to strike a match. As it flared he held the flame to his cigar and drew deeply. He shook the match and threw it into a wastepaper bin.

'All right. He can go.' He pointed the panatella at Simon and said, 'You have been very fortunate . . . this time. Stay out of Spanish politics. If you don't, you may not be so lucky next time.' The colonel's eyes met John's. 'As for you, Baron, I also suggest you do not stay too long in the area. Accidents can happen. Unpleasant accidents. Lieutenant, show these people out.'

They left the garrison as quickly as they could and sped back to the vineyard.

We listened avidly to their tale. I was pleased with the outcome but aghast at Simon's reaction.

'If they think they're stopping me, they can think again,' he said.

'Simon, are you so stupid,' his father began, 'as to think the army will not do as they say? If it hadn't been for Sir John you would be in a military jail right now facing the good Lord alone knows what. Don't you understand the perilous position you're in?'

'I shall write a complete report on the incident and

place it with my advocate. If anything happens to me he will know what to do.'

'Listen to him,' said Augustine. 'A report with an advocate! How clever! How safe! Don't you understand, you stupid boy, you'll be dead?' She spoke loudly, her anger and fear erupting.

Simon was on his feet, yelling. 'You don't understand. If we don't stop them, if we don't fight them every step of the way, the liberties that we've worked for over the last five or six years will evaporate. Pouf!' He snapped his fingers. 'Gone! Just like that.'

'*Assieds toi*!' Pierre spoke harshly. 'And apologise to your mother. She was frightened for your safety. We were armed, prepared to fight to get you back. If it hadn't been for Sir John there would have been a gunfight . . . men would have been killed. It stops now! Now! Do you understand? No more politics!'

Simon was breathing heavily, as though he had been running. He made his apologies to his mother, thanked John in muted tones and left the room.

'Phillipe,' said Jacques, 'go after him. Try and talk some sense into him.'

Phillipe, as ashen-faced as the rest of us, nodded and stood up. He quickly followed his cousin. After a moment's hesitation Susan went as well.

Augustine bowed her head. When she looked up there were tears in her eyes. 'What are we to do? He won't stop. Pierre?'

Her husband bit his lip and shook his head resignedly.

'May I suggest something?' I asked.

Every eye turned to me. 'I know how you feel. I lost a daughter many years ago and let me tell you the pain remains in your heart until the day you die.' There were murmurs of condolence and I carried on. 'Send him away. Tell Simon he must go to America on business. Perhaps a few months over there will give him a fresh perspective. And the army will know he is no longer in the area.'

'But what reason can we have for sending him?' Augustine asked with sudden interest.

'I have a reason,' Pierre answered, suddenly excited. 'We had a report in about a new canning factory in Nova Scotia. We can send him there to study it. To see what the Canadians are doing that is different to us.'

'Better yet,' said John, warming to the theme, 'send him across Canada and America to look at different processes. The countries are so big, it will take him at least six months. Even a year.'

There were more suggestions along similar lines, but the factory was thought the best ruse.

A few days later a blazing row ensued between Simon and his parents. In the end after John's intervention, Simon was made to see sense and he agreed to go to America. We had booked our passage to London for two days hence and we agreed to take Simon with us. He would take the train down to Southampton for passage to New York on the first available ship.

On the day before we departed we were at dinner. The three youngsters had gone to a restaurant in Cádiz and we sat over a leisurely port.

'I can never thank you enough,' said Augustine. 'How were you able to convince my son to go to America?'

'I appealed to the buccaneer in him. The last time he was there he spent the whole time in New York. I described the excitement of the continent. The sheer adventure of travelling across a foreign land. What he could expect to see. I suppose I captured his imagination.'

'Well done, John,' said Pierre. 'Let us hope he will be away long enough to see sense.'

'I'll drink to that,' said Jacques and raised his glass in a toast.

When we departed we sailed from Cádiz. With us we took a dozen cases of port, a gift from the Bouchers. It was to be laid down for ten years. John joked it could be drunk at his wake. Susan and Phillipe had a tender parting and I saw Susan surreptitiously wipe a tear from her eye. Young love, I thought, sure she would soon grow out of it.

The cruise back was uneventful. Again we sailed aboard one of the Buchanan Shipping Lines' vessels, this time carrying wood and spices from India and Burma.

Throughout the journey Simon proved to be obsessed with politics. It seemed there were not only the two sides of Republicanism and Nationalism but serious differences of opinion on both sides which often led to open hostility within the parties. It was a complete mess.

Susan spent a good deal of her time with Simon asking questions about Phillipe, about his childhood and particularly about any previous girl friends. She was relieved to learn that there was no particular love in Phillipe's life.

The fair weather we'd had on the voyage out was long past and we hit winter winds and gales as we ploughed through the Bay of Biscay. I had been blessed with an iron stomach and enjoyed the rough weather, although it was very tiring. I spent each afternoon taking a nap. Eventually we reached the Channel. John stood with me, pointing out landmarks – Portland Bill, the Needles and the forts leading past the Isle of Wight into Portsmouth. The forts were bastions of engineering built to repel an invasion by Napoleon in the eighteen hundreds. We sailed serenely past the white cliffs of Dover in the early afternoon and docked at Tilbury just before dinner. I had enjoyed our adventure but I was very happy to be back home.

Simon stayed with us that night and left by train from Waterloo for Southampton first thing in the morning.

After her adventure in Spain I noticed a change in my granddaughter. Susan seemed more involved than ever with politics and attended many rallies advocating the socialist cause, either under the guise of the Labour Party or more often, communism and Marxism. Many of her set espoused the same doctrine. But for all their fervour and alleged support I noticed they did not skimp on their lifestyles. They still partied until all hours, squandered money they hadn't earned and drank expensive wines, rather than stout or brown ale. 'champagne communists' I called them.

I believed the thirties would go down in history as the most momentous decade in the history of the world. The Chinese revolution led by Mao Tse-tung was well advanced, although they faced certain defeat by the Nationalist forces and began their "long march" across 6,000 miles of hostile territory to Yenan in the province of Shensi.

Sion was as excited as a child when it was announced that a new airport would open in Gatwick to relieve the congestion at Croydon. The new aerodrome, complete with shops and air-conditioning, would be linked by underground with the London to Brighton railway line. The new air traffic control tower would be able to handle six aircraft at a time. It would be the most advanced airfield in the world.

The Tories swept back to power at the end of 1935 with a huge majority, promising rearmament, although it seemed to me the voters were more interested in housing and the issue of unemployment. Stanley Baldwin was again Prime Minister.

Italy invaded Abyssinia. Mussolini, the Italian fascist leader, proclaimed the Italian King, Victor Emmanuel, King of Italy and Emperor of Abyssinia. Ethiopia was no more.

After more than twenty-five years on the throne our beloved King George V died and his eldest son, the Duke of Windsor, became Edward VIII.

The armies of the Nazis walked into the Rhineland, welcomed by its people, and Hitler proposed a peace treaty to last for the next quarter century.

34

DAVID AND JOHN arrived at our townhouse almost simultaneously – David from the Commons, John from the Lords. Both were in foul moods.

'Whatever's the matter?' I asked. I was alarmed. Both men lived and breathed politics, but I'd never seen either of them so upset before.

'You won't believe it,' said David, 'but we aren't doing anything about the Reichwehr invading the Rhineland.'

John thrust a whisky into his hand. David sat morosely in an armchair, his glass untouched.

'The French Foreign Minister, Pierre Flandin, flew in today and begged us to support France against the Germans. To enforce the Treaty of Locarno, and stop Germany re-militarising the Rhineland. It was, after all, the only guarantee we in the West had that Germany would never be able to invade France and Belgium again. Now that buffer is gone, unless we do something about it now. Baldwin is a coward. He should have stood up to Edward.'

'What has the King got to do with it?' I asked, accepting a glass of sherry from John. I was puzzled. The King had made his pro-fascist views clear enough on the occasions I had met him. According to Edward, Hitler alone stood between us and Bolshevism. I knew too that the death of his cousin, the Czar, had left him with a deep hatred of communism.

'He's meddling in things he doesn't understand,' David said. 'Hitler won't stop at the Rhineland. Two years ago

he declared that the world should consist of three major
world powers. The British Empire, the Americas and the
German Empire of the future.'

'That's outrageous! Wherever did you hear such a
thing?' I asked.

'Straight from Squadron Leader Winterbotham, late of
the Flying Corps and Head of the Air Intelligence Section
of our Secret Intelligence Service. Herr Hitler told Freddy
personally. So we know those are his true intentions.
Right now Hitler is weak and we could easily send him
back into Germany with his tail between his legs. That
would probably cause his political downfall. France is
strong enough to do the job alone. They just want our
blessing.'

'Why don't we give it?' I asked.

'Because the King has threatened to abdicate if we
don't leave Germany alone,' was David's surprising reply.
'Let him, I say.'

'Don't be ridiculous,' I said. 'We need our King.'

David gave me an impatient look, sipped his drink and
said, rather patronisingly, I thought, 'Good old Mam.
Born in poverty, now living in wealth thanks to the
republicanism of America. Yet still a supporter of the most
privileged family in Europe. At least his brother understands duty and commitment. Edward's a rake and a
fool.'

I couldn't argue there. Edward's affairs with married
women were notorious but known only in the circles in
which he, and we, moved. Lord Beaverbrook, the newspaper magnate, had entered into an alliance with the
other newspaper proprietors to keep Edward's dalliances
a secret, allowing the British people to live in blissful
ignorance. While he was the Prince of Wales, his penchant
for married women was well known and he appeared to
indulge himself whenever he could. I could never understand why the women's husbands didn't kick up a fuss.
When I raised the issue with John he said that it just

wasn't the done thing. Now that he was King, he seemed to be a bigger rake than ever.

'An abdication so soon after becoming King would be a disaster,' I argued.

'He has no intention of abdicating,' said David. 'He likes the trappings of his position too much. It's a bluff and that useless buffoon Baldwin won't call it.' Draining his glass he stood up. 'I'd better be going. It's a late sitting and I have to get back.'

'Why didn't you stay for a drink in the House?'

'I'd have stood in one of the bars and spoken too loudly,' was my son's honest reply. 'I'll keep my powder dry for the Chamber. We must make the government see that appeasement doesn't work. Winnie's the only member making sense – he needs all our support. Hitler only understands one thing and that's force.' With that he left.

'Is he right?'

John looked at me and nodded. 'I'm afraid so. Edward has threatened a constitutional crisis of the first order. Baldwin has very little choice. Damn! It certainly bodes ill for the future. This isn't the first time that Edward has interfered. He sided with Mussolini when the Italians invaded Abyssinia *and* used his influence against Anthony Eden when Eden tried to get the League of Nations to impose sanctions against the Italians. Then he was still Prince of Wales. Now he's King, he's become insufferable.'

'I thought our constitution, such as it is, prevents him from interfering too much.'

'You've met Channon a few times, haven't you?'

'Sir Henry. Known as Chips. Once or twice, yes.'

'He's a very astute fellow. He's extremely worried by Edward's pro-German stance. He wouldn't be surprised if Edward was attempting to make himself a mini-dictator. A difficult task for an English King, but not impossible.'

'If he's flexing his muscle now, so soon after his father's death, how bad will he be after his coronation in May?'

'Good question, Meg. Recently, I've been involved in

high-level talks between Hardinge at Buckingham Palace, Canon Don of Westminster who speaks for the Archbishop of Canterbury and Geoffrey Dawson, editor of the *Times*.'

'You didn't tell me,' I said, a little peeved. Sir Alexander Hardinge was a very senior official within Buckingham Palace.

'Sorry, my dear. It was all terribly hush-hush. Fact of the matter is there was little to report except they all agree that Edward would make a particularly bad King. Dawson's tasked, privately of course, with using his contacts in the Dominions to canvas the opinion of influential people in Canada, New Zealand and Australia.'

'Canvas them? You mean, should Edward be crowned King?'

'No. Would they accept him as King if he married Wallis Simpson.'

'Ah! And? What was the outcome?'

'Under no circumstances would the old Dominions accept her as queen. It's clear to us that we must use Edward's marriage as an excuse to remove him from the throne.'

'Gunpowder, treason and plot?'

John's smile was positively wolfish. 'Mmm. Speaking of which, I've promised to organise a shooting weekend at Fairweather. I'll explain over dinner.'

The majority of the shooting party arrived on Saturday morning although some had arrived the night before. They included senior civil-service mandarins, members of the cabinet and church leaders and were gathered to discuss Edward and his role as our King. Decisions had been made over the brandy and cigars after dinner on the Friday but a good deal still needed to be agreed. I, like the other women in the party, was excluded from the discussions.

Saturday evening before dinner I was sitting with John in our room. In all the years we had known each other I had never seen him so agitated.

'It's agreed,' said John. 'Edward is to be manoeuvred off the throne. The more secure he feels in his position, the more evident his pro-Nazi sympathies become. Worse, he's attempting to impose his political will.' John sadly shook his head. 'We've learned that Edward gives state secrets to Germany within hours of receiving important papers and confidential information. It's absolutely intolerable. The man has no honour. The Foreign Office withhold sensitive information from him because they can't trust the blighter and he's Head of State. It's preposterous.'

John was working himself up into a tizzy and, conscious of his blood pressure, I said, 'Calm down, John. There's no point getting upset.'

John smiled, leant over and patted my hand. 'You're quite right. What would I do without you? We now have a plan to use Wallis to unseat him and by God, if the man acts as we expect, we can be rid of him by the end of next year.'

'Is she so much a threat?'

'We believe so. She's a "friend" of the German Ambassador, Joachim von Ribbentrop, who is a Nazi to the core. Some believe the friendship doesn't stop at the bedroom door. We now have the Secret Service watching her. Ironically, the King is being spied on as a result, because he's so often in her company.'

'Is there any real harm being done?' I asked naively, my pro-monarchy upbringing resurfacing.

John's reply shocked me to the core. 'There are men and women in this country, as in every country, who support their monarch, right or wrong. If he interferes too much and the government try and stop him we could have a civil war as bloody and devastating as the one in Spain.'

'Surely not!' I was aghast.

John looked gloomy. 'I'm afraid so. War is uppermost in the minds of everyone here. Sir Oswald Mosley and his blackshirts are in open support of the idea. And look at the names of the people who visited the King and Wallis while they were cruising in the Mediterranean. A veritable Who's Who of British and continental dignitaries.'

'The huge yacht Malcolm Muggeridge dubbed The Good Ship *Swastika*?'

'That's the one. For our Head of State to be swanning around southern Europe like that was inexcusable. Especially when General Metaxas has just seized power in Greece and Italy has become a dictatorship. And look at the people he entertained on board. Muggeridge was right, as usual.'

'As long as the British public doesn't know, surely we can keep a lid on things?'

'Yes, but it won't last much longer. The cruise has been heavily reported in the international papers. It's only here in Britain that we've kept his affairs secret. And that won't last much longer.'

'Why do you say that?'

'More people have begun holidaying abroad. They're reading the foreign press and wondering what on earth is going on. Baldwin has been inundated with letters from angry and concerned subjects on the matter. They are all virulently anti-Wallis. I agree with Baldwin on this. If he marries her and insists on remaining King then the country will divide and the consequences don't bear thinking about. We need to push Edward into making a move and soon. Baldwin has been tasked to set the wheels in motion.' Much to my chagrin, John declined to tell me what they were.

In November we had a visitor. He sat with John for hours before leaving to see the Prime Minister. When he left, I joined John in his study.

'That was Esmond Harmsworth,' he told me. 'He's a great personal friend of the King's. He was sounding me out about the Lords. He's on his way to see Baldwin to ask if the government would agree to a morganatic marriage.'

'What will that mean?'

'It means that as a commoner, Wallis would not acquire the King's rank and become queen. Any children could not inherit the throne, or any of his worldly goods. It is still unacceptable. I told Harmsworth. The government is unlikely to pass such legislation. Even if they tried, the Lords would fight it tooth and nail.'

John was proven right and the morganatic marriage was refused.

Still the crisis wouldn't go away. Churchill was a staunch supporter of the King and he came to dinner the day after he'd had lunch with Edward. As usual, once he had a few ports after a good dinner, Winnie unwound a little, knowing he was amongst friends whose discretion he could rely on.

His deep voice boomed across the dinner table. 'You know the PM refused the King permission to broadcast to the people. The King visited Baldwin in Downing Street last week and announced that he intended making a radio broadcast to his loyal subjects. To appeal to them over the government. To let him marry the woman he loves.'

'Good God!' John exclaimed. 'That would mean civil war. What on earth was the man thinking?'

'Now, Buchanan, I wouldn't go as far as that,' said Churchill, 'but it did give that lazy bugger Baldwin palpitations, I can tell you.' He chuckled. 'Baldwin told the King it was unconstitutional and couldn't be allowed.'

'Good for Baldwin,' said John.

'What's happening now?' I asked.

Churchill took out his watch and looked closely at the dial. 'Now I think we should listen to the wireless. I believe His Majesty is about to make an announcement.'

'He's not crowned yet,' said John. 'He's King in name only, not fact.'

Churchill waved his cigar and scowled. 'That's all he'll ever be. Turn on the wireless.'

David stood up and switched on the set in the corner, a handsome art-deco Consolette. While the valves warmed up we speculated as to the content of the King's speech.

The national anthem sounded and then a voice came

clearly over the airwaves. 'This is Sir John Reith at Windsor Castle. I have with me His Royal Highness, Prince Edward.'

'At long last, I am able to say a few words of my own.' His voice was far from strong, the accent an odd mixture of American and Cockney. 'I want you to understand that in making up my mind I did not forget the country or the Empire which as Prince of Wales, and lately as King, I have for twenty-five years tried to serve. But you must believe me when I tell you that I have found it impossible to carry the heavy burden of responsibility and to discharge . . .' his voice faltered and then he continued, 'my duties as King as I would wish to do, without the help and support of the woman I love . . . God bless you all. God Save the King.'

We sat in shocked silence until he had finished. 'My God,' said John, 'he's done it. He's abdicated. I'd never have thought it.'

'It's a sorry day,' said Winston. 'Meg, forgive me, but I need to return to Parliament. There is a debate starting in half an hour that I must attend.'

'I'm needed too,' said David. 'If you will excuse us, Mam?'

'Of course. Though, may we come to the public gallery? Tonight will be an historic occasion.'

David looked surprised. 'I don't see why not, if you wish it. Madelaine?'

'Will you be speaking?' His wife asked him, straightening the handkerchief hemline of her dress.

'Undoubtedly. If I can catch the eye of the Speaker and am called, I will.'

'Then yes, I'd like to come as well,' she said, her pride in David apparent.

We all five settled in the car. From our house in Mayfair the quickest route was along Park Lane to Hyde Park Corner, down Grosvenor Place, and along Victoria St. When we reached Buckingham Palace Road we could hear chanting. David was driving and John immediately instructed him to turn left and go along Buckingham Gate.

In front of the gate a crowd had gathered. As we drove nearer, we saw that the police were there in force, keeping back the crowd.

'What on earth are they doing?' Madelaine asked.

'Listen,' replied John, opening a window. We could distinguish the words quite clearly.

'We want Edward! We want Edward!'

'One two three four five, we want Baldwin, dead or alive.' Growing steadily louder the crowd alternated chants.

'Who are they?' I asked. 'If they are ordinary people come to support their King, why so few women?'

'Look at their uniforms, Meg,' John said heavily.'

I looked more closely. 'Good Lord! Blackshirts!' I gasped.

'Mosley's fascist scum,' said Winston bitterly.

'Let's go, David,' said John. 'We've a busy night ahead of us.'

Approaching the Houses of Parliament, we saw another Blackshirt rally. This time they were waving placards that demanded, 'Sack Baldwin. Support our King'.

The police cordon around the House had been strengthened but we were quickly waved through the barrier. John took us to the spectators' gallery while David and Winston went through the Members' Lobby.

Unsurprisingly, the House was packed. Britain was facing its greatest challenge for centuries and people had a great deal to say on the matter. As usual when I listened to the baying of Parliament, I was reminded of a hound pack closing in for the kill. I found their antics childish, their catcalls unoriginal and boorish. The Speaker, sitting in splendid isolation at the far end of the chamber, seemed a comic figure in his wig and sixteenth century clothes. His attempts to keep order bordered on the farcical. Suddenly he lost his temper.

In a loud commanding voice he said, 'I name . . .'

In the uproar I missed what he said. I looked at John

quizzically and he leaned over and said in my ear, 'The Speaker has named a Member. He must now leave the Chamber. If he doesn't, he can be more severely punished.'

Pandemonium continued until I saw a disgruntled man eventually walk out.

The Speaker finally got the members under control like a good whipper-in with the hounds. His threat to name other MPs was effective for about ten minutes, allowing serious debate to take place but the atmosphere quickly deteriorated once more. And so it went on for the next few hours. Not only was the House divided but so was the government. The abdication had aroused huge passions.

I was sitting quietly, wishing to go back home, when I suddenly jerked upright. David's name had been called.

'Mr Speaker, we are facing the gravest constitutional crisis it is possible to imagine. Unless we move quickly and decisively we are in danger of precipitating this great nation into civil war.' The rest of his words were drowned out by his opponents. As he continued, I thought proudly that David was indeed a fine figure of a man. I only wished his father could have been there to see it. Age and tiredness were making me maudlin. I turned to John, but he'd anticipated my desire to leave. We returned home, in sombre mood, as soon as David finished.

At Stepney, rioting broke out the following morning, between fascists and socialists when Sir Oswald Mosley held a mass rally for three thousand of his supporters. Windows were smashed, people were injured and there was a rumour that the army was to be called in. Britain teetered on the very brink of civil war. Then suddenly it was over, almost as quickly as it had begun.

Newsreels and newspapers showed Edward, now Duke of Windsor, taken by car to Portsmouth. The *HMS Fury* took him across the Channel to France. He had been King less than a year – a mere three hundred and twenty five days.

Prince Albert was proclaimed King George VI nine

hours after his elder brother went into exile. The new King immediately set about his duties while the newspapers ran editorials extolling his virtues. Small intimate details began to surface. Bertie, as he was known to his closest friends, was a crack shot. He had seen action during the Great War at the Battle of Jutland and then served with the Royal Air Force. His wife was now Queen Elizabeth. If they didn't have a son, ten year old Princess Elizabeth would ascend to the throne.

The crisis passed, slowly at first, but then more quickly as people realised that fundamentally nothing had changed. Except that Britain had exchanged a poor King for a good one. Other problems resurfaced and our attention was taken up again with events in Europe.

I received a letter from the Duchess of Devonshire a fortnight later. We had been regular correspondents for many years but this epistle was of particular interest. She had been staying at the home of Herman and Katherine Rogers, rich Americans, and close friends of Wallis Simpson. Why she was there I never discovered, as I would never have thought that the Rogers were the sort she would want to associate with. Be that as it may, she was there when Mrs Simpson arrived. The letter read as follows.

Villa Lou Viei
The French Riviera

Baroness of Guildford
etc.

12 December 1936

Dearest Megan,
I just had to write. The most extraordinary thing happened last night. We were seated after dinner playing a poor hand of piquet when the wireless was turned on and tuned to the BBC. You could have heard a pin drop when the King began his broadcast.

I looked immediately at Mrs Simpson, who turned bright red then a pasty white as the speech progresses. She had been rather quiet all evening but now she was grim faced – and absolutely furious, I could tell. When the speech ended we all simply sat there for a few seconds absorbing the news. Wallis suddenly stood up. She reminded me of one of the Furies in that play by what's his name. Oh, you know who I mean. 'The fool! The stupid fool!' she said loudly. Then she did the most extraordinary thing.

She began picking up glasses and flinging them across the room in temper. She broke a vase and then a glass bowl. It was all terribly dramatic and exciting. Herman Rogers managed to calm her down and Katherine took her from the room. When Katherine returned she said she had given Wallis a sedative and put her to bed. What a delicious fuss! I wouldn't have missed it for the world.

The following pages contained more tittle-tattle about mutual acquaintances. I showed John the letter who smiled and said, 'Good. I hope the damn woman remains upset and angry.'

'Where is the Prince, do we know?'

Nodding slowly, John said, 'I suppose there is no harm in telling you, only don't breathe a word. He is at Baron Rothschild's home, Schloss Enzesfeld. We have a close eye on him, believe me.'

I was intrigued. 'How?'

'You know we keep tabs on the right-wing here in Britain.'

I nodded.

'One of our most valuable assets is Fruity Metcalf. Major Edward Metcalf, to give him his name and rank.'

'Mosley's brother-in-law?'

'The same. He's a close and long-term friend of

Edward's. He just happens to be in Kitzbühel right now, skiing. Right across the border from his old chum. Edward has asked him to go to Enzesfeld. Fruity'll keep us in the picture as to what our ex-King gets up to.'

The devious brilliance of the British establishment never ceased to amaze me. Pity it was counter-balanced almost perfectly by its crass stupidity.

Germany began to rearm after Britain agreed to a new Naval ship building programme that effectively increased Germany's navy tenfold. John muttered darkly that it was a bad day for Europe. The lives of Jews were being made intolerable by the Nazis which upset me greatly. I was further upset by the lack of interest shown in Britain about their plight.

Throughout this time events in Spain were deteriorating. A socialist member of the Assault Guard, Lieutenant José Castillo, was assassinated. His friend, Captain Condés of the Civil Guard, set out to take revenge. He went to the home of Calvo Sotelo, the monarchist leader, and invited him to the headquarters of the Civil Guard under some pretext or other. He shot Sotelo in the back of the head and dumped his body at the East Cemetery in Madrid. These two events were used by the army as proof that Spain was no longer governable. Their deaths had the effect of accelerating a military coup that had been in preparation for some time. The conspirators had been waiting for General Franco's decision to begin the uprising. In July it spread to other garrisons. The three generals, Mola, Goded and Franco were finally in agreement. Their go-ahead triggered one of the bloodiest civil wars in history.

Naturally, gravely concerned for the Bouchers, we followed events avidly from newspaper reports. The *Times* was particularly good with its coverage and even the BBC was beginning to send reports for broadcast on the wireless. Appalling atrocities were being committed by both sides. How could the Spanish people do that to one another?

David was equally concerned about other dear family friends, Jake and Estella Kirkpatrick, who had settled in Spain. The children never tired of hearing how Jake, Estella and David had been shipwrecked on a Caribbean Island twenty years earlier. Their eventual escape and return to civilisation was indeed an enthralling story. Jake married Estella and returned with her to Spain, to her home town near Barcelona. Over the next two decades we had seen them regularly and David, together with John and Jake, seemed to drag each other into one scrape after another. But their escapades were behind them now. Or so I thought.

Susan had been restless ever since our trip to Cádiz. She was tired, she said, of her set who considered an elegant outfit or a game of tennis of more concern than events in Spain. Letters had been flying back and forth regularly between her and Phillipe. I noticed that she was often subdued after receiving one of his letters, and given to dramatic outbursts if the post failed to deliver one when expected.

Convinced she required intellectual stimulation, I had recommended she begin a university course in psychology and politics, with the aim of receiving a doctorate. Susan fairly bloomed in the hothouse atmosphere of Oxford, gaining in self-confidence and, apparently, revelling in late-night discussions with her new found friends.

Then, early in 1937, everything changed. Susan, together with six other undergraduates, stole one of Sion's planes and flew to Spain.

BOOK 4

Susan's Story

35

Spring 1937

WITH UNCLE SION safely away on business, Susan had no trouble in persuading Peter Cazorla to let her take the Griffin V for a spin. A promotional flight, she said, to show her friends the advantages of owning one's own plane. They were all super rich; she might get Uncle Sion an order or two. Peter agreed. The plane was the demonstrator they used for exactly that purpose.

'Peter, dear,' Susan added, 'Frances' father owns a large estate in Scotland. I thought I would take them up there and show them how convenient it is to land on your own property. The estate's just south of Oban, on the west coast. I'll be back tomorrow.'

Peter knew that Susan was a highly experienced pilot and often flew with Mike or Sion. She had also gone solo when flying circuits around Biggin Hill. He was dubious at first but she had always been able to twist him around her little finger and this time was no exception. The plane was in the hangar and they were sitting in the cockpit, Susan running her hands over the controls, a faraway look in her eyes. She loved the far horizons, the prospect of adventure.

'What's this?' She pointed to a short metal rod hanging alongside the pilot's position.

Peter grinned and said proudly, 'That is Juan's idea. See, it is adjustable. It slides back and forth. It can be fitted to this stud on the side of the column. We call it a height control lever. Let me show you.' He demonstrated how it worked.

Susan frowned. 'Why bother?'

'You know.' Peter jerked his head over his shoulder and Susan looked behind them. She saw nothing.

'No, I don't.'

'Susan, it will hold the plane in level flight long enough to you know what.'

'I know what? What on earth . . .' she trailed off. 'Oh, I see! To use the loo!'

'Yes. Exactly.' Peter sounded relieved that Susan understood. 'The plane will yaw but at least she will not dive or climb.'

'An excellent idea. Tell Juan from me that he is one clever *hombre*.'

Peter smiled with pleasure, basking in Susan's praise of his son. Susan climbed out of the cockpit while the plane was fully fuelled and wheeled out. Susan's friends, a woman and five men, climbed on board. If he was surprised by their casual clothes and battered cases, Peter didn't show it. He knew the rich often dressed quite poorly, showing a scant disregard for their wealth and station.

While the plane was being prepared for the long flight, Susan slipped into Sion's office and rifled through his charts. She quickly found the ones covering western and southern France and Spain. Folding them up she slipped them into her flight case and went out to the plane, dressed in a leather fur-lined flying jacket as protection from the cold wind blowing from the north.

Robert Nicholson, from her politics seminar, was to sit in the co-pilot's seat. She ran through a few things with him, including how to raise and lower the landing gear or the floats, depending on which was needed.

Finally they were ready and they lined up at the end of the runway. The plane rapidly picked up speed and soared into a bright blue sky, turning north. Susan waggled the wings to Peter who was standing by the hangar. He waved back. When Biggin Hill was a small handkerchief in the distance Susan turned to starboard and headed east for five miles. Again she banked to the right and turned to a new heading. Now the Griffin was headed south.

'Robert, can you hold the plane steady for a few moments?' Susan asked him, with a smile.

'Tell me what to do,' he replied. Narrow-faced, of medium height with thinning blond hair, his accent was northern England and working class. His hands were rough and callused, the hands of a carpenter, a trade he had been in since leaving school at fifteen, ten years earlier. He had worked for his uncle, whose last will and testament was funding his degree.

'Put your feet on the pedals and keep them there. Got it?'

'Yes,' he replied tentatively.

'Good. Now take the wheel. Just hold it steady.' Susan removed her own hands and the plane's nose began to dip. 'Hold her steady, for Christ's sake!' Susan snapped at him.

'Sorry.' He took a firmer grip and Susan removed her hands. This time the plane flew in a straight line for a few seconds before diving.

'I've got her,' Susan said. She had forgotten about the height control lever and fixed it to the column, adjusting its length to hold the plane steady. She took her hands off and watched the dials. The plane flew steadily onwards and she smiled. It worked!

'Good. Now I can check the charts.' Taking the purloined charts out of her case she rifled through them, selecting one and folding it into a square that fitted across her knees. Glancing up she looked out of the cockpit window and peered at the altimeter. The plane had drifted higher by fifty feet and she made a minute adjustment to the lever by twisting a micrometer gauge fitted to the fuselage end of the rod. She kept her feet on the pedals and retained control while able to read the charts.

Susan took some measurements and spent a few minutes checking her figures. 'We'll land at Toulouse in southern France. There's an airfield where we can refuel. We'll stay for the night and carry on in the morning.'

The flight was uneventful. The height control lever was a godsend. Instead of having to make continuous adjustments with her arms outstretched she could relax more than was usual. More importantly, it made navigating much easier. An anti-cyclone over the Bay of Biscay meant no winds even at ten thousand feet, no clouds, and views that were utterly breathtaking. None of the passengers had eyes for the panorama. They were each busy with their thoughts and fears. As they flew to join the International Brigades, fighting the fascists in Spain, their overwhelming emotion was one of pride.

For weeks they had been planning. The friends were an incongruous group, with little in common except their democratic beliefs. Thrown together in classes, they had gravitated gradually to each other, excluding the more pompous element of their year from their tight circle.

Originally they had escaped to the Oxford countryside for cycling and rambles, brought together as much by their love of the outdoors as their love of politics. How Susan had looked forward to their trips, dressed in checked skirt and jaunty beret, a kerchief round her neck. Most of all she loved the discussions, talking long into the evening. Later they claimed not to know who originally had the idea of doing their bit in Spain.

Daphne, full of verve and vitality, had been the most passionate about fighting the Fascists and had wanted to come to Spain for months. A friendly, outspoken girl, she loved to debate politics long into the early hours, eager to hear others' points of view. Mark had been the opposite, prone to anger if challenged. A Communist since his sixteenth birthday, he had become a passionate public speaker on the ills of big business and the rights of the working man. He saw it as his duty to travel to Spain to help in the war.

Henry was a slight twenty-two year old, with a thatch of blond hair and a straggling moustache. He belonged to the same college as Mark, and they had met in the debating society. If Mark had been a sabre of rhetoric, smashing his points home with a forceful finger, Henry was a rapier, each point a finessing prick against the stupidity of all those who did not understand the wonderful benefits that communism would bring to mankind.

The other woman in the group was a little irritating to say the least. Susan could never understand why such an intelligent man as Henry would put up with the simpering Frances. Blonde and pretty, if a little plump, Frances had never been troubled with a sense of humour.

They were joined by Toby Stoddard, who had recently come down from Oxford with a degree in European history. He was nearly six feet tall, thick set, trying to grow a beard and failing. His parents had hoped he would go on to become a lecturer but the romanticism of the civil war had beckoned. He often said that he'd read too much about conflict and history. Now he wanted to live it. Having come down from Oxford only months earlier, he had been looking for a way to get to Spain when he had been introduced to Susan. Without hesitation, he had volunteered to join her party, even offering to help with the expenses. His idealism was tempered with a will of steel. A boxing blue, he had been tipped for the Olympics in 1936, missing selection by a hairsbreadth.

Susan hoped her uncle would forgive her for stealing the Griffin. She had written a letter explaining what she was doing. It would arrive in a day or two at Biggin Hill, addressed to him. Her trust fund would go to her when she reached thirty, in four years time, or to her estate, in the event of her death. She had willed the price of the plane to Sion. The balance was to go to numerous charities after small bequests to the family. She had also written a long letter to her father, asking for his understanding and forgiveness. This was something she just had to do.

From her charts, Susan said, 'There's an airfield where we can refuel. We'll stay for the night and carry on in the morning.'

The landing at Toulouse went smoothly and Susan arranged to refuel the plane. They piled into a battered bus which took them to a small hotel in the nearby town, where they were checked in by the friendly proprietor and his wife.

After the excitement of flying so far, dinner in the hotel restaurant was an unusually quiet affair, where little food was eaten and too much wine drunk.

'Come on, cheer up,' said Robert, whose naturally cheerful, ebullient nature could be relied on to perk the group up. 'We knew what we were letting ourselves in for before we left jolly old England. The fascists have to be stopped at all costs. Let's raise a glass in a toast to the Republicans.'

They did so, clinking glasses, 'The Brigades International,' they said, one by one.

The proprietor, Jean-Luc, entering the dining-room from the kitchen, stopped at their table, full of fatherly concern. Placing his hands on the back of Susan's chair, he regarded the small group solemnly. 'What can I do,' he asked, 'to persuade you fine young people to return home to your parents? We have so many of you passing through, going to Spain. Not many of you come back,' he added ominously. 'And those who do wish they had never gone in the first place. There is much death and tragedy down there.'

The restaurant was full, with more than twenty tables occupied. Two men sitting at a corner table, looked over at them with dislike. One said something, stood up and came across to them. He was a tall, fit, young man with a pencil-thin moustache. He looked what he was. An army officer.

'Our host speaks the truth. You should turn back now. Do not go to Spain,' he said in English. 'You are not welcome. Go back home to Britain.'

'Who the hell are you?' Robert asked, outraged at the stranger's audacity.

'My name doesn't matter. I am a lieutenant in the glorious Spanish army. I warn you merely to go home. You are not wanted in my country.'

'Not by your lot,' sneered Robert. 'Thousands of us are being made welcome in the fight against the fascist swine.'

The officer shrugged. 'And many more support the Nationalist cause. I am one of them.'

'A bully in a uniform more like. Now go away before I give you a good hiding.' Robert glowered at him.

Susan realised he had drunk far too much of Jean-Luc's vin rouge. 'Shut up, you're drunk!'

'I do not think so, *señor*. I suggest you mind your manners. I will say this once more. Go back to where you've come from and stay out of Spain's affairs.'

'Go to hell,' said Robert.

The officer smiled. 'I think you'll be there before me. *Buenas noches*. And pray *señor*, we do not meet again.' He walked away with a tight smile on his face.

'The obnoxious little swine. Who does he think he is?' Toby said, glowering after the officer.

The confrontation with the Nationalist officer put a damper on their spirits and shortly after they left the restaurant and retired to their rooms.

The following morning, at first light, they headed back to the aerodrome. First-off, Susan checked the plane. As with all civilian planes there was no way of telling their nationality or identity. Personal or company logos were often the only indication of a plane's provenance. In their case, painted on either side of the fuselage was the Griffin rampant, showing the head and wings of an eagle and the body of a lion. It was painted silver on a black shield.

Then Susan spent some time studying her charts. Every mile she flew was a mile nearer to Phillipe. She closed her eyes, conjuring up a vivid image of his animated face, the strong set of his jaw, as he looked at her, his expression expectant and so full of charm.

She should have taken them further west, like Biarritz. She saw now that she should have skirted Madrid by flying well to the west, perhaps even over Portuguese territory. There was nothing for it. They would have to go straight down the middle. She measured it. In a straight line it was 640 miles and Madrid would be fifty miles to starboard. Luckily there was very little wind and Susan hoped for an easy passage over the Pyrenees.

There were a number of peaks marked on the chart, Pico de Aneto at 11,168 feet above sea level being the highest she could see. They would be aiming for it. She checked for emergency landing sites and was perturbed to find none until they had crossed the mountain range. Ever careful, she took a pipette of fuel out of the tanks and checked for water. The traces she found were well within the tolerances set by her safety-conscious uncle.

Remembering the scene in the restaurant she was suddenly overwhelmed with doubts but resolutely thrust them aside. Scanning the charts once more, she was unaware of the man at the edge of the airfield, taking notes. Notes he would later phone through to his commanding officer in Spain.

They took-off in a steep climb in a westerly direction and banked to port and the south-southwest. In the distance they could see the Pyrenees, the peaks gleaming white with ice and snow. Flying at a steady eight thousand feet the land was gradually rising to meet them as though they were in a shallow dive. When people on the ground could be clearly seen from the aircraft, Susan took them up another thousand. Now the mountains were rearing on either side. Big, beautiful and dangerous. By her reckoning, the village below was St Girons, and the snow-capped peak twenty miles away was Pico de la Calabasse. They were following the valley of the River Lez when they hit turbulence and the plane began to rise and fall in stomach-churning swoops of updrafts and downdrafts. She was frightened but didn't show it. She had never flown in conditions like these before. Her mouth was dry, her hands sweating. Wiping one palm and then the other on her trousers, she took them higher, passing through twelve thousand feet until they were flying straight again, the turbulence below them. The valley ended and they were travelling over high mountains stretching as far as they could see. Passing Pic de Maubèrbe at 9,450 feet, they came to another valley where the land began to fall away, this time to the south. They were over the main range.

Flying between the twin peaks of de Posets and de Aneto, Susan called, 'Ladies and gentlemen, for the past five minutes we have been flying in Spanish airspace.' She smiled at Robert sitting beside her, a cheer greeting her words.

Navigation was a case of checking the plane's position against landmarks or following a river or road. Susan flew south along the Rio Esera. The plane banked twenty degrees to starboard towards the town of Barbastro. And so it went on. Small alterations, as she flew from one point to another.

An hour and a half after take-off they were over the sprawling city of Zaragoza, one of the largest and most important cities in Spain.

They had no warning. One second they were flying peacefully along and the next the cabin was being shot to pieces. There were loud screams and a plane flew past the starboard wing. Susan was too shocked to react – she didn't know how. Her instinct told her they had been shot while her brain told her it was impossible. The screaming behind convinced her it was all too real. She looked everywhere, scanning the skies. Then she saw it.

A Messerschmitt Bf109! They were in serious trouble if he came back.

Susan was a natural pilot. She had started flying as a teenager and since then had taken to the air at every opportunity. She loved to hear her uncle Sion's war stories and often talked about fighter tactics with him. Those talks saved them when the Bf109, which had been climbing, then turned leisurely back. Susan put the Griffin into a steep dive and increased speed. She knew she had a top speed of 265mph which was no match for the Bf109.

Looking over her shoulder she said, 'Are you all right, back there?'

'Jesus, Susan!' Robert yelled. 'I think they're dead!'

Susan felt the hysteria rising in her. 'Dead?'

'Mark and Daphne. There's blood all over the place and they're not moving.'

She sat, numbed in shock and disbelief. Less than two hours ago, they had been at the beginning of the next stage of their adventure, gung-ho, off to fight the good fight, on the side of the people. A thought screamed through her head – they shouldn't have come. She wanted to scream and rant. Instead, a cold fury took hold. Looking over her shoulder she scanned the sky for the enemy plane. She squinted into the sun but saw nothing. She looked the other way. There it was, lining up on them like it was a turkey shoot.

Part of her had been flying instinctively while her mind had been verging on the hysterical. Now she had it together she knew she needed to do something fast. She pulled up and headed straight as an arrow for the Rio Ebro, the river that flowed through Zaragoza. The Bf109 changed its altitude and lined up on the Griffin. Susan was now looking steadily at the plane behind them. Since she was a girl she had acquired information about aircraft at every opportunity. Facts and figures flooded her mind. The plane, German built, was powered by a Rolls-Royce 1,000hp, 12 cylinder British manufactured engine called the 'Merlin'. She guessed the plane was capable of flying somewhere between 360mph and 400mph. The Bf109's armament included four 7.9mm machine guns, two to each wing. She knew nothing about their firing ranges. When would the pilot open fire? Instinct told her he'd come close. Make sure. With an easy unarmed target, he wouldn't want to waste any bullets.

She almost left it too late. Bullets were chewing into the trailing edge of the Griffin's starboard wing when she threw the plane onto its side and pulled back hard on the wheel. The Bf109 shot past with an angry roar of its engine. Susan whipped the plane upright and looked frantically for the river. There it was, glistening behind the four tall towers of a large, imposing building. It was their only hope. Surely the Bf109 wouldn't shoot so close to civilians? She flew between the towers, almost scraping the large central dome situated in the middle of the structure. She was trying to miss the building while staying low. At the same time she needed to spot the other aircraft. Flying through the towers she turned the Griffin as tightly as she could, standing on the port wing as they turned to the left. The manoeuvre saved them but it was more by luck than judgement. The Bf109 was firing even as they turned and the bullets went wild, strafing the river, missing one barge by inches, hitting another, killing the bargee standing in the stern.

Susan saw the fighter flash skywards and knew it would come again. She had nothing left. He could keep attacking until he got them. Their best bet was to land and jump for cover.

They were mere feet above the river, going against the flow. In front of her was a single span, stone bridge. She made up her mind.

'Put down the float gear. Quickly!'

Her co-pilot, Robert had only managed to turn the gear partly down when they were nearly at the bridge.

'Faster!' Susan said urgently.

Robert cranked the handle, fumbling for the locking pins.

Toby had been keeping a lookout behind them. 'Here he comes again,' he said, his deep voice relatively steady.

Instinctively they hunched down as though the very act would ward off the enemy bullets. The Griffin hit the water hard. Susan throttled back and they passed into the shadow under the bridge. The Bf109 flew over and started another turn, even as Susan was mashing the foot pedals in a desperate attempt to keep them in the middle of the river. There were a few barges on the water but none nearby, the bargemen keeping their distance from the Griffin. The plane began to drift down with the current, slowly at first but picking up speed. But it was too slow. The bridge was still fifty, sixty yards behind them and the Bf109 was already lined up for another strafing run. They were sitting ducks.

'Get ready to jump in the water,' said Susan. 'I'll try and keep the plane from hitting the banks while you jump clear.'

'No, Susan. There isn't time,' yelled Toby. 'Here he comes. Wait! He's turning away. I can hear guns! Look! On the bridge. There's a dozen or so men shooting at the plane. He's leaving!'

A few seconds later the Griffin swept under the span of the bridge and Susan worked like fury to keep them hidden. When they drifted out from under she increased power and took them back into shelter. One thing she knew. The Messerschmitt's range was relatively poor and he couldn't stay airborne for long, not when compared to the Griffin. When they drifted into the sunlight for a fourth or fifth time one of the men shooting at the plane leant down and waved. Above the noise of the engine Susan couldn't hear what he was saying but his thumbs-up gesture made it clear that they were safe.

Susan began to shake as aftershock set in. Tears welled up. She couldn't prevent them spilling down her cheeks.

Angrily she wiped her face with the back of one hand. This was no good. She needed to do something quickly if they weren't to damage the plane on the banks of the river or get mowed down by a barge. Much as she wanted to escape from the Griffin they needed to land somewhere safe.

Opening the throttles wide she lined them up and the little plane shot across the water and was quickly lifting into the sky. Turning the plane she flew back over the bridge and waggled the wings to the waving crowd. Then she headed south. Fear moved like a live worm in her stomach as she searched the sky for other enemy aircraft. If one appeared what could she do? She had no answers, only prayers. A mantra played in her head. Please let us live. Please let me live.

Realising they were following the Rio Hueiva she looked for a flat piece of ground. She needed to land more than anything in the world. If they pranged, so what? She had to get out of the plane as quickly as possible. The stench of blood was overpowering.

A track ran alongside the river, wide enough to take the plane. If there were potholes too large to cope with then too bad. She lined up the Griffin, went in too steeply, hit the ground hard and finally brought the plane to a stop. Fumbling with her lap belt, she undid it, crawled over her seat and threw open the door. Practically falling out of the plane she made it to the verge before she threw up. On her hands and knees she heaved until her stomach was dry. She couldn't stop. Tears coursed down her face and sobs wracked her body.

Wearily, as the heaving and sobbing subsided, she turned over and sat down, her head hanging between her knees. She was aware of a presence beside her; Toby knelt down, offering her a drink of water.

Taking it she swilled her mouth and then drank thirstily. After a few moments she looked at him and asked, 'How are the others?'

'Badly shaken. Henry has a flesh wound. A bullet grazed his thigh.'

'Mark and Daphne?'

'Dead. They each have five, perhaps six bullets in them. They're a mess.' He shuddered visibly. 'I've never seen anything so ugly before. Their faces are . . . contorted. The blood is everywhere. The carpet is sodden with it.'

Taking a deep breath Susan said, 'Pull them out. Strip the covers from the seats too, if they've got blood on them. Get Robert to give you a hand to take the bodies out.'

'What do you plan to do with them?'

'Bury them,' said Susan. 'We'll use our hands if we have to and dig them a grave together.'

'But we can't!' Toby was aghast.

'What do you suggest, Toby? Take them with us? What for?'

'We need a church. A priest.'

'What priest will bury someone fighting for the government? The enemy, our enemy, are the Church and the Army. Besides, neither of them believed in God.'

'Daphne did.'

'Then she shouldn't have been here,' came the harsh reply. Seeing the hurt on Toby's face she put out her hand and touched his arm. 'I'm sorry, Toby, really I am. But we've no choice. You must see that.'

After a few seconds he raised a wan smile and nodded. 'We'll bury them under those trees.'

Frances, prone to hysteria at the best of times, objected stridently to the idea. Although she had no rational objection and could suggest nothing better she still didn't want to bury her friends in the wilderness. While she sat by the aircraft, crying and refusing to help, the others used an axe and anything else they could get their hands on to dig shallow trenches. They covered the mound of earth with rocks. Then they stood in a forlorn group, heads bowed, remembering.

Frances stood with her arms around Henry. She was sobbing quietly, making no attempt to dry her eyes or her face. She had practically forced Henry to allow her to come. She was prepared to agree to his views, to support his arguments but all she had really wanted was to settle down and have children. Henry's children. Now look at them.

They carried no bible, but Toby mumbled the Lord's Prayer over the graves. Sadly they turned away, trudging back to the plane.

'What do we do now?' Toby asked as they stood by the cabin door.

Frances' voice shrilled through the morning air. 'Do? We go home! We get out of this rotten country, Toby, and get back to England.'

The others looked at her in a mixture of surprise and shock. 'Don't talk rubbish,' said Susan. 'We aren't going back. We came to fight the fascists and fight them we will.'

'You can't!' Frances was verging on hysteria again. 'We have to go back. Two of our friends are already dead, Susan. Isn't that enough?'

Henry looked at her in bewilderment. 'But that's even more reason to stay. Their deaths, otherwise, are pointless.'

'This isn't our war, Henry. Please, all of you. Let's go back home. I don't want any more of us killed. Please.'

Susan spoke coldly. 'If you want to go home, Frances, we won't stop you. I'm here to get to Cádiz. To help Phillipe. I never hid that from you. This morning hasn't changed anything. If anything it's made me more determined than ever. A German aircraft killed our friends. That means the fascists are working together, to end socialism and communism. We have to stop them.'

'Then let somebody else do it,' Frances said bitterly.

Four pairs of eyes turned away from her with varying degrees of contempt. Susan turned towards the Griffin. 'I'm checking the damage. The rest of you can do what

you like but I'm going on.' What a waste, she thought
bitterly. She had an image of Mark and Daphne, lying
together on Mark's cramped bed in his untidy rooms,
cramming Spanish and laughing. Laughing in anticipation
of their trip and because they were in love. She shook
her head to clear her thoughts.

Frances shouted. 'There could be more of them. Out
there, waiting to attack us. Let's go back before it's too
late.'

'You go, Frances,' Henry spoke quietly. 'Walk into
town and take a train. Explain that you're a tourist stranded
in Spain and trying to get home. I'm sure you'll be all
right.'

Frances sobbed while they checked the plane. After
about fifteen minutes Susan straightened up. 'There
doesn't appear to be any structural damage. The holes in
the wings will hold until I can get them patched. Fuel is
fine. There's nothing keeping us from flying.'

They stood looking at each other for a few seconds
until Toby said, 'Shall we climb aboard?'

'We need to turn the plane,' Susan said. 'We landed
safely so in theory we should be all right going over the
same ground again.

When the Griffin was facing the opposite direction,
they climbed aboard. Frances was still standing in the
road. She was the picture of misery. Her dark blonde hair
hung lank on either side of her face, her nose and eyes
were red from crying. She stood as if frozen, unable to
make a decision.

Susan became impatient. 'Throw out her luggage and
let's go. I'm not waiting any longer.'

Henry said, 'Please, Frances. Get in.' The propeller
turned, the engine coughed, spluttered blue smoke and
burst into life. The sound appeared to galvanise Frances
into action, for she suddenly ran across and climbed
aboard. Henry closed the door and signalled to Susan.

It was a bumpy take-off but they were soon airborne

without mishap. Susan flew low, avoiding any built up areas. Instructing the others to keep a sharp watch for any aircraft, near or far, she searched constantly for landing sites as she flew, steep and narrow valleys, rivers and lakes that might help them to get down quickly and run for cover. Of one thing she was sure. She couldn't out-fly a Bf109 fighter.

36

AN HOUR AFTER take-off they passed near the town of Cuenca. Susan had been following the Rio Jucar as it flowed south out of the Cuenca Mountains, hugging the terrain. When she saw the town ahead she banked steeply to port and went around it. By her estimate they had about three hundred and fifty miles to go. Just under two hours. The weather was beginning to deteriorate, the wind from the west picking up. On the far horizon, clouds were forming as a storm blew in from the Atlantic. She didn't fancy getting caught in bad weather but hopefully storm clouds might keep the Germans out of the air. Checking the fuel she decided they had plenty and opened the throttles further. She settled the plane at 230mph and did her sums again. An hour and a half flying time. Better.

Susan was feeling tired. Not just from the effort of flying dangerously low, navigating and staying hyper-alert. Her fatigue was partly shock, the aftermath of their experience. The adrenaline rush that had fed her senses had gone, leaving her feeling battered and bruised. Her concentration was wandering and she knew that a lapse could be lethal. What she wanted most of all was a deep sleep and a hot bath. A cold glass of wine, a hot bath and a nice soft bed . . . She jerked awake. Christ! She had to stay alert, for all their sakes.

The remaining flight was straightforward. They landed on a pasture near the house at the Bouchers' vineyard. Phillipe and Simon were there to greet them. Susan's heart raced when Phillipe's eyes met hers. She was suddenly aware of her appearance, her dirty face, her bedraggled clothes. Looking at him, she was overcome with shyness. No promises had been exchanged, but whatever was between them had brought her across Europe and into a war. Because she longed to be with him. Now doubts assailed her. Uncertain of his reaction, she looked again into his eyes. How could she have forgotten the golden flecks in his irises? She scanned his face for any hint of emotion, any hesitation in his heart. He looked back at her, the same regular features she knew from photographs, the straight white teeth in his tanned face.

His smile said it all. As she jumped down from the aircraft, Phillipe took her in his arms and kissed her passionately. She could feel the relief and longing in his embrace and responded. A deluge of emotions swept through her and she held on to his neck for support. Tears sprang to her eyes. Seeing them, Phillipe was immediately full of concern.

'*Mais, qu'est-ce qu'il y a?* What's wrong, Susan? Where are the others? I thought there were seven of you coming.' Catching their mood he grabbed her by the shoulders. 'What has happened?'

In monosyllables they told their story. In a sombre mood they walked towards the house.

Simon spoke slowly. 'It was the officer at the hotel in Toulouse. That whole region of France is covered with spies looking for International Brigades supporters. He will have reported you. And that emblem on the side of the plane would have been very easy to spot.'

Susan nodded. 'That's what I thought. But the plane? Where did it come from?'

Phillipe sighed heavily. 'So much has changed since you were here last. Up till a few weeks ago, the legitimate government had military superiority. It controlled the air force and the navy. Then that swine Hitler interfered and changed the balance of power.'

'I thought,' interrupted Toby, 'that Stalin was supplying you with arms.'

'He is. Stalin has been supplying the Spanish government since last August, as part of his plan to build a united front against Nazi Germany. He sent one hundred tanks, one hundred aircraft and around five hundred experts to advise and maintain the equipment. It meant the government was technically superior to the Nationalists.'

'And now?' Susan asked.

'And now Franco has the Condor Legion. German Nazis to a man,' Simon replied bitterly. 'We've estimated there are twelve thousand Germans here, along with fighter and bomber aircraft, tanks and other motorised units.'

The information was met with stunned silence until Susan said, in a whisper, 'So many?'

'The Messerschmitts are at Seville. Sixteen Bf109Bs. They've got transport aircraft and six He51A-1 biplane fighters.'

'It was a Bf109 that jumped us,' said Susan. 'And that was nearly five hundred miles away.'

Phillipe nodded. 'They must have deployed some of them north. Matters down here have taken a serious turn for the worse.'

Susan was by now thoroughly alarmed. 'Go on.'

'The Condor Legion disembarked at Cádiz in November last year. They are controlled by a German officer named Colonel Wolfram von Richthofen. They strike fast and they strike hard and give no quarter. Already they have been responsible for the deaths of thousands.'

'Why is it we haven't even heard of them?' Susan asked.

'Unbelievably,' said Simon, 'Franco denies their existence. He says it is all Republican propaganda. Of course, he in turn exaggerates the involvement of the Russians and the other International Brigades.'

'Málaga fell last month,' said Phillipe, 'and it shouldn't

have. Here, let us sit outside. I will tell you about it over a glass of wine.'

Susan sat down heavily next to Phillipe, exhaustion sweeping through her. But it was quickly forgotten as Phillipe's tale unfolded.

'When the war started many Republicans saw it as an excuse to extract revenge for both petty and major insults and injustices. Málaga and the surrounding countryside has been dominated by the CNT. That's the *Confederación Nacional del Trabajo*, an anarchist-syndicalist trade union. They hate the Army and the Church in equal measure. In fact, they hate just about everybody. They're always squabbling amongst themselves. Once the rising started, they began to burn churches and kill priests for no reason. They also murdered many political rivals, both Republicans and Nationalists. The Italians attacked Málaga under the command of General Orate. Squabbling and ineptness amongst the Republicans prevented them from mounting a suitable defence and they were quickly overrun. It was a bloodbath. Summary trials were followed by immediate executions.'

'But why,' asked Susan, 'didn't other Republican units come to their aid?'

Simon shook his head sadly. 'That is part of the problem. Anarchists, of course, don't believe in leadership. They won't agree to any formal command structure which would allow them to fight cohesively. Málaga is linked to Almería by a narrow coastal road and there we have a Republican stronghold. Reinforcements could have easily been sent.'

'So why weren't they?' Robert asked, his glass of wine standing forgotten on the table in front of him.

'We don't know,' replied Phillipe. 'There are many rumours. Some say help wasn't asked for and others that it was refused. Whatever the truth of the matter help didn't arrive and the Nationalists took the city. Everyone in Málaga who has any sort of link with the government is being tried and killed. In the first week alone four thousand Republican supporters were executed.'

There was a collective gasp of horror. Frances turned to Henry and said, 'Did you hear that? Four thousand! For the love of God, Henry, let's get out of this country.'

Phillipe and Simon looked at her in surprise.

'I thought you came to fight for us?' Simon asked. 'And now you would leave?' His voice was rising, anger coursing through him.

Frances was momentarily thrown but Simon's anger sparked her own. 'Two of my friends are already dead,' she retorted. 'Isn't that enough?'

'No!' Simon smashed his fist on the table. 'We too have lost many friends. This is the beginning. We must fight this tyranny.'

Phillipe put a hand on his cousin's arm. 'That's enough,' he said. 'I am very much afraid, Frances, that it is impossible for you to leave Spain.'

'Why? You cannot keep us here.'

Smiling, Phillipe replied. 'I would not dream of doing so. However, I must inform you that the Nationalists have decreed that all foreigners are to be considered members of one of the International Brigades and summarily executed.'

Frances gasped, her hand going to her mouth; her pale blue eyes huge in her doll-like face.

'I am afraid that what he says is true.' Simon could not quite keep the satisfaction out of his voice.

'We are very close to Gibraltar here,' Susan said softly, looking at Simon, not hiding her dislike in her voice. 'She can go there.'

Simon snorted. 'She can try but she won't get very far. I know. Others have gone before her.'

'What happened to them?' Frances' voice was tremulous.

'They were shot. No trial. No publicity. No protest by your government. Just . . . shot. Or,' he added with a certain amount of relish, 'hung.'

'Only sides of beef and pictures are hung. People,' said Susan coldly, 'are hanged.'

Simon gave an ironic little bow across the table.

'I can fly them to Gibraltar,' Susan toyed with her glass, looking at him defiantly.

'There's no airstrip,' he said triumphantly.

Susan suddenly leant forward in anger. 'The Griffin can land on water. If Frances wishes to leave I'll take her.'

'I will not allow it,' replied Simon, white spots of fury on his cheeks. 'The aircraft is forthwith impounded.'

Susan did the only thing she could think of. She threw her glass of wine in his face.

Simon leapt to his feet and made to strike Susan but Phillipe caught his arm and stopped him. Toby and Henry had also jumped up, ready to defend Susan.

'Enough!' Phillipe yelled. 'We are working . . . fighting together. I regret Frances, you must remain here. Simon is right. We cannot allow the plane to be used to try and reach Gibraltar. It is too precious a commodity.'

Susan stood up and leant on the table, 'I'm the pilot. It is my plane. I decide where she goes and when. I and I alone will fly the Griffin. I hope that is perfectly clear.'

Simon made to protest but Phillipe gripped his arm again. 'Perfectly, Susan. You are quite right.'

'*Espèce d'idiote*,' argued Simon. 'The local council will decide about the plane. No one else. Especially not a woman.'

'Listen to me, Simon,' Susan said wearily. 'I am here to fight against fascists. We each need to know what is going on. We will then make our own informed decisions about whether we stay or leave. If Frances wants to leave I will take her to Gibraltar. I will also return. I brought her here, so I am responsible for her. I hope I make myself understood?'

Phillipe and Simon looked at her in astonishment. Spanish men were proud of their women, but preferred them to be seen rather than heard. Even in their parents' house, where their mothers were French, there was an understood role for women. In the kitchen. In the bedroom. Bringing up the children. But *not* in politics. Despite socialist feminism.

They sat in silence until Susan spoke. 'I need a bath and a few hours rest. After that I would like to be filled in on events locally and nationally. I'm sure I speak for all of us. We came here as an act of faith – to help you beat the fascists. We think this is our battle as much as Spain's.' Looking at her watch, she added, 'I suggest we meet for dinner. Say drinks at six o'clock?'

If they were surprised at the easy way she assumed control of the discussion, they didn't show it. Simon glowered as Phillipe stood up.

Susan smiled at him. 'Will you please show me to my room?'

As she moved away, Phillipe picked up her holdall, almost at a loss for words. He directed her to the right wing of the house. Susan was acutely aware of his presence and moved slightly so that her hand touched the back of his. Phillipe dropped the bag and pulled her around by the arm. As she turned to face him, he cupped her face in his hands and kissed her deeply. Clinging to him tightly, she felt tears welling in her eyes. The stress of the last hours was taking its toll. Phillipe broke away and smiled down at her while she looked up into his eyes. She examined his face again, the straight nose, his slightly cleft chin. His skin was tanned, with the colour of a man who lived under a Mediterranean sun. She examined each detail, absorbing him into her consciousness.

Her voice husky, she whispered, 'Will you come and waken me about five?'

Phillipe nodded, not trusting himself to speak. Breaking off their embrace he showed her to her room, the same room she had stayed in before. After bathing she lay awake for what seemed an eternity, but was only moments before she fell into a deep sleep. She dreamt of Phillipe. Of making love to him, of his hands on her. Suddenly she was awake with a start and knew it wasn't a dream. It was real.

Later he lay with her head on his arm, caressing her. Kissing her forehead he murmured, '*Tu n'es plus vierge. I thank you with all my heart.*' Seconds later his hands were arousing her again. In that moment Susan knew that she was completely in love, a feeling so exquisite, so painful, that there was nothing she wouldn't do for him. Nothing.

Finally she heard him whisper, 'It's time to go downstairs. The others will be wondering where we are.'

Sleepily she replied. 'I know. It's just that I want this moment to last forever.'

Reluctantly she pushed herself up on her elbow and looked down at him. He was smiling contentedly. 'You look,' Susan said, stroking his cheek with a finger, 'like the cat who got the cream.'

'Pardon?'

Shaking her hair out, she laughed. 'Nothing. It's an English saying. You look, how should I put it? Satisfied with yourself? Like you've hit the jackpot.'

Phillipe put his hand behind her head, kissed her and said, 'But I have, *ma chérie*. Know that I love you very much. For months I have been thinking only of being with you again. When I received your letter I was the happiest man in Spain. In the world!' he added gallantly, causing Susan to giggle. 'More, I want babies. Lots of them.'

'That's usually the girl's line. Aren't you forgetting something first?'

He looked at her enquiringly.

'A little thing like a wedding ring.'

Phillipe laughed. 'Oh, that! No, I'm not forgetting. It will be a big affair. We will invite all your friends and relations and have the wedding here. The local priest can officiate.'

Susan smiled back. 'Alternatively,' she teased, 'we can have the wedding in England. Knowing my family we can probably have it in Westminster Abbey.' A thought suddenly came to her. 'Religion! What religion are you?'

Phillipe looked at her in surprise. 'If forced to answer, I'd have to say lapsed Roman Catholic. And you?'

'A lapsed Protestant. Perhaps we should find a lapsed rabbi to marry us?'

The absurd notion appealed to them enormously and in the mood they were in, they thought it very funny. They both got a fit of the giggles and were soon rolling on the bed, laughing out loud. They were in that euphoric place known only to young lovers. Stopping suddenly, they looked at each other for long seconds, the reality of their situation sweeping away their mood.

Susan spoke softly. 'I want a long and happy life with you, my beloved. Perhaps we should leave Spain, as Frances says.'

Phillipe looked at her sadly. 'I cannot leave, Susan. You've no idea what it is like here.'

'Where are your parents? And Pierre and Augustine?'

'My parents are in California looking at the fledgling wine industry there, while Simon's parents are in Canada where there's a huge fishing and canning industry. My parents say with a lot of justification that they've seen enough war to last a lifetime. And a Spanish civil war isn't theirs to fight.' Shrugging, he added, 'Who can blame them? The horrors of the trenches in the Great War are enough for any sane man. They do not wish to get caught up in any more war.'

'What do they say about you and Simon? And what's he doing here? He was in America not long ago.'

'He could not stay away. His heart is here.' Phillipe paused. 'My father and Pierre tell us we have to decide for ourselves. Our mothers say we should leave and join them.'

'And what do you say?'

Phillipe was silent for a few seconds and then he shook his head. 'I don't know any more. The fascists are truly evil. It is the only word I can think of to describe them. But the communists are no better. Each side commits one barbarous act after the other.'

'Hold me tight, my darling.' Susan slipped her arm around his neck and hugged him. 'We don't chose whom we love. We just do. I absolve you of any responsibility. I'm here because I wish to be with you. It's as simple as that. If you stay, I stay. If you leave, I leave.' An image of her dead friends filled her mind and her eyes prickled with tears.

Phillipe was silent for a few seconds and then he looked down at Susan's upturned face. 'If I leave,' he said heavily, 'I would be running away. I would spend my life wondering whether I left out of cowardice or out of love. In my heart I know that fascism must be stopped – at all costs. We know what is happening in Germany. Hitler and his evil regime are strangling freedoms one by one. I feel,' his voice faltered, 'I feel I have an obligation to fight.'

Susan nodded.

'I could not love thee, dear, so much,
Loved I not honour more.'

'What was that?'

'From a poem by Richard Lovelace written about three hundred years ago. That's what it's all about – honour, decency. In all conscience we can't go back and fighting is the only way forward. So my skills – and my aeroplane – are at your disposal.' She began to caress him. 'But the fight can wait until later.'

When they went downstairs the others were already

gathered on the patio, drinking wine and talking animatedly.

Susan asked Henry, 'How's your leg?' Taking a glass of cold white wine she drank a mouthful, savouring the taste, contentment coursing through her veins.

'Frances changed the dressing. It's nothing.'

'What were you discussing?' Phillipe asked them.

'Tactics,' said Simon. 'The easiest, most effective way to undermine the fascists.'

'And what conclusions did you come to?' Susan toyed with her glass, twisting the stem in her fingers.

Simon answered. 'We attack known Nationalist targets.'

'Such as?' Robert asked. 'I mean do we attack police stations? Or army barracks? Or what?'

Simon shook his head. 'We wouldn't stand a chance if we did. Not until we're better organised.' He paused, lost in thought, gazing out across the valley and the vineyard.

'So what *are* you proposing?' Susan's exasperation was compounded by Simon's attitude.

'We rob a bank. Correction, four banks.' There were gasps of astonishment from the others. 'We have already identified the targets. With the money we can buy arms.'

'Which banks?' Susan asked.

'You do not need to know that,' Simon glared. It was obvious that he had a problem with her. She wondered why. Was it simply because she was a woman? Taking a cigarette he lit it from the glow of the one he was smoking. Simon had long tapering fingers. The index and middle finger of his right hand were stained a light brown from nicotine.

Susan returned his stare for long seconds. She spoke firmly, keeping her voice level. 'If we are to be involved we need to know what you are planning and who we are dealing with.'

'The names will mean nothing to you,' Simon glared at her.

'Granted, but you can give us their background. That's important. Do they have any skills?' She realised that what she was about to say would sound ludicrous but she said it anyway. 'To help us carry out the robberies?'

'Yes,' said Simon, smiling for the first time. 'They took a course in robbing banks at the University of Madrid.'

The flippant remark broke the tension and they all laughed. Susan blushed, before smiling sheepishly. The laughter was a little forced but it cleared the air.

Simon appeared to relent. 'We are from all walks of life. It is not good for you to know our names.'

'What do you mean?' Frances asked, fear flaring in her eyes. She was sure she knew what his reply would be.

'If you are taken by the Nationalists they will do everything they can to get information out of you.' He paused, dragged deeply on his cigarette and waited.

'Such . . . such as?' Frances asked.

'Torture. Do I have to spell it out for you, Frances?'

'What . . . what sort of torture?' Frances couldn't let go. Like a dog worrying a bone she had to know.

Simon told her, in graphic detail.

'It can't be true,' protested Robert. 'Not in Europe. It's savage, barbaric.'

'I agree,' said Phillipe. 'But what Simon says is true.' He gulped a mouthful of wine. 'Unfortunately it's happening on both sides.'

'Thanks to Franco and his pigs,' Simon swore vehemently. 'Since he arrived from Africa he's taken terror to a new level. It was bad before but now,' Simon shook his head, 'it is beyond anything we have known or seen. Women see their children killed in front of their eyes before they die. Pregnant women are bayoneted and their babies cut from their wombs. Rape is commonplace. No age is safe. It doesn't matter if you're a woman, a man or a child. Some of the animals from Africa are sodomites.'

Frances' face convinced Phillipe it was time to change the subject. 'We need to make plans. We have a great

deal to do.' The men and Susan spoke animatedly but
Frances kept quiet. She was brooding and evidently upset.
A short while later she excused herself and went to her
room. They watched in silence as she departed.

'She is a liability,' said Simon.

'She'll be all right,' Henry defended her. 'Leave her
alone.'

Blowing a long stream of smoke through his nostrils
Simon slitted his eyes and said, 'I do not think so. She
is a danger to us all.'

'What do you propose?' Susan asked. 'Sending her
home?'

'She cannot go home. It is too late.' The way he spoke
sent shivers along Susan's spine. He couldn't have meant
what she thought he meant. Looking into his eyes she
shivered. They were cold and angry. Suddenly she felt
overwhelming fear. Their sterile, academic arguments
back in England seemed puerile. If Simon wanted to take
the plane he could and she knew it. What was worse,
Simon saw the understanding in her face and smiled
triumphantly.

A dish of paella was brought from the kitchen, a feast
of rice flavoured with saffron, local shellfish and fresh
vegetables grown on the estate. Served with a fine, white
wine, it should have been a delicious meal enjoyed by
them all. To Susan the food tasted like ashes.

They split up soon afterwards. Her lovemaking with
Phillipe that night was intense and passionate. She wanted
to treasure every moment with him.

37

SITTING OUTSIDE THE taverna in a red, wide-brimmed raffia hat and pretty wrap-over chiffon dress, Susan looked for all the world like a carefree young woman waiting for her beau.

She had spent the last three days repairing the bullet holes in the plane and checking that everything worked properly. She had taken her time, ignoring as best she could the activity around her. People came and went, strangers who ignored her and the others. It was better not to know their names and to forget their faces. The less they knew the less they could be made to tell. A bank had been selected. A careful reconnaissance had been made and information collected. Friday was payday for many businesses in the area. So Thursday was the day the bank coffers were fullest. Yesterday she had been given her orders. Her task? To sit and watch. If the police or army arrived she was to warn them. How? By firing a single shot from a gun. Which gun? The one she was handed. She took it matter-of-factly, aware of the contempt in Simon's eyes. She had handled many different guns in her time, mainly shotguns, but also a few revolvers and once even a Lee Enfield. The co-ordination needed to fly could be improved by practising eye and hand co-ordination, usually by shooting at clay pigeons and live pheasants. Her father prided himself on his ability with a shotgun. She could outshoot him. Usually.

The revolver fired a .38 Special. From butt to barrel end it was nearly nine inches long. The trademark on the butt identified the maker as Arizmendi Zulaica & Co of Eibar, Spain. There was no safety device. A rapid examination told her what she needed to know and she pulled back the thumb catch on the left side of the frame and swung the cylinder out. She pressed in the ejector rod which forced in the ejector plate and pushed the bullets into her palm. She examined each one. There was no sign of corrosion. She took a cloth and wiped the gun, examining it carefully for rust. She lightly oiled the working parts and put the gun back together, working silently.

She beaded along the hammer and the foresight, her arm outstretched. The gun was old. At least fifteen years, maybe more. It had seen a lot of action. The rifling was probably worn and hence it would be highly inaccurate. An empty wine bottle stood on a table thirty feet away. She knew she shouldn't but she wanted to wipe the smirk off Simon's face. She took up the sharpshooter's stance, standing sideways on to the target, her left hand on her hip. She pulled the trigger. The sharp report was deafening in the still morning air. She'd missed. If she was upset or annoyed by the fact she didn't show it. She wouldn't give Simon the satisfaction. His smirk grew larger. The desire to aim at his head and pull the trigger was almost overwhelming but she resisted.

'The rifling is worn and the sight slightly off,' she said, regretting the words as soon as she had uttered them.

'If you say so,' Simon said his voice dripping sarcasm.

'I do. But the gun will do as a warning. Do you have any more bullets?'

Simon nodded. 'A few. Here.' He handed her a further six. Susan stuffed them in a pocket.

'Aren't you going to replace the one you fired?'

'Of course not. There's no safety.' She could see his perplexed look. 'Simon,' she sighed as though speaking to a particularly backward child, 'if the hammer is cocked and the gun falls to the ground it can go off because there's no safety device. Prudence dictates the chamber under the hammer be left empty.'

'What if you need to use the gun quickly?'

'If I need it that quickly then it's already too late.' She spoke calmly enough but her heart was pounding and her palms felt slick with sweat. She walked away, annoyed at herself for firing the gun and more annoyed for missing.

That had been yesterday. Today she was sitting alone in the sun, watching the streets and the people hurrying past. The plaza was a rectangle, two hundred yards long, a hundred wide. A street passed each end, running north to south. The long sides of the rectangle were fronted by small shops, a bakery, numerous bars and restaurants and the bank. The businesses had apartments above them, except the bank which housed offices. The ends of the rectangle comprised apartment buildings only. The middle of the plaza was a scrubby area of sun-bleached grass, stunted trees and dying flower beds. Nobody had bothered watering the plants for days, even weeks. It was the last thing on the minds of the people of Algeciras.

Diagonally opposite where she sat she could see Toby, leaning against the wall. He had arrived ten minutes earlier. On the other side, the same distance away, was Henry. He'd been there a few minutes longer. Robert appeared and took up position near the third entrance to the square. If Susan's bag had been on the table it would have warned them that something was amiss and that the raid should be cancelled. But she had seen nothing untoward and the bag lay at her feet, with the revolver nestling within. She had been praying for a reason to call off the raid but to do so without a very good reason would lead to a lot of trouble. Not with Phillipe. Possibly not even with Simon. But with some of the other, cold-eyed men she'd seen coming and going at the house. In spite of the warm day she shivered. She was in over her head. The sun was long past its zenith and was now casting a long shadow on her left. The bank would soon be closing for the night. She checked her watch. It was time. Even as the thought occurred to her she saw them arriving. Three men from different directions. Simon, another man she didn't know and . . . Phillipe! Phillipe was supposed to stay with the get-away cars. He was to have given them five minutes inside then drive along the broad pavement to the bank doors. What the hell was going on?

All three carried a carpetbag. They appeared unarmed but she knew they carried guns inside the bags. She looked around frantically. The plaza was full of people. Looking upwards at the windows on the far side of the square the sun was shining directly onto them, and reflected golden shafts of light back at her. She looked to her left but there the windows were in shadow and she could see nothing. Her heart was pounding. It was going to happen and all she could do was sit and pray.

She watched them enter through the bank doors. She looked at her watch. More than twenty, perhaps thirty people were sitting in the cafe beside the bank, huddled together in small groups, talking and gesticulating. A few pedestrians were walking along the pavement, one man with a small, fat poodle on a lead. Still nothing unusual. The car nosed into the square. No tyres squealing, no alarm. It turned slowly on the pavement and edged past the café tables and chairs. If the people sitting at the tables were annoyed they didn't show it. The car drew up at the doors of the bank. A few seconds passed. Nothing. Susan was holding her breath. Time stood still. Her pulse beat loudly in her ears.

As she watched, Phillipe and the others ran out of the bank. They jumped into the car and it took-off with a loud gunning of the engine. This time the tyres did squeal as the car shot around the corner and sped away, leaving behind a haze of dust. A bell began ringing loudly. The patrons sitting at the tables were galvanised into action. They abandoned their drinks and fled. Shutters were suddenly closed and doors locked. Within moments it seemed to Susan, the square was deserted. She and the other look-outs were suddenly very conspicuous. Susan didn't linger. She grabbed her bag and hurried away. Turning a corner she walked as quickly as she could, trying not to appear in too much of a hurry. Her heart was pounding. In the background she heard the noise of over-revving engines. Loud horns rent the air. The noise got closer and she stepped into a doorway. She was just in time. Two cars followed by a lorry full of Nationalist soldiers swept past her.

She could no longer suppress the feeling of panic that swept over her and she began to run. The street was cobbled and uneven and she almost fell. Sweat poured from her and she was soon gasping for breath. After a few minutes she was forced to stop and bend over, retching and gasping at the same time. Her confidence was shattered. She had to get away. Away from Spain and the madness. Back to England, her family, and normality. Gradually her breathing eased and reason returned. Walking on, she forced down the panic. She had been an innocent bystander. She'd had no idea what was happening. If she was picked up she could prove that she was a British citizen. Her transport was a kilometre away. She remembered the directions. By now the streets were back to normal. The incident was behind her. Most of the people she saw hurrying by weren't even aware that something had happened.

She slowed down, desperate not to draw attention to herself. She saw that she was heading in the right direction and then she found the car. The others – Toby, Henry and Robert weren't there.

What had happened to them? Had they been picked up? Were they even now being tortured and made to tell all they knew? Her imagination ran riot. The car was parked on a busy street with shops, bars and restaurants lining both sides. She was surprised that in the middle of conflict people were going about their ordinary business.

It was surreal. She sat at a vacant café table near the car and waited. Asked what she would like to drink she ordered a local brandy. She looked about her. Half a dozen tables were occupied. She registered the laughter and the normality of the people around her. Still none of the others were in sight. She was becoming worried. She was surprised to see that her glass was empty and ordered another drink. A patrol of five soldiers coming towards her set her heart fluttering wildly. They were coming for her, she knew it. Each second seemed an eternity as they walked slowly past her table, looking at her boldly, their ribald comments inaudible above the buzzing in her ears.

Where on earth were they? The chair next to her was scraped back, startling her, and Toby sat down. Without saying a word he gestured to the waiter and ordered a cold beer. His hands on the table in front of him were trembling slightly.

'Where's Robert?' Susan asked in a low voice.

'Coming. He's right behind.' Looking up he added, 'Here he is now.'

An excited Robert rushed to the table from a different direction. Out of breath he gasped, 'I went around. Boy, that was exciting. Absolutely spiffing,' he said with a mock upper crust accent. Susan was amazed that the twenty-two year old still had the presence of mind to tease the older Toby about his breeding.

'Weren't you scared?' asked Susan.

Robert looked at her with genuine surprise on his face. 'No. Why should I have been? Were you?'

'Terrified,' Susan replied honestly. 'Give me a ciggie.'

Toby offered her a cigarette, which she lit with surprisingly steady hands. Blowing out a stream of smoke she said, 'It was horrible. I thought we were going to get caught.'

Robert tensed and looked past the shoulders of the other two. He leaned towards the middle of the small, round table. 'Don't look now but there are two men at

another table taking an inordinate interest in us. I think
it's time we left.'

'We need to pay for the drinks,' said Toby.

'Leave enough money on the table and let's get the
hell out of here.' Susan spoke nervously. She wanted to
look behind her but steeled herself not to.

Robert dropped pesetas on the table and they stood up.
The car was less than ten metres away and they reached
it without any trouble. Toby drove and Susan sat in the
back. She glanced back in time to see the two men hail
a car, one of them pointing after them.

'We've got trouble.' Opening the window she threw
her cigarette butt into the street. Now that there was a
real problem she felt icily calm. Reaching into her bag
she withdrew the worn .38 Special.

'There's Henry,' said Robert, pointing ahead. As had
been arranged, Henry had walked away from town to be
picked up later.

'Don't stop,' said Susan. 'Otherwise we're all in
trouble.'

'What are we going to do?' Robert asked. They swept
passed an open-mouthed Henry who had been expecting
them to stop and pick him up. Susan did not even look
in his direction.

Susan's natural authority had asserted itself earlier and
now they looked to her for leadership. 'We don't know
who those men are,' Susan stated. 'They may be on our
side and covering us. We need to find out. My instinct is
to try and lose them but this road goes straight along the
coast.'

By now it was growing dark. Their headlights cut a
swathe through the countryside.

'Tarifa is twenty kilometres away,' said Toby. 'We could
try and lose them there.'

'If we get that far,' said Robert.

'They may try and stop us before then,' said Susan.
'But somehow I don't think so. They could have picked

us up back at the bar. They're following us to see where we're going. Who we'll lead them to.'

'That makes sense,' said Robert. 'Can't you go any faster?'

By way of an answer Toby pressed his foot on the accelerator and the car gradually picked up speed. The car was an old Seat four-seater, with front opening doors. Its springs were soft, sending the car bouncing over the smallest pothole. Though it was well used, it had a powerful engine.

'What do we do about Henry?' Toby raised his voice above the noise of the engine.

'We'll go back for him if we can. He knows what to do,' said Susan. She looked out of the back window. 'We're moving away from them. How far to go?'

'It can't be long now,' replied Toby.

The road they were on was a two-lane highway. They hadn't seen another vehicle since leaving Algeciras but that was only to be expected. Travelling at night brought all sorts of hazards, not just those associated with driving. There was no telling when you might hit a Nationalist or Republican roadblock.

The car swayed around a corner and Robert pointed.'Around the next bend is the turn-off!'

'Faster, Toby, open up the distance,' Susan ordered.

The car accelerated. The loom of the lights from the other vehicle began to fade behind them. They swayed around the bend.

'That's the turn!' Robert said.

Toby braked and swung the wheel towards the left. The tyres squealed in protest and the car rocked to the right on its worn springs. Looking back Susan saw the lights of the other car approaching the bend and leant over the front seats. She punched out the light switch and plunged the road into darkness.

'I can't see!' Toby yelled. The car swerved from side to side; tyres squealed and the crunch of gravel sounded inordinately loud. Toby jerked the wheel to the right and they bounced back onto the tarmac. Rounding the first bend, the Seat was pitching heavily as Toby fought it to a standstill. Susan was glued to the rear window watching for the lights of the other vehicle. The car swept past even as their own stopped.

'Quick,' said Susan, 'turn us around and take us back to Algeciras. We'll pick up Henry and then come back.'

Toby turned the car, leaving the lights off. The sky was cloudless and the half moon rising over Africa bathed the land in enough light for him to see, now that his eyes were accustomed to the dark. They approached the main road, paused and sped away. Once round the next bend Toby turned the lights on. Putting his foot to the floorboards he drove as fast as he dared back to Algeciras.

Susan was leaning forward, looking through the windscreen but constantly glancing behind them. In the distance they could see the lights of the town and as they rounded a left-hand bend the panorama of the Bay of Algeciras and the towering hulk of the Rock of Gibraltar were spread before them. Lights twinkled across the water and the massive rock looked bluish in the moonlight. A safe haven, it beckoned them to escape from the madness they were ensnared in.

'Though every aspect pleases, and only man is vile,' murmured Toby.

'I don't know if now is the time to be quoting poetry,' Susan said, though she was smiling.

'It's from a missionary hymn by Reginald Heber.' Repeating the quote, he added, 'And ain't that the truth.'

'Amen to that,' whispered Robert.

'Slow down,' Susan ordered. 'Henry should be hiding around here somewhere.'

Toby slowed and stopped the car. Susan climbed out. 'Turn around while I look for him.'

She wandered along the side of the road. 'Henry.' She

spoke in a loud whisper before realising how ludicrous that was. 'Henry!' She called out.

'Not so loud!' A voice spoke right next to her. Henry climbed out of a drainage ditch and dusted himself down. 'What happened?'

'Thank God you're all right,' Susan replied. 'Just get into the car and let's get the hell out of this place.'

Retracing the route they'd just taken Susan told Henry about being followed.

'I wonder who they were?' Henry rubbed the wound in his thigh. It was healing fast and now itched like the devil.

'We've no idea but we weren't taking any chances. It may have been someone Simon had watching us.' Susan spoke pensively, 'But somehow I doubt it. There's not enough manpower for that. Let's hope we never find out.'

They lapsed into silence. Susan's uppermost emotion was exhilaration, tinged with an underlying desire to get away from Spain. It was true she'd been nervous, scared even, but they weren't her over-riding emotions. If she had to use one word to describe how she felt it was excited. She couldn't wait to see Phillipe.

'Pass me the map,' she said to Robert. Opening it on her knees she took a small torch from her bag and examined the routes available to them. 'I think we want to get off the main road as soon as possible. We haven't seen another car. If we do, it could well be the one that was following us.'

'They may have guessed that we stopped and be waiting up ahead,' said Robert.

'I've thought of that. If they are we'll cross that bridge when we come to it,' replied Susan. 'The only other way is the road to Medina Sidonia.'

'Where we'd stick out like a sore thumb at this time of day,' said Henry.

'Any better ideas?' Toby asked.

'Indeed, old chap, indeed,' replied Henry. 'We hole up

for the night. In the morning there'll be plenty of other cars and vehicles around. If we're stopped and searched tonight we'll be in big trouble.' He did not have to spell it out. Each of them had a gun of some sort and if the Nationalists caught them, their futures would be grim. Their only option would be a gunfight.

'Henry's right,' said Susan. 'We cross over a river in a few minutes, the Rio Barbate. We'll look for a place to stop.'

'Here's the bridge,' announced Toby. Once across, he stopped the car.

'You stay here,' said Susan, 'while Henry and I see if we can get off the road.' Climbing out of the car they walked either side of the road.

'Over here,' called Henry a few moments later, pointing to a smooth section of packed earth that dropped down to the river about twenty metres below. 'Give me the torch and I'll take a look.' Sweeping the light back and forth he clambered down the siding. Although steep, it wasn't dangerously so. It could be a problem in the morning when it came to getting back up again. He was about to tell the others it was probably too difficult when the decision was taken away from him.

'There's a car coming,' yelled Susan. 'Come on, Toby, drive down. And switch off those bloody lights.'

The roadside was plunged into darkness. Ramming the Seat into gear with a loud, grinding crunch, Toby lurched the car across the road and over the edge. It was steeper than he'd been expecting and he slammed on the brakes. The car slid uncontrollably down the scree, bouncing over holes, scratching the paintwork on hardy shrubs that clung to the shallow earth. Veering across the gradient, the Seat bounced on its right wheels and threatened to turn over. Toby wrenched the wheel around, taking his foot off the brake. The car straightened and he gained a semblance of control. It hit the bottom and came to a dead halt, the engine stalling.

Toby sat slumped over the wheel. Susan and the others scrambled down just as the approaching car swept past. It didn't slow down but sped towards Algeciras. Susan wrenched open the driver's door. 'Are you all right?'

Toby raised his head. 'I think so.'

In the moonlight Susan could see a black mark across his forehead growing slowly.

'You've hurt your brow. It's bleeding. Let me take a look.' She assured herself that it was a superficial wound before giving him her handkerchief. 'Hold this until it stops bleeding.' Turning to the others she said, 'Let's push the car under the bridge. We'll be out of sight, just in case.'

They quickly did as she suggested.

'We need to keep guard,' she announced. 'If we keep a lookout for two hours we'll share the night. Who's going first?' There were no takers. 'In that case, we'll draw for it.' Picking up a piece of stick she turned her back and broke it into four pieces. Holding the ends hidden in her hand she offered them to each one. 'Longest has first watch, shortest has the last.' Toby drew the first watch.

'We ought to try and get comfortable for the night,' said Robert.

'We can remove the back seat,' said Susan. 'If we place it against the slope under the bridge we can lie against it.'

With three of them leaning against the seat, shoulders touching, acutely aware of each others' presence, it made for an uncomfortable arrangement. But there was warmth and some comfort to be gained from being near to each other and they fell into fitful dozes. Susan's night was fair to hellish. In the middle of the three, she knew when they each changed sentry duty, and was conscious of an ache in the small of her back but was too tired to do anything about it. She grew cold. It was almost a relief when she was told it was her turn to stand guard.

She moved her cramped, aching muscles and thought about Phillipe. How was he? Was he safely at home? In the dark hours her thoughts spiralled out of control. She had never thought about bravery, particularly her own. She had taken her care-free existence and her God-given abilities for granted. She had never known fear. But then, she realised, she had never been tested like this. It was one thing to deal with a problem when flying. It was quite another to face the idea of being shot dead at any moment. The feeling of excitement earlier was merely a memory.

The others had stood guard under the bridge. By contrast, Susan crawled up the slope to the side of the road to keep watch. It was 5am. Day was breaking when she heard a vehicle approaching. There was a loud bang followed by a crunch as a lower gear was engaged and a decrepit lorry, belching acrid smoke, lumbered around the bend. Laden down, it was leaning to one side, moving slowly. Weak headlights shone a yellow path in front of it, as it trundled past. There was not another vehicle for half an hour but then, slowly, the traffic built up until there was a car or a lorry passing in one direction or the other every few minutes. Susan realised that if they were going to get away it had to be now, otherwise they would not be able to get back onto the road without being noticed.

She slid down the slope to the others. None of them had been sleeping properly and nobody protested when she urged them to make a move.

Toby started the car and drove out from under the bridge. Aiming it at the slope he began to drive upwards. Halfway the wheels began to slide but he kept his foot down until the engine was screaming in protest. The back wheels pushed, the front slid and he was turning side on to the slope and in danger of rolling over.

'It's no good,' yelled Henry. 'Stop.'

Toby took his foot off the accelerator and allowed the car to roll back to the bottom. 'What now?' He asked the three grim faces staring at him.

'Go backwards,' replied Susan, 'and we'll push from the front.'

'What good will that do?' Toby asked curtly, lack of sleeping making him irritable.

'Trust me,' said Susan. 'The wheels will pull the car and so you won't slide to one side. When you push, as soon as you start slipping off the true, the car loses traction. The car quickly loses momentum and you're stuck. I've seen it happen before. Reversed, it won't happen. Let's give it a go. Henry, you go up to the road and keep a lookout. Once it's all clear let us know.'

Henry scrabbled up to the top and took a cautious look in both directions. Nothing was coming and strain as hard as he could, he heard nothing.

'All right!' he called down.

Toby turned the car and set off backwards at a steady pace. The Seat went smoothly past the halfway point where it had got into difficulties the first time. It was only a few metres from the top when the wheels started slipping and the tyres began to lose their grip.

'Come on,' Susan urged them. 'Push with all your might.'

She and Robert got in front of the car and put their weight against it, their feet scrabbling in the scree. The car moved a few more inches and then sent a shower of small stones and earth flying out from under. The back wheels were bedding themselves into the slope. Henry slid down the slope and joined them. For a few seconds the car didn't move and then it lurched upwards a few more inches. The left rear wheel rolled onto a flat stone covered with a thin covering of soil, gripped and pulled the car up smoothly. The two back wheels hit the lip and dragged the car onto the flat, leaving the three of them on their knees, panting.

'Hurry up,' Toby looked out of the window, 'I can hear a car coming.'

38

EXHAUSTED, THEY CLIMBED after the car, feet sliding, hands clutching at small rocks and weeds as they dragged themselves up the slope. Susan was unaware of her grazed knees, broken finger nails and dishevelled appearance as she fell into the back of the car. Toby gunned the engine and they shot onto the road and screamed around the corner, moving as fast as the car and conditions allowed. They passed a bus coming towards them and within minutes were at the turn off for Medina Sidonia. Toby took the turning too fast, overcorrected and almost put them into a ditch as the car fishtailed.

'Slow down,' yelled Henry, sitting next to him. 'There's no hurry now.'

The car slowed as it wound up into the mountains. By now the sun was breaking over the horizon and it promised to be a fine, warm day. Behind them the blue Atlantic rolled majestically into the bay, awesome in its grandeur and power, timeless in its motion.

It took forty minutes to travel the twenty kilometres to Medina Sidonia. They passed through the village without a glance of interest being shown in them.

'Not far now,' Susan announced looking at the chart.

Toby brought the car to a halt, tyres squealing. Two hundred yards ahead of them was a roadblock manned by soldiers.

'What do we do?' Henry asked, his bravado now gone.

'Keep our heads,' said Susan. 'We can turn around or we can drive up to them and try and bluff our way through.'

'If that doesn't work?' Toby asked, a laconic drawl hiding his own concern.

'We don't have much choice,' Susan replied. 'We can't let them stop and search us. They'll find the guns and we'll be in trouble.'

Her matter-of-fact voice helped to calm them, but her next words were electrifying. 'We'll have to shoot them.'

'We can't. Dear God,' said Henry, 'we can't.' Panic was in his voice and his face was a ghastly white.

'Henry,' said Susan leaning forward and putting her hand on his shoulder, 'they're the enemy and we are here to kill them. That's what it's all about. Remember Mark and Daphne.'

'How can I forget?' Henry felt the resolve wash through him. 'Drive forward, Toby.' Henry lifted his gun out of his bag.

'Drive slowly,' said Susan, 'we don't want to alarm them. There are four of them, so one each. Have you got your guns ready?'

Toby gripped the wheel as though he was trying to break it. 'Mine's in my bag beside you, Susan.'

Susan felt in the bag, grabbed the weapon and pulled it out. It was an odd-shaped Astra Model F. 'Take my gun.' Pulling the trigger, it clicked on the empty chamber. She placed it in Toby's right hand. 'It's ready to fire.'

She examined the Astra. It was the newest weapon they had. Only a year or two old. It held twenty rounds of 9mm Largo cartridges. Phillipe had shown them how to use it only the day before. She pushed forward the safety next to the hammer and turned the rotary switch on the right side of the frame to automatic fire. Nearly fourteen inches from grip to forward sight, it was a cumbersome weapon prone to jamming.

The car slowed as the four soldiers waved them down. Three were armed with rifles, one carried a revolver. They were scruffily dressed although their uniform clearly identified them as Nationalists. The man with the handgun was a corporal, the other three were privates. They looked as nervous as Susan felt.

'Keep the guns out of sight,' said Susan. Her lips were dry and her mouth parched. 'Until I say fire.'

The makeshift barrier was a red and white pole lying on top of two oil drums filled with earth. They could have smashed through easily. It had been erected without thought or proper planning. Looking at the faces of the soldiers, two standing behind the pole, two now at their side, she saw how young they were.

'Keep the guns down,' Susan said fiercely. They aren't pointing theirs at us. I'll try and talk our way through.'

She opened the window and smiled sweetly. In excellent Spanish she said, 'We're American. We broke down last night. We've only just got the car to start again. Is this the way to Cádiz? We appear to be lost.'

The corporal returned the smile and straightened up. '*Si*. If you take the next turning on your left it will lead to Puerto Real and then you are almost in Cádiz.'

'Thank you so much. You have been most kind. Please let me give you something for your trouble.' She handed him a thousand peseta note and said, 'Buy yourselves a beer when you go off duty.'

Saluting, the corporal issued orders and the pole was lifted. Toby put the car into gear and it jerked forward. In his anxiety he pressed the accelerator and they shot forward, causing one of the soldiers to leap out of the way. There were startled cries and yells and panic broke out amongst the soldiers. Susan leant out of the window and waved gaily to them, apologising. One of the soldiers waved back and then they were around a bend.

There was a collective sigh of relief in the car. 'Toby, you prat,' admonished Robert, 'why don't you learn how to drive?'

'You drive, if you're so bloody clever,' Toby yelled. 'My foot slipped, all right?'

'Be quiet, both of you,' Susan ordered wearily. 'We're

through and that's all that counts. God, did you see how young they were?'

'They may be young, but they carry sodding big rifles,' replied Robert.

They lapsed into silence, each busy with their own thoughts. Susan was nauseous. She had nearly shot somebody. A boy barely older than Richard. And if there had been trouble, they could have been killed in turn. Or wounded. Or taken prisoner. Tortured. Nothing in her life had prepared her for the crushing reality of war. She should be proud of their efforts and pleased with their good fortune.

'There's the turn-off for Puerto Real. We go straight on,' said Robert. 'It's not far now.'

They came to the entrance of the estate and stopped. Henry climbed out and pushed the heavy, wrought-iron gates open. They drove through and waited for him to shut the gates and climb back into the car. The estate was eerily quiet. Approaching the house, instead of relief, they each felt a strange, nervous tension. Nobody was about. It was already past eight o'clock and there was work to be done. Climbing wearily from the car they stood in an uncertain group, each holding their gun, nerves stretched to breaking point. The front door flew open with a crash.

'Susan!' Phillipe yelled joyfully, rushing down the steps. 'Where were you? We've been worried sick. We thought the worst.' Taking her in his arms his embrace stole her very breath.

Fighting back her tears she clung to him tightly. After a few seconds she had regained her composure and she stepped back. She ran her hand through her hair and looked around. 'What's going on? Where is everybody?'

Phillipe gave a high, piercing whistle and men began to appear from the house and the outbuildings. They carried weapons of different sorts but one thing was clear. They were armed to the teeth.

'What's happening?' Susan repeated.

'We had no way of knowing what had happened to you. So we were ready.'

Susan frowned and then understanding dawned. 'Oh, I see.'

Henry was dumbstruck, looking around at the small army that had appeared.

'You were ready to defend yourselves,' said Robert, 'in case we'd been captured. Isn't that so?' He addressed his question to Simon.

Simon stood with a machine gun gripped in his left hand. The Browning Automatic Rifle was scratched, silver metal shone through the black barrelling and the stock was cracked. He nodded nonchalantly. 'You are quite correct, my friend. We prepared for the worst.'

Frances appeared and ran down the steps and put her arms around Henry 'Let's go inside,' she said. 'You look all in.'

He allowed her to lead him away. Susan followed, with Phillipe close behind. Like an automaton she climbed the stairs, Phillipe trailing behind. He tried to speak but she held up her hand. 'Not now, Phillipe, please. I need a bath and some sleep. Afterwards.' She took no notice of his pleading look.

It was the middle of the afternoon when Susan finally awoke and sat at the dressing table mirror, regarding herself critically. God, she was a mess. She ran a brush through her dark hair and then turned her attention to her broken finger nails. Using a file, she rounded her broken nails, put clear vanish on them and blew on them while they dried. She was still seated there when Phillipe knocked and entered.

'I'm glad you're awake,' he began awkwardly. 'We're about to have another planning meeting.'

Wearily she wiped a hand over her eyes. 'What's on the agenda?'

'The next job. We have a shipment of arms arriving the day after tomorrow and we need more money.'

Their eyes met in the mirror. Susan watched his reflection as he stood directly behind her. Her dressing gown had fallen agape. She followed the direction of his gaze. She suddenly needed him very, very much.

Half an hour later they dressed. 'We're late again,' said Phillipe with a smile.

'Too bad,' Susan replied. Placing her hand on his arm she added, 'I'm sorry I was so quiet earlier. I was so relieved that you had got away safely. I couldn't bear it if something were to happen to you.'

Putting his arms around her, he kissed her upturned face, 'Nor I, you.'

There was a knock on the door and Phillipe called out to enter. Sheepishly Henry put his head around the door and said, 'Sorry. But we're waiting.'

They followed him downstairs and onto the patio. Food and wine were laid out and a ravenous Susan helped herself to a plateful of cold meats and salad.

'Ah, so glad you could join us,' said Simon sarcastically.

Phillipe spoke rapid and harsh French. Simon was about to reply when he thought better of it. His cousin was not in the mood to be trifled with.

'Let us begin,' said Simon, holding his temper in check. 'We have identified another bank at Seville. Near the railway station.'

Henry was about to ask a question. 'Don't ask me for details, Henry. If you know nothing then you cannot betray us.'

Henry was about to argue when Susan raised her hand. 'Much as I hate to say it, Simon's right. The less we know the better. Presumably the *modus operandi* will be the same as before?'

'No, this time Robert is going into the bank,' said Simon.

Consternation was written on all their faces but it was Susan who asked the question. 'Why Robert?'

'Because we need him,' said Simon. 'Three banks are being targeted simultaneously. We are short of men.'

'There are plenty of men,' argued Susan, waving her hand. 'The estate is full of able-bodied men. What's the real reason?'

'I've given it. Everyone has a role to play. That is all there is to it.'

'It's all right, Susan,' said Robert. 'I'll go.'

The next twenty minutes were exasperating. No details were discussed. Susan couldn't help feeling that Simon was being deliberately obtuse. Finally, she stood up in temper. 'This is ludicrous. Unless we know which bank we're targeting we cannot make a detailed plan. We need to identify streets and buildings. Escape routes. Everything.'

Phillipe was frowning. What she said was true.

'What's really going on?' Susan asked. 'Tell me!' She insisted.

Simon looked at Phillipe and they both appeared uncomfortable. It was Phillipe who answered. 'You returned so late. Understand, *ma chérie*, for us there is always the possibility that you were taken. That you have already betrayed us. In order to save your own skins.'

Toby sprang to his feet, the blood draining from his face. 'How dare you! We've done no such thing. We had a hellish time of it getting back. You have no right to suggest otherwise.'

'I have every right,' Simon shouted. 'I am responsible for many lives. Including everybody who works here, and their families. We cannot be too careful. Franco's soldiers are animals. They rape and kill indiscriminately. If they *had* picked you up it wouldn't take them long to convince you to help them.'

'Is that what you think?' Susan asked Simon and then turned her bleak gaze on Phillipe.

He held her eyes. 'Simon is right. We cannot be too careful. Please, try and understand.'

Resignedly she said, 'I do. But believe us we've disclosed nothing. We got away just as we told you. Now, we need a proper plan. Not a half-baked one, otherwise we're not going. Which is it to be?'

The two cousins exchanged looks and then Phillipe said, 'The bank is on the Avenue Carlos V. It is near the railway station *de San Bernardo.*'

'Thank you,' said Susan. 'Now we can proceed.'

The planning didn't take long. The idea was basically the same as before. Susan wasn't happy.

'We got away with it last time,' she argued. 'It doesn't mean we will a second time.'

'What do you suggest, *señorita* Griffiths?' Simon could not keep his displeasure from his voice.

'Something unexpected. I've been thinking,' replied Susan. 'The bank, you say, is just here.' She pointed at a map of the city. 'Get the money to us at this junction,' she pointed again, 'by the railway station. We can time it to the second, to coincide with the departure of a train. We get off down the line and pick up the cars. We'll be out of the city much faster than if we try it by car. And don't forget, there are a large number of Nationalists in Seville.'

'Thank you, Susan,' said Simon, 'but we hadn't forgotten Franco's supporters. Their presence is part of why we target the city.'

'Think, Simon,' replied Susan. 'We have to get out fast. It is too easy for them to literally close the city. What will we do then?' It was a good question and one they had no answer for. If they didn't get out it would be all too easy to be picked up and interrogated. With fatal consequences.

'We know,' said Phillipe, 'that General Queipo de Llano has a stranglehold on Seville. The only reason he has not moved out and attacked other cities is because Franco is keeping him isolated for political reasons. He has a powerful army based in the city.'

'Then why not find another bank to rob, if it's so dangerous?' Susan asked.

'Because,' said Simon, 'this is also an attack at the very heart of the Nationalists. We are making a statement which is almost as important as the money itself.'

The more Susan learned about the war and its constant change of fortunes, the less she understood. Dr Juan Negrín, the Republican Prime Minister, was trying to unite the vast array of diverse parties to the left of Spanish politics. Spain was still isolated in the world. When the war broke out, a non-intervention agreement had been signed by Italy, Russia, France, Germany and Britain. Germany and Italy had openly broken the agreement and supplied vast numbers of troops, armaments and aircraft to fight on the side of the Nationalists. Britain and France sat on their hands and only Russia was helping the Spanish government. The Russians had provided heavy tanks and advisors, who interfered in the political running of the country, much to the anger and dismay of many of Spain's citizens. Any other weapons the Spanish government wanted had to be bought on the black market and smuggled into the country. It was unprecedented for a sovereign country not to be able to buy arms openly and from whoever wished to sell them. Like the Boucher group, the Republican militias were completely fragmented and operated without a central command structure. This made it impossible to have a cohesive force against the well-ordered troops of Franco. On the frontline, men were fighting with abysmal weapons and insufficient ammunition, while back in those cities still under government control, an officer elite was lording it in new uniforms and new weapons which had never seen a shot fired in anger.

The backbone of the resistance to Franco was the 'International Brigades XI–XV'. They were recruited from sympathisers world-wide. Weapons were being bought by small units and smuggled to the Brigades to continue the fight. It was, from top to bottom, an unholy mess. Furthermore, with the Church firmly on the side of Franco and the Nationalists, there was a battle for the hearts and minds of the Spanish people being waged as well. Susan willed her thoughts back to the matter at hand.

'I take your point, Simon,' said Toby, 'but I think Susan's idea should at least be discussed.'

'So do I,' said Phillipe.

Simon was about to argue when he saw the resolute look on the faces of the others. With bad grace he capitulated. 'Certainly. Let us do so. I shall get a copy of the railway timetable.'

They planned late into the night. Eventually, even Simon had to admit Susan's idea made sense. If they did not escape the city boundaries by car within minutes then all would be lost. Looking at the map it was clear. The distances were too great. The operation they had carried out in Algeciras could not be replicated in Seville.

'It calls for careful timing,' said Phillipe for the umpteenth time. 'Before the war you could set your watch by the railway timetable. Now you cannot. If there's a derailment or other incident somewhere along the track then the trains are stopped.'

'So,' said Henry, 'we could be sitting in the train waiting to leave and the army arrives and catches us. Brilliant. What about another bank? Closer to the city walls?'

'There isn't one,' said a gloomy Simon. It galled him but they were right. The plan as it stood was far too risky.

Susan had been mulling an idea over in her mind. 'What if we were to fly out?'

'You cannot be serious,' said Simon.

'Never more so.' She proceeded to explain. When they broke up to go to bed, an hour later, a plan of action had been agreed.

That night Phillipe and Susan's lovemaking was particularly tender. Lying in his arms, thinking of tomorrow, Susan was filled with a sense of foreboding.

She waved them off the following morning. They had allowed over three hours for the journey, wary of road-blocks. In fact they had a smooth passage and arrived in Seville in plenty of time. As before, they set up observation positions and settled down to wait for the bank to close for the day.

Frances took the position nearest to the bank. Although Simon had not wanted to use her, he'd had no choice. There had been no one else he could spare. She watched as Phillipe, Simon and Robert entered the marble fronted building. Fear gnawed at her insides and her vision seemed to be coming and going. She wanted to run but couldn't. Henry was opposite her, leaning against the wall and Toby was seated at a table a hundred metres away. Both sides of the Avenue were lined with restaurants and bars. Many of the tables were occupied. A more observant person than Frances would have seen a preponderance of males, young, in twos, watching.

The door of the bank opened and the three men walked quickly out, turning right towards the river, less than a kilometre away. It happened quickly. The first thing Frances knew, she was on her feet, screaming.

Susan banked the plane and lined up to land on the *Canal de Alfonso XIII*. It was connected to the Rio Guadalquivir in the middle of the city next to the *Estación de Córdoba*. There was little current and at that time of the day very few boats or other craft moving. Sunset was fast falling. She knew that the *Puente San Telmo* was a single span bridge and she hit the water four hundred metres downstream. People stood on the avenue that followed the eastern side of the canal and pointed at her. Timing was all. The plane kissed the water and settled on its floats. Opening up the throttle she taxied to the bridge and sat drifting underneath. Whenever she drifted back into view she opened the throttle and moved back under the span. Street lights were coming on and people were gathering to look down at her and the plane. Their curiosity was inevitable. Luckily there weren't many of them. Businesses were only now closing and people heading for home. The university was nearby and some of the students ambled across to look and point. She checked her watch. They would be walking out of the bank now.

She became aware of consternation and then panic amongst the few dozen onlookers. There were screams and they began running away. Suddenly she was frightened. Very frightened.

Opening the door in the fuselage she stuck her head out. She could hear the chatter of guns, single shots and machine-guns. Something had gone wrong! What was she to do? She needed to know what was going on. Scrambling into the pilot's seat she took the plane out the other side of the bridge, hurried back into the passengers section and grabbed a rope, slinging a rifle over her shoulder. She climbed down onto the starboard float, tied the rope to the outer strut and, holding it in her hand, jumped into the water. A few swift strokes and she was at a metal ladder embedded into the side of the canal. Climbing it, she tied the end of the rope to a rung. The Griffin floated down and settled, tugging gently at the rope.

Susan found herself on the bank with the pavement and road about two metres higher. She darted up a set of concrete steps. The sound of gunfire was much louder and coming from the street directly ahead. Darkness was now falling and the streets were deserted. Nobody wanted to be caught in a gunfight. She hesitated. Ahead and to her right was the imposing building of the university. To her left and half a kilometre away she could see the Cathedral of Seville, dominating the skyline.

There was still nobody in sight and the sound of shooting had become sporadic. Bent forward, Susan ran across the road, the rifle held in both hands, ready to fire. She could only hope that the brief immersion in the canal had not affected it. The rifle was a new

Mannlicher-Carcano M1938 made in Italy and issued that year to the Italian troops fighting in Spain. It was one of a number taken from the bodies of dead soldiers or stolen from raids on armouries.

She reached the university grounds. Bushes and early spring flowers covered the area. Her heart was pounding and her mouth dry. She shivered. The light wind was cold and she was soaked to the skin. Reaching the street that lead to the railway station, she paused. Looking around the corner she stifled a cry. In the dusk, bathed in street-light, she could see a body. Staying low, she crept through the bushes that led to the main university building. There was not a soul to be seen. She heard shouting from further along the street and more gunfire.

The body lay in the middle of the road, twenty metres away. The light was too bad to discern who it was and she stopped, wondering what to do next. She heard more shooting. Taking her courage in her hands she ran out from the bushes and across the street, throwing herself next to the body. Blood stained the cobbled road. The face was turned away and as she leant forward she saw it was Toby. Even as she was feeling for a pulse she knew he was dead.

More shots made her jump. Anger coursed through her body. First Mark and Daphne and now Toby. She ran back across the street and into the bushes. The shooting had started again with a vengeance. Running alongside the university building she stopped at the corner and peered around. Opposite her, on the other side of the road, she saw two soldiers firing at a doorway. Their backs were to her and she didn't hesitate. Putting the rifle to her shoulder, she twisted the knurled safety collar at the end of the bolt, worked the bolt and fired. One soldier threw his arms into the air and collapsed, but she wasn't looking at him. She had already ejected the spent round and was aiming at the second man. He turned her way and she shot him between the eyes. A lucky shot, she had been aiming at his torso.

There were more soldiers further along the street who had temporarily ceased shooting. 'Run!' Susan yelled to the figure holed up in the doorway while she fired the last four shots she carried in the magazine at three soldiers hidden behind a parked car.

Two people came running out of the doorway towards her. She was fitting more rounds into the magazine, her fingers shaking, and risked a look at who was coming her way. She recognised Phillipe and Robert. A shot rang out and Phillipe stumbled. Stifling a scream, she pressed home the magazine and fired three quick rounds at the soldiers. They were about two hundred metres away and she had the satisfaction of seeing one hit while the other two dived around the front of the car.

Phillipe and Robert collapsed beside her.

'What happened?' Susan asked.

'Later,' was the gasped response from Phillipe. 'Thank God you came. We have to get out of here.'

'What about the others?'

'Dead,' said Robert bitterly. 'All dead.'

'Are you sure?' Susan fired three more shots and ejected the magazine.

'There's no way they could have survived. They were cut down, I tell you,' Robert's voice rose, hysteria reaching for the surface.

'Are you all right, Phillipe?'

Getting to his feet he gasped. 'Bullet in the side. Hurts like hell. You two go on. I'll hold them here.'

'You'll do no such thing,' said Susan vehemently. 'The three of us go or we all stay. Aim at the back of the car. At the petrol tank.'

Phillipe had a machine gun. He fired a short burst into the back of the car and the petrol erupted. The soldiers panicked and ran into view. Phillipe fired again and hit one, possibly both of them. They both hit the ground.

'Let's go, quickly,' said Susan. She led the way, the two men following her, Robert half-carrying Phillipe.

Staying in the bushes they hurried as best they could and reached the river without mishap. Much to Susan's relief the plane was where she had left it. 'Can you get down the steps?'

Phillipe was looking ghastly. The front of his shirt was covered with blood, his face was a pasty white, with sweat pouring down it. He was gasping for breath. A shot rang out and a bullet hit the pavement, ricocheting away. Turning and ducking, Susan put the rifle to her shoulder and aimed. There was nobody to shoot back at. Another shot hit the concrete next to her and bounced away with a loud pinging noise as the lead was flattened. She was now down behind the steps and she looked up, aimed and shot out the light that was bathing the area. The sudden darkness was very welcome.

'Hurry up!' Susan screamed 'I can't see where the shots are coming from.' She looked over her shoulder to see Phillipe climbing down the ladder.

'Come on!' Robert called to her.

Susan took one last look. A bullet hit the concrete in front of her face, peppering her with sharp splinters. It winged past her left ear. She screamed.

'Are you all right?' Robert asked.

'Yes. Untie the rope and wrap it around your wrist so the Griffin doesn't drift away.' She was by Robert's side. She looked down at the water, Phillipe was at the bottom, his face barely discernible in the black water.

The plane was bobbing on the water only three metres away. The engine was turning over, its steady sound a promise of escape.

'We'll jump. Come on.' So saying, Susan held her nose and leapt into the water. She heard an accompanying splash. Surfacing alongside Phillipe she grabbed his arm and said, 'Come on, my darling, time to go.'

She swam towards the plane, now drifting slowly away, towing Phillipe with her. Robert was suddenly by her side and swimming furiously, helping Phillipe. They reached the float. The Griffin was now floating in the middle of the canal, in danger of hitting a bridge or the side. If the propeller went in first, it would shatter and there would be no escape. Fear gave Susan added strength.

'You climb up first,' she said to Robert.

The rifle was dragging her down, sapping her strength and she shucked it off her shoulder, letting it fall.

Kicking frantically, Robert slithered up the smooth float. He grabbed Phillipe's arm. Heaving, Robert pulled while Susan pushed Phillipe over the float. Phillipe lay gagging, unable to move. The last of his strength had oozed out with his blood. The cold water had revitalised Susan and she scrambled onto the float. Somehow, between them, they got Phillipe into the cabin. How, Susan would never know.

'The plane's turned towards the bank!' Susan yelled. You'll have to go out on the wing and push us around. I can then hold her in position while you come back in. And remove the rope from the bottom of the strut!'

Robert crawled back along the wing to the float. He was leaning over when shots smashed into the plane's wing.

39

SUSAN WAS IN the pilot's seat, adjusting the controls, helping to turn the plane. She saw Robert arch backwards, his hands held towards her in supplication, before he fell into the water. She screamed, paralysed with indecision. More shots were fired, hitting the fuselage and bringing her back to her senses. She opened the throttle. The little plane passed under a bridge and rocketed along the canal. The next bridge, the *Puente de Isabel II*, had a narrower span. There was enough room to pass underneath but only just. It would be a tricky manoeuvre in daylight. In the darkness it was suicidal. She glanced at the speed dial and frowned. They weren't accelerating as quickly as they should have been. Delicate movements of her hands told here that the 'feel' of the plane was all wrong. It was dragging to starboard. She surmised that the right float had been holed and was taking in water. The sooner they were in the air the better. She pulled back on the column. The plane lifted, but too slowly. She would never make it. They would hit the bridge.

She pushed forward, settled on the water and built up speed. The *Puente de Isabel II* was coming towards her at an alarming rate. There was nothing for it. She aimed for the middle and kept going. The tip of the port wing scraped along the underside of the bridge with a loud screech, the plane veered to the left and was in danger of hitting the side when she corrected the course and flew out the other side. They were approaching take-off speed with the next bridge too close for comfort when she pulled back on the column. Do or die.

The engine screamed in protest. Sweat dripped down her face and into her eyes as she fought with the plane, praying for altitude. The floats left the water. They were being dragged to starboard and the plane was dipping to the right as the span of the bridge loomed in front of her.

'Come on, you bitch!' She screamed loudly, knowing they weren't going to make it.

The nose of the plane lifted over the wall but it wasn't high enough. Whatever was holding them down was proving too much. The floats would hit the wall of the bridge. Just then a gust of wind caught the nose and pushed them a few degrees higher. Then the leading edge of the wings felt the same lift and they swooped upwards, missing the bridge by inches. The drag to starboard was badly affecting the plane's stability. She seemed to be holding it when there was a thud and a quiver ran through the plane. They almost stalled but somehow Susan kept control and they flew on, away from the canal, gaining height all the time.

She turned to port in a wide sweeping turn, climbing away from the city as far as possible. Reaction set in. Susan found she was shaking. Angrily she wiped tears away with the back of her hand. She winced. Her face hurt. Looking at the back of her hand she saw the black smudge of blood in the moonlight.

What about the others? Simon, Henry and Frances! Were they really dead? Like poor Toby? Ruthlessly she cleared her mind of speculation. She needed to concentrate on her flying like never before if she and Phillipe were to survive. Where could she go? But she knew she had only one choice. Back to the estate. The plane was still flying like a pig but she was somehow managing to keep on the right course. Though desperate to check on Phillipe, she did not dare leave the controls. So she prayed. She begged the God she had abandoned years before to let Phillipe survive.

With a shock she recognised the lights of Cádiz ahead

and fitted the height control lever. Clambering into the back, she quickly turned down the undercarriage, regained her seat, unclipped the lever, and began working her way through the landing procedures. Finally, she adjusted the Griffin's height and course and headed for the track on the estate. In accordance with the instructions she had left, lanterns had been lit along each side of the track and hung on poles two metres high. They were clearly visible.

'Not long now, my darling,' she called over her shoulder. 'Not long now.'

As she lined up to land, she compensated for the drag to starboard. They were just touching down when the aircraft veered hard to the right. Susan was in danger of losing control. Only super fast reflexes saved her. She stamped on her left foot and kept the plane flying, though only just. They hit the earth with a breath taking force which threatened to destroy the undercarriage. Testimony to the good engineering of her uncle's factory, the plane survived the landing and kept rolling, although turning to the right with the speed bleeding off faster than usual. They came to a halt off the track, stopping in record time.

Susan sat there shaking, trying to muster some strength in her legs, desperate to get into the back to see to Phillipe. And yet part of her did not want to go and look. Part of her just wanted to sit there and cry. But move she did. She climbed shakily from her seat and into the cabin. Phillipe hadn't changed position. He lay along the cabin, wedged in the aisle between the seats. To her relief she saw that he was still breathing but only just. Each breath was shallow and ragged. He groaned pitifully and the sound of his pain pierced her heart. There did not appear to be any more blood on the floor. Susan prayed that the bleeding had stopped. She heard noises outside and a torch shone in through the door. The men had arrived to help them.

'Quickly, we must get him to the house. And we need a doctor.' Susan ordered.

Two men climbed into the Griffin and lifted Phillipe out of the plane. They lay him down gently onto the hard packed earth. One of them issued a stream of commands and some of the men began to hurry away.

'Please hurry,' Susan begged.

'What happened?' The man who addressed her was a stranger. She gazed in puzzlement at his hawkish face, with its beaked nose, thick moustache and long sideburns. He carried a gun over his shoulder.

'Who are you?' Susan asked.

'My name does not matter. I was told to meet you and collect the money.'

Susan had knelt down by Phillipe and taken his hand. 'Hang in there, my darling. Help is coming.' Phillipe groaned but said nothing.

'What happened?' This time the question was asked more harshly.

Shaking her head Susan looked up at the shadowy figure. 'I don't know. I heard shooting and went to investigate. I found only Phillipe and Robert alive. Robert was killed when we tried to escape.' Tears welled up and she knew she was on the edge of breaking down. With difficulty she held herself together. 'That's all I know.'

'And the money? Where is the money?'

The callousness of the question and his apparent indifference to her friends proved too much for Susan. Leaping to her feet she screamed at him. 'Don't talk to me about money! My friends are dead and Phillipe is probably dying. And you ask about money? Well, I didn't see any and if I had I wouldn't have brought it. I wouldn't have been able to. All I cared about was saving Phillipe and the others.'

The man stepped closer to her and looked into her eyes, his face inches from hers. 'This is war. People die. We need that money to fight the fascists. Pull yourself together, *señorita*, or it will be the worst for you.'

Susan took a step back intending to release her pent

up anger, fear and frustration, with a slap to the man's face. The blow never reached its target. He caught her hand and held it easily. 'Do not try my patience too far, *señorita*. We will help Phillipe. We will send one of our own doctors to you but be careful. I do not take insults from a woman.'

He squeezed her wrist until she flinched and said, 'Let go. You've made your point.'

'Good. So long as we understand each other.'

Just then two of the men appeared carrying a door. Placing their makeshift stretcher beside Phillipe, they lifted his comatose body onto it. They hurried towards the house with Susan by their side. Awkwardly they carried him up the stairs and into his bedroom. When he was on the bed, Susan began to strip off his clothes. A servant appeared, wringing her hands, babbling incoherent Spanish.

'Fetch hot water and bandages,' Susan ordered. The girl did not move. 'Go on! Are you deaf or just stupid?'

The girl hurried away. Susan took a closer look at the wound. A bullet had hit Phillipe in the lower abdomen and passed right through. She guessed it had damaged his stomach and by the way he was breathing, possibly a lung. He was chalk white and his breath came in ragged, shallow gasps. He was barely alive.

A servant, Mercedes, appeared with a bowl of hot water and a towel over her arm. Susan began to wash the wound, front and back. Each time she touched him, Phillipe gasped in pain. Tears of compassion sprang to her eyes and she wiped at her face.

In Spanish she said to the girl, 'Is there a first aid kit?'

Mercedes looked at her uncomprehendingly. Susan took her shoulders and gave her a shake. '*Entiende*? Do you understand?'

The girl had been staring down in horror at Phillipe's bloodied body and now she looked at Susan. 'A first aid kit. *Si*. I will get you what you need.'

While she was away Susan did her best to clean the wound. Mercedes returned with a basket. She used lint as a pad and wrapped crepe bandage around Phillipe's body, with the girl helping him to sit upright. There was nothing more she could do until the doctor arrived. She thanked the girl and ushered her from the room. Exhausted, Susan sat by the bed and looked at Phillipe's sleeping form. Sitting by his side was not going to help anybody. She needed to get the plane under cover before dawn and see what damage there was. She looked at her watch. It showed 9pm. She placed it to her ear but found it ticking as strongly and steadily as ever. It could not be! She shook it and looked again. She looked out of the window. It was dark. From downstairs she was aware of the grandfather clock stirring and she counted the chimes. Nine! It was only 9pm! Her whole life had been turned upside down in under two hours. She sat forward, put her face in her hands and sobbed.

After a few minutes she pulled herself together and climbed wearily to her feet. They weren't safe. They never would be safe as long as they stayed in Spain. Once the doctor had been she would fly Phillipe to safety. She would take them to Gibraltar that very night.

In her room she stripped off and put on a bathrobe before hurrying to the bathroom. She began to shower. Under the water her face stung and she crossed to a mirror to look at herself. Her reflection was barely recognisable. In hours she seemed to have aged years. Her complexion was grey, her eyes lacklustre and her cheeks and forehead covered in small scratches. She realised they were pepper spray cuts from the bullet that had hit the concrete in front of her face. The gash on her forehead was oozing blood and she washed it with cold water.

Back in her room she used the first aid kit to wipe each cut with antiseptic and put a plaster on the deeper one on her forehead. She dressed in trousers, a clean blouse and put on a safari jacket. Checking on Phillipe again, she called for Mercedes and told her to sit with him.

Downstairs she went into the library. Opening the cupboard in the corner, she lifted down an old brandy and poured herself a stiff drink. She took the raw spirit neat and gasped as it hit her stomach. She poured another, and had lifted it to her lips, when she thought better of it. She needed her wits about her, especially if she and Phillipe were to fly out of there later that night. But she had to see what was wrong with the plane first.

Outside the balmy evening was lost on her. The moon was well over the horizon, bathing the Atlantic in its white, reflected light. There was a distinct chill in the air but she did not feel it. She had work to do.

Nearing the plane, she wondered what on earth the problem could be. She had never encountered anything like it before and was at a loss as to why the plane had dragged to starboard as it had.

She went to the starboard side and looked at the plane but saw nothing wrong. She felt along the float expecting to find holes but found none. Moving further along, she found the strut and felt the rope she had tied off there. Strange. She had told Robert to untie it. She felt for the knot and found it impossible to undo. It was a sign of her exhaustion that she still hadn't realised what had happened. She reached along the rope and stopped. She stared. What was tied to the end? She tried to pick it up. It was heavy. Peering in the dark, she looked again. The next second she was on her hands and knees vomiting up the brandy. It showered painfully through her mouth and nose. She retched and kept on retching, even when her stomach was completely empty.

For long seconds her mind refused to acknowledge what she had seen but she knew it was true. It explained everything. The way the plane had moved, its handling. The thud when they had landed. From the waist down he was missing. Only the upper half of his torso was left. She retched again and then fainted.

She had no idea how long she had lain there but it could not have been many minutes. When she stirred and sat up, memory flooded back and she looked involuntarily at Robert's remains. She stood up unsteadily and tottered to the barn where they kept the plane hidden. Inside she found a spade. By the side of the aircraft she dug a hole two feet wide, about three long and three deep. The work helped her to stop thinking. When she was finished she climbed out, took a knife from the toolbox in the plane and cut the rope from the strut. Bile rose in her throat as she dragged what was left of her friend to the hole, looking away when she shovelled the dirt over him. When she was finished she stood with her head bowed for a few seconds, trying to pray. No words came.

Trudging back to the barn she threw the spade into a corner and returned to the house. In the kitchen she swilled out her mouth, drank copious amounts of water and washed her face, before returning to the aircraft. She resumed her careful inspection.

There were bullet holes in the starboard wing but nothing vital appeared to have been damaged. She could easily patch them up and debated with herself whether to leave them until they got to Gibraltar or to deal with them immediately. In her heart of hearts she knew the answer. With a sigh she started the engine and taxied across to the barn and went inside, out of sight. With the door closed, she lit a lamp and got to work. There were eight holes. On the top of the wing each hole was smooth but underneath it was jagged where the bullet had smashed through the aluminium. Using a hacksaw and file she smoothed the edges. She cut small patches out of a sheet of aluminium and drilled holes through them. Threading a nut through a patch, she coated it with resin and fitted it over one of the holes in the wing. She coated a second patch and fitted it to the underside before threading on a bolt and fixing the patches firmly in place. Finally she sawed off the extra length of bolt. She repeated the process until all the holes were patched. Her last task was to fill the fuel tanks. She turned the plane, ready for take-off and went back to the house. There was still no sign of the doctor.

She checked on Phillipe. He was breathing faintly and his pallor was terrifying. She was going to have to be strong for both of them. Forcing herself back down to the kitchen, she made herself a platter of cheese, green and black olives and crusty bread. She poured herself a glass of red wine and placed the bottle beside her on the table.

What if one of the others had been taken alive? Would they even now be telling the Nationalists about her and Phillipe, where they could be found? She shivered. The atrocities committed by Franco's men were legion. It would not take much to make Frances talk, she was sure of that. Frances had been sitting away from the bank, keeping guard. Susan prayed she had kept her head and been ignored. Then it could only be a matter of time before she returned. Yes, that was a possibility.

Susan had been aware of people moving around the grounds and house but had ignored them. Her nemesis, the Spaniard who had met the plane had been in and out of sight a number of times but she had taken no notice of him. Now he entered the kitchen, sat opposite her and picked up the bottle of wine. He drank it from the neck, taking deep gulps until he was satisfied. Susan watched without emotion.

'*Gracias, señorita*, that's better.' He wiped his mouth and moustache with the back of his hand. 'I hope you do not mind.' From his tone it was clear he did not care one way or another.

Susan shook her head. The man was scum. 'When will the doctor get here?'

'He should not be much longer.'

'Why are you still here?'

'I came to collect money and deliver it safely to our agent in Cádiz. He would have sent the necessary signal and we would have met a ship offshore and collected our guns. You returned from Seville with nothing. We still need money.'

Susan looked at him stony faced. She no longer cared one way or another. It was no longer her fight. She was leaving just as soon as Phillipe had been seen by the doctor.

'There is a way to get money,' the man continued. 'Would you like to know how?' Susan showed no interest. 'You should as it concerns you.'

Her heart racing, her mouth was suddenly dry. What on earth could he possibly mean?

The man placed a long thin cigar between his lips, displaying startling white teeth, and struck a match. He dragged the aromatic smoke deep into his lungs before exhaling. She noticed how blue his eyes were, the deep creases at the corners of his mouth. He had thin lips and a determined, cleft chin. He badly needed a shave.

'A ship is heading for Valencia. She will unload her cargo there. She sailed from Hamburg and the cargo is intended for Franco.'

'So how were we to collect it?' she asked in spite of herself.

'The Master is an old hand. He has two manifests. One is the correct one which he will present at Valencia if he arrives with a full cargo. The second represents the smaller cargo which he would hand over in harbour should he "unload" some of his goods to us before he docks.'

Narrowing his eyes against the smoke, he dragged again on the cigar. 'The arms and ammunition are a gift from Hitler to the Nationalist army. If we intercept them, we pay over twice the going rate. The shipping line makes an extra profit and so does the crew. They get treble wages each time they make a delivery to us, so their silence is bought at a heavy price.'

'What has the ship to do with me?'

'If the message is not sent, the ship will not come close enough for us to board her. We know the freighter is full of weapons for Franco. It is their biggest shipment to date. The Seville bank robbery was crucial.' He was glaring at her now, his passion for his cause barely controlled. 'We must stop the cargo reaching Valencia.'

'I still don't see . . .'

He held up his hand. 'You will fly us out to the ship. With your help we will attack the freighter and board her.'

Whatever she had been expecting it was not that. 'Are you mad? Are you stark, raving bonkers? That's impossible. I can't stop a freighter.' She was shaking her head while he looked at her with venom in his eyes.

'Anything is possible, if you want Phillipe to live,' he said softly. So softly in fact that Susan thought for a moment she had misheard him.

The blood drained from her face. 'What did you say?'

'You heard me. The doctor is outside. He can help Phillipe but only if I say so. If you do not agree then your lover . . .' his voice dropped to a whisper, 'will not see the morning.'

Susan's own voice was a whisper. 'He's one of you, for God's sake! He's been fighting for the Republicans since it all started.'

The man shrugged. 'That may be so. But now he is badly hurt, a liability.'

His callousness appalled her. He was sub-human. Thinking feverishly, she tried another tack. 'His wound is healing. He could as easily live without the doctor's help.'

The man grimaced, took a drag on his cheroot and shook his head. 'I guarantee he won't.'

'How can you . . .' She broke off as understanding

dawned. 'You bastard.' This time when she struck, she was too fast for him to stop her. The palm of her hand hit his cheek with a loud slap, but he did not so much as move his head. Her fingers tingled and she had the satisfaction of seeing her hand print on his cheek. He glared at her and she stared straight back, unafraid. 'You need a psychiatrist.'

'I am fighting a war for the freedom of my people. The only way we can reach the ship is by using the plane.'

'But even if we reach the ship how will we stop it?'

'It is unarmed. We will tell the Master to stop and if he doesn't we threaten to bomb him.'

'It's not as simple as that. First of all we don't *have* any bombs and secondly the Griffin cannot drop them.'

'We have bombs, *señorita*, and we have time to fit some sort of mechanism so that you will be able to drop them.'

'It's madness.'

Shrugging, he squashed the butt of his cheroot onto her plate. It lay smouldering between them. 'That may be so. But it is the best chance we have. If you give me your word that you'll try I'll have the doctor see to Phillipe.'

She glared at him for a few seconds before nodding. All that mattered right then was Phillipe's life.

The doctor proved to be a surgeon who had dealt with many bullet wounds. Since the death of his wife and son at the hands of the fascists his hatred of Franco and his men was absolute, the driving force in his life. Anxious to save the life of a Republican soldier, he quickly assessed the damage to Phillipe. With a chloroform-soaked pad, he knocked him out and then opened him up. Working quickly, he stitched together Phillipe's torn lung, a gash in the wall of his stomach and the exit wound. Finally he sutured Phillipe's front. He was an intense, small man with tiny hands.

'With rest he will be fine. Keep him quiet for a few days and when he is ready feed him small amounts of broth as often as he wants them. But not too much at a time. Do not overburden his stomach. I will come again in a week or so to remove the stitching and check on my patient.'

'Thank you.' Called on to help the doctor, she had done so albeit with a feeling of nausea throughout.

'You did well. Perhaps you should consider nursing,' was the doctor's parting words.

Looking at her watch Susan had a craving for a strong drink. It was barely midnight. She walked slowly down the stairs and got herself a large brandy. She stood in the dark room looking down the hill and out to the ocean. The decision she had made earlier had seemed so easy. To fly to Gib and then take a ship back to England. Now she was trapped by a madman whose name she did not even know. In thirty-six hours the ship would be passing through the Straits of Gibraltar. Was there enough time to do what was needed? It was obvious that Phillipe was in no state to leave, even if she somehow managed to get him to the plane. He needed rest until his wounds healed. She was trapped. She swigged the brandy, savouring its sharp taste. Her best bet was to pull off the attack on the ship and then get out. She shivered. She knew the man would not hesitate to carry out his threat to Phillipe. Then what about her? Downing the remainder of her brandy she went back upstairs. She passed a fitful night sleeping in the chair next to Phillipe's bed.

The following morning Phillipe was resting quietly and appeared to be breathing more easily. Susan showered, changed and went down for breakfast. Halfway through an omelette she had prepared, the door opened and the man walked in. She immediately lost her appetite. Pushing the plate away from her she lit a cigarette and turned her attention to her coffee.

'If you are finished, *señorita*, I will eat the remainder.'

He wolfed down the remainder of her meal. 'We have much to do.'

'Who do you have to help me?'

'Two men who are graduates from the University of Madrid.'

'In what? Accounting?'

'Of course not,' he looked affronted. 'Aero-engineering, my dear Miss Griffiths.'

His announcement took the wind out of her sails.

'There is something you must know – about Seville.'

She looked at him, her heart beating faster.

'It was an ambush. The fascists were waiting for them.'

'Who betrayed them?' Her voice caught in her throat and she cleared it before repeating herself. 'Who would do that?'

He shrugged his shoulders raising his palms in front of him. 'I do not know, *señorita*, but such a betrayal is all too common. People we have trusted from the start are forced by the Nationalists to divulge information. Their loved ones are tortured, or worse, threatened with death. It happens often. Perhaps now you understand why we are so careful. Even names.'

'My friends – is there any word?'

'As far as we know they were all killed. We know for certain that Simon Boucher is dead.'

'What about a girl? Frances.'

'I cannot say. Come. We have work to do.'

In the barn she found two men inspecting the Griffin. They each shook hands with her. As always they used no surnames, only Christian ones. The elder, aged around forty, was going to fat but his face was open and friendly. He introduced himself as Alfonso. The younger man was Gualterio. He was in his twenties and had just qualified from the university. Alfonso had been his tutor. Gualterio seemed more nervous, but Susan quickly learned that he had a sharp brain and steady hands. He had already made the connection between Susan and her Uncle Sion. It came as no surprise to Susan that he held the aviation pioneer in such high esteem.

'Can we do this?' she asked them, needing an honest appraisal of their chances.

'Very easily,' replied Alfonso. 'See the brackets we've made and fixed to the bottom of the wings. Come inside, I'll show you.' In the cockpit he showed her a new lever, about four inches long and fixed to the side. 'There are four bombs, two either side. They are held in place when the lever is upright. When the lever is pushed forward the two outside bombs, one port and the other starboard, are dropped. Pull the lever all the way back and the inner bombs are released. Watch.'

He signalled to Gualterio who waved back. Pushing the lever forward there was a mechanical clatter and two fuseless bombs landed on the floor with a thud. Instinctively, Susan winced. 'Look again.' Alfonso pulled the lever back, releasing another two.

'How many times have you tried the mechanism?' Susan asked.

'This is the third time, why?'

'Do it one hundred times,' she ordered. 'So that we can be sure it works when we need it to. Then I will take the plane into the air and practice dropping the bombs onto a target. We only get one shot at this.' She climbed out of the plane.

Without a backward glance she hurried away to Phillipe's bedside. Sitting, watching his even breathing under the white coverlet, she knew she had no choice. But if she was to survive the explosion of the falling bombs she would have to be high enough. Next, the target would be moving and that had to be taken into account, making it all the more difficult to time the drop. What sort of bombs were they? Did they have a delay after impact or did they explode immediately? If the former she would have time to get away. And what if the ammunition carried on the ship was set off? The ship would be blown to smithereens and all would be lost. What fools they were! The whole plan was ludicrous. They had to find a better way.

While she pondered on the problem Phillipe slept on, breathing easily. For the first time she dared to believe his poor, broken body, could be mended.

It was dusk when she finally stirred herself and to go downstairs. Seated in the kitchen, a cheroot between his teeth, an open bottle of red wine in front of him, was her enemy.

Without preamble, she took a clean glass and sat down opposite him. She poured herself some wine. Savouring the sharp tang on her tongue, she lit a cigarette. 'I need a name to address you by,' she said.

He stared at her for a few seconds while she returned his gaze, not in the least intimidated by his scrutiny. 'Call me Rey,' he shrugged.

'Rey? Just that?'

'It will do.'

She nodded, drank more wine and saw with surprise her glass was empty. As she refilled it, she said, 'Your amateurish plan won't work.'

His breath hissed between his teeth and he leaned forward. 'Then you will have to make it work. There is no other way.'

Susan made a moue with her lips and shook her head. With patience she didn't know she still possessed, she explained the impossibility of dropping the bombs with any accuracy. 'Did they test the new mechanism a hundred times?'

Rey nodded irritably. 'Enough so that we lost count.'

'And?'

'And it worked every time. Surely with your flying skills you will be able to target the ship accurately?'

'Spoken like a man who neither knows nor understands flying. The winds are capricious. The plane light. The target's small and it's moving. We would need a bomb aimer of some sort. Something that works out relative movement and drops the bombs where we want them. Trust me, Rey,' she spoke his name with barely disguised distaste, 'I know what I am talking about.'

He could see that she was serious and the angry retort that had sprung to his lips remained unsaid. 'Even dropping the bombs may be enough to frighten them. To make them stop.'

'If you want to take the risk it's all right with me. I warn you only because I don't want you blaming me if the attempt fails. And I don't want you hurting Phillipe as a result. I'll do my best but I'm telling you now, it won't be good enough.' She spoke with utter conviction and he knew she was right.

'What else could we do?' His question hung between them, representing a shift in power, almost imperceptible but a shift nonetheless.

'Mount a machine gun in the doorway. Shoot the ship's bridge out if you have to. I know it's not as damaging as a bomb but it should work, and it would be a lot safer. A bomb could set off the very ammunition you're trying to capture.'

Draining his glass Rey picked up the bottle and with irritation saw it was empty. Susan stood up and went to fetch another one. She waited for him to speak while he downed another glass of wine. Placing the glass on the table he looked sombre. 'If we are close enough to shoot at them, they in turn can fire at us.'

Susan shrugged with feigned nonchalance. 'Whoever is firing our gun had better aim straight.'

His reply took her by surprise. 'Which is why I'll be doing the shooting.'

'We'll be vulnerable. We'll be close enough to be shot to pieces and we won't be able to do a thing about it.'

Rey nodded. He knew she was speaking the truth but at that moment he could not think of a solution.

'There is a way,' Susan added.

He looked at her keenly.

'We use the plane to stop the ship at a prearranged spot, where our boats are waiting with men to board her.'

'We have a place.' He stopped, not wanting to give too much away.

Nodding, Susan said, 'I don't want to know. I just want to fill my side of the bargain and get out of here with Phillipe. Can you get the men and boats?'

'Yes. We can easily be ready. The ship is arriving the day after tomorrow in the Straits.'

'Good. Next problem. Have you ever fired – at right angles – from a moving platform at a moving target?'

'Naturally. Not from an aircraft. But from the back of a lorry.'

'Which is a lot slower. We'll try it tomorrow. At least you'll have an idea what it feels like.'

'Good. If there is nothing else, *señorita*, I must speak to my men.'

With relief Susan watched him leave, as long limbed and agile as a wild animal. A predator. She shivered. She did not like the man one iota.

40

SUSAN SPENT ANOTHER uncomfortable night in the chair beside Phillipe's bed. He slept peacefully until the dawn, and awoke to the sound of birds outside the window. For a few seconds, he lay there blinking away sleep. Turning his head he saw Susan sleeping. His mouth was as dry as the Sahara and he tried to call her name. He managed only a slight croak but it was enough to awaken her immediately. Her eyes instantly locked on his and she smiled broadly.

'Welcome back, my darling.'

He smiled in reply. 'Water. Please.'

She poured a glass from the carafe at the side of his bed and helped him drink. He drained the glass and then lay back, exhausted.

'That's better,' he said softly. 'What happened? How long have I been like this?' His eyes opened wide with shock as memory returned. 'Simon! He's dead!'

Speaking softly, she began to tell him her story, but halfway through he fell asleep. Stretching, Susan looked at her watch and decided it was still early enough to justify getting some proper rest herself. She went to her own bedroom, threw off her clothes and crawled under the sheets. In seconds she was sound asleep. When she awoke she felt dehydrated, a headache threatening. She felt better once she had bathed and dressed. When she checked on Phillipe, he was awake.

'I thought you'd deserted me.' He managed to smile.

'Never, my love. Never. Are you hungry?'

'Now that you mention it, yes. But I could use some more water.' He reached out for the carafe, grimaced and then groaned, his hand falling back to his side.

'Don't move,' she said in some alarm. 'I'll get you the water and then I'll see to breakfast. Scrambled eggs, all right for sir?'

'Sounds good.' He drank the water and then smiled up at her concerned face. 'Thank you. Do you know just how much I love you?'

'Regain your strength, my darling. Then,' she smiled, kissing him warmly, 'you can show me.'

Two hours later she was airborne and flying over a small lake known as *Embalse de Barbate,* an isolated area twenty-five miles to the east of the estate. Rey stood at the door of the Griffin, a mounted machine gun pointing outside the fuselage. At Susan's insistence, thin chains had been welded to either side of the gun barrel and fixed to the fuselage. A necessary caution – when the gun was swung in an arc it could not travel far enough to shoot off the starboard or tail wing. Like so much of the armoury of weapons used in the conflict, the machine gun was foreign. The French Chatellerault M1924/29 was over a metre long and weighed more than nine kilograms.

Susan flew straight and level. Rey fired the gun at an isolated tree. He missed. They went round again and this time he succeeded in chipping bark off one side.

'One more try,' Rey yelled to her.

She waved acknowledgement and turned the plane. This time when he opened fire he aimed in front of the target and fired in short, controlled bursts. The bullets struck the middle of the trunk and chipped the bark again before they were past. Rey nodded in satisfaction. He understood now what he needed to do.

Back at the estate the plane was wheeled out of sight. In the hangar she showed Rey how to change the landing-gear, emphasising the need for ensuring the mechanism was fully locked in place.

Though necessary, the practice flight had been a terrible risk. The fascists had begun to send up their own aircraft in the area. If they were seen, one of Franco's patrols would be around to investigate in no time. Susan refuelled the Griffin and went back to the house. She found Phillipe sitting up, wan-looking but it was clear his strength was gradually returning.

'I heard the plane. Where have you been?'

It was no use upsetting him. He needed all the rest he could get. *Diversionary tactics,* she thought. 'Who's Rey?'

'Rey?' He looked startled. 'Why do you ask?'

'He's here. He's convinced we were betrayed. That Franco's men were waiting for you when you arrived.'

Phillipe nodded. 'It was all so well executed. I've been lying here playing it all in my head and it's the only explanation.'

'Rey may be paranoid about secrecy, but in this instance he was right. So many people knew what we were doing. We'll never find out who it was.'

'What do you know about him?'

'His name is Reynaldo Ramon y Cajal. He was a professor of languages in the University of Cádiz.'

Susan looked at him in shock. 'A professor? You have to be joking. He ... he's the most villainous looking man I've ever seen.'

Phillipe dredged up a smile and said, 'That may be so, but he was extremely well-respected and effective, I believe. Perhaps he frightened his students into working hard.'

'What is he doing here?'

'Like so many of us he spoke out against fascism but was no activist. But many of his students were. Some of them were killed by Franco's army when they tried to stop his tanks driving into Cádiz. Unarmed kids,' he spoke bitterly, 'against a trained army. It was slaughter.'

'That still doesn't explain why he's here.'

'Franco's stronghold is the southwest. They shut the

university down and Rey escaped – just minutes before
being arrested. The other dons were not so lucky. They
were all killed in less than an hour. Shot. Rey came west
along the coast in a small boat. Since then he's been
co-ordinating the whole of the southern region against
Franco. The government has given him some title but
it's pretty meaningless. Resistance in the area has been
fractured up till now. Rey is helping to unite us. He's a
good man.'

Susan did not correct him, though she was certain
Phillipe would change his mind if he knew the whole
truth. Right now all that mattered was his recovery.

'Can I get you anything?'

He indicated the empty carafe. 'Something to eat and
more water.'

She left but soon returned, carrying a bowl of soup
and cold water on a tray. Phillipe was fast asleep. She
placed the tray within reach and stood for a few seconds,
looking down at his face, so peaceful in repose. A lock
of hair had fallen across his forehead and she could not
resist the desire to push it back. He stirred but did not
waken. Her heart soared. She had not known it was
possible to love someone more than life itself. She had
no doubt that Rey would carry out his threat if she failed
him. In a day or two Phillipe would be strong enough to
fly the short distance to Gibraltar. They would be safe
there.

She was in the kitchen drinking a cup of fresh coffee
and smoking a cigarette when Rey walked in, accompanied
by two men she had not seen before. No introductions
were made.

'We can expect the ship in about seven hours,' he
announced without preamble, helping himself to coffee.

She thought she had at least a day. The news set her
heart tripping but she was gratified to see that her hands
were as steady as ever.

'And the boats and men will be waiting?'

Rey nodded. 'They will be waiting.' He slung a khaki map case off his shoulder and onto the table, before seating himself. Undoing the straps he withdrew a map. Spreading it across the table he pointed. 'The ship is here. It will be in the Straits around eighteen hundred hours.'

'How will we recognise her?'

'We know what she looks like, but we also have a name. We'll fly across her stern and take a look.'

'What's the name?'

In answer Rey looked at her through half-hooded eyes.

'I'm fed up to my back teeth with you, *profesor*.' Susan was gratified to see a fleeting look of surprise pass across his face, before he got his features back under control.

'So, you know who I am, *señorita*.'

'I'm here because I volunteered. Stop threatening me and start trusting me. I've already proven that I am a help, not a hindrance. What is the name of the ship?'

Rey drummed his fingers on the table, staring at her. Susan held his gaze and stared back. She was determined not to break the silence.

Sighing, he said, 'All right. The ship is registered in Hamburg. Her name is *Blitzen*, which is a joke as she is a tramp steamer. Will that do you?'

'Thank you. Shall we continue?' Susan had difficulty hiding her delight at his small concession.

'After the raid,' Rey continued, 'we're abandoning this place. The workers are leaving to join some of the other militia units or relatives in the mountain villages. It's become too dangerous to stay here.'

Susan shrugged, indifferent to their plans.

They took-off at 5.15pm. The day had started blustery and overcast but now, with an hour or so of daylight left, the sky had cleared and the wind had abated. Susan took the plane down the valley to Medina Sidonia and then straight south, crossing the coast at Barbate. Only twenty-five miles away, Africa could be seen clearly.

Rey was seated next to her, a pair of battered binoculars held to his eyes. During the afternoon he had lightened up a little and had been almost pleasant by the time they came to leave. Susan cared only that the raid would soon be over. She flew low, a mere thousand feet above the water. A long swell was riding in from the west but there were no white caps. Ships dotted the sea, heading in both directions with no lane control, relying on the Rule of the Sea to avoid collision or mishap. Luckily the Straits of Gibraltar were not busy. Some fishing boats were still hard at work while those which had filled their holds were even now heading for harbour. The first boat in demanded the best prices.

'I see six, no seven, possibilities,' Rey said. After a few more minutes he shouted, 'Over there.' He pointed through the cockpit window.

Susan altered course, dropped eight hundred feet and crossed the stern of the ship. Her name was too difficult to read but she was registered in Athens. Disappointed, she looked at Rey. 'Where now?'

'That one.'

A few minutes later, 'That one.'

Finally, 'That one. *Blitzen* out of Hamburg,' he read.

She took the plane up to 10,000ft and flew towards the narrows where Europe and Africa were separated by a mere thirteen miles. Two fishing boats were wallowing in the swell, further from land than was usual for their size.

'Those are our men,' said Rey. 'Drop down and waggle your wings.'

Flying at less than a hundred feet, she did as she was told and saw a man standing on the stern of one of the boats wave back. The boats were typical of southern Spain. About thirty feet long, they had a small wheelhouse, a large hold and an engine that was good for something between seven and eight knots. The crew usually consisted of three men. She counted five on one of the boats alone, before they were behind her.

She turned to Rey. 'When do you want me to attack?'
'When the ship is within half a mile of the boats.'

Spiralling upwards, Susan was surprised at how calm
she was, now that action was so near. In the next few
minutes she could easily be killed but amazingly, she felt
no fear. She looked over her left shoulder to the west. At
that altitude, the sun was above the horizon but already
the surface of the sea was darkening.

Rey's, 'Let's go,' was superfluous. She was already
losing height in preparation for their run at the ship.

At fifty feet she brought the plane around and lined up
to run parallel with the ship. The Griffin was travelling
just above stalling speed, four, perhaps five times the
speed of the ship. As agreed, on the first pass, Rey opened
fire with the machine gun deliberately missing the *Blitzen*.
The aim was only to get the attention of the crew. Using
a loud hailer he leant out of the door and ordered the
ship to stop. He saw a fat man with a white cap on his
head, wearing some sort of uniform jacket, shake a fist
in response.

'Look out,' yelled Rey, but he need not have bothered.

Susan had already seen the crewman on the ship mount
a gun on the bridge wing and prepare to open fire. She
opened the throttle and turned the plane away, clawing
for height, passing out of range.

She dropped back to sea level and flew in front of the
ship. By now guns had been mounted on both sides and
were opening fire on them. Rey shot back, traversing the
gun from right to left, firing controlled bursts of three
rounds across the ship's port wing, into the bridge
windows and then into the starboard wing. The man on
the port gun ducked just in time. His opposite number to
starboard was hit. The plane banked around tightly, the
starboard wing tip missing the sea by what looked like
feet, before coming up the port side of the ship. Rey had
reloaded and was shooting again, using a more sustained
rate of fire as he shot the bridge to pieces. This time the

other gunner was killed. The wake behind the ship was dying as her speed bled away. Susan kept the plane circling while the two boats approached at speed. Nobody appeared on deck and she wondered briefly if they had killed the whole crew.

When the armed men climbed onto the ship she turned away, aimed into the light breeze and brought the plane down on to the sea. She taxied over to the ship. A small rowing boat pulled out from one of the boats. Rey waved to her briefly and climbed out into it. She taxied clear, opened the throttle and flew away without a backward glance. At sea level the sun had set but the higher she flew the lighter the sky became. At ten thousand feet she could see the edge of the world, a mixture of golden sunset and blue sea that caused her heart to soar with joy. The top of the rock of Gibraltar was just discernible and she itched to fly there, away from the madness of Spain. But first she had to pick up Phillipe.

She flew quickly back to the coast, navigating by the lights she could now easily identify. She was impatient, desperate, to see Phillipe again. She fittted the height control lever, adjusted it for level flight and climbed into the main cabin where she put down the wheels. The lights of the house were discernible and she lined up to land on the dark earth. Before taking-off she had lit a lantern and hung it on a pole at the far end of the track while at the touchdown she had another two lanterns, also lit, either side. There they were! She adjusted for height and course and went straight in, hitting the ground harder than she would have liked, but right in the middle of the two lanterns. She kept her eyes on the lantern shining ahead, staying on the track, rapidly bleeding off speed.

The plane came to a halt. In her desire to run to Phillipe, she considered leaving it where it was but sighed and thought better of it. She headed towards the barn. The doors were wide open, a black shadow in the wooden walls of the barn. Wearily she climbed down from the plane and went inside the barn. Lighting an oil lamp she left it hanging on the far wall before returning to the plane and taxiing inside. She climbed out, swithering whether to leave things as they were when she shook her head. It would not do. Pray for the best, prepare for the worst, was her Uncle Sion's motto and it was a good one. She turned the plane, refuelled it, removed the machine gun from its mounting and placed it on the floor of the Griffin. She'd dump it at sea. Appearing in Gibraltar with a machine gun would not be advisable the way things stood. She closed the barn doors behind her when she left.

She paused on the patio and looked up at a clear sky. The heavens were alive with twinkling stars and two planets, Mars and Venus, were clearly visible. Mars was easily recognisable by the reddish tinge it threw out. She felt at peace for the first time since the failed raid in Seville. They were safe now. She shivered and hurried indoors, eager to see Phillipe.

The kitchen door was closed. At the back of the house she could hear the gentle throb of the diesel generator and so she switched on the kitchen light as she entered. She stopped dead in complete shock.

At the table sat two uniformed men each holding a gun trained directly at her.

Recovering quickly, burying her fear in a show of aggression, she asked, 'Who are you? What do you want?'

'I am Captain Jaime Granados. I am here to arrest you, *señorita*.'

Susan was surprised that her voice was so level. 'On what charge?'

'Robbing Nationalist banks, shooting down a Nationalist plane, killing Nationalist supporters. Quite an impressive list for a young woman your age . . .'

'So I'm to be arrested without proof?' Susan stopped in horror. The machine gun was still in the plane. She should have hidden it! How could she have been so stupid?

'My men are searching the estate as I speak, looking for proof to use at your trial in Cádiz – before we shoot you.'

'I am innocent, and a British citizen.' Susan was rallying now, ready to argue and defend herself to the best of her ability. 'Phillipe, my fiancé, was shot for his support of General Franco. Take me to him.'

The captain grimaced. 'All in good time, *señorita*. But know this, your pathetic lies are useless. We have first hand information about your involvement in the bank raids, *and* about the Bouchers.'

The Captain raised his voice and called out. Two soldiers entered pushing someone in front of them. From her clothes it was obviously a woman. Her head had been shaved and her face was a misshapen, bloody pulp. She fell to her knees after a well-aimed boot to her backside. Slowly she raised her face to Susan. Her eyes were full of tears. Frances. Susan's knees buckled and she would have fallen herself if she had not been close enough to the table to support herself with her hands.

'I see you recognise your friend.'

'What have you done to her, you fiend?' Susan straightened up and stepped around the table to go to her.

A muscular arm caught her wrist and pulled her back roughly. The captain looked up at her, 'Do not take another step or she will die.'

Susan wrenched her arm free. She stepped away and froze at the sound of a gun being cocked. One of the men standing behind Frances had drawn his sidearm and was pointing at her head.

Susan screamed.

She did not notice the signal from the captain but the retort of the gun in the confined space was ear-splitting. The bullet hit Frances in the back of the head, smashed through her skull and splattered her brains over the floor. Susan moaned and gagged as blood, brain matter and shards of white skull splashed at her feet.

'Bastards!' She turned to the captain, beside herself

with rage. Before he could move she was on him. Beating, kicking and pulling his hair. He fell off his chair, with Susan clinging to him, trying desperately to hurt him. Hands reached for her but she fought them off. A stunning blow to the back of her head left her dazed and she sagged to the floor.

The captain climbed to his feet, dusting down his uniform. He straightened his tie and pushed a hand through his hair. Turning to his men he said, 'I will be talking to you shortly, *señorita*, and I want answers. I want names and plans. I want to know exactly what you communist scum are up to. And you will tell me.' He paused and then repeated, 'I promise, you *will* tell me. Throw the bitch into the cellar. She can cool off with her lover boy.'

Susan was dragged to her feet and pushed across the kitchen to the door of the cellar. The door was flung open and she stumbled down the steps. A light was burning in the middle of the vast cellar, a single bulb that lit the macabre scene before her. She sank to her knees and sobbed, staring at Phillipe as he swung from the rafter, a rope around his neck.

How long she stayed there staring at him, she never knew. Cramped legs and locked muscles finally forced her into moving. She stood up like an arthritic old crone and walked slowly towards his body. From his mottled face she knew that he had taken a long time to die. She pictured him, fighting for breath, dying slowly, in agony. She touched his hand. It was not yet cold. He could not have been dead for very long. Perhaps he had taken his last breath even while she was in the kitchen. The rope around his neck was thrown over a beam and tied to one of the racks of wine. Phillipe had been held up with his toes just touching the floor which had prolonged his death throes. She shook her head. Frantically she tugged at the knot in the rope. It was too tight and she cursed. Casting around, she searched for a means to cut him down. There was nothing.

Self-pity welled up, engulfing her. Tears streamed down her cheeks and she angrily wiped them away. All her plans, her hopes, had died with Phillipe. Next it would be her turn. How long did she have to live? A day? Two? She was not dead yet and one thing was certain, she was not going quietly.

The cellar with its earthen floor stretched almost the full length and width of the house. Along one wall were several small rooms. Running down the other were ceiling-high wooden wine racks, containing many hundreds of bottles of wine.

She went into the first of the rooms. Empty. The second contained sides of meat hanging from the beams, the third was filled with racks of port and sherry. The next room held discarded household items, tea chests full of domestic paraphernalia. In one she discovered a broken axe. The head had slipped off the end leaving a metre long handle which she picked up and hefted. It would make a good cosh. She placed it at the foot of the stairs and returned to rummage some more. She was despairing of finding anything else of use when her hand wrapped around a broken kitchen knife. The blade was about three inches long. It had broken cleanly, leaving a squared off end. She tried the blade with her thumb. It was sharp enough.

Shakily she approached Phillipe's body and tears streamed down her face as she sawed through the rope. The body fell with a heavy thud to the floor. She dropped the knife and fell to her knees alongside him, cradling his head in her arms. For a few minutes she was not quite sane. She talked to him, telling him what had happened and about the plans and dreams she had for their future. After a while her sobs eased and the tears stopped. Hatred washed through her, wiping away her self-pity, focusing her thoughts. With difficulty she dragged Phillipe's body into one of the side rooms and closed the door. She would come back for him later.

Shivering, she took stock. The stairs were wooden,

four feet high and projecting roughly four feet from the back wall. They were fixed to the left wall and supported on the right by a metal frame. Kneeling down, Susan saw there was plenty of room behind the stairs to hide. The single, bare light bulb cast its glow over the middle of the cellar, leaving the corners in dark shadow.

Tying an end of the rope used to hang Phillipe to the top of one of the furthest wine racks, she passed it through a metal ring-bolt opposite and back to the stairs. She gave an experimental tug but it stuck fast. She pulled harder and this time the whole rack teetered and for one heart-stopping second she thought it would topple right over. With a loud rattle of bottles, the rack settled back.

For her own sake, she didn't care if she survived or not. All she desired, all she hungered for, was revenge. Her reckless abandon of any thought for her own safety gave her a huge advantage over the soldiers in the kitchen. They would want to live. She placed full bottles of wine beside the stairs, took one last look around and then swung the axe-handle to smash the light bulb, plunging the cellar into pitch darkness.

There was nothing more she could do. Except wait. The knife and axe-handle suddenly seemed very puny in her hands.

41

SHE KNEW THEY would not be long in coming. The door to the cellar crashed open and a harsh voice ordered her out. The soldier called again, more impatiently this time. He said something over his shoulder and another man shouldered him aside.

'Come out! If you do not it will be the worse for you.' There was a pause. 'Come out, you bitch!' He screamed. They waited a few seconds, conferred softly and then both men came slowly down the stairs, one behind the other. The light from the door cast their shadows before them as they entered.

Susan sat with her head bowed, barely daring to breathe, hiding the white of her face. She did not dare move. The feet passed her head, one pair, a second pair, hesitating but unafraid.

They both reached the foot of the stairs and stopped. Each carried a rifle that was now cocked and pointing forward. The soldiers had stepped out of the brightly lit kitchen into the gloom of the cellar. Susan knew it was time to make her move before their eyes grew accustomed to the dark.

With her heart hammering she pulled with all her might on the rope attached to the wine rack. It shook, rattled and fell over with a huge, thundering crash. Both soldiers fired their rifles and as they did so she stood up quickly. The soldiers were two paces away, moving slowly towards the smashed bottles, the over-powering stench of wine permeating the enclosed space. She threw two bottles in quick succession into the furthest corner of the cellar. They smashed, distracting the men even further.

With all her strength she rammed the knife into the side of the throat of the soldier on her right. The man gurgled, dropped his rifle and reached for his neck. As the other soldier was turning she hit him on the side of the head with the axe handle. She was holding it left-handed and was unable to put enough energy into the swing. It glanced off his head, sending him stumbling forward. She gripped the handle with both hands and ran after him, this time swinging it from shoulder height. She hit his shoulder and his rifle clattered to the floor. She swung again, panic in her movements. This time she hit the side of his head. The blow crushed his skull and he collapsed without a sound.

The other soldier was clawing at his throat, on his knees, beseeching her help with his eyes. Susan felt a wave of revulsion sweeping through her. She grabbed the man by the hair, took hold of the knife and ripped it out through his throat. Blood gushed and the man toppled forward, dead. Susan found she was gulping for air as though she had run a long distance but then, just as suddenly, she was calm again. She still had work to do.

She grabbed one of the dead soldier's rifles and worked the bolt. She recognised the gun as a Lee-Enfield MkIII. She had fired one on numerous occasions and knew it to be highly accurate and reliable. Darting up the stairs she paused. Surely the two shots had been heard?

She looked carefully around the door but there was nobody there. Keeping low she darted across the kitchen and put out the light. She listened but could hear nothing, apart from the gentle sounds a quiet house makes in the cooling of the night, as timbers contract. Suddenly the silence was disturbed by a loud voice, calling from the other side of the house. Out the front.

She moved into the hall and up to the front door. How many of them were there? If only two were left of the

original four, she had a good chance of survival. She
looked out of the window. A lorry stood outside, with
two men sitting in the cab. The driver was leaning out of
the window, calling to his brothers-in-arms. No response.
In the moonlight Susan could see him wearily open the
cab door and climb down. She was tempted to shoot him
through the window but thought better of it. There could
be more men in the back of the lorry. If there were she
would lose in a straight fire fight.

   She still had the axe handle. Patiently and quietly she
stood behind the door. It opened and a voice called out
harshly. The soldier stepped into the hall and she moved.
Instinct must have given him a warning for he was turning
when she struck. Holding the handle in both hands, she
used all her pent-up hatred and fear. His head smashed
apart like a melon, blood and brains spraying out in an
arc, much of it on her face and clothes.

   Standing by the window she watched the cab. She could
just see the silhouette of the fourth man. She assumed he
was the captain. Becoming impatient, he pressed the horn
and it blared out, a harsh sound in the quiet night. After
a few seconds he became agitated and this time pressed
the horn harder and longer. When the night remained
silent, he dropped down from the other side of the cab
and ran, doubled-over, to the side of the house. Damn!
He was outwith her vision. But she had seen the pistol
he had been holding.

   She listened intently. There it was – a footfall outside
on the veranda. Stepping away from the door she knelt in
the darkness, her rifle trained at the doorway. After a few
seconds the door flew open and hit the wall with a
resounding crash. She held her fire. There was nobody in
the doorway. Where was he? Had he gone around the
back? The urge to call out was almost irresistible. But she
held it back. The first one to talk would be the one to die.

   'Jorge.' The whisper came from the open door. Seconds
later he repeated the name more loudly. 'Jorge!'

The captain only had to step through the door to see what had happened to his sergeant.

She was pretty sure that he was on the left of the door and trained the gun slightly that way. She held it to her shoulder, ready to fire. Her arms began to ache and the end of the rifle began to tremble. Slowly she relaxed them, bringing the rifle down from her shoulder and to her side. It was very nearly her undoing.

There was a blur of movement in the doorway and against the moonlit shadows a deeper shadow dived into the hall. She fired instinctively and had the satisfaction of hearing him scream in pain. The captain hit the floor with a thud and his gun fell from his hands and clattered across the wooden hallway. It came to rest in the middle of the pool of light cast by the moon through the window.

Susan worked the bolt on the rifle. He was holding his leg, groaning in pain. Stepping out from the shadows she silently crossed the hall. He looked at her with a mixture of astonishment and hate. His revolver was only a metre away, glinting in the moonlight, tempting him to reach for it.

'Please do,' Susan said softly.

'*Qué?*'

'Please reach for your gun. I want an excuse to kill you.'

'*Señorita, por favor*. Please help me. I am bleeding.' He was holding his knee. Dark blood oozed through his fingers. He tried to sit up. The movement brought him closer to his pistol. If he fell backwards he would easily reach his gun.

'*Señorita*, I must admit your courage is remarkable . . .' He launched himself at the pistol.

Susan's shot struck just as the captain's hand closed on the grip. He screamed as the bullet smashed through his hand and sent the gun skimming across the wooden floor.

He turned on her, screaming a torrent of vile Spanish,

holding his hand to his chest. Blood poured from the wound.

Susan worked the bolt and reloaded. Stepping across the floor she stared at him malevolently. 'Tell me, Captain, how long did it take for Phillipe to die?'

He screamed. 'I beg you, *señorita* . . .' He got no further.

Susan pulled the trigger and blew his knee cap and joint away. The captain fell unconscious. She stood looking down at him for a few seconds. Reaction was setting in and she found her limbs were beginning to tremble. Near exhaustion now, she went into the kitchen and got herself a glass of water. She was desperately thirsty and she refilled the tumbler three times. There was a low moan from the captain. She returned to the hall. The end of the barrel of her rifle was trembling and she cursed herself for being so weak. She would finish it once and for all.

He was lying in a widening pool of blood, black in the moonlight. His eyes were closed and he moaned piti-fully. Looking at him Susan felt nothing in her heart but hate. She and Phillipe should have been safe, free from this blighted land. Instead all her dreams were gone. This man had killed them. The power of her feelings caused the barrel to tremble more. She had to put the rifle down when tears obscured her vision.

The captain was coming round, moaning and crying with the pain. But already his nervous system was shutting down, turning the searing agony into a duller ache.

Opening his eyes he looked at her. 'English bitch,' he said hoarsely.

Susan smiled humourlessly, her face a rictus of hatred as she looked down at him. 'Say your prayers, Captain. What are the chances for a man such as you? What's it like to die knowing you killed innocent women and children? The world will be a better place without you – and without every fascist pig I will kill from this day on.'

'Then you too will be cursed, *señorita*,' he said softly, his strength ebbing with his blood. 'And I will see you in hell.'

Susan awoke with the noise of birds chattering and the sun streaming through the bedroom window. She lay still for a few seconds until the memories of the night before jerked her fully awake. How long had she slept? Her heart was hammering and her head throbbed to its beat. She climbed off the bed and dragged herself into the shower and began scrubbing herself clean, over and over. Four men had died at her hands. They would be missed by their unit commander. She could expect army patrols at any time. The thought galvanised her.

She dressed in a hurry, tucking her trousers into her boots, her shirt into her trousers and putting on her leather flying jacket. She went below to the cellar and stood looking at the mound of earth covering the body of her beloved Phillipe. Burying him last night had cost her all her strength.

She stood for a few seconds and then spoke fiercely. 'I had thought to give you a different vow on our wedding day, Phillipe. But this is my vow to you. Soon, beloved, we will be re-united. Till then, rest in peace, knowing that your death will be avenged. I love you and I always will. I will have my vengeance for what they did to you. I swear.'

Turning on her heel, she hurried away without a backward glance, resolve in every step she took. She collected guns and ammunition from the dead Nationalists and went outside. The day mocked her with its beauty. To Susan, the light breeze coming in from the Atlantic, the few clouds scudding across the sky meant only an opportunity to kill.

Gualterio and Alfonso had fitted the bomb mechanism to the Griffin, although it had not been used on the raid on the Blitzen. When she had flown into action, she had not carried any bombs, but now she fitted them herself. The doors of the barn were wide open and she could be airborne before any soldiers reached her as they would be clearly visible from the bottom of the driveway over a kilometre away. She had time.

The Griffin's fuselage was badly battered and scarred. Susan found a tin of black paint and a brush and began to coat the underside of the plane with it. She worked as rapidly as she could, without any finesse. When she had finished she started on the sides and then on the top. Working, she could keep her thoughts at bay. It was with a shock that she saw the morning had gone. The Griffin looked like an ugly predator in her new colours. All morning, Susan had been looking down the hill but nobody had appeared. She realised that she was hungry and thirsty. The thought of entering the kitchen turned her stomach in horror but she steeled herself.

Back in the house she averted her eyes from Frances' dead body. Flies had settled on the corpse. Picking up a towel she dropped it over Frances' head and the sound of their buzzing was instantly cut off. Sitting on the veranda steps, she forced down a mouthful of ham and cheese. After a swig of wine her appetite was gone. She was staring at the bottom of the hill, unseeingly, when the moving vehicles finally penetrated her subconscious.

She stood up with a jerk, dropping the glass of wine she had been holding, and shaded her eyes against the sun. It did not take long to make out who it was. It was the army. Franco's army.

Swallowing the nausea that had collected in her throat, Susan collected the food and bottle of wine and rushed to the barn. The engine turned over and caught instantly. She taxied out and along to the track. Opening up the throttle wide the Griffin accelerated rapidly and with a swoop climbed steeply into the air.

As she watched, three lorries came up the hill. She climbed to ten thousand feet and hung there. Soldiers disgorged from the backs of the lorries and surrounded the house. At that moment she would have given her soul for someone to man the machine gun in the doorway.

She watched some of the soldiers enter the house. The tiny figures were suddenly running back and forth like a colony of ants that has been kicked apart. More soldiers entered the house, while others headed for the barn. Her hand strayed to the release mechanism on the side of the cockpit. She toyed with it for a second and made up her mind. With the height control lever in place she retracted the wheels, aiding the Griffin's manoeuvrability.

The black plane came down out of the sun, almost invisible until it was overhead. She was flying at one hundred feet and dropped the first two bombs when she was over the house. They dropped through the middle of the roof, passed through the ceiling and first floor before impacting on the ground, one in the hall, the other in the kitchen. Both exploded with a terrific force. Most of the blast went upwards and took the house apart, but some went down, penetrating the cellar, collapsing earth and stone, creating a tomb for Phillipe's body.

The other two bombs were dropped seconds later when the plane was already fast approaching the barn. It had a steep-sided roof and one bomb missed the structure by inches. It ploughed into the earth and sat there, its tail in the air. It was a dud.

The second bomb fell to the right and clipped the edge of the roof and dropped straight down. Inside the barn was another cellar, smaller than the one in the house and carefully hidden. In it the group had stored much of their ammunition and weaponry. Amongst the explosives were a number of bombs. When Susan's bomb exploded it caused a resulting sympathetic detonation. The barn disintegrated. Soldiers who had escaped the blast from the house were caught in the holocaust now unleashed. Heavy timber rained down on them. The lucky ones were killed outright. Others were horrifyingly injured and bled to death slowly when nobody came to their aid.

Susan had banked the plane in a shallow dive down the side of the hill, more from instinct than a planned escape route. The blast from the barn flew upwards and outwards and passed her by a safe margin.

One bolt was all it took. A bolt embedded in a rotten section of the roof flew with the energy and deadliness of a bullet. The Griffin was three hundred yards away when the bolt flew past the top of the cockpit and smashed into the propeller, ripping it to shreds. Immediately the plane began to drop from the sky. The engine began to scream and shudder as all resistance to the spinning axis was lost. It was in danger of ripping itself out of the fuselage. Susan hit the emergency button. The petrol was cut off at the engine and it stopped almost instantaneously. With the immediate danger past, Susan found her training and the exercises her uncle had made her practise taking over. She knew exactly what to do. She just hoped it would be enough.

The Griffin was gliding over the cracked, dry soil of the vineyard. Tough vines clung to the hillside and Susan knew that if she put down on them the plane would most likely flip over and she would be seriously hurt. Worse, she could be trapped, with petrol falling onto the hot engine and bursting into flames. She shuddered. It was every pilot's nightmare. Luckily a slight breeze was coming in off the ocean and giving lift to the light plane. Even so she knew she could not stay airborne for much longer. There was only one hope. She had to try for the track. If she could land there she had a chance. It was a slim one as the track was on a downward slope with a tight bend, but it was the only one she had. The plane was gliding at about forty feet and would have already hit the ground if the land had not been falling away. Susan manipulated the column and rudder and the plane side-slipped to the right, towards the track. Now she was at twenty-five feet, with still a hundred yards to go. Fifteen feet and still too far away. She pulled back on the column, the plane clawed for height, in danger of stalling at any second as her speed bled away fast. The plane shuddered and was about to tumble from the sky when she pushed the column forward and continued the glide. Forty feet and fifty yards to go. Lower and closer, she willed the plane to stay in the air as the track slid beneath the fuselage.

Not a moment too soon. The plane hit the packed track, bounced, hit again and slid down the hill. The Griffin settled to port, on the float. There was a horrendous noise of metal scraping on stone as the paint and then the aluminium began to rub along the track. The sharp bend was now less than a hundred yards away, and still she was travelling too fast!

On the left side of the track there was a ditch, used for running off heavy rainwater while on the right was a low bank of small stones about a yard wide. They had been picked out of the earth of the vine terraces over the years and used to make the track. The plane was still travelling at 20mph when she went off the track. Susan pulled hard on the column and gave the wings just enough lift to take the plane over the verge of the stones. Landing on wheels, she would have had no chance. As it was the plane skidded over the land, at right-angles to the terraces, vines whipping at the fuselage, the plane bouncing and scraping slower and slower. The right float hit a drainage ditch, dropped two feet and trapped the plane. The left side slewed right, the starboard float jammed in the soil and the Griffin twisted further. There was a shocking ripping sound, the plane stopped dead and Susan was flung forward. In spite of her seat belt, she hit her head with a resounding crack. The last thing she was aware of was gratitude that the plane was still in one piece.

The sound of voices brought her back to consciousness. She groaned and sat up. Putting a hand to her forehead she winced. Memories flooded back and she looked around her, wide-eyed. She tried to swallow, fear paralysing her throat. The voices had to be soldiers. The sun was glinting on the windscreen and initially she could only make out vague shapes. What she could see did not reassure her. Men were jumping down from the back of a lorry, rifles slung over their shoulders. Suddenly she made up her mind. They would not take her alive.

Fumbling for her revolver stowed next to her seat, she cocked the gun while undoing her seat belt. She stumbled over the back of the seat and into the main cabin. Her vision swam in and out and she could make out only hazy shadows. Somehow she reached the door, opened it, knelt with the gun in her hand and prepared to fire.

A hand clamped down hard ripping the gun away.

42

WHEN SHE CAME to, Susan was lying on a blanket. Her head was throbbing and her tongue cleaved to the roof of her parched mouth. She tried to sit up and was surprised to find that there were no restraints on her. She could see the plane, looking forlorn and battered. And the lorry. And then she saw the men. She looked around her, bewildered. One came across and knelt by her side. Rey.

'Take it easy. You've had a nasty knock.'

Putting her hand to her forehead she winced. 'Water. Can I have some water, please?'

He placed a bottle in her hand and she drank greedily. Slowly she felt her strength returning and her head clearing although it still pounded incessantly. She tried to stand up but the world began to spin and she slumped back down.

'Take it easy,' said Rey. 'Can you tell us what happened?' His voice was gentle.

She told her story beginning with her return from the hijack. She spoke haltingly, her pain and anguish breaking the façade she had tried to erect. When she was finished she said tiredly, 'Frances betrayed us.' Her tone was bitter.

'Don't be so quick to condemn your friend. Stronger people have been broken. Believe me, I know.'

'What happens now?'

'Now? We go on. We were taking the arms from the ship to a safe house in the mountains when we saw the explosions.' He gestured over his shoulder.

Surprised, Susan saw that not one but four lorries had arrived. 'We've already hidden much more.'

The old Susan would have asked, 'Where?' Now she simply nodded.

'Can the plane be repaired?' Rey asked.

Susan shrugged. 'I don't see why not. If we can get it away from here. With Gualterio and Alfonso helping, it shouldn't be too difficult.'

'What'll you need?'

'A workshop if possible. A forge. Spares.' Susan put a hand to her head, pain and dizziness sweeping through her.

'We'll see what we can do. Why did you paint it black?'

'It's a her. Planes and ships are feminine.' She knew she was rambling, but couldn't stop herself.

'Why the paint?' Rey asked again.

'I wanted to hide the Griffin's identity.' She looked at the man kneeling beside her and he suppressed a shiver at the hate he saw in her eyes. 'I will have my revenge, Rey. No more leaving Spain. I mean to kill Nationalists, kill as many as I can for what they did to Phillipe. And the Griffin – well, that's my chance. I'm going to be like a vengeful angel, swooping down from the skies, wreaking revenge. A black angel.'

With an effort, Susan climbed to her feet. She stood, swaying, for a few seconds and then rallied. 'We have work to do. They could send somebody to investigate at any time.'

'I doubt it. From what you said you wiped out a whole section. They won't have enough men to send for hours, if not days.'

'What about sending one or two men to take a look?'

Rey pondered the possibility and then nodded. 'You could be right. We'll set up lookouts and an ambush. This is the only way in, isn't it?'

'By vehicle. But an army could walk through the estate. And if I was coming to take a look, I wouldn't drive in and announce myself. I'd come slow and quiet from another direction.'

'The explosion was huge. People in Cádiz probably saw it.'

Susan shook her head. 'I doubt it. Cádiz is twenty miles away. We're surrounded by hills and more importantly, most people don't want to see. No, the problem will arrive when the unit doesn't hear from its soldiers. Then they'll organise a reconnaissance patrol ...' Her voice trailed off, her head throbbing. She would have fallen if Rey had not suddenly reached out and caught her. 'Thanks. Let's go up to the house. There may be something worth salvaging.'

Rey nodded. He turned to the men and issued a string of orders. The lorries began to back and turn.

'What's happening?'

'They're going to the mountains. As soon as they've unloaded the arms, they'll be back with our aero-engineers and cutting equipment. We'll take the plane apart, load it on the lorries and get the hell out of here. I've also sent lookouts around the estate.'

Susan noticed men walking away, singly, in different directions.

Slowly they trudged up the hillside, cutting across the vine terraces, directly towards the burnt-out carcasses of what had been a fine house and outbuildings.

As they neared the remains of the house they heard moaning. Someone was calling for help. They followed the sound, walking past corpses, some badly mutilated, others without a mark.

A fire had started but had already burnt down to a smouldering black pile. Some of the walls still stood while others had collapsed. The beautiful house was utterly destroyed. Susan looked to where she thought the cellar door should be but could not see it. Rubble covered the whole area. It would take a team of men to dig their way into the cellar.

She followed Rey. On the far side of the patio they found the injured soldier whose voice they had followed.

'*La ayuda, por favor*.' The soldier was in his late twenties, perhaps early thirties.

Susan sucked in her breath and looked at Rey who was staring stonily at the man. She had recognised the uniform. The man was one of Franco's *africanistas*. A captain no less. The elite troops were renowned for the atrocities they were inflicting on the ordinary people of Spain. The men represented by the wounded captain, along with the regiment of Moors brought in by Franco, were amongst the worst of their kind.

Rey spoke Spanish to the man, which Susan followed easily.

'What were you doing here?'

'Help me, please. My name is . . .'

'I am not interested in your name. What were you doing here?'

'I came to look for the patrol that was sent here yesterday. The next moment a huge black plane dropped out of the sky and was bombing us. All my men . . . dead!' He spoke the last sentence in a whisper.

'Why had the patrol come to the estate?' Susan asked.

'Why would I talk to you, woman? Go! Get bandages and dress my wounds.' His tone was arrogant and commanding.

'Permit me?' Susan asked Rey, taking a pistol from his holster.

Rey shrugged, a gleam of considerable interest in his eyes.

Susan did not hesitate. She cocked the gun, aimed, fired and blew the right knee off the captain. He screamed in pain and shock before fainting. She was pleased with her reaction. Susan felt nothing. No remorse, no pity. Handing back the gun she walked over to the well and drew a bucket of water. She dribbled the water onto the captain's face. He spluttered, moaned and came awake.

'It's my day for blowing knees off army captains. Now we'll try that again,' Susan said in passable Spanish.

She was treated to a torrent of abuse which she let wash over her for a few moments. When there was no sign of it stopping she kicked him in his wounded knee. Hard. He screamed and fainted again. Susan repeated the water treatment. This time it took him longer to regain consciousness.

He lay silently looking at her and for the first time his face showed fear.

'Why did the patrol come here in the first place?'

He did not answer and Susan lifted the gun from Rey's holster once more. She cocked the hammer, the click a frightening sound despite the background noise of crackling timbers and falling masonry.

'I will blow off your other knee. Then each of your elbows. You will remain alive as long as it takes for you to answer my questions. It will be slow and painful and I will enjoy every second. Do I make myself clear?'

His bravado collapsed and tears ran down his cheeks. 'We were sent to find out what had happened to the four-man patrol that came here. Nothing else. I swear.'

'Why did they come in the first place?' Her voice oozed patience, as though she was talking to a difficult child.

'I do not know. I swear!' He screamed the last word when Susan aimed at his other knee. His hands covered the knee as though they could stop the bullet.

'If you leave your hands there I'll blow them away as well. Three wounds instead of one. Now remove your hands.'

'No! No! For God's sake, please. *Señor*,' he turned his begging eyes to Rey, 'make her stop. She is a devil. Help me!'

Rey shrugged. 'Answer her.'

'I swear I do not know.'

The gunshot was loud. The captain had two fingers blown off his left hand, one off his right and his knee blown away. Susan had to use three buckets of water to revive him.

As soon as he was able he spoke. 'We had been informed that this was a Republican stronghold,' he gasped, sweat pouring from his face and body. Deep lines of agony stretched from his nose to his mouth.

'Who was your informant?' Susan asked.

'I do not know. I swear it!' He screamed when she cocked the pistol for a third time. 'I think . . . I think it was an Englishwoman. But truly I do not know, *señorita*. There are traitors on both sides.'

'He's right, Susan,' said Rey, thoughtfully. 'I don't think we'll get any more out of him.'

Susan nodded and looked at Rey. 'I want him.'

Rey shook his head. 'We don't have time.' Looking into her dark eyes, for a moment he wondered if she was going to use the gun on him. 'We have too much to do.'

Susan nodded reluctantly and turned to look at the soldier. 'It is your lucky day.'

The captain sighed with relief. 'Thank you. Thank you, for sparing me.'

'Sparing you?' Susan repeated in wonder, aiming the gun at his head. He was still looking at her in horror when she pulled the trigger blowing a hole in his head. Handing the gun back to Rey she walked across to the smouldering house, found a piece of burnt timber about six inches long and half an inch wide and returned to the body. She drew a picture, in profile, of a winged angel, on the earth.

Rey looked at her quizzically.

'Call it my trademark. I want the Nationalists to know just who they're dealing with. I mean to remove Franco and all his scum from Spain, and I won't rest until I do.'

Rey shivered. The look in her cruel, compelling eyes, made even a veteran like himself fearful. He wondered what had been unleashed in that beautiful valley on that glorious day. He wondered if she was sane.

They had searched everywhere but found nothing of use or value. Everything had been destroyed.

By now the sun was well past its zenith. The swelling on Susan's forehead had gone down and the pain was easing. Although she was less pale, Rey was concerned for her.

'I could do with something to eat. Let's take another look in the kitchen,' he suggested.

The chimney wall, fireplace and stove were still standing. They found a nearby cupboard intact. Inside were cold meats, a cured ham and cheese. When Susan bit into the meat she suddenly found herself ravenous and wolfed the food down. 'I'd give my soul for a cup of coffee,' she announced.

'I fear your soul is quite safe. There is no coffee here.'

Susan kicked at a charred wooden plank. Bending, she pulled it to one side. Shards of broken pottery lay underneath. She moved some more wood and then exclaimed in triumph. Her hand burrowed down further and she pulled out an intact jar. 'Unless I am very much mistaken,' she began and untwisted the lid. 'Ah! Coffee! Perhaps my soul isn't safe after all.' She spoke without humour.

Rey lit the stove and put water on to boil. With mugs of coffee in their hands they continued exploring. The large sheds furthest from the house were untouched. In them, she knew, thousands of bottles of wine were maturing.

'We can't take them with us.' She lifted down a bottle and dusted off the cobwebs. 'I'll take this. It is one of the winery's vintage blends. I'll take it and you can drink it one day.'

'Me? When?'

'At my funeral.'

Susan led the way outside. They heard lorries in the distance. Shading their eyes, they looked down the hillside. Two of Rey's trucks were returning. 'Come on, we've got work to do,' she announced.

Rey was totally unused to taking orders yet he merely smiled and followed. In truth, he was intrigued. He regarded Susan as a psychological experiment, an academic issue. Rey decided to let her have her head. And he would observe. She could prove to be a useful ally or a serious liability. If a liability, the problem was easily dealt with. His face betrayed none of his thoughts as he accompanied her back to the crash site.

They worked ceaselessly, Gualterio and Alfonso directing half a dozen men as they took the plane apart and stowed the pieces on the trucks. The Nationalist trucks had been damaged beyond repair but they too were soon cannibalised and the parts packed onto the lorries. Other trucks appeared and the work went quickly.

They removed the wings, the engine, the floats and the undercarriage, shipping and despatching each lorry as it became laden. Finally, all that was left was the fuselage. So far they had managed to manhandle everything but the fuselage proved too heavy for them.

'What do we do now?' Alfonso put the question. It was an indication of her standing within the group that they looked to Susan to answer it.

Wearily she shook her head. She was dog-tired. 'We build a tripod. Over the fuselage. We can use the rope and wheel from the well to lift the fuselage onto a truck when one returns.' She looked to the west and the dying sun. 'We'd better hurry. It'll be dark soon.'

They sawed rafters from the roof of the big shed and carried them back to the crash site. Susan followed in the rear, with the rope and wheel from the well. Luckily it was brand new. The one inch manila would have lasted decades before it ever needed replacing. They propped three fifteen feet long rafters, each six inches by four, against one another, lashing them at the top. They fashioned a sling around the fuselage and tied the end of the rope to it. The wheel was hung and the rope threaded. There was nothing more they could do until the trucks returned. It was a long wait.

Susan fell into an exhausted sleep on the packed earth. She was awoken hours later and told it was her turn to stand guard. Groggily she stood up and went over to the vantage point they had selected. From there she could see down the valley. Anybody approaching by vehicle would easily be spotted. She lit a cigarette, looked at it with distaste and threw it away. Her mouth tasted foul.

They had lit a fire against the chill of the evening and Susan threw dry twigs on it, watching the flames hungrily coming back to life. The previous night's coffee sat in a pot and was quickly warmed through. Although it was bitter, the caffeine gave her the jolt she needed. With a deep, aching sadness she sat and looked up at the clear sky and down at the distant ocean. Grief ate at her soul. The thought of being deprived of Phillipe for evermore was incomprehensible to her. Since they had met, her identity had been inextricably woven with his. She had never felt so alone, knowing they had shared the same feelings, the same hopes for the future, the same ideals. Now she was trapped. Held, she knew full well, by her hatred and desire for vengeance.

The moon had risen and cast a white light over the landscape. It was all so beautiful. The stars, the night smells and night sounds. She lowered her head to her arms and fought back the tears.

Although she was only meant to spend ninety minutes on watch, she stayed until dawn. The sun was rising when she heard the sound of motors in the distance and woke the others. They made ready to either fight or flee, depending on the size of the force coming their way. With a collective sigh of relief, they saw it was two of their trucks.

They wasted no time. One lorry manoeuvred into position, the end of the rope was tied to it and the fuselage raised as high as possible. The second truck backed underneath and the fuselage was lowered, before being secured and covered with a tarpaulin. The sun was barely over the horizon when they were on their way. Susan had no idea of their destination, nor did she care.

They travelled for two days, leaving the coast far behind, going deeper and deeper into the mountains. Susan was thoroughly lost. A small convoy of vehicles had joined them, along with more men and some women.

At one of their rare stops, to refuel from cans of petrol and to take a natural break, she asked Rey where they were headed.

'Into the Sierra de Segura.'

'That's a large area.'

'It's all you need to know.'

'Look Rey, don't you trust me yet? You're taking secrecy to the verge of paranoia.'

'Which is why I am still alive and Simon and Phillipe are dead.'

She stepped back as though she had been struck. 'What do you mean?'

'Precisely that. They were well-meaning amateurs.' Rey sighed. 'We are fighting a well equipped, fully-trained army that has seen a good deal of action in Africa. Our army is led by a bunch of dandies who sit in their city barracks and leave the fighting to the peasants. They dress in popinjay uniforms, go to balls and hold parades.' Shaking his head in disgust he added, 'We cannot win unless our government has a major shift of attitude.'

'Then why fight? Why continue?'

'Because,' came the bleak reply, 'I have no choice. This way at least I'm trying. And what's the alternative? We *have* to fight.'

They travelled at night, holing up during the day, resting and hiding. They saw airplanes to the south of them but none came near. Susan identified them as Junkers, from the German Condor Legion based in Cádiz.

Eventually they were travelling down a beaten track that clung precariously to the side of a mountain, when a valley opened before them. In the distance lay a long and narrow lake, with an island at its southern end. It was an inhospitable part of the world, secluded, remote. Susan was seated next to Rey who was driving the lead truck. Dawn had broken two hours earlier but they had kept going.

'Is that our destination?'

'Yes. We have hidden bases all over Spain. Here we bring our wounded when we can or we come for a rest from the firing lines. We have learnt that we cannot stay in the front-line without a break. Those of us with families or friends in the towns and cities still under government control can go there. Those from the rural areas that have been wiped out by Franco we bring here – and to dozens of other places like it.'

Susan saw a number of wooden buildings through the morning haze, some complete while one or two were under construction.

When they drew up they were greeted by a group of armed men and women, as well as Gualterio and Alfonso. Susan was shown to a hut which contained two double bunks, a table and hard-backed chairs. She tumbled exhausted onto the bunk she was allocated. Within a few minutes she was fast asleep.

It was late afternoon when she awoke and went outside. She urgently needed a toilet and a shower. She counted ten huts laid out in an orderly fashion and constructed under high pine trees. Camouflage netting was suspended from the trees and draped over the huts, hiding them from enemy aircraft.

The hut furthest away was the latrine. It held unmarked cubicles with sacking tacked over the doorways to afford some privacy. Toilet paper was torn from various newspapers. She learned that if she wanted a hot shower she would have to boil her own water. It was poured into a galvanised container over the shower, which was operated by a chain. She opted for cold water and regretted every second she was under the icy cascade.

By the time she found Rey she was feeling fresh and

rested. Her head had stopped hurting and she was hungry
again. One of the largest huts was a communal dining
room. There were thirty or forty people in the hut talking,
exchanging war news, eating a stew supper. There were
half a dozen women, all of whom appeared older than
her. A lit range supplied heat for cooking and a table
served as a counter. Large trestle tables were lined up and
down the room and she saw there was room for at least
another twenty or thirty people to sit and eat. She sat
opposite Rey and began eating with gusto. The stew was
rich with vegetables and a dark meat. Someone had been
heavy-handed with the garlic which explained the fragrant
breath of her compadres. The bread was fresh and delicious and she was almost replete when she turned to Rey.

'How soon can we get to work on the plane?'

'Straight after you've eaten. We've been bringing in
supplies all day. There should be enough to get the plane
back together again. Alfonso thinks so anyway.'

'Good. The sooner the plane's fixed the better,' said
Susan. She finished eating and pushed her plate away.
She reached for a cigarette, looked at the empty packet
and threw it with disgust onto her plate. 'It's time I
stopped, anyway. I don't really like the taste.'

Leaving the hut with Rey and the engineers, she was
soon in the clearing where the plane was laid out. The
fuselage had been slung beneath a tripod and hung three
feet off the ground. Laid out beneath was the undercarriage, including the bent and battered parts. The wings
were lying on the ground on either side and the engine
sat on a bench in front. The engineers had found the spare
propeller Susan had brought with her and had already
attached it.

Susan thought longingly of her uncle's works at Biggin
Hill. 'Let's get started,' she said.

43

IT TOOK FIVE days. Oxy-acetylene torches had been purloined, along with a complete set of welding gear. A furnace was built to heat the metal so it could be beaten straight. The undercarriage was repaired first, then the fuselage attached. The wings were replaced, followed by the floats. Work went on for eighteen hours a day. The last item was the engine, expertly fitted by Alfonso and Gualterio. At Susan's insistence the Griffin was given a fresh coat of black paint.

In that time people had come and gone from the camp. News was brought in by word of mouth and week-old newspapers. They made depressing reading. Atrocity was piling on atrocity on both sides of the divide. The government held show trials before executing the prisoners, many of whom were innocent. Old scores were settled against the clergy and the owners of large farms, estates and companies. With no evidence other than hearsay, usually voiced by disgruntled workers and envious peasants, men were given long prison sentences, hanged or shot before a firing squad. The communists and anarchists were particularly busy in this direction, oblivious to the condemnation being heaped on them by the outside world. Since they were recognised as supporters of the Republican government, their involvement did not bode well for the future of Spain.

Germany and Italy were becoming more belligerent by the day. With fascism now rife across Europe, the Spanish government had thought they could automatically rely on support from other European countries, especially Britain and France. In political circles throughout the continent, war was considered inevitable. The Republicans saw themselves as natural allies of the non-fascist countries. But because of their communist allies and anti-clerical stance, Spain's ruling parties were gradually losing the propaganda war. The government had disbanded the army. Local militias had sprung up all over Spain. Their loyalty, naturally, was to local leaders. The government's lack of cohesion had allowed the better led, more united Nationalists to prosper. A recent event, however, had led to the balance of power being tipped in the government's favour. The Republicans introduced conscription of all males over the age of eighteen. At last the Republicans began to turn the tide of war against the Nationalists. The news merely added to Susan's determination.

The plane was fuelled and the engine run up. It sounded as sweet as it had ever done. The ground had been cleared and land around the lake flattened to allow the plane to taxi to the water. The Griffin bobbed on the water while Susan carefully watched the gauges. After a few minutes Susan taxied further out onto the lake, waved to the throng watching her and accelerated away. The plane lifted elegantly into the air. Susan circled the lake once and then climbed high. She put the Griffin through a series of exercises, each one more daring than the last. Finally satisfied, she returned to the lake, landing with barely a bump.

Taxiing to the shore she climbed out, smiling. 'She seems fine. We need to give her another thorough check but all being well, we're ready.'

Gualterio, Alfonso and Susan went over the plane with a fine-tooth comb. They checked nuts and bolts, welded seams and all connections until they were as satisfied as they could be.

'I've been working on an idea,' Gualterio announced over their evening meal. Exhausted from the day's labours, the words did little to arouse their interest. 'About the plane,' he added. That got their attention. He explained.

'Will it work?' Susan asked.

'The German Messerschmitts and the British Hurricanes fire that way. It's relatively easy to fit.'

'I'm not sure I like the idea of firing through my own propeller. Is there no other way?'

'We could drill out the propeller hub and fire through that. Then we fix guns to the wings.'

'That'll spoil the aerodynamics of the plane,' protested Susan.

'The guns are inside the wings. There's a belt feed along the wings. Usually two guns each side. Believe me, the easiest way is synchronised firing through the prop. Although the propeller is spinning and looks solid, in fact the blades only take up six to eight degrees of space at any one time. It's easy to fit a cut-out switch when a blade is almost vertical that allows firing as soon as it is past. Trust me. It was part of my specialisation under the professor here.' It was news to Susan that Alfonso had been a professor and the information gave her a certain amount of comfort.

'If it goes wrong and I shoot off the prop we won't be flying anywhere. I don't have another spare.'

Alfonso was quick to reassure her. 'It won't happen. But Gualterio, we don't have the necessary equipment.'

'If you get me a lathe I can make it work,' he replied eagerly.

'Can you get a lathe?' Susan asked Rey.

'It's not beyond the realms of possibility. But you need electricity to run a lathe. That we don't have.'

'So it's a no go,' she said to Gualterio.

His face had fallen with disappointment but he wasn't prepared to give up. 'In that case, I'll go to the lathe.'

They discussed the options. A factory in Quesada, thirty-five miles down the valley, could give them what he needed. The two aeronautical engineers left just after dusk.

For Susan it meant a period of inactivity, wasted time she could have used to attack the enemy. She helped out around the camp, cooking, cleaning and helping with some of the wounded. A doctor and a nurse visited the camp most days. Sometimes they were called away to treat the wounded in other places.

Her thoughts turned often to home. She had written twice since arriving in Spain and wondered if her letters had reached England. How she longed to see the family and tell them what had happened. She wondered how Richard was doing. He had confided in her more than anyone else. At thirteen she knew that he idolised her. What a responsibility, she thought, aching to see him again. And Dad. And Madelaine. And dear Gran. Images tumbled through her head.

The news was good. With conscription, for the first time, the Republicans had began to beat the Nationalists. Supplies were arriving from Russia in ever increasing quantities and battles were being won against the better trained and hitherto better armed *africanistas*. The heartening news filtered through the camp.

Gualterio and Alfonso returned three days later in triumph. They worked feverishly to fit the new device. Not only had they made a timing belt for firing a mounted machine gun through the propeller, but they had also designed and made a system to fire through the wings.

'If we could fit a 20mm cannon to fire through the prop hub,' Alfonso announced, 'you'd be as well armed as a Messerschmitt Bf109.'

She test fired while the plane was on the ground and facing over the lake. The guns worked like a dream. A stream of bullets spat out in three devastating lines.

'Remember,' said Alfonso, 'short, sharp bursts. You'll conserve your ammunition and reduce the chances of overheating and jamming.'

Susan took to the air with Rey as a passenger. She put

the plane through a series of manoeuvres before diving at a copse of trees situated on the island at the southern end of the lake. She opened fire. A makeshift sight was aligned to the centre gun, offset to account for the fact that she sat to one side. When Susan pulled the trigger the hammering made the plane shudder, which surprised her so much she held the trigger down longer than she had intended. The copse was shredded.

Rey sat with binoculars glued to his eyes and asked, 'Which tree were you aiming at?'

'The big pine in the middle.'

'In that case you win the coconut. The bullets from the middle gun hit the tree. Gualterio's idea works.'

'Why don't we go and fight in Madrid?' Susan asked. 'That's where Franco's to be found.'

'The General's a long way from Madrid,' replied Rey. 'Besides, there's heavy fighting going on there. Our best bet is to hit and run. Guerrilla tactics all the way. The armies are lined up along different fronts all over Spain. The government hold the cities while the Nationalists control vast amounts of the countryside. Already food is getting scarce in some Republican areas. If we join up with the government we will come under the control of the communists. That would mean a disaster.'

'Why?'

'Because, Susan, their ideology prevents them from seeing reason. They lost tens of thousands of men at Huesca, two hundred kilometres west of Barcelona. They were under two communist generals, Enrique Lister and El Campesino. They cannot agree which day it is never mind how to fight a battle.' Rey spoke with some bitterness and Susan wondered what personal experience he'd had of the two men. 'The British Battalion led by Fred Copeman of the XVth Brigade was also there. Thanks to them the government troops won the battle.'

'That's good.'

'It didn't end there. The usual squabbling allowed

Franco to call up his reserves and win in the end. Franco's men captured three hundred prisoners and killed them – by severing their legs.'

'My God, that's awful.'

'Be assured, Susan, they would do a lot worse to you before they killed you.'

'So we stay away from the main army?'

'Most assuredly. I have an idea to strike terror into the enemy.'

'Are you going to share it with the rest of us?'

Rey grinned wolfishly. 'All in good time.'

For the next two days Susan occupied herself around the camp while she waited to be told their first target. Her patience was rewarded when Rey disclosed it to her. It was ideal.

The city of Granada lay eighty miles to the south. On its outskirts was a small aerodrome, used by Condor aircraft, mainly Junkers and other, older bombers. Perimeter defences were medium to heavy but the field itself was laid out as for an inspection during peace time. Rey would lead a diversionary attack while she went for the aircraft. She would be carrying four bombs, as well as the machine guns. In the passengers' cabin Gualterio, with a machine gun fixed in the open doorway, would add to the firepower.

'The secret of success,' said Rey, 'is timing. You all know what to do?' There were murmurs of agreement and he said, 'Good. Then it is time we left.'

The small convoy of one lorry and a jeep travelled overnight. By the time dawn was hinting at a new day they were in position, hidden and prepared to wait until nightfall. The airfield was two kilometres away, on open, flat ground, surrounded by a perimeter fence. Every five hundred metres they could see sandbagged positions, with two men manning a machine gun. There were twenty guns around the field. A barracks held another fifty men. Alongside the men's quarters was an ack-ack gun which was only manned during the day. On the other side was the pilots' mess. Sergeants and officers mixed together, their common bond their chosen profession. The soldiers went off-duty at sunset.

The plane lifted gracefully into the air and Susan turned onto a southerly heading. She took them up to fifteen thousand feet, checked that the undercarriage was stowed and then fired a short burst on the guns. As she flew, Susan was brimming over with energy and confidence. Everything was exactly as it should be. Remembering her comrade she called back into the aircraft. 'Are you all right?' She knew it was the young engineer's first time into combat.

'*Si*. I am well, *señorita*, but I will be better when we're back at camp.'

'Relax. The worst that can happen is that we die.' On that reassuring note she concentrated on arriving at their destination at exactly the right time.

'There's Granada.' She pointed to the lights in the distance, still few in number as dusk was only now settling over the land.

Circling downwind she checked her watch. 'Time to go. Ready?' she asked over her shoulder.

Gualterio was now at the passenger door. He was strapped in a complex array of belts behind the machine gun. No matter how Susan flung the plane around the sky he would be kept safely in place.

A mile from the target, Susan cut the engine and drifted like a black bird. Her dive took her over the soldiers' barracks and the pilots' mess. In spite of the conflict the whole place was lit like a Christmas tree. Perimeter lights were on, there were no blackout curtains and doors were opened and closed without concern.

Inside the cockpit it was eerily silent apart from the whistling of the wind around the plane and through the passengers' door. Even though both of them were dressed warmly they could feel the cold. They flexed their fingers, ready to begin.

Susan pushed the bomb-release lever forward and the first two bombs dropped clear. At the same time she made ignition contact, started the engine and continued the dive, dropping the next two onto the pilots' mess. Simultaneously a firefight began at the southerly edge of the perimeter as Rey and his men attacked.

Both explosions blew out the walls causing the roofs to fall in on the men inside, maiming and killing. All but a handful were injured in some way or another. Turning to follow the perimeter fence, Susan fired her guns into the first dugout. The soldiers died under a withering burst of fire. She changed the plane's aspect, gained a little height and attacked a second and then a third dugout. The fourth was not so easy. A light machine gun opened fire on them and she jinked the plane hard to port. This brought the dugout onto their starboard side and Gualterio opened up. He managed to kill one sentry and wound the second.

It was time to buzz the buildings they had just bombed. Turning sharply, Susan put the plane into a shallow dive and aimed at the now burning buildings as some of the injured men crawled out and others went to their rescue. She thought of Phillipe as she pulled the trigger and sent short, deadly bursts into their midst.

The Griffin headed across the field and towards the southern perimeter. She saw a petrol tanker being driven away and hit it with a short burst. It erupted into flames. As it did she reached down by the side of her seat and threw several small, flat, black aluminium figures out of the window. They fluttered and twisted in the air before scattering across the field below; profiles of a winged angel, her calling card.

Before turning north again they shot up two more dugouts which had been targeting Rey and his men. Her adrenaline was up and she wanted to continue but knew that she shouldn't. The old adage came to mind. It was a good maxim to work by. She fully intended to live and fight another day.

She took the plane up to fifteen thousand feet and made a small adjustment to their heading. She would be in her bunk soon, while Rey and his men would need most of the night to get back.

The attack was the beginning of her reputation. When the third airfield was similarly destroyed the press learned about the angel silhouettes she scattered during every attack. The headlines in Spain were **'El Angel Negro de la Muerte'** and across the English speaking world they were **'The Black Angel of Death'**. She relished the sobriquet.

She suffered bouts of sickness after each raid and put it down to nerves and the relief she felt at returning safely to their hideout.

Following the third attack Rey arrived at the mess tent late in the morning. 'We have to leave,' he said without preamble.

Susan looked at him in some alarm.

'The Nationalists are coming up the trail. They are two hours behind, no more.'

'Damn!' Susan spoke with feeling. 'We have eight wounded men here. Taking them over the mountains means a slow and painful journey. Some of them won't survive.' The only road out was the one to the south, along which the Nationalists were coming.

Rey unfolded a map of the region and pointed. 'This lake is only forty kilometres away. Straight over this high ridge and down the other side. Start ferrying people and equipment while we try and hold back the army.'

'Gualterio,' Susan raised her voice and the young engineer came running to her, like a puppy eager to please.

'We've got to leave. Tell everyone to strike camp. I want two of the women to help me with the wounded.'

'You'd better take Alfonso as well. He's needed for the aircraft,' said Rey.

'How much time can you buy us?'

Rey shrugged. 'Not enough. We have accumulated valuable supplies which I fear will be lost.'

'Get the men you don't need to begin ferrying them to the island. We've enough boats and rafts out there.'

As spring had passed into summer they had swum in the lake and built a number of rafts which were easily hidden when not in use.

'Prioritise the supplies and the equipment,' Susan said. 'I'll cram the plane with everything I can.' She rushed out and began giving orders. From the beginning, Susan had inspired trust in the men. Such was her status now that nobody questioned her. The legend growing up around her had quickly become part of their identity. She was their mascot, their black angel, and they loved her for it.

Susan checked the plane. She had refuelled as always when she had returned the previous night. She was flushed. As she swept her hair from her face she was aware that she was being watched. Looking over her shoulder she saw Rey who smiled and waved to her. She waved back.

Within fifteen minutes she was taxiing across the lake. The plane was dangerously overloaded and sluggish. The day was completely still and hot. There was not the faintest of breezes to help give her lift. They passed the southern island and were approaching the narrower half of the lake when she felt the floats rise and fall. It happened a second time and then they were airborne, skimming low over the tall pines that lined the lake. She kept at tree top height, hugging the hills and following the contour of the land. The highest mountain was six thousand feet. They passed over with little room to spare and dropped down the other side. Susan side-slipped to starboard, keeping as low as she dared, and followed the river that led to the lake Rey had indicated. Within minutes the broad expanse of water opened before them.

'Welcome to *Embalse de la Fuensanta*,' she said to Alfonso, sitting in the seat next to her. They overflew the lake while Susan looked for the best spot to put down. They needed to unload as quickly as possible, no easy task with eight wounded people and only four able bodies.

Making her decision she lined up and took them in with a heavy thump. The plane slowed quickly and she taxied to a small beach they had spotted. Grounding the floats, they helped the wounded down and onto dry land. Tents, utensils and food followed. The plane had been jam-packed with as much as they could squeeze in, but it represented only a tiny amount of the supplies back at the camp. Supplies they needed to survive the coming autumn and winter. They removed the machine gun.

Alfonso and one of the women pushed the plane into deeper water and in seconds Susan was heading back.

She made two more trips, each time carrying a mountain of goods and ferrying the women and younger children to safety. She was landing back at the camp for the fourth time when she heard gunfire. It was still a way off but helped to underline the urgency of their position. This next flight would consist of food and cans of petrol, many cans of petrol. If she crashed this time she would not be walking away. She would be incinerated to a crisp. Carrying petrol was every pilot's nightmare and she handled the plane particularly carefully, this time travelling alone. She need not have feared. Within the hour she was back once again.

Rey and his men had been in slow retreat against the superior forces advancing up the trail. It had cost them dearly. Time, she decided, to get involved.

By now the firing was close, less than a kilometre away. Although they had ferried most of the bombs over the mountain she had purposefully left four at the camp. Gualterio helped her to attach them to the underside of the wings.

'I'll come with you,' he said. 'I can fire my machine gun out of the door.' He held an old French Hotchkiss M1922/26 that had been manufactured just after the Great War. There had been less than ten thousand made, as it was not very reliable, but it was better, Susan thought, than nothing. She nodded and he happily climbed into the harness in the doorway.

Once in the air Susan took them high, anxious to see what was going on. The trail followed a series of hairpin bends before reaching the valley bed. There were trucks backed up the trail for nearly a kilometre. Some were towing field-guns and, even as she watched, she saw the forward gun being unhitched and turned to point into the valley.

She identified the areas where Rey and his men were hiding, sniping at the enemy, moving back, losing ground and men all the time.

The Griffin dived out of the sun, straight at the forward trucks. With her guns hammering, she walked the plane along a third of the convoy before being forced to gain height. Climbing, she dipped the starboard wing and gave Gualterio a chance to fire. She could hear the machine gun and smell the acrid cordite as he poured fire down on the troops. Some attempted to return fire, although most dived for cover. Within seconds they were past and away.

'Are you all right?' She called over her shoulder.

'*Si*. Do we go round again?'

'This time I'm lobbing the bombs into the cliff face.'

'I don't understand.'

'You will,' she yelled.

She took the plane high and turned towards the cliff which towered above the convoy. On the ground the Nationalists were already moving damaged vehicles and regrouping to charge onto the valley floor. She aimed for the middle of the cliff. It rose a thousand feet above the plane but she held steady, the stone face filling the windshield.

She released all four bombs in a smooth movement, throwing forward the lever and hauling it back as soon as the first two bombs were gone. With the lightened load she hauled back on the column, opened the throttle full and prayed. The cliff face was so close she could see individual cracks and tufts of grass clinging tightly to the rock. She knew she wasn't going to make it.

44

THE PLANE WAS flying almost vertically, still too close to the rock face. In desperation Susan turned to starboard where the cliff fell away slightly but she knew it was not enough. Then the explosion occurred. The blast lifted the light aircraft up and away from the wall of rock with its force. The Griffin tumbled backwards, falling from the sky, upside-down.

She twisted the aircraft around, felt the wings begin to bite into the air as they swooped away from the cliff face and down the valley floor towards the lake. Shakily she pulled back on the column and gained height. She found that her hands were trembling.

'Are you all right?' she yelled.

'*Gracias* . . . I think so.' Gualterio's voice was less than certain.

'Hold tight. We're going in again.'

The plane turned in a tight circle and headed back for the track. But it was no longer there. Susan saw that the cliff face had collapsed, taking the convoy with it, burying most of it under thousands of tons of rock and rubble. One lorry and a handful of soldiers had survived at the front of the convoy and Rey and his men were already attacking them. She joined in and with three controlled bursts from the plane's guns, finished them off.

The plane followed the track around two bends and found the remainder of the convoy. Four trucks unscathed, Franco's men standing uncomprehending by the devastated track. She began firing. Some of the soldiers dived for cover while others returned fire. She felt bullets thud into the side of the Griffin but kept shooting. Two of the lorries erupted in flame and then they were past, turning, gaining height, going around for another pass.

Almost automatically Susan called over her shoulder to Gualterio. There was no reply and she glanced back. With a shock she saw his bloodied form hanging in the sling. His machine gun still in his hands, he looked at her, smiled and died.

All thought of further attack was gone and she headed back to the lake. She landed as quickly as she dared, stopped on the water and climbed into the back. It took her only a second to know she was too late. He was gone. Tears sprang to her eyes as she stroked his face. Dear, sweet, funny Gualterio – she had known how he felt about her. For all her faults, her impatience, her temper, he had been completely accepting and supportive. She had hoped he would find some nice girl, one day. Damn them! Damn them all to hell! Damn this pointless war!

She taxied the plane to the water's edge and waited for Rey to join her. She sat dejectedly on a float, her feet in the lake, her boots full of water.

'What is it?' Rey called to her as he approached.

'Gualterio. He's dead.'

Rey nodded, almost matter of factly. 'We lost seven good men today. Eight including Gualterio. And we've two more wounded, though not seriously.'

'God, how can you be so emotionless? Don't you care about human life?'

'I care. I care very much. But if you waste too much energy on your emotions you have nothing left with which to fight.'

Susan shook her head. 'You're an uncaring machine. You would have killed Phillipe, just to get your own way.'

'Would I? How can you be so sure?'

His words gave Susan food for thought and she said nothing. He sat by her and offered her a cigarette.

She waved it away. 'No thanks. I've decided I don't like the taste. The first one in the mornings has been making me nauseous so I think I'll stop.'

After a few seconds of silence, he spoke. 'That was incredible flying.'

'It was sheer blind luck,' she retorted. 'I nearly bought it.' She looked down at her hands and was faintly surprised to see that they weren't shaking any more. 'I miscalculated badly.'

'Maybe so, but you not only survived, you saved us. We would all be dead if it hadn't been for you.'

She reached out, took the cigarette from him, and drew deeply before handing it back. She held the smoke in her lungs for a few seconds before exhaling. 'Help me cut him down.'

They buried their dead. No prayers were spoken over the graves, just small farewell messages to men who could no longer hear.

Much of their equipment had to be abandoned. They left behind their lorries, three jeeps and a diesel generator. The rest of the gear they ferried out by plane. It took the remainder of that day and all the next, but finally they had all that they could reasonably move. The loss of Gualterio was felt acutely. He had been the linchpin in the plane's maintenance schedule and had got to know the aircraft intimately. Now the work fell to Susan and to Alfonso, who helped with bad grace. Used to being treated with deference by Gualterio, he did not take kindly to orders from a woman, even one as revered as Susan. As a result most of the work fell to her. Filters had to be changed and cleaned in petrol, oil checked and changed regularly, worn parts inspected and replaced or repaired. As each flying hour was added more work was required.

At the new base they lived under canvas. Only in autumn would they think of building more permanent accommodation to see them through the winter. Right now they had other problems to contend with. They were running low on supplies of petrol and food. They had plenty of guns and ammunition, but were miles both from civilisation and the war, with no means of travelling to either.

A week after they had quit their old base, they held a council of war. Everyone took part. They sat in the warm evening air, sipping glasses of wine or brandy, their spartan meal of fish flavoured paella lingering on their taste buds.

'The river,' Rey began, 'leads down to the coast and reaches the sea between Cartagena and Alicante. Both are Nationalist strongholds. So we have plenty of targets to choose from. We need supplies and most of all we need transport.'

There were murmurs of agreement. There were forty-three of them in the camp, ten wounded, four seriously.

'We need to survey the route and see if we can get out of the valley,' said Susan. 'If there's no suitable track then we can't stay. We'll have to find somewhere else.'

'Or go and join up with the regular army,' called one of the men. There was a chorus of assent.

Rey raised his hand and eventually they listened. 'If that's what you want to do then we won't stop you. But know the facts. The regular army is cowering behind the lines, holed up in towns and cities while the International Brigades lead the fighting. Instead of fighting the fascists, the communists argue with the anarchists who cannot agree with anybody. We have all seen it for ourselves. Which is why there are many groups like ours fighting the Nationalists all across Spain. But it is up to each and every one of you to decide what you want to do.'

The men and women looked at one another. They knew Rey spoke the truth. The war was a shambles. Good intentions and well-meaning individuals did not win wars. Training, discipline and weapons did. The death toll across the country was horrendous. It was to be a fight to the finish, the winner taking all.

'What else can we do?' a voice asked.

Susan replied. 'Walk down the valley. All the way to the first road, see if we can bring vehicles in. If we cannot we either find somewhere else or we dig out the track.'

'What with?'

'Our bare hands, if necessary,' replied Susan holding hers up. 'I may as well break my last fingernail.' Her nails and hands were ingrained with old oil, almost impossible to remove without scrubbing the skin off. The comment earned her a laugh.

'What about flying down the valley and taking a look?' someone suggested.

'I won't be able to tell enough from the air. And besides it's a waste of flying time. Let's put the plane to better use.'

'Killing Nationalists,' somebody yelled amidst more laughter.

Shortly afterwards, with full night blanketing the valley, they went to their beds. Susan shared a tent with two other women. Although tired she found she couldn't sleep and went to sit on a rotting log at the side of the lake, throwing stones at the water. Crunching gravel made her turn around.

Rey sat down beside her. 'Are you sure you're up to going down river tomorrow?' he enquired.

'Sure. Why not?' She threw another pebble into the water, the sound barely disturbing the night.

'I thought you might like to rest,' he said awkwardly.

'That's the last thing I want. I don't want to think. I don't want to play the game of what if.'

'What if?'

'What if I hadn't come to Spain? What if Phillipe had come to England? What if he hadn't been killed? What if, what if, what if, until I feel I'm going mad.'

He reached out and touched her shoulder. 'It's not too late, Susan. This isn't your war. You can leave anytime you like. A quick dash to Gibraltar and you'll be safe. Because of who you are the British government would probably even send a warship to take you home.'

Susan laughed mirthlessly. 'I doubt it very much. Anyway, I would be letting down too many people. Like it or not this is my war.'

'Is that the reason? Or is there something else?' Rey asked quietly.

Susan threw more stones before replying. 'I honestly don't know anymore. Nor do I care. I'll fight until there's nothing left to fight with. Then I'll throw rocks at General Franco.'

Rey chuckled. 'I think you would too. Okay, we'll set off at dawn and see what's what.' Climbing to his feet he bade her goodnight.

Susan returned the pleasantry and listened to him walk away. She suddenly felt very alone.

At dawn four of them set out. Susan, Rey, an eighteen-year old named Jorge and a man in his early fifties called Zebadiah, a Spanish Jew who joked with Susan that his name was Hebrew for Gift of God.

Susan and Zebadiah walked on one side of the river, the others on the opposite bank. They stayed in sight of each other but had not gone more than a few hundred metres when Rey called. Susan waved acknowledgement. She had seen it too. A well-defined track crossed in front of them, fording the river and vanishing left and right. They stood and conferred.

'You go right and we'll go left,' said Rey. 'Meet back here in an hour.'

'Right. One hour.' Susan and Zeb, as he was known, walked away. Rey said he had been a lawyer. He was fit for his age, with a shock of white hair, a weather beaten face and badly scarred hands. When Susan asked him about his hands all he said was, 'Franco.' It was enough.

They walked less than two kilometres before they hit a tarred road.

'Which way?' Susan asked. Zeb shrugged so she turned left.

There were no vehicles on the road and nothing passed

them as they walked for half an hour. Susan reckoned they had been walking in a southwesterly direction and Zeb agreed.

'We'd better go back if we're to be on time for Rey,' said Susan and they began retracing their steps. They had not gone far when she held up her hand. 'Listen. Sounds like a horse.' The words were barely out of her mouth when a donkey appeared, slowly dragging a battered cart with an old man walking by its side.

Zeb greeted him and after an exchange of pleasantries, learned what they wanted to know. Five kilometres further along, the road petered out in the village of Yeste. The other way lay Elche de la Sierra, a further forty kilometres away. They thanked the old man and walked on. If he was curious he did not show it. Curiosity could prove fatal.

Rey was late. Nearly an hour late. Susan and Zeb were becoming concerned when he and Jorge finally showed up. They briefly told him what they had found and he nodded. 'We found another river which I think is the *Rio Tabilla*, but although we followed the track we didn't get as far as a road. We found a small village to the south of here called *Los Belmontes*. But we didn't stop to talk to anybody.'

'So there are plenty of ways in and out of here,' said Susan.

'Is that a good thing?' Jorge asked.

By way of reply, Rey shrugged. 'It's getting late. We'd best return to the camp.'

'At least we can bring in vehicles,' said Susan. 'And all the equipment and supplies that we need.'

'But we have to steal them first,' said Rey, with a smile.

Back at the camp they made plans. Rey's maps showed the main features of the area but no details. The nearest large towns were Cieza to the south east and Albacete to the north. The latter was further away but three or four times larger.

'That's our best bet,' said Rey. Susan agreed. 'Only it'll take days to get there.'

Susan frowned. 'It's less than fifty miles by air. We'll be there in under twenty minutes.'

'It's too risky to take the plane,' protested Rey.

'It is not as risky as a gang of armed men wandering through the countryside in imminent danger of being spotted. No, we take the plane.'

'Where will we land?'

'How the hell do I know,' she replied irritably, 'until we get there?'

There was no time to waste. They took-off that evening. The sun was setting but there was still enough light to land safely as they approached Albacete. There were a few cars and lorries around but the traffic was light. As elsewhere in Spain, it was as if an unofficial curfew descended around sunset and remained in force until daylight.

Rey switched the undercarriage and Susan landed the Griffin on the road to the south of the town. The raiding party disembarked quickly and in seconds the plane was rolling and clawing her way back into the sky. She landed at their new camp in time for supper.

At first light Susan flew into a glorious dawn. She circled at fifteen thousand feet, high over the mountains and plains of La Mancha, the wine producing area of the province of Albacete. Flying directly north, following the road that led to Albacete she had already seen a number of lorries and other vehicles heading south. She had dropped down low and buzzed each one. Two of them acknowledged her signal.

A car and a lorry came out of a side road and drove hell for leather down the road that led towards the camp. It did not take her long to spot the trouble. Behind the stolen vehicles followed two jeeps. When she dropped down to take a closer look she saw they were manned by uniformed soldiers. Each jeep had a fixed machine gun in the back. The front jeep rounded a bend, saw the truck in front and opened fire, missing the target, but closing rapidly.

Susan didn't hesitate. She swooped down out of the skies and opened fire from behind. Her first burst blew the trailing jeep apart. She missed the other target when the jeep swerved and skidded to a halt, the gunner aiming at her. She turned tightly and was quickly out of range. Just then the sun broke over the horizon and she flew low, putting it behind her before attacking again. The jeep's occupants didn't see her until it was too late. A short burst and the driver was dead. The jeep hit a wall and the gunner was thrown out, breaking his neck on impact. Susan overflew the position of the wrecked jeep and dropped two of her silhouettes. Riding shotgun, she stayed high until she saw the trucks driven off the main road. Minutes later, she landed back in camp.

The vehicles arrived to joyful cheers of welcome. There had been a large hardware shop in the town which they had emptied. They had practically everything they needed to survive for weeks if not months, including cured hams and cheeses, olives, wines – even a case of brandy. In a local garage they had found a portable generator, which they had somehow manhandled onto the back of one of the lorries.

'Any trouble?' Susan asked Rey over a breakfast of fresh bread and cheese.

'No. One man caught us in the garage. We left him with a sore head.'

'You were lucky.'

'I agree. Last night in the bars I picked up a handful of newspapers and heard some of the news. Most of it isn't good.'

Susan visibly tensed.

'There's been a minor civil war in the Republican camp. In Barcelona. The government have outlawed POUM – the Marxist party, and the CNT – the anarchist trade union. The result is Russia's influence is stronger than ever.

If only,' Rey hit the palm of his hand with his fist, 'they stopped squabbling amongst themselves we might be able to beat Franco.'

Susan sipped more coffee in an attempt to settle her queasy stomach. 'What else did you hear?'

'Bilbao has fallen, which means the Basque Provinces are effectively in the hands of the Nationalists. The fighting around Madrid is vicious. It's only thanks to the Russian tanks and Russian Chato aircraft that the city hasn't fallen. But the losses on both sides have been huge.'

'Perhaps we should go and help them. Excuse me.' Susan stood up hurriedly and left the tent. She found a quiet spot and vomited up her breakfast. This, she thought, is ludicrous. Anyone would think . . . Dear God, no! She couldn't be! She sat down heavily on a log. Yes! It was nearly seven weeks since her last period. A baby! She was going to have a baby! Babies were supposed to be born in safe, loving environments, protected and cherished. Susan closed her eyes and prayed for help. She couldn't tell anyone. Not yet. She had to keep it a secret.

When she returned to the tent, Rey asked, 'Are you all right?'

'Yes. Something I ate or drank, that's all. I've been thinking,' she said, anxious to change the subject. What she really wanted to do was consider her own plight but for now she would ignore it until later. Much later. 'There's a German Condor squadron at Murcia.' She indicated the front cover of one of the newspapers. 'We should take it, as we did the others. We need to keep up the pressure. We've established a good strategy and we should take advantage of it.'

Rey picked up the paper. 'It says here that twenty Junkers are on the base and that it is heavily defended.'

'So we plan better and attack harder.'

Rey slitted his eyes against the smoke rising from the end of his cigarette. 'The reality is we're a support team for the plane.'

'Is that a problem?'

He thought for a few seconds and finally shook his head. 'I guess not. Can we use the plane more often?'

'I doubt it. Maintenance would become a problem. It already is, truth to tell.'

'So what do we do?'

'We need more engineers. Perhaps fitters. The professor can take care of the aero side of things but Gualterio was a hands-on mechanic as well as an aero-engineer.'

Rey nodded. 'All right, I'll make that a priority. How airworthy is the plane?'

'I'd say very good. For now. But with use it deteriorates rapidly.'

'Can we make it more effective as a fighting machine?'

'I'll need to talk with the Prof about that.'

'How good would you be in a straight fight with a 109?'

'Not very. My best bet would be to turn and run, like a lame rabbit being chased by a greyhound.'

Rey sat silently for a few seconds and then said, 'We need to take a close look at Murcia. I'll do a recce while you and the Prof work on the plane.'

Rey was away from the camp for two days. During that time more tents were erected under cover of the pine trees and camouflage netting was strung over the whole encampment. Susan and the Prof set up an engineering workshop, making a rough trestle table to work on. They examined the entire aircraft for wear and tear, effecting repairs as best they could. Whilst they did so, they talked about ways of making the Griffin a more efficient killing-machine.

'We can't cut a hole in the top,' said Alfonso. 'The strain would prove too much – the plane would break its back.'

'What about shooting through the port window?'

'I see no problem. But how badly will the plane's flying capability be affected with two apertures?'

'We can only try it and find out.'

'What if we welded a baffle on the front and kept the wind away from the hole?'

'That could work.'

They removed the port window and Susan took the plane up. Even before she left the surface of the water she could feel an unaccustomed drag. The wind whistled through the cabin, making flying particularly unpleasant but she kept going. Minutes later she landed again.

They cut and shaped a piece of aluminium to fit the length of the starboard door. It protruded by four inches, at an angle of forty-five degrees. They repeated the procedure with the port window and tried again. The difference was startling. No wind whistled through the cabin and the plane behaved almost as though the door and window were closed.

Luckily the door was forward of the window. When they installed machine guns on either side, with harnesses, there was no danger of the gunners getting in each others way. Chains were fixed to the barrels and the plane, restricting the movement of the guns. This eliminated the possibility of the Griffin being shot by her own bullets.

'Is there any way that we could carry more bombs?' Susan asked during a well-earned coffee break.

'I do not think so. Bigger and better bombs could be carried, but we have the fifty pounders and nothing else.'

'And blessed few of those. Where did they come from?'

Alfonso shrugged. 'I do not know. I think Rey got them from our army, but I cannot be sure. Speak of the devil.'

Rey drove into the camp and parked under the netting. Five figures climbed down from the truck. Two were strangers. Rey made the introductions.

'This is Chester. He's been fighting with the Abraham Lincoln Battalion and was at Málaga. He can tell you his story later. He was a mechanic at a Ford garage. And this is Consuelo. She escaped from Málaga and has been travelling with Chester.'

Susan felt an almost immediate distrust of the young Spanish woman. 'Any skills?' she asked.

'Pardon?' Consuelo looked to be in her mid-twenties. She was of average height with dark, bedraggled hair hanging to her shoulders. Her eyes were brown, her nose thin and straight, her lips full. Beneath the surface she seemed to crackle with tension.

'What do you do?' Susan asked.

'I am a nurse. Before the war I specialised as a midwife. Now I tend the wounded.'

Susan nodded and turned to Chester. The American was tall and skinny. At least he wouldn't eat much. 'What did you do at the garage?'

'Bit of everything. Don't worry – I'm a good mechanic.' He spoke without boasting and Susan smiled at him before shaking his hand.

'You're very welcome.'

'That's not all the good news,' said Rey. 'We've brought another generator and a lathe. As well as more petrol and oil.'

Susan clapped her hands with joy. 'Wonderful. That will make all the difference. Come on, Chester, I'll show you the Griffin.'

Over supper, at Rey's prompting, Chester told them about the battle in Málaga that had taken place four months earlier. 'I'd been sent from Madrid as a sort of liaison officer. I gotta tell you folks what I saw was a shock. Hell, I'm a communist but I don't hold with no burning of churches. There was arguments all the time between the top brass. Army fighting politicians non-stop. It was the Eyeties who attacked. They were really well equipped. All the latest stuff, including planes and tanks. I was sent to Valencia to ask the army to attack from behind, but they refused. I tried to get back to Málaga but couldn't. I met Connie here on the coast road between Málaga and Almería and we sort of hitched up. She can tell you what's happening in the city.'

'It was hell on earth. When the Italians entered the city Franco's men followed. They killed thousands of our supporters after summary show trials. You could hear the firing squads shooting non-stop.' Consuelo shuddered and placed her hands over her face.

'Take it easy, kid,' said Chester, putting an arm around her. 'Connie was raped. One of them made her pregnant.'

'Pregnant?' Susan said, her eyes darting to Consuelo's stomach.

'I lost the baby three weeks ago.'

'I'm sorry,' said Susan, an automatic reaction strengthened by her own difficult situation.

Consuelo removed her hands and wiped away the tears. 'Men held me down. After the tenth one did . . . did,' she shook her head. 'Believe me, this way is better.' She was shaking and Chester led her away until she calmed down.

He returned a few minutes later. 'She's had a rough time.'

The others nodded, their sympathy no less this time than the countless other times they had heard such a story.

'What did you think about our chances at the airport?' Susan asked Rey.

'The place is well guarded. It lies to the southwest of the city, at a place called El Palma. I counted twenty-two Junkers in all. Nothing else. There's a perimeter fence about three metres high. It's chain-link and easy to cut. There don't appear to be any dogs, but a foot patrol walks the whole way round. It takes them forty to fifty minutes. Every four hundred metres or so there's a dugout with an anti-aircraft gun. There are six down each side.' Taking his map case, Rey removed a detailed pencil drawing. 'These are the buildings and the hangars. This one is for the guards, this one for the pilots. They still haven't learnt their lesson. At night the planes are lined up, ready to go. All the pilots need do is run to their aircraft, start their engines and taxi two or three metres onto the runway and they're off. I saw them scramble and they were away in ten minutes.'

'At night or during the day?' Susan asked.

'During the day.' Rey grinned.

'What if we attack at night?' Susan suggested.

'You mean dusk?' Rey asked.

'No. I mean at midnight.'

'But you won't see the targets and you won't see to land once you're back here. It would be too dangerous.'

'We've thought of that. I've landed at night on a field with lights.'

Rey pointed out the obvious. 'Here you would be landing on water.'

'The Prof and I had an idea. We've taken some of the oil drums and cut them in half, length ways. Filled with wood chippings soaked in a mixture of oil and petrol, they'll burn brightly for about five minutes. We can place four on the lake and I can land between them. They don't need to be lit until I'm overhead. We think it will work.'

'Maybe. But what about the target? You won't be able to see the planes.'

Susan pointed at Rey's diagram. 'The Junkers are lined up along here. If you take out this emplacement and the one opposite and set them on fire I can line up between them and attack down the line.'

'You'll wander off the line as soon as the first fire is behind you. What we need are two beacons at one end. You can keep them in a straight line easily enough. It would then be a matter of judgement as to when you drop the bombs. But why fly at night?'

'Because there'll be no fighters around to pounce on me.'

'But the risk . . .'

'You haven't heard the worst of it.' Alfonso turned almost shame-facedly to Rey. 'The plane will be slower, less manoeuvrable than usual. We've rigged the Griffin to carry petrol bombs slung underneath the plane.'

45

TAKING-OFF WAS HIGHLY dangerous and Susan had her heart in her mouth as the plane accelerated across the water. Strapped to the bottom of the fuselage and running the length of the passenger's cabin was a net. It was pegged along the floor, with a peg every eighteen inches. Inside the net sat five-litre cans of petrol, held widthways. There were twenty in all. Should a stray bullet hit, they would go up in a ball of flame. For a second Susan wondered if the risk was worth it and then put the thought out of her mind. She concentrated on the beacon at the end of the lake, keeping it in the middle of the windscreen. As they passed take-off speed she pulled back on the column and the plane lifted gently into the air.

Apart from the women and the wounded, the camp was deserted. Every able-bodied man was taking part in the attack. Rey had increased the stakes. He wanted to wipe Murcia off the face of the earth.

In the back were two men, strapped into the webbing seats and manning machine guns pointing either side of the fuselage. They had practised on three previous occasions. Susan was confident they knew what they were doing. Another man sat in the only remaining seat in the cabin, ready to undo his seatbelt and start releasing the net and petrol bombs. As ever, timing was of the essence.

Rey's men had split into teams of two. Each one was armed with grenades and automatic weapons. They had driven to within a few kilometres of the airfield, hidden the trucks and other vehicles and approached on foot.

Rey's first target was the southeast corner ack-ack dugout and its two occupants. He and the man with him were less than a hundred metres away. The airfield itself was dark but lights shone from the windows of one building. He looked up at a cloudless sky. It took a few seconds to identify the changing stars, flashing in and out. The aircraft was where it should be. He smiled without humour. Susan was as reliable as the sunrise.

He had been in position all afternoon, hidden in the woods that lined the valley on both sides. The airfield was near the *Rio Sangonera*, which bisected the mountain ranges of *de Espuña* to the northwest and *de Carrasco* to the southeast. Fixing a signal to line up with the laid-out bombers had been child's play. Now it was time.

The Griffin dropped from the sky. At the same time each team ran towards the ack-ack emplacements. The soldiers manning the guns were already looking for the plane, trying to identify it, wondering whether they should open fire. Small arms fire started and then came the loud bang of a grenade being thrown.

Susan saw the two beacons of burning wood in the distance, the lower one a few degrees to the right of the higher. She adjusted course. She could make out the buildings but only just, as there was only a sliver of moon and that was already sinking beyond the horizon. Tiny pinpricks of light sparkled around the airfield as guns were fired at the ack-ack emplacements. To her surprise and great relief none of the anti-aircraft guns fired at her.

Lights were already coming on in the other buildings as she dropped the first two bombs, followed a full minute later by the second two. She banked the plane in a tight circle and went round again. The bombs had done their job. Two fires had started, one in the second aircraft in the line, the other at the end. More good luck than judgement, she realised.

'Standby,' she called over her shoulder. 'Now!'

In the back, the crewman had slipped his seatbelt and

knelt on the floor. At the signal, he pulled the first two pins, counted two seconds and pulled another two. The net beneath the fuselage peeled away, dropping a can of petrol which burst on impact on the row of planes. The petrol reached the already burning planes and exploded along the line with a huge surge of flame. Susan realised there was a gap. A plane was missing!

Inside the Griffin, the port-side gunner had been firing down at the buildings and the airmen running to their planes. He stopped as Susan twisted the Griffin savagely on its side. She wanted to get sight of the other plane before the pilot managed to get it airborne. There it was, taxiing onto the runway, already approaching flying speed. She turned the Griffin to port and followed the Junkers. First the tail and then the main part of the fuselage came into her sights. The Junkers began to rise in the air. Susan inched further along and then opened fire. The Junkers lurched, hit the ground, bounced, caught its starboard wingtip on the earth and flipped end over end before bursting into flame. Already she was turning, bringing them back around to attack the buildings. Her blood was up. She wasn't going to stop until the whole place ceased to exist. If Franco's terror tactics were good enough for the Nationalists they were good enough for her. Besides, Rey and his men would be needing help.

The fires were burning fiercely, lighting up the field, making it a turkey shoot. She went down the middle, firing at anybody she saw while the machine-guns on both sides of the passengers' cabin rattled away furiously. Devoid of emotion, she watched the pilots and soldiers of the Condor Legion die, pass after pass. Each time there were fewer shots fired at the plane.

In the meantime Rey and his men moved slowly and cautiously forward, picking off the troops and the pilots, staying away from the path of the Griffin, mopping up any resistance. Finally there was no more shooting. The Griffin came around for one last pass but there were no more targets. Rey was standing near a fire, waving a white cloth. As she overflew the field she dropped a handful of her black silhouettes. Turning north she bolted for the sanctuary of the camp. With a shock she realised that the whole attack had taken less than twenty minutes.

She flew once over the lake and by the time she had lined up to land the four floating barrels had been lit. The Griffin landed with a gentle bump and taxied to the shore, where it was covered with a camouflage net, rearmed and refuelled. Susan dragged herself to her tent. Within minutes she was fast asleep but, her body fuelled by adrenaline, she snapped awake after an hour, reliving the attack, seeing every second in her mind's eye. Each man she had killed died again. She saw the Junkers tumbling over the ground. She heard their silent screams and she thought of Phillipe.

So the legend grew. Together, she and Rey planned attack after attack. Each one was different, a variation on a theme, the targets changing as required. They included a Nationalist train full of troops heading for the war around Madrid; a bridge with a convoy of Italian tanks on it; and General Queipo de Llano's headquarters in Seville while Franco was visiting. Both generals escaped death by seconds.

A price of $100,000 was offered for the capture, dead or alive, of 'El Angel Negro de la Muerte'. Valuable foreign currency was being used to stop one deadly individual.

Newspapers wrote yards of columns about her exploits. The Republicans called her 'a saint' and the Nationalists 'a murdering devil'. One thing they had in common was their belief that the angel was a man. And so the reputation grew. The angel was often reported in different parts of the country at the same time.

The attacks on Nationalist army barracks, airfields and convoys were quick and deadly. Summer was at its height when they dropped bombs on a German freighter carrying munitions to Cádiz, blowing it out of the water. There was the first hint of autumn in the air when they took out a bridge with a convoy of soldiers guarding Franco and other members of his high command. Franco's staff car narrowly avoided falling into a hundred metre ravine. Franco upped the ante, by increasing the reward, dead or alive, to $150,000.

Although she had taken to wearing loose clothing, Susan's bump was now becoming more pronounced. She was tiring more quickly and the stresses she was putting on her body made her worry for the baby's safety.

Consuelo, now known to everyone as Connie, had proven invaluable helping to tend the sick and the wounded and an unlikely friendship had begun to build between the two women. She had quickly realised Susan's condition but wisely said nothing. Susan would have to tell her when the time was right. Weeks on, when it looked as though that was not going to happen, Connie decided to broach the subject.

They were alone in the mess tent. 'I think it is time, Susan, that you shared your concern.'

Susan was genuinely perplexed. She had developed the ability not to think of her condition for days at a time, putting all thoughts of it away, only to be dusted down and examined in the wee small hours when she lay sleepless, thinking of Phillipe.

Connie looked Susan in the eyes and then nodded at her belly. 'The baby.'

Susan sat in silence. Minutes earlier they had been discussing the probability that they would have to move to another location soon. The change of topic left Susan speechless.

'I don't wish to talk about it.' Susan stood up abruptly and walked to the trestle table that held the tub for washing dishes. She swilled out her cup and placed it on a shelf. Leaning against the table she pugnaciously crossed her arms.

Connie watched her, seeing the fragility beneath the

façade, the chinks in her armour of resolve. 'But talk about it we must. You are four, perhaps five months pregnant. You must take it easy. Slow down. Or you will endanger the baby.'

Susan swallowed hard, each word a dagger in her heart. Her eyes misted over and she hung her head. Connie was immediately at Susan's side, her arm around her friend. Susan let out a sob.

Connie let her cry for a few minutes. 'It's not the end of the world. Hush now. We have to make sensible plans for the baby's sake. Rest, eat well – do less flying.'

'But they rely on me so much.'

'This war will continue for a long time. Babies are being born everyday, and every one is precious. You must do everything in your power to protect your unborn child. For Phillipe as well as yourself.'

'Who told you about Phillipe?'

'Rey. He is very concerned for you, Susan.'

'He doesn't show it.'

'That is just his way. Believe me, Susan, he cares. He cares very much.'

Something in Connie's voice made Susan look at her sharply, but seeing her friend's calm face she dismissed the notion.

'What do you know about having a baby?' Connie asked.

Susan shrugged and then said sheepishly, 'Not a lot.'

'Come and sit down. First of all, you need to know that there is nothing to fear. Women in some cultures give birth in the fields and almost immediately return to work. You are not ill. You are not an invalid. You are merely having a baby. You need to eat better than you do. I have been preparing a proper diet regime. We need to look at the way your seatbelt crosses your lap. It needs to be rigged differently, so that you are not putting a heavy pressure on your belly.'

'You have been thinking about me!' Susan exclaimed

gratefully, her feelings of loneliness and isolation dissipating.

'Once a midwife,' Connie smiled, 'always a midwife.'

'What will we tell Rey?'

'He already knows. You and he will have to discuss the aircraft and what happens to it in the future. In two months maximum, you will have to stop. Once the baby is born you can fly again. Perhaps, when the baby is born, it will be time for you to leave. Perhaps,' she offered hesitatingly, 'you should leave now.'

'No!' Susan said with vehemence. She had spent long nights thinking the same thing. The thought of being with her family was torment, but she couldn't leave.

'Susan, revenge will not bring Phillipe back,' said Connie softly. 'A personal vendetta is no reason to go to war. Hatred will sour you. Think of your child. It's time to leave the past behind, to think of the new life in your belly. Have faith again. Love again.'

Susan's eyes were blazing. 'Thank you for your advice.' In a whirl, she left the tent. Was Connie right? Was she becoming embittered? Was she capable of love any more? Would she be able to love the baby? She realised with a shock that she had no feelings for the life inside her. Were her feelings dead? Hatred she knew. If anything her hatred of Franco and his *africanistas* had increased.

She found herself by the Griffin and decided to check on the latest maintenance schedule. Work, as always, helped to block out her thoughts.

Rey found her with a spanner in her hand and a grease mark down her cheek, taking apart a brake shoe. He stood watching her for a few seconds, until she became aware of his presence. She looked up at him and smiled.

'I've been talking to Connie,' he began, without preamble. 'What are you going to do?'

Susan shrugged. 'I don't know. I can continue for now.'

'But not for long, loath though we are to lose you. Your reputation is growing, Susan. You have given our people hope. The angel is revered across Spain. You are an icon.'

'An icon with a price on her head. Someone will betray me, sometime.'

'Never!' Rey spoke fiercely. 'Whoever did would not live long enough to enjoy the money.'

'That's a comforting thought.' Susan smiled at him. Her initial, fierce hatred of him was hard to comprehend now. His protectiveness was, she thought, quite endearing. 'What's the next target?'

He recognised her desire to change the subject and went along with it. 'A railway siding. A munitions train will be travelling to Madrid from Málaga. Half the train carries weapons and ammunition, the other half soldiers. Troops from the Moors regiment and the Foreign Legion.'

'Those vicious bastards? They're worse than animals. Have you read what they did at Málaga?'

'Chester wasn't exaggerating. They're heading north to reinforce the army around Madrid.'

'When?'

'In two days. Will the plane be ready?'

'Whenever you need it. What do you intend? Attacking in Málaga?'

Rey took out one of his maps and spread it on the trestle table that doubled as a work bench. 'This is the route I've chosen.' He traced it with his finger. 'In Málaga itself there are too many anti-aircraft emplacements and far too many troops. But just here, about twenty kilometres to the north, is a steep and narrow gorge.'

'How narrow?'

'Don't worry. There's plenty of room to fly in it. See here, the road is on one side and the rail track on the other. This is a wooden bridge across the river. It's a hundred metres high. If we get it just right we can blow the bridge and send the whole lot to hell.'

'What do you need me for? Why not just put explosives on the bridge and blow it when the train passes over?'

'The Nationalists aren't that stupid. The whole line is regularly checked by a special train. Engineers will comb the bridge a few hours before the train departs and when it gets there it will stop and another search will be carried out. So planting explosives won't work.'

'How strong is the bridge?'

'Very.'

'Are you sure that bombing it will do the trick? What if I miss the bridge?'

'Then we'll have failed.'

'What if I hit the bridge and the bombs don't detonate?'

'Come on, Susan, what is this? You know the answer as well as I do. We'll have failed.'

'So we need a better plan.'

Rey looked at her in exasperation.

Susan explained her alternative idea.

The train was due to depart at sunrise. At that time of the year it was early, four thirty-eight. Susan and those left in the camp were up well before then, checking and double checking. The train would be heavily guarded. Rey had left two days earlier. He had over three hundred kilometres to travel, often on bad roads, some of which were in hostile territory. Susan would attack only if she got the signal to tell her that Rey and his men were in position and ready.

The plane was fully fuelled, fully armed and both machine gunners were in their webbed seats. They took-off in the grey light of dawn, taxiing over the flat calm lake and rising into the breathless air. It promised to be a hot day once the morning mist had burnt off.

Her direct route covered a distance of one hundred and fifty air miles and would take forty five minutes. Most of the way was over barren land and mountains and so she did not expect any trouble from patrolling aircraft. Nonetheless, she kept a good lookout, quartering the sky continuously, her eyes flicking ceaselessly between the gauges and the world outside the cockpit.

At fifteen thousand feet the sun was already over the horizon. Below, the earth was cast in deep shadow, only the tops of the mountains lighting up as the new day began. She saw the river first and then the railway line. The track was a single line, with passing points on the plains and in some of the valleys. The trains travelled to a rigid timetable, the despatchers at either end in contact by telephone. As yet there was no sign of the train. She prayed that she had not left it too late.

The Griffin descended to five thousand feet above the landscape. Looking behind her she called, 'Watch for Rey's signal.'

The two gunners waved in acknowledgement, both staring out of their respective sides. The one to port spotted it and yelled out.

Susan caught the flashing light and waggled the plane's wings. She flew higher, edging south, searching for the train.

Nothing. Around another peak and there it was, smoke billowing from its stack as it slowly climbed the steep incline, following the tracks that wound around the mountains.

Susan headed back to where Rey and his men were hidden, waggled the plane's wings, received a flash of light in acknowledgement and took up position ready to pounce out of the sun, which was now ten degrees above the horizon. The bridge had been checked during the night by troops from the Nationalist army, who had already moved on to the next danger point. Rey and his men had moved in shortly afterwards and placed large amounts of explosives on the two centre spans. Looking closely at the bridge it was obvious to Rey that Susan had been right. Even if all four bombs had landed at the right place, and had gone up, there was no guarantee the bridge would have collapsed. It was constructed skilfully from massive timbers, well seasoned, held together by huge bolts and metal staples. Already over fifty years old it looked like lasting another hundred at least.

When the train reached the bridge it would stop and

a team of engineers would disembark to examine the bridge again. Just in case. When they did, the team would find the explosives. During the past year or two they had been caught out too often by the Republicans.

The train rounded a bend, sounded its whistle and was slowing down when the Griffin came flying out of the sun, banked sharply to starboard and began strafing the front of the train. Susan deliberately missed the engine, aiming for the carriages behind. Their intelligence was good. Susan knew there were twenty-four carriages in all. But she was unprepared for the onslaught of heavy fire aimed at her from the roofs of the carriages.

Bullets slammed into the Griffin's wings as she turned the plane on its side, the port wing pointing vertically down. More bullets hit the fuselage as she opened the throttle and followed the bend in the ravine, finally escaping the murderous wall of fire they had encountered.

'Are you all right?' She yelled back.

'Jorge has a flesh wound in his shoulder.'

'We'll drop the bombs,' Susan called, banking the plane, rising above the narrow ravine and turning back. A fire-fight had begun. Rey, on the other side of the ravine, had built a barricade of logs to hide behind. There were twelve men in all, including Rey. The road they had travelled followed the railway for much of its route, separated by the ravine. At this point it was a mere sixty metres away and paralleled the line for about two hundred metres as far as the bridge. Already the train was slowing down to drop off the search engineers.

The carriages were intermixed, so as to make an attack on the munitions carriages more difficult. After the engine and tender came a troop carriage and then a munitions carriage and so on, all the way to the last segment which was full of soldiers. They had opened up a blistering attack of small arms, shooting at the wooden barricade forcing Rey and his men to keep their heads down or have them blown off. The Republicans were no match for the overwhelming firepower that was pouring down on them. As soon as Rey or one of the others tried to shoot, bullets would smash into the logs. Already the barricade was beginning to shred under the fierce firestorm.

On the top of each manned carriage sat a two-manned machine gun post surrounded by sandbags. These too were firing at Rey and his men, the plane all but forgotten. Susan began strafing the train, firing short, sharp bursts, aiming at the machine gun posts. Gunners on the last carriage died as she turned to fly along the length of the train. When her bullets passed through the roofs and hit some of the troops inside, their attention was drawn from Rey and his men. Some of the gunners turned to fire at the Griffin. This enabled Rey's troops to shoot, grateful for the diversion. By now the train was barely crawling, its reduced speed rendering it an easy target. Susan dropped her first two bombs. One was a dud. The second landed by the side of the track, its explosion rocking a carriage full of troops.

The engine was less than fifty metres from the bridge when a second ambush began. The front of the train was targeted. The driver was hit in the arm just as he was reaching up to pull down the brake that would finally bring the behemoth to a complete stop.

Susan was relentless. Several bullets hit the Griffin but many missed as the troopers wavered between targets. Then she was flying over the engine and bullets from her guns rattled around the cab. The engineer panicked. He pushed the brake off and opened up the steam valve. The train inched forward, faster and faster, heading for the bridge.

Susan felt more jolts along the fuselage as the Griffin turned away from the train and she flew out of gun range. A quick glance at the gauges told her that everything appeared to be still working. The engine sounded steady and the fuel level was as she expected.

'Are you all right?'

'*Temo que haya muerto,*' the starboard gunner shouted. Jorge was dead.

The plane was back round and was levelling off when the explosives erupted with a huge bang. Track flew into the air and then collapsed down into the ravine, taking away two of the three arches that spanned the river. The engineer slammed on the brakes but it was too late. As though in slow motion the train began to fall over the edge, dragging the carriages behind it. Screams rent the air as the troopers realised what was happening. They began to abandon their positions, leaping onto the side of the track, many injuring themselves when they fell.

It took a full two minutes for the last of the train to be dragged down into the ravine, and be smashed to pieces on the rocks below, scattering bodies and munitions all along the river bank and in the water.

Rey and his men fired on the Moorish troopers who were trying to find cover behind the rails and on the far side of the track. Some of them had retained their weapons and were returning shots, although ineffectively. They knew that the Republicans could not remain where they were indefinitely. Sooner or later the railway would send somebody to look for the train. Probably a strong army unit. But Rey and the others couldn't move position either. The road was a few feet lower than the track and if they tried to escape they would be easily shot down. As it was, three of Rey's men were already dead and another wounded. One or two at the second ambush site were also hit. Rey did not know whether or not they were dead. But they all would be unless Susan came to their aid.

Lining up with the sun behind her she identified the strongest contingent of troops and dropped on them like an eagle out of the sky. The Griffin's black shape strengthened as she drew nearer and some of the troopers opened fire at her. The windscreen shattered just as she released the final two bombs and pulled up. Her starboard gunner was shooting, spraying a deadly hose of fire onto the cowering men while Rey and his men stood up and attacked from the side. The exploding bombs wiped out most of the surviving Nationalist troops.

One of the last bullets fired at the Griffin sliced through Susan's belly like a red hot poker.

46

SOMEHOW, SHE TOOK the plane up out of the ravine and high into the sky. Although the aircraft had been riddled with bullets, still the little Griffin flew as sweetly as ever. Flying by the hand of God, or perhaps with the luck of the devil, Susan struggled to remain conscious.

The single strap of the still unmodified seat belt lay across her abdomen. She reached down, groaned and brought her hand up to her face. It was covered in blood. The pain was intense and Susan realised it was probably stopping her from fainting.

The baby. Please, don't let anything happen to my baby. For the first time Susan felt a connection with the unborn life she was carrying. After weeks of flutterings which she had refused to acknowledge, now the baby, *her baby*, was kicking as if he was angry. And she couldn't blame him. For months now she had viewed him – she felt sure the baby was a boy – as a messy inconvenience. Now, as she slowly bled to death, he was suddenly her only focus.

Her training kept the plane in the air. With the instincts of a homing pigeon, she knew automatically which way to go. She also knew that she had to get there quickly, if she was to save the baby.

The demands on her body were too great. Drained, exhausted, she was aware of someone at her shoulder, shaking her. Coming awake with a sudden jerk she saw that the plane was in a shallow dive and pulled it up.

The lake lay ahead.

Relief gave her renewed strength but she knew she had only one chance. She didn't think she would be able to take them around a second time. So it was straight in.

She went through the check list in her head. Angle of descent, flaps, speed, heading, look up. Aim for the middle. Too fast, too high, lose speed and height. Water cascaded through the shattered windscreen as the plane ploughed in, stood on its nose for a second and dropped back, miraculously remaining upright. Cutting the engine Susan gave in to her pain and exhaustion as she drifted into unconsciousness.

When she awoke, Consuelo was sitting by her side. Susan moved her head and tried to sit up, but immediately Connie was leaning over her, pushing her back.

'Take it easy, Susan. You mustn't move.'

'My baby. Is he safe?'

Connie smiled warmly. 'At last you care for your child. He is all right. The bullet cut across your stomach but did not touch your womb, as far as I can tell. I have listened hard and I can hear the little one's heart beating as strongly as ever. You got here just in time. I was able to stop the bleeding.'

'Rey? Where is he? Did he get back? How long have I been out?'

'One thing at a time, Susan. Yes, he's back. You have lain here two days. Sleep now. If you need anything, ring this little bell.' She indicated the bell on a stool by the side of the bed. 'There is water in the glass. When you next wake we'll get some broth into you.'

Susan drifted off, barely aware of the voices outside the tent.

'Is she okay?' Rey asked, concern evident in his voice.

'Yes. She needs rest, but she'll pull through. She's a tough one all right. And now she has something to live for.'

'The baby?'

Connie nodded. 'It was her first thought.'

Rey nodded with satisfaction.

'Her second thought was for you. Interesting, heh?'

For a week she rested. By the end of seven days she was restless. She wanted news of the war. From Rey she learned the remainder of their men had escaped, while the Nationalist troops had been virtually wiped out. Their own dead Rey dumped into the river, to let the bodies be swept away by the fast flowing current, pounded and disfigured by the rocks. Unrecognisable even by their loved ones, leaving no clue as to where they had come from.

Susan was irked about one aspect of the attack. She had been unable to throw down her angels' silhouettes, as was her custom.

Rey comforted her, patting her hand. 'They will know it was you. Believe me.'

And they did. The attack fed another frenzy of speculation in the newspapers as to the identity of el Angel Negro de la Muerte. Franco increased the reward yet again. $200,000 plus immunity. A safe passage to another country. Anywhere in the world. Suddenly the offer was tempting. Very tempting indeed. For the first time Susan was scared.

By now she was up and about, her strength returning. All she had to show for her ordeal was an eight-inch red scar across her belly. If she bent and straightened, she pulled on the stitches and Connie was often making her sit down and rest. Food was what she needed and food was what she was given. Five small meals a day, rich in protein, with olives and bread and watered red wine. The stitches were made of gut and after two weeks Connie announced they could come out. The scar healed, an angry red mark, vivid and hard to the touch. Susan thought she would hate the scar but in a way she was thankful for it. Her baby still lived.

At Rey's insistence, she was no longer flying. She

admitted, but only to herself, that she was relieved. Risking her own life was one thing, risking the child's was another. She yearned for England. To be back with the family, where she knew she would be welcomed with open arms. The stigma of an illegitimate child would mean nothing to David and Madelaine. After all, the baby was a Griffiths.

Winter was fast approaching and it was becoming cold. Talk of moving was in the air. But where could they go? No one had the appetite to join with other Republican bands. And with the total ineptitude being displayed by the government's forces, none of them wanted to join the new conscripted army.

As Susan's time approached she began to fret. Unused to inactivity, she complained bitterly. Her back ached, her ankles were swollen. If this was a precursor to motherhood, it stank.

Connie had heard it all before and treated Susan with love and kindness. She often reduced Susan to giggles recounting stories of some of the other pregnant mothers she had known in the past. Susan, knowing she was being unreasonable, would behave. For a while.

In November some of the men and women in the camp began to drift away. Professor Alfonso left with them. He had been unhappy and discontented for some time. Susan thought that she would miss him or at least his skills. But Chester came into his own without Alfonso's interference and soon had everything under control. He was never happier than when up to his elbows in grease.

Those who remained did not like the thought of winter in such bleak and desolate surroundings. By the end of the month there were a mere dozen people left. They stayed because they had nowhere else to go. No families and no friends still alive. All they had was each other. Christmas was a bleak affair and when the new year came, Rey called a council of war to discuss their options.

Rey started the meeting. 'We can't stay here any longer.'

'Why not?' Connie asked the question, concerned for Susan's welfare.

'Because,' answered Susan, 'of me.' Her hand on Rey's arm stopped his protests. 'The price on my head is too tempting. We need to go and we need to go soon.'

There was little argument. The problem was – where? Stories of Russian interference in the Republican's campaigns were legion. Orders were given by people who could not speak Spanish to people who did not understand Russian. The errors would have been farcical if the results hadn't been so devastating. If they were to live and fight, they must do so independently. The Griffin was the secret of their success. It was agreed that they would run and hide for a month or two. Then they would be back with a vengeance. They would have to abandon all the equipment they had painstakingly collected a second time.

'So we do it a third time,' Zeb called out. His words were greeted with laughter. Now the decision had been taken, there was an air of festivity about the camp. Possible safe havens were suggested, locations discussed back and forth. Malta, still under British rule, was put forward by Chester, but dismissed as being too far away. Finally it was decided. They would head for France.

'Let's get planning,' Rey said, his voice clear and decisive.

'Before we do, I have something to tell you all,' said Susan, hesitatingly. Her voice rallied and she went on. 'Once we are in France and the baby is born I intend taking him back to England. I will teach one or more of you to fly before I go. I'll leave the Griffin and I'm sorry, but this is no life for a child.'

Her announcement was like a bombshell and they sat in stunned silence for a few seconds.

Rey recovered fastest and gave Susan a hug. 'You have done so much for us. Now it is time to think of yourself and the baby. Only come and visit us once the war is over.'

Strained laughter greeted his words and they got back to the task in hand.

Two days later, with a heavy rain falling and a wind gusting over forty knots from the north, Susan made her first sortie out. They had repainted the plane. Instead of a gleaming black, the fuselage was now silver with a red stripe down both sides. Seats were replaced and the port and starboard guns removed. The Griffin looked like a civilian aircraft once more.

Susan and Rey spent time discussing the best route to take. To cross Spain meant dodging the Condor Legion's pilots and their German fighters. There was no reason why, in their new colours, they should be attacked but it wasn't worth the risk. If they were forced to land it would only take a matter of minutes before the enemy discovered that they were not as innocent as they appeared.

'The best route, I think, is to make a dash to the Mediterranean and follow the coastline all the way,' Susan said.

'It's over four hundred and fifty miles.'

'I know. But we can carry spare fuel in the cans. I'll fly half our people out and land them at Perpignan. They can look for somewhere to hole up, while I come back for the others. We'll only be able to take our people. None of the supplies. Not this time.'

'You're right. Okay. While you're gone we'll bury as much of our equipment as we can. It should still be here when we come back.'

All the next day they toiled. The lathe and other heavy equipment were wrapped in tarpaulin and buried in a big pit. Careful note was taken of its location. They hid some of the weapons, including the heavy machine guns, along with boxes of ammunition and explosives.

On a Sunday morning, the second in January, Susan was ready to depart.

'You've forgotten something,' Rey said with a smile.

Susan frowned. 'I have? I don't think so.'

From behind his back he took a bottle and waved it in front of her. 'Your bottle of wine. The one we were to drink at your funeral.'

Susan smiled. 'How melodramatic I was! Now we can drink it after the baby is born.'

Rey gave a formal little bow and presented it to her. 'Then don't break it,' he admonished.

The Griffin departed with six passengers and as much gear as they could fit in, including personal weapons, ammunition, a box of hand grenades and two tents.

Dawn hadn't yet broken but it wasn't far off. She took the plane high, over eighteen thousand feet, in a sharp spiral before turning northeast and dashing for the coast. She was planning to fly across the *Golf de Valencia*, between the villages of *Gandia* and *Cellera*. Flying time was half an hour. Although it was cold, the wet and windy weather of the last few days had disappeared and in its wake was an anticyclone. The high pressure created a region of light winds and sunshine but to the south, where the anticyclone passed over the Mediterranean, the sky was overcast with low cloud giving an occasional light shower. But it was, thought Susan, a wonderful day to be flying. She smiled at Connie who was seated next to her. Her response was more tentative. This was her first time in an aeroplane.

As was her habit of late, Susan talked softly to the baby. She told him about his father, his grandparents and Uncle Richard. About the joys of flying, about the sheer wonder of being alive. Even, she added the painful caveat, in times like this.

The plane streaked over the land and crossed the coastline without any problems. They stayed on the same heading, flying out to sea until the coast of Spain was a dark streak on the horizon to port. They turned to a heading that paralleled the land and flew over a tranquil sea, hardly a wave rippling its surface. They were now cruising at fifteen thousand feet. As always, Susan was quartering the sky. She had instructed Connie and the others to do the same. They did not expect to get jumped by an enemy aircraft but nobody was taking the risk.

The flight droned on uneventfully. The sun had long risen and they could see tiny ships passing far below. Many were heading towards Spain, to the port of Barcelona. The plane drifted closer to the land as they passed *Cap de Begur* and then *Cap de Creus* a few miles north. These were the most easterly points of Spain and meant that France was minutes away.

Susan let out a whoop of joy and announced, 'France! We're there!'

Excitement swept over them. They had escaped! Susan had examined her charts closely and, although nowhere nearly as detailed as the maps used by Rey, they were ideal for flying as mountain heights and landing places were marked. Now they passed Perpignan and headed for the coastal lake of *Etand de Leucate ou de Salses*, separated from the Mediterranean by a narrow strip of coast. There was no activity on or around the lake and they landed gently on the water. Taxiing the plane to the north she took them into an inlet with a gently sloping beach. Two of the men leapt out and checked the beach for stones and other obstacles. When they were satisfied they waved Susan up on to dry land. At that time of the year there were no holidaymakers and, if they had seen by any locals, nobody came to question them.

Sitting so long and in such a cramped position had played havoc with Susan's bladder and she could tell the baby did not like it as he began kicking his protest. She put her hand on her belly and spoke to him. 'Not long now, little one. Not long now. Just two more flights and you can come and see what you make of this ridiculous old world.'

It was obvious that the journey had taken a lot out of

her and Connie persuaded Susan to rest, to sleep on the floor of the plane while they went to look for somewhere to stay. They all thought longingly of warm beds, hot baths and properly prepared food. They knew that there were plenty of hotels in the area as this was a popular spot in the summertime. Most of them would be closed for the winter, or so they thought, but would surely open if they could guarantee a full house. And money was no object. The bank jobs had been extremely lucrative.

Susan slept fitfully on the floor of the passengers' cabin. She left Chester to refuel the plane and check everything was in order. Her need for sleep was overwhelming.

To the south a second anticyclone appeared. It pushed the other northwards until they settled down in equilibrium, creating a ridge of low pressure in between. This ridge, known as a col, resulted in very light winds and dense fog. Susan woke to a sea of white. At first she was disorientated but quickly realised where she was. When she saw the weather she groaned. The damnable thing was that as little as a hundred metres away it could be a clear day. A sodding col, she thought bitterly. Why now, when everything had been going so well?

She called out and heard Chester's disembodied voice.

'Yell again,' Chester called. 'I haven't a clue where you are.'

On the fifth shout he stumbled into the plane. 'Ouch. Christ, I've never seen anything like it.'

'It's damnably common at this time of the year. Where are the others?'

'Still looking for a place to bed down. The town is full. No room at the inn, not even the stable, so to speak. A lot of Spaniards have crossed the border to escape the war. And there are plenty of naive fools waiting to go south to fight.'

'So no hotels, hot baths or decent food?'

'Not so far, Susan. I guess we'll have to move away a bit further.'

'Let's fly in Rey and the others first. Then we can decide. Luckily we brought the tents with us. We can still get some sleep tonight.'

'You can't fly in this,' Chester stated the obvious. 'It came down awfully fast. One minute it was as clear as crystal and the next, bam.'

'It can go just as quickly. If I remember my meteorology it's worse in the evening and at dawn. It should clear sometime tonight. As soon as we can see we'll rig a beacon for me to aim at. I can get airborne and land on the sea. I'll go back just after dawn tomorrow.'

She fretted all evening and well into the night. By 1am it was obvious that she had badly miscalculated – the fog was here to stay. Reluctantly she tried to get some sleep. The others had returned and put up the tents in the late evening, disappointed not to have found a hotel and a comfortable bed but resigned and uncomplaining. A guard was posted to keep an eye on the weather, but at dawn it was as bad as ever.

The whiteout lasted all day, each passing minute making them fraught and anxious. Though no one mentioned it, another problem was looming rapidly. Susan was due to give birth at anytime. Once she did she wouldn't be flying anywhere.

That second night she was awoken a few minutes after 4am by Chester saying gently, 'Susan, the weather's cleared. The fog vanished as I was coming on watch.'

Awkwardly she climbed to her feet, her back aching. Chester, the dear that he was, put a cup of hot coffee into her hand and let her waken properly. The night was clear. A myriad stars and a new moon greeted her.

'I sent one of the others to put up the beacon. He'll light it as soon as he hears the engine start up.'

'I urgently need a pee and another coffee, in that order. Is the plane ready?'

'Sure. We can have you away in minutes.'

'Good. Connie? What are you doing?'

The pretty young Spaniard was packing a travel bag. 'I'm coming with you.'

'No, you aren't. There's not enough room. We've already discussed this.'

'Susan, be reasonable. You're due any time now. What will you do if you have contractions while you're flying? Or when you're with Rey and the others? They don't know what to do.'

They argued for the next fifteen minutes, but Susan was adamant. When she finally started the engine the passenger seat was empty.

The take-off was smooth and fast. She retraced the steps they had taken two days earlier. After an hour the baby began kicking hard and she put her hand on her womb and talked gently to him, telling him to take it easy, to be patient. It was still dark although there was a hint of light in the sky far away to port, like an oyster being chiselled open. It promised to be a fine day, although there had been a light frost on the ground when she had taken off.

She was offshore Barcelona when she had a desperate urge to urinate. Within minutes it had become an excruciating force within her that needed attention. Awkwardly she unstrapped her seatbelt, put the height control lever in place, clambered out of her seat and squatted over a bucket that Connie'd had the foresight to put on board.

The sun was behind her when she crossed the coast and headed for the valley. She felt her heart quicken and realised that she was looking forward to seeing Rey again. There was something about his dark, sardonic looks that appealed to her. Stop it, girl, she told herself. She was heavily pregnant and looked awful, but her hormones were jigging about in her body like live wires. It was ludicrous.

Then she saw it. The lake. She made a pass but saw no one. The sun had not yet reached over the mountains, but it was light enough to land by. She lined up and touched down with a gentle kiss of the floats. She was almost at the end of her taxiing when a wire snagged around the floats and stopped the little plane dead. She jerked forward but caught herself in time, her hands hitting the instrument panel.

A hail of bullets smashed into the back of the plane, chopping out chunks of the Griffin's tail, blowing away the rudder. Another fusillade took out the engine and shattered the propeller.

Soldiers appeared and swarmed into the water, pulling the plane to the shore. The door was ripped open and Susan was grabbed roughly and dragged out.

Thrown to the ground, she saw a pair of highly polished boots in front of her and looked up. The officer's features were arranged in a smile, a smile Susan knew sealed her fate.

'Is this the infamous *Angel Negro de la Muerte*?'

'Yes. That's her.'

Recognising the voice, she turned her face and looked into the eyes of Alfonso. He turned away from her and then said to the officer, 'I want my money and my safe passage.'

'All in good time,' said the officer. 'What of the others?'

'Their bodies lie over there,' Alfonso whined.

Despair washed through Susan.

'All of them?'

'Except their leader,' said Alfonso.

Susan heard the words and looked at him with hope in her heart.

A shot rang out. Alfonso's face turned to astonishment as he tottered backwards. A second shot knocked him to the ground, while the soldiers around her dived for cover.

She heard Rey's voice calling out but did not understand the words. She looked up. He was standing on a craggy ledge, waving to her. A hail of bullets smacked into the rocks and into his body. He tottered for a second and then fell head first into the gorge.

The officer standing in front of her began to bark orders. Susan was thrown into the back of a truck where she lay on the metal floor. Her waters broke and she felt warm liquid pouring down her legs. She shivered, from fear and cold. What would happen to her baby? She knew she would be summarily executed as soon as possible. And the baby? Once he was born would he be killed? Or allowed to die? Would they abandon him and let him fade away? Hot tears spilled down her cheeks. Fear for her unborn child overwhelmed her.

Outside the truck, the officer was issuing brisk commands, ordering his men to pack up without delay. 'We'll take her to Cádiz. She can stand trial there.'

BOOK 5

David's Story

47

January 1938

THROUGHOUT THE YEAR we had received only two letters from Susan. It was as though she had vanished off the face of the earth. I had sent out feelers to everybody I knew but to no avail. Her last letter, received in the summer, had told of her devastation at Phillipe's death. Since then, nothing. It had become my habit to rise early and walk the quiet streets of London, thinking and praying. I had no idea where to start searching. I had been in contact with Jake Kirkpatrick in Spain and he was pulling out every stop to find her. All we had discovered so far was that the Bouchers house had been completely destroyed.

Despite the warmth of my fawn gabardine overcoat and fedora hat, it was cold in the bitter wind that was blowing from the north. A heavy blanket of snow lay everywhere and train and road travel had been badly disrupted. I had my hands in my pockets and my head down as I trudged over the compacted snow which crunched beneath my feet. Christmas had been a joyless time although we did our best for the sake of Richard. I tried to enter into the spirit of the thing but it was hard work. Madelaine understood and helped me through my bleakest moods. I couldn't bear the feeling of helplessness. I had spent my life tackling problems, surmounting obstacles. Knowing Susan was in danger filled me with anguish. My precocious, independent, utterly infuriating daughter – I had never loved her more.

I had inveigled my way onto the Non-Intervention Committee based in London and manned by the Foreign Office. It consisted of representatives from Britain, France, Germany, Italy and the Soviet Union and was set up to monitor the sale of arms to Spain. In effect, to stop any arms from the countries on the committee being sold to the Spanish. In spite of the certain knowledge that Germany and Italy were supplying the Nationalists and the Soviet Union the Republicans, still we sat on our hands. The whole thing was a farce. Britain and France vacillated first one way and then the other. The resulting fudge enabled others to take advantage of the situation.

After the summer of 1937, the huge iron-ore resources of the Basque territory became available to the Nationalists. These were exchanged for foreign aid, particularly arms and ammunition from Germany and Italy. The Nationalists bought cotton for tyres and guns from Britain and our colonies, and petrol from Shell and Standard Oil. The Rio-Tinto mines of Spain were British owned. Pyrites were exported to Nazi Germany from 1936 without protest. Our hypocrisy knew no bounds and I was sickened by it. But I also used it to my own ends. I used every possible contact to find Susan. I was beginning to fear that she was dead.

I picked up my usual newspaper, tucked it under my arm and returned home. It was too early for any of the servants to be up and about, so I made myself a cup of tea. I opened the paper and stared unseeingly at the print. As the phone went in the hall I glanced at the lead photograph. The headline above it read 'Captured. The Black Angel of Death stands trial'.

Knowing the call would be important at that time of the day I hurried to pick up the phone, praying as always, that it was Susan.

'David? It's me.' I immediately recognised my brother's voice. 'They've found her! I just received a telegram from Jake.'

'That's wonderful news . . .' I began, but he interrupted me.

'You don't understand!' His tone was bleak. 'She's being tried as a Republican sympathiser and will be shot. She has been denounced as the Black Angel of Death.'

The photograph! Could it be? 'Hang on.' I dropped the receiver and ran back to the kitchen. I looked closely at the grainy grey photograph. The room reeled. It was indeed Susan.

I made it back to the telephone. 'Sion? Christ! What are we to do?'

'Hang in there, David. Jake will move heaven and earth now. He has a good deal of influence with Franco and you know what he's like. He won't take no for an answer.'

The thought gave me some comfort. Jake was a Nationalist. He hated the Republicans with a passion, loathing the communists and the anarchists to an equal degree. The anti-Christs he called them. Their views on the church justified some of his comments. Now my daughter, his enemy, depended on his help. But at last I had something to do. I was no longer floundering around in darkness. I felt myself coming alive again. I knew what was needed and there were few people better placed to do it. That was not a boast. It was a fact.

'Get a plane ready. We go in twenty-four hours,' I ordered.

'Why so long?'

'We're going armed to the teeth.'

'Guns won't do us any good, David.'

'Not with guns. We go armed with diplomatic immunity. A pile of letters of introduction and a pile more of threats. I'll get onto John. If Franco kills my girl I'll fight him and his fascists all the way. He'll lose a lot more than the life of one individual.' My voice was full of hope. 'I'll call you later.'

I ran up the stairs, the paper in my hand, calling for Madelaine. She woke in alarm when I burst into our bedroom.

'We've found her,' I said excitedly.

Even though roused from a deep sleep, Madelaine was out of bed in a second. 'That's wonderful. Where is she?' She slipped on a robe, belting it around her waist.

So I told her. Her excitement changed to grave concern and then to fear as we read the newspaper article. Her thoughts matched my own. The journalist wrote of a quick trial and an even quicker death. Dear God, was I already too late?

The telephone rang and I rushed downstairs to answer it. It was the telegram service with a long message from Jake. I dictated a reply asking for more information and praying, most of all, for confirmation that she was still alive.

Next I telephoned John at the lodge at Fairweather. His annoyance at being woken so early quickly faded when he learned why I had rang. 'Leave it to me, David. I know exactly what we need. Who will be travelling with us?'

Us? I couldn't help grinning. There was nothing on earth that would induce John to stay behind. 'You, me, Sion and Mike.'

'The usual suspects, in other words,' he said and broke the connection.

I spent the day begging and cajoling letters of intro-duction from my contacts throughout the government and industry. Lord Saltmore, the peer who was the chairman of the Non-Intervention Committee, gave me the most trouble.

'I cannot agree to your wishes,' he said in his adenoidal, cut-glass accent. 'I'm sorry, Griffiths, my position doesn't allow it.'

'I'm only asking you for a letter to Franco, advising him that if he doesn't help me to save my daughter the Committee would put its weight behind supporting and supplying the Spanish government. And that all aid to the Nationalists would be cut off.'

'I cannot and will not do any such thing.'

'Saltmore, use your wits, man, and your influence for once. We're supposed to be non-interventionist and nothing could be further from the truth. Everybody is breaking the agreement. The Russian communists will have a stranglehold on Spain if the Republicans win. We don't want that. And if Franco wins there'll be another fascist state we'll have to deal with. He'll be in the German-Italian orbit and when we go to war . . .'

He interrupted me. 'What war? Don't talk nonsense. There will be no war with Germany.'

'Winnie says . . .'

'Damn and blast Churchill. The man is a buffoon. He has no idea what he's talking about. There will be no war with Germany.'

Politically, I was obviously on a non-starter. Instead, I tried pleading with him, appealing to his feelings as a father. 'Imagine if it was your daughter.'

'Don't be ridiculous. Geraldine would never have got herself into such a situation. She behaves,' he looked down his nose when he said it, 'as a proper young lady should. Not as the daughter of an upstart from the Welsh valleys.'

So that was it. His refusal had nothing to do with Susan. This was about me. I was beginning to lose my temper and raise my voice. 'Give me a letter, damn you, or else.'

He was quivering with fury and I knew I had blown it. 'Or else what? Get out of my house, Griffiths. Get back to your coal mine with the rest of the peasants. You have no place in society. Go before I have you thrown out!'

'You wouldn't dare, you little popinjay,' I snarled back at him and stalked from the room. I grabbed my hat from the stand and slammed the door behind me. Damn the man! A letter from him would have been invaluable. I smiled. It still could be.

As a Member of the House of Commons I had access to all areas, apart from private offices. I quickly made my way to the room where Saltmore's committee met every two months. In a stationery drawer I found what I needed. Headed notepaper with the committee's details and names of the members, including my own.

The House was still in recess and so very few people were around. In my own offices I whipped the cover off my secretary's typewriter and sat down to compose a letter to General Franco. It contained a brief reference to Susan's situation and the committee's inevitable displeasure should she be harmed. I included veiled threats, vague promises of political intervention and the possibility of supplies withdrawn. I had no idea what the chairman's signature looked like but then I didn't think for one second that Franco did either. I signed with a flourish, Lord Saltmore, Chairman.

By the time I arrived home it was late. There was a telegram from Jake. Susan was being held incommunicado at an Army barracks in the very heart of Cádiz. She was alive and as well as could be expected. The next words on the telegram came as a total shock. 'Baby well also.' What the hell was going on? Susan had a baby? I was a grandfather? Jesus H. Christ.

I looked at Madelaine who smiled tightly and shrugged. 'She's a chip off the old block all right.'

'What do you mean?'

'In one scrape after another. Headstrong, pigheaded and always in trouble. And now she has a baby, the poor darling.'

'It couldn't get much worse,' I said, examining my feelings as I tried to come to terms with the thought. Vanity won the day. 'I'm too young to be a grandfather.'

That set Madelaine laughing so hard I thought she would cry. Richard came to see what the noise was about and I explained that he was now an uncle.

He clearly understood the danger Susan was in. 'Bring them back safely, won't you, Dad?' he said seriously. He paused, frowned, then added, 'I'm not going back to school till they're safe.'

I was about to argue but saw the look on his face. I nodded agreement.

Madelaine hugged him closely. 'Don't worry, Richard, if anybody can do it, it's the Griffiths family. Trust me, I know what I'm talking about.' She became business-like. 'I've packed a portmanteau and a hamper. John will be round to pick you up at six. Sion says he'll be ready to leave at eight, just after daybreak. Jake has arranged for you to land at the military airfield on the outskirts of Cádiz. So far nobody knows the true purpose behind your visit. Only that you're important members of the British government desiring an audience with *Generalissimo* Franco.'

'Has Jake arranged a meeting?'

'Not yet. But don't worry, he'll get you in. Jake and Estella have all the right connections. I have been in touch with her myself. She has already spoken to Franco's wife. There is a reception at Franco's house on Friday. You're invited. So one way or another you will see him.'

I mustered up a semblance of a smile. 'Well done, my love. What would I do without you?'

'I've also included a dinner jacket amongst your things. John has letters from the chairmen of,' she consulted a list, 'Rio Tinto Mines, British Petroleum, The Anglo Colonies Group, The Anglo Australian Mining Group . . .' She rattled off another half dozen names. I recognised them all. They were amongst Britain's biggest companies, all with significant interests in Spain. Over a third of the Nationalist supplies came from Britain, ninety-nine percent from the companies named. John, as always, had come up trumps.

I had a restless night and awoke early. Madelaine had risen with me and I was kissing her goodbye when, much to my surprise, John arrived with Mam. The plan had been to meet at Biggin Hill.

'You know your mother,' said John. 'She insisted on being here with the family.'

Mam looked haggard, worry lines etched in her face. She took my arm in a tight grip and said fiercely, 'Bring my granddaughter home, David. Do whatever it takes. Money. Threats. Leave no stone unturned.'

I smiled at her. 'Don't worry, Mam, you can rely on us.' I wasn't sure for whose benefit the words were, hers or mine.

Beech was driving, which enabled us to sit in the back and discuss our plans and strategies. Luckily it had not snowed in recent days and what was lying was already melting. We skidded a few times and on one occasion nearly came a cropper but we eventually got to Biggin Hill well before 8am.

Sion and Mike were ready and packed. Kirsty had prepared a giant hamper to which I added my own offering. Farewells were made and we climbed aboard the Griffin V, modified to fly us all the way to Spain in one hop without the requirement to refuel.

We waved to Kirsty and the Cazorlas, who had come to see us off. Peter had wanted to come but, as Sion said, he was of more use holding the fort.

We flew into a blustery wind and a cloud-laden sky. I was sitting in the passenger section with John; Mike and Sion in the cockpit. Once we were at the right height and on a level flight path, Sion gave the controls to Mike and joined us.

'What about weapons?' I asked.

Sion grinned. 'Full. Every nook and cranny. I even managed to get hold of some of those new silencers for the Star MD.' The Star was a Spanish, 9mm handgun, capable of single and automatic firing. It took an eight, sixteen or twenty-five round magazine and was a little gem to use.

'I thought,' said John, 'that this was to be handled in a diplomatic way.'

'Oh, it is,' I replied airily, 'but let's talk soft and carry a big stick.'

John shook his head at me, smiled and settled down to a doze. Sion and I exchanged worried glances. He was looking old and Mam had said that he should not be gallivanting across Europe like this. I was under strict instructions to make him take it easy. Fat chance of that, I thought.

We had over eleven hundred miles to travel. Sion's modifications to the Griffin meant that she now had a top speed of 380mph. He and Mike kept near to that speed all the way. It was barely 11.30am when we saw the city of Cádiz sprawled out below us. Sion, well prepared as always, flew unerringly towards the airfield. It was still ten miles away when he called out.

'Stand by to be jumped. Fighters left and right.'

We looked out of the window. A fighter had taken up station on either side of the Griffin and led us all the way to the field. We landed with barely a bump although there was a crosswind that shook the plane when we came to a stop. A jeep appeared and beckoned for us to follow. We stopped on the other side of the airfield, near to brick offices. A small gathering of officers was there to greet us. Four of them. All army.

As we climbed down they saluted and led us inside the building. The welcome was reserved but friendly. The highest-ranking officer was a colonel, whose typically long, Spanish surname I forgot as soon as I heard it. He checked our passports and John handed him a letter of introduction from our Prime Minister for Franco.

We looked at him in surprise. The old fox had kept

that up his sleeve. But how in hell he'd got Neville Chamberlain to part with it was beyond me. When I asked him later, all he did was tap the side of his nose and wink.

I was in a blue funk to get to Susan but knew that I must keep my powder dry at all costs. There was no doubt that Susan, or what she had come to represent, was hated by the Nationalists. They would be up in arms if they learned of our real mission. Were our cover blown, it would not surprise me if they took her out and summarily executed her before Franco gave the order to release her.

It was then that Jake Kirkpatrick stalked into the room. He casually acknowledged the army officer's salute. Normally when we met we embraced warmly. We had known each other for years, although it only seemed like yesterday we had met in a drunken brawl in New Orleans. He was almost as close to me as Sion, so I was surprised when he kept the greetings formal, offering his hand, shaking ours. Something was up and we played along with it. No matter what the politics of Spain, Jake was first and foremost a friend. And a good one at that.

Sion made arrangements to put the Griffin into a hangar while we loaded our gear into Jake's two cars. Sion was some time but when he returned he was carrying another bag, which was obviously heavily laden. He slung it into the boot of the four-door Plymouth sedan Jake had imported from America and we all piled in. Sion was with Mike in the following car, another Plymouth Six.

'Who's the other driver,' I asked.

Jake chuckled. 'That's Dom.'

I looked out of the rear window and waved. My godson waved back, a wide grin on his face. Christened David Dominic Rodriguez Mendoza Kirkpatrick, a hell of a mouthful for a little boy, he had quickly become known as Dom. I had helped deliver him when Jake and I had been stranded on a desert island with Estella and her brother, also named Dominic. 'He's grown up.'

'They all do,' Jake said heavily. 'He's the reason I have grey hairs.'

We exchanged the smiles of beleaguered fathers everywhere. Over the years we had been through a great deal together and our friendship knew no bounds. 'What's the situation with Susan?'

'To be honest, not good, David. They've been after her for nearly a year. Catching her has been a great coup for the Nationalists. Her trial,' he looked me squarely in the eyes, 'her execution, would greatly help the Nationalist cause.'

'Thank you for being so honest. And thank you for all your help. I know you support Franco.'

He shrugged. 'I think it is a question of choosing between the devil and the deep blue sea. The Republicans kill priests whenever they get a chance. Estella is deeply religious – her faith dictates her politics. Initially, there was no question as to whose side we'd be on. I hate everything the communists stand for. They burnt our stables and killed eight of our horses and threatened our workers and my family. That was why we decided to get out of Barcelona and move to Cádiz. Franco, well he's power crazy, David. The man's frightening. But politics aside, Estella is horrified about the whole situation and wants Susan safe. Like she says, nothing will be gained by Susan's death.'

'That's kind of her,' I said gratefully. 'If we get Susan out she won't be coming back to Spain. I promise you that.'

'Does anybody know Susan's real identity?' Jake asked.

'Not to my knowledge. And the photograph in the papers is so grainy it's virtually impossible to recognise her. Also . . . she appears to have changed a lot.'

'Good. Let's hope we can keep it that way.'

'I won't argue there,' I agreed. 'Remember our run-in with the fascists in Germany? They aren't nice people.'

Which was probably the biggest understatement of the year.

'This is all out war, David, and one Franco means to win. And I think he will. Provided he continues receiving arms and ammunition and other foreign aid.'

'That's why we intend playing on Franco's weakness. Threaten to withdraw British supplies.' I began to outline our plan and the weapons of words we had brought with us. Jake nodded in agreement and satisfaction, as I laid it all before him.

'It could work. I have a condition, though. I don't want any of my people killed. Dom will insist on it. He's helping out of regard for you but I have to tell you he is very unhappy about it.'

'Fair enough.'

'I'm still trying to get us in to see Franco but he's away for the next twenty-four hours. However, he will be back in time for the reception at his house.'

'That's two days away.'

'I know,' he spoke heavily, 'I'm sorry David.'

'That's okay. Have you seen her?'

Jake nodded slowly. 'Yes. I have.'

'How's she looking?'

'Not good. But then I don't suppose I would be at my best, knowing a firing squad was only a few days away.'

'And the baby? We had no idea until your telegram arrived.'

'Phillipe Boucher was the father. He was killed by Nationalists. Susan and the men she teamed up with killed them in revenge. You have read of some of her exploits but believe me she has done a lot more than you think. She has become a legend amongst the Republicans. Hence the reason for the trial and a quick execution. Your daughter is a beacon of Republican hope and there is a real danger that her supporters will launch an all out attack to rescue her.'

'And the baby?' I prompted him.

'A week old. She has been allowed to keep him with her.'

'That's kind of the authorities,' I said dryly.

Jake's tone was gentle. 'David, when the firing squad opens fire, the baby will be in her arms.'

48

AT THE HOTEL we were greeted like visiting royalty and shown to our suites. Each of us had a bedroom and a sitting room, with a balcony-view down to the harbour and the sea beyond. We met in my room ten minutes later for a council of war.

Dom Kirkpatrick was taller than any of us, a fine looking young man, with a firm handshake, tanned regular features, and black, curly hair like his father's. He had a determined mouth, wide shoulders and an air of responsibility about him. He also wore the uniform of a major in Franco's army.

In spite of the hampers we'd been supplied with, we had eaten little on the flight over and so I ordered room service. While coffees and sandwiches were being brought I thanked Dom for meeting us and asked him what he knew.

'Susan is held in a cell at the barracks, about three kilometres from here. She is guarded day and night. They dare not risk her escaping. If the Republicans come for her the guards have been ordered to kill her and the baby.'

Seeing my stricken expression, Sion asked the next obvious question. 'When's the trial?'

'I think it's starting on Monday.'

'You think?' I asked more harshly than I'd intended. 'I'm sorry, Dom, please go on.'

'That's okay, Uncle David.' I was touched that he still called me that and I smiled in appreciation. 'The trial hasn't been officially announced. I'm afraid that the situation is impossible. She will only walk out of there if Franco pardons her but, I hate to say it, I cannot see that happening. The army would revolt. Especially the *Africanistas*. They want her dead so badly that they talk of nothing else.' He paused.

I could see that he was troubled by something and so I prompted him. 'What is it, Dom?'

'You know I am helping reluctantly. Because of the great affection our families have for each other. For our history together. But Susan has been responsible for the deaths of many of my comrades. My helping you has cost me many troubled moments. I wanted you to know that.'

'Thanks. We appreciate it, believe me.' It seemed strangely comforting that this man, whom I had held in his first moments on this earth, should be the key to my own grandchild's survival.

Dom had confirmed my worst fears. There was no way we could reach Susan and bring her out alive. And what he said about the *Africanistas* was bad news. Franco needed a free hand if this was to work and it didn't sound as though he had one. Somehow, we had to deal him one.

We debated possibilities all afternoon. John excused himself around 4pm and went to rest while we continued our discussion. It seemed hopeless. We were getting nowhere, until Mike had an idea. 'Are you attached to the barracks?' He looked at Dom.

'Yes. I command a tank regiment.'

'The firing squad. Who are they?'

'On the whole they are from the regiments of the *Moors* and the *Africanistas*.'

'How many make up a squad?'

'Normally six men. I expect it will be the same for Susan.'

We were casually discussing the death of my daughter and I felt utterly helpless.

'Your men. Are they *Moors* and *Africanistas* too, or are they locals?'

Dom answered without hesitation. 'Locals. I raised the troops to form a mechanised unit, which rapidly became a squadron. Hence my rank of major. Most at my age are mere captains.' It was not said boastfully, only as a statement of fact. 'Why do you ask?'

'Are your men loyal to you?'

Dom thought about it for a few seconds and then shrugged. 'I would say they are loyal. But not enough to help Susan escape, if that's what you're thinking.'

Mike slapped his knee. 'I'm not. But I have a plan that might work.' He sketched his idea and we sat for a few minutes in contemplation. 'What do you think?'

I grinned. 'Brilliant, Mike. Bloody brilliant. But would it work, Dom?'

Dom shrugged. 'If I fully understand you, we substitute my men for the firing squad. They are to use blanks, or shoot over Susan's head. The volley would be heard followed by the single shot of the *coup de grâce*, administered by me. Suppose we manage it. What happens afterwards? How do we keep the silence of six men?'

'We pay for it. Ten thousand dollars each,' I said.

'You do not know soldiers, Uncle David. They will get drunk and boast what they have done. The information will reach the wrong ears and it will be curtains for us. For all of my family. Franco is an unforgiving brute.'

I nodded. It was true and I could see that. Yet there had to be a way. 'In that case it's back to blackmailing him. Unless he wants to lose one hell of a lot of support, support he can't do without, he had better find a way to let Susan escape.'

'Mike's idea can't work anyway,' said Dom. 'Most executions are done in private with only the firing squad and sometimes a priest in attendance. Susan's is to be in public. In the bullring. There will be thousands watching.'

'What!' I exclaimed.

'Because of who she is and what she represents,' said Dom.

We talked, argued and discussed some more. If all else failed I was determined to attack with the Griffin and try and rescue her. Sion had already said he would go with me.

'I need to get in to see Susan,' I said.

'Impossible,' Dom said immediately. 'No visitors are allowed under any circumstances.'

'Can *you* get in?' I asked.

He thought for a few seconds before replying. 'I think so.'

'Will you be able to talk to her in private?'

'I don't see why not.'

'Good,' I said and left it at that. I did have an idea forming but needed more time to think about it. 'Now, gentlemen, I need a drink. Do we have dinner here or do we go in search of a restaurant?'

We decided to eat in the hotel. I phoned down to the concierge to learn that dinner was either uniform or black tie. We changed and went down to the bar. It was packed. Many of the men wore uniform, army and airforce. The army were all Spaniards, the airforce, Germans. I watched the pilots strutting around in their ludicrous uniforms, their arrogance and air of superiority grating on my already jangling nerves. We kept ourselves to ourselves, in a corner, away from the rest of the room. Despite their dialects, I had no difficulty understanding some of the conversations that were taking place around us. At every table the topic was the same – my daughter – The Black Angel of Death. They were positively gloating over her capture and I had a hell of a time keeping my temper.

John saw what was going on and tried to distract me. But it was no use. I stood up, excused myself and went outside to cool down. I walked around the block, then round again. Finally I got my temper under control. And what helped was the firming up of my plan. It was risky, but when all said and done it stood a better chance than Sion and I storming in by plane. It was so audacious and idiotic it could work! Mike's idea had been the right one. With one change.

I walked back into the hotel. Never before had I had so much riding on so many unknowns. Susan meant more to me than all my fortune. And now there was the baby. I stopped dead. My grandson! The baby would cry! It was inevitable. We had to find a way to get him out of there before Susan stood in front of the firing squad. An appeal to Franco? It might work though I doubted it.

Although there was a good deal of laughter and ribald humour at the other tables, it appeared forced to me. I couldn't help catching snippets of conversation from some of the louder-mouthed boors and it was all about the trial and execution of Susan. One German officer, a particularly fat braggart, having boasted about the supremacy of the Condor Legion went on to describe what he would like to do to my daughter – in no uncertain terms.

My emotions were simmering once more like a volcano. Jake grabbed my arm and squeezed, shaking his head. 'Don't rise to it, David. We know that these people are scum. We've fought and beaten them in the past. We need them now but I can tell you, once Franco has won, he will not be supporting Germany. Trust me. I know for sure. When war comes to Europe once more, Spain will stay neutral.'

I nodded. Jake's information was useful and just the sort of intelligence our government could use. I filed it away. Eventually we were served. In spite of the war and its deprivations the food was superb, or so the others said. I picked at my plate, disinterested. Thoughts of Susan, alone in her cell, kept flashing through my mind. My hands trembled slightly as they held my knife and fork. And in the background, that blasted German, going on and on.

I heard a chair scrape back and his hectoring voice calling out, '*Wo ist . . .*'

I didn't hear any more as I was also scraping back my

chair. The German staggered down a flight of stairs towards the toilet and I followed. I could feel the eyes of my friends on my back. I was being reckless and I knew it but I had to vent my feelings somehow and the fat German had drawn the short straw.

Another German officer stood at a urinal when I followed his colleague inside, but he left shortly after, leaving us alone. Standing with a hand on the wall, supporting himself, the German fumbled with his trouser buttons. My instinct was to grab his head and smash it into the wall. Watching him stand there, a ludicrous mediocrity, the wave of anger and despair passed. I came to my senses. Venting my feelings would not help Susan. She was my priority, my *raison d'être*. I walked past, made use of an urinal myself, washed my hands and departed. The fat German stumbled along behind me. The looks of relief on the faces of the others would have been comical if the situation had not been so fraught.

John left the company early. He was looking tired and wan, a little grey around the gills. I felt an early night would probably do him good and, truth to tell, we weren't long behind. Once in my room, I poured myself a large brandy and soda and sat, cigar in hand, looking out of the balcony window at the city and harbour, catching a glint of the sea in the dark night. I thought over the plan again. There were so many flaws, it made my blood run cold. And there was still the possibility that Franco would pardon her. The snatches of conversation from the restaurant played in my mind – the crowds of Nationalist supporters baying for my daughter's blood. It would be too dangerous for Franco, politically, to let her go. I stubbed out half the cigar, drained my glass and climbed into bed. I didn't think I would be able to sleep but I woke up with a weak sun streaming through the windows. My head and mouth felt foul and I tottered into the bathroom.

After breakfast Sion and Mike returned to the airfield to get the plane refuelled and ready for an immediate take-off. In the meantime I explained my idea to John, Jake and Dom. This time there was no argument from Dom only a slight smile and a nod. It was possible. Small refinements presented themselves until, in the afternoon, we agreed there was no more to be said. We received one piece of news that afternoon. Susan's trial was confirmed for Monday.

Franco had commandeered a huge house within walking distance of the hotel we were occupying. That evening, armed with our letters and invitations, we sauntered along the pavement, following other well-dressed men and women, many of the men in uniform. A country at war with itself doesn't have petrol to waste driving short distances even to such an important event as this one. Austerity was the order of the day. Until we reached the General's address. Rooms were lit all over the house and hundreds of people thronged around the hall and the ballroom. A line of dignitaries met us, shaking our hands, murmuring the usual insincere words of welcome. At the end of the queue was the man we had come to see. Short, overweight, downright ugly, with a ludicrous moustache, Franco, I had to admit, possessed a certain charm and charisma when he smiled. One did not become a General in the Spanish army without ruthless ambition and skill. Franco was not to be underestimated.

'General Franco, I would be grateful for an opportunity to present my credentials later this evening,' John said, shaking the General's hand. 'On behalf of the British government. It is of the utmost importance.'

If Franco was surprised he didn't show it. I guessed this night was not about entertaining functionaries and friends, it was about alliances being born and nurtured. This was a show of power aimed at the international community. Britain was represented by our party. Franco had to see us, for form's sake. He muttered something to John and we passed on.

'He'll see us in the second floor library at ten pm.'

We moved into the body of the crowd. Amidst the babble of languages, I recognised Spanish, Italian and German. A loud American was boasting about the amount of petrol Standard Oil was supplying to the Nationalists. John and I mingled and exchanged small talk. I saw Jake and Dom in the crowd and then, to my great pleasure I caught sight of Estella. John and I crossed the room, he to shake her hand, me to give her a big hug and kisses on both cheeks. All these years on, she was a stately beauty. Her black hair was streaked with grey and her figure owed more to her corsets than used to be the case. Her face had developed crow's feet around the eyes, but they still sparkled with warmth and humour and occasional flashes of the strong-willed individual I knew and loved. It was clear that she was glad to see us and we settled into a corner where I could bring her up to date on all the family news. Naturally we wanted to talk about Susan but deemed it safer not to. There was no way of telling if someone might overhear. Estella simply wished us good luck. No censorship, no berating the idiocy of youth for supporting the Republicans, just hoping with all her heart that we would manage to save her. I loved her more for it.

John tapped my shoulder and pointed at his watch. With Estella's best wishes ringing in our ears we went upstairs to the library. Much to our surprise Jake joined us.

We approached a door with two guards posted outside. They saluted Jake and opened the door. To our surprise there were only two people in the room, Franco in uniform and another man, dressed in black tails and bow tie. He was introduced as Franco's secretary.

Franco spoke good, though highly accented English. The occasional word he had difficulty with, Jake translated. We presented our credentials, which Franco did not even glance at as he handed them to his secretary.

'May I ask the purpose of your visit?' Franco smiled.

Here it comes, I thought. 'We have come to secure the release of my daughter from prison. Her name is Susan Griffiths.'

'I see no problem,' said Franco, 'it shall be done immediately.'

'You know her as *el Angel Negro de la Muerte*.'

The transformation that came over Franco was astonishing. We had been sitting in a group of armchairs, at ease, Franco with his legs crossed under a low table. In his agitation his leg jerked and he sent the table flying. He leapt to his feet and began pacing the room.

'Impossible. Your daughter, Sir, is a murderer, a she-devil who has been responsible for the deaths of many of my men.' He ranted on for several moments, listing the atrocities which had befallen the Nationalists at Susan's hands. Finally he stood before us, panting, his hands on his hips. 'Release her? Never!'

It was what we had expected so we weren't surprised. If he let her go he would be committing political suicide. Now we'd start applying the pressure.

'I want you to read these.' I began handing him the letters I'd brought. The doctored one from the Non-Intervention Committee brought a gasp to his lips. He was literally shaking with surpressed fury the more he read.

He finally looked up at me. With anger and dislike contorting his features he said, 'You cannot do this, Griffiths.'

I stood up, towering over him and pointed a finger at him. 'I assure you, General, the British companies who supply your movement with munitions and other vital equipment will withdraw their support at our behest. Many of them bank with us. They need us. These are not idle threats. I want my daughter and my grandson and I'm going to have them. Co-operate or we will move heaven and earth to fight you. If we switch our aid and commerce to the government forces your fight will be all the harder.

May I remind you, we are travelling with diplomatic immunity. I am a member of His Majesty's Government. Baron Guildford is in the House of Lords. Between us we have a great deal of influence and power. Tell him Mr Fitzpatrick.'

I sat down again, regaining my composure while Jake rattled away in Spanish. It went on for some time. As he listened, Franco stopped looking angry and became more pensive. He asked numerous questions, as he paced the room.

Finally he said, 'There will be certain conditions.' In that moment I knew we'd won. Or so I thought.

Franco's secretary was ordered to deliver the letters we needed the following morning to our hotel. Jake was told to wait behind and we went downstairs, the farewells distinctly frosty.

Sion and the others were eagerly awaiting our news but I warned them with a shake of my head that it was too dangerous to speak. Secrecy was everything.

When Jake came down we collected Estella and departed. Once outside, Jake began. 'He's not at all happy, which is only to be expected. We'll have to be careful. I don't trust him an inch.'

'What can he do?' Mike asked.

'The man is cunning and ruthless. He doesn't like losing and he certainly doesn't like being told what to do. He's a bad enemy.'

'Are you in trouble?'

'I don't think so. I'm very useful to the General. I have an effective network of spies across Spain who passionately want the Republicans defeated. He ranted and raved at me but is unaware of the personal connection between us.' Jake gave a sardonic laugh.

He and Estella were staying at a house not far from the hotel, and so we retired there.

'If Franco does as we ask then we get Susan and he's off the hook. Monday morning we can collect the baby before the trial begins. At least he'll be safe and that's one problem taken care of. Once we leave Spain no one will ever know what we've done,' I said.

John, a large brandy in his hand nodded. 'But Jake's right. I don't trust Franco.'

It was midnight when the telephone rang. Surprised, Jake answered it, listened and replaced the receiver with a thoughtful frown. 'Like I said, Franco cannot be trusted. That was Dom. The trial has been brought forward to tomorrow.'

I sprang to my feet, slamming my glass down on the mantelpiece at my elbow. 'He can't do that.'

'He can and he has. Of course he's denied it has anything to do with him. He claims the court acted independently and he has only just found out himself. If Susan is found guilty, she will be shot in front of a capacity crowd on Sunday, just before the bull fight. Dom is on his way here now. He was called in to Franco's secretary to be given the letters you asked for. That's when he was told. The secretary expressed much regret, but we could see that the General was doing all in his power to keep his side of the bargain.'

When Dom arrived he handed the letters to Jake, who quickly read them. 'It's all here. This is the authorisation for Dom to take charge of the firing squad. This letter gives him access to supply Susan with clean clothes for the court appearance and this one to take her food on the morning before she's shot. There's a caveat to the letter,' he added dryly. '*If* she is found guilty. The last one is to allow you,' he handed me the letter, 'to remove her body from Spain, as requested.'

'And the baby?' I asked.

Jake sighed and waved the last letter in his hand. 'This releases the baby into your care,' he saw the hope in my eyes and quickly added, 'on Monday. By which time it will be too late.'

'The swine,' I said with feeling. 'It's just as well we

didn't confide all of our plans to him. Dom, can you go in early in the morning with the clothes?'

'Of course.'

'Estella, we need to raid your wardrobe.' I explained what we wanted.

She nodded, stood up and said, 'Leave it to me.'

We left a short while later. On the way back to the hotel I said, 'If Franco can do this . . .' I began, but was interrupted by Sion.

'. . . he can do anything. I think we need to keep a watch on the plane. If it blew up while we were flying out of Spain, all his problems would be solved.'

'He won't know when we're leaving, so timing will be a problem. But shooting us down won't be. He could have a squadron of fighters up there ready to pounce,' John said.

'Okay,' said Mike. 'So we tell the authorities that we're flying directly to Portugal but make a bee-line for Gib instead.'

'Sion, Mike, that's your department,' I said. 'Keep an eye on the plane and plan an exit route. Can you find a reason to be at the plane from tomorrow onwards?'

'Sure. There's a problem with the dynamo,' Sion said. 'We can find other good reasons to be there. Leave it to us.'

I was awake before dawn and at Jake's house with the others by seven thirty. Dom was ready to go. If he was nervous he didn't show it. He was dressed in uniform, had the letters and my portmanteau. Inside it were a change of clothing, a bottle of milk laced with laudanum and fixed with a teat, and a life sized baby doll that Estella had conjured up from somewhere. Both the doll and bottle were covered by the clothes.

We watched him leave. The following hours were the longest of my life. Breakfast was served but we had little appetite. Almost two hours later we heard the front door slam open and Dom stalked in, a beaming smile on his face. He gently placed the bag on the kitchen table and opened it. And there he was, my grandson, fast asleep.

I had a lump in my throat when I reached in to carefully pick him up. His face was puckered in a scowl, and his little fists clenched. He had a thatch of black hair and Susan's nose and chin. We all stood round in wonder, gazing at him. He opened his eyes and looked at us angelically. An almighty fart and accompanying odour brought us down to earth. Estella took him away. Much to our relief he appeared none the worse for his escapade. We had been unsure what dosage of laudanum such a tiny child could survive.

'Tell us everything,' I begged Dom.

He shrugged, puffed out his cheeks, poured a cup of coffee and sat down. 'Getting past the guards was easy. The letter worked a charm. I had more difficulty with Susan.'

'Why? What happened?'

'I had to convince her who I was. She didn't seem able to take it in at first. Then I told her a few stories from our childhood holidays and she began to rally round. I told her what we planned to do. She came alive then. More animated. We didn't have a lot of time so she gave me the baby to feed, while she got changed. Her clothes were no more than filthy rags.' He didn't have to tell us. We could smell them in the bag.

Dom suddenly smiled. 'I was useless with the bottle. She took over and got some into him before the guard came and asked how much longer I was going to be as the prisoner was due to leave for the court.' He shrugged. 'She kissed the baby, put him in the bag and I walked out. I left her with the doll wrapped in a dirty blanket, walking up and down, cooing to it.'

'Nobody asked to search you? Or tried to stop you?' I asked.

'No one. Everybody was relaxed almost to the point of sloppiness. Bringing the trial forward has boosted morale. They know it's not a real trial. It's an army tribunal. There's no evidence in her defence, although Susan will be allowed to make a statement on her behalf – or her lawyer can.'

'She has a lawyer?' John asked.

'If you can call him that. He's an army officer. The fact of the matter is, she has no defence. She has admitted who she is and that's that. She's been condemned out of her own mouth.' Dom stood up and stretched. 'I need to go. I still have to get the magazines and bullets over.'

I held my hand out to him. 'I cannot thank you enough,' I said. 'If there is ever anything that I can do for you, you need only ask.'

He looked embarrassed, and then said, quite formally, 'I do it for my family's honour. Once this is over I never want to see Susan again. She and the rest of the International Brigades should never have become involved with my country's struggle.' On that note he left.

Now all we had to do was await the verdict of the trial. I thought about going for a walk but then dismissed the idea. I wanted to be there when Jake took the call from the barracks. It came in the middle of the afternoon.

He replaced the receiver. 'Guilty. Death by firing squad, tomorrow at noon.'

49

THOUGH THE VERDICT was expected, it still came as a shock. We sat in stunned silence for a few seconds and then all began to talk at once. There was nothing we could do, except carry on with our plan. So far it had worked. Dom would be returning to the prison in the morning with the remainder of the props Susan needed, while we completed our preparations.

In the middle of the afternoon the carpenter arrived. He had brought with him the coffin we would use for Susan's body. It was an ornate affair and stood on four short legs. The bottom was drilled full of air-holes. A pillow was placed at one end but she would have to lie on the bare wood as we did not dare risk her suffocating.

The next tradesman to arrive was the butcher. He brought bottles of pigs' blood and two sheep's bladders. We experimented with one of them until we were satisfied. The second we filled with blood and Estella sewed it inside one of Jake's waistcoats.

'Are you sure,' I asked, 'that it will fit under her dress?'

'Have no fears, David,' replied Estella, 'I made certain. And she will also have a *rebozo* around her shoulders, made of white, Spanish lace. It will show the blood up beautifully. Don't worry,' she added fiercely, 'it will work.'

It must work, I thought.

The strain was telling on me and the others though we tried to be patient with each other. We envied Dom as he had so much to do. In the evening we did have something to occupy us. We sat at the kitchen table, removing the lead from the bullets of the rifles that would be used by the firing squad. It wasn't difficult. We sealed the ends with small pieces of cardboard. When the trigger was pulled there would be a loud noise, a puff of smoke and nothing else. Dom doctored his pistol in the same way. A blank would be the second bullet in each of the magazines. Mike's idea of replacing the firing squad wouldn't work for the reasons given by Dom. So we intended using a firing squad of *Moors*, known to hate Susan and the Republicans.

It was Dom's task to get the firing squad to replace their magazines in their rifles with the ones we were preparing. He would order them to do so but at the same time explain it was to prevent a mis-fire, something not uncommon with the Nationalist Army, as each bullet had been specially checked. If any man asked him why it mattered he was going to reply, 'Do you want to be the one whose bullet doesn't kill the whore? You will be laughed at by your comrades forever.' It was a compelling argument. I hoped it was compelling enough.

But that raised another problem. Any soldier feeding a magazine into his rifle will look at the bottom of it. Inevitably one of them would notice the doctored bullet. There was no mistaking it. So the first bullet had to be a live round. Sion had thought of the solution to that problem.

We would be at the bullring, waiting with the coffin. Jake had drawn us a map of the layout. We would be behind one of the barriers that the bullfighters ran behind when escaping the horns of the tormented beasts. Susan would be less than five yards away.

The night was sheer hell. I gave up trying to sleep around 3am and sat looking out of the window. When you're in danger of losing a loved one you think of all the things you should have said or should have done, or wished you'd done differently. I shook my head in frustration. I

had to keep a clear head for what the morning would
bring.

I must have dozed because I jerked awake to see a
grey morning breaking. The sky was lightly overcast but
didn't look as though it was going to rain. I stood up
wearily, stretching aching bones, and glanced at my watch.
It was seven-thirty five.

Sion and Mike had stayed with the plane all night,
making use of the hampers of food we'd brought with us
from England. A number of base personnel had been over
to see what they were up to but, on the whole, they were
left alone. Sion had returned to the hotel in the evening,
to collect their gear.

I was tying my tie when my hand froze. I stared in
shock at my image in the mirror. We had thought of everything except one vital item. How were we to take the
coffin from the bullring to the airfield?

With a shaking hand I reached for the telephone to
ring Jake but then thought better of it. Instead I hurriedly
finished dressing and practically ran all the way to his
house. When I got there I gasped out my oversight,
berating myself for a fool.

'David, David, take it easy.' He spoke soothingly. 'Sit
down, have a coffee. It's all been taken care of. The coffin
will be placed in the back of an army truck. Dom will
travel with it. I'll follow in the car with you and John.
We go straight to the airfield.'

'Why didn't I know about it?' I wondered for a moment
if I was losing my grip on reality.

'You were out when we discussed it. It took very little
in the way of planning. Dom has his own regiment's
transport, so it hasn't been an issue.'

'God,' I groaned, 'how could I have forgotten to even
bring it up?'

'You've had so much on your mind. Now, you'd better
go back to the hotel. Take one of the cars. Pack, pay your
bills and come back here. We've still a lot to do.'

I did as I was told. Dom returned around mid-morning.
'How is she?'
'Bearing up, now she knows the baby is safe.' He
paused and then added, 'Uncle David, she asked one
thing. If she doesn't make it, will you name the baby
Phillipe Griffiths?'
I didn't want to think about failure, but I nodded. 'Tell
her I'll be proud to stand with her at the font when
he's christened. And that goes for Madelaine as well.'
I swallowed the lump in my throat.
'Does the waistcoat fit?' Estella looked up from trying
to feed the baby some milk.
'Yes. No problem there.'
'And the baby? Has anybody noticed the substitution?'
John queried.
'No, I'm sure they haven't. She holds it, rocks it and
talks to it. The guards just leave her alone. I've given her
the small bag of blood to take in her hand and helped
her to fit one behind her head, under her hair. She's placed
the white *rebozo* around her forehead and is letting it hang
down her back. It holds the bag of blood in place and
hides it.' Almost wistfully he added, 'She looks beautiful.
Like Madonna and child. Every eye in the bullring will
be on her today and they will see exactly what they
expect to see.' On that encouraging note, Dom left to
return to the barracks. He would be escorting Susan to the
bullring.
Jake turned to Estella. 'Are you all set?'
'Yes. I'll be at the airport in plenty of time. I've got
a crib for the baby and I've boiled some milk in case
Susan needs it. He seems quite happy with the bottle now
but no doubt he'll take to Susan's breast again.'
At last it was time to leave. The whole range of
emotions that had been stirred up inside me over the
last few days – fear, anger, despair and hope, were now
horribly concentrated deep in my guts. How much worse
must Susan be feeling?

When we arrived at the bullring it was already full, with more people crowding in to the amphitheatre. Although the day was cold, the rain had stayed away and there was a festival atmosphere about the place. I was shocked to see so many children amongst the crowds.

Jake, with his impressive height, shouldered his way through the crowds who quickly parted when they saw John and me with a coffin between us. We placed it behind the barrier, against the wall, hidden from prying eyes. Unknown to the others, inside was a machine gun. If Dom failed to substitute the magazines for some reason I'd know about it and I was going to attack, kill Franco and make a wild dash for freedom with Susan. I'd probably fail, but on the other hand in the ensuing chaos who could tell what could happen? I was determined to die trying. There was a stir of interest amongst the crowd when two men walked out carrying a mannequin between them. Two posts had been erected and the porcelain dummy was tied to one. Incongruously it was dressed like a woman, down to a white shawl over its head.

As the clock approached twelve noon there was a great roar from the crowd and we looked out to see Franco and an entourage arrive. I was also armed with a sidearm hidden under my coat and my fingers itched to draw it and shoot the perfidious swine.

A murmur went up and a deathly silence fell across the arena. I looked out and saw my daughter walking across the width of the bullring. She walked slowly, head erect, her arms in front of her, cradling what to all intents and purposes was a baby. She looked achingly beautiful and my heart almost stopped in my chest. Turning to him, I saw John wipe a surreptitious tear from the corner of his eye.

Susan stopped in front of the wooden post and looked around defiantly. She could not see us where she stood, as we were behind her. And we didn't dare draw any attention to ourselves. This was the moment of greatest danger.

Dom marched up to her with a black kerchief in his hands to wrap around her eyes. Disdainfully she shook her head. He threw it to the ground where it fluttered in the breeze. Relief flooded through me. That was the signal. He had made the substitution. The crowds gasped at her courage and became utterly still. Dom saluted her and walked back to the firing squad. He wasted no time. Drawing his sword, he held it in his right hand, forearm parallel to the ground and gave the orders.

'Firing squad,' he called in a loud voice. 'Load your guns.' We heard the sound of the bolts working, the breaches opening and closing.

'Take aim!'

There was the sound of guns being raised to shoulders, stiff webbing moving and then an even deeper hush fell over the crowd.

'Fire!' Dom shouted the order and at the same time dropped his sword.

The bullets smashed the mannequin to pieces and the crowd roared its approval. The sheer drama of it held them enthralled. I had been watching Susan and seen her flinch but she held herself proud and I admired her courage more than ever. Again a hush fell over the crowd.

Dom repeated the orders and this time the guns were pointed at my darling daughter.

'Fire!' Dom brought his sword down and the volley thundered out, the six shots sounding as one. I flinched, my heart in my mouth as I watched Susan sway, blood bursting out of her chest and over the white lace shawl. She collapsed to her knees. Her left hand, clutching the doll's head, spurted blood and she toppled on top of it and lay still. The crowd remained silent, shocked to its very core. Dom marched smartly across to her, sheathed his sword and removed his pistol. He fired one round into the back of her head, scattering more blood the cardboard in the bullet bursting the bag hidden there. Now the crowd erupted. They were on their feet, screaming with delight, yelling, pointing.

John and I were already hurrying into the arena with the coffin. We placed it by Susan's side, removed the lid and lifted her into the box, laying hcr on her back. When she opened her eyes, smiled at me and winked, I thought I would yell out with joy. I had no need of the machine gun. With fumbling fingers we quickly secured two butterfly nuts. We lifted the box and walked away as fast as we could. Already men were in the arena throwing sand on the blood, preparing for the bullfight. I saw one of them pick up one of the empty cartridge cases and pocket it, to keep as a souvenir or sell to some other sick soul who wanted a keepsake of this day. The crowd were now chanting Franco's name and 'Death to the Republicans'. It was utter bedlam and perfect for our purposes.

We placed the coffin in the back of a lorry and Dom climbed in with it. We found Jake already waiting for us with the car and we scrambled into the passengers' seats. We set off immediately. The silenced pistol I carried in a specially made holster dangled butt-down under my left armpit. It dug into my side and I moved it to a more comfortable position. I checked a final time for Franco's letter allowing us permission to remove Susan's body from Spain.

At the airfield the letter worked its magic and we were waved through. We did not dare to hurry. We had come this far; speed could be our undoing. The Griffin was ready to go, the engine warmed through. In a crib, tucked behind the pilot's seat, the baby was sleeping peacefully. Estella was there to say goodbye. Our farewells were brief. There were no words of thanks adequate and none necessary. We hugged, shook hands and piled into the plane. The two vehicles then departed.

We taxied towards the runway with Sion calling the

control tower for permission to take-off. We were unscrewing the coffin lid and helping Susan out when I realised Sion was arguing with the tower.

'What is it?' I yelled at him.

'They told us we aren't cleared for take-off and to return to the hangar and await further instructions.'

'Forget it,' I yelled, 'just go.' The words were hardly out of my mouth when two jeeps came tearing into view. One pulled up in front of us and one to the side. They began herding us around, like cattle.

'If I don't do as they say,' Sion said loudly, 'they'll damage the Griffin and we won't be going anywhere.'

Susan was already nursing the baby. She looked at me, terror in her eyes.

'Don't worry, my darling, we'll get out of here,' I said trying to hide a tide of rage rising within me. So Franco had had a further change of heart and reneged even more on our deal. Well he'd picked on the wrong people this time.

There were two men in each jeep. One driving, another carrying a rifle. The rifles were pointed clearly at Sion.

We stopped with a jerk. An officer indicated that we open the door and step down. I nodded, raising my hands and then dropping them from sight as I operated the door handle. I opened the door, stepped down then pointed behind the soldiers. As they turned to look, I drew my silenced Star, flicked the safety to automatic and pulled the trigger. I remembered my promise to Dom. No deaths.

The bullet hit the officer in the shoulder. I waved the gun at the other soldiers who, with alacrity, raised their hands. Gesturing for them to climb down they leapt nervously to the tarmac. I indicated they should pick up the officer and move away from their weapons and jeeps. Nervously they did so, the officer with a hand to his wound, blood seeping through his fingers.

Sion was already gunning the engine when I piled back

in and slammed the door behind me. I could hear Sion talking to the tower. He was thanking them for being allowed to take-off and informing them that we would be heading for Portugal once we were airborne. He grinned and passed the earphones to me to listen. I heard the man in the tower screaming with rage, ordering us to return, but I merely shrugged and gave the earphones back to Sion. He continued talking drivel while we lined up and accelerated down the runway. Vehicles were starting up and giving chase but they were far too late. We were airborne and turning northwest and still the tower was yelling orders at us.

We were already over the Atlantic and climbing fast when I looked back. Two Me Bf109s were lining up on the runway. We didn't stand an earthly against them. We had personal firearms, including a machine gun, but nothing else. I pointed them out to Sion who looked back and swore.

'Mike, you know what to do.'

'No problem, Sion.' O'Donnell climbed into the passengers' cabin, ripped open a hidden compartment in the floor and took out a handful of grenades. While he worked, Sion was turning the Griffin and swooping back towards the airfield. I could hear him telling the tower that we were coming in to land as instructed, demanding to know why the two planes were blocking our path.

I suspected confusion reigned down below. We saw the Bf109s slow down and then begin to pick speed again. A plane is at its most vulnerable when landing and taking-off, committed to a course and speed and unable to manoeuvre. Mike had the door open and was leaning far out with me holding his feet to steady him. He pulled the pin on the first grenade and dropped it. One followed the other as fast as he could pull the pins. Two exploded in front of the lead plane, a third over the cockpit and two underneath the second aircraft. Both planes blew up with a thunderous roar as we turned skywards once more.

The runway was completely blocked. No more aircraft would be taking-off from there for a while.

We were climbing past twelve thousand feet when Sion said, 'Trouble.'

'What is it?' I asked.

'A squadron of Junkers is approaching from the north. They've been diverted to head us off.'

'How far away?'

'Ten minutes flying time. Tally ho!' Sion yelled, turning the plane on its wing and diving towards the sea, heading south and easing around to port. Just above wave height we flashed over the coast of Spain. Only seventy-five miles to Gibraltar, approximately twelve minutes flying time. We were around *Tarifa*, the southernmost point of mainland Spain, in ten minutes. Gibraltar was dead ahead. With relief I lowered the floats.

There was no sign of pursuit and we landed safely outside the harbour wall, in a long, low swell, amongst the anchored ships of a Royal naval squadron.

We taxied very slowly past the ships and in through the southern entrance. The harbour was one of the most secure in the world and certainly one of the finest anywhere in the Mediterranean.

We anchored near the Old Mole in the top right hand corner and waited for the harbour master to come out to us. We didn't have long to wait. A black and white fast patrol boat approached, bristling with marines carrying rifles. The HM hailed us and we waved the boat carefully alongside. John came into his own once more. He handed over his diplomatic passport, had a few words with the man, received a salute and sat back in his seat. He looked exhausted and I was immediately concerned about him but he shooed me away.

'A small boat is on its way. I've sent word to Rex that we're here.'

'Rex?' I queried.

'Sir Rex Coward. He's the Governor. We were at Eton

together. He fagged for me. A good man to know in a tight spot.' I realised John was labouring for breath and helped him undo his tie and top button. He slipped a pill into his mouth and, after a few seconds, his breathing eased and colour returned to his cheeks.

'Are you all right?'

'Better. Better. Just need to rest for a few minutes. Here comes the boat.'

A small row boat came alongside and began ferrying us and our belongings ashore. Much to my surprise a large, black limousine drew up and a hearty, red faced man climbed out. There were warm greetings between him and John and introductions were made. The Governor shepherded us into the car and we drove off, leaving Mike and Sion to follow. It wasn't far and Sion knew the way to Government House.

Throughout the journey I held Susan's hand. She was horribly thin, hardly recognisable as the glamorous young woman who'd disappeared from our lives a year before. I was desperate to talk to her, to hear all that she had to say but we needed privacy. I also needed to send a telegram to Madelaine. We had already made up a small code and as soon as we arrived at Government House I sent it off. All it said was 'All goods safe'.

Susan was clearly exhausted and we had her put to bed as quickly as possible. The baby slept next to her, in his crib, and when I crept out of the room I saw her lying back, smiling down at him, talking softly.

I found the others with the Governor in his study. They each had a large glass of whisky in their hands and were standing awkwardly in silence. John, by contrast, was sipping a glass of water.

'I can't tell you, Rex old boy. It's need to know, I promise you that.' John's chuckle was laboured. 'But we're travelling on diplomatic passports on government business.'

'What sort of business?' Coward looked intrigued and not a little annoyed at being kept in the dark.

John tapped the side of his nose. 'Monkey business. Best not to know. National security and all that.'

Coward changed his questioning. 'What are you doing here?'

'We had to leave Spain in a hurry. Damn Nationalists tried to shoot us down.'

'What!' Sir Rex was aghast. 'Did they know you had DI?'

'Yes. But Franco didn't seem to care.' John sipped more water.

'Blasted scoundrel. Though it doesn't surprise me. We have, as you saw, the fleet in, on their way back to Blighty. We have a reception tonight, followed by dinner for the captains. I regret there's no room at the table for all of you. Perhaps you, John, and you, Sir David, would care to join us?'

John smiled tiredly. 'I think not. An early night is called for.' He looked at me. 'What about you, David?'

I shook my head. 'That's very kind but I need rest as well. The last few days have been rather trying.' I was physically and emotionally exhausted. The Governor was evidently relieved and excused himself, while he went to check on the arrangements for the evening.

'How are we going to get home?' Sion asked. 'We can't exactly fly over Spain.'

'We'll hitch a lift,' I replied airily. 'Didn't you see what was in the harbour?'

'Of course,' replied Mike, 'the aircraft carrier.'

'The *Ark Royal*. All three million pounds worth of her and less than a year old. And I happen to know the Captain.'

'How come?' Sion asked.

'His son is at school with Richard. Luckily,' I chortled, 'it's a small world.'

When I looked in on Susan she was fast asleep. I sat next to her for a while and looked down at her beautiful face. Even in repose I saw the pain that was etched there.

I sat by her bed for some time. As she slept, I saw tears trickle out from under her eyelashes. Silent tears, the sort that show when you hurt far down in the depths of your being. I ached for her.

50

THE GOVERNOR'S RECEPTION was in full swing. I ate sandwiches and drank half a bottle of wine in my room. Though I could hear the laughter and frolics taking place downstairs, I had no desire to join them. I fell onto my bed and slept heavily all night. There was a rumpus sometime in the small hours, but it passed me by. I had no interest but to sleep.

Having stayed at official residences previously, I knew breakfast would be kept warm on hot plates in the dining room. At 10am it would be cleared away and preparations made for lunch. I wandered in around nine to find Sion and Mike already seated and tucking into bacon and eggs. It smelt wonderful and I began helping myself to a large plateful.

'Did you hear the explosion in the night?' Sion asked.

'I can't say I did,' I paused then remembered. 'Actually, I did hear something.'

'That was the Griffin.'

'What!'

Sion grimaced. 'Afraid so. Somebody blew it to pieces. It looks as though they blew themselves up as well, judging by the bits of body we found around the area.'

'Damn!'

'Look on the bright side, David. If they hadn't been so incompetent, the bomb might have gone off when we were on board or even flying. It could have been a hell of a lot worse.'

'That's an understatement.' I sat down morosely but

then shook myself out of it. My reaction was ludicrous.
We had Susan and my grandson back safe and sound and
we were all fit and in one piece. What did the loss of the
Griffin compare to that? I would take my fight with Franco
back to Parliament now, where I could do some good.

'Has Susan been down yet?' I asked them.

'No. She's having breakfast in her room. She said she'll
be down shortly.'

'What about John?'

'Seen neither hide nor hair of him. I expect he's having
a lie in,' said Mike.

I thought no more of it and tucked into my bacon and
eggs. I was ravenous and quickly polished them off, along
with a second cup of coffee.

Susan joined us, with the baby, and we sat making
idiotic noises at him until she announced it was time for
his feed.

As she reached the door, she paused and looked back.
'Thank you all for everything. For saving us. It ... it
seems so inadequate ... I can't find the words,' she
faltered.

I nodded, swallowed hard and said, 'I'm proud of you,
Susan. Everything's going to be all right.' And proud I
was. But fearful as well. She had been through a great
deal. She had seen and experienced more than was good
for her. She had faced death on countless occasions, seen
her friends killed, her lover tortured and killed and she
had killed many people herself. It was a heavy burden to
carry. Did she have the strength? The thought haunted
me.

It proved unnecessary for me to talk to the captain of the
Ark Royal. Sir Rex had already spoken with Vice Admiral
Sir Peter Carbonne, whose flag flew on the aircraft carrier.
He had made it clear that he would be delighted to take
us back to England.

I met with Susan a short while later. The baby was

being cared for by a maid who was pleased to have the opportunity to nurse him and skive-off from her normal duties. We walked up the square onto the main shopping street in Gib, appropriately called Main St. We were well wrapped up against a cold wind blowing from the north-east. The clouds, having dumped their fill of rain and snow, had vanished and it was a clear, crisp, winter's day. I began with a simple question to introduce a difficult topic.

'Have you finally decided on the name for the baby? Phillipe what? Griffiths? Boucher?'

She smiled a troubled smile and put her hand through my arm. 'He'll be a Griffiths. Should any man be daft enough to tie up with me in the future I can see about a name change then.'

'Any man would be lucky to have you,' I argued.

'Spoken like a true father.' She gently shook my arm. 'I'm soiled goods, Dad. It will be a long time before any man will want me, I know.'

I changed the subject, which was making us both uncomfortable, by pointing at a small dress shop. We spent the next hour shopping, an activity I normally detested. Susan made the morning a delight though she had changed greatly, I realised. In a weird way it was like getting to know a stranger, albeit one I knew a good deal about. I gently began to question her about her time in Spain. It transpired she had written home every month, but we had only received the two letters. She was truly upset to learn that we had been so much in the dark about her, but did admit that she had not mentioned the baby.

We purchased a good many items, for Susan and the baby, which were being delivered by the shopkeepers to Government House. Entering a small, hospitable-looking inn, we ordered hot chocolate, laced with rum and topped with cream.

'This,' Susan chuckled delightedly at me, her upper lip smeared with thick cream, 'is so wonderful.' She licked her mouth in a most unladylike manner. I saw a flash of the little girl I knew and loved so much. 'If only' . . . The two saddest words in the world. If only I could wave away her pain, because in spite of the laughter, I could see shadows lurking behind her eyes.

We sat there for a long time. Susan began to open up, recounting her exploits in Spain. Such bravery, audacity and skill would have been astonishing in a man, but in a young woman . . . I was awed. I could see it was doing her good to unburden the memories but when she came to the part where they had fled Spain, she gasped aloud. 'Connie!'

'Your friend?'

'I must let her know I'm alive. I must get word to her. Oh, Dad,' she said, the picture of misery, 'I must tell her. She'll think I'm dead.'

Reluctantly I shook my head. 'As far as Spain is concerned, you *are* dead. It was part of the deal with Franco.'

'But he broke his word. You said so.'

'I know. But I'll fight him in Britain with sanctions. The man made it clear what he would do if word of your escape surfaced and embarrassed him.' I paused. There was no easy way to say it. 'He'll send a hit squad to kill you and the baby.'

There was a sudden flash of her fighting spirit. 'I'm not afraid . . .'

I held my hand up, forestalling her. 'That's not the point. We won't be able to protect you all the time and his men would get to you eventually. You *and* the baby.'

That was the clincher and I saw the defiance leak out of her. 'But I must tell Connie. Please, Dad.'

I thought about it for a few seconds and nodded. 'I'll see what I can do.'

The door to the inn flew open and a marine rushed in. He stopped at our table and saluted. 'Sir, we've been looking for you everywhere. The Governor wants you back straightaway.'

'What's the problem?' I was standing up already, reaching for my overcoat.

'It's the Baron, sir.'

John had passed away peacefully in the night. His face looked serene, as if life had decided to leave him and had quietly slipped away. He was lying on his back, his eyes were closed and his manicured fingers, always a small vanity, lay outstretched before him.

I sighed heavily. My immediate thoughts went to Mam and what I was to tell her. There was no question of going back with the Royal Navy now. It would take a week. We needed a faster route. And I didn't want Mam to learn of her husband's death by telegram or from the newspapers.

'Can we keep this quiet?' I asked Coward.

He looked uncomfortable. 'I suppose so, but not for long. Why?'

'Consideration of the relatives. I would like to tell his wife. She's my mother.'

'Oh! I had no idea. All right, I'll see what I can do. But I won't be able to keep the news from escaping indefinitely. The servants and the men will gossip and there are plenty of newspaper reporters who'll be onto the story in a flash.'

'I know. I'll go and speak with the Vice-Admiral.'

Before I did, I found Sion and Mike. They sat with long faces in the library, cold coffees on the tables before them. John's death had hit us all very hard.

'I need to get back to England to tell Mam,' I began, 'and as fast as possible.'

Sion nodded. 'That's what we figured.'

'Any ideas?'

'Without the plane, not really, unless the navy will help.'

I nodded. 'I'm sending a telegram to the Minister for the Navy. I'll explain what we require.'

Just then the door opened and a signals rating appeared. 'You sent for me, sir?'

'Yes. I need to send an encrypted signal to Whitehall. Can you do that?'

'Yes, sir.'

'Good.' I dictated a brief message. 'Got that?'

He read it back and I nodded in satisfaction. 'As soon as you've got a reply bring it to me.'

'Yes, sir.' He saluted and withdrew.

Sion spoke up. 'For form's sake, David, someone has to travel with the coffin and I'm sure you'd rather stay with Susan and the baby. I know you're the elder, but this time I'll go.'

We argued over that one but I suppose in my heart of hearts I knew he was right. It made more sense. Susan and the baby needed me and Sion was as capable of telling Mam as I was.

Reluctantly I agreed. 'There's one more thing.' I briefly outlined what I would like them to do, if it was at all possible.

By the middle of the afternoon we were approaching the side of the Ark Royal. At twenty-three thousand tons she was a huge ship, with formidable fire power and carrying a squadron of swordfish fighters. She was also the first flat-top ever built, though the third ship to carry the name '*Ark Royal*'.

We arrived alongside the quarter-deck and the main ladder. Four ratings had been sent ashore to handle the coffin, the flags were at half-mast and a Royal Marine bugler played as we stepped aboard. The quartermaster's desk at the top of the gangway was in front of us. Lined up on either side was a welcoming guard and the ship's senior officers, including the Admiral. The guard presented arms and the officers saluted. I noticed the ship's crest, an old-fashioned Noah's ark, surmounted by a gold crown with the king's crown above. In a curly banner underneath was the ship's motto, 'Zeal does not Rest'.

Admiral Peter Carbonne stepped forward and offered his hand. He was a tall, spare man, with a cleft chin and intelligent brown eyes. Introductions were made and we followed him to his cabin. John's coffin was taken in a different direction. I paused for a few seconds and watched it go, tears misting my eyes.

In the luxurious cabin that befitted a man of his rank we were offered drinks. I accepted a whisky.

'I have a signal here from Whitehall,' Carbonne began without preamble. He had discarded his hat to show a thick shock of white, wavy hair, 'and its instructions are quite clear. I am to give you every assistance, short of endangering my ships and the lives of my men. That's pretty *carte blanche*, so what do you want to do?'

I explained and he nodded. 'That presents no problem as all,' he said with evident relief in his voice. 'Derek?'

'No problem, sir.' Derek Entwhistle was the ship's captain, who I knew in passing, from Richard's school. He was in his early to mid-forties, a tough-looking, competent man with brown hair, sideburns turning grey, and a fading tan around blue eyes. 'I'll get onto it right away.'

'Madam,' Carbonne turned to Susan, 'I have arranged for you to have my day cabin.'

'I don't wish to put you to any trouble,' Susan began.

'It's no trouble. There's a bedroom through there with a shower and heads. Eh,' he blushed, 'toilet facilities. Sir,' he turned to me, 'you will have the cabin directly below. It's the Commander's, but he's already shifted his berth.'

'Thank you.' I knew enough about the Royal Navy to know that all this was strictly regimented and that protesting was unnecessary, even boorish.

'Gentlemen, in view of what Sir David has told me you won't be staying long.'

Sion and Mike nodded. 'The sooner we can get away the better. Once we get to France it'll take a full day to get the train back to England.'

'That won't be necessary,' said the Admiral. 'My instructions mean that I can do everything in my power to expedite your return and so I shall. You will fly all the way. Along with the Swordfish torpedo planes we also have a four-seater seaplane. It has a range of over a thousand miles and we use it as a spotter plane in front of the task force.'

We were thanking him when someone knocked on the door. A nervous head appeared around it. 'You sent for me, sir?'

'Come in, Lt Cdr Braithwaite. Let me introduce you.'

Braithwaite was early thirties at the most. He was short, with black hair and an anxious smile. His handshake was firm and when he was introduced to Sion he exclaimed, 'Sion Griffiths? The aircraft manufacturer?'

Sion looked embarrassed for a second or two as he nodded.

'Gosh, the boys will be so pleased to meet you, sir.'

He said something else but I had tuned him out. A few moments later, Mike, Braithwaite and Sion left. They were being taken to the pilot officers' briefing room where I learnt later the whole squadron turned up to listen to Sion and Mike talk about aviation and its future developments.

'We'll be underway at eighteen hundred precisely.' The Admiral looked at his watch. 'In just over two hours. When it comes time to depart I shall have you escorted to my bridge, which is situated just under the Captain's bridge. You'll have a fine view from there. Is there anything else I can do for you?'

'No, thank you, Admiral. You have been kindness itself. I appreciate all the trouble you're going to and I'll let them know in Whitehall.'

He smiled. 'Thank you, Sir David.'

'Please, just David.'

'In that case you must call me Peter.' He excused himself, as he had work to do. Susan and I were left alone.

We weren't to know it then but that day was the beginning of a friendship that would go on for many years, a
friendship that would stand us in good stead in the dark
years ahead.

Half an hour later, Sion and Mike returned. 'We're all
set,' Sion announced. 'We're leaving now so we'll reach
France before it's dark. We've come to say cheerio.'

We were taken up to the flight deck, where we watched
the sea-plane being lowered into the water, Sion and Mike
waving to us as they dropped out of sight. The plane was
twin-engined and could carry bombs or torpedoes if
necessary. On this occasion they only had a nose-mounted
machine gun for self-defence. Sion was sitting next to
the pilot. There was one empty seat.

The little plane, tiny now from our vantage point on
the flight deck, was released from the crane as soon as
the engines started and taxied across the bay. It was soon
in the air and flying east, into the Mediterranean.

There was bustle all around as the ship prepared for
sea. Last minute fresh provisions were being brought on
board, libertymen collected from the bars that were open
all day in Gibraltar and announcements were sounding
non-stop over the ship's tannoy system, none of which I
understood.

Finally we were standing on the lower bridge watching
the spectacle of a fleet going to sea. The minute synchro-
nisation of events was stupendous and brought a lift to
my very soul on this sad occasion. I knew that John would
have loved it.

Flags flew up and down masts across the whole fleet.
They moved as though controlled by one hand. The red
and white squares of the flag uniform controlled the
evolution of raising anchor. Peter Carbonne stood with
glasses glued to his eyes, his flag-lieutenant by his right
shoulder and two signalmen at hand. He issued a stream
of orders, reprimands and expedites. One reprimand was
to the Commanding Officer, *HMS Ark Royal*. I never did

work that one out seeing as he was on the bridge above us and only five feet away.

At nineteen-thirty precisely a steward knocked on our door and entered. 'Sir, the Commander's compliments, but the wardroom was wondering if you would like to join them for a pre-dinner drink?'

Susan and I had changed into evening clothes. Susan wore a fetching coral pink dress with tiny pearls sewn on the bodice with matching jacket while I wore my dinner suit. It was one of the outfits she had bought in Gibraltar.

She hesitated in front of me. 'Dad, I know I shouldn't be wearing this, but I've nothing black.'

'John would have wanted you to look as beautiful as you do now.' Motherhood had given her beauty a maturity that went straight to my heart.

She smiled tentatively. 'I'll just check on the baby. A junior steward has been sent to watch him. Incidentally, I've decided on his name. It's John Phillipe Griffiths.'

I was inordinately pleased and I knew John would have been proud.

The wardroom spanned the width of the ship and faded into the distance. There were hundreds of officers only a fraction of whom we met. Susan was immediately surrounded by a large group of them. I was whisked away to talk politics and navy with the more senior officers, all of whom held the rank of Commander. I gratefully accepted a brandy and ginger ale, a horse's neck in RN parlance and frequently had a tray of 'small eats' thrust in front of me, the naval description for *hors d'oeuvres*.

Three-quarters of an hour later, Susan and I were escorted back to the Admiral's cabin. The table was beautifully set with a white linen cloth, crystal glasses, and an array of cutlery. The Admiral and Captain were in attendance.

Dinner was four courses, all of them excellent. The

conversation was good, particularly the talk of international politics and naval issues. Towards the end of the
meal we heard baby John demanding attention and Susan
excused herself and went into the sleeping cabin. I didn't
see her again until the following morning.

The days blurred. We received a signal informing us
that Sion had arrived safely at Portland, the Royal Naval
port in Dorset. Other messages passed back and forth,
but on the whole we were left in peace.

The navy exercised continuously. Aircraft landed and
took-off, guns fired and, to my untrained eye, chaos
reigned. In truth we had the privilege of watching one of
the world's most competent fleets in action.

On the second day at sea, as we dipped into a heavy
Atlantic swell, I asked to be taken down to the storeroom
where John's coffin was stored. I sat there for a long time,
my hand resting on the hard oak wood. In my head I said
a lot of things to him, wishing I had said them while he'd
still been alive. I wondered if he knew how much I had
loved him – almost as much as my own father.

Eventually, hunger drove me back to the world of the
living. I didn't return to see the coffin again until it was
unloaded at Portsmouth.

The day was wet and blustery. Bands played, bunting
and flags flew, and the ships' sides were manned and
cheered as we passed. The fleet had been away for
eighteen months and the ships' companies were desperate
to get back to their loved ones.

It had been agreed that we would stay in the background
until all the fuss had died down. Hours after we docked,
a hearse appeared along with two other cars. I was standing
at the top of the gangway when I saw Mam alight. She
was dressed in black with a heavy veil over her face.
She was accompanied by Madelaine and Kirsty. I saw
Sion and Mike. There was a stranger with them, a woman.
I guessed immediately who she was. Sion had succeeded
after all.

The coffin was saluted over the side. I shook hands with some of the officers, confirmed the meeting Carbonne and I had agreed on in London, and followed Susan down the side. I caught up with her as she burst into tears and threw her arms around the woman.

'Oh, Connie, Connie, I can't believe it's you.'

51

THE FUNERAL TOOK place in a small church in Guildford, John's home town. Mam was looking frail but bore up well under the circumstances. I was proud of Richard. This was his first funeral and he behaved superbly, hardly leaving Mam's side the whole time. His eyes, though, rarely left his sister, his devotion clear to all. Life settled down for a while. The trust John had arranged years earlier was invoked and I found that I was about to become the Baron of Guildford. The news sent Churchill into apoplexy.

He needn't have bothered trying to argue with me. I let him splutter on for a few minutes before interrupting him, 'Winston, I agree. I'm not taking the title. It's been arranged with my solicitors. The trust can remain and the title can be preserved. If Richard wants it when he's grown up, he can take it. If he doesn't,' I shrugged, 'it'll wither on the vine, so to speak.'

Back in the House of Commons I fought Franco every step of the way. I argued that, as the legitimate government of Spain, the Republicans deserved and warranted our support. I pleaded with the other Members of Parliament to take heed that it was the fascists who were our enemy, not the Russians. But I failed. Miserably. The financial clout of big business was just too great for the representatives of democracy. The global power of some of the companies was awesome and they called on their government to support them. What's good for business is good for Britain was the mantra.

Susan, with Connie's help, settled down. On the surface Susan appeared to have come through her ordeal amazingly well, but I could tell that she was hurting. Beneath her smile was a brittleness that manifested itself in tear-filled eyes and she would hurry from the room for no apparent reason. I was down at Fairweather on a bright winter's day and looking forward to the week-end. I found Connie walking baby John in a perambulator along the garden path. We had hired the charming Spanish girl as a nurse, ostensibly for the baby. But she was also a great comfort to Susan. They had been through so much together and shared such memories that nobody else could possibly comprehend the true affection they had for each other. Susan's friends, whom she had left behind when she went off to war, seemed frivolous by comparison.

'Where's Susan?'

Connie looked at me bleakly. 'She has been in her room for the past twenty-four hours.' She hesitated and like a true friend said, 'Perhaps it is a chill.'

'Perhaps.' I hurried away. I knocked on her door but received no answer. I went in. The curtains were closed but I could see Susan lying on her bed, on her back, her arms by her sides. 'Are you all right?'

There was no reply. There was plenty of light filtering through the curtains and I could see that her eyes were open, staring at the ceiling.

'What is it, sweetheart?' I sat beside her and took her hand in mine. It was cold and limp but I could see that she was breathing regularly. There was no reply and I looked closer. Tears began to roll down the side of her face and onto the pillow. 'Hush, Susan, don't take on so.' There was no reply, no reaction. She seemed almost catatonic and I recognised the same symptoms we discovered in many men returning from the front after the Great War.

I knew she needed help but I didn't know what to do.

I began to talk about the family and what we had been through while she had been away. I talked about war and its horrors and its necessity when all else failed. I don't know how long I sat there but it was while I was talking about Richard that I got the first response.

She turned her head and looked at me. 'I killed brothers and fathers and uncles. Many of them boys hardly more than Richard's age. What kind of monster can do that?' She began to sob, her hands to her face, making a horrible keening sound I had never heard before.

I put my arms around her and did my best to comfort her. Madelaine appeared, saw Susan's distress and went to fetch a sleeping draught. Eventually she fell asleep. Within twenty-four hours I had the best advice money could buy and I arranged for a psychiatrist to see her. Susan's recuperation was slow but we could see her improving slowly. The baby helped a good deal. His dependency on her brought Susan out of herself and she behaved normally, going into fits of depression less and less. We even managed to get her to attend a ball or party from time to time, though she usually left early. Throughout, Connie was a great help, uncomplaining and adept at gauging Susan's moods.

Outside our safe little world at Fairweather, storm clouds were gathering. Horrendous events were taking place across Europe in quick succession – events that would determine the future of the world.

In March Hitler walked into Austria and signed the annexation agreement.

In Czechoslovakia the Sudeten region was handed over to Germany by agreement of the British, French, Italians and Germans. No Czechs were present when the treaty was signed.

On the 30th of September Chamberlain was seen arriving from Munich waving a piece of paper bearing Hitler's signature which promised peace in our time. Even then I thought him a bumbling fool.

A week later Hitler's troops marched into the Sudeten-land and Polish troops moved into the Czech region of Teschen-Silesia.

In January 1939 Barcelona fell to Franco and the war in Spain was all but over. A month later Franco was recognised by the British and other governments as the leader of Spain, much to my bitter chagrin.

About that time I noticed a real improvement in Susan. She was livelier, more like her old self. My relief and happiness at her recuperation lasted only until Mam announced her bombshell.

She and I were sitting in the living room in the London house. It was early evening, a Sunday, the last in February, and a heavy slush lay on the ground outside. Mam was looking more tired than ever, thin to the point of emaciation.

'David,' she began without preamble, 'I'm dying. I have cancer.'

I knelt by her side and kissed her hand. In my heart I'd known for some time, but had not wanted to admit it. Her loss of weight, the transparency of her skin, her weakness, all pointed to one thing. I began to weep. I couldn't help it.

'Don't take on so, *Dai bach*. It comes to us all in the end, one way or another.' She stroked her hand through my hair and smiled at me. I saw her through a blur of tears. 'Shush now. Remember, tears are for pillows. I'm glad I have this time though. I want you to know how immensely proud I am of you and Sion. No woman could have better sons.'

'Mam, the family . . .'

She put a finger to my lips. 'Your Da laid the found-ations for our family's achievements, but you drove them to unbelievable heights of success. Let us hope and pray,' she said with insight, 'that the following generations can continue to succeed and be as happy. But the future lies in the hand of God. Now, we have to be practical. Do sit down, there's a dear. I've made up my mind about certain things and I won't be dissuaded. I hope you understand that.'

I nodded. 'Sure, Mam, whatever you want.'

Whatever I expected, it wasn't what she said next. 'I am returning to Wales, to Llanbeddas.'

'What! Mam, you can't!' I protested.

'David, *cariad Dai*.' Darling Dai, the name she had called me when I was a small child. 'It's not for arguing. I have thought long and hard and wish to go back to my roots. To where it all started. I want to hear Welsh again, go to chapel and be buried alongside my darling Sian.' There were tears in her eyes and she used a cambric handkerchief to irritably wipe them away. 'I had made up my mind a long time ago should John predecease me, that was what I would do. The arrangements have been made in Llanbeddas. The cancer just makes the decision all the easier.'

'If that's what you want. I'll see about a house for Madelaine and me.'

She looked at me in utter astonishment. 'Who said anything about you? My dear boy, I don't want you there.'

I looked at her in amazement. 'But . . .'

She smiled. 'Don't look so surprised, David, I am currently taking small amounts of morphine. The doses will get heavier as the cancer advances and I become weaker. I will not have you fussing and I will not have you seeing me deteriorate. My doctor has told me what I can expect and I won't have you worrying over me. You all have your lives to lead – important work to get on with. Chamberlain is a fool. There will be war with Germany in the next twelve months and you're going to be needed at the heart of things.'

'Where will you stay?'

'It's all arranged. I have rented a small house in Llanbeddas, one of those that leads up to the chapel. On Heol-y-Graig. Number four, I think it is. Betty has the details. She made the arrangements.'

'Who will look after you?'

'I'll have a full time nurse as well.'

'Who?'

She smiled. 'Why, Connie of course. She and Susan and the baby will be there. I want to see as much of him as I can before I die. He'll not remember me, but it will be something for me to take away with me.'

'Do the others know?'

'Not yet. Only Susan and Connie, of course. I've seen the darkness in my granddaughter's soul and hesitated asking her at first. Then I realised how much she needs to be wanted. She didn't hesitate. So it's all arranged.'

I knew then why Susan had started to get so much better. There had been a strong bond between them ever since Da had died. I nodded.

Mam smiled at me and nodded, understanding my thoughts. 'Precisely. It will do her the world of good. Better than drugs and doctors.'

'When are you going?'

'Wednesday.'

'But Mam . . .' I began again and this time she interrupted me with a flash of her iron will.

'No buts, David. None. I wish to do this and I will. Now would you help me to get everything organised that I need? My will is with my solicitors. Fetch me a sherry, please.' I walked to the sideboard, feeling numb.

I watched her sitting in the firelight, and tried to capture her image forever. For me she had come to symbolise all the qualities that I had come to recognise as heroic – integrity, strength of character, fearlessness, dedication to family and friends. I wanted to uphold the values she, Da and John had passed down to me. But this was too sudden. I wanted Mam near me for a lot longer. I saw the far-off look on her face. I wondered for a moment who she was thinking of, Dad or John? I was ashamed of my selfishness and thrust my thoughts aside. I needed to be as strong as Mam.

*   *   *

Mam travelled down to Wales and ensconced herself in
the tiny house. She had many visitors who had known her
when she had lived there with Da. She was no longer the
grande dame, but Megan Griffiths, ex-school teacher and
wife of a coal miner. I went down as often as I could but
not as often as I'd have liked. Thanks to Sion, we were
able to fly to Cardiff and travel up the valley to Llanbeddas
whenever we could. Mike O'Donnell was usually with us
and even I, blind idiot that I am, noticed his growing
friendship with Betty. I learned that they were 'stepping-
out together' and though she had tried to resist his charms,
Betty had finally given in once her divorce from Dafydd
was finalised. They became engaged to be married.

Each visit was more painful than the last. Mam was
fading but clinging to life with the tenacity I had come
to expect of her. She and Susan talked a great deal and
I learnt later that Susan was compiling notes on Mam's
life, details that not even I knew about. Susan and the
baby thrived. She would never again be the carefree spirit
of the past but I sensed there was so much more she
would accomplish. She had written to the Bouchers in
California and sent them a photograph of their grandson,
resplendent in a knitted suit. In return she had received
a long and loving letter with an invitation to visit them
as soon as it was convenient.

Spring was in the offing when Franco finally took
Madrid and the Spanish Civil War was declared over. My
time was split between the bank and Parliament. I came
to realise how much I had relied on John. I was swamped
with work and needed to get rid of a load before I was
driven into an early grave.

Italy and Germany signed their 'Pact of Steel' and the
country lurched ever closer to war. I was in the House
of Commons when the telegram arrived.

The chapel was full to overflowing and every nook and
cranny was filled with flowers. People from all over

Britain had made the pilgrimage to this small, coal-dust covered village in the hinterland of Wales. There had never been anything like it in the valleys and there probably never would be again. Royalty stood outside in the sunshine rubbing shoulders with the miners who were there in their flat caps and white silk scarves around their necks. Luckily the weather was lovely, a glorious July day. A street party had been organised to celebrate Mam's life, the plans made months earlier. Under Susan and Connie's control, it went off without mishap. There were trestle tables laden with food and drink and it seemed half the people of the Taff and Rhondda valleys appeared. There were no speeches. It wasn't appropriate.

Madelaine stayed by me, whilst Richard was away meeting cousins he didn't know he had. I had a quiet word with Betty about the factory, which was doing well, and thanked her for all she and Myfanwy had done for Mam. I knew them to have been very regular visitors.

Her reply was, 'It's family, David. Family comes first.'

It was a sentiment dear to my heart.

I had been at the graveside when Mam's coffin had been lowered alongside Sian's and now I wished to go and have a last word before we left. I excused myself from Madelaine and she understood. At the graveside I stood alone, head bowed, looking inward with my thoughts when I felt a presence by my side.

'Mind if I stand with you, Dad?' Susan asked.

'Of course not.'

She took my hand in hers. 'Gran told me so much about the past. She was an exceptional woman. I only hope John inherits his great grandparents' zest for life. Sometimes I lie in bed wondering what the future holds for him.'

I gave her a hug. 'We shall have to see.'

I looked down the valley to where the new school now stood. All those years ago, all those tears. I shook off my mood and smiled. 'It's time we rejoined the others and made our farewells. We've work to be getting on with.'

Less than two months later World War II started with the German invasion of Poland.

Epilogue

TIM HUNTER SAT quietly with Sir David Griffiths in his study. The *Time* magazine reporter was sipping a peaty malt whisky while Sir David drank a herbal tea. After a few moments the octogenarian broke the silence, 'Bah! Get me a malt, young man. I can't stomach this rubbish any longer.'

'But, sir, your wife . . .'

'Never mind my wife. What she doesn't know won't hurt her. Be a good fellow.'

'Yes, sir.' Hunter did as he was directed, adding a cube of ice and a dash of soda, just as the old man liked it. Not for him the convention of a drop of water to bring out the flavour.

'How far are you with the archives?' Sir David asked, with a nod of thanks.

'Your mother's just died and you've returned from Wales. The Second World War is about to start.'

Sir David nodded with satisfaction. 'You'll find the next bit very interesting. Especially about the Duke of Windsor.' His eyes hardened. 'The damn scoundrel was a traitor to his country.' He calmed down and forced a smile, 'But you'll see that for yourself.'

'Susan's exploits in the Spanish Civil war were incredible,' Hunter said, sipping his whisky, enjoying every moment he could spend with the old man.

'Yes, they were. Rightfully she should have had medals galore and been a senior officer.' Sir David sipped his drink, winced as it burnt its way down his gullet, and then added, 'Actually, in any other war, she would never have seen action. As she found out later.'

'Sir?'

'You'll have to wait until we get to the story. It's something though, I can promise you. She is a very formidable woman.'

'So I gather, sir. Can I ask you about the gold?'

'Of course. Ask away.'

'You took a huge gamble. If you'd been discovered you'd have been disgraced. Probably imprisoned.'

Sir David nodded, remembering. 'Yes. But everything was at stake as it was. It's impossible to survive a run on a bank. The sums of money are too great. John and I would have been destitute. So we felt we had no choice. It worked, though, that was the main thing.'

Hunter nodded. 'No one can argue with success.'

'How are you and Sian getting along?' The old man didn't wait for a reply but went on, 'She has her mother's passion, that one. For life and love.'

'Yes, sir. I mean, no, sir.' Hunter was flummoxed until he saw the twinkle in the old man's eyes. Damn him.

'Don't look so worried. She's a wonderful girl. She has her mother's courage and her father's brains. She and her brother have caused a few grey hairs, I can tell you.'

At that moment the door opened and Sian walked in. Her black curly hair was tied behind her head and she looked exhilarated. 'I've just been driving the new MGB. Wonderful. Tim, can we go out for a spin?'

'Yes, of course, if that's all right, sir?'

Sir David waved an airy hand. 'Of course it is. You young things go off and enjoy yourselves, don't mind me. If you see Madelaine ask her if she'd like to join me for a drink, will you? And tell her I don't mean blasted herbal tea.' Sir David took a defiant swig of his whisky and watched the two young people depart.

So much more to do, he thought, *and never enough*

time. On that philosophical note he heaved himself out of his leather armchair and went to refresh his glass. At least his wife wouldn't be able to wrest it from him. She might refuse, though, to top it up.